C

MAURICE BARING (1874–1945) was educated
at Eton, at Trinity College, Cambridge and, for
two terms, at Oxford (where he was not attached
officially to any college). In 1898 he entered the
Diplomatic Service, followed in 1903–4 by a time
at the Foreign Office in London. In 1904 he
resigned and went to Manchuria as correspondent
for the *Morning Post* and then, from 1905–8, to
St. Petersburg as a special correspondent. In 1909
he was correspondent in Constantinople and, in
1912, he worked for *The Times* in the Balkans. In
1909 he was received into the Roman Catholic
Church.

In the Great War he was a member of the Royal
Flying Corps, and gained an illustrious reputation,
being made an Honorary
Royal Air Force in 1925
After the First Worl
full-time novelist, publis
of fiction from 1921 to
novels include *C* (1924
Daphne Adeane (1926). *T*
The Coat Without Seam (1929).

The last ten years of Maurice Baring's life were
severely marred by the onset of paralysis agitans,
and he died at Eilean Aigus in Inverness-shire in
1945.

EMMA LETLEY has spent several years teaching
literature at the University of Hong Kong. She
now lectures in London and writes on nineteenth-
and twentieth-century literature. Her publications
include editions of novels by Robert Louis Stevenson;
and she is at present working on a biography of
Maurice Baring.

MAURICE BARING

C

WITH A FOREWORD BY
EMMA LETLEY

Oxford   New York
OXFORD UNIVERSITY PRESS
1986

Oxford University Press, Walton Street, Oxford OX2 6DP

Oxford New York Toronto
Delhi Bombay Calcutta Madras Karachi
Kuala Lumpur Singapore Hong Kong Tokyo
Nairobi Dar es Salaam Cape Town
Melbourne Auckland

and associated companies in
Beirut Berlin Ibadan Nicosia

Oxford is a trade mark of Oxford University Press

Foreword © Emma Letley 1985

First published 1924 by William Heinemann Ltd.
First issued, with Emma Letley's Foreword, as an Oxford
University Press paperback 1986

British Library Cataloguing in Publication Data

Baring, Maurice
C. — (Twentieth-century classics)
I. Title   II. Series
823'.8[F]   PR6003.A67
ISBN 0-19-281942-9

Printed in Great Britain by
The Guernsey Press Co. Ltd,
Guernsey, Channel Islands

FOREWORD

BY EMMA LETLEY

Maurice Baring's first novel was not published until 1921 when he was forty-seven; *C*, arguably his best book, appeared in 1924, Baring's fiftieth year. This novel and its successors (the best-known are *Cat's Cradle* and *Daphne Adeane*) come after a very varied, versatile career as diplomat, journalist and war correspondent, and Staff Officer in the Royal Flying Corps in 1914–18. During this time of action he had also already published poetry, essays, verse plays, fantasies on literary and historical characters, criticism, fairy tales, and important books on Russia and Russian literature; but, only then, his first attempt at a novel.

Passing By (1921), the account in letters and diary-form of a young man's social and spiritual struggles (leading eventually to his conversion to Roman Catholicism), with its international world of parties, embassies, affairs, and unfortunate liaisons, combined with the most painful theme of renunciation, sits somewhat oddly amongst the main prose publications in England in 1921—for example, Conrad's *Notes on Life and Letters*, Galsworthy's *To Let*, Aldous Huxley's *Crome Yellow*, George Moore's *Héloïse amd Abélard*, D. H. Lawrence's *Psychoanalysis and the Unconscious*, and Virginia Woolf's *Monday or Tuesday*. *C*, published three years later, also has little in common with the more notable literary events of the 1920s; it cannot readily be compared with Woolf's *Jacob's Room* (1922) or *Mrs Dalloway* (1925), nor with

Joyce's *Ulysses* (1922), a book which Baring confessed to a Russian friend he found not only 'indecent' but also 'very boring'. Although he was a friend of writers such as H. G. Wells and Arnold Bennett, Baring is dissimilar to both; and he cannot entirely comfortably be placed as a member of the Catholic Literary Revival together with Hilaire Belloc and G. K. Chesterton (although he is often associated with them and is commemorated in their company in James Gunn's portrait, currently in the National Portrait Gallery in London). In his own time, his reputation was assured by the widespread success of his books in France. André Maurois, whom Baring met in 1925, was one of his most perceptive and appreciative readers, finding comparable pleasure to reading *C* only in the work of Tolstoy and Proust (recent critics also draw attention to the Proustian quality of the novel). As J. B. Priestley put it, Baring 'is one of the most interesting "cases" we have. He is brimful of talent of every kind, and there runs through everything he does a streak of real originality.'

Particularly characteristic of Baring's literary personality, is the way the novel is presented. In *C* we have, as a contemporary critic in the *New Statesman* remarked, 'The novel approximating to the memoir'; the book purports to be the 'biography' of C., otherwise Caryl Bramsley, written by one Walter Wright, and merely passed on to Baring for publication. Baring is fond of this kind of literary game and of experimenting with different fictional forms, but there is more to it than that. *C* is also, in part at least, the author's own story (the novel draws on Baring's childhood in London and the country, his time at Eton, his travels, his literary discoveries, and his brief experience of diplomatic life); and Maurice Baring, although well-known for his sociability, his wit and humour, and the vast range of his friends and acquaintances, was ultimately a very private man. He came too, from a milieu where such privacy could be very closely guarded by, for instance, a special family language, sometimes known as 'The Expressions', and used amongst relations and particular intimates in both conversation and letters. This language, originally created by Baring's mother and her sister when they were children, is arcane and almost impenetrable to outsiders who would doubtless have been bemused to discover that *Robespierre* meant *shabby*, that *Ibsen* meant *ordinary* or *straightforward*, or that a *dentist* was a *heart-to-heart talk*.

Baring had published his autobiography, *The Puppet Show of Memory* in 1922; this was well-received and according to G. B. Shaw, 'unique as a record of a happy childhood', but it had left out a great deal about its author's life, in particular his emotional and spiritual life. In *C*, Baring not only negotiates with the process of conversion (reduced in *Puppet Show* to a single sentence), he also turns his innate reticence and aesthetic preference for the understated to great artistic effect in his portrait of Caryl Bramsley (nicknamed 'C.'). C. is a quintessentially reserved man, an aspiring writer who cannot be fully articulate about his feelings: commenting on the *Vale* he had written on leaving Eton, he regrets that 'He had left out everything that had mattered to him, his thoughts, his dreams, his friendships, all that Eton had meant. He had left it out because he couldn't say it.' Of his later years, too, C.'s papers give the putative author only a 'few illuminating details' and 'suggestive silences'. This reticence is typical of Baring's fictional heroes; also typical are C.'s cultured, cosmopolitan, leisured background, his sensitivity to music and poetry, and the inevitably sad ending to his life.

The style of the book is carefully modulated to suit such a man (both author and protagonist). A contemporary critic in the *Saturday Review* highlighted this typical quality of Baring' novels:

Mr. Baring has developed a technique of his own: in various novels he has put an apparently plain unvarnished tale in the mouth of this character or that—or of several characters—and out of what they betray by what they *don't* say, as much as out of what they do say, has indicated his events.

In one way, this reticence looks unmodern, even Victorian, and there are some definite silences about the sexual relationship between C. and Leila (the reader can judge for himself, for instance, the effects and implications of the break in Chapter XXXIV). On the other hand, *C* has a curiously modern look in its attention to writing itself and to the ways that a 'biography' can be constructed from letters, notes and fragments, with occasional interventions from a fictive editor. Baring is both Victorian and modern, a tension that enriches the novel. In *C*, as in all his major novels, he is also quite deliberately writing of events set well back in the past (from the 1870s to the turn of the century, or, in some cases, to the 1914–18 war) from a more contemporary perspective.

Characteristic too of Baring's education and of his fiction is *C*'s strong classical flavour. Several critics in the 1920s pointed out that the story of C. and Leila was very like that of Catullus and Lesbia, the notorious Clodia Metelli; it was 'an expansion of the tragic story told in Catullus's poems', a turbulent romantic history, beset with rivalry, renunciations, and reconciliations. Like all Baring's best novels, *C* is a very unhappy love story indeed, and the title of one of his most moving novellas, *Comfortless Memory*, could be the sub-title of most of his fiction. Although he was surrounded by friends and by beautiful women (Lady Diana Cooper, Lady Desborough, Countess Benckendorff, and Lady Lovat, among others) throughout his life, Baring never married; and this probably accounts for the pervasive sadness of much of his fiction. His unhappy plots are also explained by his dedication to Belloc in *Cat's Cradle* where he quotes Cervantes:

"Love is too strong to be overcome by anything except flight, no mortal creature ought to be so presumptuous as to stand the encounter, since there is need for something more than human, and indeed a heavenly force, to confront and vanquish that human passion."

Flight, either into a religious life or by means of death, is in the majority of his novels, the only possible solution to the dangers of passion.

These dangers are most skilfully dramatized in *C* in the character of Leila Bucknell and her destructive influence. Baring often brings the same people into several of his books, showing them working out their social and spiritual destinies in new formations and patterns. Leila is a particularly telling example; in *Cat's Cradle*, published a year later than *C*, in 1925, Leila appears right at the end of the novel when the protagonists have some chance of happiness; she is a sign to the reader that the future of the characters is by no means as assured as it appears. Leila captivated her creator in much the same way as she entrapped C. C. himself fluctuates between two kinds of women, found in Beatrice, the good woman and the romantic love of his early manhood, and Leila, the siren. Beatrice, as her name implies, is something of a saviour but she cannot save C. He is too enmeshed with Leila; she is always the 'drawback' to his happiness and, indeed, we may infer, to his conversion. Decidedly and sentimentally 'Low Church', Leila is emotionally and culturally shallow (she cannot share in any of the fervid excitement of C.'s literary and musical discoveries); her taste is appalling, except in the matter of personal dress, and she is associated with the poisoning of C.'s hopes and ambitions just as the classical Lesbia was believed to have poisoned her husband.

Yet, Leila is a wonderful creation. The contradictory response of women who read the novel in 1924 is proof enough of Baring's consummate skill in characterisation. Ethyl Smyth, the composer and friend of the author, reports the reaction of certain *femmes du monde*: some felt

that 'so wicked a character could have been produced by
the Victorian epoch alone, and no longer existed'; others
thought Leila charming, and 'a certain lady professed to
believe that she had been taken as a model for Leila; and
behind simulated indignation peeped out manifest satisfaction!' Models have been suggested for Leila: the
famous beauty Pamela Plowden, later Lady Lytton, is
one favoured candidate; and a recent writer has suggested
that C. and Leila have much in common with Maurice
Baring's brother John (Lord Revelstoke) and Etty (Lady
Desborough), two members of the Souls who conducted
a long affair in which one of the many aliases used in
their correspondence was 'C.'. It is impossible to know
for certain: Baring, in any case, does not like this kind of
labelling; in his life-time he avoided making direct
identifications and insisted that his characters were
composites.

We might, however, wonder if the 'satisfied' lady had
not, perhaps, been taken in by Baring's flat, low-key style
and been eluded by his dry wit. There are, after all, some
fairly devastating comments about Leila:

What she would have liked would have been love poems
written in the style of the *Christian Year*.

and

Every now and again C. would send her poems that he wrote,
and she ended by treating these like bills; they got lost almost
before she had looked at them.

The danger signs are all there in Baring's portrait of

Leila: the veneer of culture, the philistine taste in (music and) books, the lack of enthusiasm for almost all music, the petty subterfuges and affectations, and there is, too, the most painful sense of timing in the way Baring handles her reappearances in the novel. Towards the end of the book, C. has a final chance of happiness with Beatrice. Passionately he resolves to 'break down all obstacles and opposition' and insists that she marry him. At that moment, before Beatrice can reply, C. receives a telegram, a summons from Leila. It is the end of any future hope for C. and Beatrice. C. is 'incurable'. Throughout the book there is the sense that C. should have been a 'remarkable person' and that he had real talent as a writer. His failure and his premature death are attributed to the fact that he is caught up in Leila's story. She is the women who killed the memory of C., losing all the poems that he sent to her—all those, that is, that he had not already burned. Leila thus not only undermines C.'s life but also destroys the possibility of even a posthumous success for Caryl Bramsley.

Leila and C.'s story is enacted against a very vivid backdrop and in a fully-realised social world, with an 'intangible web' of family and social obligations, parties, balls, financial crises, and diplomatic postings. There is a bustling, and often humorous, sub-plot, largely staged by Lady Hengrave (one of Baring's best comic creations), with her single-minded attention to marrying off her daughters to men of property and status; and involving the misalliance of her son, Edward, with 'a vulgar little American'. Then, too, there is the return of C.'s black-sheep brother, Gilbert, from South Africa, and the reclaiming of the family home at Bramsley from the diamond-rich South African, Sir Alfred Rooter (here, Baring draws on his own experience: the Barings' family home at Membland in Devon had been sold after the 'crash' at Baring Brothers in 1890. In fiction, a wish can be fulfilled and Bramsley, unlike Membland, is restored to its original owners). This world, together with vignettes of diplomatic, literary, and artistic life at the turn of the century, Baring creates with ironic wit and without nostalgia, giving his reader a life-like impression of the pace and texture of that 'golden swan-song of European life before the First World War.'

The darker tones of the book's romantic plot are also balanced by Baring's skill in evoking childhood and youth: his own early years had been, as he tells in *Puppet Show*, exceptionally happy. There he writes of 'the fairyland of childhood' and of a first half at Eton that was 'like Paradise' (in this, he is unlike many of his contemporaries). Throughout his life he had a great affection for children and an ability for telling them stories, such as the memorable *Forget-me-not and Lily of the Valley* (1909). In *C*, using ingredients from his own life but creating a very different atmosphere from that he had himself known, Baring carefully dramatises the child's sense of time and the child's viewpoint; the decision as to C.'s future career, made prematurely but definitely by Lady Hengrave on her son's eighth birthday, the boy's reaction to a set of terrifying nut-crackers given to him as a birthday present, and the 'murder' of his sister's favourite doll, Joséphine, are all wonderfully imagined; so also, later in the novel, are events of C.'s schooldays, such as the unfortunate visit to the wrong Mr. Swinburne. As J. B. Priestley commented, 'the book is packed with good things'—'good things' that a modern reader can still thoroughly enjoy today.

INTRODUCTION

It was in January, 1923, that I received a letter from an old friend of mine, a journalist and a traveller, whom I will call Walter Wright, from which the following is an extract :—

New York. July, 1922. . . . You will remember my telling you about Gerald Malone's papers two or three years ago—if not, you will understand what happened if you read the introduction to the manuscript I am sending you to-day, registered and under separate cover. I tried to do what he wanted, and, now it's finished, I want you to read it and tell me whether you think the story could possibly be published as it is. If not, could you re-write and re-cast the whole thing on the basis of the material (all Malone's papers) which I am sending you with what I have done? Should it ever be published I should like it to appear in England.

W. W.

I wrote back saying I thought the story should be published as it stood ; that I would not hear of re-casting, re-writing or altering it. Should I try to find a publisher ?

He answered by cable : "Go ahead. Married yesterday."

By the next mail I received a short letter from him telling me of his marriage, and that all his plans had been changed. He and his wife were starting at once for the South Seas, Australia, the East Indies, and Japan, and other places. The journey was to be combined with writing and business, and might probably last several years. It was impossible for him to do anything more. He gave me absolute control over the MSS., and asked me to do what I could with, and for it.

That being so, I endeavoured to comply with his wishes, and the result is the publication of the story as I received it from Wright, without any alteration on my part.

I have heard nothing further from Wright, with the exception of a picture postcard from Sumatra.

MAURICE BARING.

1924.

WALTER WRIGHT'S INTRODUCTION

In the autumn of 1919, almost a year to a day after the declaration of the armistice, I received a letter from an old college friend, Gerald Malone. He said in his letter that he was ill and that he wanted to see me on an urgent matter.

I had not seen Malone since the end of the war. At Oxford I had known him well. He was thought to be exceptionally gifted, but all the promise that he showed was destined to come to nothing. He took a disappointing degree and he worked for a time at law, but he was never called to the Bar. His father died, leaving him a small competence, which he rapidly got rid of by spending it. When his fortunes appeared to be at their lowest ebb and his situation and prospects seemed to be precarious in the extreme, and he was starting for the Colonies to begin life afresh on a ranch, he was left some money by a distant relation—not a large fortune, but enough to live on—and almost immediately after this he was offered the job of publisher's reader by a firm of publishers. He was not the only reader to the firm—he was to read novels only—and the salary he was given was not a large one. The work did not interest him, but, curiously enough, he did it well. He was successful. He now seemed to have reached smooth waters, but he made an unfortunate alliance, which resulted materially in his life being a long struggle to make both ends meet, and morally in ceaseless friction and permanent domestic misery. He fell in love with a woman of loose morals, violent passions and inflexible tenacity. They lived together for a time ; they quarrelled and separated. They were reconciled again and quarrelled again. He could neither live with her nor without her. She could not be faithful, and she would not abandon him. Finally he married her, and this made the situation worse than ever. She never deserted him, nor did they have a day's happiness together. This state of material strain and moral friction lasted until his wife's death. The release, instead of making him happier, led him to the brink of despair, and I think he would have certainly taken his life had it not been for the good offices of a noble and good woman, a Mrs. Fitzclare, who had been a friend of his greatest friend, and who helped him to tide over this period of hopelessness. Then came the war. Gerald enlisted as a private, and was subsequently promoted. He served in various capacities and in various countries. He returned home after the armistice unwounded, but broken in health.

I went to see him and found him in the rooms at Gray's Inn which he had occupied since his marriage. He looked ill, indeed ; his face, as well as his hair, was grey.

He was lying in a bed in a comfortless, untidy bed-room.

" I'm dying," he said, " and I have asked you to come because I am leaving you something and I want to give it you before I die."

He handed me a large parcel.

" In this parcel," he said, " you will find a bundle of unsorted papers. You are not to open it till I die. They contain not the story, but materials for the story of C."

C. was the nickname of a common college friend of ours who had been Gerald Malone's greatest friend at Oxford, and whom I had afterwards also known in a curiously intimate way.

" I want you to write his story," he went on. " I want you to write it as a novel, not as a biography, but write it you must."

I said that although ever since I had left Oxford I had been an intermittent journalist and had written several books, and had even dabbled in romantic themes, I had never written a novel, nor did I feel capable of doing so. I agreed that a biography was out of the question. We were too near the story ; but we were, also, I thought and said, far too near to turn it into fiction. Some of the actors in the drama were still alive.

" No," he said, " the principal actors are dead. C. is dead, and Terence Bucknell is dead, and that's all that really matters. But you needn't publish it till you think fit. You needn't publish it for years. Not, if

you like, while you are alive, or as long as any one else
of that lot is alive.   As a matter of fact they are nearly
all of them dead now.   But you *must* write it.   C.'s
story must be told.   It must be put on record, and not
as a dry, lifeless biography with everything left out,
but as a living novel with everything put in, *everything ;* the story, in fact, of his life, which is just what
is generally left out in biographies.   I haven't told it.
I haven't attempted to tell it.   I couldn't.   I have
read too many novels to write one myself.   But I
should like it to be told as a novel.   A biography—one
of those stiff tombstone eulogies—would deaden it.
You can do it.   You are the only person who can do it.
You are the only person left alive who really knew
him."

I pointed out that he, Gerald, was C.'s greatest
friend, a far greater friend than I was.

"Yes," he said, "that is true.   I was a greater
friend, but when you knew him he *talked* to you, he
told you more than he told any one.   He knew me too
well to want to tell me things.   You knew him more
intimately than I did, although I was a nearer friend.
He often told me this himself."

"But surely," I said, "the interesting thing about
C.'s story is its truth, and to turn it into fiction would
be to falsify and to desecrate it."

"I don't want you to write an ordinary novel," he
said, "I want you to tell the story of C. as you saw it,
in the first person.   What you don't know you can fill
in from the papers I have left you.   You can, if you

like, say at the start you are doing that. In that way you will be able to tell all that there is to be told, all that we know. That will be enough. The main facts are enough. You will understand when you read my notes. I want you to begin quite straightforwardly to tell how you met him for the first time ; then life at Oxford and in London, and all that we knew and felt about him, and spare Leila nothing."

" I don't think I can do it," I said.

" I beg of you as a dying request to try," he said. " My ghost will haunt you unless you try. Do what you can. You must try."

I said I would try, as I saw that my resistance was making him worse. We were then interrupted by a visit from the doctor. I waited in the sitting-room while the doctor visited him.

Gerald's sitting-room was an epitome of his life. The room was most untidy. Over the chimney piece there was a large map of the city of Rome and a crucifix. On the chimney piece a small photograph of his wife as she had been when he first knew her, and a lot of pewter cups—school and college trophies of sprinting. On the single bookshelf which ran round the walls were books of all kinds : Dante, Plato, *Sherlock Holmes*, *Alice in Wonderland*, Theocritus, *Monte Cristo*, *Chess Strategy*, Herrick's poems, Boswell, Mommsen, Catullus, Gregorovius, *The House on the Marsh*, *The Mysteries of Paris*, Gibbon, *The Diary of a Nobody*, Ganot's *Physics*, *The Time Machine*, and Jules Verne, but no novels. On the table was a bottle of brandy and a half-smoked cigar in a tray full of ashes, and an almost finished, rather mouldy-looking tongue. On the open piano there was the score of the *Geisha*, which had been his wife's favourite opera. In the corner of the room there was a broken gramophone. The chintzless armchairs had many holes torn and burnt in them. The carpet was threadbare and covered with stains. There were no pictures on the walls except a large photogravure of a lady playing the organ near a stained glass window, which I imagined must have belonged to his wife. I waited till the doctor came out, so as to have a few words with him. The doctor told me he thought Gerald was very bad. I mustn't stay long—it was bad for him to talk. I asked if there was no one looking after him. The doctor said that Gerald appeared to have no relations alive, but there was a Mrs. Fitzclare, who was nursing him. She had become a nurse during the war, and had remained one ; she had left him a message saying she would be back immediately, and asking him to wait ; she was admirable. It was she who had sent for him some days previously. She had been with Malone all the day before and all night, and had only just gone out to fetch something, and he was expecting her now at any minute. I could stay till she arrived if I liked. The doctor looked into the bedroom and said that Gerald was dozing. He waited for about five minutes in the sitting-room ; then Mrs. Fitzclare arrived. I had known her for years, and I will anticipate nothing by saying anything about her now. I waited in a small ante-room while the doctor gave her a few instructions. He then left us. She told me that she thought Gerald was dying, and that she was not going to leave him. There would be another nurse coming in the evening for the night, but she would be here as well. Gerald had been born and baptised a Catholic, but during his life he had worried little about religion until latterly, but now he wanted to see a priest, and there was one coming presently.

"Gerald was very anxious to see you," she said; "it will be a great load off his mind now that he has seen you."

I then left his rooms with my parcel. Mrs. Fitzclare promised to let me know how he went on. That evening I got a telephone message from her saying that Gerald was a shade better, but there was no hope. He had seen the priest and had received the last Sacraments. She would ring me up in the morning. The next morning she telephoned to me that Gerald had died at four o'clock in the morning.

A requiem Mass was said for him at a church in Maiden Lane. Mrs. Fitzclare, myself and a Major Jackson, with whom he had served in the war, were the only people present. I asked Mrs. Fitzclare if I might call on her, as there were several things I wanted to ask her about Gerald, but she told me that she was just starting for France.

"I have another sick friend there," she said, "and I only delayed starting because of Gerald. We may meet later, but I am almost always abroad now." But we never have met again, as I lived in one continent and she in another.

I opened Gerald's parcel on the afternoon of the day he was buried. It was a large, untidy parcel, done up in an old map—Gerald was always passionately fond of maps—and tied up and sealed. I opened it while it was still daylight, and as I opened it a great quantity of papers of every size, shape and substance, came tumbling out. The papers were all unsorted and in an incredible state of confusion. They consisted of letters, envelopes, old programmes, signed menus, telegrams even, fragments of diaries, notes, some sketches of incidents in his childhood, descriptions of places, pencil sketches, some water-colours, interrupted fragments of narrative, hints for possible stories or poems, isolated sentences and dates. No chronology was observed, and no order, but separate items were sometimes conjecturally dated in pencil. There were letters from C., letters from Gerald, letters from other people, some faded photographs of people and places, some kodak films, photographs of college groups and places in England and abroad. I turned over one item after the other, reading a bit here and a bit there, and I suddenly realised that it had become dark. I had some tea, and read on and on till it was past dinner-time, and then, after the briefest of meals, I went on reading till far into the night.

As I read these faded papers a host of slumbering, long-forgotten memories crowded round me. Many little absurd incidents which I had not thought of for years rose up clearly before me, and I saw faces I had not thought of for years, and wandered once more in once familiar scenes, and heard voices and accents of friends and acquaintances some of whom were dead, others of whom were still alive somewhere, but lost sight of in the changes of life. I was hypnotised by this poignant melancholy peep-show. And through it all the figure of C., his face and his voice, kept coming back with startling vividness. A thousand aspects of him came to life once more, and as I sat brooding over all these dead scraps the story that was revealed, or half revealed, was, I thought, a strangely moving one.

It was one o'clock in the morning when I had finished the greater part of the papers, and as I sat thinking over all the story the most vivid of all these peeps into the past was the occasion of my meeting with C., an incident which he alluded to in one of the letters. It was purely by accident that I made C.'s acquaintance.

I had passed the necessary examination at school admitting me to the University, and to be a member of X—— College, but I had not been able to go up when the time came, owing to an attack of rheumatic fever. When the Michaelmas term came I decided that it would be waste of time to go up to the University. I spent the autumn till Christmas at a crammer's in London. The crammer, Mr. Spark, urged me to go up to Oxford in January, even if I only stayed there a year. He said that nothing made up for the loss of

University experience. I had then in my own mind decided not to take his advice. I spent Christmas with my family in Sussex, and when Christmas was over I accepted an invitation to stay with some friends of my family, Mr. and Mrs. Roden (this is not their real name). Mr. Roden was a retired business man. He was very well off, cultivated, and a patron of the arts. His wife was the sister of C.'s father. I did not know this at the time. I had not seen the Rodens since I was a child. I was surprised at receiving the invitation, but my parents said I must accept it, and assured me that I should enjoy myself. I remember starting full of scepticism as to their forecast. Gerald's papers brought back that visit now, which after so many years was completely blurred. I remembered as if it was yesterday the shyness and apprehension I felt as I drove from the station alone in a one-horse brougham, and I remembered that the coachman seemed to shut his eyes tight when he addressed you. It was the first time I had ever been to a country-house party. The house was modern, and I felt once more the impression of comfort you received directly you entered the front hall. I was often invited to the house subsequently, but I have quite forgotten the details of those many other visits. But as I looked at C.'s handwriting on paper stamped with " Elladon House, Southampton," I saw the large hall or gallery in which there was a bright wood fire burning, some oak pillars, and many modern pictures : Corot, Daubigny and Rossetti. At a large tea-table the family and guests were eating tea loudly and noisily; the cracker stage had been reached; some one was wearing a paper cap. Mrs. Roden walked up to me, bubbling with welcome. She was older than I remembered her to be. Her hair was white, and she wore a long, trailing, sage-green tea-gown and a white fichu. She was handsome and picturesque. Mr. Roden, with his bald, shiny head, his grey hair rather longer at the back than most people's, greeted me in his rather squeaky, piping voice.

I remember coming down to dinner in a frantic hurry, thinking I was late and finding myself the first, except for Mrs. Roden, a married niece of hers, and a grown-up boy who was standing by the fireplace looking down into the fire. He turned round and smiled at me, and said : " How do you do ? " and I suppose it was taken for granted that we knew each other already. In reality I had never seen him before, and I did not find out till the next day that he was a nephew of Mrs. Roden. This was C.

I wondered whether I ought to know who he was and whether I had seen him before. I felt convinced of the contrary, and yet I had the impression that I knew him already, and that I knew him quite well. There are some people like that. When you see them for the first time you feel that you have known them all your life.

I took into dinner a tall, dark girl, dressed in black, who was the daughter of a well-known painter, Sir Gabriel Carteret. She was studying painting, she said, and meant to devote her whole life to it. She would never marry ; she intended to give up her whole life to art. She was, I afterwards learnt, a girl of great talent. She drew and painted in a masterly way, and she had already exhibited some pictures which people said were superior to her father's. But, after an artistic career of three or four years, she fell in love with a Polish pianist, married him, and never painted another picture. She is still alive and, I believe, still extremely happy with her Polish pianist, who tours the world giving concerts from Brussels to Tokio and from Aberdeen to the Cape of Good Hope. C. sat on the other side of Miss Carteret, and I saw him now once more as I turned to my right-hand neighbour, trying to make conversation with the lady artist. He seemed to be not exactly shy, but at his wits' ends for something to say. I caught his eye once or twice, and it twinkled. I wondered then more whether I ought to know who he was, and whether I had possibly ever seen him before, and at the same time I knew I hadn't.

After dinner, when the move was made and the men were left to drink their port and smoke, I found myself next to C., and the first thing he said to me was : " I did admire the way you talked to that girl." He meant Miss Carteret. " I couldn't think of anything to say to her."

We then talked of other things. He told me he was at Oxford, and that he had gone up at Michaelmas, and had just finished his first term. I told him how I had been on the verge of going there myself ; how it had been put off, and what the crammer had said ; and how I had settled not to go. He swept all that aside and said I must, of course, come to Oxford, and I must come to X——, which was the jolliest college at Oxford, the only college, the best college.

Mr. Roden, who was inquisitive of the conversation of others, overheard this remark, and said to us :

" It is like all other colleges in that respect."

Then he went on with another conversation.

C. went on about Oxford. He poured out the advantages. He said I would regret it all my life if I didn't go there. I said I thought that I had missed my opportunity ; that I had dropped out of the running, and would no longer find myself with my contemporaries. I was afraid I had missed the right moment. C. said that was all nonsense. I *must* go up, and that was an end of it. Then some one on his other side claimed his attention, and another picture came before me : C. listening with courtesy and deference to an old man who was not, I think, very amusing. At the time it didn't strike me that his face, or that anything about him, was remarkable. All that I was conscious of then was that I seemed to know him, and that he seemed to know me, and that as far as I knew we had never met before. I certainly did not give his appearance a thought at the time. I merely wondered who he was.

A salmon-pink programme enclosed in C.'s letter to Gerald summoned up another picture before me. It was the programme of a village concert which we all went to one night. I heard once more the uncertain unison of the glee singers, and a village maiden who in a pianoforte solo seemed always on the point of reaching the top note of a difficult run and never attaining it ; a sailor singing a sentimental song of which the refrain was " For greed of gold," and the vicar, apprehensive of indelicacy, stopping his encore after the third verse ; the Rodens' butler singing " To-morrow will be Friday," and the chaos of the toy symphony at the end, with a cuckoo that cuckooed backwards.

It was at that concert that C. and I were introduced to some friends of theirs who were staying in the neighbourhood, whom I will call Lord. They were there with their daughter, and I sat next to Mrs. Lord at the concert, whose conversation was bewilderingly disconnected.

" Are you at Oxford or at Cambridge ? " she asked me, and when I said I hoped to go to Oxford she said it was so interesting to have been at both.

I only listened with half an ear to Mrs. Lord's rambling discourse. I thought all the time what an exceedingly beautiful creature her daughter was. She sat a little further up in the row, not far from C. She had corn-coloured hair, sky-blue eyes, a dazzling skin, and a celestial smile. Could that radiant creature really have been the same person as the Mrs. Fitzclare whom I had seen and talked to that very morning at Gerald's funeral ? Yes, the eyes were the same, and the smile was, if anything, more beautiful, but life had rubbed out all the radiance and joy with a hard piece of pumice-stone. Perhaps the sharpest of all the pictures these papers evoked was that of C. at that concert looking at Miss Lord. What a fresh look of undisguised, devout, complete, enthusiastic, unmixed admiration !

It was owing to that visit that I made C.'s acquaintance, and had I not met C. I should not have gone to Oxford. My parents thought it unwise, but Mr. Spark, the crammer, persuaded them it was the wiser course.

After living through all that early meeting once more, I could hardly bear to look at the papers again. I put them away and went to bed. The crowd of ghosts was too thick ; the ghosts were too real.

The next morning, in the sober light of day, I tackled the papers once more in a serious manner, and I began the business of sorting them. The work took me about a week. Then I was able to sum up my impressions and face the question of what was to be done with them.

The disconnected facts and dates and scraps of this disordered, rambling, chaotic record enabled me to focus what I knew already, and what I had guessed had taken place. I regretted that Gerald had not co-ordinated the papers himself ; that he had not himself tried to mould an organic whole out of the rich material. There was something in the matter, as it told itself fragmentarily, that I from the outside, with my comparatively cheap journalistic experience and stereotyped habit of writing, could not hope to achieve.

Nevertheless I felt bound to try and keep the promise I made to my dying friend.

The question arose, How was it to be done ? I agreed with Gerald that a biography was impossible if the story was to be told. I had no experience of novel-writing. On the other hand, I felt, after reading the papers, that it was not possible to do what Gerald suggested, namely, to tell the story from my point of view in the first person. If fiction it was to be, it must, I thought, be *direct* fiction based on the material that Gerald had provided for me. That material would be more or less the limit of my field of knowledge. I must work it out as best I could, inventing as little as possible.

I finally settled, after thinking it over, to try and tell the story in the shape of direct fiction. A novelist, when he does this, is, as far as his characters are concerned, omniscient. I am not. I am well aware that in this case my omniscience is limited to Gerald's papers, and yet, to make the story coherent, I shall have to try as far as possible to get into C.'s mind and tell his story from that point of view.

It is not possible to tell the whole story, because nobody knows it. C. on certain matters was the most reticent man in the world. He was one of those men who can tell the whole world, as some poet says, what he dared or would not tell to his dearest and nearest friends. He would have told—and I believe he did tell—the world through the medium of the written word ; but the record of what he told is, as far as we know, at present irretrievably lost, so that all we have now are the few and disjointed facts of a brief and troubled life : the stray jottings of one friend ; a few letters and the surmises of another friend, who is conscious of the uncertainty of his intuition and of his total inexperience in presenting fact in the guise of fiction.

I have, of course, changed all the names of persons and places ; even the names I have mentioned so far are fictitious, but I have tried to keep to the facts.

I may have omitted much that is vital. At least, I have invented no data of my own.

WALTER WRIGHT.

New York,
  July, 1922.

CONTENTS

VOL. I.

CONTENTS

CONTENTS

per te poeta fui.
                DANTE.

CHAPTER I

LORD AND LADY HENGRAVE had a house in London and a house in the country. The London house was in Portman Square, a gloomy building originally Adam in style, but entirely redecorated in the reign of William IV. Their house in the country, Bramsley, was in Easthamptonshire.

Lord Hengrave had started life by being a younger son, and had been sent into a cavalry regiment. He had spent some years in India, and while serving there his elder brother died. He was recalled home by the death of his second brother, and found himself the heir of a title, two houses and a considerable amount of property. He was at that time thirty years old. He married, the same year he arrived in England, the fourth daughter of a retired admiral, who came from an old Suffolk stock. He had been extremely hard up all his life, and the allowance that he drew and his pay were just enough to enable him to live in the army. The result was, he was heavily in debt. The debts were paid, but no sooner was he married than fresh debts began to accumulate. He was a gambler by nature, and he played cards for high stakes, but, although he was fond of racing, he never betted on the turf. He had an invincible prejudice against the turf as a business, and maintained that it was not a thing a gentleman could do with clean hands.

He was a staunch Tory, but cared little for politics, and never held any public appointment, with the exception of the Lord-Lieutenancy of the county and for a brief period a minor Court appointment. He was a kind husband, unfaithful with discretion and decorum, and he never let his affections interfere with the even tenor of his life. He was fond of country life and of fox-hunting, fonder still of yachting, and at one time possessed a racing cutter, which he was soon obliged to sell.

During his early married life he spent money quickly and carelessly. He entertained; he yachted; he gambled; he bought; he built. He was fairly culti-vated, and fond of old pictures and prints. He liked claret and port, and soon became a martyr to gout, which he treated by drinking more port and cursing the doctors. In his youth he had been extremely good-looking, and he maintained a look of great youth through his middle age and beyond.

There soon came a time, as his family increased, when he realised that he was up to his neck in debt. He mortgaged his property, sold some pictures and some furniture, and gave up yachting. Henceforward his life was a perpetual compromise between excessive expenditure and makeshift arrangements for meeting it. He never ceased to be in debt, and nobody under-stood how the Hengraves managed to make both ends meet. The simple solution was that they didn't.

He gave up gambling, and from time to time, in moments of extreme stress, he sold something. This would have been a satisfactory solution if he had not at the same time increased his expenditure by buying something else.

He was always immaculately dressed, and his clothes looked as if they had grown on him. Lady Hengrave was at home to luncheon every day, even in the days when the financial situation was at its worst, and the food there was always better than that at the houses of other people. Lord Hengrave went to the Derby every year, and to the Omnibus Box at Covent Garden. He rode in Rotten Row in the evening. He always wore a white flower in his buttonhole, and his pocket-handkerchiefs were undemonstratively exquisite.

Lady Hengrave faced the uneasy conditions of her married life with calm and determination. She was well aware of her husband's infidelities and ignored them. She accepted his gambling propensities and his extravagance as she accepted the march of the seasons, and she devoted herself to the task of driving the rickety coach of the family fortunes as safely as possible under the conditions. In her youth she had been greatly admired. She was not tall, but beautifully proportioned; she had a fair, dazzlingly white skin, pale blue eyes, fair hair parted in the middle, determined lines of decision round the mouth and chin, and beautiful sloping shoulders. She was an ideal Winterhalter. As a girl she had been a prominent figure in London, and no party had been thought complete without her. It was expected that she would make an ambitious marriage and become a leader in the political world. Her marriage, which on the face of it, at the time it occurred, was a good one, was thought disappointing. She had been strictly brought up by a violent-tempered father and a Continentally educated mother, who had instilled into her an undying respect for the classics in politics, literature, art and music. Lady Hengrave had no talents ; she was neither literary nor artistic, but consciously or unconsciously she handed down to her children the traditions of culture and the respect for the classics in all the arts which she had absorbed in her youth. She was sensible and practical, and accepted life with a shrewd, calm philosophy. She was undemonstrative, and with the exception of Gilbert, a " ne'er-do-weel," and Harry, the youngest boy, was not particularly fond of her children. She disliked children in general, and she had been born grown up. She had certain rigid and inflexible standards which concerned small as well as large matters. Certain things could be done, indeed, must be done, certain opinions accepted, and certain books could be read ; others could not. When in talking of two people being engaged to be married she would say that " there was no money," one felt the couple in question had somehow been extinguished. When she would talk of some one being poor, but having pretty daughters, one felt that the daughters were being appraised at their exact market value. If she talked of the books from the circulating library, they were divided into three categories : those which were pretty, well written, and disagreeable. The first two categories were read, must be read ; those which belonged to the third category were not to be mentioned. And yet in all this there was nothing snobbish or hypocritical, as people who were used to a different layer and a more liberal atmosphere might have thought, and sometimes did think. It was the result of a certain definite, rigid way of looking at things, which was the direct offspring of the eighteenth century, with its worldly wisdom, its sceptical acceptance of the realities of life and the nature of society, and its horror of enthusiasm.

She had a marvellous memory for the genealogies of all the people she knew, and could trace the correlatives of any family of her acquaintance ; she always knew who anybody, who had a legitimate claim to her acquaintance, " had been " before her marriage. Here again there was food for misunderstanding, and those who should think of her as one of Thackeray's snobs, poring over the peerage, would be wrong indeed. Lady Hengrave divided people into those you knew and those you didn't know. The genealogies of those she knew were as familiar to her as the multiplication table. She no more bothered about the rest than she did about the Esquimaux.

The Hengraves had a family of six children. The eldest, Edward, was sent to Eton and Cambridge, whence he passed through the militia into the Brigade of Guards. After one of the financial crises which periodically occurred in the Hengrave family, he left the army and obtained a billet in the City, in which he gave satisfaction. He married an American wife, who, although far from being a millionairess, was well enough off, so the problem of Edward's subsistence was satisfactorily settled.

Very different was the fate of the second son, Gilbert, who was said to be Lady Hengrave's favourite child. He was an attractive, sharp boy, and his parents destined him for the diplomatic service. He passed his examination, but unfortunately he had inherited all his father's gambling propensities, and none of his father's rigid principle in such matters. There was a scandal : he was accused—falsely, some said— of cheating at cards ; but although it was doubtful whether he had cheated, it was certain that he had lost over ten thousand pounds, which necessitated the sale of the Bramsley Gobelins. He quarrelled with his father, left for Canada and started life on a ranch. His father and mother never set eyes on him again.

Next to Gilbert came two girls—Julia and Marjorie— and after them came Caryl, who from his earliest years was called C. A younger son, Harry, was born two years after Caryl.

After the third of the financial crises which afflicted the family, the Hengraves lived perhaps a little longer in the country, but their London house was never let, and they always spent some months in London, even before the girls came out. The girls, although quite nice-looking and exceedingly well dressed and neat, had no real beauty, whereas the boys were all of them, in different ways, remarkable for their looks.

The two eldest children were brought up by a series of French and German governesses, none of whom stayed long, as they found the naughtiness of the children to be unendurable, and they all of them prognosticated a sad future for Gilbert. Their souls proved only too prophetic. When the two elder boys went to school, Lady Hengrave abandoned for a time the idea of foreign tuition, and engaged an English governess to live permanently in the house, in whom she thought that at last she had found a treasure, relying on outside classes for their French and German. But the treasure, Miss Meredith, left the family, for reasons of her own, after she had been with them for a year, much to Lady Hengrave's annoyance. She was succeeded at first by an Alsatian, Mademoiselle Walter, who was intelligent and violent-tempered, and combined French logic and German discipline.

The Hengraves always spent Christmas at Bramsley. They would go up to London at the beginning of February and stay there till Easter. For Easter they would go back to Bramsley and after Easter come back to London and stay there till the middle of July, and they would perhaps go down to Bramsley for Whitsuntide. From July onwards they remained at Bramsley, sometimes paying a fleeting visit to London in the month of November.

CHAPTER II

C.'s earliest recollections were centered round the nursery in Portman Square, which was presided over by a brisk and rather sharp-tongued Nanny called Mrs. Brimstone, whom the children called Brinnie. With the help of two nursery-maids, Jessie and Eliza, she ruled over the nursery and the washing and dressing of C. and Harry. Brinnie shared Lady Hengrave's preference for Harry, but in reality she cared nothing for the younger children compared with what she had felt for the elder boys, especially for Master Gilbert. She was fond of Harry because he was the youngest and the last baby she had had charge of. She was old, and her temper was worn out. C., she considered, as did the rest of the household, to be an irreclaimable young ruffian, and if ever Harry was naughty she said that it was Master C. who had led him into mischief.

C. learnt to read in the nursery when he was six, and at the age of seven he was soon promoted to lessons in the schoolroom, but he continued to be taken for the morning walk in the park, or to play in the square with Brinnie and Harry after the promotion had taken place.

C. used to look forward to his birthday throughout

8

the year. It was the only day in the year on which he seemed to play a part of any importance in the family. Lady Hengrave recognised birthdays and encouraged the celebration of each of her children's birthdays with undemonstrative impartiality. There was a birthday cake at the schoolroom tea, with candles on it, and generally his aunt, Mrs. Roden, who was also his god-mother, would come to luncheon and bring him a present. C.'s eighth birthday, which occurred in March, when the family were in London, began auspiciously. He was given some toys in the morning, and a new shilling by his father. He was allowed a holiday in the schoolroom, and all went well till luncheon-time. Just before luncheon Brinnie and Jessie scrubbed Master C. and Master Harry with extra vigour, and extra time was spent in curling Master C.'s curls with a tail comb and in sprinkling them with rose-water, and Brinnie was more than usually caustic in her comments on those curls, which were always refractory, and more than usually gloomy in her forebodings as to the immediate fate of the clean starched pinafore that she tied round him. She hoped, to be sure, he would be good, as his aunt, and his godmother into the bargain, Mrs. Roden, was coming to luncheon. Her ladyship had sent up word to say so. C.'s heart leapt when he heard this news, as this would be sure to mean a present. Brinnie had no fear of Master Harry behaving badly : he was always good, " and it is a pity," said Brinnie to Harry, " that she isn't your godmother instead of Master C.'s. Master C. doesn't really deserve a godmother, what with his naughtiness and his leading others into mischief who are too young to know any better."

Brinnie ignored the fact that Harry had a godmother of his own.

Punctually at two o'clock a loud bell rang through the house up the reverberating back staircase, and C. and Harry, under a volley of final exhortations, ran downstairs, joining up on their way with their two sisters, Julia and Marjorie, who came down from the upper floor in charge of Mademoiselle.

The children trooped down to what was called the blue room, on the ground floor, and which was next to the dining-room. It was a comfortable room, full of prints, and their father used it as a smoking-room and study, but it was there guests were received before going into the dining-room.

Lord Hengrave was out to luncheon. He only had luncheon at home on certain days of the week, and this was not one of them. Lady Hengrave was standing up in front of the fireplace talking to Mr. Dartrey, who always came to luncheon twice a week. He was an M.P. and the director of a railway company, and the children thought him inexpressibly dreary, especially as, being friendly and well disposed towards them, yet at the same time completely removed from the world of childhood, he thought it necessary to make conversation with them. C. was always scolded after his visits for having been rude to Mr. Dartrey.

Lady Hengrave shot an enveloping glance at the

children and at Mademoiselle as they came into the
room, and asked in French after the lessons.

"*On a été suffisament sage*," Mademoiselle said
laconically. She was not the least afraid of Lady
Hengrave, as so many other people were. The girls
were frightened of her, and she maltreated them and
made them, obstinate as they were, learn their lessons
and speak French. She preferred the boys to the girls,
and she thought C. showed promise of intelligence.
This made her none the less severe. She rapped the
children's knuckles with a ruler till they were sore, but
neither the girls nor C. ever complained to their
parents. They had already had a long and eventful
experience of different governesses—French, German,
Swiss and English—and they knew now that their
present lot might be exchanged for a worse one.

Harry alone of the family was well treated by
Mademoiselle, but he did not return her affection, and
he bitterly resented her treatment of his elder brother.

Lady Hengrave asked whether C. had been behaving
properly.

"*Il perd son temps, comme toujours; il pourrait
travailler très bien s'il voulait*," said Mademoiselle.

Lady Hengrave gave an almost inaudible sigh. Mr.
Dartrey tactfully changed the conversation by saying
that the trains on the line of which he was a director
reached a greater pitch of perfection in punctuality
every day.

At that moment Mrs. Roden was announced.

Mrs. Roden was Lord Hengrave's sister. She had

married a partner of a large City firm, who was
extremely well off and fond of modern pictures. Mrs.
Roden was fond of artists, and this was a characteristic that Lady Hengrave deplored. Mrs. Roden was
a handsome, picturesque woman, who had been
painted by several of the most famous painters of the
day. She was amiable to the extent of being gushing.
C. preferred her to all his relations. Lady Hengrave
never took any of the children with her when she
stayed with her sister-in-law, as she feared the effect
on them of what she considered to be a Bohemian
atmosphere.

Mrs. Roden swept into the room, pouring out
apologies for being late. She kissed C. and gave him
her present, large wooden nut-crackers. The two
crackers as they shut formed a black nigger's head,
and as you shut them small white teeth opened and
shut, and the empty sockets revealed two gleaming
eyes.

"Thank your aunt Rachel," Lady Hengrave said
to C., and, addressing the company in general, "He's
had too many presents already."

Just before they went into luncheon another guest
was announced. This was Lady Hengrave's brother,
Captain Farringford, whom the children knew as
Uncle William. He was a sailor.

They went into luncheon, and, as usual, the
children's physical characteristics were discussed as if
they had not been there.

"Harry grows more and more like Charles every

day," said Mrs. Roden. Charles was Lord Hengrave. " He's grown so much ; so have the girls."

" Do you see a look of Aunt Jessica in Julia ? " Lady Hengrave asked.

Aunt Jessica was a great-aunt of the children. Mrs. Roden, after a careful scrutiny of Julia's face, said, yes, she could just detect in it a distinct look of Aunt Jessica. Julia blushed. But as it was C.'s birthday, he became, for the time, the centre of the conversation.

" What are you going to be when you grow up ? " Mr. Dartrey asked him point-blank.

C. blushed scarlet and was about to stammer something when his uncle William, who was loud-voiced, breezy and boisterous, answered for him. " He's going to be a sailor, of course ; and that's why I've brought him this knife." And he produced from his pocket a large clasp-knife, which he said he would give to C. after luncheon.

" Would you like to be a sailor ? " asked his god-mother.

Lady Hengrave answered for him. " We have settled," she said, " to send him into the Navy if he can pass into the *Britannia*."

C. was conscious that he had no voice in the matter of the choice of his profession.

" The examinations are so difficult now," said Mrs. Roden.

" Yes, very difficult," said Lady Hengrave, shutting her eyes as if to rid herself of such a disagreeable vision.

And thus it was that C.'s career was settled for the time being. Apart from wearing a sailor's suit and from having been violently sick on a penny steamer, he had not yet shown signs of any particular vocation for the sea.

C.'s birthday, for a birthday, passed off fairly calmly. The children did not break all his toys, and Mademoiselle quelled one or two incipient quarrels between C. and his sisters.

As C. was eight years old, Lady Hengrave had settled that he was no longer to sleep in the night nursery with Harry, but in a little room by himself on the floor above. As he was to go to school next year, it was time, she said, that he should get used to sleeping by himself.

C. was a nervous child, afraid of the dark, and prone to nightmare. He often talked, and sometimes walked, in his sleep, but Brinnie would not admit this, and Lady Hengrave was told nothing about it. Nor, if she had been told, would she have understood. She did not like C., and she did not understand him.

The chief excitement of C.'s birthday had been Mrs. Roden's present. It was the most exciting present that any of the children had ever yet received, even from Mrs. Roden, who was famous in the schoolroom and the nursery for the unexpectedness and the glamour of her presents. The girls were, of course, agreed that C. was too young for such a present, and that he would break it before it had lasted a day, and they were well in the way of breaking it themselves when C. snatched it from them and rushed upstairs with it to his room.

Tea went off quietly; the birthday cake was satisfactory, and all went well till bedtime came, and for the first time C. was to sleep by himself in his lonely little bedroom.

Eliza, the nursery-maid, undressed him and put him to bed, and then he was left alone. A night-light was burning on the washing-stand.

C. was still excited after the events of his birthday, and he did not feel sleepy. The incidents of the day began to flit before him, like pictures on the slide of a magic lantern, slightly distorted as they are apt to be when the brain is on its way to sleep. He thought about his uncle and the clasp-knife, and whether he would ever be a sailor, and whether he wanted to be one. He was not at all sure he had any such wish. Then everything else was blotted out by the sudden thought of his godmother and of her startling present, the nigger nut-crackers. They were in the room now, in the corner of the room near the washing-stand, where he had hidden them from his sisters.

But instead of being pleasantly thrilling as they had been all day, and an object of delightful interest, the nut-crackers now seemed to be a very different thing. First of all, they had become much larger; he knew this without looking at them, for he dared not look even in the direction where they were hidden. Also, the nigger's head was alive, the eyes had returned to the sockets without any one touching the crackers, and the jaws were opening and shutting, and showing their gleaming teeth. He hid his head under the bed-clothes and prayed for the vision to depart, but it did not depart ; it became more and more portentous. He thought the nigger was now walking across the room, and now bending over his bed. The nigger's head had become enormous. His eyes were glowing like live coals. C. shook with terror. How could he escape from this awful thing ? At last he made a great effort and crept out of bed, and ran blindly to the door, which had been left ajar. What was he to do next ? He dared not go to the nursery, where Brinnie and the nursery-maids were having their supper, as he knew Brinnie would be extremely cross and pack him off to bed again. Downstairs there was company. The children had watched the guests arriving through the banisters of the staircase. He knew vaguely it was about nursery supper-time, between nine and half-past. He decided to try the housekeeper's room, and he ran right down the stone back staircase to the basement, to the housekeeper's room, where he found Mrs. Oldfield, the housekeeper, a stately figure in large swishing skirts, having supper with the upper servants. There, too, was Miss Hackett, Lady Hengrave's maid, who was a friend of C.'s. Brinnie was jealous of Miss Hackett and detested Mrs. Oldfield, so C. felt a fearful joy at being safe in the enemy's camp.

"Well, I never !" said Miss Hackett. "Whatever is the little boy going to do next ?"

Miss Hackett took him on her lap ; Mrs. Oldfield gave him a sponge cake, some white grapes, and said :

" A glass of ginger wine will do the child no harm. His feet and hands are as cold as ice."

" And to run all that way without his dressing-gown and slippers ! Whatever will Mrs. Brimstone say ? " said Miss Hackett.

" Don't tell Brinnie," said C. " Please, Hacky, don't tell her."

Miss Hackett promised not to tell ; she saw that he had been frightened by something, and it was settled that she had better take him upstairs again before his flight should be discovered. She took him upstairs, and when she had put him to bed C. confided to her the cause of his fears : the nut-crackers ; the nigger's head. She took the nut-crackers away and put them in her own room. She then went back and stayed by his bed till he fell asleep, which he soon did, as he was very tired.

Nothing was discovered, but the next night the same thing happened again. C. was put to bed and fell asleep almost immediately. He was then visited by a nightmare in which the black head played a large part, and before he was awake he was half-way down-stairs. He was again welcomed in the housekeeper's room and received comfort and refreshment, and he was again taken back to bed by Miss Hackett. C now made a regular practice of visiting the house-keeper's room at night, although he was not conscious of wishing to do so, or even of starting to do so. He

was urged on by the vision of the nigger's head,
although he had not set eyes on the nut-crackers for
some days. One night Eliza met him on the staircase
as he was returning from one of his expeditions, and
the secret was out. A battle royal ensued between
Miss Hackett and Mrs. Brimstone.

" The poor child is frightened out of his wits by that
nigger's head," said Miss Hackett.

" Nigger's head and fiddlesticks ! " said Mrs.
Brimstone. " I shall go straight to her ladyship." And
straight to her ladyship she went.

Lady Hengrave was annoyed, and said gravely that
if ever C. was to run downstairs again he would be
whipped. Nobody, not even Miss Hackett, realised
that when he started on these expeditions he was still
asleep and did not know what he was doing, nor that
he was being urged by the spurs of a nightmare. In
spite of all Lady Hengrave said, and of an icy threat
from Mademoiselle, C. did the very same thing the
next night. Fortunately, Mrs. Brimstone was out.
Miss Hackett took him back to bed and soothed him
(he was in a flood of tears), and, what is more, promised
to destroy the nut-crackers. The nigger's head was
destroyed the next day, and its destruction seemed to
break the spell, for after this his nightmares took a less
active form, although he still suffered from one recur-
rent dream. He dreamt he was alone on the deck of a
derelict vessel which was buffeting the waves without
progress in a blanket of mist. He was aware of a
waste of bleak, desolate and moaning waters, and

somewhere in the thick salt mist a fog-horn was sounding dolefully. He could taste the salt in the air and feel the sting of the fog, and what sounded like a fog-horn was really the cry of some one or something in gigantic pain. Yet he had only rarely seen the sea. He had once been taken to Ryde, and he had spent a week with Mademoiselle and the girls at Broadstairs to recover from the chickenpox.

CHAPTER III

THE life of the children at Hengrave House and at
Bramsley was conducted rigidly according to plan
both during the half-year that was spent at Bramsley and that which was spent in London. The
children saw little of their parents. The two boys
were brought down to say good-morning after breakfast in the nursery, or later in the schoolroom, a
meal which was ready punctually at eight, and all
the family met at luncheon. The rest of the time
was spent by the children in the nursery or the
schoolroom.

C. joined the schoolroom soon after his sixth birthday, and became a minor, obstinate and rebellious
satellite in the system of lessons which revolved immediately round the severe and arid moon of Mademoiselle, but which was none the less under the perpetual
influence of a remote but effective sun, namely, Lady
Hengrave. For although the children seldom went
downstairs, Lady Hengrave frequently visited the
schoolroom, and she kept a sharp eye on the course of
her children's lessons. She herself drew up the scheme
of lesson hours and of the subjects and books to be
studied, and she insisted on the children learning
passages of Shakespeare, Schiller, and La Fontaine by

heart, which they were sometimes made to recite
before people.

C., although fond of story-books and fairy tales,
detested these incursions into literature. He learnt
the passages like a parrot and had no idea what the
words meant, nor any idea that they could by any
stretch of imagination be poetry.

He pretended to learn them with much greater difficulty than was really the case, as his memory was in
reality quite remarkably good. German and French
he detested still more, and allowed as little as possible
of either tongue to penetrate into his mind. Nevertheless by the time he went to school he knew a great
many speeches from Shakespeare's historical plays by
heart, and a great many of La Fontaine's fables,
besides passages from Pope and Dryden, all of which
were far too advanced for him to understand.

The routine of lessons was the same for the children
in London and in the country, and lessons, save for the
interruption of a walk, took up all the morning, an
hour in the evening before tea, and a certain amount
of time for "preparation" after tea.

Towards the end of July the nursery and schoolroom passages were obstructed by large shiny leather
boxes, which meant that the family were going to
move down to the country. "We're going to Bramsley," the children would shout in the passages and
down the staircase.

Bramsley Hall was in Easthamptonshire, only a
little over an hour's journey from London. It was

situated in rather a bleak stretch of country, and the west front of the house looked out on the high-road to London. The nursery looked out on this road, and on Sundays C. used to watch from the nursery windows the high velocipedes whizz by; and sometimes a regiment of red-coated soldiers would march past to the music of drums and fifes and "*The Girl I left behind Me.*" There was a "park" which had once boasted of fine trees and deer, but the finest timber had been cut down, and all that was left of the park was a walled-in approach. The garden was still stately, and the house had a shabby dignity of its own. It was an old house, but had been made more modern at three different epochs. The prevailing style was Early Victorian, although there were still scattered traces and solid remains of many periods, Caroline, Queen Anne and Georgian, and it had escaped the vandalism of restoration.

The move to Bramsley was an event which would have been hailed with excitement by the children, and especially by C., who greatly preferred the country to London, if life at Bramsley had not been marred by several permanent drawbacks. In the first place, there was Mademoiselle, and Mademoiselle and lessons in general were far more irksome in the country than in London; in the second place, there was a neigh-bouring family, the Calhouns, which played an important part in their lives; and in the third place, there were the uncles and aunts who stayed in the house for long periods at a time. Lessons at Brams-

ley seemed to C. in the summer an almost unbearable
tyranny.

It was hard to pore over problems in arithmetic,
to learn by heart the fable of *Les Animaux
Malades de la Peste*, to grapple with rules of French
past participles, while outside at that very moment
there was a bird in the raspberry nets waiting to
be caught ; minnows waiting to be fished in the
stream which ran through the kitchen garden ;
peaches hanging ripe on the sunburnt wall, waiting
to be stolen ; while the breeze, through the open
windows, brought with it sights and sounds from
the world which was at present forbidden and shut
from view even by the red and yellow Venetian
blinds : the rhythmical music of the mowing machine,
and the smell of the warm flowers on the terrace, and
the cries of Harry, who was not yet a thrall to the full
discipline of the schoolroom, as he raced down the
lawn. It was in moments like these that C. hated
lessons with a bitter fury. He saw no possible
redeeming feature in them anywhere, and as he pored
over the speech in *Absalom and Ahitophel*, which he
was learning by heart, he wished that all authors, and
especially the French and British poets, were at the
bottom of the sea.

Mademoiselle Walter was intelligent enough to know
that C.'s education was being conducted on radically
mistaken lines. The English governess who had preceded her, Miss Meredith, had likewise understood
C.'s mentality far better than Lady Hengrave did and

had alleviated the aridity of his classical education by letting him have a whiff of Longfellow and a *soupçon* of Southey. But then Miss Meredith had left just when she might have been a friend for C.

Mademoiselle Walter divined in C. a possible future love of literature, and cleverly allowed him to read the lyrics of Victor Hugo, which he delighted in, in secret. But such was his dislike for Mademoiselle that he never admitted he learnt these poems by heart for his own pleasure. On the contrary, he pretended that he hated them, and he never lost an opportunity before Mademoiselle of decrying the French; only since she was Alsatian, and in order to make quite sure of offending her, he decried the Germans as well. There was only one ecstatic moment in schoolroom life at Bramsley, and that was when Mademoiselle Walter went for her holidays; this happened sometimes in the month of August and sometimes in the month of September. The second cross of the children's life at Bramsley were their neighbours, the Calhouns, a family who lived ten miles off, and consisted of a retired soldier, an energetic wife, three daughters, who were the bosom friends of Julia and Marjorie, and two boys, Albert and Freddy, one of whom was older than C. and the other the same age. They were his playfellows, and were always held up to him as an example of what boys should be. They did their lessons well; they were said to be, and what is more, they *were*, extremely intelligent; they rode well and they played cricket well. It was this last fact which was destined to mar two of the principal pleasures of C.'s life at Bramsley, namely, hunting and cricket.

C. had been taught how to play cricket by Mr. Hatch, the under-butler, and in company with James, the footman, Alec, the groom, and Teddy, the gardener's son, and every now and then a few further recruits from the servants' hall, the stables, and the garden, C. used to enjoy ecstatic games of cricket in the summer evenings with a single wicket on the roughest of pitches, a patch of ground near the stables.

C. was for some time successful in keeping these games dark from Mademoiselle and the drawing-room. Experience had taught him that it was wiser never to mention a treat. If one did, the chances were that for some unaccountable reason it was forthwith forbidden. This had happened so often to C. that he had become prudent and cunning in the concealment of his secret treats, hiding them behind plausible substitutes.

Mrs. Calhoun had sometimes suggested that C. should go over and play cricket with their boys, but to C.'s infinite relief the distance made it inconvenient, and Albert Calhoun, who was at school, did not press his mother to invite a raw novice. So somehow or other it was taken for granted that C. did not play cricket.

Unfortunately, one evening Colonel Calhoun, riding back from a visit in the neighbourhood, happened to ride down the secluded lane which fringed the improvised cricket ground where C. was playing. Colonel Calhoun was an enthusiastic cricketer, full of theory, not only as to how the game should be played, but also as to how it should be taught.   He watched the game with equanimity for some time, but at last he could bear it no longer, and he shouted to C., who was batting :—

"Play forward, play forward, you're not playing with a straight bat."

He then cantered to the house and asked to see Lord Hengrave.   Lord Hengrave was in the garden. The Colonel left his cob in charge of the footman and sought Lord Hengrave, who was busily engaged in pulling the bindweed out of the phlox on his terrace border.   After mutual salutations were exchanged, Colonel Calhoun went straight to the point.

"I have just seen your boy playing cricket near the stables.   They're teaching him to play very badly. He's not playing with a straight bat.   They'll ruin the boy's style.   Nothing is so important as to be taught right at the beginning."

"Ah, yes," said Lord Hengrave thoughtfully, as he espied another piece of bindweed.   "Of course, the boy's small," he added.

"He's not too small to learn," said the Colonel. "Now I have a professional over from Carbury twice a week to teach my boys."

At this moment Lady Hengrave appeared on the scene, and Colonel Calhoun began again at the beginning.

"Can't the boys come over," he suggested, "on the days that the professional comes to us ? "

" Harry is too small," said Lady Hengrave, " and C. doesn't care for cricket."

" But," said the Colonel, " I have just seen him playing." And he told the story all over again, dwelling on the faults of style that were being implanted in him, and how he was not playing with a straight bat. " It's better," he said, " not to be taught at all than to be taught badly."

" I'll see that he learns properly," said Lady Hengrave.

She determined at that moment that, if cricket was played, she would put the game on a proper basis.

Colonel Calhoun, after declining to stay for dinner, went away feeling that his words of wisdom had not been spoken in vain. Colonel Calhoun's visit was the seed of a large organisation, namely, the Bramsley Hall Cricket Club, and end of C.'s fun as a cricketer.

Lady Hengrave interviewed Oldham, the gardener, and Wilkes, the coachman, who were both of them enthusiastic cricketers, and the result was that a field was made into a cricket ground. The village schoolmaster became the honorary secretary of the Bramsley Cricket Club, and the professional who visited the Calhouns came over to Bramsley once a week and bowled to C. at the nets, and insisted on his playing forward and with a straight bat, and Colonel Calhoun rode over every now and then to see how he was getting on. C. was given some small cricket pads and small cricket gloves, and made to score during the matches on Saturday afternoon, and taught how to keep the bowling analysis. Bramsley was soon able to challenge Frimpton, where the Calhouns lived, and Albert and Freddy Calhoun came over and played. Theirs was always the winning side.

As for C., he imbibed a hatred for the game which lasted for the rest of his life, and the only incident of all the cricket matches which subsequently occurred with regularity at Bramsley and Frimpton which he recalled with any pleasure was one occasion when Freddy Calhoun's front tooth was knocked clean out of his mouth by a swift ball. That was exciting enough in itself, but it was nothing to what happened immediately afterwards. The tooth was lost on the cricket pitch, and Mrs. Calhoun advanced swiftly from among the public, searched for and found the tooth, and replaced it in its socket with dexterity and firmness, where it solidified, grew, and remained firm and sound. This seemed to C. miraculous.

During the summer there were no guests at Bramsley but with the autumn a few relations and old friends arrived for the hunting season and for such shooting as Lord Hengrave was able to offer, but never many at a time until Christmas. The children called this the uncle-and-aunt season, and they all of them disliked and feared it.

There was Aunt Harriet, a widow of a brother of Lady Hengrave's, a formidable old lady in a peaked cap, who was a rigid churchwoman on the Low side, and who invariably asked C. whether he had learnt last Sunday's collect. Learning the collect and the

Catechism was one of the Sunday duties of the children, and C. learnt the collects with ease, and till the end of his life could repeat them all word-perfect; but when his Aunt Harriet was present he could not bring the first word of any one of them across his lips.

At Christmas there was always a family gathering, consisting of such uncles and aunts as were in England and free. The Rodens never came. They had Christmas gatherings of their own. But Uncle George, a younger brother of Lord Hengrave's—a grey-haired, grumpy, very upright old gentleman—always arrived punctually on the 20th of December. He took the opposite line to the rest of his family on every topic under the sun. Because his elder brother was a Tory, he was a Whig, and if he went out walking with his younger brother, Harold, who was a clergyman, he spat if they chanced to meet a bishop.

Uncle William, the sailor, came if he was in England, but he was generally in some far-off station.

Far more formidable than the uncles were the aunts. Lady Hengrave had two sisters older and one younger than herself. The eldest sister, Aunt Louisa, had been the beauty of the family. She had been radiantly fair and elegant in her youth, and she maintained her elegance when she grew older by natural, and the fairness of her complexion and the glitter of her hair by artificial means. She had made a runaway match with a younger son, who, on marrying her, had left the Army for the Stock Exchange. They had a small house in Stratford Place, and they had difficulty in making both ends meet, which they achieved by living largely on their relations and friends.

The second sister, Aunt Fanny, married Cuthbert Transome, a Fellow of All Souls, who wrote history and contributed to the *Nineteenth Century*. They had a large house in St. John's Wood. Aunt Fanny was extremely cultivated and well read, but her taste was forbiddingly austere. She read German philosophy and gave musical afternoons at her house every now and then, where only the severest classical music was tolerated. C. was sometimes taken to these entertainments by his mother, and had to sit through quintets and trios in which not a repeat was spared. He suffered acutely. Aunt Fanny and Uncle Cuthbert spent Christmas at Bramsley regularly.

As Uncle Cuthbert was an atheist, neither he nor Aunt Fanny went to church, even on Christmas Day, and Lady Hengrave used to explain this to the children by saying that the church was draughty, and Uncle Cuthbert had a weak chest; but the children were not taken in, nor would they have been, even if Mrs. Oldham, the housekeeper, had not carefully explained to C. that there was no fear of Aunt Fanny and Uncle Cuthbert not going to hell for their unbelief.

Lady Hengrave's third sister had married a diplomat and lived almost always abroad. She seldom came to Bramsley and never at Christmas time. C. detested all his aunts equally and cordially. He did not know which he detested most, Aunt Louisa, who found fault with his seat on horseback and the cut of his clothes,

Aunt Fanny, who asked him questions in geography and the dates of the Roman Emperors, a list of which she said was always on her dressing-table, or Aunt Emma, who on her comparatively rare appearances at Portman Square, criticised his French accent and found fault with his manners.

C. and the girls were taught to ride when they were quite small, and were soon allowed to go out hunting. They all inherited their father's horsemanship. C. rode well and easily, but here again the Calhoun family intervened and turned this pleasure to bitterness. It was always being pointed out to him that the Calhoun boys rode so much better than he did, which was true, and every time he went out hunting he had to face a fire of hostile criticism from Colonel and Lady Calhoun. Mrs. Calhoun hunted herself, and never a meet passed at which she did not criticise C.'s deportment on horseback. Lord Hengrave, too, was a formidable critic, whether on horseback, or, if his gout was too bad, in a carriage, and sometimes he would shout at C. at the top of his voice. C. did not mind this, but what he did mind was the expression of unconcern on the faces of the two Calhoun boys, while the criticisms were being made in public. C. knew that they were greedily drinking in every word.

CHAPTER IV

WHEN C. attained his eighth birthday his child-hood had become crystallised, and the main facts of it were these.

He was frightened of his father and never knew what to say to him. He did not get on with his mother, who did not like him and did not understand him. He was a nervous child, frightened of intangible things, and reckless and over-bold in the daylight.

Prematurely intelligent in some ways, but in great need of direction, and since he received just the very guidance that was ill-suited to him, he became rebellious and sullen.

He was an outcast in the nursery, and a rebel in the schoolroom. In none of the governesses who looked after him did he find a friend or a companion, and his relations with his two sisters were perpetually strained, and often violently explosive. His sister Julia was four years and his sister Marjorie two years older than he was. Julia was a model of convention and pro-priety, but she was capable of great naughtiness. She was small, she had tight thin features, a clear complexion and flaxen hair. Marjorie was larger and darker, and had fine grey eyes. She was completely self-possessed and brimful of assurance. In reality she was just as conventional as her sister, but she had wilder spirits. She was musical and had a natural sense of rhythm. The two sisters spent all their time quarrelling, and sometimes they beat each other with umbrellas, but they always combined against C.

There were brief interludes of neutrality, as, for instance, when C. invited his sisters to join in his surreptitious games of cricket, which they managed to do when Mademoiselle was on her holidays, until Colonel Calhoun intervened with his professionalism. The most violent rupture between C. and his sisters occurred at Bramsley during the Christmas holidays, after his eighth birthday.

Mrs. Roden had sent all the children a Christmas present. To Julia, Marjorie and C. she had sent the same present, namely, the materials in a large card-board box for making out of paper a model farmyard. Christmas went off quietly enough, devastated for the children by Aunt Fanny, Uncle Cuthbert, Aunt Louisa and Uncle George. After the New Year the guests departed, and the children felt they might play with their toys without fear of criticism.

One evening, after tea, they settled down to under-take to construct Aunt Rachel's, otherwise Mrs. Roden's, model farmyards.

The lamps had been brought to the schoolroom; Mademoiselle was engrossed in a French novel which had a white paper cover shrouding its title and yellow cover from inquisitive eyes, and which happened to be Zola's *Germinal*. The children sat round the large

tea-table which had been cleared for games. They
opened the red cardboard boxes and read carefully the
printed sheet of directions which they found in the
box. After so doing they each of them went in search
of starch and scissors. The problem was to make a
model farmyard, including buildings, outhouses, cows,
poultry, trees, pig-styes and pigs, in three dimensions.
The means were a large sheet of paper on which the
houses, animals and other accessories were printed in
colour. You had to cut out the house, tree, animal,
or implement, and fold it till it assumed a concrete
shape ; then stick the folded edges together and stick
the base of the object in question, so that it stood upright on a solid board. That evening all went well.
They did not get beyond cutting out. Mademoiselle,
who was finding Zola's new book engrossing, complimented them on their quiet, and blessed Mrs. Roden
for having given them so absorbing a present.

Each of the girls and C. were engaged in making a
rival farmyard. The second evening they reached the
sticking stage. The great silence of the night before
was punctuated on this second evening by fragments
of absent-minded, disconnected talk, such as " Your
tree's crooked," " Which tree ? " ; " Your wall's too
large." " What wall ? " but everything passed off
quietly, and Mademoiselle was not interrupted in her
reading. She was getting more and more interested
in *Germinal*. The farms had progressed. All of the
children had got the walls up and the trees, and
several of the animals, but as yet not one of them

had succeeded in sticking on a roof to the walls of the farm building itself. This was an operation which required peculiar dexterity, and when clearing-up time came they had not one of them succeeded in achieving it. The two girls railed at C. for being clumsy; nevertheless, they had not themselves been successful in dealing with the difficult problem of the roof.

The third evening was almost entirely consecrated to the roof problem. Mademoiselle had reached the most enthralling part of Zola's book, and the children were silent from the intense effort of trying to stick on the recalcitrant roofs. But their tempers were on edge. The girls had tried and failed over and over again, and every now and then they jeered at C.'s efforts. Suddenly C. gave a wild shriek. Mademoiselle dropped her book and lost the place, and breaking into English, which she only did under the stress of strong emotion, she said :—

" You naughty boy, what do you make such a noise ? "

" I've done it," said C. " Look, look, Mademoiselle, my roof is on ! The whole house is there ! It's finished ! "

There was no gainsaying the fact. There was the farmhouse solidly established, stuck firmly on the cardboard, and perfectly roofed. The girls looked at each other with silent stupor, and black jealousy entered into Marjorie's heart. She said nothing. C. danced round the room, clapping his hands, till Mademoiselle said :—

" *Veux-tu te taire*, vill you be quiet ?   *Je te mettrai au pain sec.*"

But no threats could overcome C.'s soaring ecstasy, the rapture of the successful creative artist.   The girls went on working sullenly.

" We shall do it presently," said Marjorie.   " It's quite easy really."

But they knew in their hearts this was not so.   They worked on for a few moments in silence and then Marjorie said :—

" Aunt Rachel gave C. that one because it's the easiest.   It's not a grown-up one like ours ! "

" They're all exactly the same," said C.

Marjorie chuckled almost inaudibly.

" We were quite right," she said in a just audible aside to Julia, " to let him do his first, and to think it's the same as ours."

" Quite right," said Julia.

" It *is* the same," said C.

" Oh, yes," said Marjorie, with great and exasperating calm.   " Just the same."

C. felt a wild wave of passion surging within him.

" At any rate," he said slowly, " Aunt Fanny said she was afraid you were going to take after Aunt Maria."

Aunt Maria was a great-aunt who for some reason unknown to the children was a black sheep, and whom they imagined to be ugly, but who in reality, merely had the drawback of being old.   Marjorie affected not to listen.

"We won't do ours till to-morrow," said Marjorie to Julia, ignoring C. "It would spoil the poor little boy's pleasure."

"Well, at any rate, I don't cry when I'm bowled at cricket," said C.

It was an undeniable fact, and one of the bitterest recollections in Marjorie's life, that she had cried publicly at a cricket match on being bowled out first ball. The shaft went home. She said nothing. C., satisfied with his triumph, left the schoolroom. Mademoiselle had finished *Germinal* and at once violently urged the children to tidy the schoolroom. She left the schoolroom herself. While Julia was putting her box away Marjorie took C.'s handiwork and tore his farmhouse from the board. A few minutes later C. entered the room.

"Mademoiselle says you're to tidy," said Marjorie, "and you didn't do the farmhouse after all."

C. looked at his devastated handiwork and said nothing. For the moment he was completely stunned; then his thoughts slowly moved towards revenge. Marjorie had a doll she was particularly fond of. It was called Joséphine, and it was respected by the whole household. It was a china doll and opened and shut its eyes. Even Lady Hengrave recognised the existence of Joséphine and tolerated Marjorie's affection for it. C. tidied his toys, put them back in the cupboard, and left the schoolroom in silence. He then went upstairs to the girls' bedroom and took Joséphine from her bed, where she had already been put to sleep, and shattered her head against the coal scuttle. Marjorie was unaware of the tragedy till she went to bed, although C.'s apparent calm frightened her. When she went to bed and realised what had happened, her screams re-echoed through the house and brought Lady Hengrave from her bedroom, where she had gone to dress for dinner. She was put in possession of the facts, or rather of a one-sided version of the facts, by Marjorie. Mademoiselle Walter, who was appealed to, said she had not witnessed the incident as she had been in her room at the time, but remarked icily that Marjorie was " *très taquine.*" The calamity of the death of Joséphine was thought too awful for punishment or even for comment. C. was treated like a murderer. Even Miss Hackett said to him :—

" You've never been and *killed* Joséphine."

C. felt that he had indeed committed murder. Nobody sympathised with him ; everyone shunned him. Lady Hengrave said :—

" I shall have to tell your father, and I don't know what he will say, and I shall tell your brother Edward as well."

This last threat was the worst of all, for, although in their experience their brother Edward had never once intervened in the domestic affairs of the schoolroom, the children were frightened of him, and C. felt overcome with shame at his being told of his deed. Nobody mentioned the ruined farmyard ; nobody could see that the two acts were on a par. The farmyard, in the eyes of the grown-ups, was simply a bit of paper. They did not realise the triumph C. had felt in his effort of successful creation; the intense mortification he had experienced when his handiwork had been destroyed— the result of so much painful labour of so sudden a final inspiration. All that was swallowed up by the more prodigious fact that Joséphine was no more. His sisters would not speak to him. Mademoiselle merely said, "*Voilà ce que c'est que d'être méchant*," and Harry was at that time too young to sympathise. Mrs. Brimstone not only gave him a long preliminary scolding, but brought the subject up on every fresh occasion, and C. was a pariah in the household. Lady Hengrave promised Marjorie a new doll, but Marjorie was inconsolable. Joséphine was taken to the toy shop and a new head was given to her, but Joséphine's original head had been made in Paris, and her new head, which was bought in Sloane Street, was a different affair altogether, besides being slightly too small. Joséphine had lost her elegance for ever, and Marjorie never forgave C.

Curiously enough, C. did not feel that he was in any way justified by Marjorie's destructive act. He shared the view of the family that the two acts were altogether disproportionate, and he felt that he was indeed a criminal and had committed an act which would certainly never be forgiven in this life, and probably not in the next.

It was a long time, a long time that is to say measured by the standards of childhood—in reality about a fortnight, and morally about an æon—before

C. lived down the murder of Joséphine, for, after the subject had been dropped at Bramsley, it cropped up again when the family returned to London and Joséphine was taken to Sloane Street for her new head, which proved, alas! to be so poor a substitute.

Although C. preferred the country to London, he often experienced a feeling of relief when the family returned to London, because life in London, on the whole, was freer and less exposed to the criticism of relations and neighbours, or, rather, outside criticism was less permanent and less intimate. He did not mind the comments of the guests who came to luncheon as much as the more prolonged criticism of the neighbours and relations whom he endured at Bramsley. Besides which some of the guests who came to luncheon from the outside world were entertaining and amiable.

There was Countess Felseck, a Swedish lady, who had something pleasantly frivolous about her as well as radiant and apparently un-aging hair. She used to come to luncheon very often, but, curiously enough, never when Lord Hengrave was at home.

In addition to Mr. Dartrey there was another regular and constantly recurring luncheon guest, who came to luncheon once a week, but never on the same day as Mr. Dartrey. This was Mr. Cecil Whitelaw, who owned racehorses and wore clothes subtly different from those of other people, talked in a loud voice, and was often sulky; but he took little notice of the children.

As far as other children were concerned, Aunt

Louisa's boys were older than C., and were already at a public school when he was in the schoolroom. Aunt Fanny had one overgrown, red-haired, spectacled boy who, she said, whenever he was left in a room, "snatched at a Shakespeare." He despised C., and C. kicked his shins whenever he had the opportunity. The Roden children were not encouraged. Harry was two years younger than C., but he was big for his age and was as tall as C. He was the favourite of the nursery and the drawing-room, and the various governesses into whose orbit he was attracted were all of them fond of him. C. was not in the least jealous of Harry. He accepted the fact that Harry found greater favour as a natural thing that could not well be otherwise, as Harry was obviously more amiable, so much better behaved, and so much nicer. Everyone admired him and said, "What a pretty boy!" C. was considered to be the ugly duckling. Their companionship was the main factor of the inside life of his childhood, and they kept the full quality of it a secret. The various governesses and Mrs. Brimstone used to see them play together and witness their noisy fun and their frequent quarrels, but what was kept from the world was that C. told Harry all the stories he read in story books and invented others of his own, which Harry listened to with breathless interest, especially as he was no reader himself. The stories were translated into action, and took the shape of exciting and dramatic games. So completely did Lady Hengrave misread the situation with Harry that she thought the boys got on badly together, and imagined them to be living in a state of perpetual feud. She was perpetually scolding C. for being rough, one of the reasons of this being that, whenever they suggested they should do anything together, C. used always to make a pretence of indifference, and the keener he was to do the thing the more indifferent he pretended to be, because he feared that any treat might share the fate of single-wicket cricket.

As to treats, Lady Hengrave never took the children to the play or to any entertainment—not on principle, but from economy—although C. and his sisters were sometimes allowed to go to tea at the Rodens' house in Kensington. Julia and Marjorie had plenty of girl friends, who used to be asked to tea in the schoolroom, but on these occasions they never let C. join in their games, especially after the murder of Joséphine. Sometimes all of them went to children's parties, but C., rightly or wrongly, acquired the reputation of being rough, and after a time the girls were more often asked by themselves. The net result of this was that, until he went to school, C. had no friends and no companions, either at home or outside, with the exception of his brother Harry and Miss Hackett. The only happy hours he spent were in the house-keeper's room, where he played cribbage and Old Maid with Miss Hackett and the housekeeper, and sometimes long whist with the butler and others, or playing with Harry, or reading a book by himself in the nursery. He never read in the schoolroom, as he

did not like his sisters to see him reading. He pretended to them and to the world in general that books
were babyish things, and fit only for girls. In reality
he was passionately fond of fairy tales and all stories of
adventure.

On Sunday afternoons Mr. Dartrey sometimes took
the children to the Zoo, and once a year a friend of the
family, a quaint old man with a beady eye, called Mr.
Short, whom they all adored, took them to the circus,
and sometimes to the pantomime. As Edward, the
eldest son, had been in the Eton eleven, the Eton and
Harrow match was considered a function that could
not be missed, and they went to Lord's every year.
This was the greatest treat of the year for C.

When the family returned to London after the
memorable Christmas holidays, which were dated in
C.'s mind by the murder of Joséphine, C. was not
far off from his ninth birthday. His birthday was in
March. It was settled that he was to go to school in
September, and during the last lap of his pre-schoolday
life, two events of importance happened to him.

One of them was the departure of Mademoiselle
Walter. This was a dramatic event which was
brought about by the unconscious intervention of
Harry.

It was a rainy day in February. There was no question of going out, and C. and Harry had planned and
had arranged with the cook to make toffee in the
kitchen, and possibly a gingerbread cake. Just before
luncheon C. committed some minor fault in the

schoolroom, for which he had been told by Mademoiselle that he must write out the phrase " *Je suis un enfant désobéissant et mal élevé,*" twelve times before tea. Soon after luncheon C. and Harry went down to the kitchen and became engrossed in the manufacture of toffee and treacle, and assisted in the making of a gingerbread cake which proved to be successful, save for a large damp hole in the centre of it.

C. forgot all about his punishment, and when Mademoiselle asked him for it at tea-time, he was silent. Mademoiselle, who had been severely tried by the girls all the afternoon, was in the worst of tempers. She rapped him on the knuckles with a ruler and sent him to bed. C. bore this with stoicism. Not so Harry, who considered that he was to blame. After he had spent the first fury of his grief in a paroxysm of tears, he rushed downstairs to Lady Hengrave, who was giving tea to Mr. Whitelaw, and declared dramatically that he wanted to go to school. When pressed for his reasons the whole story came out, and Lady Hengrave drew the conclusion from it that not only C. and the girls were maltreated by Mademoiselle, but that possibly Harry was liable to the same treatment, although he had made no such accusation. The result was that Mademoiselle Walter left the house.

She was replaced by a kindly German, Fräulein Setzer, a South German, with a passion for children and a great talent for teaching them. Julia and Marjorie took advantage of her kindness and teased her unmercifully, but she was quite indifferent to this and went on steadily through the routine of lessons, and in spite of everything managed to teach the children something. C. liked her, but he knew in his heart that she was far less interesting than Mademoiselle Walter, who had been so unkind to him.

After Easter, in the summer of the same year, another treat came for an all too brief period into his life.

Ever since his eighth birthday and the incident of the nigger's head, although he no longer walked in his sleep, he had frequently been tormented by nightmares, and especially by the recurring dream of the ship and the mist and the fog horn. Something now happened which drove these nightmares away for ever. C. conceived one of those romantic adorations that children sometimes have for grown-ups, love for a girl some years older than himself. This is how it came about.

He was allowed for the first time to join his sisters when they went in the evenings to play games with other children in Hamilton Gardens. The children were nearly all of them older than C., and the contemporaries of his sisters. There were not many boys. It was considered a great favour that he should be admitted to the games, and his sisters were opposed to it. Kind Miss Setzer, however, insisted on C. being allowed to go. C. enjoyed himself for the first time with other children, and made friends with two girls. One was called Freda; she was very dark and had large black eyes. The other, Leila, was fairer, with a promise of great beauty and melting violet eyes. They were both of them several years older than he was. For about a month everything went smoothly. C. enjoyed himself ecstatically, and his sisters were forced to admit that he was an asset on whoever's side he played, as he ran faster than any of the other boys. Leila and Freda were not always there together, and he got to know both of them intimately. But it was Leila he loved best. He confided everything to her. He thought her the most ravishing creature who had ever been born, and the vision of her face and of her violet eyes banished the nightmare from the limbo in which his mind wandered just before dropping off to sleep.

One evening, it was a radiant evening towards the end of June, and the Park was crowded with people, C. was looking forward more than he had ever done to the game of flags and to a meeting with Leila. The children arrived in Hamilton Gardens. On the way they had passed their brother Edward, who was on horse-back on his way to Rotten Row. A band somewhere was playing *Estudiantina*, a valse. Sides for flags were picked. Freda was on the same side as C., and Leila was on the opposite side. Never had the game been more exciting. At one moment Freda was captured by the enemy, and C. raced across the lawn and succeeded in rescuing her. As they ran back together C. said something to Freda and laughed.

At that moment Leila rushed past them.

When the game was over C. walked up to Leila, whom he had not seen for some time, and spoke to her. Leila looked at him and turned away.

"What is the matter?" asked C.

"Nothing," she said, "only you had better go and talk to Freda as you like her so much better," and she turned away and wouldn't speak to him again.

"I thought you were her best friend," he said.

So she was. C. never forgot that moment. It was connected in his mind with the strains of the *Estudiantina* valse and the ringing clatter of hansom cabs, and the intoxicating atmosphere of gaiety that hung about evenings of the London season.

The next day Leila's governess complained to her mother that Caryl Bramsley spoilt the games by his roughness. Leila's mother complained to Lady Hengrave. Lady Hengrave said it was high time he was going to school, and forbade him ever to be taken to Hamilton Gardens again. That was the bitterest moment in C.'s life before he went to school.

CHAPTER V

In his ninth year C. was sent to a private school. Lady Hengrave had been recommended an excellent school in Berkshire, where the boys were well taught and obtained scholarships at public schools. As C. was destined for the Navy, and had to pass what was considered a difficult examination to get into the *Britannia*, it was important that he should be well taught. But in the summer of C.'s ninth year the Headmaster at the Berkshire school died, the staff of the school split up, and the school came to an end. One of the masters started a school of his own near Oxford, taking with him one of the assistant masters ; another, who, although the least intellectual, was considered to have the greater organising capacities, started a school near Brighton. Lady Hengrave, who had inspected the school and made the acquaintance of the masters, made up her mind that Mr. Forsyth, who had migrated to Brighton from the Berkshire school, was preferable, and C. was sent to the seaside school. There were only nine boys under Mr. Forsyth's charge during C.'s first term, and that was thought to be an advantage. Lady Hengrave thought the boys would get more attention, and consequently work harder. Mr. Forsyth was a brisk, breezy, rather burly man. He understood boys, knew how to manage them, and how to amuse them, but he was not a scholar in any sense, and he left the intellectual education of the boys to his staff. At the Berkshire school he had only taught the smallest boys the elements of French and arithmetic, as well as drawing and music to the whole school.

At the new school he took no classes at all, but contented himself with organising and pervading the whole, which he did very well. Indeed, if the acquiring of knowledge had been of no importance, " Forsyth's," as the school was called, would have been one of the best schools in England. The staff was not over large. Mr. Cartwright, who was practically Mr. Forsyth's partner, although they were not co-equal (Mr. Cartwright was called an assistant master), lived in the house and dealt with mathematics, modern languages, history and geography. His interests were purely athletic. He had been a Rugger blue at Oxford, and he looked upon work as an interruption which had to be borne patiently in the serious business of school life, which was games.

Mr. Forsyth was unmarried, but Mr. Cartwright was married, and Mrs. Cartwright lived in the house, looked after the boys and played the part of matron.

Mrs. Cartwright came from the North ; she was one of the many daughters of a well-to-do minister. She had a fuzzy, reddish fringe and a delicate, little, white, freckled face, and a refined Glasgow intonation. She was kind to the boys, but took little interest in the school. Her heart was in the columns of the *Queen* newspaper and the *Court Journal*, and she sometimes read *Modern Society* in secret. She had a passion for the news of the world of fashion, and she followed the movements of every member of the Royal Family with enthralled interest. C., being the younger son of a peer, had great prestige in her eyes, and her only regret was that his sisters were not yet out, and that she could not read their names in the lists of guests at the balls and parties that were chronicled in the *Morning Post*.

Latin and Greek were taught by an anæmic, pale and bearded man with worn-out trousers and frayed linen, who came in from Brighton every day. Although his name was Porson he had only a superficial knowledge of the classics, and little authority over the boys.

Another visitor taught the boys English literature.

Music was encouraged, and the boys were also taught sketching in water colours and in oils. At the end of his first term C. took home a water colour of a mill which was supposed to be by his hand, but it had a grown-up Royal Academy quality which would have been surprising in the work of a boy of nine. Mr. Birch, the drawing master, wore a velvet jacket, and lived in a house furnished entirely with unsold Academy pictures, some of which had been hung. He always finished off the boys' pictures, feeling that it was more satisfactory to all concerned, which it was ; for, although the parents must have known that the pictures were not their son's unaided work, they liked to think that progress had been made, and that some of the work was perhaps authentic. Some parents, indeed, bravely maintained the illusion that the sketches were entirely their boys' work.

The boys played Association football with a neighbouring school. They went twice a week to a gymnasium, where they learnt gymnastics. They went out riding on the Downs on ponies from a riding school. They attended a swimming bath once a week, and had swimming lessons. They had a thoroughly enjoyable life and learnt nothing. At the end of his first term C. went home for the holidays, taking with him a handsomely bound copy of *Stories from Livy*, a prize for modern languages. He took with him as well a report saying that he had been most satisfactory in every respect, and that he was making excellent progress in all subjects. He was, perhaps, a little weak in freehand drawing.

Lady Hengrave was delighted, but Fräulein Setzer shook her head after cross-examining C. about his German lessons, and came to the conclusion that he had not learnt much; for, although music at Forsyth's school was taught by a German, German was taught by Mr. Cartwright, who had never been to Germany, and who had the slightest acquaintance with the language. He could not construe the simplest German poem without the help of a translation.

When C. went back after his holidays, for his second term, the number of boys had increased; there were now fourteen, and before C. left the numbers increased to twenty-nine. Mr. Forsyth had joined the volunteers, and the boys were now drilled by a sergeant in a drill hall, were taught to form fours, and were sometimes, as a great treat, allowed to pull a string which let off a gun.

Athletic sports were the excitement during the Lent term, and C. won the hundred yards race in an open competition for various schools. He was tall for his age, and the committee were inclined to think that his reported age was incorrect. This was not the case. C. made friends with a boy called Arkright, who introduced him to the works of Harrison Ainsworth, and to *Oliver Twist* and *The Old Curiosity Shop*. He soon reached a position of importance in the school, and became the captain of the football eleven, but he never took to cricket, in spite of Mr. Cartwright's exhortations, and used, whenever he could, to go out sailing on the sea. This the boys were allowed to do; and, as C. was destined to be a sailor, the Headmaster thought it fitting and appropriate that he should get used to the sea as soon as possible and overcome an unfortunate tendency to sea-sickness.

When he learnt to swim, Mr. Forsyth said that the first step in his naval career had been reached, and he prophesied that C. would one day be an admiral. His reports became more and more glowing; and at the end of every term he took home more and more prizes, among others the works of Josephus, in two volumes, bound in red calf. He was nearly always at the top of his division, and both his father and mother were astonished at the apparent fertility of what they had considered to be a difficult and unprofitable soil. Nobody at home had any doubts about the situation except Fräulein Setzer, who had a shrewd suspicion that C. was learning very little, but she was too frightened of Lady Hengrave and too fond of C. to say anything.

C. had little aptitude for mathematics, and, although he had not in him the makings of a scholar, his mind responded to classical subjects, and he had been well grounded in French at home. Unfortunately, the teaching in Latin and Greek, and still more in modern languages, at Forsyth's was not only negatively inadequate, but positively harmful ; and, instead of learning Latin, French and a little Greek, C. gradually forgot the Latin that he knew, and would have completely forgotten his French if Fräulein Setzer had not compelled him to talk French in the holidays. The reason that he was so easily first in his classes and won so many prizes was that the little knowledge he acquired was greater than what was picked up by the other boys, and in the kingdom of the blind the one-eyed was king.

Apart from the work which formed the daily routine C. met with no stimulant which acted on his mind in any way in the teaching of his masters, or in his intercourse with them. He read the works of Henty and he discovered the genius of Rider Haggard, but, apart from that, the world of fancy was a closed

book to him, for the lessons in English literature at
Forsyth's were delivered by an expert in Pitman's
shorthand, whose highest ideals were the most fluent
and stereotyped form of journalese and the scrupulous
avoidance of prepositions at the end of a sentence.

Mr. Forsyth used often to take the boys to the local
theatre, and there C. made his first acquaintance with
the more melodramatic and sentimental branches of
the English drama. He saw a dramatised version of
The House on the Marsh, and several other melo-
dramas of the same nature. These plays sometimes
renewed for him the nightmares of his childhood, but
he did not confess the fact to anybody.

C. behaved fairly well during his schooldays. He
did no work, but he gave no trouble. He ragged Mr.
Porson during the classical hours, and burnt pills called
Pharaoh's serpents during his class which, when lit,
developed into brown coiling and rather nauseating
snakes. He got on well with the Headmaster, and
he was on amicable terms with Mr. and Mrs. Cartwright, but he took no interest in them. He was
good at games but cared little for them, a fact which
baffled Mr. Cartwright. He collected stamps and
worked hard in the carpenter's shop with his friend,
Arkright. Together they made a quantity of brac-
kets and other ornamental pieces of furniture with a
fret-saw. He made no other great friends, but the
last two years of his private school life were enlivened
by the arrival of his younger brother. He and Harry
shared a room together, and fought over the bath

religiously every day. The boys respected C., as he
was easily the best football player and athlete at
the school, and he was supposed to be the best scholar.
During one of the summer terms C. went through an
emotional experience. A French company came down
to Brighton and gave a flying matinée at the Theatre
Royal. The company was a scratch one gathered
together round a star from the Paris *Gymnase*, named
Fanny Talbot, who was French in spite of her English
name. The play she appeared in was *Le Maître
des Forges*, familiar to the public of London under
the name of the *Ironmaster*. Fanny Talbot was an
abrupt and rather violently emotional actress. But
her sudden fame and instantaneous popularity were
due to her great and unusual beauty. She had delicate, rippling, fair, *cendré* hair with natural golden
lights in it, and mysterious brooding eyes, a statuesque
presence and the expression of a somewhat peevish
sphinx. Mr. Forsyth took the boys of the first
division to see this play. He said it would be good
for their French. He wanted to see the actress whom
London had been raving about. As for C. he fell
instantly and madly in love with Fanny Talbot, and
the performance of the *Ironmaster* opened for him
a door on to the kingdom of romance. He had no
idea such beauty could exist, and in some way she
reminded him of Leila, the heroine of his romance in
Hamilton Gardens. He bought several photographs
of her which he concealed, and he confided his passion
to Arkright, who was sympathetic, but said it was a

great pity she did not speak and act in English. For his part he preferred Violet Cameron.

With the help of Arkright—that is to say, aided by the advice of Arkright as far as the sentiments were concerned (for Arkright knew little French)—C. composed a letter to Miss Fanny Talbot, which, after many rough copies, drafts, alterations and emendations, finally read thus :—

Deux anglais élèves à l'école de Forsyth's, Brighton, désirent mettre à vos pieds leur profounde admiration, aux pieds de Fanny Talbot, la plus grande actrice du monde et la plus belle entre toutes les belles. O prodige Incroyable !

La plus belle entre toutes les belles was a phrase that C. had once heard Mademoiselle Walter make use of, and the final apostrophe was a quotation from a speech in Racine's *Athalie*, which C. had known by heart for some years.

Miss Fanny Talbot answered the letter by sending a visiting card on which she wrote a civil phrase thanking her English friends for their kind appreciation. They tossed up as to who should own the card, for Arkright, although his passion for Fanny Talbot was less violent, collected autographs, and the personal autograph of so great a celebrity would be the flower of his collection. He won the toss, but most generously he insisted on C. keeping the autograph, for, as he said, " It's one thing for a chap to collect autographs and another to have a lifelong passion for a great actress, and, although I admire her very much,

I do prefer Violet Cameron, both as an actress and a beauty." C. yielded to this argument, and hid the little visiting card in the same box which concealed four different photographs of Fanny Talbot, three of them in costume, and one of them *en ville*.

Arkright was an amateur of the theatrical life and knew a great many actors and actresses by name, as his parents took him to the play quite often during the holidays. Up till now C. had taken little interest in this taste, but now Fanny Talbot had changed all that, and C. took an interest in the stage for her sake, and read the theatrical news in the *Daily Telegraph*, in the hope of seeing her name. He even had a fight with Baily major because Baily slighted her. This is how the incident occurred. C. had bought a new photograph of Fanny Talbot and was showing it to an interested but critical group, with that desire of universal confirmation and that apprehension of a possible want of appreciation that an idol inspires.

"It's of course not a bit like her," he said apologetically, meaning that it was not nearly beautiful enough.

"That's a pity," said Baily major, "because if it had been she would have been rather good-looking."

The group tittered. Baily major was famous for his sarcasm.

"All right," said C., "we'll fight it out in the playroom."

And fight it out they did, with gloves and seconds. The first three rounds were indecisive. In the fourth round Baily major's nose bled and his face had grown very red. He was slightly the more powerful of the two, and neither of them were skilful boxers ; but C. had behind him the fierce drive of his overwhelming passion for Fanny Talbot, and a raging desire to avenge her, so that in the fifth round, after a few wild swings, he managed to pound Baily major's head till the latter admitted defeat in tears. They shook hands, but before doing so C. demanded that Baily major should apologise for having slighted Fanny Talbot.

"I never said anything against her," Baily said between pants. "How could I know that you'd get so waxy over a photograph ?"

"Well," said C., "Fanny Talbot is the most beautiful person and the greatest actress in the world, and I'll fight any one who says the contrary."

Nobody disputed the sentiment.

This was the most emotional experience C. had at his private school, but perhaps the school incident which impressed him the most, and which gave him the greatest cause for thought—an incident which changed him and shifted him to another centre, so to speak—was the following.

One afternoon towards the end of the summer term the first division were engaged in doing sums. Mr. Cartwright was out of the room. The sums in question were decimal fractions of an exasperating kind, and none of the boys, not even the best mathematicians, could cope successfully with all of them. Through the

open window came the voices of a nigger party singing
in the street and the smell of the sea, and the distant
noise of a merry-go-round. It was a radiant afternoon
towards the middle of July. The room was hot and
stuffy ; a few wasps buzzed along the window frames.
The black arithmetic books seemed more than usually
dismal, the ink in the ink pots of the wooden desks
more choked with blotting paper and more stagnant
than ever. The black steel pens seemed more than
ever to have feelers as of some strange sea beast.

Suddenly C. voiced public opinion by saying out
loud :—

" I shan't do another stroke of work."

" Nor shall I," said Baily major.

" Nor shall I," said every one else in chorus, and a
feeling of exhilarating desperation pervaded the
division. The boys shut their books and began making
pellets with blotting paper and flipping them at each
other. The room began soon to hum with noise.
Some one dropped a book. Some one else banged down
the lid of a desk. One boy threw a book across the
room. The noise almost grew into a hubbub.
Presently Mr. Cartwright swept into the room and
shut the door with a bang. A deadly stillness ensued,
and immediately all the boys automatically closed
their desks, took their pens, and went on tackling
their decimal fractions in the most docile manner
imaginable—all of them except C., who kept his word
and did not go on with his work, and did not even open
his book.

" Bramsley major, why aren't you working ? " said Mr. Cartwright to C.

" I can't do these sums, Sir," said C.

" Rubbish," said Mr. Cartwright good-humouredly, " try again."

C. said nothing, but remained looking obstinately in front of him, his book still closed, his pen idle.

" Bramsley major," said Mr. Cartwright, " go to bed at once ! "

C. walked off to bed, but he had kept his promise and had not done another stroke of work more that day, and as he lay in bed supperless that night, he dimly pondered long over the cowardice of human nature : the secret of corporate action, the mystery of people not being able to combine, the brief nature of revolutions, and the subjugation of the majority by a minority of one. Puzzling questions all of them, and destined to recur and occur to him often in after life.

CHAPTER VI

C. WENT up for his naval examination in Michaelmas term of his third year at school. Mr. Forsyth
and the whole staff of " Forsyth's " were optimistic
as to the result, and the news of his complete failure
fell like a bombshell both upon home and school.
Mr. Forsyth attributed the failure to a bruise on his
shin he had received in the football field just before
the examination. Fräulein Setzer attributed it to the
incapacity of his teachers, but she kept her opinions to
herself. It was settled that he should stay two more
terms at school and then go to Eton. His name had
been put down for Winslow's when he was quite small.
Eton was a part of the religion of the Hengrave
family, and they considered it unthinkable that a
member of their family should go to any other school.
As C. could not become a sailor, it was thought that he
might perhaps be able to pass into the Foreign Office,
or possibly, better still, get " something in the City."
There would be time to think of that later.

When the time came for C. to go to Eton, Winslow's
was full up, and Mr. Winslow could not take him, nor
could one or two other house-masters whom Lady
Hengrave would have preferred, and C. was sent to
Pringle's. It was a good house, but not conspicuous

for stars either in the athletic or the intellectual world. The house boasted of only one boy in Sixth Form, and of no member either of the eleven, the eight, or even the Victory, and of no member of Pop.

In the house cup matches Pringle's never got further than the second ties, and did not always reach that stage. On the other hand, Pringle's was respected as being quite a "decent" house. This was largely due to Mr. Pringle's personality. There was something fundamentally gentlemanlike and urbane about him. He was polished, Attic, rather highly-strung, and given to nervous brain storms in school ; an electric teacher, stimulating to boys he liked and got on with, but blighting to those whom he did not like, and a master of light but stinging irony.

When C. reached Eton he was still called at home the Ugly Duckling. And there was something at this epoch rather uncouth and overgrown about him, something immature and yet overripe. He was too big for his age and showed little promise of good looks, although there was something rather striking about his dark eyes and undisciplined hair. He was lanky and thin, and looked as if he had grown up too quickly. He was untidy, too, and his hair and his clothes looked as if they had never been brushed.

He took Upper Fourth on arrival, which was another shock both to Forsyth's and to Lady Hengrave, as they had confidently expected him to take Remove.

At the end of his first half the lower master whom he had been up to wrote in his report that he had been taught " small Latin and less Greek," and Mr. Pringle took a pessimistic view of the effects of his irreparable past on the future.

C.'s Eton career was a curious one. He was perfectly happy, enjoyed the life, did his work just well enough to pass trials and just not well enough to achieve ordinary distinction. He was sufficiently idle and disobedient to get into trouble every now and then, but sufficiently reserved and obstinate to weather rows with equanimity and without disaster.

It has been already recorded he was considered to be the best athlete at his private school. At Eton he passed athletically into a phase of total eclipse. He was naturally a good football player, and had he been at a house that was good at games he would have forcibly been pushed up the ladder of success. As it was, he played with bad players, and did what he found the others doing. He took the line of least resistance and conformed to his surroundings. He had no athletic ambitions. He was a wet bob. But it was a long time, and then only by accident, and at the instigation of one of the masters who had taken him out one day downstream, that he put his name down for Novice Eights. He ultimately got into the Lower Boats, but there he remained rooted. His Eton life was a curious life within a life. He had his own little circle, which escaped the notice of the crowd, and in that little circle he was happy.

When C. had been at Eton two years his brother Harry joined him ; he was not sent to Pringle's, as there was room for him at Crutchleigh's, an athletic house which boasted of the presence of the Captain of the Boats, the Keeper of the Field, and two members of Sixth Form. Harry's career was very different from C.'s. He became a shining star in the cricket world, got his sixpenny his first summer term, and ended by playing at Lord's and being Master of the Beagles. He moved in a different universe to that of C.

C. looked on at the dawn and promise of these triumphs with admiration untinged by envy, and the two brothers would go for a walk together regularly every Sunday afternoon. They never criticised each other. Each accepted the other as inevitable, and Harry's success amply made up to Lady Hengrave for C.'s obscurity. In fact, C.'s obscurity enhanced Harry's success in her eyes. Had it been the other way round she could scarcely have borne it, and C. knew that.

C. did not get on very well with his tutor, Mr. Pringle. Mr. Pringle suspected in him a lurking spirit of opposition, and felt that he was more intelligent than his work showed him to be. He was sarcastic, and C. met his sarcasm with sullen silence. They just missed getting on. During his first half C. had nothing to do with his tutor as far as work was concerned. Mr. Pringle had no room for him at first, and sent him in company with two other new boys, to Mr. Oxley's pupil room, who acted as his tutor for the time being. It was only when he got into Remove that they came into direct contact, and at first there was little friction between them. Mr. Pringle used to call him a scamp and accuse him of " trying it on," but there was nothing more than that. It was when C. reached Upper Remove that a little incident dug an irreparable breach between C. and his tutor, although Mr. Pringle was quite unconscious of the fact.

One day the boys were construing Homer in pupil room, *The Odyssey*. C. was fascinated by *The Odyssey*. They were construing in the Tenth Book, a passage which tells how Odysseus came to the Palace of Circe in the Island of Æææa. C. was put on to construe at line 211.

This is how he translated the passage :—

" They saw in the glades the well-built house of Circe, of polished marble, in a conspicuous place, and around were mountain wolves and lions which she had subdued by enchantment, since she had given them wicked herbs."

" ' Wicked herbs,' that's good," said Mr. Pringle. " Very good." Then he caught himself up and said " You may be taking me in, you probably are taking me in."

" Wicked herbs " was Dryden's rendering, and quoted in Pope's *Odyssey*, a book which C. had read at home. C. was profoundly hurt by his tutor's bantering distrust, and that was the last time he made the slightest attempt to construe a passage well in pupil room.

Another time C.'s tutor had told his boys to learn

for *private* a passage from Pope, the famous passage about Addison, which C., as a matter of fact, had known ever since he was nine years old. It was a passage that Lady Hengrave had insisted on her sons learning in the schoolroom.

"Go on, Bramsley," said Mr. Pringle to C. C. hesitated for a little and then began to spout :—

> Peace be to you!

"No, no," said Mr. Pringle, in an agony of impatience,

> Peace to all such!

C. began again :—

> But were there one whose fires,
> Peace to all such!
> True genius kindles and the blame inspires.

Mr. Pringle buried his face in his hands, and then lifted his head as though shattered by the nerve-wracking experience.

"Don't you see that besides murdering the verse you're talking nonsense ? " he said.

"I don't know what it's all about, Sir," said C.

"It doesn't matter whether you know or not. You must take it from me that it's good, as good as verse can be, and if you don't like it, dub yourself a fool."

"Yes, Sir," said C. calmly, and went on massacring the lines with perverse ingenuity, saying, for instance : "Brook no arrivals to the Turkish throne," instead of "Bear like the Turk no brother near the throne."

And " Damn with vain praise assent without a tear," till Mr. Pringle could bear it no more.

" Dub yourself a fool, dub yourself a fool," he said, and he put some one else on.

C. was perfectly consistent in his conduct with regard to all the masters. With the French masters he pretended not to understand a word of French, and with the German master, not to understand a word of German. This deceived some of the French masters but not all of them. M. Bué, who was a man who stood no nonsense, told C. that he saw through his British accent, and that he was not going to stand it, so C. was reluctantly obliged to modify his feigned ignorance, although he managed never to reveal the full extent of his knowledge or capacity. With the mathematical masters he was able, without pretence, to maintain an attitude of invincible ignorance. With the classical masters he assumed an attitude of respectable mediocrity, which on the whole met with toleration, if not with approval.

C. made no great friends at his tutor's, with the exception of one boy, whom he messed with, called Weigall. This was a matter-of-fact boy, who came from Yorkshire. Weigall was C.'s greatest friend in the house. The link which bound them was natural history. Weigall was an ardent naturalist and an impassioned bird's egg collector, and C. and Weigall spent hours together at a taxidermist's shop in Windsor, where they learnt bird-stuffing. Weigall had come to Eton the same half as C., and they had gone up to the school together. They messed together ever since their first half, and had always been in the same division, and they both read and revelled in the works of Marie Corelli. C. thought her works were quite entrancing, and he enjoyed the fierce satire and vehement sentiments of that authoress as much as her daring imagination. His tutor, when he used to come round in the evenings after prayers, used always to find at that time a book by Marie Corelli on the table, and when he saw it he used to snort. C. used to put it there on purpose, knowing that the bait was sure to get a rise.

"How can you read such stuff?" Mr. Pringle would say.

"Oh, but, Sir, it's awfully good!" C. used to say.

Mr. Pringle begged him to read the works of R. L. Stevenson, and C. obstinately refused to do this, although he had read and enjoyed *Treasure Island* in secret. He was not ashamed of admitting to his admiration for Rider Haggard. He had been en-thralled by *She*, when he read it at his private school, but he was still more enthralled when he re-read the book three years later at Eton, when he was sixteen. He thought it the most wonderful book that the human mind could imagine, a vision of thrilling beauty and a soul-shattering tragedy, a world epic. When asked by one of the division masters, Mr. Cobden, who was the greatest English author, he said, without hesitation, Rider Haggard. Mr. Cobden, who liked originality and hated the conventionality of boys, was not displeased, and said it was a great thing to know one's mind. C. was sixteen years old when he was up to Mr. Cobden in the summer half. This master had a powerful effect on him. Mr. Cobden saw that C. was not the average boy he pretended to be, and found out that he had a queer storehouse of disjointed, out-of-the-way knowledge in him. Under his tuition C. consented to recognise quotations from Shakespeare, although he had not yet read any of the plays, and knew no more of them than the passages he had learnt by heart as a child. But Mr. Cobden interested him, and he showed his interest and answered the master's questions. Mr. Cobden called him an idle brat, but he was interested, and said in his report at the end of that summer half that C. was " an uncommonly sharp and thoughtful lad." His tutor was astonished to learn that C. was at the top of his division that half, and had been presented by Mr. Cobden with Boswell's *Life of Johnson*, bound in white vellum, *honoris causa*.

" Have you ever read this ? " asked Mr. Cobden, as he wrote C.'s name in it.

" No, sir."

" Well," said Mr. Cobden, " it's the best book in the world."

C. felt quite certain that Mr. Cobden was speaking the truth.

CHAPTER VII

IT was in the Michaelmas half of his fifteenth year that C. underwent a startling mental change. In the summer holidays, one Sunday in church the vicar had mentioned the poet Shelley with disapprobation, and C. had wondered who he was. When he went back to Eton he was laid up shortly after the beginning of the term with a bad chill, and he stayed out for a week. He was kept in bed for three days, and when he was allowed to get up he sat in his Dame's room and discussed books with Miss Derwent, the matron. She was a great novel reader, but she did not care for verse. He asked her if she had ever read the works of Shelley, as, knowing that she was very High Church indeed, he had an instinct that there might be something in Shelley likely to rouse or to shock her ecclesiastical susceptibilities. Miss Derwent rustled and creaked all over at the name, and said that Shelley was a dreadful unbeliever.

" Was he a clergyman ? " asked C.

" No," said Miss Derwent, " he was not so bad as that—not so bad as Renan."

C. resolved to read the works of Shelley.

As soon as he was up, he went to the school library and asked Burcher, the librarian, for the works of

Shelley. Burcher produced three small volumes
bound in red morocco, published by Moxon, in 1857.
C. took home the third volume with him, which
seemed to contain shorter poems.

He had just finished tea. He was sitting with
Weigall in his room, which was one of the smallest
and most encumbered of all the rooms in the house.
It possessed a mantel-board covered with blue cloth
and embossed with gilt nails, and a set of coloured
hunting pictures bought in Eton, an ottoman, a
bureau, slightly damaged by red-hot poker-work, and
a table on which there was a maroon-coloured table-
cloth covered with candle-grease stains, which C. and
Weigall used to begin to remove when they became
excessive, with a red-hot poker and a piece of blotting-
paper. Tea had been cleared away. They had begun
to sap. The room was stuffy from the heat of too
many candles. It was a Thursday evening. Verses
were done with, signed and written out. But both C.
and Weigall had an *Extra work* looming in front
of them. C. had done one sum, grappled with it for
some time, and then after looking up the answer at the
end of the book, put a large " W " meaning " wrong "
next to it, thus admitting absolute and final defeat.
He had drawn a line under that sum and begun another,
which being easy he had solved almost at once. A
triumphant " R," meaning " right," was put alongside
of it, and a line drawn underneath it. Then C. had
begun another sum and had become hopelessly stuck
in it. He felt he could go on with it better after a

slight interval of relaxation. Weigall was almost in exactly the same position. He had finished three sums of his *Extra work* (his was not the same as C.'s as they were not up to the same mathematical master), and had got stuck in a third. He, too, felt the imperative necessity for a slight interval. He fetched a paper bag from the sock cupboard, and the two mathematicians each consumed a banana. From the passage came the tempting sound of a game of football, but they resisted the call.

" We can't," said Weigall, " we've got far too much work to do."

" Yes," said C. " *Far* too much work to do. I've almost done an hour's work," he added. " The Friar says we need only do an hour's work, and I've done over half an hour."

" I've got stuck," said Weigall. " I can't get this equation out. There must be something wrong with it."

" Probably a misprint," suggested C.

" Piggy never takes that for an excuse," said Weigall dolefully.

" I think I shall do mine better a little later on," said C.

He walked up to his little bracket bookshelf and took from it the volume of Moxon's Shelley he had taken from the boys' library. He sat down in the solitary armchair in the room—a basket-work, rather diminutive, armchair stuffed with blue material. Weigall followed suit and fetched *Three in Norway*, a book he had read over and over again.

C. opened the volume of Shelley and came across *The Cloud*, which is at the beginning of the third volume, on p. 19. He read and experienced for the first time in his life what the printed words upon a page are capable of. He seemed to be caught up in a chariot of fire. Time and place were annihilated; one gorgeous vision after another swept him with dewy, rainbow wings; celestial bells seemed to be ringing in the air, and when it was all over something ineffable had been left behind. He was dazed. He thought he must be mistaken. He read the poem through slowly and silently again from the beginning until the end. Yes, it was all there. He had opened the gates of an undiscovered magical kingdom. He was bursting with the wonder of his discovery.

"Weigall, you must listen to this," he said. And he began to read it out.

Weigall put down *Three in Norway*, and listened in silence. He was quite interested, if a little puzzled. When C. came to this passage—

> As on the jag of a mountain crag,
>   Which an earthquake rocks and swings,
> An eagle alit one moment may sit
>   In the light of its golden wings

he paused.

"Isn't that wonderful ? " he said.

"Yes," said Weigall, " but I don't think an eagle *would* do that."

"Why not ? " said C.

" Oh," said Weigall, " because an eagle's wings aren't golden."

C. suddenly realised that Weigall was not quite as sympathetic an audience as you could wish for this music, but he went on reading till the end. When he had finished Weigall said :—

" Listen to this."

And he read out, by no means for the first time, the tragedy of a salmon which some one had failed to gaff after an hour of desperate playing.

" Children aren't salmon," said Weigall with a sigh, quoting from the book.

C. went on with Shelley, and every now and then he read an extract to Weigall, who tried to be as sympathetic as possible, although Shelley's natural history shocked him. At last he said, after rather a long excerpt from *The Witch of Atlas* :—

" I must go on with my *Extra work*.

" Well, I suppose I must too," said C., and they both raced through three more sums, none of which could be solved correctly.

It cannot be said they expended much effort over them, but a " W " was written against each uncompleted sum, and then Weigall said with a cry of relief :—

" I've done an hour's work, let's go and play passage football," and they went.

But C. had entered a new world. He felt he must talk to some one who would understand the nature of the marvellous discovery he had made.

That half he was up to a dry, prim master with a

quiet sniggle and a current of gentle irony, and a general air of Miss Austen's novels about him. There was not much sympathy to be looked for in that quarter, and C. would rather have died than let his tutor, who, as a matter of fact, appreciated certain kinds of verse greatly, know that he read and enjoyed poetry. However, the supply, as so often happens, was soon destined to respond to the demand. C. found what he was looking for close at hand, in the acquaintance and companionship of a boy in the same division as himself, whom he almost immediately after this made friends with. This was a boy called Calmady, who was at a Dame's house. He was an idle and irrepressibly high-spirited boy, to whom work came quite easily, who had a facile talent for writing Latin verses without thinking of what he was doing. He was too lazy to excel in games, although he had a latent talent for cricket, which remained entirely undeveloped.

Calmady introduced C. in his turn to a friend of his called Bentham, who was in a division above them. Bentham was a Colleger. He was an alert and original boy, full of brains and mischief, and always carrying on a half-concealed war with authority. These three soon became inseparable, and formed a Triumvirate, an association of idleness. On long after-fours when they were not playing football, they would stroll up town to Califano's and drink chocolate and whipped cream, and Bentham would bait " Cali " till the latter threatened them all with a carving knife.

Bentham organised a small society called the S.F.T.P.O.C.K., that is to say, the *Society for the Prevention of Christian Knowledge*, and besides the Triumvirate in question, one or two outsiders were allowed to be honorary members. Bentham had drawn up an elaborate book of rules. The first rule was : " No member is allowed to do his own verses or his own *Extra work*." The second rule was : " No member is allowed to prepare a Latin or Greek construe without the aid of a word-for-word translation " ; and the third rule, which would have been the most irritating and monstrous of all in the eyes of the classical masters with a tradition, was : " No member, in translating English into Latin, is allowed to use the Latin-English Dictionary."

Bentham was a poet, a satiric poet, and he wrote pointed satires in the heroic couplet.

Calmady had imbibed considerable education at home. He came from a large family where French and German had been spoken, and his father possessed one of the finest libraries in England. His tastes were literary and musical, but he was an incurable dilettante. He learnt the violin, but resolutely refused to practise. In Calmady, C. found a willing ear into which to pour the discovery he had made of the poet Shelley. Calmady was steeped in the poetry of Byron, to which he introduced C., but up till this moment he had never read Shelley. C., up to the moment when he had discovered the three little red volumes in the school library, had never read nor looked at a line of more modern poetry. He had regarded all poetry as an unintelligible jargon which had to be learnt by heart. In the summer half before he had made Calmady's acquaintance, he had bought at Ingleton Drake's, and heaven knows why, a book of selections of verse and prose for recitation. In this book, alongside *The Bells*, by Edgar Allan Poe, and *Count Robert of Sicily*, by Longfellow, there was Keats's *Ode to the Nightingale*. C. had read this through one evening when he was changing, and had not understood one word of it. He had wondered what it was all about.

He now consulted Calmady about books in general. He found that Calmady was most understanding and shared his tastes. Calmady was also a passionate admirer of Marie Corelli, but Byron now was his chief idol, and he was greatly incensed because his tutor did not like Byron. He told C. about Byron. C. said rather solemnly that he had promised his mother not to read *Don Juan*, but he supposed he could read the rest. He remembered hearing her speak with respect of *Childe Harold*. He bought a selection of Byron in the Canterbury Poets, which he soon devoured. He then resolved to make discoveries for himself. These discoveries proceeded slowly at first. After the discovery of Shelley and a partial discovery of Byron they remained more or less stationary for a time. C., Calmady and Bentham had many other things to think of, and when they had any money to spend on books they usually bought novels. They each of them read *Jane Eyre*, and Weigall read it,

too, and was enormously struck by it, and Fräulein
Setzer gave C. *Les Trois Mousquetaires* as a Christmas
present, and introduced C. to the magic of Alexandre
Dumas.

C., Bentham and Calmady decided to collaborate
in a novel or a romance, and later on to edit
a newspaper. The novel was to be historical and
to deal with the epoch of the French Revolution.

" But, of course," said Calmady, " we must read up
the epoch."

With this object in view, C. began to read Carlyle's
French Revolution, but he could not get beyond the
first chapters. He consulted Miss Derwent on the
matter, and she said she also found Carlyle's style
dreadfully difficult, but fearfully interesting once you
got into it. They searched the boys' library for works
on the French Revolution, and they found a book of
memoirs by Croker, which, however, was not quite
what they needed. It assumed a certain knowledge of
the period on the part of the reader. Nevertheless,
the novel was begun. Calmady and C. were to write
it, and Bentham was to write incidental lyrics and the
verse at the beginning of each chapter, as in the
Waverley Novels. Weigall was to do the illustrations
of those parts which dealt with incidents in natural
history. The title of the novel, which was to be in
three volumes, was to be *Clorinda*, the reason for
the Italianate name being that Bentham said that, if
the novel were to dramatised and turned into an
opera (there was a boy in college, he said, who would

write very good music for it), it was simpler to begin by having an Italian name, at least for the heroine. So the heroine became an Italian by birth, although domiciled in France. The whole of this novel was actually written, mostly in the boys' library, but some of it in school, in a black notebook bought at Williams' by Bentham, who wrote the whole of the text as well as the lyrics. It was profusely illustrated by Weigall, who insisted on the mother of the heroine being of Scottish descent—a Jacobite—in order to give him scope for some sporting scenes in the Highlands.

Bentham was allowed to take it home for the Christmas holidays, but at the beginning of the holidays he caught measles, and the novel, *Clorinda*, was burnt when his effects were disinfected, and so joined the poems of Calvus, the sonnets of Raphael, the original version of the first volume of Carlyle's *French Revolution*, Dante's picture, and other rare things that have irrevocably vanished. The authors did not feel the loss greatly; they were too intoxicated with the fumes of what Balzac called "enchanted cigarettes," that is to say, the planning and discussing of books to be written in the future.

When C. went back to Eton after those Christmas holidays he was sixteen, and he entered upon what proved to be the most enjoyable year of his school life.

CHAPTER VIII

C. was now at the top of Lower Division. He had so far accomplished nothing brilliant nor noteworthy, either at work or at play. He had no friends besides the few which have been mentioned. He was not known in the school at large, and he made friends with none of the masters. Calmady's tutor, Mr. Carr, was literary, and extremely anxious and willing to help and encourage any signs of literary taste in the boys. He would get Calmady and some others to come and read poetry in his house. C. was asked to join the group, but he resolutely refused to do so. Nevertheless, Calmady used to bring back scraps from the feasts of poetry that were held on these occasions.

C. was up in the Lent half to D. D. Keanes, an energetic teacher, unconventional in manner, but conventional at the core, and a thorough Philistine. Keanes saw there was something in C., but his indifference and slovenliness irritated him to madness.

" You're not the fool you pretend to be. You've got *some* brains," he used to say to C., " but you're as obstinate as a mule, and your scholarship is *miserable*."

One day Mr. Keanes told the boys they were each of them to write down the name of his favourite poet, and C., without thinking of what he was doing, wrote

Dryden. He would have put Shelley, who was then his favourite poet, but he did not like to desecrate his admiration by proclaiming it. Mr. D. D. Keanes was astonished and thought C. was posing.

" Dryden ! " he said. " Quote me one line of Dryden."

Upon which C. mechanically, automatically, as if in the schoolroom at Portman Square, began to spout :

> Of these the false Ahitophel was first ;
> A name to all succeeding ages curst :
> For close designs, and crooked counsels fit ;
> Sagacious, bold and turbulent of wit ;
> Restless, unfix'd in Principles and Place ;
> In Pow'r unpleas'd, impatient of disgrace :
> A fiery soul, which working out its way,
> Fretted the Pigmy-Body to decay,
> And o'er-informed the Tenement of Clay.
> A daring pilot in extremity. . .

until Mr. Keanes had to tell him to stop.

" Where did you learn that ? " he said.

" At my first school," said C.

This, although it sounded plausible, was totally untrue, as he had learnt it at home in the schoolroom.

" Well," said Mr. Keanes, " if you can quote Dryden, you ought to be able to learn your saying lessons decently, and I shall see in future that you do."

C. was conscious of an error in tactics, and saw that in future it would be useless for him to pretend to have a memory as bad as the one he had hitherto taken pains to be credited with. During the Easter half he used to enjoy running with the Beagles when the trees of the playing fields were just tipped here and there with green; he delighted in the vistas of fallow country and the fresh furrow, the brown earth, the grey skies with a gleam of blue, the meet at Ditton Cross Roads, or Salt Bridge; he enjoyed, too, the pleasant exhaustion afterwards; the hot bath, and the long, lazy tea with sausages and boiled eggs and strawberry jam, while Weigall read aloud *Three in Norway*. But even here, while taking part in an occupation that he liked, he seemed to take trouble not to distinguish himself, and he purposely and successfully escaped notice, although he probably put in as much hard work as any one else.

It was not that C. was really without ambition. Ever since he had made friends with Calmady a tiny seed, *un grain d'ambition*, began to swell in his heart, but his ambition was not of an ordinary kind, and as soon as it was born he felt it was destined to be thwarted. He gradually realised during the last two years that he spent at Eton that there was a want of harmony between his values, between what he thought was important, unimportant, desirable, undesirable, fun or no fun, good or not good and the values and tone of those who surrounded him both at school and at home.

He realised that he had always felt this unconsciously at home, but he had never been able to put it into words. He did not even now put it into words.

He was merely conscious of a kind of uneasiness, of a misfit, of being either too square or too round for the hole in which he had been placed.

His second summer half in Fifth Form opened out for him a new era of enjoyment. Calmady's tutor took him out with one other master and Calmady one day down-stream. They rowed past the Bells of Ousely to Runnymede. C. rowed extremely well, and Mr. Carr asked him why he wasn't in the boats. He had never put down his name for *Novice Eights*. Mr. Carr told him he must do so at once.

Calmady was a dry-bob, and took no interest whatsoever in the boats, and only a platonic interest in cricket, but since he came from a cricketing family he thought it would be treason not to be a dry-bob.

The next evening C. put down his name for *Novice Eights*, and went through the ordeal successfully. He ended by getting into the Lower Boats.

All this time, and all this summer, he was living in fairyland. Spurred on by Calmady, and his accounts of the poetry sessions at Mr. Carr's, C. was making fresh discoveries for himself in the boy's library. He discovered another little volume bound in red morocco, namely, the works of Keats, published by Moxon, in 1863. He read again the *Ode to the Nightingale*, which he had found unintelligible when he had come across it in a book of recitations. Now it was unintelligible no longer. It touched unguessed-of springs in his nature, and opened the door on to another province of the fairyland into which he had already entered with the magic password of Shelley; a wonderful limbo of dreams and desires—colour and sound.

Then followed after this, the discovery of the romantic poets, of Walter Scott, Coleridge, William Morris's *Defence of Guenevere*, which he found, too, in the boys' library, and the Ballads of Rossetti. But with the exception of Calmady and Bentham, whose scholarship was more advanced, and whose taste was already on the severe side, there was no one whom C. wished to talk to on the subject of his discoveries.

If Bentham was less extravagant in his enthusiasm, and more circumspect in his literary adventures, Calmady made up for it by his unlimited exuberance, and his undisciplined extravagance of expression. Calmady kept the loud pedal pressed down on C.'s enthusiasms, and one day, when C. confided to his friend a great secret, namely, that he wished one day to be an author, Calmady said there was no doubt that he was destined to be one of the greatest of English authors. He knew it for certain. But Calmady's violence of expression did not only take a literary direction. He and C. were up during that summer half to a mathematical master called Smythson. Nothing could be slower or more dreary than the routine of arithmetic, algebra and Euclid carried on on a hot summer's afternoon under the influence of Mr. Smythson's ponderous personality. Calmady became more and more restless, and less and less attentive, till at last Mr. Smythson remonstrated with him fiercely, and threatened him with divers punishments. Calmady, stung to the quick by what he considered the injustice of the proceeding, rose to his feet and delivered a fiery oration. He carried the attack into the enemy's camp, and took the offensive. The disorder and misrule during the mathematical hour was Mr. Smythson's fault, he said, and not the boys' fault.

"We none of us do a stroke of work," was his peroration. "Everybody cribs. You teach us *nothing*. In point of fact," and here his voice reached a high pitch of hysterical frenzy, "you're the rankest beak in Eton!"

Mr. Smythson was so dumbfounded at this outburst that he did nothing. He merely wrote a note to Calmady's tutor afterwards, telling him that his pupil was apt to get dangerously excited and to lose self-control. He supposed it was the hot weather.

Calmady's literary enthusiasm took the shape, firstly, of composing, with the help of C., and again, of Bentham, a fantastic romance modelled to a certain extent on Marie Corelli, with reminiscences of Marion Crawford and Rider Haggard, called *The Opal Ring*, and, secondly, of writing long letters to distinguished authors discussing their works, and the works of other authors. C. was asked to join in this correspondence, but all he consented to do was to make suggestions; he refused, except on one occasion, either to write or even to be the co-signatory of a letter either to Mr. Andrew Lang, Mr. Swinburne, Mr. William

Morris, Mr. Gladstone, or Mr. Walter Pater. But Calmady wrote to some author of note about once a week. One of the masters having said that *Jack the Giant-Killer* was not an English story, Calmady wrote by the next post to Mr. Andrew Lang on the subject of *Märchen*; told him what he thought about his works, and received a civil answer.

In the Christmas holidays of C.'s sixteenth year, Calmady was given, as a Christmas present by one of his relations, Swinburne's *Atalanta in Calydon*. He brought it back with him after the holidays, and he and C. both revelled in this work.

" Why," they said, " have we never been told of Swinburne before ? "

Calmady wrote at once to Mr. Swinburne himself, and told him of this sad neglect in their education. Here was one of the greatest English poets alive and still writing, an Etonian into the bargain, and they had never heard his name mentioned by one of the masters. It was true, they discovered, that *Atalanta in Calydon*, *Erectheus*, and some of the poet's later works were in the boys' library, but it was an amazing thing that they should have been kept in ignorance on so important and vital a subject.

" I am not the only person," wrote Calmady, " who considers you to be one of the greatest of English poets."

To this letter Calmady received no answer, and C. expressed the opinion that he feared the great poet had considered the letter to be cheek.

They were both of them unaware of the existence of *Poems and Ballads*, which was not on the shelves of the school library, until C. happened to find the volume in question, which belonged to his brother Edward, at home. Lady Hengrave saw him looking at it and she promptly burnt the book.

In the holidays C.'s life proceeded with unvarying monotony. At Christmas the aunts and the uncles arrived. The hounds would sometimes meet at Bramsley. The Calhouns would ride over. One of the Calhoun boys was now at Harrow, one at Eton in circles removed from those of C., and the girls were out. In the summer there were cricket matches and lawn tennis. Marjorie and Julia were now both of them out, and the Hengraves spent more time in London than they had been used to do hitherto. Fräulein Setzer had gone, and the schoolroom *régime* was at an end. Marjorie and Julia affected to be very grown-up, and talked disdainfully of C. and of Harry as the " boys."

The finances of the Hengrave family were undergoing one of their periodical crises, and Lady Hengrave told C. during the Christmas holidays, of his sixteenth year, that the next year would have to be his last year at Eton, as they would not be able to afford to keep him there any longer.

It was during the same holidays that C. made a discovery. In one of the turrets of the old part of the house at Bramsley there was a small room full of books. It contained all the British poets, from

Chaucer to Byron, and most of the Elizabethan
dramatists. C. discovered that now that he had tasted
of modern verse, that the verse of the older epochs
was readable too, and did not only consist of dreary,
unintelligible passages that had to be learnt by heart.
He read the works of Milton and delighted in *Paradise
Lost*. He discovered that he could even read the
classics of the eighteenth century—Pope and Dryden
—whom he had learnt to dislike as a child, with
pleasure. He spent a great deal of time in this turret,
and found it a refuge, a sanctuary, especially when the
house was full of relations and guests, and Julia and
Marjorie were indulging in noisy chaff with their contemporaries, and sarcastic remarks at the expense
of C., his brother, and of schoolboys in general.

Lady Hengrave had settled that they could not
afford to send C. to the university, and the question
of his profession was discussed, and for the time being
settled. Harry was to go into the Army. That had
to be at all costs. He was to go to Sandhurst from
Eton, and that being so it would be impossible for C.
to go into the Army as well. Besides, he was not
fitted for it. He was not himself consulted. The
question was, what remained ? It was thought
unlikely that he would ever pass the examination into
the Foreign Office. There was an off-chance of his
passing into the Diplomatic Service, should he chance
upon an examination in which his fellow candidates
were not of the most exalted intellectual calibre, but
even then, could they afford to have a son in diplo-

macy? The answer was in the negative. He was not clever enough to pass into the Indian Civil Service. The Bar was out of the question. All that remained was the chance of Edward getting him "something in the City," or the doubtful and frankly miraculous supposition that C. might suddenly develop capacities and brains.

Finally, Lady Hengrave settled, and Lord Hengrave assented to the following arrangement. C. should stay one year longer at Eton. He should leave at Christmas, before his eighteenth birthday. He would then go abroad for a time and learn some foreign language sufficiently well to qualify him for employment in the City, or for any other profession that might possibly turn up.

All these arrangements, which for the time being C. ignored, were based on the reports that Lord Hengrave received from Mr. Pringle. They were to the effect that C. was getting on fairly well, but that he left much to be desired. He was not a scholar and never would be one. He did not take enough trouble, and did not do nearly as well as he could do. Sometimes he distinctly showed signs of greater ability than his average work manifested. The masters who had to deal with him were all agreed that he could do better if he tried. They all agreed that he did not take pains. His tutor admitted that he was frankly puzzled by the boy. Some masters gave him an excellent report; others could make nothing of him and do nothing with him. The science masters praised him without qualification. His science abstracts were admirable, and yet he took not the slightest interest in science, and did badly in the subject in trials. The truth was that science abstracts gave C. a rare opportunity of writing English, of composing, which he did much better than the other boys. Sometimes he was praised by other masters for his English in translations, but rarely, for, in common with many people, when he translated he did not write so well as when he wrote out of his own head.

Mr. Pringle put down the unsatisfactory nature of the results achieved by C. to his companionship with Calmady, who, so he wrote to Lady Hengrave, was an exceedingly idle and, to his mind, an exceedingly tiresome boy.

Lady Hengrave, who knew Calmady's father and mother, who were both in her eyes thoroughly right in every respect, took no notice of this. His friendship with Calmady was, to her mind, the one bright spot of C.'s Eton career.

She sighed, when she read these reports, and settled in her mind that it was useless to expect anything either useful or brilliant from C., and that he would be fortunate if he obtained " something in the City." That was, however, what she determined he should achieve, unless it were possible to find some private secretaryship for him.

CHAPTER IX

WHEN C. went back to Eton after Christmas to start on the last year of his school life, he was nearly seventeen years old. He had grown rapidly during his last year at Eton, and now looked less loose and less immature; his thick hair was a little less unkempt; his eyebrows beetled a little less, and he had faint indications of an embryo moustache.

His younger brother was taller than he was, and far better looking. He had already made a name for himself as a cricketer and a football player. C. was in the Lower Boats, but that fact summed up all his athletic achievements so far. In any other house he certainly would have had his house colours by now. He was in Upper Division. He did German for Greek. His intellectual career had been, up to this point, of the most ordinary. He had never got a " distinction," although he had sometimes got a " class " in Trials. He had never been sent up for good ; on the other hand, he had never failed to pass Trials. His last year was destined to be the happiest of his school time, possibly the happiest of his life.

He had changed. In the first place he was much tidier. Instead of his clothes being covered with candle-grease stains from head to foot, and instead of his hat being always brushed the wrong way, there was a certain smartness and finish about his appearance, his clothes, his socks, and his ties, which he was unconscious of, and which he inherited from his father, but which other boys noticed. His tutor, too, noticed it immediately, and congratulated him satirically on his elegance. This enraged C., and he no longer wore the new socks he had chosen, which were somewhat audacious in design, except when he went on leave. The boys at his house did not even call him " lush," as they would any other boy, for C.'s smartness was subtly different and they did not criticise him, they accepted him, and confined themselves to laughing appreciatively when in *pupil room* at *private* Mr. Pringle made pointed jokes at the expense of C. and of his handkerchiefs. Mr. Pringle tried to foist the name of " Beau Brummel " on him, but it was too late. C. was already known to the house and outside it as " C.," and nothing can displace a nickname once it is there.

It was during C.'s last summer half that Mr. Carr suggested that his name should be put up for the literary society, on the strength of what Calmady had told him, but the literary society would not hear of it. They considered C. to be an absolute Bœotian.

Bentham, in the meanwhile, had printed a small book of satirical verse, and was contemplating the editorship of a periodical. It was to be called the *Weekly Scug*, but his tutor got wind of it, and exercised preventive censorship, so the newspaper was written out for private circulation only, and had only one number.

The romance, *The Opal Ring*, in three volumes, but only 100 pages of MS. was sent to a whole series of publishers, and to an equal number of magazines for serial publication, but it was always returned with thanks. Calmady, smarting under what he considered to be the injustice of these refusals, sent it to Madame Sarah Bernhardt, with a view to its being dramatised. He never heard if it reached her. It was certainly never performed.

C., in the meantime, partly on his own initiative and partly under the indirect influence of Calmady's tutor, which reached him through Calmady, continued to make discoveries in English literature. He discovered Wordsworth; Matthew Arnold, and Marlowe, as well as the later Elizabethans, and lastly, he made the astonishing discovery that Shakespeare's verse was intelligible—that it *was* verse.

During C.'s last summer term the ninth jubilee of Eton was being celebrated. There was an exhibition in Upper School of Eton relics and banquets of old Etonians were taking place, and there was a feeling of excitement in the air. But C. spent all his time either on the river or in the boys' library. He had an out-rigger and he enjoyed sculling up to Monkey Island after six, and the sights and sounds of the river on the long summer evenings, or bathes at Athens, and feasts of cherries and squash-fly biscuits on the bank. C. did not know this was to be his last summer half.

Had he known it, it is probable that he would have liked the world to stand still on one evening which he spent on the river, and which he never forgot in after life. He was sculling back from Surly in his outrigger, taking long, sweeping strokes. The threat of a thunderstorm had turned the sky grey. There was not a breath of air, and the water of the river was as still and seemed as even as glass. Every reflection in it was distinct and clear-cut. In spite of this there was nothing oppressive in the air, only an enveloping soft summer warmth. By the time he had sculled past Athens and reached the Brocas, and Windsor Castle came into sight, the sky seemed like a warm, grey curtain made of an even silken texture, unfurrowed and without a ripple in it. And this infinite greyness seemed to be faintly, but only just faintly, suffused by the softest pink tinge, as if somewhere behind the curtain there had been a gorgeous sunset ablaze which shone through it. The storm did not break. A few large drops of rain fell, and that was all. The storm floated or drifted away stealthily to the sound of a far-off murmur of thunder, and instead of the rain, a tall, vast rainbow presently encircled Windsor Castle, and by the side of it shone another fainter ghost of its sevenfold glory.

The effect was magical ; the elm trees of the Brocas, the grey walls of the Castle, the little houses and the roofs below the Castle, seemed to have become more unsubstantial than their reflections in the water ; as unreal, as fantastic as that great round rainbow itself,

and to be of the same stuff as those castles that are
faery, that hang for a moment like many-coloured
gems in the morning air and then vanish at the call of
an unearthly bugle.

As C. skulled past the Brocas it seemed to him that
he had entered into an enchanted space, and that he
was released from the bonds of time. " Stay," he could
have said to the fleeting moment, " for thou art in very
truth so beautiful." That was one of the impressions
of school life which was destined to remain with him.

Another equally strong one was the school concert of
the same summer half, which was held on the evening
of June 23rd. Neither C. nor Calmady belonged to
the musical society, and they went to the concert
together. Shelley's *Arethusa* was sung first to music
by Goodhart, and C. and Calmady both enjoyed
hearing the words of their favourite poet, for he was
to them at that time the poet of poets ; his verse
was for them on a different plane to that of all others,
however magnificent those others might be, sung out
by the fresh young voices.

C. remembered reading that lyric for the first time
after tea the same evening he had discovered *The Cloud*.

" Shepherding her bright fountains " struck him
as being a wonderfully beautiful image. He had
never thought about it before. The music pointed
it out to him.

> The loud ocean heard,
> To its blue depth stirred,
> And divided at her prayer,

moved him inexpressibly, and the vision of the worlds
beneath the sea––

> Under the bowers
> Where the ocean powers
> Sit on their pearled thrones.
> Through the coral woods
> Of the weltering floods,
> Over heaps of unvalued stones,

touched, as it already hảd done when he read the poem
for the first time, a spring in his mind that opened a
door on to a kingdom of wonder ; but most of all he
enjoyed the last stanza :––

> And now from their fountains
> In Enna's mountains,
> Down one vale where the morning basks,
> Like friends once parted,
> Grown single-hearted,
> They ply their watery tasks.

He wondered whether friends, really great friends,
could or did ever part, and whether, if they did, they
grew single-hearted once more. The words and the
music steeped him in a curious day-dream, full of
questions and shot with wonder ; but the end of
the lyric soothed and rocked his anxious doubts and
uneasy questionings to sleep.

> At sunrise they leap
> From their cradles steep
> In the cave of the shelving hill ;
> At noontide they flow
> Through the woods below
> And the meadows of Asphodel ;

And at night they sleep
In the rocking deep
Beneath the Ortygian shore ;
Like spirits that lie
In the azure sky,
When they love but live no more.

There was a wonderful peace about this ending, a
final beatitude in the suggestion that love would
endure when the turmoil of life was over ; and the
sense of the poem and the sound of the music both
of them left something behind them that remained
long after they had ceased to be heard.

Arethusa was followed by the *Eton Ode*, of
which the words were written especially for the
occasion by Swinburne, and set to music by Parry.
The music was essentially English ; English in the
same way as Shakespeare's chronicle plays and
Herrick's lyrics are English, with nothing shoddy or
vulgar about it.

Shelley's name is mentioned in the poem. " Shelley,
lyric lord of England's lordliest singers." This pleased
C. and Calmady, especially as Calmady had asked
their division master if he liked the poem, and the
master had said that the introduction of the name of
Shelley had given him great pain. This had made
Calmady and C., to whom he had retailed the story,
furious. They were incensed at a master daring to find
fault with Shelley, but this offence was wiped out by the
triumph they felt in hearing these words sung in public
by a large chorus, and in noting the gratifying fact
that the master in question was singing in the chorus

himself and paying tribute with his lips, if not with his heart, to the genius of Shelley.

But when the ode reached its close—

> Still the reaches of the river, still the light on field and
> hill,
> Still the memories held aloft as lamps for hope's young
> fire to fill,

C. became conscious of a thick lump in his throat. He suddenly realised that he must leave Eton one day, that all this must come to an end ; he suddenly became conscious, and for the first time, that he was the part of something large, of a corporate body, of a long tradition, a note in an endless series.

> Bright with names that men remember, loud with
> names that men forget,

they sang, and he knew that, if his name was not destined to increase the blaze of the long record, it would, at any rate, be one of those obscure notes that contribute to the volume of continuous sound. And at the thought of the brief nature of the longest Eton school life, that it might come to an end almost at once, and then for ever, C. felt an intolerable pang, and bent his head lest Calmady and others should see that he was crying.

That same week he tasted a sip of Eton's outward and visible triumphs in the procession of the boats, which had been put off from the 4th of June. He went up for long leave for the Eton and Harrow match, and Calmady's people had a coach, where

Calmady and C. enjoyed their luncheon, but they neither of them enjoyed the cricket, which was not exciting. C. and Calmady were taken to a Gaiety burlesque on Saturday evening, and up till then all was great fun, but when C. found himself wandering aimlessly about the gaunt rooms of Hengrave House, or sitting in an empty back drawing-room, where the furniture was covered with brown holland, fearful of disturbing his father, and afraid of finding visitors in the drawing-room, and ultimately taking refuge in the schoolroom, and even there liable to come across a *tête-à-tête* between one of his sisters and a girl friend, he was glad on the whole when his leave was over and he got back to Eton.

He left Eton at the end of the summer nursing a secret project about which he had spoken to no one, not even to Calmady; and this was to win the Shakespeare prize. Four plays had been set—*The Tempest*, *Henry V.*, *As You Like It*, and *Julius Cæsar*. C. was perfectly determined to get this prize, and he set about to study these plays, which he had read already, till he knew them almost by heart. He did not say a word about it.

When he went back to Eton at Michaelmas he still did not know it was his last half. Lady Hengrave wrote the momentous decision to Mr. Pringle, and asked him to communicate it to C. This he did shortly after C. arrived. C. was just out of first hundred. If he stayed until the summer he would be in the Upper Boats. He would in all probability get his house colours, unless Pringle's did impossibly badly in the house cup. He was up to a rather severe master, Mr. Whitethorn, but he liked him. They understood each other. Never had Eton life seemed more pleasant or more promising. It was just beginning, he thought, to be really enjoyable. C. was just about to emerge from his shell when the blind Fury had come with the abhorred shears to slit his thin-spun Eton career.

C. at once confided the news to Calmady.

" And what are they going to make you do next ? " he asked.

" They're going to send me abroad to rub up my French. They don't know that I know French now as well as I shall ever know it in my life."

" And then will you go to Oxford ? " asked Calmady.

" No ; they say it's too expensive. They are going to send me into the City into my brother's office, if he can find a place for me."

" Well," said Calmady, " I don't expect they'll let me stay much longer either. They want me to go up for the Diplomatic Service, and I shall have to go to a crammer's or abroad."

And then they spoke of their ambitions and their projects for the future. Calmady wanted to be a composer, and to study music in Leipsig or Berlin, or, failing that—his appreciation of the arts was catholic— to be an artist and to study in the *Quartier Latin*. Unfortunately, he knew little of music, had no ear, and could not draw at all. C. wanted to be a writer—any kind of writer. He would have liked to begin at once at the lowest rung of journalism, in the most humble capacity, but he knew it was not the slightest use to suggest anything of the kind to Lady Hengrave.

"You will be a writer," said Calmady. "I am quite sure you will. My tutor corrected some of your papers last Trials, and he said you were one of the few boys he had ever come across who wrote good English. He said he was quite sure you would write some day if you wanted to."

C. then told Calmady about the Shakespeare prize. Calmady was delighted. He was himself going in for the Prince Consort's prize for German, but had no chance, no chance at all, of winning it. C. swore Calmady to secrecy about the Shakespeare. Later, however, he was obliged to let his tutor know, as his name had to be sent in. His tutor was agreeably surprised and greatly astonished. He thought at first for a moment that there was something behind it, that C. was doing it to avoid a school or to shirk work of some kind, but he did not say this. He contented himself by asking in a mildly bantering fashion how long C. had been a Shakespeare student. C. was inclined to answer "All my life," which he felt was only too painfully true, but he wisely said nothing. He went in for the prize. He thought he'd done very badly and answered wrongly questions which he could have answered perfectly well at any other time. But to his immense surprise, and to the still greater surprise of Mr. Pringle, one day, when he had for the moment forgotten all about it, a large sheet of paper with the well-known blue ink writing caught his eye on the school board, and he stopped to look at it and saw the words " Shakespeare prize." He felt quite dizzy for the moment, and could not read the rest of the words, which seemed to be blurred. Then through the mist he caught the words " Shakespeare Prize : Prizeman, Bramsley major." He walked away, chewing the cud of the great news to himself in silence. Presently he was met by Calmady, who had seen the news, and who greeted him with a shrill scream of triumph. They both walked up town together, and, as though celebrating some old time-honoured ritual, they walked into Califano's, and ordered two choco-lates. Calmady's joy was completely disinterested and all the more unaffectedly sincere from his having failed even to be mentioned among candidates for the Prince Consort's prize.

" I knew you'd get it," said Calmady. " My tutor told me this morning. He set the papers, and he said yours were far the best."

Mr. Pringle was astonished, and as annoyed at having been taken in by C.'s pretended ignorance as he would have been had he been deceived by an assumed knowledge. But he congratulated him warmly, nevertheless, and told him that a man who could quote Shakespeare would never be dubbed a fool.

" You've been taking me in for years," he said. " I thought you were a dunce, and you were a knave all the time. However, I prefer a knave to a dunce," he said graciously, and he gave C., in addition to the book which he was going to present him with on leaving, a Shakespeare Concordance.

The end of C.'s last half went by with incredible rapidity. He was given his house colours, but Pringle's did not get beyond second ties in the matches for the House Cup. Then came the end: the last school concert; the last breakfast at Little Brown's; dinner with his tutor; the choosing of his prize at Ingalton Drake's. He chose the works of Shelley, in four large red volumes, Buxton Forman's edition, and some little books. Mr. Pringle gave a slight snort when he saw the books, and said:

"Why don't you choose something you'll like when you're older?"

Then came the last school concert. The deafening roar as the swells walked up the school hall with their coloured scarfs. The melting voice of Digby, whose voice was just about the break, singing the most sentimental of all sentimental songs, *Lay your head on my shoulder, Daddy*. The boating song, spoken more than sung by the Captain of the Boats; and the *Vale*, which C. had enjoyed so often before when the fact of leaving had seemed so impossibly remote, but which was now almost unbearable.

The last morning in Chapel.

Lord, dismiss us with Thy blessing;

sang the choir. How often C. had wondered what it would feel like when the well-known words

Let Thy Father-hand be shielding
All who here shall meet no more;

would apply to him. They had always given a feeling of sadness, but, on the whole, it was a pleasurable sadness; and, now for the first time in his life, he learnt the difference between the tears that are luxuriously shed in tasting an emotion that does not belong to you and the tears of recognition that respond to the call of actual experience.

The final packing; the last walk through Eton with Calmady and Bentham, neither of whom were leaving yet. The last morning; the scurry. And then farewell to *Mater Etona*. A sad farewell for C., the saddest of all, for what he was leaving had been a home, and the home to which he was returning was a place of exile.

CHAPTER X

BEFORE C. left, Calmady, Bentham and he had a little sheaf of verses printed at New's, the stationer's, consisting of ten short lyrics. The pamphlet was called : " In the Boys' Library and other Poems," printed for private circulation. Most of the lyrics were written by Bentham, but Calmady contributed an *Ode* (in the Spenserian stanza) *to Algernon Charles Swinburne*, and C. wrote a *Vale*. Only a few copies of this pamphlet were printed, and the joint authors enjoyed correcting the proofs enormously, but their proof-correcting was more enthusiastic than accurate, for the only fragment of this pamphlet which is still extant is a stanza from a poem which had been stuck by C. into a notebook, and subsequently torn, so that all the remains of it is this :—

> Wsulsoroven 'co tell the tale,
> His triumph, love and tragedy,
> . . . Colchian shore set sail.

This and the incomplete and undated title page, torn likewise :—

> " In the Boys' Library and other Poems "
> by
> C. B., R. L. C., and E. B.
> Printed for Private Circulation,

is all that remains of the printed work, and it must be
admitted that the fragment is one which even a
German Shakespearean commentator would find
difficulty in reconstructing, and he would have grave
doubts which of the three possible authors to attribute
it to.

C.'s *Vale* survived in MS. He had showed it to his
tutor, who had written on it : " Good, but there were
others at Eton besides Poets."

Here is the *Vale* which was found in Malone's
papers :—

VALE

Farewell, this is the first, the worst Farewell,
    Good-bye to the long dream ;
I hear the tolling of my boyhood's knell,
    And I must cross the stream.

Good-bye, South Meadow, Athens, Cuckoo Weir,
    Good-bye, tall Brocas trees ;
To me you are more sacred and more fair
    Then the Hesperides.

Good-bye, dear Library, dear musty shelves,
    Worn books and marble bust,
Where over tables scholars skipped like elves,
    And raised a cloud of dust.

But there I saw—as through a misty veil,
    A chalice of white fire—
The light of Shelley's song, and heard the tale
    Of his divine desire.

'Twas there I read how, led by fatal chance,
    A mortal loved the Moon ;
And thus I learnt the language of romance,
    And heard the magic tune.

The little book was like a silver key
　　To many-coloured lands,
Where wondrous harps upon a ghostly sea
　　Are swept by a mermaid's hands.

To-morrow I shall be beyond the spell,
　　The fields behind ; the road
Before me ; banished from the wishing-well,
　　And on my back a load.

Yet none can steal the tasted happiness,
　　And if I meet dark hours,
Dear Mother, I will turn in my distress
　　Back to thy chiming towers.

Though pangs begotten of sweet memory
　　Make worse the present woe,
I'll turn to thee and say : " At Eton I
　　Was happy long ago."

" What can I give thee, Mother, in return
　　For all thy gifts to me ?
What if no laurel shall adorn my urn,
　　Nor deed of high degree ?

" Others with honour, glory and green bays
　　Shall brighten thy bright fame ;
I, with no more than love, can swell thy praise
　　With one forgotten name."

His tutor complimented him on it in a bantering
tone, repeating what he had written on the copy, and
hinting that C. had left out everything that made
Eton important. C. felt this was only too true in
another sense. He had left out everything that had
mattered to him, his thoughts, his dreams, his friendships, all that Eton had meant. He had left it out
because he couldn't say it.

During the Christmas holidays after his last half

at Eton, C. realised more sharply than he had ever done before, what a gulf there was between himself and all the rest of his family with the exception of Harry.

Julia and Marjorie, since they had been out, had become models of crystallised convention. They had their father's pride, without his dignity and case, and their mother's rigid limitations, without her culture. C. felt there was no one now at home whom he could talk to about anything that interested him, and he felt more than this. He felt it was impossible to say what he really thought about any subject under the sun. If he got near to doing so before his sisters a misunderstanding would be sure to arise, and this would quickly grow into an argument, and from an argument into a quarrel, which would rage until Lady Hengrave would intervene and put a stop to it by telling C. not to tease the girls.

Towards the end of the holidays the Hengraves went up to London as usual, and C. and Calmady were able to meet. C. was in the flush of the full and complete discovery of Swinburne, and he was intoxicated with the beverage. He thought, as so many people have thought on making the same discovery in the days of their youth, that there was no such poetry in the world ; nothing like it at all ; nothing to be compared with it, and Calmady and C. chanted *The Hymn to Proserpine*, and *The Triumph of Time*, and other poems as they walked down the London streets or in the parks. They felt a great desire to express the homage they felt for the poet in some tangible way. They wanted to see him and tell him— no, tell him they would never dare—but express the fervour of their worship to him by their silent and reverent awe. It seemed a pity, as so many poets were dead, that one who was alive and so superior to all the rest should not receive the homage that was due to him from the living.

Calmady had already written to Mr. Swinburne a year before, but had received no answer. A bolder project now took shape in their minds. This was to call on Mr. Swinburne, and to take with them a letter asking him if they might have the supreme honour of shaking hands with the greatest poet of the age. They discussed the matter for hours, but as C. was going abroad and Calmady was due to return to Eton, time was short, and whatever was to be done would have to be done quickly.

The Sunday before Calmady was due to go back to Eton, C. was asked to luncheon with Calmady's people in Grosvenor Place, and after luncheon they determined to put the long-talked-of and daring project into execution. They looked out Swinburne in the Court Guide, and found that C. A. Swinburne lived in a flat in Hyde Park Mansions. They were faintly astonished to find that his initials ran C. A. instead of A. C., as on the title pages of his books, but they thought that perhaps A. C. were his initials as an author, and C. A. his initials as a private gentleman. They then composed a letter, a very brief letter, asking if they might be allowed to shake hands with the author of *Atalanta in Calydon* and other immortal poems. Armed with this missive they set out for the flat in Hyde Park Mansions. It was a large building. They arrived at a hall where there was a mahogany board with an immense array of names in slots, show-ing who was in and who out. They found a hall porter in uniform.

Did Mr. Swinburne live there? they asked in trepidation.

Yes, he did.

Was he at home?

Yes, he was.

They were shown into a lift, and were whirled up to an upper landing. They rang an electric bell. A dignified butler opened the door; not quite the kind of butler you expected in a poet's household. There was nothing Bohemian about him, and his face had a mask-like calm, his shoulders a military squareness.

Was Mr. Swinburne at home?

He was.

Would he kindly give him this letter and ask for an answer?

The butler acquiesced with perfect deference and departed with the letter. The boys scrutinised the little ante-room with awe. It was hung with trophies of sport; antelopes' horns, stags' heads, riding whips, and some prints of a naval battle.

" His father was an admiral," whispered Calmady.

They waited a moment and then a dignified, very

upright, military gentleman with white hair and kind, grey eyes walked into the ante-room, holding the letter in his hand.

" I am afraid I am not," he said, " my illustrious namesake, but I shall be delighted to shake hands with you."

C. and Calmady blushed scarlet, and wished the earth might swallow them up.   They shook hands, but they were not able to speak, and they left the building not knowing what they were doing.

" Wasn't it awful ? " said C.

" Awful ! " said Calmady, " what must he have thought of us ? He didn't seem to mind," he added.

" No," said C.   " That's what made it worse, his being so awfully jolly. I don't expect he'll tell anybody."

" I hope he doesn't know my people," said Calmady.

C. shivered at the possibility.

" Nor mine.   Mine would be worse, as Mother hates Swinburne."

" So does Mamma," said Calmady, " but nobody need ever know."

" Those are just the sort of things that leak out years afterwards when one has forgotten all about them," said C., remembering dramatic, belated disclosures in novels.

Calmady groaned, and agreed.

" Yes," he said, " like in a Greek tragedy or Hall Caine."

And the two boys felt that from henceforth a

Nemesis would hang over them, and that they had sown a fatal seed, as the members of the House of Atreus were wont to do, which was bound to bear some dreadful fruit.

The next week Calmady went back to Eton, and C. started for France. It was settled that he should spend three months at Versailles in the house of an old musician, whose wife had been in old days a friend of Lady Hengrave's, and who had known better days; then, perhaps, three months in Germany. After that it was to be determined by a competent judge whether he had any chance of passing into any public office, or whether his brother Edward could find him something in the City. It was thought that in either case foreign languages were a necessity, and as he already knew French and German fairly well he would only need to rub them up a little. It would be out of the question, it was thought, for him to go to the University. That would be sheer waste of time, besides being impossibly expensive.

C. had never been abroad before in his life. He felt a certain excitement, not unmingled with apprehension and a sickening longing to go back to Eton.

He asked to be allowed to spend one Sunday at Eton before he left, so as to say good-bye to Harry. This favour was granted. He went down on one Saturday afternoon to Eton and stayed with his tutor. He arrived about tea-time and strolled through the familiar passages. He found Weigall, who had just finished tea, and who now messed with a boy called

Sims.   They were discussing questions that concerned
the Beagles and the House Debating Society, and they
could not pay any attention to C., so absorbed were
they in the immediate facts of the present.

C. realised with a pang that he no longer belonged
to the life that was going on ; that he was of yesterday.
He went out and strolled to Calmady's house.   There
was a riotous game of passage football going on, and
Calmady greeted him cheerily, but could not leave it.

He came back and went to see his Dame, Miss
Derwent. She was very glad to see him, and they
discussed novels, as usual, and when she heard he was
going to Versailles she said he would enjoy the park in
the summer, and that it was conveniently near Paris.
She, herself, was perhaps going to spend Holy Week
in Paris. She preferred France to Germany ; in
Germany there was the music, of course, only she did
wish they would not do so much Wagner.

They talked about Tennyson's latest poem on the
death of a royal personage, which Miss Derwent said
she thought might have been a little more personal.
C. said it was a pity Swinburne wasn't Poet Laureate,
upon which Miss Derwent said that he was a republican
and had written very unpleasant things.

" But he wrote much the best *Jubilee Ode*," said
C., " and he's not a Home Ruler."

Miss Derwent admitted that not to be a Home Ruler
was something, and she thought he was sound on the
subject of Mr. Gladstone, but, nevertheless, he had
written some unpardonable things.

C., finding the conversation was becoming dangerous, said he must go and dress for dinner.

At dinner there were four Eton masters, and C. was shy and silent. They talked about R. L. Stevenson all through dinner, capping each other's quotations. C., who had only read *Treasure Island*, felt out of it. Mr. Pringle approved of C. going to France and deplored his having to go to Germany. He said that the Germans were barbarians, and that their language was excruciating. There was nothing to read in German, but Mr. Whitethorn, who was there, said he would enjoy the music in Germany, and that he would be able to hear a Beethoven symphony for two marks. C. had never heard a Beethoven symphony, nor even of one, although he knew that Beethoven was a phenomenon that Lady Hengrave approved of. But he reflected that if it was anything like the kind of music he had heard at his Aunt Fanny's house he should not spend two marks on it. C. had heard little music in his life, but Lady Hengrave had instilled a certain respect for Mozart and the Italian opera into him, and he had a genuine love of tune.

On Sunday he went to chapel, and after luncheon he went out for a long walk with Harry, as their custom had been while they were still at Eton together. They had always been for the same walk. Up the Long Walk, round the spurless equestrian statue of King George, and home.

C. knew that this was the last time that he and Harry would ever be together on the old terms, and even now that he had left the situation was no longer the same. It was the *finale* of a long piece of music which, while it had been going on, had passed unnoticed.

Harry was now in Army Class. He had already got his house colours, and he was in *upper sixpenny*. He was extremely popular both with the boys and the masters, and his career showed every sign of exploding into a blaze of Eton triumph. The two boys talked about the future, and they talked about the past; the tyranny they had mutually suffered at the hands of Mademoiselle Walter, and of their detestation of the Calhoun family.

Harry asked C. what he was going to be, and C. said he had no idea. He loathed the idea of the City. He loathed the idea of a Government office.

"Wouldn't you have liked to go into the Army?" asked Harry.

"I should never have passed the exam.," said C.

But this wasn't true. He knew that his mother would never have let them both go into the Army, and it was, of course, right that Harry should do so in preference to him. They got back in time for chapel, and C. remembered, as he heard the last hurried, frantic beats of the chapel bell, the old panic he used to have of shirking chapel. Those final hurried beats of the bell had seemed to him the most ominous sounds, fraught with inevitability and doom, in the world. And now he would not hear them in that same way any more.

He went back to London on Sunday night, so as to have a whole last day in London before starting for France.

He started from Victoria Station on Tuesday morning for Paris and Versailles. At the station there was another Eton boy, whom he had known by sight, bound for the same destination. His name was Pelly. They greeted each other shyly, but on the boat they made friends. They were both violently seasick during the whole of the crossing, and both of them swore that they would never cross the Channel again. They arrived at Paris rather late in the evening, and C., who was by way of going straight on to Versailles, put off going till the next day, so as to spend the evening with Pelly, who also desired to have one free evening before joining his *pension*. They both of them sent telegrams to their respective hosts.

During the journey C. and Pelly had made great friends. Pelly was a quiet, cultivated scholar, and he was about to study French in Paris before going to the University. They went to a small hotel in one of the side streets off the *Rue de Rivoli*. C. knew the name of it, because Miss Derwent had told him she always stayed there. It was dark and cheap, clean and stuffy, and had no bathrooms and no electric light, and wooden bedsteads with curtains.

After they had unpacked their things, and washed and tidied themselves, they felt extremely hungry, and they thought they would like some dinner. They strolled up the *Avenue de l'Opéra* till they passed, on the right-hand side, an unpretentious-looking restaurant, on which they saw the name *Bignon*.

"Let's go and have dinner here," said C.; "it looks quite decent."

Pelly agreed that the place seemed inviting and not too crowded. They sat down at a table, and a friendly waiter suggested that they would, no doubt, fancy "*des hors d'œuvres et quelques huîtres*," a nice, plain *consommé Milanaise*, and, perhaps, a *truite meunière* to follow, and a plain roast *poularde* with a little salad. That sounded simple enough. Another waiter, with large side-whiskers and black apron, hinted with aloof disinterestedness at the wine, and C. said he thought some claret, just an ordinary Bordeaux, would be the thing. The waiter agreed. There was a *Hautbrion* which he was certain would meet the case. He came back presently bearing with reverence, and yet with the intrepid familiarity of those who are used to handling sacred things, an old cobweb-covered bottle, slightly tilted in a basket. He uncorked the bottle without shaking it.

The food proved to be simple and excellent. The wine, too, was soothing, so much so that they ordered another bottle.

They began by discussing Eton, the boys and the masters, recent events and happenings; they went on to discuss books and poets, and C., after a few glasses of the *Hautbrion*, declaimed reams of Shelley and Swinburne to the surprised but interested Pelly. They sat on talking until late. They finished up with

coffee, and the waiter suggested a "*verre de fine.*"
This proved to be also very pleasant and soothing,
and not at all fiery. They repeated the dose. They
then asked for the bill. It was unobtrusively brought,
face downwards, and amounted to 251 francs 35 cen-
times. C. was aghast. This represented his monthly
allowance. He would only just have enough money
to get to Versailles, and he doubted whether he would
have enough money to pay his hotel bill. Pelly was
anxious to pay half, but C. insisted that he had
invited him. Luckily Mrs. Roden had sent him a
cheque before starting, otherwise he would not have
been able to pay the bill at all.

He put down on the plate 250 francs in paper and
20 francs in gold. The waiter indicated by his gesture
that he would fetch the change, but C., half as in a
dream, and half feeling that if he was in for a penny
it was better to be in for a pound, and that the tip
was only on the scale of the rest of the extras, waved
him away, and left him in possession of the lordly
tip. The waiter took the twenty-franc piece like a
lamb, with perfect composure, indicating that the
transaction which had just been accomplished had
been between gentlemen and men of the world who
understood each other perfectly, and C. wondered
whether all restaurants in Paris were as costly as this
one. Fortunately his hotel bill proved to be unexpectedly moderate, and he had just enough money left
to travel to Versailles.

CHAPTER XI

THE family to which C. was now introduced consisted of an old man and an old lady called Maartens. The professor and his wife were both Dutch by birth, but they had lived many years in France, and the French people simply called them Martin. They had once been well-to-do landed proprietors, but they had lost all their money in a financial crisis, and were obliged to receive pupils in order to live. Professor Maartens gave music lessons, and his wife taught French. The professor had only adopted the title of Professor since the change in his fortunes. He was not a professional musician, but he was intensely musical, and he played the pianoforte with a soft touch and great delicacy of feeling. He had composed a barcarolle which had been published and publicly performed in happier days before the Emperor Napoleon III. They lived in a small flat in a side street on the left-hand side of the palace. It was small, but scrupulously clean. Madame Maartens had been brought up from her earliest years in France, and she had not only known Lady Hengrave, but Lady Hengrave's mother, who had lived in Paris. She was refined and cultivated and devoted to the pupils she received in her house.

She took to C. at once. When he arrived at Versailles he had not finished growing, and he was
already tall for his age, but he had lost the look of
immaturity and awkwardness that had seemed to
hang about him during all the end of his Eton career.
Nobody now would have called him the ugly duckling.
In fact, Madame Maartens was extremely struck by
his looks, and in writing to Lady Hengrave congratulated her on having a son who promised to be so good-
looking, and who was " *plein d'esprit.*" Lady Hengrave was astonished by these comments, and thought
that Madame Maartens must be suffering from senile
decay. A photograph of C. as he was in those days is
still in existence. He looks in it curiously old for his
age, and almost like the hero of an 1830 romance, with
a touch of Balzac and Dickens about him. In real life
he probably did not look as old as that, or did not look
old at all, but Madame Maartens frequently remarked
that he was old for his age, and said on one occasion
that at times he behaved like a child of ten, and at
others he reasoned like a man of forty.

He was very dark, his hair was thick and undisciplined, his cheeks a little hollow, and his eyes very
bright and very dark. His manners were shy, reserved
and diffident, and the French people liked him at once.
He was happy at Versailles, and felt once more that he
had found a home which might, to a certain extent,
make up for having left Eton so prematurely.

His life settled down into a regular routine. Madame
Maartens gave him a French lesson every day, and

three times a week he had a lesson from a French schoolmaster, Monsieur Jollivet, who lived at the other end of the town—rather a long tram drive—in a neat little villa. Monsieur Jollivet taught him French literature and French composition. The other pupil in the Maartens' house was a French boy called Henri Marcel, to whom Madame Maartens was teaching English.

Madame Maartens suggested that C. should from time to time go to Paris, dine there, go to the theatre, and come back by a late train ; but C. made excuses. The truth was that he had no money, and would not have any till the end of the month. He had not even enough money to pay for the bi-weekly tram journey to Monsieur Jollivet's house, and every time he went there during the first month he was obliged to walk, which meant starting three-quarters of an hour before his lesson began.

Monsieur Jollivet was a small, dark, bearded, fiery and lucid teacher, with a great contempt for his own countrymen and a great love of what he called *real* French literature, which meant Molière, Racine, La Fontaine, Voltaire, André Chénier, and Guy de Maupassant, but not Zola.

Lucidity, simplicity, logic and ease were the qualities he rated highest. He made C. read Corneille and Racine, and was stupefied to find that he was already familiar with both these authors, and could quote them by the yard. The fact gave him great satisfaction, as he was able to use it against the class of French boys he taught at school.

"*Pas un de vous n'est à la cheville de cet Anglais*," he would say to them.

He made C. read the plays and write analyses of them afterwards, and also translations and compositions of his own.

Monsieur Jollivet did not despise all the modern poets. He thought that Victor Hugo had sinned colossally against the canons of taste and the laws of proportion, but he would sometimes say: "*quand il est grand, il est grand comme le monde*," and in support of this he would quote the lines from *Napoléon II.*:

> Demain, c'est le cheval qui s'abat blanc d'écume.
> Demain, Ô conquérant, c'est Moscou qui s'allume,

Foreign literature and languages he ignored.

One day he asked C. to translate something from one of the English poets, and C. tried his hand at Swinburne's *Garden of Proserpine*.

Monsieur Jollivet was not pleased by the result.

C.'s version of

> " And gathers all things mortal
> With cold immortal hands."

"*Et cueille toutes choses mortelles de ses mains froides et immortelles*" shocked him.

"*Ce n'est pas clair*," he said, "*et c'est d'un goût douteux*."

Monsieur Jollivet advised him in the future to confine his translations to the English prose authors. On the other hand, he was pleased with C.'s French prose, which he said was pure, except on one occasion,

when C. unfortunately used a phrase of current
journalistic slang, "*le* clou *de la pièce*"—harmless
enough, one would have thought. This incensed
Monsieur Jollivet, who went so far as to say that it
was the fabrication and use of such idiotic, meaningless and vulgar expressions which had caused the
French to lose the Franco-Prussian War.

In politics Monsieur Jollivet was a pessimist, and
was for ever prophesying disasters to his country.
Were the French to fight the Germans to-morrow,
he would say, the latter would walk into France
"*comme dans du beurre*," and he attributed this to
the incurable vanity, complacency and frivolity of
his countrymen.

Curiously enough, he introduced C. to the name of
Wagner. At least he made C. realise that Wagner
was an out-of-the-way phenomenon. Monsieur Jollivet
said he seldom went to the theatre—the modern plays
were so stupid, and the modern actors massacred the
classics—but he did go to the opera, whenever Wagner
was performed, and the *Valkyrie* and *Tristan* had
stupefied him.

"*Cette musique*," he went on repeating, "*qui ne
resemble à rien.*"

C. checked this opinion by asking Professor Maartens
and his wife what they thought about Wagner, and
both the Professor and Madame Maartens (and she
was extremely musical as well as her husband) agreed
with Monsieur Jollivet that Wagner was a great genius,
and that evening after dinner the Professor played C.

some selections from the *Ring*, which impressed him greatly.

" You must go to Paris the next time they do one of the operas," they said, " and hear one."

" Yes," said C., blushing and thinking of his straitened finances.

And they, too, said they had no wish to go to the theatre, but they did enjoy more than anything else an evening at the opera, only——

C. felt they could not afford it, and felt, too, the right thing for him to do would be to take them to Paris one night, and give them the treat they so greatly enjoyed. However, the state of his budget made it, for the moment, quite impossible. Pelly wrote to him, and asked him to meet him in Paris and share his delightful discoveries. C. was only too willing, but he felt cramped at every turn for want of money. At last he thought of selling something. He had a gold watch-chain and two pearl studs which had been given him by his godmother. He spent his last francs in registering these and posting them to a silversmith in London. He asked him to make an offer for them. The silversmith sent him back a cheque for five pounds and kept the jewels—this, for the moment relieved the situation. On receipt of the money he wrote to Pelly, and suggested they should meet and go to the play. He did not suggest dinner, as he was still under the impression that to feed at a restaurant in Paris was a pleasure which could only be indulged in by the very rich. Pelly accepted the invitation and met him at the station, and suggested that they should go and have some food somewhere, but C. said he thought it too expensive.

Pelly had now gained sufficient experience of Parisian life to be able to convince C. that cheaper restaurants than *Bignon* existed. They went to a *Bouillon Duval*, where they had an excellent meal for two francs fifty. After dinner they decided to go to the play. In looking through the list of theatres in the newspaper, C. caught the name of Fanny Talbot, his early adoration. She was playing in a historical drama. He said they must go and see her, so they went to the *Porte Saint Martin*, where the drama was being played.

Fanny Talbot's art had improved in the interval, and although her hair had been dyed a dark colour, and her face had lost its look of youth, she was still strikingly beautiful, perhaps the most beautiful, and certainly the best dressed actress on the stage at that time. But she was not the same person to C. as she had been when he had first seen her at Brighton. Then he had not thought of her as an actress at all. He had identified her with the romantic, proud and persecuted personage she had interpreted on the stage. He had thought of her as the embodiment of youth, thwarted romance, and outraged virtue. Now he looked at her as a beautiful and finished actress, and her art, although competent enough to deserve the praises of the French critics, was neither sufficiently inspired nor artistic to sweep these two boys off their feet, nor to make up for its commonplace setting. The play in which she was appearing was a historical melodrama which was more like a series of *tableaux vivants* than anything else, with not sufficient life in it to afford one thrill. The two boys enjoyed themselves nevertheless. Pelly was by this time a great theatre-goer, and he said that C. really must see the great actors of Paris, the artists of the *Comédie Française*: Got, Bartet, Barctta, Samary, as well as Réjane and Dupuis, and also the adventurous pioneers of the *Théâtre Libre*.

When C. told Monsieur Jollivet that he had been to see Fanny Talbot in the historical drama of *Malmaison*, he snorted with contempt. He advised C., if he *must* go to the play, to try the *Théâtre Français* on a night when they were not playing Racine ; in Molière there were still a few passable actors who knew how to speak, but there wasn't one who could interpret Racine. Nowadays directly an actor made the slightest success he was obliged to have a troup, if not a theatre, of his own to tour in America and round the world, to gather dollars and exaggerate his effects, and cheapen them until his art became as coarsened and travel-stained as his much labelled travelling trunks.

The age of art was rapidly fading away. Few people know how to write French, and still fewer how to speak it. In twenty years' time French written in the classical tradition would be unintelligible, and what was it replaced by ? A shoddy journalese in prose— expressions such as *le clou*—and cryptic and senseless mystifications in shapeless verse.

In the meantime, C. was making discoveries for himself in French literature. M. Jollivet made him read the classics, but he surreptitiously read the moderns as well—novels: Zola, Daudet and Flaubert; and Pelly brought him echoes from the *Quartier Latin*, and of the enthusiasms of the young generation; the names of obscure symbolists and decadents, few of whom were destined to achieve more than a passing notoriety.

Pelly also got wind of Norwegian literature. Ibsen was just emerging above the European horizon, and *Hedda Gabler* was being acted at the *Vaudeville*. The *Théâtre Libre* introduced him to Paris by producing *Ghosts* two years before. Pelly was immensely interested, but failed to find great response in C., who was drawn to the more romantic drama, and was revelling in Victor Hugo and Alfred de Musset. One night C. and Pelly watched a performance of *Hernani* from the gallery of the *Théâtre Français*, and they were moved to tears. The time went on, the winter, which was a long and cold one, began to show slight signs of surrender before the invasion of spring.

With the exception of occasional visits to Paris, C.'s life was a monotonous one. He would work all the morning. In the afternoon he would go for a walk with Henri Marcel, the French pupil who lived in the house, who was a conscientious, unassuming, industrious, but unimaginative boy. Twice a week he had lessons from Monsieur Jollivet, and on Monday afternoons he would attend Madame Maartens' day. She

would sit in a red silk and somewhat faded armchair,
dressed in mauve velvet, which was her one dress for
occasions, and receive the guests, who were varied.
They consisted of members of the Versailles aristocracy, with a sprinkling of musicians, and on one
occasion a French-Canadian Professor of Christian
Science. Madame Maartens was proud of C., and
liked showing him off to her friends. Some of these
used to invite him to breakfast or dinner, exquisitely
served meals in small panelled dining-rooms, on
smooth polished mahogany tables without table linen,
presided over by an old retainer, who would dangle a
bunch of keys.

On one occasion Madame Maartens took him to dine
with two American old maids who lived in an apartment on the top story of a house near the *Hôtel des
Réservoirs*. When they entered the drawing-room
Madame Maartens announced C. solemnly as " The
Honourable Caryl Bramsley," and the two old maids
each made a low curtsey. They came from a Virginian
family, and seemed to belong to an older and more
refined civilisation. They were cousins. They seemed
to be the living ghosts of pre-revolutionary Versailles,
and the mother of one of them had been born
seventeen years before the Revolution, so that her
links with the past went back to an incredible
distance, and she herself remembered Napoleon at
Trianon, and the *Cent Jours*, and the Battle of
Waterloo with perfect distinctness.

They were both beautiful to look at, with exquisite

lace frills, lace caps and cuffs, and one of them took snuff with a little gold spoon from a tiny gold snuff-box. They had lived at Versailles all their lives, and so had their parents, even through the Revolution and the Terror. The mother of the eldest remembered seeing the Dauphin playing in the gardens of Versailles. They spoke of the *Place de la Concorde* as the *Place Louis Quinze*, and Rachel seemed to them a modern, a revolutionary actress.

They spoke exquisite French, and still more exquisite English, and they were delighted with C. He called on them after he dined there, and they offered him preserved fruits, and entertained him with anecdotes and reminiscences of the past.

CHAPTER XII

As the spring progressed, C. continued to make discoveries in French as well as in English literature, but he had nobody with whom he could share them. Pelly was engrossed in art and in the discovery of Norwegian plays and Russian novels, that C. thought unreadable, nor did his friend passionately care for verse, and as for Monsieur Jollivet, he had bounded in his seat when C. told him that he had been reading Zola. It was not the questionable morality nor the indecency of Zola's work that offended him, but the lack of proportion he displayed. Zola's work, he said, was all false ; his pretence of realism absurd, his talent one of distortion ; he was a painter of exaggerated panoramas, and one of the least *French* of French authors. C. had also admitted to Monsieur Jollivet that he had read Baudelaire and Verlaine, and here again he had come up against uncompromising opposition. Monsieur Jollivet maintained that C. was beginning at the wrong end ; that it was impossible for him to gauge the merits of such authors before he had formed a standard by being thoroughly familiar with the classics. Baudelaire no doubt had written some fine verses, but he was affected and perverse, an exotic. Verlaine had a lyrical gift, but C. should seek the garden and the

fields, all of them full of natural flowers, before studying the artificial products of the hothouse ; and as for
all the symbolists and decadents, they were *de
simples fumistes*, or, what was worse, they often used
what might have been a genuine talent to debase and
disfigure the French language.

" You can't," he said, " be obscure in French."

" *Tout ce qui n'est pas clair n'est pas français.*"

He worked himself up into a fever, and ended by
saying the greatest of French poets, and, indeed, the
greatest not only of all French writers but of all writers
in all the world, and of all times, was La Fontaine. C.
confessed to finding the fables tedious.

Monsieur Jollivet sighed.

" When you are forty," he said, " you will agree
with me."

To C. this seemed to be impossibly far off.

" Well," said Monsieur Jollivet, " at least if you
read the moderns, read the best ; read André Chénier,
Alfred de Vigny, Musset, Heredia, and in prose read
Sainte Beuve, Maupassant and Flaubert ; they all
write *French ;* but do not waste time on the *gali-
matias* of Mallarmé and such people. All that is *du
chinois.*"

C., who had been profoundly impressed by the music
and the imagery of Baudelaire's poems, and whose
heart was captured by the intangible charm and the
intolerable poignancy of Verlaine's wayward min-
strelsy, felt it was no use discussing these things. And
the vision of a small yellow copy of La Fontaine, out of

which he used to learn the fables by heart with Mademoiselle Walter, rose up before him, and filled him with nausea.   He wondered whether one day he would in reality come to agree with Monsieur Jollivet. Possibly about the old things, he thought, but not about the new.   He would always admire Baudelaire and Verlaine.

It was on an afternoon in March—one of those surprisingly balmy days when you feel that winter is dying—after one of his lessons, which generally began with the analysis of a play of Racine or Molière and ended by a discussion on general subjects, during which Monsieur Jollivet always managed to rail at the authors who dared to try and obscure the glorious lucidity and the inviolate logic of the French language, that C. walked to the Park of the Château and sat down on a stone seat and, putting away from him all thoughts of French literature, took out a pocket Keats and began reading *Endymion* straight through.   He was soon engrossed in the poem, which, in spite of its subject and its setting, brought back vividly and poignantly to his mind the sounds and smells of English lanes and English fields, and the colour of English hills and English skies.   He was so absorbed in his reading that he did not notice that a man had sat down beside him till he heard a faint grunt.   He looked up and saw, sitting at the other end of the long stone seat, rather an untidy man on this side of the middle-age barrier, and not more than thirty-five years old, but having certainly left behind

him all his baggage of early dreams, youthful ambitions and illusions. He was large without being fat,
His hair was shaggy and rather long. There was a
slightly Johnsonian look about him ; his clothes dark
and untidy, but you did not notice his clothes at all.
They seemed all right. What you did notice were his
great broad forehead and his eyes, which were pene-
trating and clear. You seemed to know at once that
this man had a good eye for what was good. He, too,
was reading in a small book, and every now and then
emitting a snort, which might have been pleasure, or
which might have been pain. As a matter of fact, he
was reading Homer. It was probably the thought of
what some people might say about the book rather
than anything which he found in it which made him
snort.

The stranger suddenly put down his book, looked at
C., who smiled and turned a little red.

" Do you think Homer was written by a committee ? " the stranger said.

" My tutor at Eton," said C., " used to tell us that
it was very difficult to believe that the same man had
written the *Iliad* and the *Odyssey*."

" Yes, he would say that," said the stranger.
" Why do they think they know better than Aristotle ?
He was probably the wisest man who ever lived, and
more than two thousand years nearer to the times of
Homer. Are you going to Oxford ? "

C. said he was not destined for the University.

" Well, if you do, don't go to Oxford, go to Cambridge. On the whole it will do you less harm. It's getting cold ; let's walk."

They got up and walked a little in silence. Then the stranger began to talk of the places they were passing. They were near the *Grand Trianon*. He pictured the last days that Louis XVI. and Marie Antoinette spent at Versailles, and Louis XVI.'s last day's hunting—October 5th, 1789—and Marie Antoinette sitting for the last time in the *Trianon* during that rainy morning till the King summoned her.

" It was a pity the French monarchy fell. What a tragedy ! " the stranger said. " Do you know Greek ? "

C. said he had learnt a little, but had forgotten. He had done German instead.

" You can learn Greek now," said the stranger. " You've plenty of time. You're young. You can learn German later, or not at all. It won't do you much good. You probably know enough now to read all that's worth reading : *Faust*, half a dozen lyrics of Goethe, and Heine. There's nothing else ; only it's worth it for that—well worth it. But Greek is endless. I met some of the young Oxford poets and essayists in London the other day. They said that Greek was useless ; Homer a superstition ; Æschylus unintelligible ; Sophocles dry, and Euripides affected. I asked them whom and what they admired. They said Flaubert and Turgenev. But the owls did not understand that the reason they admired these people (if they did, if they had read and understood them, which I greatly doubt), the reason they are at all admirable, is for conforming to the Greek standard of excellence, and to no other. They are admirable as artists, and admirable only in so much and in so far as they attain that standard—set by the Greeks. Turgenev tried to write Greek tragedy. He had the form, but not the power—no *estomac*. Flaubert had the *estomac*, but hadn't the restraint. He could paint, but he couldn't really draw. The principles of art, like the principles of strategy, are eternal. It doesn't matter if you fight with bows and arrows, or if you fight with torpedoes and the *mitrailleuse*. It doesn't matter if you write a sonnet or an epic ; if you make a statue of Apollo or paint a picture of the Thames Embankment. The principles are the same, and when you apply them well, the result is good art, or good verse—a victory ; and if you apply them badly, the result is bad art, bad verse—defeat.

"But the best verse of all is Greek—Homer. Nothing has ever touched it. Do you remember when Priam goes to Achilles to ransom the body of Hector ? " And here he began to quote :—

"Ὣς φάτο, τῷ δ᾽ ἄρα πατρὸς ὑφ᾽ ἵμερον ὦρσε γόοιο·
ἁψάμενος δ᾽ ἄρα χειρὸς ἀπώσατο ἧκα γέροντα.

"But the words so stirred the heart of Achilles that he wept, thinking now of Patroclus, and now of his old father at home, and Priam wept, thinking of his dead Hector."

"That is how Church translates it in *Stories from*

Homer, and, as usual, he does it best, only he leaves out one line :—

" And he touched the old man's hand and gently moved him back."

And the stranger repeated the Greek lines again, and as he did so he looked towards the lowering sunlight which was reflected and shone on the large window panes of *Trianon*, and at the sky which, for the first time that year, was spring-like. It was lilac and green, and the trees were soft and dewy. In the East, great snowy, cold clouds were piled up one on another, faintly reflecting the light in the West. A black-cap was singing somewhere. The stranger's eyes filled with tears, and there was a new light in them, and of the same quality as that of the evening sky. C. felt they were for the moment on holy ground, and that it was good for him to be there. So do great verse and the words of the mighty poets transfigure the semblance and the manner of ordinary mortals, for nothing could have been more prosaic than the appearance of the stranger. All at once the spell was broken, and the stranger said :—

" I must go. I have got an appointment. My name is Burstall. I live 4, *Rue de la Gare*. Where do you live ? "

C. told him his name and address.

" I am generally in to breakfast at twelve. You must come some day. I'll send you a line."

With these words Burstall left C. and walked away briskly. C. waited a moment longer in the garden and then he, too, walked away in the opposite direction, wondering who the stranger was, and fearing to force himself upon the stranger's society.

A week passed without C. hearing anything from his new acquaintance, and C. had almost forgotten all about the incident when he received a card, written in a diminutive and clear scholarly handwriting, asking him to breakfast on the following Saturday. He accepted and went. He found Burstall occupied three small rooms on the fourth floor of a large building. The rooms were untidy and littered with books and papers. An old woman, immensely hardy and sturdy, a peasant called Suzanne, with grey hair and the makings of a grey moustache, looked after him and cooked for him. After C. had been sitting for a few moments on the only available space that was not covered with books, Suzanne put her head into the room and announced that "Monsieur" was "*servi*."

Burstall leapt up and shouted, "What about the omelette?" he trusted that was not *servi*. It was not. There was on the dining-room table, covered with *toile cirée*, only some *hors d'œuvre* in the form of radishes, sardines and olives.

"I always make the omelette myself," said Burstall.

He disappeared into the kitchen, whence there issued during the next few moments the echoes of a heated argument.

"*Mais non, Monsieur. Ce n'est pas comme cela qu'on fait une omelette.*"

Presently Burstall came out very red in the face, and said :—

" She never will cook an omelette on a hot enough fire. However, I have let her do it just for this once to pacify her."

This was, as C. found out later, the usual ritual at Burstall's luncheons. He always announced his intention of making the omelette himself. Suzanne let him begin, then made objections. The result was he would argue, shout, and drop an egg, and finally let Suzanne cook the omelette herself, which she did quite admirably.

They sat down in the dining-room, which had no pictures on the grey *boiseries*, and no ornaments save a glass of narcissi and violets, lilies-of-the-valley and one little alien rose, put there by Suzanne.

Burstall fetched a bottle of burgundy, and they sat down to their breakfast. Burstall talked about Paris ; what was going on. He had seen Musset's *Fantasio* at the *Odéon*.

" Professional actors spoil Musset," he said. " Children would do it, only, unfortunately, they are not children's plays ; or amateurs, if amateurs could only speak and move and not be self-conscious. Delaunay was the only professional actor who could act Musset. His plays are meant for drawing-rooms. So are Racine's, as to that. There has only been one perfect performance of Racine, I expect. At *Saint Cyr*. I should have liked to have seen it. Actors shout and rant Racine now. That's all wrong. I suppose you were taught at Eton to despise Racine ? "

C. said he had been brought up at home to admire Racine, but he confessed the plays bored him. He had never seen one acted.

" I'll take you some day," said Burstall. " Sometimes you get a decent performance, and you want to hear the verse spoken. The dons and the critics in England despise Racine for one simple reason. They don't understand French. They understand *sometimes* what the words mean, but not always ; they are capable even then of the most ludicrous blunders, but they don't feel the *values* of the language. The French don't feel the values of English—of Shakespeare and Milton ; they don't see why

> Smooth-sliding Mincius crowned with vocal reeds

is a good line, but they don't go about saying the English can't write verse. They say they can't understand English and don't want to. It's all they can do to compete with their own language, which, as you know, is an exacting one. The English see no difference between Voltaire's plays and Racine's ; they don't see why lines like

> J'ai voulu devant vous exposant mes remords,
> Par un chemin plus lent descendre chez les morts

are the lines of a great poet, that they are as good as they can be. They talk rot about it not being Greek. It isn't ; it's French. Phèdre is a practising Catholic Christian, slightly tinged with Jansenism, and she talks the language of Versailles. But she is a living being, and the language she talks is quite perfect.

"Don't believe a word they tell you about anything French. They know nothing about it whatever. Because Matthew Arnold talked nonsense about French verse, which he didn't understand, they think they can do the same thing safely. Some day, if ever they give a *matinée* of *Phèdre*, we'll go. You're bored with Racine now. That's because they've spoilt it for you at home or at school, or at both, but once you hear the lines properly spoken you'll understand that it is great verse."

C. told Burstall about his lessons with Monsieur Jollivet, and of the want of appreciation that Professor professed of the modern authors.

"A great deal of what he says is true," said Burstall. "He's quite right about Zola not being French. He's got what they call a "*gros talent*"; he can set crowds going, but he can't write French; not French such as Maupassant writes. As to the modern verse, your man is annoyed by the *fumistes* I suppose. There always are a lot of those about, because literature in Paris is a living thing. People care for it, care for it enough to make jokes about it and in it, and to understand the jokes that are being made about it and in it. But Baudelaire is good, as good as he can be, and of the living poets Verlaine is about the best thing in French lyrics since Villon, and Heredia is first-rate. You've read him?"

C. hadn't.

Burstall quoted some lines from a poem on a Greek subject, a funeral epigram on a shipwrecked mariner.

"That's as good as possible," he said, " only it takes him fourteen lines to say it.   A Greek would have said it in four.   Heredia would have written a perfect sonnet about those flowers that Suzanne has put on the table.   Rufinus did it in six lines ; they are his flowers, too.   'I send you Rhodocleia, this garland, the lily, the rose, the moist windflower, the wet narcissus, and the dark-eyed violet.   Crowned with these flowers, put pride away, for you shall fade, you as well as the garland.'   I'll lend you a Heredia when you go away."

Then they talked of English books and of English verse, and to C.'s delight there was nothing that Burstall did not seem to know.   He quoted Webster and Donne ; Dryden and Keats ; Pope and Byron.

"Of course," he said, " you are at the stage when you think Swinburne is the greatest poet who ever lived.   But you won't think that for ever.   He is a damned good poet at his best.   For the moment at a certain epoch of one's life he's like Wagner's music, he annihilates everything else.   Have you ever heard Wagner's music ? "

C. shook his head.

"Well, you'll have to some day, I suppose.   You must get through it like measles.   Don't go to it here ; they can't do it.   It's poisonous, neurotic stuff, and it's all wrong ; but you'll have to experience the disease.   Don't think I'm saying you're wrong to like what you like. You're young, that's the great thing, and I'm not, and the young are often right in admiring what they do admire. It's a great thing they should admire anything. When people get older they see nothing in Shelley or Swinburne; the colours seem to have faded out of these things, but they haven't really. The colours are there, only they are too dry and too crusted to see them. Only remember, there are other poets as well, and if they tell you that Pope is not a poet, or that Byron couldn't write verse, don't believe them. There is not a young man now alive writing who would now give both his hands to be able to write one line as good as any line of Pope, or one of Byron's good lines, and they could no more do it than fly. Pay no attention to them, neither to the dons, and still less to the professsional writers. You don't know any? Thank God for it, and don't. I suppose you write yourself?"

C. blushed scarlet.

"Yes," he said, "I have tried to write a little."

"Well, you must show me what you've written. I shall tell you what I think, and I shan't talk nonsense to you. Whatever the stuff is like you are writing now, if you are keen about it, and go on, you will end by writing something good." He paused, and added with a sigh: "It may be something quite different from what you imagine. When I was young I thought I should like to write an epic on King Arthur, and a tragedy about Helen of Troy, and God knows what— a century of sonnets, hymns like Ronsard's. Actually

I make my living by writing in journals that nobody reads, and about people like Donne, and Rabelais, and Villon, that nobody cares about except pedants who don't understand them—or anything else. We live in an illiterate age, and in a country that cares nothing for art and literature, and it's becoming—although this wasn't always so, and certainly not in the eighteenth century—a good thing when they don't; because those who do tend to become nauseating. Here, in France, there is a public which does care about those things. I don't say they are better. I don't say they are even more intelligent. In some ways they are not, but they do care about those things; they care for literature, art, and the stage, only they take no interest in our country, or our literature, or in any country except their own. They are like the Chinese, and they have a stiff brick wall round them. But if you do care for such things, for good prose, good verse, good pictures, and good music, you will have a lonely time of it in England, and the more you keep it to yourself, the better."

They had finished breakfast by now, and Suzanne brought in some cups of steaming, fragrant coffee. Burstall offered C. a *Bock* cigar, and wandered round the untidy room, picking up a book here and a book there, and carrying on a disconnected running comment. He was a book collector. And looking for a quotation from *Phèdre* he took up from an untidy litter a small volume, and showed it to C., saying :—

" That's a first edition. I picked it up for two

francs. These things do happen sometimes. Adventures in book-collecting happen sometimes—even to the adventurous."

He began reading to himself, and he stopped and cried out :—

" My God, how good it is ! " and his eyes were wet.

CHAPTER XIII

C. LEFT Burstall's house in a flutter that day. What filled him most with excitement, not unmixed with apprehension, was the thought that Burstall might one day read the attempts he had made at writing. During his last year at Eton he had written long ballads, in which the influence of Coleridge, Walter Scott, William Morris and Rossetti was paramount, but he had burnt all of these, except what had been printed in the pamphlet started by Bentham, entitled *In the Boys' Library and Other Poems*. But since leaving Eton the influence of Robert Browning, Victor Hugo and Baudelaire was beginning to make itself felt, and he attempted several longer dramatic poems.

He dared not show Burstall his Eton pamphlet, and he was doubtful about what he had written since. He had shown some of it to Pelly, who had been sympathetic and encouraging, and had even sent one of the poems home to his father, who was a highly-cultivated Government official. What his opinion had been was not known, but Pelly's sister wrote that "They"—meaning the family—"had thought the poem very bad."

"Probably," C. thought, "Burstall will forget all

about it." In the meantime he bought Heredia's *Trophées*, and under the influence of that impeccable craftsman he began to write sonnets on classical themes.

Burstall asked him to go for a walk with him several days later, but he did not mention C.'s writings on this occasion. They saw each other frequently during the month of April, but, in spite of their frequent meetings and their long talks, C. acquired astonishingly little information about his new friend, that is to say, about the facts of his life.

Burstall poured out a flood of ideas, opinions, comments, judicious criticism blent with blatant prejudice, violent abuse and enthusiastic praise, but he seldom talked about himself; neither of his present occupations nor past adventures. C. had no idea where he had been at school. He gathered he had been at Cambridge, and had studied in Germany; that he had travelled in Italy and Greece, and in the Near East; that he knew French and German extremely well; that he was saturated with the classics; that he had some knowledge of painting, sculpture, architecture and music; and that he was engaged in writing a long and erudite work on Villon and his epoch, and that he contributed to the more serious reviews.

One afternoon he took C. to the Louvre.

In the picture gallery he spent most of his time looking at the pictures of Ingres.

" He is the greatest draughtsman who has ever

lived," he said. " You can't appreciate it now. You don't care for line at present ; you only care for colour."

C. admitted that he preferred the *Fête Champêtre* of Giorgione. Pelly had recently lent him Pater's *Renaissance*, and he had found it intoxicating. As he stood in the *Salon Carré* with Burstall he quoted a phrase from this book.

" Sticky, sickly stuff," said Burstall ; " it's like the paste on a wedding cake. You can digest it now all right, just as school-boys can eat ices without stopping, but there is no life in it and no rhythm. It is mosaic, a pattern of different-coloured woods. Prose ought to be alive with rhythm, however simple or however complicated it may be. Take any sentence of Thomas Browne, what he says about sleep, for instance " ; and he declaimed in sonorous voice : " ' A death which Adam died before his mortality ; a death whereby we live a middle and moderating point between life and death ; in fine, so like death, I dare not trust it without my prayers, and an half adieu unto the world, and take my farewell in a colloquy with God.' "

" But surely," said C., " there is a rhythm in Pater's prose too ? "

" No rhythm at all, no play of life, no bones, and no flesh and blood," said Burstall. " It's all sugar and patchouli—decadent stuff."

C. wondered why on earth Burstall couldn't admire both, and he was frankly puzzled at what he thought was a wilful blindness.

"When you're as old as I am," said Burstall, "Pater will make you vomit."

"But," stammered C. rather shyly, "isn't the end of the essay on Leonardo jolly good? Do you remember the end, about Leonardo's love of precise forms: hands, flowers or hair? and something about the 'vague land and the last curiosity?'"

"It's musty," said Burstall, "like

> Faint sweetness from some old
> Egyptian's fine worm-eaten shroud
> Which breaks to dust when once unrolled.

Do you know that? It's Browning—one of the only decent poems he ever wrote."

"Yes," said C., and he went on with the quotation in his mind:—

> Or shredded perfume, like a cloud
> From closet long to quiet vowed,
> With mothed and dropping arras hung.

He did not dare to say it aloud.

They left the Louvre and walked across the river down the quays. Paris looked extraordinarily beautiful and elegant in the clear air of the March evening. C. made some remark to that effect.

"Yes," said Burstall, "but it's not London." And he seemed, as he said that, to be looking for and at something far off and out of reach with infinite desire and acute homesickness.

They walked down the Quays. Burstall made a few purchases at a booth; he bought a small Rabelais and a Horace. He had, he said, dozens already, but this one pleased him. Then they walked slowly back again and watched the sky, which had spread a rose-red glory behind the *Arc de Triomphe*, and they crossed the *Place de la Concorde*, and Burstall accompanied C. to the *Gare Saint Lazare*.

C. was puzzled by Burstall's violent dislikes and his equally violent likes. He couldn't abide Wordsworth. He cared little for any of the modern poets except for a few fragments of Browning and Tennyson, and a little of Swinburne's earliest work. He didn't care for Virgil; he was indifferent to Shelley. On the other hand, he was a fanatical admirer of Catullus, Byron, Verlaine and Racine, which at first sight would appear to be a mixture full of contradictions.

Before the end of the month C. had a series of small experiences which opened fresh cells in his mind and coloured his thoughts with a new dye. Pelly took him one night to a studio where a Polish artist, who was a friend of his, was entertaining a few fellow artists and other friends. The party began early—about nine.

The guests were most of them foreigners, that is to say, not French people, although there were one or two French students and a Madame Valmont, who was well-known in the literary world of Paris. Burstall was there. He knew the host, whose name was Vegas, well. Vegas was a little man with a sallow face and very long, dark hair, and quick understanding eyes, vivacious gestures and an insinuating welcoming manner. He painted strange landscapes and fashioned rather shapeless statuettes, but they found favour with the connoisseurs of the town, and he was able to live by his art.

Burstall snorted at his work openly and frankly and to his face, and said it was utterly preposterous, but he liked Vegas, and his criticisms were taken in good part. Vegas welcomed C. warmly; he introduced him to Madame Valmont, and to a Miss Church, a young American from California, who was studying sculpture, and to a Russian lady with an Italian name, Madame Orioli.

It was a large, high studio, lit by Chinese lanterns. On one of the walls there was a fine unfinished oil-colour sketch of some people in a boat on the Seine in flood, by a friend of Vegas, some of his tortuous and puzzling impressions, a drawing by Lorain, and a huge photograph of Michael Angelo's *Adam*. There were two large divans, one in one corner, the other against the opposite wall, heaped with torn and shabby coloured cushions; at one end of the room there was a platform with a grand pianoforte on it, an old and decayed instrument which had seen better days, and an easel with a picture concealed by a drapery. There were chairs scattered all over the place; a table with books and palettes and brushes lying about, in comfortable chaos, and a long table with supper :— saucisson de Lyons, sardines, sandwiches, salad, radishes, pickled caviare, *Barsac*, lemonade, beer and *Cassis* and *Anisette*—and chairs all along one side of it only, stretched right across the whole length of one wall. The room was warmed by a stove and pipe

which disappeared through the ceiling, but the evening
was warm, and the stove was hardly necessary.

Madame Valmont, a middle-aged lady with a decided
face and a brisk, precise utterance, beady eyes and
black clothes, and a lace mantilla, sat bolt upright in a
wooden armchair, surrounded by a crowd of men, and
Madame Orioli reclined on one of the divans, smoking
little yellow cigarettes with long mouthpieces. She
was a large, dark-eyed, lazy-looking person, with a
swarthy complexion, and she looked like a handsome
Indian idol. Miss Church was standing up in a group
of American students ; she was quite young, very tall,
almost impossibly fair, with the lightest of blue eyes,
and the most regular features. She looked as if she
had been carved out of crystal. Her mother had the
same regular features, but neither the height nor the
eyes, and her face was ravaged by years of travel,
ceaseless anxiety and incessant poverty. She was
weather-beaten and weary, but she still kept up a
gallant fight, and meant to do well by her daughter,
Alice. She watched her incessantly, without appearing to do so, and seemed to be engrossed in the conversation she was carrying on with a Frenchman about
the latest developments in art. Burstall was roped
into Madame Valmont's circle, and very soon dominated it. Every now and then Madame Valmont was
heard to say that " *Burstall est impayable.*" He had
the reputation among the French of being a *pince
sans rire.*

C., after having been introduced to four or five

people, suddenly found himself isolated in a crowd of strangers without the sheet-anchor of Burstall. He felt helpless and lonely. Madame Orioli noticed his plight, and said something to Vegas, who was standing up at the corner of her divan. He gave C. a quick look and then walked up to him, and said :—

"I want to introduce you to a great friend of mine, Madame Orioli," and he led him up to the divan.

"Sit down there," said Madame Orioli, and she gave him a cigarette. "Make yourself comfortable. I don't expect you know who any of these people are. I will tell you."

C. blushed and admitted that he knew nobody. Madame Orioli made a remark in Russian to a man who was sitting on the other side of her. He said "*Da, da.*" Then she turned to C. and said :

"You don't speak Russian ? " C. assented. "You must learn it some day. It's an interesting and such a convenient language. This is the first time you have been to Vegas' studio ? "

"Yes, the first time."

"It is always very amusing. He can't paint, but he knows how to receive and entertain. He is very charming. Do you want to know who all the people are ? If I recite to you a string of names you will be not much the wiser. You have been introduced to that American. She is beautiful, but she has no money, and she and her mother go from *pension* to *pension* like characters in Henry James. You have read Henry James ? "

" No, I am afraid not."

" Well, when you do read him you will find them like that. The mother may try and catch you, but she will make enquiries first. She will take nothing for granted."

" Who is that just coming into the room ? " asked C.

It was a girl with very dark hair and large dark blue eyes. She was young, and dressed in black, and she might have been French, or Italian, or Irish.

" She is an English girl," said Madame Orioli, " the daughter of a musician, a Miss Burke. She is studying singing. She will go far, but not I think in art. She is too good looking. She will make *un beau mariage dans le monde.*"

C. agreed that she was most beautiful.

" She sings very nicely," said Madame Orioli, " but not well enough I find. That man who is talking to her is a French student, Dorant. He is a natural, untaught musician and a charming singer, with a very pleasing voice. They will both sing to-night, and we shall have some gypsy music, too. You have never heard Russian gypsy songs ? You will like them."

At that moment there was a slight stir near the doorway, and a lady made an *entrée*. She created a wake like a swift, sailing vessel. She was not very tall, but her perfectly-proportioned figure and her erect carriage made her look tall. She trod the ground like a thoroughbred horse, with the assurance that only those have who are used to take admiration for granted. She took the stage without hesitation, and she moved magnificently. And yet she was not a great beauty, not a beauty at all, some people would have said. She was fair, but her hair was colourless and without radiance ; her eyes were pale blue, hard and without lights ; her features small, too regular, and unimportant ; her complexion a little faded. It was her figure, her magnificent shoulders, and the way she held herself and walked that gave her, perhaps, more than she deserved of the world's attention. Directly she came into the room everybody looked at her, and nobody paid any more attention to the crystal moonshine of Miss Church or to the liquid dark beauty of Miss Burke. She was very simply dressed in black, relieved by one flashing slash of yellow satin, somewhere near her waist and was wearing a bunch of yellow daffodils ; but her clothes seemed to grow on her, and had an undefinable stamp of elegance and neatness about them. She was followed by a tall and rather sulky-looking, fair-haired man about thirty, who looked younger than she did.

" Who is that ? " asked C.

" That," said Madame Orioli, " is Lady Ralph Dallington. The French people call her Lady Dallington as they cannot master the *nuances* of your English titles. She lives in Italy, in Rome, and sometimes she comes here. Her husband lives in England or Scotland. They are not divorced, not even separated, I think, but they live apart. I have never seen him. I know her very well, as I, too, live in Rome most of the year. She is what you call a very good sort, with a great deal of *aplomb* and pluck. She has one daughter. She is much admired in Rome."

" Why is she here ? " C. had put the question owing to a sudden whiff of Bramsley that the appearance of Lady Ralph had brought with her.

" Well, it is complicated. I like her very much, and she is a very good sort, as I said, and that is all you need know."

" Who is the man who came with her ? " asked C.

" That is a Russian," said Madame Orioli. " He was in a cavalry regiment in Petersburg, and he rides very well. He is often in Rome, and he sings gypsy songs. You will hear him presently."

C. was enjoying his conversation with Madame Orioli, and he was greatly disappointed when Mrs. Church sailed up to him in a determined manner, and said that she wanted him to talk to her daughter. She led him away to the opposite side of the room, which was becoming more and more crowded, and hotter and hotter. C. sat down on another divan next to the fair and transparent Miss Church. Vegas, at that moment got up on to the platform, and asked for silence, as he said the music was about to begin.

CHAPTER XIV

THE first person to sing was Miss Burke. She sang *Si mes vers avaient des ailes* and *Ah! si vous saviez comme on pleure* to a tune of Tosti's, and as an encore, a song, the refrain of which was *Les coccinelles sont couchées*.

She sang with a limpid, clear voice; her French accent was perfect, her diction faultless, but the performance was totally uninspired.

" What does a *coccinelle* mean ? " asked C.

" I guess," said Miss Church, " it's a kind of bug."

" A dragonfly ? " hazarded C.

" No, a black-beetle," said Miss Church.

They both laughed. The music had begun again and they had to control their laughter as best they could.

Some one was playing the piano—playing Chopin with so much expression that he was scarcely audible. The audience listened inattentively, a spontaneous whispering crept up in various parts of the room, and they clapped with relief when he had finished. Then the fair-haired young man who had arrived with Lady Ralph Dallington got up on to the platform and tuned his three-stringed *balalaika*. As soon as he was ready he began to sing some grating, bittersweet, intensely sentimental and piercingly melancholy gipsy songs.

C. was entranced.

After the first song three other singers joined him, a soprano, an alto, and a bass, and they sang a quartette ; also the same kind of song about delirious moonshine and cold dawns, " fierce midnights and famishing morrows," the intoxication and briefness of love, the sadness of spring, the satiety of summer, passion lightly come and gone, lasting heartache and unsatisfied longing—unsatisfied, permanent longing.

C. and Miss Church looked at each other as these people sang, and as they drank in the music they enjoyed and shared each other's pleasure. They both wallowed in the voluptuous melancholy; they both enjoyed the luxury of idle tears. They longed for the singers to go on for ever. They did sing again ; they sang two or three songs, songs with a passionate wail in them, and one with an insistent, swelling refrain that grew louder and fiercer, like the howling of a pack of wolves.

" Aren't they wonderful ? " said Miss Church.

Her lovely cool-blue eyes were wet with tears. C. was deeply moved as well.

" I should like them to go on all night," he said.

" So should I," she said, and they looked at each other, and C. went on looking at Miss Church.

They stopped, however, after the fourth or fifth song, and they were followed on the platform by Dorant, who sang a seventeenth-century song with grace and great purity of tone. His voice was slight, but true. Dorant was a professional painter, and, although only an amateur musical composer and performer, he was an amateur in the best sense of the word. He made music for pleasure. His range was not wide, but what he tried to do he accomplished with unerring tact and discretion. After the old French he sang a love-song by Augusta Holmès, and then a lyric of Théophile Gautier, with music by Fauré :—

> Avril est de retour.
> La première des roses,
> De ses lèvres mi-closes,
> Sourit au premier beau jour ;
> La terre bien heureuse
> S'ouvre et s'épanouit ;
> Tout aime, tout jouit,
> Hélas ! J'ai dans le cœur une tristesse affreuse !

And once again C. and Miss Church shared the luxury of melancholy, a melancholy they had not yet experienced. They were, therefore, able to enjoy it to the full, and to shed happy tears ; all the more so perhaps because Dorant sang the song in the same mood and without a trace of the sorrows that hurts and the passion that sears.

> Les buveurs en gaité,
> Dans leurs chansons vermeilles,
> Célèbrent sous les treilles
> Le vin et la beauté ;
> La musique joyeuse
> Avec leur rire clair
> S'éparpille dans l'air.
> Hélas ! J'ai dans le cœur une tristesse affreuse !

En deshabillés blancs,
Les jeunes demoiselles
S'en vont sous les tonnelles
Au bras de leurs galants ;
La lune langoureuse
Argente leurs baisers
Longuement appuyés.

Hélas ! J'ai dans le cœur une tristesse affreuse !

Moi, je n'aime plus rien,
Ni l'homme, ni la femme,
Ni mon corps, ni mon âme,
Pas même mon vieux chien.
Allez dire qu'on creuse,
Sous le pâle gazon,
Une fosse sans nom.

Hélas ! J'ai dans le cœur une tristesse affreuse !

" I liked that one best of all," said Miss Church, when he had finished.

" So did I," said C.

There was a general move towards the supper table. C. wanted to sit next to Miss Church, but, to his surprise, Vegas asked him to take " Lady Dallington " to the supper table.

" I used to know your father and mother very well," she said as he walked up to her, "and I know your Aunt Emma in Rome. Let's sit right at the end of the table. I don't want to sit next to a Frenchman. It's such a comfort to see an Englishman after all these frowsy foreigners. I don't count Americans as English."

They sat down. On the other side of Lady Ralph there was a shy American student, who, however, was firmly taken in hand by his neighbour, Mrs. Church.

Lady Ralph sipped a small glass of anisette, and poured out volumes of quick, metallic talk to C. She was on her way back to Rome. She loathed it as a place and she detested Roman society, but one must live somewhere, and it was cheap and warm in winter.

"The Italians are monkeys," she said. "I always wear black and yellow, and when I went to the races at Milan last year, and the Italian women saw me dressed in black and yellow, the next day they all copied me. They were all in black and yellow. I just looked at them and said 'Monkeys!' If you come to Rome you must come and see me. I like seeing Englishmen. Of course, there are English people in Rome, but not my sort."

And so the conversation rattled on, and they sat a long time at supper. When, at last, it was over, C. made an attempt to have another talk with Miss Church, who he saw was looking at him, but it was too late. The plan was again thwarted, by Mrs. Church this time, who carried C. off to one of the divans and talked to him about serious subjects in an undertone, while Dorant sang some songs by Lully. And then it was time to go, for, although the party lasted till far on in the night—past midnight—Burstall and C. had to leave to catch the last train to Versailles.

C. was steeped in melancholy as he left the studio. He had wanted to talk to Miss Church. It would be too strong an expression to say it had been a case of love at first sight, but it had been a case of sympathy and admiration at first sight, one of those little love

affairs that are the false dawn of real ones, but further
progress had been impeded by the intervention of
Lady Ralph Dallington, and C., unfortunately, had
not reached quite the right age to be charmed by her.
Moreover, she had plunged him into the atmosphere
of Bramsley once more. As Burstall and C. travelled
back in the train C. spoke of the music.

" I liked the Russian songs best," he said.

" Barbarous, nasal, Oriental wailings," said Burstall.
" Dorant was good."

" Yes," said C. " I liked that song of Gautier's. I
had never come across those words."

" Yes," said Burstall, " you would enjoy that *now*."

But even the thought of that song was evidently
painful to him, and an expression of pain passed over
his face, but he brushed away the evidences of his
melancholy by humming one of the Offenbach tunes
that Dorant had sung.

" That's better stuff," he said. " It's as good as
Sullivan—the only modern English composer."

They parted at Versailles Station, and as Burstall
said good-bye to C. he said to him :—

" By the way, you never sent me your verse. Send
it along."

The words were like an electric shock to C. He slept
little that night. First of all the vision of Miss
Church's clear complexion and light blue eyes rose
before him obstinately, and fragments of the music,
the long-drawn-out wail and the howling, insistent
chorus of the Russian singers, the finished grace of

Dorant when he sang seventeenth-century music,
he tang and rattle of Lady Ralph's conversation,
which had brought him back to Bramsley and to the
Hengrave atmosphere, and the look of pain on
Burstall's face when he had spoken of Gautier's poem
—all these things shone and moved before him like
the facets of an ever-changing kaleidoscope. And
Burstall's request that he should send him his verse!
Did he mean it? Of course he did, otherwise he
would never have mentioned it. What would he
think? What should he send? Not everything
he had written. The sonnet *Medea* perhaps, or the
series of sonnets on *Resolution*, or that lyric? No;
Burstall would think that crude. Perhaps he had
better not send him anything, and yet he would so
much like to know.

Towards morning he fell into a restless sleep, and he
woke up again earlier than usual, when the birds were
singing and the sun not long been up. He got up early
and went out. When he came back, and had his *café
au lait*, he took out his MSS. from a drawer, and he
made a selection of those poems which he thought
were least likely to displease Burstall, and put them
into a large envelope. He was very *distrait* all that
morning as he sat at his books and read aloud to
Madame Maartens. She noticed it and said to herself
" The boy is in love. *Tant mieux.*" She had a homely
fund of romance.

In the afternoon, he had a lesson from Monsieur
Jollivet, who was in an irritable frame of mind, and

underlined several mistakes he had made in his composition, " A letter to a friend describing a visit to Paris,"
ferociously. When the lesson was over Monsieur
Jollivet calmed down slightly. C. ventured to ask
him whether he admired Gautier.

Yes. Monsieur Jollivet said that Théophile Gautier
had written some very good verse, but that he was too
romantic and not a patch on André Chénier. He
took the works of the latter from the shelf and read out
La Captive from beginning to end. C. didn't listen.
He was thinking of a thousand other things. On
his way home C. left his MSS. at Burstall's house,
and in so doing he felt he had committed an irreparable
act. He had arranged to spend the next day, which
was Sunday, with Pelly in Paris. It was the only day
of the week on which Pelly was free.

Sunday was a day of luxury to C. It was sheer
bliss to him no longer to be obliged to go to
church. Sunday at home at Bramsley had always
been a nightmare; the long Morning Service, the
Litany, the Ante-Communion Service, the interminable
aridity of the sermon, the long luncheon afterwards,
beginning with roast beef and ending with seed cake
and sherry; and then the Sunday walk in which the
whole family and any guests who happened to be
there joined, the inspection of the stables and the
garden.

Now he felt he need never go to church again unless
he wished to, and yet, in spite of this, he never once
questioned the orthodox beliefs he had been taught at

home, and the Church of England seemed to him as solid and as unchangeable a fact as the solar system. As for Catholicism and other religions, they were, of course, all very well for foreigners, but he could no more imagine changing his religion than becoming a Hottentot.

He found Pelly in his *pension* and they went to a Duval and had *déjeuner*.

They talked first of the party at Vegas'. C. talked of Burstall. Pelly had never seen him before.

" I expect he's tremendously clever," said Pelly.

" Yes, he is, tremendously," said C. " He's read everything."

He felt more uncomfortable than ever at having sent Burstall his MSS. He would have consulted Pelly, only he knew that Pelly was engrossed at this moment in pictures and art.

After luncheon they went to the Luxembourg and Pelly took C. to see Whistler's picture of his mother, which he said his artist friends told him was the greatest of all modern pictures, and one of the finest pictures in the world.

" They say," he said, " that it's all nonsense pretending that modern art isn't just as good as what the old masters did. They say that picture is every inch as good as a Velasquez. I don't know. I agree with them about modern music. Think of Wagner."

He had been, he said, to a wonderful concert where a great deal of Wagner had been performed, and he was full of it.

"The next time there is a really good concert you must come with me."

"Yes," said C., feeling that he would be an inadequate companion, and remembering the classical concerts at Aunt Fanny's house. "But I'm not musical," he said, "I don't understand classical music. I like the sort of music those Russians sang the other night."

"Yes," said Pelly, "but you should hear Wagner. He isn't classical. It's like nothing else in the world. After you have heard it you can't listen to any other kind of music. You can't bear Mozart. At any rate, I'm a Wagnerite."

They left the Luxembourg after Pelly had taken C. through room after room discussing the pictures, comparing notes on this and that painter. They walked through the network of streets on the south side of the Seine past the *Odéon*, and as they passed rather a big church, Pelly said :—

"We might go in there; the music there is very good. There is a man at my *pension*, called Winslow, he took me here."

They went in, but there was no service going on. It was a large, late Renaissance, neo-classic building. A few women in deep mourning were kneeling here and there in the deserted Nave. In front of a side altar a multitude of candles were burning. As they stood there a young woman dressed in black and heavily veiled bought a tall candle from an old woman and placed it on a spike with the other candles. She then knelt down and said a prayer. Over the altar there was a gaudy statue of a Saint, holding a bunch of lilies and the Infant Saviour in his arms.

There was a palpable silence in the church, and C., who had never been inside a Catholic church in his life, and thought of them, in the light of Mrs. Brimstone's and Miss Hackett's stray remarks, with a feeling of dread and horror, was surprised. The church seemed to be much less empty and different from those to which he had been accustomed.

As they went out Pelly said :—

" Winslow takes me here on Sundays."

" Is he an R.C. ? " asked C.

" No," said Pelly, " but he's very High Church. He knows exactly what to do and how and when to cross himself."

" Will he become an R.C. ? " asked C., remembering the views of his family on conversions.

" No," said Pelly. " He says the Anglican Catholic Church is an older branch than the Roman."

" And are you High Church, too ? " asked C.

" No," said Pelly. " I'm not a Christian."

" Oh," said C. interestedly.

It was the first time he had heard any one he knew make such a confession, although he knew that his Aunt Fanny had the reputation of being in the same position.

" Have you ever read the Song of Solomon in the Bible ? " Pelly asked, after a light pause.

" No," said C., " I haven't."

" Well, you must. It's wonderful. It's much

better than Swinburne. It's the most wonderful,
passionate, burning love song ever written. Well, in
the Bible, they say it's all a symbol of the Church, the
Christian Church. Well, that must be nonsense, and
if that is nonsense, why should any of it be true? It's
supposed to be all true." The problem did seem a
difficult one. " But I like the Catholic churches and
the services, all the same," said Pelly, " and the Latin
words. It's very old and dignified."

" But you couldn't become an R.C. ? "

" Well, I don't think Catholicism is anything to do
with Christianity, I could never make the mental
gymnastic necessary to fit them together, and I think,
too, one must be born a Catholic to be one."

They talked of other things. C. went back to
Versailles for dinner, and that night, when he went to
bed, he read the Song of Solomon in the Bible that
Lady Hengrave had given him when he first went to
school. Pelly was right. It was, indeed, a wonderful
poem. It was like Swinburne, but if anything, better.
And the commentary on the top of the pages, talking
of what it symbolised, must be nonsense. Pelly was
right. It *was* nonsense. Then why was any of it
true? Was the whole thing imagination? People
had made up the story and believed it because they
wanted to. Yes—but it had convulsed the world, and
thousands of people had died because they believed in
it. But what did that prove? Only two days before
he had read in a book that a cause was not necessarily
true because people died for it. People had died for

every kind of cause, and often for worthless causes. There had been martyrs for the Stuarts. There were people who thought Mr. Gladstone was the antichrist. And it suddenly occurred to C. that the religion he had been brought up in was more a social and political code, a standard of decorum, than anything else ; that his father and mother went to church in the same way as they went to Lord's, or to the House of Lords, or to Ascot, but there was little real religion behind it all. They weren't religious at all. The whole thing was a sham. Then why bother ? Pelly was right. Pelly had said quite simply that he wasn't a Christian, and that solved the matter. Well, he wasn't a Christian either. And having made this discovery, C. felt relieved and quite easy in his mind. That question was settled, and he need not give any thought to the matter again. He wondered what Burstall thought about such things. He had never heard him mention anything to do with religion. He felt that he would certainly never dare to broach the subject to him, nor did he now feel the need of doing so, for he considered that he had settled the matter in his mind once and for all.

This walk with Pelly, the visit to the church, and the conversation that followed it, and the fruits which that conversation bore, was the second of the little episodes that occurred to C. during that month, which changed or modified the pattern and the colours of his mind.

CHAPTER XV

C. was longing to talk over this religious discovery with Burstall. He regarded it as an emancipation which seemed to have lifted a load that, unknown to himself, had been weighing on him for years. Pelly had mentioned the writings of Renan, and C. bought the *Vie de Jésus*, and this seemed to clinch the matter. Christianity, he thought, was a dead thing, the observance of which was kept going and kept alive by society because it was convenient and expedient, and as a social observance. The people who thought and studied for themselves, and who went into the matter like Renan and Ibsen, for instance (and Pelly had told C. all about Ibsen), obviously thought it was all nonsense, but very few people thought for themselves, and the majority loved convention and ready-made ideas, and could not bear the even surface of accepted doctrine to be ruffled or disturbed. He felt that Christianity was just one of the many conventions upon which the life of the people among whom he had been brought up, and whom he knew best (his parents, his uncles and aunts, and the Calhouns, and the Eton masters), was based and built up. It was like the cult of athletics at school, the observance of social rules and conventions at home.

This discovery did not worry him in the least. On

the contrary, he felt he had attained an unguessed-of freedom. He did not wish to proclaim his need, or his absence of need, to any one, but he had a certain curiosity to know what Burstall thought about these things. All the knowledge he had of Burstall consisted of certain incomplete sidelights on tastes and opinions in literature and art, and these were perplexingly contradictory. Besides this, all he knew was that Burstall was an uncompromising Tory, who was in favour of the power of the Crown being increased; who thought that the Whigs had been the bane of England, and should be killed *en bloc*, and that Gladstone was a traitor, a hypocrite and a self-deceiver, and he had heard him say that he hoped the Emperor of Russia would never give way to the aliens and to the demagogues. That was all he knew of his opinions on **political** matters. He had never heard him mention religion. The nearest he had ever got to it was to say that Cobbett's book on the Reformation was fundamentally true, but C. had never read it and had never heard of Cobbett. He made up his mind that the next time he saw him he would ask him what he thought of Renan as a writer, and this might lead to further revelations.

Two days later he received the following letter :—

VERSAILLES, RUE DE LA GARE,
April, 18—.

DEAR BRAMSLEY,
  I have been called back to London. I am obliged to start immediately, and I have no time to bid

you good-bye. I have read your verse. It is difficult to
give an opinion on the work of the very young, and you
are—and I hope you thank God for it every day—still
very young. There are extremely few instances in the
whole history of literature of men afterwards destined
to become writers of good verse whose work written at
your age showed any promise beyond that of being able
to write something. You have facility. That is all
that the young Pope and the baby Keats and the infant
Shelley showed signs of in the work of their 'teens. I
seem to detect something else. I should not be sur-
prised if one day you were to write verse or prose of the
first excellence, but I may be wrong. My judgment is
bad, and I am no critic, and still less of a prophet.
But I do say this, whether you write good verse or bad
verse, or no verse at all, I feel sure that write you will,
and you cannot do better than to persevere. I have
marked what I considered to be some good lines in your
work—good not only in the sense of promise, but of
performance. Remember that verse is the blossom of
many minds, the fruit of few. But go on writing
whatever you feel inclined to write, and when you are
older you will have command of the tools, and you will
be able to express whatever your particular message is
destined to be. Read the classics in all the languages.
If possible, learn Greek, but don't believe a word you
are told by the professors. I do not know how long I
shall be away, nor when I shall return, if ever. These
things are on the knees of the gods. I shall always be
pleased to hear from you, and I wish you success.

Letters sent to the MINERVA CLUB, LONDON, *will be forwarded to me.*

> I am,
>> Yours always,
>>> ANDREW MICHAEL BURSTALL.

C. was immensely cheered by this letter, but grieved that Burstall had left. The element that had made life most interesting had suddenly been removed, for Pelly, although he was a charming companion, had none of the fire, nor the energy, nor the salt and the savour, that made Burstall's company and companionship interesting and exciting. A chill feeling of inexpressible gloom, disappointment and emptiness settled upon him. The world seemed for the moment to be a much greyer place. As to his writing, what Burstall told him cheered him, and he felt justified in continuing. He wrote a series of poems about the pictures in the Louvre, and a lyric addressed to an anonymous unknown, in which there was a reflection of his impressions of Miss Church. He burnt a great deal of what he had written since he left Eton, keeping only those poems in which some lines had been marked by Burstall.

Soon after Burstall's departure Pelly wrote to him saying that he had been given two tickets, *billets de faveur*, for a *matinée* that was being held at the *Trocadéro* for some charity. The programme was not especially interesting, but a famous actress who was passing through Paris was said to be going to recite.

This, however, was doubtful. He urged C. to accompany him. C. accepted with alacrity. The *matinée* took place on a Sunday afternoon, so that Pelly was able to go without difficulty. They were well placed in the huge hall, near the stage, but Pelly was forced to admit that the programme was not of the most attractive. The orchestra played the overture to *Coriolanus;* a famous pianist played some elaborate fantasias which showed off the dexterity of his fingers to its utmost advantage ; a gigantic and massive contralto sang the Gounod's *Ave Maria* with violin obligato ; there was a violin solo, and several songs were sung by a tenor from the *Opéra Comique*, and the first part of the concert ended with the *Intermezzo* from the *Cavalleria Rusticana*. So far C. had not enjoyed anything very greatly. The second part of the concert began with a patriotic recitation by one of the male artists of the *Comédie Française*, which was immensely applauded, but which left C. stone-cold. Then came more solos, a duet from Gounod's *Romeo and Juliet*, more instrumental playing, till the long expected and partially deferred number was put up which announced the appearance of Madame Madeleine Lapara.

" She is coming after all," C. heard his neighbours say.

C. had heard about this actress during his schooldays. She had appeared in London, and his mother went to see her act religiously, but never took the children. The plays she appeared in were said to be unfit for the young. C. had seen photographs of her in the Paris shop windows, and he had admired what seemed to be the poetic semblance of a great and rare personality, but when he had mentioned her to Monsieur Jollivet all the latter had said was "*Je l'ai vu jouer Hermione dans Andromaque et elle y était exécrable.*"

"Is she very wonderful?" he said to Pelly.

"I have never seen her," said Pelly, "but one of the art students at the pension says that, when she chooses, she is the greatest artist who has ever lived, and he says he would walk barefoot to see her in *Phèdre.*"

There was suddenly a breathless hush, then a great storm of applause, and Madame Madeleine Lapara was led on to the stage. She was not tall; she wore a large black hat, which seemed to be in the way, and a long, loose, dark brown cloak, plentifully trimmed with fur, and a fur boa round her neck. She carried a large bunch of violets. She put the flowers on the grand pianoforte, and then, taking a little piece of paper in her hand, she walked to the edge of the platform. C. was disappointed in her appearance. He had expected a romantic princess, instead of which, on the platform, there stood a lady who might have stepped out of an artistic fashion plate. She seemed to be intensely Parisian, ultra-modern, an *article de Paris.*

She paused a moment, looking down at the piece of paper in her hand. And then she said, "*Obsession

de Sully Prudhomme." And as she spoke the title
C. already seemed to feel a change in the moral
temperature of the air.

> Un mot me hante, un mot me tue.
> Je l'écoute contre mon gré :
> A le bannir je m'évertue,
> Il me suit, toujours murmuré.
>
> A l'ancien chant de ma nourrice
> Je le mêle pour l'assoupir,
> Mais, redoutable adulatrice,
> La musique en fait un soupir.

She sighed the words, speech seemed too coarse and
music too definite a word for the soft, rippling cascade
of syllables which filled the large hall.

> Je gravis alors la montagne
> Pour l'étouffer dans le grand vent.
> Jusqu'au sommet il m'accompagne :
> Il y devient gémissement.

She raised her voice, her arms and her eyes ; she
lifted the soft pedal. The mystery took wings ; her
voice sounded clear and silvery, and the audience
scaled that mountain with her, and felt the buffet of
the great clean wind, and all at once the undying
sadness following her even to the mountain top—it
dimmed the glory and darkened the sun.

> Je demande à la mer sonore
> De le changer en bruit de flot.
> Plus plaintif et plus tendre encore,
> Hélas ! il y devient sanglot. . . .

In the first two lines an abrupt modulation enlarged
the sighing utterance ; it became grave and deep, and

then she pressed an ethereal pedal on her voice ; it was once more unimaginably soft and caressing, and something more than soft : there was something subtle about it which defied analysis, like the scent of a flower at night.   As she spoke the word *sanglot* there was a break in her voice, and it was her piteous eyes that seemed to be speaking.   A murmured acclammation escaped from the audience, and here and there whispered *bravos* were heard.   A well-known critic, commenting on the recitation in his *feuilleton* the following Monday, said there was no search after effect in it and nothing time-taking, " *point d'effets cherchés ni de temps pris ; cependant que de nuances indiquées, d'un simple trait de voix courant !*" and he spoke of the tremor of applause.   " *C'etait un frémissement continu dans la salle ; . . . un murmure d'admiration et de plaisir qui coupait le vers.*"

> Je tente, comme un dernier charme,
> Le silence enchanté des bois ;

You could have heard a pin drop.

> Mais je le sens qui devient larme
> Dès qu'il a cessé d'être voix.

The accent on the word *larme* trembled a little and stabbed the listeners, who had been taken to secret woodways and to lofty aisles of green trees.

> Ce qui pleure ou ne peut se taire,
> Est-ce en moi le remords ? oh ! non :
> C'est un souvenir solitaire
> Au plus lointain de l'âme . . . un nom.

The last stanza seemed to float by as swiftly as a

puff of smoke. They were said almost before C. was aware she had begun ; and far away, infinitely far away, from the starless end of the soul, the last word was sent to sound and softly die, leaving something behind that lingered after its death. And through all the plaintive sighing music there was something else, something which made itself felt, a poignant note, a stab, an immense sadness.

" Yes," the accents said : " I know how sweet it is, and I know, too, how very bitter is that sweetness," and as she ended, her eyes were full of the sorrow of all the lovers in the world. It was as if she had laid bare a secret wound, a wound that every one had suffered and every one had concealed, and that she had touched it with a divinely magical, healing finger.

There were a few seconds of silence and then the audience burst into a great roar. C. didn't any longer know where he was nor what he was doing.

In the meantime Madeleine Lapara had bowed her way from the stage, but the audience stood up and shouted till she came back. She bowed from the corner of the platform and pressed her face against her bouquet of violets, but the enthusiasm of the audience when they saw her, rose into a frenzy, and there was one loud roar of *bis*.

She left the platform, but she was recalled again and yet again, but she showed no sign of being willing to repeat the performance. The roar of the audience became more insistent and more imperative, and all at once she apparently either changed her mind or made

it up. The expression in her eyes seemed to say :
" Well, if you want it, you shall have it."

She walked up to the pianoforte and she took off her
hat, which was transfixed and held in place by a long
dagger-like pin. This freed a great mane of picturesque
rebellious hair. She put the hat down and the flowers
as well, on the pianoforte, and she took a cane chair
and dragged it right to the extreme front edge of the
stage. Then she sat down, and said in ordinary commonplace tones, as of a schoolgirl saying a lesson :
" *Le Songe d'Athalie.*" There came a gasp, partly of
surprise, partly of expectation, from the audience, and
C. felt that he was back in the schoolroom at Hengrave
House. He saw Mademoiselle Walter, her determined
jaw and the square, black ruler on the long polished
table.

" *Caryl, tu perds ton temps,*" he heard the sharp
reminder again.

Madeleine Lapara clasped her hands and bent her
head. Then she raised her head again and looked
straight in front of her and murmured to herself :

> Un songe (me devrai-je inquiéter d'un songe ?)
> Entretient dans mon cœur un chagrin qui le ronge,
> Je l'évite partout, partout il me poursuit.

Ominous apprehension and the shadow of a coming
nightmare descended upon the audience.

> C'était pendant l'horreur d'une profonde nuit.

As she spoke the line she opened her eyes wide,
and they were full of fire and dread, like those of a
frightened wild beast.

In the row in front opposite there was a little boy about nine years old sitting next to his mother, a large prosperous middle-class lady dressed in bright magenta.

" *Maman, j'ai peur*," he whispered.

She took him on her knee, kissed him and quieted and soothed him. He buried his face on her shoulder and remained quite still till the end of the performance.

As Lapara spoke this first line her voice had the depth and sonority of a great bell, and C. suddenly felt how infinite in suggestion were these bare, bald words. He understood what Monsieur Jollivet, what Burstall, what the whole French nation meant when they said Racine was a great poet.

> Ma mère Jézabel devant moi s'est montrée,
> Comme au jour de sa mort pompeusement parée.
> Ses malheurs n'avaient point abattu sa fierté.
> Même elle avait encor cet éclat emprunté,
> Dont elle eut soin de peindre et d'orner son visage,
> Pour réparer des ans l'irréparable outrage.

The words were hammered out in icy, low, metallic tones, in a matter-of-fact voice, but a matter of tremendous fact, as of some one who had been the eyewitness of a ghastly tragedy, and who had not yet recovered from the shock of the spectacle. The words had the ring of truth and the accent of calamity. She was telling the bare facts, and as she did so the fallen Queen appeared to that vast audience in all her undiminished pride. The image evoked was horrible, and great, and piteous, as well as horrible ; for she had come

back with a painted face from the dead, and taken
pains to make up even in the region of Tophet. And
her arts had proved ineffectual, her pretence of youth
a mockery. The reciter seemed to grow a hundred
years older as she said the lines, and C. thought of
Froude's description of the executioner holding up
Mary Stuart's severed head, grown grey and suddenly
that of an old woman, at Fotheringay. (He had read
this at Eton in the Boys' Library.)

> "Tremble," m'a-t-elle dit, "fille digne de moi,
> Le cruel Dieu des Juifs l'emporte aussi sur toi.
> Je te plains de tomber dans ses mains redoutables,
> Ma fille."

A soul in hell seemed to be shrieking a warning with
all its feeble might.

There came a change of key.

> En achevant ses mots épouvantables
> Son ombre vers mon lit a paru se baisser,
> Et moi, je lui tendais mes mains pour l'embrasser.
> Mais je n'ai plus trouvé qu'un horrible mélange
> D'os et de chair meurtris, et trainés dans la fange,
> Des lambeaux pleins de sang, et des membres affreux,
> Que des chiens dévorants se disputaient entre eux.

There was a decrescendo in tone, but the horror it
expressed went on increasing in pitch. She suited the
gesture to the words, and she stretched out her hands.
She stood up as she spoke, and became a classic figure.
C. beheld the ghosts in Virgil, on the banks of the
Styx, stretching their arms towards the forbidden
shore. In the last four lines of the speech the voice
rose to a high pitch of horror, and ended with
a cry and a gesture—as though she were warding off

the vision with her hands—of terror, pity, disgust—
unendurable pain. The audience felt they were in the
presence of a brutal catastrophe. C. remembered the
first time he had been in at the death out fox hunting,
and as he looked at the actress he saw reflected in her
eyes the horror at an unbearable sight; and then she
seemed to change and to become herself the fallen
Queen at bay, Queen Jezebel, in all her borrowed
youth, her malignant majesty and evil glamour,
turning and snarling defiance at the murderous
pack, and finally defeated, pulled down, chawed and
mangled, and he seemed to hear a human cry drowned
and stifled by a merciless baying and yelping. The
audience, he felt, were all of them in at the death, and
they knew it. It was a hideous *hallali*, and the quarry
was an old painted queen. The audience swayed
towards the platform; and C. noticed, in one brief
second, that right up at the right-hand corner of the
top gallery, two members of the *Garde Républicaine*
were straining over the heads of the people in the back
row, immobile, fascinated, spellbound, as every one
else. The audience were shouting now, not with a
clamorous enthusiasm as after the first piece, but with
determination and in a rhythmical disciplined chorus,
" *Bis, bis, bis,*" that would take no denial. She
said it all over again, beginning this time at

> C'était pendant l'horreur d'une profonde nuit,

and C. was hardly conscious when it was over that she
had begun, or that it had all happened twice; he was

still in the vision; still on the spot of the tragedy; still in the presence of the murdered and mangled queen; still under the pressure of the prodigious nightmare. She was silent; and once more the audience, like one man, insisted on hearing it all over again. It seemed as if both they and the actress had been caught as workmen are caught by the flying wheel of a machine. Genius had escaped and got beyond control, and had maddened the audience beyond frenzy to a cold, relentless fury. They were determined to have their way. It was as though the actress had become the hunted quarry, and they the remorseless pack of hounds—or were they the quarry and she the inspired huntsman? A vicious circle of inspiration and enthusiasm had been forged from which there was no escape, and to which there could be no end.

C. had no idea how many times Madeleine Lapara repeated the passage, but, at last, he was conscious that the audience had risen to its feet, and that every one was leaving the hall in silence. The dream was over. She had, so Pelly said, repeated the sixteen lines five times running. It was, they said afterwards, unheard-of in the annals of the stage.

The programme was by no means exhausted, but the concert, by universal consent, had come to an end, for the audience, after what they had heard, were unable to listen to anything else, and Madame Lapara tottered from the platform under a final deafening farewell of acclamation—a shattered, exhausted shell— a sibyl who had been bending too long over the cauldrons of Doldona.

In the vestibule of the hall C. met Burstall.

"I came over for this, last night," he said. "She promised to recite if I came over. She bet me a hundred francs I wouldn't come. I am going back to-night by the night train, and I can't stop and talk to you now. I'm going round to see Madeleine. She knows I'm here. She saw me when she was recalled after the first piece. She knows I like Racine. My God! What a woman! and what a poet!" and he rushed off snuffling.

CHAPTER XVI

THE three experiences that dyed the colour of C.'s mind during his stay at Versailles, besides his acquaintance with Burstall, were the evening party given in Vegas' studio, the conversation he had with Pelly about the Song of Solomon, and the recitation of Madeleine Lapara. It was, curiously enough, this last experience that confirmed and expressed what the other two had only dimly adumbrated and foreshadowed. As soon as Madame Lapara opened her lips, C. entered into a new world. The experience was on a larger and a deeper scale than that which he had already felt when he had heard Fanny Talbot at his private school. But the sentiments that Madame Lapara inspired him with were as different from those he had felt when seeing Fanny Talbot, as the thoughts of a boy of thirteen are different from those of a boy of eighteen. He did not fall in love with Madeleine Lapara, although he felt he would give worlds to see her again, but he fell in love with *love*, with an imaginary person, based more or less on Miss Church, whom he felt he would give worlds to see again. He was like some one who had seen the object of a quest in a vision and who must henceforth roam the world till he is face to face with the incarnation of his dream—and must tear the masks from the faces of all till he finds the one face he is seeking for.

But this was not the only effect the recitation at the *Trocadèro* had. It sealed not only what he had begun to feel in the studio, but also what he had felt after his conversation with Pelly about the Song of Solomon ; it ratified the emancipation he was enjoying. He felt he now had the entry into a free Pagan world and that the forts of convention and social prejudice had all crumbled and had fallen before the blast of magic trumpets. This new world was all before him. He had only just crossed the boundary, and he felt there were wide fertile provinces and infinite riches to be discovered. Paris, he felt, was a wonderful springboard from whence to leap into undiscovered seas, and he was looking forward to exhilarating adventure when all of a sudden an unexpected revolution took place in his career.

C.'s aunt, Mrs. Roden, Mr. Roden and the two girls spent Easter in Paris that year, and C. was invited to have *déjeuner* one day and to dine another evening with his cousins, the Roden girls, and to see *Le tour du monde en* 80 *jours*, at the *Châtelet*, which was the only play going on at that moment which was thought to be quite safe for the female young person.

One day C. was asked to *déjeuner* at the Hotel Meurice, where the Rodens were staying, and he found Mrs. Roden alone. The girls had gone out, she said, with their father.

" I wanted to have a talk with you alone," she said.

She then explained to C. that a family council had been held in London about him and his future. It had been settled that he was to try and pass into the Foreign Office, possibly into the Diplomatic Service, although there were difficulties about that. The difficulties meant the expense, of course.

Mr. Spark, the crammer, had been consulted. He knew all that there was to be known about these examinations. He was of the opinion that C. should spend at least a year at Oxford or Cambridge. Mrs. Roden said she had persuaded Lady Hengrave to consent to this plan. What she didn't say was that she had undertaken to pay for C.'s university education.

Lady Hengrave had then written to Mr. Pringle, C.'s former tutor, and had asked him whether C. would be able to pass into Oxford without difficulty. There was, it appeared, a tiresome little examination called Smalls, which had to be faced. Mr. Pringle had written back to say that, owing to C.'s having done German for Greek during his last year at Eton, he would need some extra coaching in that subject ; he was also extremely weak in mathematics, and the sums needed in Responsions, although easy, had to be solved correctly if the candidate was to pass. He had made inquiries about C.'s proficiency in modern languages, and the French masters had all agreed that his French was far above the average. The German master, on the other hand, said that his German sadly needed brushing up. He considered, therefore, that C. was wasting his time in France, and it would be far wiser for him to spend a few months in Germany, and then a month, or possibly two months, at a crammer's. He recommended a certain Mr. Owen, who lived at Bournemouth, and was a specialist in preparing boys for Oxford and Cambridge.

Mr. Spark's establishment did not open in the autumn till the middle of September, nor did he specialise in this branch of cramming. Lady Hengrave had consulted Mr. Spark once more, who had said that C. should undoubtedly brush up his German, and recommended a family at Alterstadt, near the Harz Mountains. He advised, after that, a year at Oxford, and he would then receive him into his establishment, and he could begin the serious business of cramming.

Lady Hengrave consented to C.'s going to Oxford, but she thought it was quite unnecessary for him to go to Germany at present. She was led, however, to change her mind. Her sister Emma was *en poste* at Rome, and she mentioned in a letter to Lady Hengrave that she had seen Lady Ralph Dallington, who had just come from Paris, and who had spoken of C. as being a nice boy and obviously in love with a very pretty but penniless American called Miss Church, whose mother was well-known to be a determined woman and an intriguer. She warned her sister of the danger, adding that C. had probably inherited his dear father's susceptibility. Lady Hengrave was alarmed, and resolved that C. must not stay a day longer at Versailles than was necessary.

As a matter of fact, Lady Hengrave's fears were

probably quite groundless, for Mrs. Church made no overtures to C. It was well known that she investigated the circumstances of any possible husband for her daughter most carefully before taking action, and the younger son of an impoverished peer with a large family and a standing harvest of debts was not what she was looking for. All these plans had been discussed, it appeared, more than a month before Easter, and as soon as Lady Hengrave heard from her sister Emma she had prudently already given Madame Maartens a month's notice. Indeed, Madame Maartens' fees were paid in advance, so C. was to leave at the end of April and take the train for Hanover.

"I had great difficulty in persuading your mother about the Oxford question," Mrs. Roden said.

So she had, until the financial side of the problem had been solved. After that, with the unconscious aid of Aunt Emma, the rest had been easy.

The Rodens left the day after this interview took place, and before saying good-bye to C. Mrs. Roden pressed a five-pound note into his hand.

"— And if ever you are badly in need of money," she said, "write to me. Don't write to your father or to your mother; it would upset them and be bad for your father's gout."

The advice was hardly necessary, as C. could not imagine writing home to ask for anything, money least of all. He went to see Pelly as soon as he could, and told him the news. Pelly was leaving at the end of the month, and they settled to travel together to Hanover. There their ways parted.

Madame Maartens had known of the plan for long, but she had not been certain that it would materialise ; she had not reckoned on the fairy godmother in the person of Mrs. Roden, so she was surprised when C. announced the news to her. She sighed.

" I suppose it's a good thing," she said. " You certainly know as much French as you would ever learn here, and Monsieur Jollivet says you are ' *très fort*,' besides which it is good for you to learn German, to see Germany, and you will hear some beautiful music."

C. invited M. and Madame Maartens to go to the opera with him at Paris. He would have liked to have treated them to an opera of Wagner. Unfortunately no Wagner was being given, so he took places for *Carmen* at the *Opéra Comique*, and they dined beforehand at the restaurant *Marguery*, which was Monsieur Maarten's favourite restaurant, and they ate some *Sole Marguery*, which was Monsieur Maarten's favourite dish.

They listened to the opera from a small box in the third tier, and they all enjoyed it, although Monsieur Maartens slept peacefully during the last act.

The next day C. spent in saying good-bye to Monsieur Jollivet and other friends, and in taking a last look at Versailles. Monsieur Jollivet was sorry to lose his pupil. He wished, he said, the French boys he had to teach showed one-tenth of the application

and good sense and intelligence that C. had given
proof of.

"*Travaillez bien, et vous irez loin, mon enfant.*" he
said. "*Vous avez le sens de la littérature. Tâchez qu'on
ne gâte pas votre goût avec toutes ces saletés modernes et
réalistes,*" and he snorted at the thought of them.

He gave C. as a parting gift, the poetical works of
André Chénier.

It had been a cold, late spring, and a bitter east wind
was blowing on the day C. left Versailles. And when
he and Pelly arrived in North Germany it was colder
still. There the spring seemed to have scarcely begun.
The skies were grey, the trees were, many of them, still
bare, and the wind cut like a knife. C. and Pelly
arrived at Hanover late in the evening. The contrast
after France and Paris was great. They went to
Casten's Hotel and, ordering what they thought would
be two small cutlets, found they had to face two
enormous chops large enough for six people. The
dining-room was full of officers in blue uniforms,
drinking *Sekt* out of tall, thin glasses. C. recklessly
ordered a bottle of *champagner*, and it turned out to be
sweeter than syrup and consisted almost entirely of
bubbles and foam.

The next morning Pelly started for Dresden, and C.
for Alterstadt. They travelled for an hour together,
then C. had to get out and change. They were sorry
to leave each other, and they exchanged promises not
only to write, but to meet later on somewhere in
Germany.

Alterstadt was a little town which might have come straight from a Grimm fairy tale. The houses were, many of them, of wood, with pointed red roofs and beams let into the walls. As C. drove from the station he reached a square in which a large grey church rose towering out of a crowd of little houses, which nestled close under it. It was like a scene from *Faust* and he expected to see Mephistopheles slink round the corner and cower at the church door, or Gretchen walk with book and rosary to church.

The house where his prospective hostess or hostesses lived, the two Fräulein Berchtold, was a small red-brick villa, two-storied, and standing in a garden in the more modern part and the outer circle of the town. They were two old maids, and their brother-in-law was a Professor who gave lessons in German to stray foreigners in his spare time. The elder of the two, Fräulein Lili, taught. She was an intellectual, full of stifled literary ambitions, and she had written in secret a cycle of love poems in which she had told the adventures and the ultimate shipwreck of her volatile heart. The second sister, Fräulein Anna, looked after the household, and her principal distraction was to look at coloured views of the Alps through a stereo-scope, but she was fond of the stage, and every now and then made an expedition to Hanover to hear an opera or a classical drama.

Besides C. there was one other boarder in the house, a German boy called Fritz Decker.

C. found the change abrupt, and the contrast

between life at Versailles and life at Alterstadt sharp,
although not disagreeable. His hostesses were exceedingly kind. His German was rusty, but the founda-
tions of it were there, and he had learnt the elements of
the language in his childhood, and this made it all so
much easier. Fräulein Lili gave him lessons, and
when he confessed to her that he enjoyed reading
poetry, she confided to him that she, too, was a poetess,
and she showed him a ballad of an emotional description of which the refrain was *Die Rosen blühen auf
Tyburn's Höhe*, or words to that effect. She warned
him before she gave it to him that he would find it
stimmungsvoll, which he did.

C. began to make for himself enchanting discoveries
in German literature. He bought the lyrics of Heine
and never did he enjoy anything in literature more
in his life than that first reading of the *Buch der
Lieder*, while there was still a thin mist of slight
difficulty and a lingering veil of intangible mystery
over their words. It was not a fog caused by an imperfect mastery of the language but a mist breathed by
the gradual dawning remembrance of what he had
once known and subsequently forgotten. It was
like going back into childhood. The words had a
strange freshness for him as if they had just been
coined and had come straight from the mint for his
enjoyment. This particular impression wore off
almost immediately ; in a week's time the words had
lost all sense of unfamiliarity and strangeness, and the
mystery which the partial veil of oblivion had lent

them in the period of dawning recomprehension, but
they never lost their charm.

C. thought Heine was the most wonderful writer who
had ever lived, and he learnt poem after poem by
heart. They sang in his head all day as he walked
about the narrow streets of Alterstadt or climbed the
rather bleak, fir-clad hills in the neighbourhood. It
was still cold ; there were patches of snow on the hills,
and biting showers of sleet and hail. But the house
was warm and cosy and the large stoves gave a friendly
warmth. The boarders had a sitting-room between
them where they did their work, and in the evening
Fritz Decker would smoke a long cherrywood pipe.
Fritz Decker was a schoolboy in the *Prima* Class of the
local *Gymnasium*. He was already a philosopher, and
he was deeply versed in questions of geology and comparative anatomy. It was on such evenings that C.
learnt the meaning of the word *gemüthlich*. There was
an indescribable comfort and moral cosiness about
them. Sometimes a fellow schoolboy of Decker's
would look in and the three would play *skat*, smoking
and drinking a little beer from time to time.

Sometimes the two Fräuleins would receive company
downstairs, and after the oldest and most exalted lady
of the company had been beckoned to the sofa, a flat
cake with apple inside it and powdered with sugar on
the top would be presented, and a bottle of white wine,
and then Herr Kuni, the son of a neighbouring *Musik-
Direktor*, would be asked to sing. He would shake the
rafters with his rendering of *Die Rothe Hanne*.

There was one other foreigner at Alterstadt at the
time ; he was a young Scottish doctor, and he was
living with another family.   C. made his acquaintance
and they would go out for long walks together.
Fräulein Anna was for ever urging C. to go to
Hanover and enjoy a nice classic play, *Die Piccolo-
mimi* or possibly *Die Jungfrau von Orleans* or a fine
classical opera, such as *Der Freischütz*.   But C. felt
no desire to do so.   At last, seeing that he was
really wounding Fräulein Anna by appearing to slight
her favourite pastime, and to be casting reflections on
what she considered to be the finest theatre in the
world, he resolved to go the very next time Fräulein
Anna suggested such a thing.   So, when one day
Fräulein Anna, after perusing the newspaper, announced that *Tannhäuser* was going to be given,
with Herr Brünning in the chief part, C. asked her
whether he might accompany her.   She was overjoyed ; Fräulein Lili was asked whether she would
like to go, but she had one of her headaches, and
Wagner's music was, in any case, too much for her.
They took the afternoon train and walked from the
station to a little shop where Fräulein Anna had a
particular friend who sold her tickets, and, after par-
taking of a *Butterbrod* and a glass of beer, they entered
the large theatre.

C. had never heard a note of Wagner, nor did he know
what *Tannhäuser* was about.   He looked forward to
a painful evening, and to having to endure the kind
of music he used to hear at his Aunt Fanny's.   Then

the orchestra began to play the overture.   Never did
he receive a more violent electric shock.   This was,
indeed, something different from chamber music.   He
did not follow all of it, but he was swept away.   The
curtain went up, and to his astonishment C. found
himself in the heart of the kingdom of romance, on
familiar ground.   There was no difficulty in following
the story, and when he was transported to the Venusberg, he felt he was witnessing a poem of Swinburne's
in action.   The second act was less exciting and at
times operatic, conventional and a little tawdry, but
C. enjoyed the outburst when Tannhäuser sang the
Venusberg song at court, and the idea of this appealed
to him immensely.   He would like, he thought, a
crashing, thunderous Venusberg song to be sung before
all his aunts, which would cause their conventions,
creeds, prejudices, morals and ideals to come crashing
to the ground.

C. was not then, nor later, particularly musical, nor
was he ever destined to become a Wagnerite, he was
too innately classical.   He did not even want to
repeat his experience ; but Wagner's music heard for
the first time hypnotised him ; laid bare his nerves,
and heightened his receptivity and sensitiveness to
artistic impressions.   He felt as if he had put on new
armour, and was ready to go and fight the world in
defence of freedom, and of the joy of life.   He wanted
to shatter the world's false idols, and break the walls
of the established temples.   It was a fresh landmark
in his progress of emancipation.   He felt now that he

had found the banner and the watchword he needed. He was ready to storm the forts of folly.

They took the last train home as soon as the performance was over, and Fräulein Anna kept on repeating, as she unfolded a parcel of *Butterbrode* which she had providently brought with her for C. and herself, "*Wunderschön war es, wunderschön.*"

C. returned, too, brooding over his new landmark in rapture. Alas! there was no one with whom he wished to exchange ideas on the subject, and he was bursting with excitement and unexpressed ideas.

CHAPTER XVII

AFTER C. had been a month at Alterstadt, Fräulein Lili said that he was sufficiently well advanced in German to take lessons from her brother-in-law, who taught more-advanced pupils. Her brother-in-law, the husband of her deceased sister, was a Professor Kaufmann, who taught English at the *Gymnasium*. He was a large, genial, grey-haired man, who had spent some years of his life in England, and he spoke of English manners, customs, institutions, art and literature with a kindly tolerance, and delighted in pointing out to English people the folly of so many of their ideas, habits, customs, and tastes. He thought the habit of eating muffins especially pernicious. C. found it as difficult to discuss English and German literature with him as it had been to discuss French literature with Monsieur Jollivet.

Professor Kaufmann thought that Shakespeare was an English superstition, and, although, no doubt, a fine dramatist, on the whole grossly over-rated. He found Milton tedious, Keats lacking in *moralische Ideen*, and he had no patience with Tennyson.

" Who do you think is the greatest English poet of the nineteenth century ? " he asked C. one day.

The answer was : " Shelley."

But another (German) pupil who was present said Tennyson.

"Shelley," said the Professor, "no doubt had ideas, but Lord Byron is the greatest English poet of the nineteenth century. And as for Tennyson, he is a dwarf," said the Professor, "a dwarf compared with Lord Byron, who is a giant."

In German literature Schiller was the only poet who satisfied him. He could not read Goethe's *Faust* because he found the Gretchen episode too painful. He considered Heine unhealthy and morbid. One day the Professor was drinking coffee with the two fräuleins, and C. was present. They were all sitting in the garden in a little summer house (*die Laube*). A volume of Heine was lying on a garden seat.

"That is no doubt Mr. Bramsley's," said the Professor, "and I am willing to wager that he himself is writing poems in the style of Heinrich Heine."

C. blushed, but made no admission.

"Is that not true?" asked the Professor. "Am I not right?"

"Ah, but you do not admire Heinrich Heine?" broke in Fräulein Lili, "and yet you must admit that he is a great poet.

> Das Meer hat seine Perlen,
> Der Himmel seine Sterne,
> Aber mein Herz, mein Herz,
> Mein Herz hat seine Liebe.

What grand thoughts! *Das ist doch grossartig.*"

"Ah, well," said the Professor, "we were all young

once, and you, Fräulein, have remained young ; but
I will quote you something better than that :—

> 'Tis true, your budding Miss is very charming,
>   But shy and awkward at first coming out,
> So much alarm'd that she is quite alarming,
>   All giggle, blush, half pertness and half pout ;
> And glancing at Mamma, for fear there's harm in
>   What you, she, it, or they, may be about,
> The nursery still lisps in all they utter,
> Besides, they always smell of bread and butter.

There are good verses for you. They are by Lord
Byron, and from *Beppo*. That is saner than Heinrich
Heine."

It was when taking part in conversations such as
these that C. longed for some one of his own age with
whom he could discuss all these things, some one who
would understand what he meant.

At the beginning of June he received a letter from
Pelly saying that he had left Dresden and that he was
now established at a *pension* in Heidelberg. He
suggested that C. should pay him a visit. C. was to
go home at the end of July. Mrs. Roden had written
to him suggesting that on his way home it would be
advisable for him to visit one or two other places in
Germany besides Alterstadt. She suggested in a
gushing letter his not leaving Germany before seeing
the Rhine, and advised him to return *via* Frankfort
and Cologne. She backed up her advice by a little
cheque sufficient to meet the needs of a short *Rundreise*. C. waited till the end of the month, and he
then bade farewell to Alterstadt. He had enjoyed his

time there, but he had lived entirely within himself, and he had been thrown back on to himself. He was too reserved to assimilate German life and to make intimate friends with the German boys of his own age. As he had no fellow-countrymen there except the Scotch doctor, who had left soon after he arrived, he had grown rather weary of the grown-up social life, the picnics in the woods, the concerts in the beer garden, and the evenings at the Fräuleins' house when they received company, although all this had exercised a soothing influence on him and given him time to think. He had made good progress in German. He knew Heine by heart, and had read a certain amount of Goethe and Schiller, although he was too young for Goethe and too old for Schiller. He had read a great many English books, and he had been spellbound by George Meredith.

Besides reading, he in his spare moments had tried to write. He had written under the influence of Heine and Uhland several romantic ballads, and under the lingering influence of Heredia and the dawning influence of Wagner a whole series of classic and romantic mythological sonnets. What he wrote at this time was either burnt by himself or lost afterwards, and nothing remains but a few fragments.

He wrote to Pelly saying that he hoped to pass through Heidelberg, and that he would let him know his plans more definitely as soon as he started. He did not wish to commit himself to any definite programme, but he allowed Fräulein Anna the treat of planning and of calculating the cost of his *Rundreise*, while he inwardly decided to commit himself to nothing as binding as a *Rundreise Billet*. Fräulein Anna planned the journey with care, and it was decided that he must stop at Frankfort first and sleep the night there, otherwise he would not arrive at Heidelberg until past midnight, which would be bound to cause inconvenience to some one, and perhaps result in his finding himself without a lodging for the night. C. always looked back on the morning on which he left Alterstadt as one of the most melancholy occasions of his life. Fräulein Anna, Fräulein Lili and Decker accompanied him to the station. They all four of them sat in the station restaurant and drank a glass of beer. Fräulein Anna toasted C. and wished him a fortunate journey, and every one else joined in the toast. There was something solemn about the ritual.

The conversation flagged.

" You must be sure to visit the Opera House at Mannheim," said Fräulein Anna.

" When they perform a play of Schiller's," said Fräulein Lili, standing up for literature as against music.

" Life at Frankfort is said to be very dear," said Decker.

" When you order coffee," said Fräulein Anna, as if to make up for this drawback, " order the *Portion* and not the *Tasse ;* it is much cheaper."

" And be sure to visit Goethe's house," said Fräulein Lili.

"And do be careful of the draughts," said Fräulein Anna, who considered that all *Sehenswürdigkeiten* were always draughty.

"And send us a postcard now and then," said Fräulein Lili.

A bell rang. The time for getting into the train had come. Fräulein Anna pressed a parcel of home-made *butterbrode* into C.'s hand. Fräulein Lili gave him a little book, *Der Trompeter von Säkkingen*. He got into the railway carriage, a third-class carriage.

"*Leben sie wohl! Auf weidersehen!*" they all said in chorus.

He said good-bye to Alterstadt. He was destined never to see it again.

Fraulein Anna and Fräulein Lili wept. They both of them felt a presentiment that they would never see him again, and they were both of them extremely fond of him. Some years later an Englishman was staying at Alterstadt in another family, also for the purpose of learning German, and he made the acquaintance of the two Fräuleins. They talked of nothing but C., and when they discovered that this stranger actually knew him they bubbled over with joy.

"So nice," said Fräulein Anna (*So nett*).

"So gifted," said Fräulein Lili (*So begabt*).

"He took me to see *Tannhäuser*, said Fräulein Anna.

"He gave me Platen's poems," said Fräulein Lili.

"He was so fond of *Gänsebraten*," said Fräulein Anna.

" He read Goethe's *Tasso* after he had been here four weeks," said Fräulein Lili.

" He had such a good heart ; was so modest " (*So bescheiden*), said Fräulein Anna.

" So good looking," said Fräulein Lili, with a sigh (*Ein so hübscher Mensch*). " Let us hope that the world may go well with him."

" I hope it will," said Fräulein Anna.

" I fear he will have sad things to experience," said Fräulein Lili, scenting a broken heart.

He arrived at Frankfort late in the evening, and as he was walking up and down the platform wondering what he should do, a notice mentioning trains to Italy caught his eye. A remark in Lewes' *Life of Goethe*, which he had just been reading, passed through his mind. Something about Goethe having been tired of the cold, wet German summers. He, too, was tired of the cold, wet summer. It had been raining at Alterstadt steadily all through the month of June, and when he had gone for a lonely walking tour in the Harz mountains he had found it so cold and bleak that he had returned after two days. He had a sudden, overwhelming *Sehnsucht nach dem Süden*, and the idea, the wild, insane idea, entered into his head that he must see Venice. He felt it was a case of now or never. If he did not see Venice now he would never see it. If he did go, he would not be able to stay long, for it would never do for them to hear at home that he was careering through Italy, besides which he doubted whether his finances would allow him even to

get there and back and then home afterwards. He
went to the booking office and asked the price of a
second-class return ticket to Venice. It was too
expensive. He decided to stay the night at Frankfort,
and to go on to Heidelberg the next day.

He asked at the hotel what was going on at the
Opera House, and they told him *Tristan und
Isolde*. He strolled out to get some dinner at a cheap
Wirtshaus. At the table next to the one where he had
sat down a young Frenchman was sitting. He also
had been studying German and was on his way home.
C. told him he was going to the opera, and he said he
would like to accompany him. They talked of Paris.
The young man took a lofty view of things there, and
when C. mentioned Madeleine Lapara he made a
spluttering noise and shrugged his shoulders, saying,
no doubt she had been good in her day, but now . . .
C. asked him whether he had often seen her, and it
turned out that he had never seen her except by hear-
say. They got places at the Opera House, high up in
the third circle of the *Logen*.

C. had no idea as to how Wagner had treated the
subject of Tristram and Iseult, which he only knew
from Swinburne and Matthew Arnold.

Once more, and more powerfully this time, he was
hypnotised by the music ; the singers were not
romantic, the Tristan was positively senile and had
only the ghost of a voice. Isolde was massive. And
yet after a few moments that was of no consequence.
It hardly mattered more than the footlights or the

scenery. C. could follow neither the words nor the music, but he was utterly spellbound, intoxicated, shipwrecked on an ocean of uneasy ecstasy, and yet oppressed; he felt at one moment as if he were drowning in heavy seas, at another as if he was alone in a sultry desert, and always in a stifling twilight.

At the end of the first act the French boy who was with him got up and, turning to the audience, exclaimed:

"La musique m'a déplu absolument!"

He then said he had had enough of it, and would meet C., if he liked, at a *Bierhaus*. But C. remained till the very end of the performance, and when it was all over he felt as if he had awakened from a long trance; he was scarcely aware of more than that, he felt he had never heard anything like this before, it was totally different even from *Tannhäuser*, and M. Jollivet's phrase came to his mind, *Cette musique qui ne resemble à rien*, and he felt as if he had entered a thick enchanted forest from which there was no escape, and that he, too, had drunk of a fatal cup, but who had shared it with him he knew not. He was haunted by a hidden face and pursued by an undiscovered name.

He went home soon after the opera was over. He could not face the conversation of the young French man again. The next day he went to Heidelberg, and found Pelly living in a crowded *pension* kept by the wife of a retired Colonel, and full of Americans, male and female. Heidelberg was gay and dry in the summer heat. C. and Pelly spent a day exploring the sights of the town, the garden, and the castle ; the next day they took a boat and made an expedition up the Neckar, to Neckarsteinar and the *Schwalben Nest,* and on the third they started on a four days' walk through the woods up the valley of the Neckar.

C. poured out to Pelly all his recent experiences in the concrete world of Alterstadt, and in the unsubstantial world of books and of music, and he hinted at his dreams and ambitions. They tired the sun with talking and compared notes, and laid the foundation of a friendship that C. thought would be lifelong. But that was not to be. After a week both left Heidelberg together and started in a steamer for Cologne. C. confided to Pelly that his ambition was to be a writer. He had no desire to work for examinations, still less to pass them. Life in a Government office he thought would be intolerable. Pelly was destined for the Indian Civil Service, and C. sadly reflected that he would most certainly pass, as he had an admirably equipped intelligence, and was capable of working without effort. He had distinguished himself at Eton, and would most probably do the same at Cambridge, which was his immediate destination.

C. and Pelly talked of Wagner, Ibsen and the English poets ; of Maupassant, Hardy, Meredith, Kipling and the novelists, and they both agreed it was high time some one should sing the *Venusberg* song all over England and shatter the walls of Philistinism. They had no idea of the solidity of these walls.

Shortly after they had left Coblenz they were sitting on a seat on the deck of the steamer, and C. was pouring out a flood of indignant rhetoric on the sins of Philistia.

" Everything in England wants reforming," he said. " The House of Lords, what is the use of it ? And the House of Commons is *worse*. The Church is dead ; the army is an expensive, inefficient machine ; the stage is childish ; literature is gagged, and art is muzzled, bound by the code of the schoolroom. Nobody dares say what they think in England. If you do you are talked down. It is the triumph of Philistinism. It's Philistinism that we must fight, *you* and *I ;* and we must get others, and never stop." And he began to declaim the end of a favourite poem of Heine :—

> Tausend Ritter, wohlgewappnet,
> Hat der heil'ge Geist erwählt,
> Seinen Willen zu erfüllen ;
> Und er hat sie muthbeseelt.
>
> Ihre theuere Schwerter blitzen,
> Ihre guten Banner wehn !
> Ei, du möchtest wohl, mein Kindchen,
> Solche stolze Ritter sehn ?
>
> Nun, so schau mich an, mein Kindchen,
> Küsse mich, und schaue dreist ;
> Denn ich selber bin ein solcher
> Ritter von dem heil'gen Geist.

Just as he finished the last lines a man and a lady walked past C. and Pelly. The man wore a covert coat and a tweed cap, and the lady a dark serge coat and skirt. The man was smoking a pipe. They might both of them have stepped from the front hall at Bramsley. The lady sat down on the side of the steamer, and the man arranged a rug on her knees.

The man walked up to C. and said to him, alluding to the General Election :—

" I say, I hope those damned Radicals won't get in."

C. blushed and murmured something which, if it did not give the impression of assent, certainly did not express any violent dissent.

And this was his first encounter with the forces of British Philistinism since he had enrolled himself among the knights of the Holy Ghost. He reflected ruefully that it was a decided victory for the enemy's forces.

CHAPTER XVIII

C. AND Pelly travelled to London together *viâ*
Cologne, and said good-bye to each other at Victoria
Station. They were both of them bound for their
respective homes. They promised each other to meet
very often in the future, and to correspond with
unfailing regularity. The last promise they to a
certain extent fulfilled. The first one was decided for
them differently to their expectations, for they never
met again. Pelly went straight into the Indian Civil
Service instead of going to Cambridge, as he had
intended to do. He passed brilliantly, went to India,
and disappeared from C.'s life, except in so far as he
was represented from an occasional letter from some
remote spot. But C. did not realise this, either at the
time of separation or afterwards. He always felt that
he might be on the verge of meeting Pelly round the
street corner; he could always write to him easily,
and he sometimes carried on imaginary conversations
with him in his head.

C. spent a fortnight at home, and thence proceeded
to Bournemouth, where Mr. Owen guaranteed to get
him into Oxford. There is no record of C.'s life at
Bournemouth. He never spoke about it or mentioned
it later. It was an epoch that seems not to have

counted in his life, nor did he ever mention any one he had met there, and yet Mr. Owen's establishment was always full to overflowing. In any case the sojourn at Bournemouth fulfilled its purpose, as C. passed Smalls and proceeded to Oxford, and became a member of X. College. He arrived at Oxford shy and a little bewildered. By going abroad he had broken the thread which united him to his contemporaries, and the few men whom he recognised as having been at Eton at the same time as himself were at other colleges, and took no notice of him.

His first interview with the Master was not very satisfactory. The Master asked him in in the evening. He seemed just to have begun his dinner, and was nibbling a piece of fried sole when C. was shown into the dining-room. He looked wise and comfortable, like a white owl. The Master told C. to sit down. Later on he offered him a glass of wine. He asked after Lord and Lady Hengrave, and then said, " And your brother ? How is your brother Gilbert ? " Gilbert was the ne'er-do-well. C. blushed scarlet and said :—

" He's abroad."

Whether the Master was conscious or not of his lapse we shall never know until the Judgment Day, and then there will scarcely be time ; but the silence caused by the remark lasted a long time.

" Have you read Boswell ? " the Master asked at last.

C. said he had not. Nor had he. The silence lasted till the Master said :—

" Good-night, Mr. Bramsley.   Read Boswell."

The Master little suspected at the time that C., although he had never read Boswell, had done a far rarer thing, namely, to read Johnson, even the dictionary.

His tutor asked him to breakfast with several other undergraduates, and during the meal C. did not utter a word, but there was one undergraduate present who never ceased talking, and told anecdote after anecdote about his experiences with Custom House officials abroad.   C. did not know who this talkative individual was, nor did he ever get to know him afterwards.   It was during his first fortnight at Oxford that one evening, when he was walking across the Quad, he met an undergraduate who was whistling to himself very loudly.   C. had already noticed him before in Hall, and had wondered who he was.   He looked like a Spaniard.   His hair was black and his eyes were clear, dark and slow.   His name was Gerald Malone. He came from the West Country.   He was a Devonshire man, the son of a doctor, who lived near Dartmoor, and he had an Iberian strain.

Malone nodded to him, and C. expressed semi-recognition.

" Come up to my rooms," said Malone ; and they strolled up to the rooms on the second floor in silence.

When they reached the rooms, which were entirely bare except for a dilapidated rep sofa, a standing bookcase full of serviceable books, and a map of Rome over the chimney-piece, they found several other

undergraduates engaged in making some kind of brew
with a kettle and some lemons. Everybody there
seemed to take C. for granted, and he mixed quite
naturally with them, and soon found himself taking an
active, not to say a violent, part in the conversation.
Every one was talking at once, and nobody was listening. Suddenly C. heard Malone say that all poetry
was rot, but that the rottenest of all poets was
Shelley.

"He's the best of all the poets," C. heard himself
saying quietly and decidedly.

"The rottenest of all *rotten* poets," said Malone,
who was just then squeezing a lemon into a glass of
hot water.

C. took the lemon from his hands, and threw it into
the fire. Malone looked at him, and then went for him
calmly. They were soon both struggling on the floor
in a long, hard-fought, silent, infinitely arduous
and painstaking struggle of the Homeric kind, where
first one and then the other of the combatants gets
the better of the contest. At one moment C. was on
the top, and thought the victory was in his hand.
Malone had another piece of lemon in his hand, and his
object was to rub C.'s nose with it. The piece of
lemon became the objective of the fight. Then
Malone got the upper hand, and forced C.'s head to the
floor, but just when victory seemed to be in his grasp
C., by a supreme wriggle and jerk, managed to neutralise
the position. He could not win, for strong as he
was, Malone was still stronger, but he could avoid the

humiliation of the lemon rub. Finally the piece of lemon in the scuffle was released from Malone's hand, and then a desperate struggle began for who should reach it first. C. was lying half on his back. Malone had more or less the upper position, but both bodies wriggled, turned and struggled so much that they were seldom in the same position for more than two seconds. Malone had pinioned one of C.'s arms, but C. managed with the other to snatch the piece of lemon and throw it towards the fire, when another under-graduate sententiously remarked that the struggle was one of those Pyrrhic battles which were neither lost nor won, and, so saying, he threw the piece of lemon into the fire. Malone got up and said :—

" You are an ass, Blades, you've spoilt the whole fight."

They had neither of them lost their tempers during the struggle, and yet each of them had fought with all the concentrated violence he was capable of. That little episode was the beginning of C.'s friendship with Gerald Malone, which was to last him all his life.

Malone inspired C. with hero-worship, less by his gifts, which were above the average, both in matters intellectual and athletic, than by his audacious high spirits and his thirst for enterprise, if possible, dangerous enterprise, and his desperate determination to go through with things. He was, in daily life, quiet, and not even very talkative, but on especial occasions, whenever there was a rag, or an enter-prise in the air, he assumed command and inspired the proceedings with the energy of a demon. He had been educated at Dulwich, and he was a good oar and a good classic scholar, but entirely without ambition, and the Master, who liked him, said upon one occasion : " I'm afraid that Malone will make a mucker of life," an unusual expression to fall from his purist lips.

C. very soon began to settle down at Oxford. He did not go in for rowing, but he played Rugby football with success. He avoided the hunting world, as he could not afford to hunt, and the more things at Oxford were like his home the more he avoided them. Curiously enough, his literary, as apart from his intellectual life (that is to say, his work), seemed to have come to an abrupt end. He was reading for Mods.

The first time he read an essay to the Master, the subject was unsympathetic to him, and he did not do himself justice. The Master piped like a bullfinch, while C. read out his platitudinous discourse, but at the end he said to him : " The English is good."

C. kept the secret of his literary tastes and aspirations to himself. It was not that he did not hear books discussed around him ; he heard endless literary discussions, but they disconcerted him. Malone had read a great deal, but it was only the Greek and Latin authors that moved his admiration. As for modern literature, he enjoyed Dumas, *Alice in Wonderland*, and *Sherlock Holmes*, but not only nineteenth century, but all English verse was a sealed book to him. He talked with laughing contempt of

Shakespeare, Milton, Shelley and Keats, and of all the poets whom C. admired most.

All his friends put C. to shame in this matter in different ways. There was Wilfrid Abbey, who seemed never to have read, nor to read anything at all, as if a well-educated man knew all that was necessary without reading a book. He could always cap a quotation, and never missed an allusion. He seemed to have absorbed his culture from the air. But he had no love of books, and it was impossible to discuss such things with him. There was Oliver Hallam, a dynamic personality, with an irregular face, uncertain in temper, and ever shifting in mood, who discussed long and loudly what was good and bad, in a way that was above C.'s head.

Then, beyond his particular sphere, there were the intellectuals : Keeley, who absorbed knowledge without difficulty, and who seemed to have got beyond the stage when it was necessary to read ; and Edmund Blades, the son of Christopher Blades, the historian, and of Rachel Ellman, the once-famous *Lieder*-singer, who said that the time had not yet come for him to read modern verse. He had not sufficiently formed his taste on the old. For the present, he was reading Thucydides. Separate from the intellectuals, there was a small musical and artistic set, into which C. penetrated from time to time. It contained a fabulously rich Israelite, called Goldmann, who collected Oriental china, which was broken in his rooms after bump suppers, and an extremely superficial, voluble, but good-natured being, named Bently Jones, who, for some reason, was called Pope Joan. He was florid in dress and demeanour, and collected obscure modern French verse and pictures from Munich. C. could not understand what or whom he was talking about when he discussed books. He seemed to inhabit a province he had neither visited nor heard of, and to have read books whose existence he had never even suspected at Versailles, either from his conversations with Burstall or from the echoes that Pelly used to bring him from the *Quartier Latin*.

C. thought for the moment no more of literature. There were plenty of other things to occupy him, and he enjoyed himself ecstatically.

He went home at the end of his first term and spent Christmas at Bramsley, where there was a large gathering of uncles and aunts. Mrs. Roden had written to his mother, asking that he might spend a few days at their country house as soon as Christmas was over. Lady Hengrave thought this was a good idea.

When he arrived at Elladon, the Rodens' house, he was enormously struck by the quality of the atmosphere there, so different from that of his own home. The Corots, the Daubignys on the walls, the noisy teas, the games, the rambling discussions about everything and every one, where apparently you could say what you thought about a book or a person without being considered odd, were a sharp contrast to him, after the rigid tenour of his family life. There was a large party staying in the house. There was some hunting and a little rough shooting. C. made friends with a boy called Walter Wright, who was working for the Indian Civil Service. He had just determined not to go up to Oxford. He passed his examinations in order to do so and had meant to go to the same college as C. a year before, but he was prevented from doing so by an attack of rheumatic fever, and he went to a crammer's instead. The crammer, however, was all in favour of his going to Oxford. C. entered into Wright's case with fire, and said he must certainly go to Oxford, and Wright settled to do so.

It was at Elladon, at a concert given in the village, that C. and Wright made the acquaintance of a family called Lord, who were staying at that time with some neighbours of the Rodens. Mr. Lord was an elderly, nervous man with grey hair, and wore a pince-nez on a broad ribbon. In his youth an unsuccessful painter, he had invented a new kind of pottery, which had likewise proved a failure, and designed a flying machine which never got further than the tracing-paper stage. With Mr. and Mrs. Lord was their daughter, Beatrice. C. sat in the same row during the concert, and was spellbound by the few glimpses he had of her beauty. She was not eighteen years old, then ; there was something indescribably noble about her. Nothing stiff nor Juno-like, but something authentically celestial ; something in her very soft, azure eyes that suggested a floating, loving ocean ; something magical in her smile ; something

strong and proud in her chin that was too pronounced, and in her eyebrows, that were too
boldly pencilled, and in her mouth that seemed
carelessly finished ; something indescribably shining
and winning in her whole appearance ; everything
about her seemed to shine—her hair, her complexion.

> Her pure and eloquent blood
> Spoke in her cheeks, and so distinctly wrought,
> That one might almost say her body thought.

C. fell in love at first sight, but he was not conscious
of the fact. He was only conscious that he wanted
to look at her. He could not manage to do so
without being uncivil and staring. He hardly saw
her, and when he was introduced to her at the end of
the concert there was no time to speak or look.

On the way home he said to Wright :—

" Isn't she beautiful ? " and his eyes were charged
with dream. He didn't allude to her again, and
shortly afterwards, the next day or the day after, he
left for home.

When C. went back to Oxford for the Lent term he
had a new friend in Walter Wright, and he introduced
him to all his friends. Wright had been educated at
Winchester. He was not a classical scholar, but
he was fond of books, and had read a great deal.
Above all things he was sympathetic and intuitive, and
he detected C.'s taste. C. was aware of this, but for
some time he did not mention to Wright, or to any one
else, that he was himself fond of reading and had read
a great quantity of English verse. With some of his

contemporaries he was ashamed of his ignorance; with others of his knowledge. It was quite by accident that he broke through the barrier of reserve with which he had hedged himself on this subject. One day Wright was sitting alone in his rooms.

"What are you reading?" asked C.

"Tennyson—*Maud*."

"I've hardly read anything by Tennyson since I was a child," said C. "My mother won't admit that Tennyson is a poet, and at Eton my tutor laughed at him, and the Germans despised him, and I've only read things like the *Charge of the Light Brigade* and the *May Queen*."

Wright handed him the book, and C. began at the beginning, and then went on without stopping. Wright did not disturb him. He went on with a piece of work he had on hand. C. read till past midnight, when he finished the monodrama. He then left the room abruptly and went to his rooms. The silvery, flute-like music, the warm passion, the luscious landscape, and the glowing imagery, had caught him and whirled him away into another sphere. It moved him in a new manner. It was the first time he had heard English verse speak in the accents of his time and express what he might have felt himself. So far poetry had kindled his enthusiasm, his admiration, his imagination, his love of romance; this kindled the dawning emotions and passions of his heart. He did not go to sleep for a long time that night. He was like a man who had taken hashish. Strings had been touched

in him which had never been stirred, and tremulous
thoughts and dreams were crowding his mind, and
there was a glimmer which had never been there
before. Something had lit a new lamp within him,
and all that night vision after vision haunted him.
The birds in the high hall garden calling, the ocean
foam in the moon, the swell of the long waves, the
noiseless music of the night ; and he murmured to
himself over and over again :—

> All night the roses have heard
> The flute, violin, bassoon.

CHAPTER XIX

ALTHOUGH C. made a new friend in Walter Wright, he did not, even after the incident of his first reading of *Maud*, confide to him any of his literary aims and ambitions, nor share with him his literary tastes. This was odd, as Wright was nothing if not literary and bubbling over with enthusiasm for books and for new discoveries in literature. C. kept all this to himself and threw himself into the active life of the college. He was insensibly becoming a leading member in the small group to which he introduced Wright, to which Abbey and Hallam belonged.

They called the outside world, that is to say, the Rowing Set, the Intellectuals, the Artistic, and the ordinary undergraduate " Limbo," and they only admitted one member of it—a red-haired, matter-of-fact, rather thick-headed and extremely painstaking, conscientious man called Baines, and nicknamed Socks—into their intimacy.

But the group itself was a fairly large one, and the college authorities frankly detested it for its covert insubordination and for the obscure rags it was perpetually organising. Wilfrid Abbey, who was shy and quiet, a refined Etonian who hardly ever spoke in company at all and was lazy beyond description as far as any mental effort was concerned, was a prime leader in these escapades.

One evening he came up to C. and said to him :

" You have been put up as a candidate for the *Quadranglers*."

" What are the *Quadranglers* ? " asked C.

" You shall see," said Abbey, and he took him to his rooms, which were on the ground floor of the college. There he found a table spread with dishes of oysters, some tankards of beer, some bottles of different-coloured wines, and in the middle of these dishes a large book, sumptuously bound in crimson crushed morocco and with the words *The Quadranglers* beautifully tooled on it. " That," said Wilfrid Abbey, " is the book of minutes, and no minutes are ever to be entered into it, and the rule of the club is that you are to eat and drink as much as you can in three minutes and then jump out of the window. If you perform this satisfactorily you become a life member."

C. performed the duty satisfactorily, and became a life member of the *Quadranglers*.

On another occasion they explored the colleges of Oxford by climbing from roof to roof, and on a third occasion they turned the Quadrangle into an imitation of the park of Versailles by bedding out flat tin baths full of gold-fish.

The college authorities were for sending down Malone, who had been thought, and rightly so, to be the ringleader in this affair, but the Master would not hear of it. He contented himself by saying that he did not think it humorous and gating him. A more serious escapade happened a little later, when, during a rag in the Quad, C. damaged a bath-chair which belonged to the Master's sister. The authorities took a very grave view of this incident, as they said it was a breach of courtesy and an insult to the old. A college meeting was held, and the Dean opted for the sending down of C. The Master opposed it and said :

" I don't think he meant to be discourteous. I don't think he meant to insult the old." And so nothing was done.

C. went home for the vacation, having enjoyed his second term even more than his first. During the vacation Lady Hengrave suggested that Walter Wright should be asked to spend a Saturday to Monday at Bramsley. She knew his people, and C., as it was not his own idea, but his mother's, had no objection. He had once proposed such a thing himself, but he would never do so again. It had been a lamentable failure.

On the Saturday on which Wright had been invited there was a typical gathering at Bramsley : the Bishop of Barminster, who had married a cousin of Lord Hengrave's, a florid and alarmingly conde- scending ecclesiastic, with a large beard and a fund of anecdote, whom Lady Hengrave thought transgressed the code of decency by being High Church. He wore a large gold cross, which she thought " odd," and he turned to the east when he said the Creed in church, which she said was against the law. With him was his apologetic, blond and explanatory wife.

Lord Hengrave, at one end of the long, crowded dining-room, which had some fine Dutch pictures, looked extremely dignified and young for his age; he was carefully dressed, and he walked assisted by a tortoise shell-headed cane. Lady Hengrave, at the other end, still " so handsome," with firm lines about the mouth and chin. It was impossible to imagine her unbending. Both C.'s sisters were there, both of them ultra-neatly dressed and rather stiff, with every pin in its right place; neither of them pretty, and neither of them bad-looking. There were several other relations and one or two neighbours staying in the house.

On Sunday morning everybody went to church, an old-fashioned church with high shut pews, in which the Hengraves knelt on large red hassocks, and followed the service in large red prayer books. The service was long and the Bishop preached, and Lord Hengrave slept through the sermon. C. felt that he was looking at Bramsley for the first time through the eyes of his observant friend. He wondered what Wright thought of it all, how Bramsley struck the outside world. They must think it a hideous house, he thought. As a matter of fact, Wright was struck by the curious and comfortable mixture of shabbiness and splendour, and he noticed the fine books in the long library, the one or two exceedingly fine pictures—the Romney on the staircase, the Lawrence and the Raeburn in the drawing-room—mixed with indifferent family portraits.

Just as the party sat down to luncheon on Sunday C.'s brother arrived. He was in the triumphant phase of his last year at Eton. He was flushed with embarrassment and tingling after a long, cold drive in an open dogcart. He was like C., but taller and better-looking ; you noticed his looks at once, and it was impossible to help thinking of Hotspur, Prince Hal, Shakespeare, and every kind of symbol and embodiment of gallantry and youth when you saw him.

Wright was sitting next to Miss Broxton, the daughter of a neighbouring master of hounds.

She read Wright's thoughts as he looked at Harry's entrance and watched him shyly take his place at the other end of the table.

" Isn't he good-looking ? " she said. " His father must have been just like that when he was young."

Wright looked at Lord Hengrave, and compared father and son. They had the same short nose and long chin, the same ease of carriage, although Lord Hengrave was a little bent and half crippled by gout, and the same distinction.

" The eldest boy was good-looking, too," said Miss Broxton, " but now he is fat. But I think Caryl is the most interesting-looking of them all."

Wright looked at Caryl critically for the first time, and appraised his looks. He had his father's distinction, he was dark like his mother, but there the likeness ended. He saw no look either of the father or of the mother, either in his features, his general appearance, or his expression.

" I suppose Caryl would be considered good-looking, too ? " he said.

" I think," said Miss B., " that he is really the best-looking of them all. Edward, the eldest, is rather gross, and Harry is a wonderful specimen of youth and health, but his face means nothing. Caryl has such a well-cut face. He reminds me of a Renaissance bronze, and those dark deep-set eyes are most interesting. I am a kind of portrait painter, a poor one, but still a portrait painter, and I look at him from that point of view—but I think it is an unhappy face and even a tragic one."

At that moment Caryl was talking and smiling easily, and, as Wright thought, happily to one of the guests. He looked singularly untouched by the cares and troubles of life.

" Why ? " he asked, " How do you read his character ? "

" Well," she said, " there is a dangerous question in his eyes, and his chin isn't strong like his father's and Harry's. I daresay I am wrong, but I think he will have a lot of trouble in his life. He looks like—I can't think of it now—I shall think of it later."

" Do you know him well ? "

" Very little, although I have seen him here for years, ever since he was ten years old. I know the others best."

After luncheon, Lord Hengrave took all the guests

for the family walk round the garden and stables.   C.
was silent and hardly spoke at all.   After tea, Lady
Hengrave showed Wright her sitting-room, over the
chimney-piece of which there was a large portrait of
a young man in uniform.

"That is Edward, my eldest boy," she said, " as
he was when he was in the Guards.   The boys," she
added, with a sigh, " have got all the looks, and they
don't want them."

C. was, during the whole of the day, desperately
uncomfortable for his friend's sake.   He kept on
thinking that Wright must be being cruelly bored—and
must be thinking everything awful.   His fears were
unnecessary.   Wright was quite comfortable at
Bramsley, but he felt, nevertheless, that the atmosphere had something chilling about it.   Lord Hengrave
was as courteous to him as it was possible to be.
Lady Hengrave was exceedingly kind, but, from time to
time, he did have a slight sense of oppression.   There
was something, he thought, desperately final about all
their judgments, and C. was more aware of this than
ever, and felt acutely what his friend must be feeling.
They both felt that life was conducted, that people
were judged, that things were done, opinions accepted,
books read according to certain rigid and inflexible
standards and codes.   When some one mentioned a
certain new musical comedy which had just been
produced, and had achieved an instantaneous
success, Lady Hengrave said with solemn decision,
" Edward couldn't get places, but we will go directly

we get to London," Wright felt, and C. felt that he was feeling, that to see this particular play was looked upon as a kind of sacred duty, like going to church on Sunday, which it would be a gross breach of decorum not to fulfil.   She said about something else, " I saw it in the newspaper," and they knew it meant only one newspaper, a Conservative one, and that that settled the matter.   And at tea-time, when some one asked her if she had read a certain Liberal politician's speech, she said, " I never read *his* speeches."

But Wright was afforded a glimpse of Lady Hengrave's respect for the classics, which she respected in the same way as she respected everything established from the Church to the acceptedly good acting of a well-known comedian, when she asked him if he knew German.   He said, " Yes," and she said to him, " Schiller's plays are beautiful," and she confirmed the remark with an affirmative sigh.

" The boys, " she added later, " have forgotten their German.   It's a great pity."

Late on Sunday afternoon, C. took Wright up into a turret, and said he wanted to show him his retreat. It was the octagonal room, full of old books.   There was no fire, and it was rather cold, for although it was April the wind was cold.   However, they sat there and smoked for a long time.

"I come here," said C., "when I want to escape from everybody."

As they smoked and talked, Wright looked at the books.

" Have you read all these ? " he asked.

" Yes," he said, to Wright's surprise, " *all* of them."

And C. spoke out for the first time. He told Wright he had a passion for literature, especially for poetry. His father and mother respected the classics, and had insisted on all their children reading Shakespeare, Dryden, Pope and Sir Walter Scott, but as they had been made to do this when they were far too young to understand what they were reading, it had only had the effect of making them cordially dislike the name and sight of these authors. But C. said he had dis-covered other poets by himself, and the romantic poets, Shelley, Keats and Coleridge, at Eton. Their works were not to be found in the library at home. Wright realised at once that he was deeply acquainted with all the earlier English poets, the Elizabethans, the Carolines, and the poets of the eighteenth century, not only as few boys of his age, but as few professional literary Englishmen. Wright discovered that he knew reams of the obscurest poets by heart ; that he had a photographic memory. He had cherished all this as a secret, and he said that Wright was not to tell a soul. Wright felt there was something else behind all this, and asked him, at last, if he had ever tried to write anything himself. He said he had tried, but he had torn up most of what he had written, and then he confessed that his great ambition was to be a writer some day ; that he would give anything to go in for journalism directly he left Oxford, he knew that this would not be possible ; he might just as well suggest being a highwayman or a pickpocket to his parents.

" They won't let me stay long at Oxford," he said. " At the most two years. They won't be able to afford it, and then I shall be dumped down in the City, or in some Government office for the rest of my life, and there will be an end of all that."

" Anthony Trollope," Wright objected, " wrote all his books while he was a Government official. I am sure you would always find time to do what you wanted to do, if you really felt keen about it."

" Yes," said C., " if one really has the gift, but I don't suppose I have ; I would rather be a journalist and learn to write leaders and the police news than be in the City or in a Government office."

They talked in that room for over two hours, and every now and then C. would take down a book from the shelves, and say, " Read that ? " or " Do you know this ? " and Wright seldom knew the passages which he pointed out to him. At other moments he would say, " Do you know this thing ? " and he would recite a passage from Donne, Campion, or from one of the Elizabethan dramatists. He had a passion for Webster and Ford, and he knew Shakespeare better than any one else Wright had ever met before or since. Talking about Shakespeare, he said :—

" It's curious that I should appreciate Shakespeare, considering how I loathed being made to read him when I was a boy, and didn't know what it all meant. But I don't regret it now, because in that way I learnt a whole lot by heart, as an unintelligible rigmarole, which now gives me immense pleasure."

On Monday morning, Wright left Bramsley and travelled up to London in the same carriage with Miss Broxton. She talked to him about C., and said that she was very glad C. had got a friend. Wright said he had plenty of friends at Oxford.

"Yes," she said, "but a friend he can see at Bramsley. He once brought a friend of his before, and it was a great failure. I expect it was Lady Hengrave who asked you."

Wright said this was the case, and she said she felt sure C. would never ask any one again of his own accord.

"The Hengraves know your people and accept you."

"Are they very difficult to please?" Wright asked.

"They don't understand anything outside their particular orbit, and C.'s friend was rather rough. They don't understand him very well. He has always been thought to be the black sheep of the family. They wanted him to be a sailor, but he failed to pass the entrance examination. He is supposed not to have done well at Eton, and to have learnt nothing there. I expect it was his own fault. He's very obstinate. They would never have sent him to Oxford, only his uncle, Mr. Roden, offered to pay for it."

"Are they so badly off?" Wright asked.

"All the property is mortgaged, and nobody knows how they manage to live, but they've got a house in Portman Square, and they live at Bramsley at Christmas, Easter, and in the summer. Nothing is ever let. Edward has done fairly well in the City, and he married an American who is quite well-off. Julia, the eldest girl, has been out two years; Marjorie, the second, one year. There was, you know, a second son, Gilbert, who got into some money scrape. He lives in Canada, and they never mention him. I believe the only one of the family Lady Hengrave really cares for now is Harry."

"Did she like Gilbert ? "

"I think so. I think he probably was the only one of the family she *loved*, but we shall never know that. She never alludes to him. She never got on with C. She doesn't understand him. I know what C. reminded me of yesterday, a Giorgione in Lord Holmby's collection.

Wright said he had never seen it.

CHAPTER XX

WHEN C. went back to Oxford in the summer, he passed through a rapid phase of development. He acquired intellectually a certain amount of inner confidence that he had till then been devoid of, or uncertain about. During his first two terms at Oxford he had been overawed by comparing himself disadvantageously with his friends in college. He had been dumbfounded by what he considered the superior culture of some—a man like Hallam, for instance, and even by the solid scholarship of Malone, and these were men he liked, and who treated him as an equal; and he had been humiliated by some of the intellectuals (men he disliked, and who looked down on him), and had felt a slightly withering blight in the company of others, like Blades (whom he liked), while he despised the superficiality and the affections of the artistic set.

On the other hand, intellectual intercourse with Wright was too easy. He distrusted Wright's opinions, views and tastes because they seemed to him to be too easily understood, and it was so easy to talk books and poetry with him that C. did not do so at all.

One day he showed Wright some verses he had written in Germany, and Wright genuinely admired them. He even praised the Eton *Vale*. This convinced C. that Wright's admiration could not count for much, and he classed him in the same category with Calmady, his old Eton friend. Thus it was that during his first two terms he had kept his literary tastes and ambitions to himself and had played up to the idea that he was a Philistine and an ignoramus. The situation was entirely changed by two new factors. One was the discernment of the Master, who, although he often had little patience with " enthusiasm," had the keenest scent for the seeds of literary talent, and detected in C.'s essays a gift for style and a foundation of wide and quite unusual reading. The Master encouraged him discreetly and tactfully, used to send for him in the evening when he was finishing his dinner, and talk to him about books. He had recommended C. to read Boswell, and he was surprised when he discovered how much more C. had already done in the way of Johnsonian study. The Master deplored his reading history, and urged him to take Greats. C. didn't care for history, and the Master realised this and said he was made to understand Greek literature. C. had considerable knowledge of Latin, which he had learnt as a child, but only an average knowledge of Greek. But even such Greek as he possessed had shown the Master that he was capable, if not of distinguished scholarship, of exceptional appreciation, and it was a thousand pities that he should not cultivate it. The Master wanted him to give up history and take up the classics in earnest. C. was only too willing to do this, but he said it would be no use. However, he consented; and so the matter rested.

Wright was perpetually urging him to produce, but with the exception of the essays he wrote for the Master it is doubtful whether C. wrote anything new during this period. He may have written some verse, but if he had he destroyed it and never showed it to any one. Nor did he ever contribute to any of the local magazines. He belonged to one or two debating societies, but during his first two terms none of his speeches attracted any attention. All his inner life was dormant and slumbering. But a spark was waiting to turn the smouldering, flickering ashes into an incandescent blaze. The spark was not slow to fall. It was the second new factor that changed the current of C.'s life.

About nine miles from Oxford there was a house called Bilbury, which belonged to a retired colonel, a bachelor, who often let it. It was too big a house for a bachelor and too small for most families. It was an old, rather ramshackle and picturesque building with a disused moat round it and an uncared-for garden. It was close to the river. This summer it was taken by Mr. and Mrs. Lord, who thought it would be a good thing for their daughter to have some country air, and possibly to see a little of Oxford life. They had let their London house for May and June. Bilbury was to be had cheap. Mrs. Lord, who was entirely unpractical, decided to take it at once because of the fireplace in the hall, which she said was so convenient.

As they were only going to live there in the summer,
it was difficult to know what she meant ; but take it
they did. One morning Mrs. Lord had come into
Oxford to do some shopping. She was dawdling in a
bookshop and her daughter, Beatrice, was with her.
C. strolled into the shop, but he did not at first notice
the Lords. They were on one side of a large upright
bookcase, and he was on the other. But he heard
Beatrice saying to her mother, " What a lovely copy,
and so cheap ! I think I must buy it," and Mrs.
Lord answering, " I'm sure your father will give it
to you another day if it isn't sold by then." Where
had he heard that voice before ? The concert in
the village, when he was staying with the Rodens,
flashed into his mind, and the vision of that girl, the
girl whom he had been introduced to, but whom he
had hardly been able to look at. He didn't dare come
forward, and he didn't dare come away. Would they
leave the shop without his being able to have a glimpse
of her ? No, fate settled otherwise. Mrs. Lord
walked round to the other side of the shop, and C. was
face to face with her. She recognised him.

" Beatrice," she called, " here's Mr. Bramsley, the
nephew of dear Mrs. Roden. You remember we met
him at the school feast—I mean the penny reading ;
or was it at the meet ? "

Beatrice came forward and shook hands with C.
She was more beautiful than he had fancied her to be.
He remembered thinking her the most beautiful
apparition he had ever seen, but he had not been able

to look at her enough, and he had exchanged no words with her except the briefest " How do you do ? " and " Good-bye," all in one, at the end of the concert.

Mrs. Lord was overflowing with hospitality and welcome.

" We have to come into Oxford next Sunday morning for Mass," she said. " Won't you come back with us to Bilbury, and bring any one you like, on your bicycle ? "

She talked of a bicycle as if it were an omnibus. C. did bicycle. He did not, however, feel equal to bringing any one on his bicycle.

On the following Sunday he met Mrs. Lord, Mr. Lord and Beatrice outside the Catholic church after Mass, and they all bicycled back to Bilbury. It was six miles from Oxford.

It was a wonderful Sunday. There are some Sundays in early summer that, if it is not pouring with rain, seem finer and more beautiful than any other days in the week. There seems to be a special grace about them. C. thought of a poem of Uhland's he had read at Alterstadt, which ends up " *Das ist der Tag des Herrn*." The lilac and the laburnum were out and the may, and there was a profusion of pink and white blossom. The fields were startlingly gay with butter-cups, and impossibly green. The country seemed to have been just created. C. felt as if he were bicycling through Paradise. When they arrived they found several other undergraduates awaiting them, all of them quite unknown to C., and all of them from other colleges. They were Catholic boys from Catholic schools, the Oratory at Birmingham and Stonyhurst. There were also some friends and relations of the Lord family. Luncheon was supposed to be at one, but it was not ready till some time after half-past one. At last they sat down to a long refectory table in a high stone hall. C. had no idea who all the people were. They talked for the most part of people he had never heard of and of things which meant nothing to him.

C. was sitting next to Mrs. Lord, and he found it impossible to keep her talk in one channel for long.

One of the young men said that some one was very " holy." Mrs. Lord said she dropped her rosary during the Last Gospel.

" I always lose my rosary," she said, " they are so brittle. The new stained glass window is not a success. It is surprising that nobody makes beautiful glass now. Have you ever read a book called *Phantastes* ? "

C. had never heard of it. Mrs. Lord drifted on from half one topic to another half. Every now and then Mr. Lord joined in the conversation from the other end of the table, and had a little monologue on his own.

Had any one guessed the acrostic in *Vanity Fair* ? There was one light which was a great puzzle. T. and T.

Not ever said to ears polite.

What could it be ?

" Termagant," Mrs. Lord suggested. " Is it uncivil to say termagant or top-knot ? Last quarter we sent

them in, but this quarter we haven't guessed one.
Wilfrid sometimes makes them up. T. and T.
Perhaps that is a word in itself, like G.P.O. or V.R.
They do that sometimes. But does T. T. mean any-
thing? Perhaps it's a catch, or perhaps one ought to
add something. I must buy a *Phrase and Fable*.
Aren't the bookshops in Oxford fascinating, Mr.
Bramsley? We spend so much time in them, don't
you?"

And so she rambled on, but she never stopped
talking. Mr. Lord asked him questions across the
table every now and then :—

"You are at X. College, and do you see the Master
often? I remember him years ago as an undergraduate.
He always wore a nankin waistcoat. We used to call
him Bosky. Nobody knew why, but it seemed to suit
him. It's dropped out. They don't call him that
now."

"He's very like his sister," said Mrs. Lord. "In
fact, very like all his family. You know his sister,
Mr. Bramsley? She is a Dante scholar. She is going
to write about him some day. Last winter Beatrice
went to a Dante class, but never got beyond the Fourth
Canto. The *Paradiso* is so difficult; so theological.
We went to Florence for Easter. Do you know
Florence?"

C. said he had never been to Italy.

"It is so nice to have Florence to look forward to,"
she said, "but you know Rome, of course?"

"I've never been to Italy at all," said C.

"Not at all, no, of course not," echoed Mrs. Lord, smiling. "I was thinking of Charles Fry."

C. wondered who Charles Fry might be.

After luncheon they split up into groups and went down to the river. C. was left with Beatrice, and they sat in a field and watched the pageant and listened to the noise of Spring. There was no cloud in the sky, and the river was even of a deeper blue. The bank opposite them was a long violent line of yellow butter-cups. Three beech trees were still brown and feathery, but against the blue they seemed pink. There was a large shrub of white may just under a huge elm which was wearing its freshest, greenest apparel. Its reflec-tion made a lovely green smudge in the blue water. Everything was humming with life, and every now and again you heard voices from the river. Mrs. Lord had suggested that Beatrice and C. should go out in a boat, and they had gone down to the river with that intention. A boat was there ready for them to use.

They talked of Geramny. C. described Alterstadt. Beatrice loved Germany, German music, and German fairy tales.

Wagner was mentioned. C. described how he had heard *Tannhäuser* and *Tristan und Isolde*. Beatrice did not like Wagner except the Pilgrims' Chorus in *Tannhäuser*. She had been to Bayreuth and heard *Parsifal ;* she said it was too difficult, but she meant she detested it.

C. said he would have given anything to have gone to Bayreuth.

"I don't think I'm at all musical, but I like those sounds," he said.

"I'm not musical, either," said Beatrice, "and I probably don't understand it, but his music gives me the feeling of being suffocated, like laughing gas."

They talked about laughing gas and dentists and dreams. They compared Germany and France. Beatrice had lived for years in Paris. They compared notes, they argued, they disagreed, they agreed. They talked about Madeleine Lapara. Beatrice had seen her play in Shakespeare's *Antony and Cleopatra*.

"Wasn't she wonderful?" she said. "There was a scene when she did nothing, just listened."

C. said you got that sort of thing in France, but not in Germany. Beatrice said she didn't care for art really, not for artists, nor for books. She never read anything.

C. was astonished, but a little later several books were mentioned: *Les Misérables*, *Vanity Fair*, Kipling, and she had read them all.

"I'm not literary all the same," said Beatrice. "I've never read any poetry—hardly any, that is to say."

"Have you read Heine?"

"Yes," she said, "German poetry; German poetry's different; it's so simple. Isn't Heine perfect?"

"Do you remember a poem called the *Wallfahrt nach Kevlaar*?" said C.

"Yes. Do you know it by heart?"

C. began to repeat that most untranslatable of all untranslatable poems. They both knew it by heart.

The tale of the youth whom his mother took to Kevlaar because his heart hurt him so, for thinking of little dead Gretchen, their neighbour. For at Kevlaar the Mother of God was wearing her best clothes, and the pilgrims were bringing her little feet and little hands made of wax, and whosoever offered a wax hand, the wound in his hand was healed, and whosoever offered a wax foot, his foot was straight-way made whole. The mother took a wax taper and moulded with it a heart :—

> Take that to the Mother of God,
> And She will heal thy smart.

The son took the wax heart, sighing, and went sighing to the Holy Image of Our Lady, and tears welled from his eyes as the words welled from his heart.

He told his story to the Queen of Heaven :—

> I was living with my Mother
> At Cologne, in the town,
> The town that has so many
> Hundreds of Chapels and Churches.

As C. repeated the lines in German :—

> Ich wohnte mit meiner Mutter,
> Zu Köllen in der Stadt,
> Der Stadt, die viele hundert
> Kapellen und Kirchen hat,

Beatrice said, " He is bribing her."

" Yes," said C., and went on (only in German, and
not translating) :—

> And next door to us lived Gretchen,
> But Gretchen now is dead,
> Mary, I bring thee a wax heart,
> Please heal the wound in my heart.
>
> Heal Thou my heart that is ailing,
> And I will, early and late,
> Devoutly pray and sing to Thee,
> " Gelobt seist du, Marie ! "

" He is bribing her again," he said.

Then C. repeated the poem to the end, to its
beautiful close, when, in the little bedroom where the
mother and the son were sleeping, the Mother of God
came stealing in and bent down over the sick boy
and laid her hand on his heart and smiled. And the
mother saw all, and more, in her dream, till the
barking of the dogs woke her up ; and there lay
her son, and he was dead, and the red light of the
morning played on his pale cheeks, and the mother
folded her hands.

> Ihr war, sie wusste nicht wie,

Devoutly she softly sang the words of praise :—

> " Gelobt seist du, Marie ! "

" You know what gave Heine the idea ? " said C.
She didn't.

" When he was at a Franciscan school at Düsseldorf,
and learning to read, he sat next to another little boy

who told him that his mother had once taken him to
Kevlaar and offered a wax foot for him to Our Lady,
and that his own ailing foot had been cured. He met
the boy later in the upper class at a *Gymnasium*, and
reminded him, laughing, of the wax foot, and the boy
became serious and said that he would offer a wax
heart now. Heine forgot all about him, but later, in
the Rhine country, one day, when he was going for a
walk, he heard the song of the Kevlaar pilgrims in
the distance, singing :—

Gelobt seist du, Marie !

And when the procession went by he noticed among
the pilgrims his schoolfellow with his old mother.
But he looked very pale and ill."

"What a heavenly story," she said, "and what a
poem. I think it's the most beautiful poem in the
world."

"But then you *do* like poetry," said C.

"I've hardly read any," said Beatrice. "I can only
read things where the book does all the reading for
you. Heine does that. I've never read any of the
classics."

"But Shelley and Keats and Swinburne," said C.,
"do you call those classics ? "

"I don't know ; I've never tried. I don't think I
should understand them."

"And French poetry ? " said C.

"I can't bear the classics I used to be taken to see
at the *Théâtre Français*, and which were supposed to

be proper. But I do like Victor Hugo. For instance, do you know that bit about the swallows :—

> Vite à tire-d'ailes !
> Oh ! c'est triste de voir s'enfuir les hirondelles !
> Elles s'en vout là-bas, vers le midi doré.

" I believe you've read everything in the world."

They got back to French and German differences and made comparisons again. C. said it must have been so wonderful for her to live among artists in Paris, and so different from the horribly dull London world. Beatrice was afraid of disillusioning him and kept to the amusing, lighter side of things, and she turned the talk on to Germany and to the enjoyment she had had there. They talked of German children's books and fairy tales. They compared notes about the books they had read in their childhood.

" My favourite book when I was a child was a book with a green cover, called *On a Pincushion*," said Beatrice.

" That was my favourite book too," said C., " especially the story called *The Seeds of Love*. Do you remember the little candles the two sisters had to burn to get one wish ? "

" On a night when there was neither moon nor star," said Beatrice. " And the story of vain Lamorna, who lost her reflection ? "

" Which was pulled down by the water elves with ropes of sand," said C.

Fairy tales led to other memories of childhood. They compared notes as to how far back they could each remember, and about experiences with governesses and schoolroom books.

Time rushed past them. Tea-time had passed and the sun was low when they remembered that they had better be going home. They remembered little of their talk when it was over. If they had been asked what they had been talking about, they could not have answered. They walked back in silence towards the house through a shrubbery and the long, untidy garden. No comment was made on their lateness. Mrs. Lord merely said that supper was nearly ready. As a matter of fact, it was not nearly ready.

They sat outside till it was ready; Beatrice, C., and the other guests, in basket chairs, and enjoyed a long rambling general conversation about nothing in particular.

Then they went in to a cold supper. After supper the night was so warm, the garden was so inviting, that they walked a little under the trees. It was dark; there was no moon, and every now and then through the trees you heard the bell of a bicycle, and you discerned a ghostly figure flitting by on the neighbouring road. The party had again divided into groups. C. again was left with Beatrice for a little while. There were pauses in their talk now, and they said little, but their speech and their silences became part of the spring evening.

Beatrice was dressed in white, and C. thought he saw her eyes shining in the darkness. He seemed to be on tip-toe with expectation. He was knocking at a new and magical door.   Everything that had seemed most new and wonderful up to this moment had been, he thought, leading him to something else and something better, something imminent.   There had been hints before—summer evenings at Eton, Shelley, Keats, Madeleine Lapara, *Tristan und Isolde ;* but now something else was surely coming, some new mysterious thing which perhaps might even now be about to be. He did not put all that into thought, still less into words.   He hardly spoke ; he didn't think ; he only felt ; he only wanted the moment to stay ; he could not think of the future ; and Beatrice ? Beatrice, surely was wondering ; she was lost in wonder ; she, too, was on tip-toe, and expecting something—although she was unaware of it.   They had both of them forgotten the world for the moment ; they were walking hand in hand like children through an enchanted country, and they were taking the wonder, the surprise, the magic of it, the curiosity, for granted ; they were like children afraid of asking questions, lest by a rash word they might break the spell.

How long this lasted they were unaware, but they were recalled to earth by a loud shout from Mr. Lord.

" Beatrice, where are you ? They must be going back."

It was time to go home so as to get into college before twelve.

" Good-bye," said Beatrice.

" Good-bye," said C.   " May I come again ? "

" Yes," said Beatrice, " please come again."

And that little minute seemed again to take them farther, to open the door a little wider, and like all partings, even the happiest, it had a slight shiver lent by the shadow of death, but it seemed so slight that it was almost like a blessing. C. bicycled home with the other undergraduates. They talked to C. every now and then, and C. answered with one part of his mind. He felt so happy that he would have liked to sing.

He felt no sorrow at the evening being over; before him was the certainty that it would happen again and again, and quite soon. Who knew how soon ? When could he ask her and her mother to luncheon in his rooms ? How soon would it be possible to do it with decency ? At any rate, Mrs. Lord seemed to approve of him, and so did Mr. Lord ; but they were both so absent-minded. They seemed hardly to have been aware of his presence. He must introduce Malone to the Lords. Wright knew them—at least, he thought he did. He thought he remembered having been introduced to them at that concert. The concert came slowly and vividly back to his mind. He lived it all over again. He remembered the songs, and what all the performers had looked like. He remembered his unavailing efforts to get a real look at Beatrice without seeming to stare, and how it had been practically impossible. And then, as they met outside, and they did talk to each other for a moment, he had scarcely dared look at her. Did he know then that he would ever see her again ? He had known, he felt now, without knowing, in a strange way. He knew, and yet he

had hardly thought of it, nor of her again, till the
morning he had met her again in the shop, and yet now
her presence seemed to have been there the whole time,
only behind a veil. He never forgot that bicycle ride
in the night.

He did not go to sleep till late that night. He lived
the afternoon and the evening all over again many
times. He wondered what she had been thinking
about, what she thought now. The next morning he
told Malone that he was going to give a luncheon party
in his rooms, and he asked him to be one of the guests.
It was fixed for the following Thursday, and he sent off
a civil letter to Mrs. Lord, asking Mr. and Mrs. and Miss
Lord to luncheon. The answer seemed all too long in
coming. When it did come it said that Mrs. Lord
would be delighted to bring Beatrice, but that Mr.
Lord was unfortunately obliged to go up to London
that day on business.

C. was overjoyed ; all his thoughts were concentrated on one idea, and that was on how he could
manage to see Beatrice before Thursday, which
seemed such a long time off.

CHAPTER XXI

On Tuesday afternoon he bicycled as far as Bilbury, but he did not dare ring at the door. He bicycled up and down in front of the house once or twice in the hope that some one might come out, but nobody came, and so he reluctantly went home.

Thursday seemed to be an interminable time in coming, but it came at last. Malone, Hallam and Wright were all of them asked to meet the Lords, and C. bought flowers and tried to make his rather bare room more cheerful.

The Lords were late. It was almost a quarter to two, and there was no sign of them. C. felt that something had happened to prevent their coming, and walked up and down the room in a fever of anxiety.

" They've probably had to go to London," he said.

" They would have let you know," said Wright.

" They've forgotten. I'm sure they've forgotten all about it," said C.

" Nonsense, your clock is fast," said Hallam.

" They have gone to the wrong college," Malone suggested.

" They may think I said Friday instead of Thursday."

And so the conversation went on, bristling with

250

every kind of improbable suggestion, until Mrs. Lord
and Beatrice were seen walking across the Quad.

"There, I told you so," said Wright. "They're
really hardly even late."

The luncheon was a great success. Hallam entertained Mrs. Lord so unceasingly that C. was able to
enjoy some prolonged snatches of talk with Beatrice,
and Malone, Hallam and Wright, all three of them,
gazed with undisguised admiration at Beatrice, who
in her summer muslin (it was an extremely hot day),
looked like the symbol and expression of the month
itself. C. felt that she was being admired. He felt,
too, that she had exceeded their expectations. He
had told them all about Miss Lord's beauty, and,
except on the part of Wright, who had seen her
already, he had been conscious of an unexpressed
scepticism. But there she was, smiling and talking,
fresh and cool and lovely. After luncheon they went
down to the river and went out in a punt. C. was able
to speak to Beatrice on the way down there, but on
the river itself he was obliged to work, while Mrs. Lord
and her daughter sat in the stern. They stayed out
till tea-time, when Mrs. Lord said they had to be
going. Arrangements were made for the future.
Hallam, Wright and Malone were all of them invited
to Bilbury on the following Sunday, to come to
luncheon and to stay for supper.

And this is how a new and settled routine began in
the life of C., which was shot with all the colours of the
rainbow.

Malone, Hallam and Wright had all of them fallen in love at first sight with Beatrice Lord, but they all of them silently agreed that C. not only had the prior claim, but the dominant right and position. They all took it for granted that Beatrice had singled out C.

C., Malone and his friends were asked to Bilbury every Sunday. During the week, the Lords often came into Oxford, and the intimacy between C. and Beatrice grew rapidly. He poured out to her his dreams and ambitions, ideas and opinions, hopes and fears.

" But you have written things already ? " she asked him one day as they were bicycling to Bilbury.

" A little, a few things, nothing that counts."

" Won't you show them to me ? " she asked.

" They are not good enough. Some day, if I ever do anything better, I will show it to you."

C. felt a great disgust for everything he had written so far. There was not a thing he felt he wanted to show to Beatrice ; nothing that was good enough for her. At the same time, he felt quite incapable of writing anything else for the present. His happiness seemed to have dried up the springs of fancy and expression. He felt there was nothing to say. Life was so wonderful that there was no time to do anything else except to live. Yet when he saw Beatrice he would talk a great deal of all his literary plans for the future.

She listened sympathetically. She could give him the rarest understanding and lend him her imagina-

tion, which was sandalled with strong wings, but at the
same time what C. told her of his hopes frightened
her. She saw that although he lived in the world of
art, that is to say, the world of books, literature and
poetry, the world of artists was unknown to him.
That was a world which she knew all too well. She
had lived in it ever since her childhood, and she had
known more than enough of it. She had seen a sordid
side of Bohemian life, which had kindled in her a
violent reaction. Her father and mother were both of
them natural Bohemians. Their friends were nearly
all of them Bohemians, and, for the most part, unsuccessful artists, forgotten musicians, unpublished
poets and unplayed playwrights. They knew, it is true,
some successful artists and some well-known authors,
but they drew the unsuccessful and the needy towards
them like magnets. Uncouth, talkative, shabby,
hard-up, easy-going people were constantly in and out
of the house, and Beatrice had often said to herself,
" Philistia, be thou glad of me," only the trouble was
there was no chance of getting anywhere near
Philistia. She knew that C. knew nothing of all her
world. She saw plainly that he imagined the world
of artists and writers to be an ideal framework for all
that was finest in art and literature, and to correspond
to that. He imagined it to consist of nothing but
completely disinterested, devoted and self-sacrificing
Paladins, who were working, all of them under great
difficulties and at great personal sacrifice, for the good
and glory of mankind, and living masterpieces as well as

painting and writing them. He mentioned artists with bated breath, as if they belonged to a higher sphere into which he would never be allowed to set foot. Beatrice, who knew the reality, foresaw that he would scarcely be able to avoid disenchantment and disillusion. She judged by what she had gone through herself. It could not be said that she had lost her illusions about such things, and such people, for she had never had any. From her earliest years she had lived in that world, and had learnt a series of saddening object lessons. As she grew up she had acted like a buffer between her father and a host of idle hangers-on who exploited his vanity, and a crowd of needy relations. It was she who now managed the household, kept the household accounts and ordered meals. Her mother, in spite of her vagueness, was not entirely unpractical. She had moments of inspiration sometimes in matters of organisation, but anything like settled routine or a continuous life of thought and action was foreign to her. They had always been poor. Mr. Lord made money by fits and starts in various ways, by painting and writing, and even in business, but he generally lost what money he made in fantastic schemes and unsound speculations. They had had one or two windfalls. Twice Mrs. Lord had been left substantial sums of money, and both the legacies had almost instantly been frittered away; but, fortunately, she had a marriage settlement that could not be touched. They were always in the position of trying to make both ends meet, and Mr. Lord was as optimistic as Mr.

Micawber. But they managed to live, and they somehow floated on an uneasy stream of debt and makeshift, and Beatrice did what she could to keep the family affairs in some kind of order, and to prevent her father from embarking on more than usually egregious follies.

The mode of Beatrice Lord's life and the nature of her circumstances had thrown her back on her religion. She and her family were all of them devout practising Catholics. C. was puzzled by this factor and never discussed it with her. It was to him frankly inexplicable. The only ideas he harboured about her religion were those he had imbibed in his childhood from Brinny, his nurse, and from Miss Hackett, and although he was willing to believe that their views on the subject were neither final nor exhaustive, he could not understand a grown-up person bothering about religion. He accepted the fact. They were born Catholics, and it was natural, he thought, that they should remain Catholics, and yet it puzzled him more than he could express. He looked upon the Catholic religion as Anglicanism pushed further and reduced to the absurd : Anglicanism run riot. If Anglicanism failed to satisfy, Catholicism *à fortiori* must do so in a higher degree. But he did not discuss the matter with Beatrice during this period. A summer of radiant, unimaginable happiness had begun for him. They both of them floated ecstatically down a tide of enjoyment, amusement, high spirits, beautiful weather, fun, picnics, laughter and song. Every day seemed to be more beautiful than yesterday, and less beautiful than to-morrow. Mrs. Lord looked on and smiled. She seemed to notice nothing, and she encouraged C. and his friends to come to the house. She lived in a world of her own and hardly noticed what went on around her.

At the end of June the Lords' tenancy of Bilbury came to an end. They were going back to London, but hoped to be back at Oxford during the Michaelmas term. But, before doing so, Mrs. Lord and Beatrice had been asked to stay for a fortnight with Sir Gabriel Carteret, who had a house on the Thames, near Datchet. The Lords and the Carterets were great friends, and Mrs. Lord corresponded regularly with Lady Elizabeth Carteret. In her letters she had mentioned C. more than once, and C. had met the Carterets at the Rodens. The Carterets invited him to stay at their house as soon as the Oxford term was over, at the beginning of July. C. was expected back in London, but he wrote to his mother and announced his intention of accepting the invitation. Mrs. Roden happened to be with Lady Hengrave when she received the letter, and she said the Carterets would be useful and valuable friends for C. Sir Gabriel Carteret was famous not only as a painter, but as a personality, and he was extremely well off, while Lady Elizabeth Carteret was of such as were accepted without question by Lady Hengrave. She wrote and told C. that as long as he was home for the Eton and Harrow match he could do what he liked.

C. went down from Oxford at the beginning of July, a few days after the Lords left Bilbury, and he went straight to Windsor. It was with a thrill that he arrived at Windsor station. He left his luggage to be called for and he walked through Eton on a July afternoon of one of the hottest and most unbroken summers that England had ever known. He walked to the playing fields, and he was greeted by a well-known shriek. He turned round and saw Calmady, who was on his way to absence. They went together to the schoolyard and C. met several acquaintances among the masters and a few among the boys. He suggested tea at Little Brown's, and he and Calmady walked into the back room and ordered cold salmon, cucumber and strawberry messes, and some iced coffee. It was Calmady's last half at Eton. He was going abroad to study French, to a family in Normandy.

"I'm almost in Sixth Form," he said, "and I've come to the end of my Eton career without being expelled, which my tutor says is a triumph," and he shrieked with laughter so loud and so long that Phœbe, who was busy dealing out teas to a lot of clamouring Lower boys in the front shop, put her head into the back room and told Calmady that if he made so much noise she wouldn't serve him.

"Come, come, Mr. Calmady," she said, "one would think you were a Lower boy by the way you go on."

When they finished tea, and each of them had eaten two large strawberry messes, C. said he must be going, and Calmady was going to play cricket. C. took a fly, picked up his luggage, and drove to Datchet.

Chestercombe, the Carterets' house, was right on the river. Opposite it there were two gaudily painted house-boats. It was a large panelled house, painted for the most part sage green and partly sealing-wax red, with a panelled oak staircase. It was more like a series of showrooms than a house. It contained some exquisite Old English furniture; a great many silver sconces and convex mirrors, and many pictures; a few sketches in crayon by Sir Gabriel himself, and more important oil colours by English and foreign contemporary artists. In the low panelled hall there was a large and most elaborate grand pianoforte of carved wood, inlaid with mosaic work. There were several other musical instruments lying about in the rooms, including a small green Irish harp and a spinet, but neither Sir Gabriel nor Lady Elizabeth Carteret, nor their daughter, Hester, played any of them. There were one or two little rooms in the house which were only for show presumably, as they were too small to sit down in unless you chanced to be a pigmy, and a library in which there were no books except a complete set of *Punch* bound in white vellum.

C. was greeted by Lady Elizabeth Carteret, who was a small, dark, refined, ladylike woman, completely natural and rather untidy. When she married Sir Gabriel he had been a penniless student, and it was considered by her family (her father was a marquis with about a dozen different titles and two large

estates) that she had made a runaway match of the
rashest description. It had, however, all turned out
for the best, and Sir Gabriel was considered an ornament to any society. Sir Gabriel himself was florid,
bearded, and had a passion for making puns. He
painted kind, dignified portraits and soothing landscapes, and exhibited something once a year at the
Academy and sometimes at the Salon. He was an
officer of the Legion of Honour, and had received
decorations from most of the European potentates.
They had one daughter, Hester, a tall girl with
black hair and large, black eyes, who was studying
painting.

" She is determined to take the bread out of her
father's mouth," Sir Gabriel would say jocularly.

Lady Elizabeth took C. into the garden, where Sir
Gabriel, Mrs. Lord, Beatrice and Hester Carteret were
sitting in basket-chairs and watching the people on the
river. Mr. Lord was not there. He had, as usual,
found pressing business to do in London.

C. had arrived on a Thursday evening. It seemed to
him that he had been separated from Beatrice for
years, and his joy at seeing her again was undisguised.
At dinner he sat between her and Lady Elizabeth, and
his happiness was beyond all expression. Lady
Elizabeth was romantic. She had apparently read
all the novels in the world, and she invested her
friends and acquaintances with romantic qualities,
and attributed sentimental and passionate adventures
to them, which she related to C.

The next day C. spent the morning at Eton, walking about looking at the shops and visiting the Boys' library with Beatrice, and in the afternoon they all went for a sketching expedition to Burnham Beeches.

They were to spend the whole of Saturday afternoon and evening on the river, and go for a long expedition to Runnymede. Never had Eton looked more beautiful; never had the river seemed so tempting, so placid and so cool; never had the loosestrife on the banks been more luxuriant.

They started out on Saturday in two boats. Two Eton boys joined them. C. and an Eton boy took Hester Carteret and Beatrice in one boat; Sir Gabriel and another Eton boy took Lady Elizabeth and Mrs. Lord in another boat. Hester Carteret took her sketching things, and when they arrived at Runnymede settled down to serious business in impressionist water-colour. Her art belonged to the opposite school to that of her father, and was very bold and wet. Mrs. Lord prepared the tea, made a fire, and organised the picnic, for which she had a peculiar and unexpected practical talent, and she baked some potatoes. Sir Gabriel toyed with a sketch and Lady Elizabeth entertained the boys, so that Beatrice and C. had an uninterrupted talk to themselves. They stayed out late, and the boys got back to Eton just in time for lock-up. They found a cold supper and strawberries waiting for them, and a male cousin of the Carterets, who was in the Foreign Office and had come down to

spend Sunday. The next morning Mrs. Lord and
Beatrice drove into Windsor for Mass, and they took
C. with them. C. went to Eton Chapel for the first
time since he had left. His happiness was increasing
every moment. He wished Beatrice could have come
to chapel with him. He had pointed out so many
things at Eton to her, and here was one thing he could
not share with her. C. and the Lords had luncheon
at Leightons, and spent the afternoon in the playing
fields. When they got back to tea C. was extremely
astonished to find a telegram waiting for him. It was
unexpected to receive a telegram on Sunday, and it
must have been sent off very early. It was from Lady
Hengrave, and it said : " Beg of you to come London
to-morrow in time for dinner we are giving for Prince
of Saxe-Altenburg. Your father wishes it." Rumours
had reached Lady Hengrave of a flirtation—nothing
more—but a flirtation with a penniless friend of the
Rodens who was staying with the Carterets. To be
a friend of the Rodens at all was a bad mark in
her eyes, but to be a penniless friend of the Rodens
was unpardonable, and a thing to be dealt with at
once.

" I suppose I must go," said C., " but I will come
back if you will let me."

The Carterets had asked him to stay till the end of
the week.

Lady Elizabeth was greatly distressed. She had
seen at a glance what was happening to C., and was
determined to encourage the romance with all the

means at her disposal. Throughout the picnic she had carefully arranged to throw them together, and she had made up her mind that it would be an excellent match. She knew, too, that it would annoy Lady Hengrave, and that was to her not the least pleasing facet of the situation.

"You can't possibly go," she said. "You've only just come, and I've got such lovely things for all of us to do next week."

"I suppose he must go if it's a dinner party," said Mrs. Lord. "It might make them thirteen, and that would upset his mother and his father; otherwise they would scarcely have telegraphed so early on Sunday."

"Well," said Lady Elizabeth, "why not go up for the dinner and come back here on Tuesday, and stay for the rest of the week?"

It was settled that he should go up the next day and come back as soon as he could. The Lords were staying on another week. Beatrice and C. were silent that evening during dinner, and Lady Elizabeth felt in complete sympathy with them. After dinner she managed matters so that Hester should show the kitchen-garden, which was separated from the house and at some distance from it, to the young male cousin, while Sir Gabriel talked to Mrs. Lord; she herself had some letters which "she must finish." C. and Beatrice went out on to the lawn.

It was a hot, breathless, beautiful night. There was no suspicion of thunder in the air, but every now and

then, in the distance, a glimmer of summer lightning
flickered across the sky. They walked down to the
bank of the river and sat down on a white wooden
garden seat. Some people were sitting on the top of
the house-boat. It was too dark to see them clearly,
but Beatrice and C. could hear what they said quite
distinctly. They could distinguish a girl in white, and
a man was just finishing whistling to banjo accompaniment an out-of-date lullaby from a Gaiety burlesque,
Ruy Blas, which had a great vogue when C. was
at Eton. There was a burst of applause, and the
singer said :—

"Now it's Harold's turn to oblige."

But Harold protested that he could neither sing
unaccompanied nor accompany himself. There was a
heated argument, in which every one appeared to take
part at once. Beatrice and C. heard the noise of a
bottle being opened, and the singer jocularly remarked
that he deserved a drink after all that. There was
a pause for refreshment. Some one named Elsie was
called upon for a song, but she protested that singing
in the night air would damage her voice. There was
something undefinably theatrical about the tone of
that conversation. They were actors, thought
Beatrice, who were staying with the inmates of the
house-boat. The original performer, whose name
turned out to be Walter, was asked to sing again, and
he consented.

"I'll give you what I gave them at Devonshire
Park," he said ; "and I was encored, you know. Of

course, it wants the accompaniment ; but I'll see
what I can vamp on the banjo.

> As the flight of a river
>   That flows to the sea,
> My soul rushes ever
>   In tumult to thee.
>
> A twofold existence
>   I lead where thou art ;
> My heart in the distance,
>   Beats close to thy heart.
>
> Look up, I am near thee,
>   I gaze on thy face ;
> I see thee, I hear thee,
>   I feel thy embrace.
>
> And absence but lightens
>   The eyes that I miss,
> And custom but heightens
>   The spell of thy kiss.
>
> It is not from duty
>   Tho' that may be owed,
> It is not from beauty,
>   Tho' that be bestowed.
>
> But all that I care for
>   And all that I know,
> Is that, without wherefore,
>   I worship thee so.

The singer put an immense amount of vehemence
into the song. C. and Beatrice felt that the veins on
his head must be bursting, but Beatrice thought, too,
that, in spite of the smart, stagey professionalism of
the performance, which was as shiny and glossy as
wet paint, and hideously competent (while utterly

lacking in all that makes anything artistic), there was
in it a genuine note of passion. She felt as if they
were having a peep into one of those little dramas
that go on behind the scenes in theatrical life, and she
felt so more strongly still when, as the song ended,
she heard a female voice say :

" I never cared for that song, Walter. The words
are so high-falutin'. Do sing us something sensible
with a chorus."

" You always hate whatever I sing. I've done—for
this evening at any rate."

Presently there was a bustle, a gathering up of
wraps, and a chorus of good-byes. Some members of
the party, and among them " Walter," were leaving.
A boat was got ready, and the people got into it.

" Come again next Sunday," said a female voice.

" No such luck," said Walter. " Next Sunday I
shall be at Glasgow."

The banjoist was in the boat, and they rowed away
up-stream towards Windsor to an accompaniment
of laughter, shouts, chaff, argument and banjo-
strumming.

" Actors, I suppose," said Beatrice.

" I suppose so," said C.

The noise of the chattering people in the boat grew
fainter and fainter. Suddenly the " Last Post "
sounded from Windsor and died away.

The flashy rendering of the song they had just been
listening to had a curious effect on C. It made him
feel inclined to say, and it made it possible for him to

say, all sorts of things that up till the present he had never dared say. It had unlocked a door.

"To-morrow night I shan't be here any more," said C.

"I wonder whether you'll be able to come back," said Beatrice.

"Of course I shall come back"; but there was an unexpressed fear in the tone of his voice.

"Fancy!" said Beatrice. "When I first heard about you and heard you called ' C. ' by Mrs. Roden, I thought it was S.E.A. I thought it such a funny name."

"At the concert?"

"Yes, at the concert."

They both laughed.

"Do you remember the concert?" asked C.

"Every moment of it. Do you remember that song, *For Greed of Gold*?"

"Yes, and the fat man who sang *To-morrow will be Friday*. I didn't dare look at you. I thought I was staring too much. I thought you would think me so rude."

"I knew we would be friends."

"I thought so, too."

The moon had risen. The trees and the shrubs seemed unreal. It seemed to C. that years had passed since the first evening they had walked down to the river after the first Sunday he had spent at Bilbury. A dog barked somewhere. It was quite still, and yet the stillness was composed of a hundred little sounds : the breaking of a twig, the rustling of a leaf, the note of a bird, then a ripple on the water. The summer night touched them with its spell, and C. poured out his love for Beatrice in a flood of inconsequent whispers, and asked her to be his wife. Beatrice said " Yes " quite simply, and they promised to love each other for ever and ever, whatever might happen. They made good the promise with their first kiss. The night, the stars, the moon, the river, the willow trees, and all the muffled noise of the midsummer night seemed to witness their declaration and to seal the sacrament.

They walked to the house, hand in hand, in silence. When they went to bed Beatrice went up to her mother's room.

" I am engaged to be married to C.," she said.

Mrs. Lord cried a great deal and clasped her child in her arms. She was genuinely, overwhelmingly surprised. Then she suddenly exclaimed :—

" But, my darling, he'll never change his religion, and your father will never hear of your marrying some one who isn't a Catholic ! "

" We'll discuss that later, darling Mummy," said Beatrice.

CHAPTER XXII

MRS. LORD had been brought back with a sharp jerk to the world of reality from the vague country of dreams in which she had been wandering, by Beatrice's announcement. She had never faced the possibility of Beatrice being engaged. She thought she was far too young, and she still looked upon her as a baby. As for C., she had never thought of him except as a schoolboy. She slept little that night. The marriage seemed to be altogether impossible for a multitude of reasons. There was the financial question. Both the children were far too poor to marry. It was possible, of course, that C.'s wealthy relations, that Mrs. Roden, for instance, might help; but it was improbable. Mrs. Lord did not know the Hengraves, but she took disapproval for granted from that quarter. Then there was the religious question. Her husband, in spite of his vagueness and affability, and his unbusinesslike, meandering habit of mind, concealed in his soul a little hard kernel on the subject of religion, and there were occasions and moments when he saw red on the subject. It would be impossible to discuss the matter quietly and reasonably with him. He became violent, too, when crossed and excited. But then Beatrice was a determined girl.

Altogether, Mrs. Lord thought that " it was all very
uncomfortable."

The next morning she braced herself to have a talk,
first of all with Beatrice, then with C.

She detailed the reasons which she said made the
marriage difficult.   She did not use the word
impossible.

The extreme youth of both of those concerned.

The want of money on both sides.

The difference of religion, which would be regarded
as an obstacle probably by the Hengrave family, and
certainly by Mr. Lord.

Beatrice did not discuss the financial side, but she
did say that mixed marriages often occurred, and often
seemed to be quite happy.

"Yes, but your father!" said Mrs. Lord, and
Beatrice felt that argument to be unanswerable.

"What does C. feel on the subject?" asked Mrs.
Lord.

"I don't know. We have never discussed it. I
know he is fond of Eton Chapel."

"Ah," said Mrs. Lord, " that's just it! You see how
difficult it is. We will say nothing to your father at
present.   After all, there is no hurry, you are both of
you so young, so absurdly young."

"Not younger than you were, Mummy, when you
married," said Beatrice.

Mrs. Lord sighed.

"I married far too young," she said.

Then she had an interview with C.

C. admitted that the financial prospects were poor, that his parents would probably be difficult at first; as to the religious question, he waved it aside.

"Mixed marriages happen every day. After all, it's practically the same religion. You only believe a little more than we do. That's all. It's not as if I was a Turk. My godmother might help us. She has always helped me so far. And then we can wait. I am willing to wait for years, so anything may happen. I can go into the City and make money. My eldest brother is in the City, and he can take me into his office. After all, when the Carterets were married they were both of them penniless."

"Yes," said Mrs. Lord, "but Sir Gabriel was exceptional, and even as a student he showed great promise. He was born for success. I don't mean, my dear, that you will be unsuccessful."

But, although she was not aware of it, that was exactly what she did mean. C. had a horrible feeling that she was right.

"All I say is," said Mrs. Lord, "do not let us do anything rash."

She felt it was fearfully difficult, practically impossible, to discuss the matter with C. He swept aside the material objections; as for the others, he did not understand them.

Luncheon passed off sadly. The Carterets put this down to C.'s departure, and Lady Elizabeth tried to enliven him by dwelling forcibly on the necessity of his immediate return. C. assented, but he felt at the back of his mind that the return might not be quite as speedy as he hoped. Mrs. Lord said nothing about the matter to Lady Elizabeth, but Lady Elizabeth suspected that something had happened. What it was she was not quite sure. She at first suspected a lovers' quarrel, but after a moment's thought she got near to the truth.

C. had one last long talk with Beatrice in the afternoon. Lady Elizabeth saw to that. They walked together round and round the kitchen-garden.

It would be interesting to know what the immortals, the angels, the devils, and the head clerk to the Fates think and say when they overhear conversations such as Beatrice and C. held on this occasion about their future.

" Father and Mother will mind at first," said C., " but they will come round in the end. Aunt Rachel will persuade them. You see, she has often said to me that, having no boys of her own, she considers me to be her son."

" But," said Beatrice, " won't they all of them mind my being a Catholic ? Mrs. Roden just as much as the others, in fact more ? She's very High Church."

" I thought," said C., " that High Church people approved of Roman Catholics. Our Dame used to at Eton."

" They do in a way, and to a certain extent," said Beatrice, " but sometimes they are the most anti-Catholic people in the world. I suppose your Father and Mother would think it awful."

" I'm afraid they would think it a drawback," said
C. " My uncles and aunts and cousins certainly
would.   They'd say I'd been got hold of by the priests,
and what's so odd is that those who mind most are just
those who care least about religion—those who haven't
really got any religion at all.   At any rate, your Mother
didn't seem to think it was a difficulty that couldn't be
got over."

" Did she say anything about Father ? "

" No, she said nothing about him."

" You know he would mind more than anybody."

" Would he really ?   I can't understand why.   He
couldn't think I would want you to change your religion or to interfere with it in any way."

" He wouldn't reason about it at all.   Father's an
extraordinary mixture.   You know he's half Irish, and
he's so gentle and vague and affable, and suddenly he
sees red about a thing, and it's no good arguing or
saying anything.   It's not so much that he'd mind me
marrying a Protestant as that he would want me to
marry a Catholic.   It would be unthinkable to him
that I shouldn't marry a Catholic."

" But aren't there mixed marriages every day ? "

" Of course, but that wouldn't affect Father."

" Do you mean he would forbid it ? "

" I don't know that he would actually do that, but
he would certainly make it difficult."

" However, whatever the difficulties are, if we are
determined to get over them, nothing can prevent us
getting over them."

"We shall have to be very patient and careful not to make things more difficult. Whatever we do we mustn't make them angry."

By *them* Beatrice meant the Hengrave family.

"I have a feeling it will all come right in the end. I shall go and see Aunt Rachel directly I get to London, and I am sure she will pull us through. You see she loves you."

"You mustn't be disappointed if Mrs. Roden isn't as enthusiastic as you expect her to be."

"But she is a great friend of your Mother's, isn't she?"

"Yes, but I feel sure she wouldn't like to do anything which would annoy your Mother, or which she thought would be likely to make difficulties between you and your family."

"We must hope for the best. I'm sure I can persuade her."

"We must hope for the best," said Beatrice; but she knew from the first moment that she had talked to her mother and had thought over the whole matter calmly in her own mind, that short of a miracle there would be little chance of the marriage being sanctioned on either side. "Miracles," she thought, "do sometimes happen, only this is too nice a miracle to happen. But she kept her doubts to herself. She implored C. to be very gentle and tactful with his family, and to respect their prejudices and not to arouse their opposition. C. promised to be as gentle as a lamb and as reasonable as a serpent. They went over the whole story again and again, and again, and then, after many protestations, and promises and assurances, and sacred, beautiful, foolish nothings, they said good-bye.

Lady Elizabeth said good-bye to C. affectionately. She conveyed to him indirectly that she knew what was happening, and bade him be of good cheer. Mrs. Lord said good-bye to him tearfully, and indirectly conveyed to him that he must not be too optimistic.

"We shall expect you to-morrow at tea-time. If you can, get down in time for luncheon," said Lady Elizabeth.

"I expect he will want to spend the morning in London," said Mrs. Lord.

"I shall come back as soon as ever I can," said C.

Sir Gabriel, who was always glad of an excuse for going to Windsor, said he would drive C. to the station, and they started off in a dog-cart after an early tea. C. was glad of Sir Gabriel's cheerful affability and flow of mild puns. Sir Gabriel left him at the South-Western station, and as he said " good-bye " to him, he said suddenly, quite gravely :—

"If you find you can't come back as soon as you wish, don't worry. Things turn out sometimes to be more difficult than they seem to be at first, but they often come right in the end," and with these words he hurried away.

C. arrived at Hengrave House about half-past seven. He found the house in a state of commotion. The girls were dressing. Lady Hengrave had gone to dress. There was a red carpet outside the front door, and an awning. The staircase was full of flowers, the front drawing-room was empty of furniture save for gilt chairs. There was, he learnt, to be a little dance after dinner. He found a pencil note from Lady Hengrave begging him not to be late for dinner, and telling him that he was to take in to dinner Alice Woburn, the daughter of Lord Woburn. She was just out. He was also, said Lady Hengrave, to be sure to be civil to Lady Harriet Clive, who was to be on his other side. Lady Harriet Clive was a lively old lady who liked the literary, the original, and the young, and she had asked Lady Hengrave to let C. sit next to her, as she had heard of him (oddly enough from Burstall, a fact she did not mention to Lady Hengrave). C. ran upstairs and dressed in a hurry. Minor mishaps occurred ; he lost his collar-stud, and spoilt three ties in the tying of them, so that he was only just in time. Dinner was at quarter past eight, and as the Prince of Saxe-Altenburg was dining, everybody was punctual. When C. came down he found that most of the guests had arrived, and Lady Hengrave, in black velvet, trimmed with artificial poppies, and a forbidding tiara, looked at him reproachfully, but with relief. The Prince of Saxe-Altenburg walked into the room as the clock struck a quarter past eight. He wore a star and a red ribbon, and he shook hands slowly with all the guests, and said a word to each. To C. he said nothing, but favoured him with an august twinkle.

It was a large dinner party. Sixteen people sat down to dinner. C. took Lady Alice Woburn down towards the end of the procession. He found her shy and silent, and their conversation took the form of a question, a pause, and a monosyllable; then another longer pause, another question, and another monosyllable. Towards the middle of dinner Lady Harriet turned a beady eye on him, and said that she had heard a lot of him from a quaint friend of hers, Andrew Burstall. C. was astonished, but delighted at his name coming up into the conversation.

"He thinks a lot of you," she said.

"Where is he now?" asked C.

"Oh, he's so tiresome—always away. It's impossible to get hold of him. He's an impossible man, but so clever and agreeable. But a dreadful Tory." Lady Harriet was a Whig. "But I suppose you are a Tory like the rest of your family. Your mother and I never discuss politics, but I do have battles with Andrew Burstall whenever I see him. He's abroad now, finishing his book."

"Was he ever married?" asked C.

"He is married now, but the marriage was an unfortunate one. He and his wife don't get on. She lives in London. They're not separated, but they quarrel dreadfully, and yet they cannot keep apart for very long. They both come to see me, but always separately. She's a clever woman, but very bitter, and she had some money. Next time I can get him to luncheon you must come and meet him. He spoke very highly of you, and he seldom does that. You must have impressed him. He said you wrote so well."

C. got very red and could scarcely believe his ears. He felt an inward glow of pleasure.

Lady Harriet asked him where he had been, and when he mentioned the Carterets she said she knew them very well.

" Such a charming man, and dear Bessie Carteret just as foolish as ever, I suppose. And who else was there ? "

" Mrs. Lord and her daughter Beatrice," said C., and he felt a great, a new, rare and exquisite pleasure in saying the name of Beatrice Lord. He tried to say it in a detached way, but the practised ears of Lady Harriet detected the quality of the interest.

" Yes, the Lords," she said. " I have met her. She was a Cartwright. He's half Irish, I think, an inventor who is always inventing things that never answer, and only end in some one going bankrupt. They say the girl's pretty. Is she ? "

Lady Harriet gave C. a piercing glance.

He tried hard not to blush, but he could not help it.

" Yes," he said, " she is very pretty—very tall."

" No money, of course," said Lady Harriet with a sigh. " They are all Roman Catholics ; and that won't make it any the easier for her to find a husband outside the old Catholic families."

" I suppose she'd have to marry a Catholic ? " said C. tentatively.

" I believe they are rather bigoted," said Lady Harriet, " but, you see, it's not every one would like their son to marry a Roman Catholic, especially if she is penniless. That would be the difficulty. I don't suppose they'd mind. If Mrs. Lord is a sensible woman she would be delighted for her daughter to marry any one."

She gave C. another piercing glance, and noted the intense interest that his expression betrayed in the topic they were discussing. "Could it be that?" she thought.

"I suppose you had never met the Lords before?" she hazarded.

"Oh, yes, I met them at Aunt Rachel's last Christmas."

He said nothing about Oxford.

"The boy is in love with her," thought Lady Harriet. "That's a marriage which will certainly be thought to be out of the question. Poor boy! poor girl!" She pictured to herself her friend Georgina Hengrave's feelings if C. proposed marrying a penniless Papist.

"Anyhow, the girl's far too young to think of marrying now," she said, and then they talked of other things.

Lady Harriet was interested in C., but she seemed to foresee rocks and shoals ahead of him in his relations with his family, and with the world in general.

"You must come to luncheon with me soon. Come next Sunday," she said.

C. became immensely embarrassed.

"I should like to very much, but I am not sure

whether I will be here. The Carterets asked me to go
back, but——"

Lady Harriet understood the situation at once.

" You will let me know. There's no hurry," she
said. " If you are in London come at two o'clock.
I'll try and get some pleasant people."

The men remained a long time over the wine when
dinner was over, and C. found himself next to two
elderly politicians, who discussed a Bill that was or
was not going to be passed that session. C. thought
their conversation would never come to an end. On
the other side of him a young guardsman, who had
sat on the other side of Lady Alice, had found a
congenial companion in another fellow guardsman, and
they were deep in shop. The politicians included C.
in their audience and acted as though he were taking
an intelligent interest in their conversation. C. was
praying for it to end.

Lord Hengrave had moved up at the end of dinner
to the opposite end of the table, and was talking
racing to the Prince of Saxe-Altenburg, who every
now and then nodded his head and sometimes said, " I
agree with you." The port and the old brandy had
both been round twice, and, after drinking a final
glass of old brandy (1848), the Prince of Saxe-
Altenburg said reflectively :—

" Ze wines are good. I have drunk zem all," and
he looked interrogatively at his host, giving him the
tacit signal for rising. Lord Hengrave and the Prince
rose from their seats, and C. rushed to open the door.

As they went upstairs C. heard the strains of a string band playing a valse he had heard in Germany, *Donauwellen*, and he passed a crowd of young men who were putting on white gloves in the cloak room. Lady Hengrave was standing, very erect and dignified, at the top of the staircase, receiving the guests. C.'s two sisters had already found partners and were twirling round the room. They were certainly better dressed than any of the other girls present. Lady Hengrave had seen to that, and C. thought he noticed a triumphant expression on the face of his eldest sister, Julia.

He was bewildered. There was hardly any one he knew by sight in the room, and the people he did know were just those whom he would like to avoid. He saw that his sisters had noticed his arrival, and would probably soon introduce him to some one. He was an unskilful dancer, and he looked upon talking to a partner as worse than dancing. He would have liked to have run away, but there was no escape. Between him and the door which led from the landing to the back staircase stood Lady Hengrave. He caught sight of his sister-in-law, his brother Edward's American wife, and he felt she was walking towards him with the intention of introducing him to a suitable partner. C. was desperate. He looked around him and wondered whether there was any means of escaping before his sister-in-law could reach him. There was luckily rather a crowd on the landing, and at that moment Lady Harriet came to his rescue. She seemed to guess what he was going through.

" This is your first ball, isn't it ? " she said. " Do come and talk to me for a moment."

C. was overjoyed at this solution. She led him through the ballroom, in which as yet only a few couples were dancing, into the back drawing-room, where there were chairs and sofas.

" You can leave me," she said, " whenever you want to go and dance."

" Oh," said C., " I hate dancing, and I don't know any one."

" Presently," said Lady Harriet, " I'll try and find you a partner who won't bore you, and in the meantime you can talk to me."

Lady Harriet knew exactly what C. was going through. She also knew what would be expected of him from his family, and she determined to see him through the evening. She had taken a great fancy to him and, from what Burstall had told her, she felt that C. was an exceptional person.

As they sat down the ballroom seemed quite empty. There were about four couples dancing, but they had not been talking for more than ten minutes when the staircase had become crowded and the ballroom was full of dancers. Just as when you pour hot water into a basin or a bath and you feel at one moment as if it will never get hot, and then in one undefinable second the basin or bath from having been a basin of cold water becomes one of boiling water, too hot to bear, so did the rooms at one moment seem as if they could never be filled and at the next were overflowing with people.

" You'll have to dance with some girl, once," said Lady Harriet, " or your mother will never forgive either you or me."

" But I can't dance," said C. " I've never danced since I went to school."

" Then you must sit out," said Lady Harriet. And as she said the words the band began to play an arrangement of Lancers from *Cinder-Ellen up-to-date*, a Gaiety burlesque.

" Lancers," she said, " You can dance the Lancers. You must dance them with Alice Woburn. She hasn't got a partner, and you sat next to her at dinner. She's standing up there next to her mother."

C. did as he was told, and got through the dance without mishap. In fact, he enjoyed it. When the dance was over he sat on the staircase with his partner. Guests were still arriving. His Aunt Rachel and her two daughters passed him. She greeted him warmly, and when the music began, and he had taken his partner back to her mother, he at once approached one of the Roden girls, and suggested that they should go and have some lemonade downstairs. He was quite happy with his cousin. She, in her turn, introduced him to other unalarming partners, so that by supper-time he had got through the evening fairly well. He took Lady Harriet down to supper, and as they were sitting at a round table, and eating quails, a murmured confidence seemed to spread through the room and make a ripple of excitement. It was a piece of news, namely, that Julia Bramsley was engaged to be married to Lord Holborn, only " it was not yet announced." By the time the piece of news had circulated throughout the dining-room the phrase " not yet announced " had lost its meaning, and by the time the first guests to come down had finished their supper and gone upstairs the marriage was considered to be announced, and Julia and the young man, who had ten thousand a year, was twenty-seven years old, and an eldest son, were receiving the congratulations of their friends.

When C. returned to the ballroom with Lady Harriet, who bade him go and congratulate his sister, he felt rather at a loss what to do. Julia was nowhere to be seen. He came across Marjorie and said :—

" I suppose it's true about Julia ? "

" Oh, that's stale news ! Do you mean you didn't know ? Of course, to Tommy."

" Where is she ? " said C.

" They've gone down to have supper," said Marjorie, and at that moment a partner came and claimed her. C. felt sentimental towards his eldest sister, and wanted to make some manifestation, but he looked round the room and saw no one with whom he felt inclined to communicate anything. He felt that he was in extreme jeopardy, that at any moment some one might come and introduce him to a partner. The ballroom was now not so crowded, as many of the dancers were having supper. He walked into the back drawing-room, and there he caught sight of Mrs. Roden. He walked up to her.

"Have you had supper?" he asked.

Supper seemed to him a providential oasis in the Sahara of ballroom life. No, she hadn't.

"May I take you down?"

Mrs. Roden was extremely hungry, and delighted to go. As they walked through the dining-room to a table at the far end of the room they passed Julia and her *fiancé*, who were sitting at one of the nearer tables. C. bent over and whispered to her, "I do congratulate you." He felt a new and unwonted wave of fondness for his sister. She smiled back ecstatic thanks at him, while Mrs. Roden overwhelmed her in a gurgle of felicitations.

"How delightful it is about Julia!" Mrs. Roden said as they sat down. "Delightful in every way."

"Aunt Rachel," said C., "I have got a secret to tell you. I am engaged to be married to Beatrice Lord."

C. poured out the whole story into his aunt's astonished ears, and asked her advice. What was he to do? Had he better tell his mother himself? If so, when? Or would she do it?

"Don't do anything in a hurry," said Mrs. Roden. "Come to luncheon with me to-morrow and we will talk it over."

C. had been looking forward to going back the next day to the Carterets in time for luncheon. Nevertheless he thought it best to accept his aunt's invitation.

When C. and Mrs. Roden returned to the ballroom they found it greatly thinned. They had been a long time at supper. It was nearly half-past three. Mrs. Roden's girls were still dancing ; Julia and her *fiancé* were still enjoying their long, uninterrupted *tête-à-tête* in the tented balcony of the back drawing-room. When the dance came to an end Mrs. Roden said that she must take her girls home, as they had a ball every night that week.

" Mind, nothing rash," she said to C., " and luncheon to-morrow at two."

The room suddenly emptied as quickly and as imperceptibly as it had filled at the beginning of the evening. Soon the only people left were Julia and her *fiancé*, Marjorie, Edward and his wife. Lord Hengrave had gone to bed some time before. Lady Hengrave walked upstairs from a belated supper with Cecil White, whom the lateness of the hour had rendered peevish. She gave a sigh of relief as she noted the emptiness of the ballroom.

" Where's Julia ? " she said.

" They're still on the bálcony," said Marjorie.

" You might fetch them," said Lady Hengrave to C., " from the balcóny," correcting her daughter's pronunciation, " It's all over now."

Even the band had gone to enjoy a well-earned supper.

" It's certainly very satisfactory," said Lady Hengrave to her daughter-in-law, " about Julia."

Good-nights were said. Edward and his wife, the

last of the guests, said good-bye. Lady Hengrave said good-night to her children, and the evening seemed to have reached a peaceful close, and would have done so if on the way upstairs Marjorie, referring to her sister's engagement, had not twitted C. with his being too young to understand such things.

" As a matter of fact," said C., " I am engaged to be married myself."

Marjorie laughed sceptically.

" I suppose you haven't told mother yet ? "

" No, but I'm going to now," he said, and he ran down the back stairs to his mother's bedroom, which was on the first floor, next to the back drawing-room.

But when he got to the door his heart failed him.

" After all," he said to himself, " Aunt Rachel begged me to do nothing rash," and he walked upstairs again slowly.

On the way he passed his two sisters, who were still talking in the passage at the door of Julia's room, which was open.

" Well," said Marjorie, " have you told Mother of your engagement ? "

C. laughed and said :—

" I believe you were taken in."

" Not in the least," said Marjorie.

They all went to bed.

CHAPTER XXIII

THE next morning Lady Hengrave came down to breakfast punctually at nine-thirty as though nothing unusual had occurred in the house the night before. Julia and Marjorie were expected to have breakfast in bed after a dance, and were not to be called till they rang. C. and his father and mother met at the breakfast table. The front hall was full of workmen taking things away : plants, gilt chairs and red baize shelves which had been used for the hats and coats of the guests. The furniture was being put back in the drawing-rooms. Lord Hengrave was reading *The Times* in silence.

"Your father and I are dining out to-night," was Lady Hengrave's first remark after C. had said good-morning, " and Edward is taking the girls and Tommy Holborn to the play, and I've arranged for you to go with them ; they want another man. After the play they are all going on to Stuart House, where there is a dance, and you are asked. To-morrow your Aunt Rachel has got a dinner and expects you, and on Thursday we have been given a box at the opera. Friday is the Eton and Harrow match. One of the Holborn boys is in the eleven, and Albert Calhoun is in the Harrow eleven. On Friday night there is a large family dinner at Holborn House and a dance, and they expect you. So you see, my dear boy, you will have a very full week."

" But I have promised the Carterets to go back there to-day," said C.

" I will write to Bessie Carteret. She will quite understand when she hears of the engagement."

" Won't she think it very rude ? "

" I will explain everything. She will understand perfectly. Won't she, Hengrave ? " she appealed to Lord Hengrave.

" Of course the boy can stay," said Lord Hengrave, thinking that C. was about to sacrifice the pleasures of London for a duty visit to the country. " He must go out and enjoy himself now he is here."

Lady Hengrave talked of the dance. She said :—

" I think they enjoyed themselves, and the supper was hot. It is very satisfactory about Julia. He's a nice boy."

She then went over the list of the week's entertainments once again and found some new items. There was a new Italian actress appearing in London. They ought to see her, and then C. ought to go to the new play at the St. James's. He must be sure, too, to go and see his aunts.

" I will write to Bessie Carteret directly after breakfast, but I think it would be civil for you to write her a line as well."

C. said he would do so. He did more than write a line. He wrote eight pages to Beatrice and four pages to Lady Elizabeth, and he sent Beatrice a telegram. He made up his mind that whatever should happen he would find some means of going down to Windsor, if only for half an hour.

Marjorie and Julia came into the back drawing-room, where he was writing. Lady Hengrave was sitting in the front drawing-room, writing letters also, and C. wondered whether Marjorie would allude to his " joke " of the night before. She looked at him as if she were about to do so, but at the last moment she refrained. It was not only fear of Lady Hengrave, but a certain schoolroom loyalty, which influenced her.

C. went to luncheon with his Aunt Rachel.

She took him aside and said, " Well, I hope you have done nothing rash."

" No, it's all right, Aunt Rachel," he said, " except that I had promised to go back to Chestercombe to-day, and I did want to so much, and mother has made arrangements for me every day this week. I haven't told her yet. I thought it wasn't the right moment. But will it ever be the right moment ? "

They were interrupted by the arrival of guests, and luncheon was announced.

After luncheon Mrs. Roden took C. into her sitting-room, and they had a long and serious conversation. She saw at once that all argument was useless. It was like arguing with a waterfall. She also saw that he had no idea of the reality of the situation ; that is to say, of the impossibility of the marriage. She was willing to give C. an allowance, but it would not be nearly enough for him to marry on, and she was loth to do something which she knew would be contrary to the wishes of his mother, and above all things she wished to avoid a quarrel between C. and his family. She undertook to speak to Lady Hengrave, because she knew that Bessie Carteret was a gossip and fond of mischief, and that if she were to meet Lady Hengrave she would be certain to let drop some hint that might do infinite harm. She promised to see Lady Hengrave that very afternoon. She felt, indeed, that there was no time to be lost, but she let C. understand she would not help him to take a line contrary to his mother's wishes.

When C. got home he looked up the trains in the A.B.C. to find out whether it would be possible for him to go down to Windsor and get back before dinner. His brother was dining early, and he found the scheme was not practicable, so he contented himself with sending another telegram to Beatrice.

That afternoon Mrs. Roden had a momentous interview with Lady Hengrave. Mrs. Roden approached Lady Hengrave with the utmost care. She had promised C. to do her best for him. She was genuinely fond of the boy, and genuinely sorry for him, but she knew in her heart that she would be fighting in a battle that was already lost.

Mrs. Roden told the story. She said that Beatrice Lord was a charming girl. A Roman Catholic it was true, but, after all, such marriages sometimes turned out well. It was true there was very little money, but Mrs. Roden regarded C. almost as a child of her own. He was her godson, and she would continue the allowance she was giving him now after his marriage.

"You see, I should leave it him in my will," she said, "and he is welcome to it now; only by itself it, of course, wouldn't be enough for him to marry on."

Lady Hengrave listened in silence.

"The Lords are impossible people," she said. "Mrs. Lord was a Cartwright. She's a very silly woman, but there's nothing against her, and I'm sorry for her; but as for him, he's impossible. And then the children would have to be Roman Catholics; and there's no money at all. Of course, dear Rachel, it's very kind of you to say you'd help, but I should look upon it as an act of great unkindness if you were to assist the boy to marry some one whom Hengrave and I could not help disapproving of as a wife. I don't want to say anything against the girl, but you know as well as I do that Hengrave would never hear of this marriage, and that it is quite out of the question."

"I was afraid you would think so," said Mrs. Roden. "Poor C.! He will take it very badly, I'm afraid."

"They are far too young, both of them, to know their minds," said Lady Hengrave.

"They are very young," said Mrs. Roden plaintively. She saw clearly that there was nothing to be done. "I hope C. will do nothing rash," she said, thinking of the well-known obstinacy and the violent outbursts of temper which were recognised traits of the Hengrave blood.

" You need not be afraid, Rachel. You can leave all that to me. I think I shall be able to arrange matters," said Lady Hengrave.

Mrs. Roden woefully reflected that this was all too true.

" There must not be, and there shall not be, any mismanagement. Bessie Carteret is quite capable of making mischief," Lady Hengrave said firmly. " I will write to Mrs. Lord to-night, and I shall go and see her as soon as she comes to London. As for C., you needn't be afraid. I understand the boy perfectly."

Mrs. Roden then left the house, sadly reflecting that Lady Hengrave was under a complete delusion in thinking that she understood her son. But she also knew that Lady Hengrave was not likely to make a mistake in the management of any worldly affair.

That evening, before dinner, Lady Hengrave spoke to C. She was unusually amiable. She said that she had heard all about what had happened from his godmother. She knew Beatrice Lord was a charming, a very charming, girl. Of course, they were both of them far too young to marry at present, and then there was the money question and many other difficulties. She did not know what Beatrice Lord's parents thought of it. She knew his father would be upset—greatly upset—at the thought of such a marriage as things were at present. The great thing was to do nothing for the moment. She would go and see the Lords as soon as she could.   For the present she begged C. not to do anything.

" I suppose I may see Beatrice ? " he said, " and write to her ? "

" But she's not in London."

" The Carterets expected me to go back as soon as I could."

" Stay here this week in any case.   If you went away we should have to tell your father.   He wouldn't understand why you were going just when you've arrived in such a full week, with Julia being engaged and so many things going on, and so many invitations accepted for you ;   and then I should have to explain everything to him, and that would be a mistake."

" I shall write in any case."

" There is no harm in that, only there must be no question of an engagement just yet."

" But we are engaged," said C.

" Yes, I know, my dear boy, but I meant a public engagement. There is plenty of time.   All I ask you is to wait a little, and we will see what can be done."

" I must see Beatrice."

" Of course you can see her," said Lady Hengrave. " All I am asking you is to be reasonable and not to make things more difficult than they are already."

C. acquiesced.   But he had a horrible feeling of being caught in the threads of an intangible web.

He wrote a long letter to Beatrice that evening, begging her to let him know if he could see her at

Windsor or in London. He must see her, he said, at
once. He went to the play that night like a man in a
dream. It was a translation of a play of Sardou's.
C. was unaware when it was over what it had all been
about. When it was over he accompanied his sisters
to what was called by the hostess a tiny dance, and
what turned out to be a large ball at Stuart House.
Here, again, he was just like a man in a dream. He
carried away the impression of a great crowd of
people packed like sardines on a large staircase, at the
top of which stood a young and radiant hostess, as
lovely as a flower, welcoming her guests with matchless
grace and a smile that reminded him of Beatrice.
Dazzling as this apparition was, he thought her far
less beautiful than Beatrice. He was soon lost in the
crowd. He knew nobody. He did not want to know
any one. He found a corner near a pillar at the top
of the gallery, where he could see the guests arriving.
Nobody noticed him. He was glad of that. He had
never felt more completely alone. The people seemed
to him like waxworks. He had only one wish, and
that was to get away, to escape.

He was just thinking how he was best able to do so,
when he heard some one saying to him :

" Aren't you dancing to-night ? "

He looked round and saw Lady Harriet Clive. In
spite of everything it was nice to hear a friendly voice.

" I don't know any one," he said. " I can't dance,
and in any case there's too great a crowd to get into
the ballroom."

"Let's go and sit down," said Lady Harriet.

She led him along the gallery into a large square room, full of beautiful pictures. She liked the boy and he interested her. She saw at once that he was in an absent-minded mood. She bothered him with no questions, but she kept up herself a running comment on different topics, and she told him who the people were.

"Who is that standing up in the doorway, dressed in yellow, talking to the man with a red ribbon round his neck ? " he said absently.

The face reminded him of some one, or something ; he could not think what.

"That is Leila Bucknell," said Lady Harriet. "The man she is talking to is a diplomat, Teddy Broughton. He's a Minister somewhere. She is pretty, isn't she ? "

The name Leila touched a cell in C.'s mind. He wondered whether she could be the Leila he had known and played with in Hamilton Gardens. He looked at her again. Yes, she was pretty, very pretty, just the right height. Yes, her eyes were like the violet eyes of his Leila, melting and appealing. She had a beautifully modelled face ; she was exquisitely made, as delicate as a Tanagra statuette, and yet not too small.

"I wonder who she was before she married," he said.

"She was a Steele, a daughter of Lord Fairleigh," said Lady Harriet. "She was married about six

years ago to a man called Terence Bucknell. He is
at the Foreign Office."

"I believe I used to know her a long time ago,"
said C.

Presently a dignified nobleman with a star and a blue
ribbon came and claimed Lady Harriet to go down to
supper. She left C. with a smile and said :—

"Don't forget I expect you to luncheon on Sunday."

C. walked through the room, and as he did so he
passed Mrs. Bucknell, who was still talking to the man
with the red ribbon round his neck, but they were now
sitting on a sofa. There was no doubt about it at all.
She was *his* Leila. He smiled at her, and made as if to
say how-do-you-do, but she did not recognise him ; she
nodded almost imperceptibly, and gave him a look of
blank non-recognition. C. felt himself grow scarlet,
and he hurried away through the room embarrassed
beyond words, and smarting with a sense of extreme
humiliation. He only wished to escape immediately.
This he managed to do. He found a way downstairs,
and managed to get away without being caught by
any of his relations or acquaintances. He continued
to have a sense of burning humiliation till he got
home. He hoped there might be a letter from
Beatrice awaiting him on the hall table, but there was
nothing but a bill from a hatter and a copy of the
Eton Chronicle. He went to bed, and when he got to
bed he once more blushed scarlet when he thought of
the incident. He knew it was foolish. Why should
she, how could she have recognised him ? But he

felt he had done something foolish, that he had made a fool of himself, and his cheeks burnt with shame.

The next morning all this was forgotten, because he received a letter from Beatrice in which she said that she and her mother were leaving Windsor and coming up to London that very evening. Her father needed them in London. She would be in all the next day in their house in Ovington Square, or if he were to come at three o'clock they would probably be able to talk undisturbed, but the morning would be better. At tea-time, she knew, Lady Hengrave was coming to see her mother, and Lady Hengrave had said in her letter that she hoped Beatrice might be there. What had happened was this : Lady Hengrave had written to Mrs. Lord as soon as Mrs. Roden had left, saying that it would be advisable for them to meet, and asking her when she could find her in. She wanted to go to Mrs. Lord, not Mrs. Lord to come to her, and she made it plain. Mr. Lord was clamouring for his wife's and his daughter's presence in London, and Mrs. Lord was as anxious to see Lady Hengrave as Lady Hengrave was anxious to see her, so when she received Lady Hengrave's letter she wrote to her that she would be in the afternoon after her arrival (Thursday) at five o'clock, and would be delighted to see Lady Hengrave then. Lady Hengrave telegraphed that she would call at five.

C. would have liked to go to the station to meet them, but Beatrice had not said what train they were coming by, nor did he even know which line they would take,

Great Western or South Western—from Datchet they used both. So he spent the whole of Wednesday in feverish agitation. The Hengraves had guests to luncheon, and in the evening he dined with the Rodens. The next morning he drove as soon as he decently could to Ovington Square, and there he found Beatrice by herself. Her father was in the City, and her mother had gone out. It was a curious fact that Mrs. Lord quite unintentionally did things which had the appearance of being done with intention, and some-times as if with a subtle purpose, when this was far from being the case. For instance, during the whole time she had spent at Oxford, while C. and Beatrice had gradually got to know each other, an outside observer would have deduced from her conduct that she was doing everything she could to throw them together, yet when she was told of the engagement she was honestly, genuinely astounded. And on this occasion, again, you would have thought, since Beatrice had told her she expected C., who had explained his movements in a long telegram, she had gone out on purpose to leave Beatrice and C. together in the exceedingly untidy room that Mr. Lord called his studio, and which did duty for drawing-room and everything else, but Mrs. Lord had gone out because she always went to Mass at Farm Street on Thursdays, and did a little shopping on the way back.

Beatrice and C. had a great deal to say to each other, and they were able to say it. They had matters of pressing urgency to discuss.

"Mother is coming here this afternoon. Will you be there?" he asked.

"I shall come in at the end; I think your mother wants to see me."

"The moment she sees you it will be all right."

Beatrice shook her head sadly.

"There are great difficulties. It is all far more difficult than you imagine. Father has not been told. Mother would never dare tell him, and I should find it difficult."

"All because of the religious difficulty?"

Beatrice got a little red. That, she knew, was not the only difficulty.

"Father is a very strange person," she said. "He's not very religious, and not what you would call fanatical, but all the same he expects me to marry a Catholic; he couldn't conceive my marrying any one else but a Catholic; and then, you see, there are other difficulties."

"Money?"

He told Beatrice exactly what Mrs. Roden had said. He had already told her the substance of the conversation in a letter.

"She will only help you if your mother consents," said Beatrice. "Your mother will never consent. She will say just what Mother says: that your father would never hear of it, and that she can't tell him."

"Then do you mean we must just give in, and give everything up?"

" We can't do it unless they consent. Neither of us can. Neither you nor I."

" But we'll get them to come round in the end. At first there always are difficulties, but no difficulties really matter if you and I are quite determined. If we are determined to be married, nothing in the world can stop us."

" It would be folly for you to quarrel with your father and mother ; if you did that it would mean in the end quarrelling with your Aunt Rachel as well, and then everything would be more impossible than ever."

" So what do you think we must do ? "

" I think we shall have to wait patiently."

" Wait, wait, that's what they all say."

" If we do anything rash we may spoil everything."

" After all, Sir Gabriel Carteret married Lady Elizabeth when they were both penniless, and he was only an art student."

" Yes, but she had very rich relations, and they did not really object to the marriage, except for the money question. Our case is far more complicated. Your family will never consent to your marrying a Catholic, and my father would only consent to my marrying a Protestant if . . ."

" If what ? "

" If he thought there were such overwhelming advantages *for me* that they outweighed everything else."

She laid stress on the " for me," but C. felt, and the

feeling gave him a chill, that it was a case of "for him" far more than "for me."

"One never knows ; all sorts of things may happen," he said.

"Yes, but the important thing is, that we mustn't do anything foolish."

"I know ; I know ; but, at the same time, we must be quite firm."

"You are so young," said Beatrice. "In a year's time you will probably be much fonder of some one else than you are of me."

"What nonsense !" said C. "You are just as young as I am, as to that."

"Yes, but much older in experience—years older. I feel as old as the hills."

So they talked, and they went over the same ground over and over again, Beatrice making reasonable objections and C. sweeping them impetuously aside. Beatrice liked C. to sweep them aside, but she estimated the force of his impetuosity and his revolt at its true value. She knew that it could but count for little against the formidable array of circumstances.

They discussed the religious question again.

"After all," said C., "I could become a Roman Catholic. I would become a Hindoo to marry you."

"Instead of making it easier, that would make it quite impossible as far as your father and mother are concerned."

"My father and mother may have prejudices, but

that's only against Catholics in general. When they see you and know you they would change their mind."

"People don't change their mind about that sort of thing," said Beatrice.

"What can it matter," said C. impatiently, "what church one goes to ?—if one thinks it necessary to go to church."

"Catholics think it does matter," said Beatrice.

"Yes, but Protestants don't," said C. "That's the beauty of being a Protestant."

"Yes, but although they don't mind anything else, they do mind Catholics," said Beatrice. "They think it doesn't matter what sect you belong to, but they think it does matter if you are a Catholic. There is no getting round that. As far as our Church is concerned, they are in a rut of prejudice, and they see it at a wrong angle, and it is very difficult to get them out of the rut and to change their angle."

"But it is all the same religion," said C.

"It's too difficult to explain. I can't explain it to you. You see, you don't think religion matters one way or the other. We think religion matters more than anything else in the world. And people like your father and mother . . ." she stopped.

"Call something else religion," said C. "I have always known that. I know *that* isn't religion at all, only it's just as strong. I mean, they think going to church is like leaving cards, only that doesn't prevent them thinking it tremendously important. Only I can't see why they should mind your doing the same thing in your way."

" But you know they do," said Beatrice.

" Yes, they do," said C.

" We must face it."

" Yes, we must face it," he repeated. " And do what we can."

" And not do anything to make it worse," said Beatrice.

C. and Beatrice went on talking till past one. She said that her father was expected back to luncheon, and C. knew that she meant that under the circumstances he had better not stay. So after making elaborate arrangements for meeting on the following days, he left the house. On the doorstep he met Mrs. Lord, who greeted him with the same kind and welcoming friendliness as usual.

CHAPTER XXIV

THE same afternoon, at five o'clock precisely, Lady Hengrave drove in her Victoria to Ovington Square. She was not impressed by the butler who opened the door. He was an affable, talkative Irishman, named Terence, slightly bald, and quick, but he was not very clean (he was an intermittent, irregular shaver). "*Domestique de mauvaise maison*," she murmured to herself. She was still less impressed by the "Studio" upstairs, in which there seemed to be all the superfluities that disfigure and none of the realities that redeem a studio.

Mrs. Lord greeted her and offered her tea.

"Cuthbert," she said (Cuthbert was Mr. Lord), "is out and won't be back until late. He will be so sorry."

Lady Hengrave was relieved. She had no wish to see Cuthbert. Tea was brought in by Terence (who was also man-of-all-work). Strangely enough, it was hot and extremely good, and the tea-cakes were hot and crisp. Mrs. Lord always managed to have hot tea and crisp tea-cakes, and Lady Hengrave noted the fact and gave her a good mark for it.

Mrs. Lord talked of random topics, and Lady Hengrave, realising at once that Mrs. Lord was capable of talking during the whole of her visit on side topics, went straight to the point.

"My son Caryl tells me," she began, and she marshalled the facts with order and perspicuity.

Mrs. Lord listened, seemingly attentive, and when it was all over, and Lady Hengrave had proved with masterly logic and unmistakable clarity that neither her husband nor she could think of allowing the match to come off, said :—

"If only Cuthbert didn't happen to feel so strongly on the subject of mixed marriages, and hadn't set his heart on Beatrice marrying a Catholic, I'm sure everything could be arranged."

Lady Hengrave made her points all over again. She made them more clearly this time, and more forcibly.

"In any case I have told Beatrice that we mustn't do anything in a hurry," she said calmly, with a smile.

Lady Hengrave gave it up. "It is no good talking to her," she thought. "Either she's not listening, or she's not quite right in the head." She asked if she might see Beatrice before she went.

"Oh, yes," said Mrs. Lord, "she would so much like to see you," and she rang the bell. "She's in the dining-room writing her letters. Ask Miss Beatrice to come up," she said to Terence, as soon as he appeared.

Lady Hengrave and Mrs. Lord talked of the topics of the day, and Mrs. Lord suddenly, on the subject of current events, became alert, practical, and vivaciously to the point. Beatrice came in.

"The girl has certainly got looks," thought Lady Hengrave. "If she had money——"

"Lady Hengrave wants to have a little talk to you," said Mrs. Lord, and she swept out of the room, leaving them together.

This action on the part of Mrs. Lord astonished Lady Hengrave more than anything else. Beatrice, too, was slightly taken aback, used as she was to her mother's sudden actions.

Lady Hengrave marshalled her facts for a third time.

"I know," said Beatrice. "I quite understand. My father would not like the marriage either. He would not like it even if there were no other difficulties. He would dislike it as much as you would." (Lady Hengrave had touched very lightly on the religious difficulty; nevertheless she had made herself clear on the point.) "What do you want me to do?"

"I want you *not* to see him."

Beatrice reflected. It seemed to her like a situation in a book, a Montagu and Capulet situation—even more difficult in its essentials—with a lot of sordid money details thrown in.

"As long as we are both in London it will be very difficult. The less I see him the more he will want to see me."

"Yes," said Lady Hengrave with a sigh, "that's true. But you might gradually see him less and less. It would be for his good. It is for him I ask you to make the sacrifice."

"He's very young," said Beatrice. "I am ready to

do anything for him, only I will not be untruthful to
him, and I will not deliberately do anything to hurt
him, nor anything which I think will make things
worse."

"But if he knows your father would not hear of
it ? "

"Father knows nothing about it."

"But couldn't you tell him ? "

"Mother would rather not. Perhaps it will all
settle itself," Beatrice added. "A letter one doesn't
answer so soon answers itself. People so often make
things worse by taking steps."

Lady Hengrave wondered at the calm way in which
Beatrice talked. "Can she really be fond of him ? "
she wondered.

"Don't you think the best thing is to let things be,
Lady Hengrave ? Very likely we shall be going away
soon, and I suppose you will be going away, so we shall
not be able to meet, and C. will have plenty of things
to distract him," she said with a smile. "If you tell
him to wait, he will be reasonable. If you tell him he
must never see me again you will touch his obstinacy,
and, as you know, he can be very obstinate."

"Yes," said Lady Hengrave, "but a girl can do so
much. If you could gradually let him see——"

"I'm afraid I'm incapable of acting a part, Lady
Hengrave. I quite understand what you feel. I knew
it must be like that. I am very sorry for you it has
happened. These things happen before one knows. I
daresay it was my fault, but I can't help feeling what

I feel. You can be sure of one thing : I will never encourage C. to have illusions about what I know is impossible. I haven't done so as yet. I told him from the first that our marriage would be regarded as impossible both by his family and by mine, for every reason. But it is useless to reason with him. I think the only thing you can do is to ask him to wait."

" I am very much obliged to you," said Lady Hengrave. " I must be going." And she rose from her chair.

Beatrice called her mother, and Mrs. Lord came back and went on with the conversation as if it had never been interrupted. She rang for Terence, and Lady Hengrave was shown out.

" I don't think C. is at all like his mother," said Mrs. Lord. That was the only comment she made on the visit.

Lady Hengrave went away with food for reflection. The mother, she thought, was a lady ; there was that to be said. The girl was very pretty, well brought up, and sensible, but all the more dangerous on that account. However, she didn't think she would be likely to do anything without her parents' consent.

That night the Hengraves had been given a box at the opera. It was not a Wagner night ; in fact, the opera was nothing more original than *Faust*. Lady Hengrave took C. and Marjorie. Julia was dining elsewhere, and her husband went in the omnibus-box, which he preferred. During one of the intervals Lady Hengrave received a visit from Ralph Bodmin, who was one of the private secretaries to the Foreign Secretary, and who had the control of the minor diplomatic appointments. C., after having been introduced to him, vacated his place and left the box. He had caught sight of Mrs. Roden in the stalls, and he went downstairs to try and speak to her.

" I had a letter from your brother-in-law," said Bodmin, " to-day, from Rome. He wants another secretary or an attaché very badly. The Ambassador —Lawless—is here on leave. George, who has been left in charge, says they are short-handed and over-worked. But they all say that. There's nothing going on now in Rome, and he's got two secretaries. However, I can't send him any one ; we can't spare him any one at present. I'm afraid he finds the heat trying."

" Yes, he does," said Lady Hengrave. " Couldn't you send him an honorary attaché ? " she asked, and an idea was born in her mind. She looked upon the appearance of Ralph Bodmin as the direct intervention of Providence.

" Yes, of course, I would gladly send one if I knew any one who would want to go. But it's difficult to find any one who wants to go to Rome in July."

" My boy Caryl—you shook hands with him just now —is at Oxford. He's going to Spark's later, and then I want him to try for the Diplomatic Service. But before he begins all that cramming, which is dreadfully expensive, I should so much like him to have a little experience of diplomatic life, to see whether he takes to it, and whether he would be likely to do well. I suppose you couldn't send him out to his uncle? Emma would be delighted, of course."

" Nothing would be easier, Lady Hengrave," said Bodmin. " I'm having luncheon with Hedworth Lawless to-morrow. I'll talk to him about it. I'm sure he would be delighted. And he could probably live in the Embassy. There's no one living there at present, and he could learn Italian. Does he know a third language yet ? "

" No," said Lady Hengrave, " only French and German so far."

" But it would interrupt his University career."

" He's been a year at Oxford, and as there's no chance of his taking honours or anything of that sort I think it's long enough ; and Spark said a year would be enough for him in any case, so I should have to send him abroad, and he would have, as you say, to learn a third language ; and as George and Emma are now at Rome, what could be more suitable ? "

" I'm afraid he would find Rome rather dull just at present."

" He's not *blasé*. He's never been to Italy. July and August will soon be over, and Rome is delightful in September. He will have great fun in the winter. I really should be most grateful if you could arrange this. You would be doing me a *real* service. And George and Emma will be very grateful to you too. I should like him to go *now*. It would be more con- venient in every way."

" Yes, they would be very grateful. Well, I will let you know to-morrow evening."

" You're not going to Lord's to-morrow ; you're too busy ? "

" I shan't be able to get away."

" Here is the boy." C. came back into the box.

" So you're going up for the Diplomatic Service," said Bodmin, rapidly sizing him up. (Good-looking and quite decently dressed, he thought to himself, and nice manners.)

" I hope to have a try, said C.

" You haven't begun to cram yet, luckily for you. I know no more disagreeable position than that of a cramming candidate ; one always has to be at half-cock waiting for the chance of an examination," said Bodmin affably, and, as the curtain was going up, he left the box.

Lady Hengrave had said little about her visit to Mrs. Lord to C. She did mention it. She said that Beatrice Lord seemed to be a nice, well-brought-up girl. It was a pity they were so poor and lived in such squalid surroundings.

C. turned crimson at the mention of Beatrice's name, and feared that the visit had not born much fruit, but, on the whole, he thought it might have been worse. Beatrice, at any rate, had made a good impression. From Lady Hengrave such words were great praise. He had talked to his aunt in the *entr' acte*. She had recommended patience.

" You would have to wait in any case," she said.

" Don't let your mother think you are being impatient, and that you want to rush things ; do whatever she sugests."

The next day was the Eton and Harrow match. It was impossible for him not to go to that. His mother looked on it as one of the most sacred festivals of a well-spent life.

But he went to see Beatrice first on the way, and stayed with her all the morning. She was not going to Lord's. Her mother couldn't take her. They compared notes about his mother's visit.

" Mother was hopeless with her," said Beatrice. " She never thought of her point of view at all. The only thing she thinks of is father. Perhaps, after all, she is right. I'm not sure the difficulties on our side are not greater than on yours. Your mother was very nice to me, but she made it quite clear that she thought it impossible."

" At present."

" Always, I'm afraid. I really don't see what could make any difference. If you became a millionaire she still wouldn't want you to marry a Catholic."

" I should do what I chose then, and she would have to accept it."

" But there is so little chance of your becoming a millionaire."

" Not much, I'm afraid. Your father hasn't been told yet ? "

" No," said Beatrice, laughing, " and I suppose yours hasn't either. They are afraid of telling the fathers.

I think they are right. Both the fathers would see red. All we can do is to wait."

" And to see each other as much as possible. I wish this beastly cricket match wasn't going on. I shall have to go there to-morrow. To-night we've got a large family dinner."

They made arrangements to go to the Italian play on Saturday evening. They wanted to see the new Italian actress La Zechetti. Ralph Bodmin, very smart in a frock-coat and a gardenia in his button-hole, came to see Lady Hengrave late that evening, when she got back from Lord's. He had seen Sir Hedworth Lawless, and Sir Hedworth had appeared delighted that C. should go out to Rome as Honorary Attaché. Sir Hedworth was going to the Holborns' dance, and he would speak to her himself about it, and he wanted to make C.'s acquaintance. When would C. be ready to go ?

" I want him to go as soon as possible," said Lady Hengrave. He has got nothing to do, and he hates London."

Bodmin understood there must be some potent motive behind Lady Hengrave's words. He guessed the nature of the difficulty, but discreetly left it alone.

Lady Hengrave then prepared her husband. She didn't tell him everything ; but she hinted at the danger of a most undesirable alliance, a penniless girl, an impossible father, and a foolish mother.

Lord Hengrave at once said he couldn't afford to send the boy to Rome. As he was at Oxford, let him stay there.   The Rodens were paying for his education, and it was sin to waste it.

Lady Hengrave said she was sure Mrs. Roden would continue the allowance while he remained at Rome. She was going to talk to her about it that very evening. Mrs. Roden, she said, thought the possible match as undesirable as she did herself.

" But it will delay his going up for his examination," said Lord Hengrave.

" Not nearly as much as Oxford does," said Lady Hengrave.   " They do nothing at Oxford except play football and row and have suppers."   Besides which, it was necessary for him to learn a third language, and he would learn Italian at Rome.   It would be cheap, because she was sure Sir Hedworth Lawless would let him live in the Embassy.

Lord Hengrave gave in.   " But supposing the boy doesn't want to go to Rome ? " he said.

" If he wants to pass his examination he must go either to Italy or Spain," said Lady Hengrave. " Ralph Bodmin says it's essential that he should know three languages."

" What damned nonsense these examinations are ! " said Lord Hengrave.   " They make one spend a mint of money cramming the boys, and then they arrange among themselves at the Foreign Office who is to get in.   It's all waste of time and waste of money."

That night—directly after dinner at the Holborns'— Lady Hengrave spoke to Mrs. Roden, and put the whole case before her. Mrs. Roden agreed that the plan was excellent. She would, of course, she said, continue to give C. his allowance. She meant from henceforward to pay for his education, and she didn't mind whether it was carried on at Oxford or abroad. It was most desirable that he should go abroad for a time, but it was a great advantage for him to know Italian. Lord Hengrave spoke to Mrs. Roden, too, after dinner.

"I thought it rather nonsense sending the boy to Rome," he said, "but they say he's got to learn Italian. I think it's silly sending him out of the country just because he happens to be in love with a girl. I should have thought a little intrigue with a married lady might have been arranged," he said, with a smile.

Mrs. Roden laughed and said :—

"I expect that will happen all too soon without any arrangement on our part."

C. was, of course, quite unconscious of all these manœuvres. He sat at dinner between one of his Roden cousins and a shy, silent *débutante*, and he talked little.

After dinner there was a ball. It was a large ball for girls. C. was utterly miserable. There was not a soul in the room he knew except his cousins : the people, although they looked the same, seemed to have been dealt from a different pack of cards from those he had seen at Stuart House or at his mother's dance.

Lady Hengrave saw him standing disconsolately at

the furthest end of the ballroom, and directly Julia and Marjorie were taken away by their respective partners, she went up to him and said to him gently :—

" I want you to sit out with me a little, C. ; I have got something I want to tell you."

They walked through the long Adam ballroom into a little round library that had been turned into a sitting-out room, and they sat down on a sofa.

Lady Hengrave approached the subject discreetly, retrospectively and prospectively. It was necessary for him to have a profession. His parents could, alas! allow him very little, but his Aunt Rachel, who up till now had paid for his Oxford education, was willing to go on giving him an allowance while he was working for his examination, and (should he pass) during his first year in the Foreign Office or the Diplomatic Service. The Foreign Secretary had promised his father that he should have a nomination. He could go in for whichever he liked.

Here C. interrupted, and said he would prefer the Foreign Office.

But whichever he did, Lady Hengrave continued, it was necessary for him to learn a third language besides French and German. Italian would, of course, be the most useful. The sooner he learnt Italian, the better. He could not learn Italian at Oxford, and Spark, the crammer, had told her that if he was to pass the examination before he reached the age limit, it would be impossible for him to stay at Oxford for more than a year altogether.

And now a wonderful opportunity had presented itself. An Honorary Attaché was wanted at Rome, where his Uncle George was now First Secretary, and at this moment in charge. Sir Hedworth Lawless, the Ambassador, had consented to his being sent there. What did he think? Didn't he think it would be an admirable idea? He could see what diplomatic life was like, and he would then have some data for making up his mind which he preferred, the Diplomatic Service or the Foreign Office. He would see Italy; he would learn Italian; he would not be away long—only a few months.

"Can't I stay at Oxford another year?" he asked.

"Your father won't hear of it," said Lady Hengrave. "He already thinks it waste of time your having been there at all, and he says that if you stay on there any longer you will never be able to pass the examination, and Mr. Spark says the same."

"Then, if I didn't go to Rome, what should I do?" said C.

"If you didn't go to Rome," said Lady Hengrave, "you would still have to learn Italian or Spanish, and we should have to find you a *pension* or a family somewhere in the north of Spain, as it would be impossible just now in summer to find anything in Italy, and you would not be nearly so comfortable. You see, your father is getting anxious. He thinks you have wasted too much time already."

"The Master didn't think it waste of time," said C.

"It wouldn't be, if it wasn't necessary for you to

work for an examination," said Lady Hengrave.
" You see, it's so much better and more convenient,
and more comfortable in every way. In all probability you will be allowed to live at the Embassy. You
will have your Uncle George and your Aunt Emma
to be kind to you ; you will see diplomatic life and
Italy under the best possible conditions, and you will
have time to yourself for work and for learning
Italian. The Ambassador, Sir Hedworth Lawless, is a
charming man, and Lady Lawless is very kind. I am
sure you would be happy at Rome."

C. understood that the verdict had been pronounced,
and that there was nothing for him to do but to accept
it. His doom was sealed. What could he do ? Say
that nothing would induce him to go in either for the
Foreign Office or the Diplomatic Service ? Say that
he would like to go into a newspaper office at once ?
He knew that his mother would then answer :—

" What do you propose to do, and how do you propose to do it ?   What will you live on ? "

There was one ray of silver behind the cloud.
Rome was the kind of place that the Lords were likely
to visit. Mrs. Lord often alluded to their frequent
visits to Italy, which sometimes seemed to have been
protracted.

" When do you want me to go ? " said C.

" Well, Ralph Bodmin says that Uncle George is
crying out for some one, and that the sooner you go,
the better. Sir Hedworth Lawless is coming here
to-night, and I want to introduce you to him."

Lady Hengrave was relieved at C. having taken matters so calmly. C. felt desperate, but, at the same time, instinct told him that the only chance of his ultimately winning his battle was not to fight his mother over points about which she was obviously in the right.

The idea to him was appalling. He hardly knew his Uncle George. His Aunt Emma he merely recollected as being one of the oppressive critics of his childhood. But all that was nothing. What mattered was leaving Beatrice.

" If we are determined to marry," he thought to himself, " nothing can prevent us. I will go to Rome, but they will find when I come back that I haven't changed my mind."

" I'll go whenever you like," he said.

" I must go back to the ballroom and look after the girls," said Lady Hengrave.

A little later Mrs. Roden managed to have a word with C. She told him she had heard of the Rome project. It was an excellent thing, and he had been wise to accept it at once. To have refused to go would have been fatal.

Sir Hedworth Lawless arrived, and the first person he spoke to was Lady Hengrave. He was enchanted that C. should go to Rome. He should, of course, live at the Embassy. There was no one at present occupying the Secretary's rooms in the house. He would be back himself in October—possibly in September. He would like to see the boy so much. Lady

Hengrave caught sight of C. in the doorway, and beckoned to him.

Sir Hedworth was not at all what C. expected. He was rather short, with dark hair, slightly silvered, and light grey eyes ; there was nothing florid nor affected about him, not even an eyeglass string. He welcomed C. charmingly.

" So you're coming to Rome ? Believe me, the best time in the Diplomatic Service is before you get in. People say Rome is hot in summer, but I assure you it's never too hot. The Embassy is very cool, and the evenings and nights are delicious. I wish I was there now myself. I'll send your mother letters to some friends who stay all the summer in their villas."

C. stammered out his thanks.

" You know Italian ? "

" No, not yet."

" You'll learn in no time. There are some excellent teachers."

The Ambassador gave a quick look at the staircase. Then, after a few more civilities to Lady Hengrave, he drifted away. C. thought him charming. He noted, too, a very curious expression in his eyes. The same thing he had noticed in Burstall the first time he saw him. It was as if Sir Hedworth was looking over your head at some one, or for some one very far away, some one who was not there, and who was out of reach ; but there was this difference between Sir Hedworth and Burstall, that whereas Burstall seemed to be looking at or for *something*, Sir Hedworth seemed to be looking at or for *some one*.

"Well, that's settled," said Lady Hengrave. "You had better go next week. Tuesday would be a good day. If one is going I always think the sooner one starts, the better."

Lord Holborn at that moment advanced to take Lady Hengrave down to supper.

C. looked about for a partner whom he could take to supper. He saw no one. The few girls he knew were all of them dancing. He walked on to the landing. Lady Harriet Clive was sitting there.

"Will you come down to supper?"

"You ought to be dancing," she said, "with one of the girls, or at least take one of them to supper, and not an old woman like me."

"Please come," he said.

They went downstairs. Supper was in a long Adam dining-room. At the next table to them was his sister, Marjorie, and with her was a rather heavy-looking man about thirty.

"Who is that talking to Marjorie?" asked C.

"That," said Lady Harriet, "is Sir Harold Ducane. He is immensely rich—he owns a tar factory, or something."

C. told Lady Harriet about the revolution in his career. She saw exactly what had happened. Lady Hengrave was sending him away so that he might get over that unfortunate love affair.

"Don't forget to come to luncheon on Sunday,"

said Lady Harriet. " I have asked some people you'll like."

At that moment Sir Hedworth Lawless walked into the dining-room, leading on his arm a young, dark and beautiful lady.

" There's your Ambassador," said Lady Harriet.

" Who is it with him ? "

" That is Madame San Paolo, the wife of one of the Secretaries at the Italian Embassy."

That night at the ball Sir Harold Ducane proposed to Marjorie for the third time; she had refused him twice. This time she accepted him. She did not dare tell her mother that she had refused him a third time.

CHAPTER XXV

C. WONDERED at the calm with which he was taking the situation. The truth was, it was so bad, it was to him such a prodigious calamity that he was numbed rather than hit by it. Even if there had been no question of Beatrice, to leave Oxford just as he was beginning to enjoy it so immensely, and to go to Rome, and live day by day with an uncle and aunt who represented to him the embodiment of all that was difficult to bear in life, would have been bad enough ; and on the top of this the separation from Beatrice ! But hope was not altogether extinct in his breast. He must get Beatrice to come to Rome. If that could be managed, it would be still better than seeing her in England, because he felt that in Rome there would be more freedom and fewer obstacles.

It would be better to be in Italy with the chance of Beatrice coming there than to be in England separated from her, and he felt that if he remained in England he would be separated from her. It was, perhaps, he liked to think, a blessing in disguise. Perhaps it was Providence's way of making things easier, although it seemed at first sight as if Providence was going out of its way to make things impossible.

Early the next morning he flew round to Ovington

Square.   He poured out the news to Beatrice breathlessly.

" You must come there with your mother.   You told
me you often used to spend the winter in Italy.   Why
not come to Rome for the winter ? "

Beatrice said that everything depended on her
father.   They never knew for long beforehand what
their plans were going to be.   She saw clearly that C.
was being sent out of the country in order to remove
him from her, and very calmly and dispassionately
she analysed the situation to him.

" I think," she said, " we had better give up all
thoughts of our marriage ever being possible.   There
are too many difficulties.   There is too much to fight
against.   Your aunt is against it as well as your
mother."

" Of course, if you take that line," said C., " it will
be impossible, but if we take the line of being utterly
determined to go through with it, whatever happens,
then it will happen.   Nothing can prevent it."

" How can we do that ? " said Beatrice.   " How
can we marry on nothing at all ? "

" Not now," said C., " but in a few years' time, everything may be different.   I don't care how long I wait."

" You may be different by then," said Beatrice.

" I shall never change."

" You think so now, but everybody always thinks
that."

They went over the familiar ground and argued the
case again and again.

C. swept Beatrice away by the force and fire of his arguments. He would not hear of any final and ultimate objections. But the more forcible and plausible his arguments were, the more completely unconvinced Beatrice became.

"You see," she said, "you don't really know Father. And I don't think you understand how fundamentally your mother is opposed to it."

"Well, at any rate, promise that you will come to Rome if you possibly can," said C.

Beatrice promised.

Their *tête-à-tête* was interrupted by Mrs. Lord, who came in with trepidation and said that Mr. Lord wanted the studio, as he had a business interview of great importance. C. was obliged to go. He again went to the Eton and Harrow match.

On Saturday evening he dined with the Lords. Lady Hengrave knew of it, and made no objection. Mr. and Mrs. Lord, Beatrice and C. all went to see the new Italian actress, Maria Zechetti, who was playing the part of Marguerite in *La Dame aux Camélias*. C. had told his mother that he was going to the play, but he had not said which play, since the point had been raised at home whether Julia and Marjorie might see *La Dame aux Camélias*, as it was in Italian, and Lady Hengrave had decided that they could not do so, although they might see *La Traviata*. It had not occurred to Beatrice's father and mother to discuss the point, so Beatrice said. She had always been allowed to see the plays that her parents saw. And

it would never have occurred to Mrs. Lord to think
that there could be anything reprehensible in a play
which was acted in Italian, besides which Mrs. Lord
said Maria Zechetti was different from other actresses
and did not make up.

Beatrice did not enjoy the play. The art of Zechetti
left her, so she said, quite unmoved, although
she knew Italian thoroughly. There was to her no
glamour about the artist's personality. C., who did
not know Italian, found the beginning of the play
teasing to the verge of exasperation. He seemed to
be looking at it through a mosquito net, to be battering
at a door that was always about to open, but which
remained resolutely shut. The more natural and
realistic the acting, the more acute his irritation
became. But the Third Act, in which the interview
between Marguerite and the father occurs, interested
him in a different manner. Here the situation, the
forcible separation of the two lovers, reminded him
of his own situation, at which he found himself looking
on with interest, wondering why he was not more
moved. It should, he felt, have touched him on the
raw. And surely there was a note of genuine passion
in Zechetti's cry of "*Impossibile!*" And what could
be more tragic than those haunting eyes, those exquisitely mobile hands and that subtle interplay of look,
gesture, accent and movement? But to his own
astonishment he felt that he was experiencing no
emotion, but interest, admiration and curiosity. The
play and the acting were a looking-glass that reflected

his own actual intimate situation, and yet, to his own inexplicable surprise, he did not feel in the least moved. He experienced nothing like what he had felt when he had heard Madeleine Lapara recite, but rather as if he were looking on at an exquisite piece of clockwork. It was, he thought, the barrier of the language. He could not feel the value of the words. Mr. Lord was enraptured, and said it reminded him of *La Traviata* and of Italy, and he hummed snatches of Verdi from time to time. Mrs. Lord said she thought it a pity that Zechetti, and indeed all actresses of note, chose such sad plays. During the *entr'acte* C., as he went to fetch a programme, met Andrew Burstall. He was enjoying the play.

" Her acting," he said, " makes one feel a cad, as if one were looking through a keyhole at things one oughtn't to be seeing. And she is still better, still more wonderful, in comedy, in *La Locandiera*."

He had only been in London a day or two, and was going back to Versailles.

Next to the Lords there was an Italian lady, who said : " *Peccato che non ha voce.*"

Beatrice repeated the remark to C., who agreed that he found her voice nasal and unmusical, but he had attributed this to his not understanding the language. But Beatrice said she felt the same.

The last act, played as it was with poignant simplicity, matchless reserve, infinite subtlety, and divine economy by Zechetti, saddened Mrs. Lord still more profoundly, but C. still complained that the barrier of the language prevented real response on his part, and Beatrice denied being under any spell.*

" I admire the acting tremendously," she said. " I don't suppose any one could *act* better, but it leaves me cold, and I never forget I am looking on at acting, although it seems the most natural acting in the world."

On Sunday morning C. accompanied his mother and his two sisters to church, an orthodox church in May-fair, which was neither high nor low. After church they went for a walk in the park and C. went to have luncheon with Lady Harriet Clive, who lived in Curzon Street.

" I've got a surprise for you," said Lady Harriet.

Several guests arrived ; some elderly politicians whom C. recognised from having seen pictures of them in the newspapers, a well-known explorer who had just come back from Upper Burma, and Sir Hedworth Lawless and a pretty Italian lady, who was at the Italian Embassy. When all these had arrived the butler announced :—

" Mrs. Garrick and Miss Lord."

" That was my surprise," whispered Lady Harriet to C.

C. sat next to Beatrice at luncheon. Lady Harriet had asked Mrs. Garrick, who was an artistic lady and an intimate friend of the Lords, to bring Beatrice, and

* In a letter of C.'s which comes outside the scope of this story, he records a very different impression of Zechetti's acting, after seeing her several years later, when he understood Italian.

she had told her that it was to be a surprise. She had
heard all about C.'s coming move to Rome, and she
had resolved to give the young people a treat.

After luncheon, when the men were left alone, Sir
Hedworth talked to C. He told him about Rome.
He said he hoped he would like the life. He mustn't
expect too much at first. That was the secret of life,
to put everything at its lowest value at first, then
things often turned out better than you expected.
He would enjoy Rome, especially in the hot weather.
He himself thought it was really the best time.

C. took an instant fancy to Sir Hedworth. He
thought him most amiable, but sad-looking, and he
imagined that he could probably be alarming if he
chose.

"I shall be back in Rome myself at the end of
September, so will my wife. She's at the seaside at
this moment for her health," said Sir Hedworth.

He asked C. when he was starting, and C. surprised
him by saying the following Tuesday.

Sir Hedworth made a correct guess at the cause of
all this manipulation of plans, and he felt sorry for C.
He guessed that Beatrice was the heroine of the
romance, and he thought her a charming girl. He
knew what the attitude of Lady Hengrave would be,
and after luncheon, when every one had gone, and C.
had accepted with alacrity an invitation to take Mrs.
Garrick and Beatrice to the Zoo, Sir Hedworth
remained with Lady Harriet and asked her about C.

She told him all that she knew.

"He is to go to Rome to be cured?" said Sir Hedworth.

"Exactly."

"He will probably be cured this time, but when he catches the illness a second time, I think it will be very difficult to cure him."

"When he's older?" said Lady Harriet.

"Yes. He seems a nice boy."

"Yes, and I'm sure he's clever and original. Andrew Burstall said that the amount he has read is extraordinary, so much poetry."

"Really. I wonder where he gets his literary tastes from," said Sir Hedworth.

"Not entirely from his father and mother," said Lady Harriet. "Georgina was very well educated, but she's not exactly a literary enthusiast. Andrew Burstall thinks this boy will go far, and may some day be a very good writer."

"Not if he makes diplomacy his profession," said Sir Hedworth.

"I should have thought," said Lady Hedworth, "that in diplomacy he ought to have plenty of time to write."

"That's just it; but let's hope for his sake he won't stay in diplomacy long."

"You are all like that, whatever you are—soldiers, sailors, writers, Prime Ministers—you all rail at your own profession. I believe the only happy people are actors and photographers, and its ungrateful of you, of all men—the youngest Ambassador—to talk like that. Don't think it takes me in. I believe you would be miserable if you left the Service."

"I swear to you quite solemnly," said Sir Hedworth, " that I detest it, only, as some one said, it may be a great mistake to go into a profession, but it is a still greater mistake to leave it once you are in it."

C., after an exceedingly sad afternoon at the Zoo, dined with his family. Julia's wedding was fixed for the end of August, and Marjorie's engagement to Sir Harold Ducane was to be announced in the *Morning Post* on Monday. They were to be married quietly in September, as Sir Harold was a widower. Lady Hengrave regretted that C. would not be present at Julia's wedding, which was to take place at Bramsley, but diplomats, as she pointed out, were always liable to be sent away at a moment's notice, and at incon- venient times. She talked of C. as if he were a diplomat already.

On Monday C. had a great deal of shopping to do, and his final arrangements to make. He had planned, nevertheless, to spend most of the day with Beatrice, but on Monday morning he received a letter from her saying that her father was obliged to go to Eastbourne to see a man on business, and so as not to travel alone he had decided to take her with him. There was no escape ; she would have to go. She did not know when they would be back.

C., after a day of gloomy shopping and aimless wandering in the streets of London, called at Ovington Square at five. He was met by Mrs. Lord.

" Beatrice will be so disappointed," she said, " to
have missed you, but she and her father will not be
back till dinner, and we are all dining out and going to
a musical party in Chelsea."

C. went home and wrote Beatrice a long letter.   The
next morning he started for Rome.   At the station,
Terence, the Lords' Irish servant, brought him a pencil
note from Beatrice.   She had wanted to come herself,
but it was not possible.   Her father had pressing
letters to dictate to her.   She just had time to scribble
this note.   Perhaps it was better.   Good-byes at a
railway station were unbearable.

CHAPTER XXVI

IT was after dark and late in the night when C. arrived at Rome. It was very hot, and his first impression as he drove from the station to the *Porta Pia* was that he had come to a city that was haunted by ghostly waters. The great splashing fountains he passed seemed to welcome him to the city of so many shadows and so many ghosts. Nothing can describe the acute heartache that C. felt on arriving in Rome. Yet he was glad that it was summer, that Rome was empty. He was introduced to the Chancery and to the two secretaries the next morning by his Uncle George, who arrived early to welcome his nephew. C. felt just as he did when he first went to school. He had not seen his Uncle George for some years.

George Maitland, who was now First Secretary at the Embassy at Rome, and for the moment Chargé d'Affaires, was the younger son of a country squire who had possessions in the west of England. He was a good specimen of an honest, sensible, orthodox, sound Englishman, and a long sojourn abroad at various European and extra-European capitals had given him a slightly incongruous cosmopolitan polish that one would like to have rubbed off. He was one of those people who seem to have been born middle-aged; he

333

was rather shiny and very neat. He greeted C. kindly, and informed him that he intended to let Farr, the younger of the two remaining secretaries, go on leave as soon as C. should have got the hang of his duties.

Farr was small, quick, alert and intelligent; there was something Southern, nimble and Latin about him. The other secretary, Wakefield, was slightly the senior. He was British in appearance, rather pale, and very fair, and one felt instinctively that he was like his mother; he was most civil to C. and took obvious trouble to help him and to make things smooth for him, and yet C. felt that he was infinitely aloof and impenetrably reserved, more British than Farr, but refined, observant, critical, yet somehow different from other Englishmen.

Rome was supposed to be empty, and yet C., as he sat at his writing table and copied out a despatch he had been given to " write out," with a quill pen, on a sheet of folded grey foolscap paper, gathered, from the stray remarks that passed between the two secretaries, that some of their friends were still in that city.

" I thought Katinka was rather cross last night," said Farr.

" She always is when Mrs. Winslope is there," said Wakefield.

" They don't get on ? "

" They hate each other."

Then, after a pause :—

" Donna Maria was in great form ; so was Alice."

" Miss Morgan is still staying with her. She told me she only liked Rome in the summer."

" She says things like that ; but, as a matter of fact, she was here most of the winter."

" Charleroi is going on leave," and so on.

After C. had finished his despatch, which did not take him long, he felt he ought to be doing something else, but he did not know what to do. Every now and then his Uncle George came in from the next room and asked a question and fetched a paper. Twice during the morning strangers called—Italians—who had to be interviewed in the next room.

A dapper, businesslike little man, Mr. Hodge, walked into the Chancery once or twice to ask a question. He was the Ambassador's personal private secretary, who kept the accounts. He was not in the Diplomatic Service. He was married and seldom went on leave.

Farr and Wakefield appeared to be quite busy, and C. felt that he was in the way, and yet doing nothing.

Wakefield every now and then gave him a little bit of information as to where things were kept and what had to be done with certain papers.

" Are you dining with the Belinskys to-night ? " said Farr.

" No, with Bessie."

" Mrs. Tremayn is going to Naples to-morrow."

After a time another short despatch was found for C. to write out. When he had finished it, Wakefield said to him :—

" You had better not blot your despatches when you write them out.   Let the ink dry, because if they have to go to the Queen she says she can't read them if the ink is *faint*."

A little later the military attaché, Colonel Hogarth, strolled into the Chancery and smoked a cigarette and exchanged a little gossip and news with the two secretaries.   C. was introduced to him, and Colonel Hogarth at once asked him to dinner on the following evening.

At one o'clock Maitland came into the room and said to C., " I'm going to take you to lunch."

Out of doors the sunlight was dazzling, but the heat not unpleasant.

C. said something about it.

" They always exaggerate those things in England," said Uncle George.   " July's the pleasantest month in Rome.   It's only just beginning to be warm."

The Maitlands lived in an apartment in the *Via Tritone*.   C. had not seen his Aunt Emma since he had been at Eton.   She was not, he found, greatly changed.   She was younger than Lady Hengrave and more talkative, very decided in her opinions, and very sure of herself ; rather good-looking and slightly peevish.

" I flatter myself " was a phrase which often crossed her lips.   She did.

She was affable to C., and said she was sure he would like Rome.

" One gets very fond of it," she said, " and I always

say that the summer is the nicest time, when the
Romans are away. Not that *that* makes any difference, as they never ask one to anything, but one has
to go to their days. In the winter everything is such
a rush, and then George likes to go on leave in the
autumn for the shooting. It's a pity there's no more
real shooting at Bramsley. But we hardly get any
leave now. George is owed about six months' leave
as it is. They are so unreasonable at the F.O."

She asked after the family and talked a great deal
about the engagement of his sisters.

"We shan't be able to go to the wedding, but that's
the worst of diplomacy. It entirely destroys all one's
family ties."

She asked a great many questions, but she paid
small heed to the answers.

"I'm sorry we can't ask you to dinner to-night,
we're dining out, but I daresay the young men will
look after you."

C. assented, but he knew, and he was relieved to
think, they were both dining out.

When luncheon was over and they had had one
smoke in the cool, dark *salone*, which was plentifully
embellished with large signed photographs of English
and foreign royalties, Maitland told C. that he had
better go back to the Chancery, as it was his first day.
As a rule, it was not necessary for more than one of
the staff to be there in the afternoon; he himself
would be coming later.

"There's been rather a lull to-day," he said. "Last

week we did not know where to turn. You'll find Embassy life isn't all milk and roses. But you've just happened to arrive on an off day."

C. went back to the Chancery and found Wakefield there by himself, studying the *Tribuna*.

" There's no reason why you should stay," he said. " There's nothing going on. If you look in about five o'clock, that will do. There may be a telegram then."

C. took advantage of the permission and called a cab and drove to St. Peter's. He wanted to lose no time in seeing the major sights of Rome.

The city was deserted. Everybody was taking their siesta. C. enjoyed the baking heat, and when he got to St. Peter's and walked up the steps and pushed the heavy leather curtain he was glad suddenly to find himself in the immense cool world of that church.

A woman was kneeling in front of one of the side altars. He thought he would walk up to that altar, which, at first, seemed to be a few paces off, but when he came to do it he found he had to walk some way, and he then, and thus, gradually, realised the immense size of the place. It was, he thought, a satisfactory monument. He did not stay there long, but drove to the Colosseum, and from there to the Protestant cemetery, where Shelley and Keats are buried. He picked a blade of grass from Shelley's grave to send to Beatrice, and then he drove back to the Chancery. There he found Wakefield and Farr having tea, and the same conversation that had been going on in the morning seemed to be continuing.

Presently his uncle returned, and, after opening some letters in his room, burst into the Chancery, and said that they would all have to go to a Requiem which was being held the next morning at the Greek Church for a member of one of the Balkan royal families who had died a few days previously.

A little later a telegram was despatched to the Foreign Office, and C. was taught how to take down the figures of the cypher. After that nothing happened, and C. wrote a long letter to Beatrice, describing his journey and his first day. Farr and Wakefield said they were sorry they were both dining out, and advised C. where to dine. He did not, however, take the advice of either of them—which was contradictory. He dined at a small restaurant in the *Porta Pia*, where there were little tables out of doors, and he went to bed early, and so his first day at Rome came to an end. It was the same as many days that followed.

The staff were to go to the Greek Church in uniform, and C. had, before leaving for Rome, made it an excuse for delay that he would not be able to get a uniform made in time, and he had been told that a uniform was essential by the Ambassador himself. But this difficulty had been got over in a curious way. Lady Hengrave had discussed the point with Bodmin, and he knew of a young man who was just back from Paris, where he had been Honorary Attaché, but who had left diplomacy for good, and was going to plant tea in Ceylon, and would be willing to let C. have his uniform for a trifling sum. The boys were about the same height, and C. had been reluctantly compelled to admit when the uniform arrived that it fitted perfectly.

So C., dressed in his blue uniform (with sword), went to the Greek Church, where he met the whole of the *Corps Diplomatique*. Most of the Ambassadors were on leave, but he was introduced to the various Chargés d'Affaires, and his uncle told him that he must be sure to lose no time in leaving cards on all of them. The service lasted over an hour, and everybody stood up the whole time, bearing wax tapers.

The next day the whole staff had to go to the railway station at half-past six in the morning in top hats and frock coats to meet an Indian potentate who was arriving at Rome, and two days later the staff attended a Requiem Mass which was sung at one of the smaller churches for an English lady who had long been a resident at Rome.

This was the first time that C. had ever attended a service in a Catholic church. He could not follow what was happening, and when it was over and he was driving back to the Embassy with his uncle, the latter said :

" Did you notice the faces of the people, all of them either fools or fanatics ? "

C., thinking of Beatrice, was annoyed. He dined with his uncle, where he met diplomats several times ; he dined with Wakefield, who had a large apartment, and with Farr, who was married to an American and who had a small apartment ; and with Colonel

Hogarth and his wife, who had a middle-sized apartment. At Wakefield's he met the Swedish Minister's
wife, who was an American and very amiable, and at
Farr's he met a Polish lady and another American, and
at the Hogarths' he met still another American lady,
who entertained a great deal at Rome, and the
Russian Naval Attaché. And then he dined with
them all again and met the same people over again.
During his first three weeks he did not meet a single
Italian. They were, so his uncle said, all of them
away.

He soon got to know his fellow secretaries very well,
up to a point, but he found intimacy was impossible
with either of them. They were both of them completely different from any one he had known at Eton
or at Oxford. Each of them was intelligent and
competent, quick at his work and efficient in business
matters; both of them easy, affable and good-natured;
but Farr was engrossed in his family life, newly
married, and very much in love with his wife, who was
young and pretty; and Wakefield did not seem to wish
to know any one well, although he had, so C. heard,
many friends among the Italians, and the *Corps
Diplomatique*. He seemed to be cultivated and well
read, but he did not take any interest in the things
that interested C., and literature, as C. understood it,
was a closed book to him. There appeared to C. to
be very little work to do in the Chancery, not more
than two people could easily manage, and yet it was
necessary to be there nearly all day. His uncle kept

on talking of the great rush of work there had been, and there would be, but the actual present seemed to be full of leisure. At his uncle's house he met several of the foreign diplomats, the French, the Russians, and the Germans. After he had been three weeks at Rome, with the exception of the Forum and the Palatine, he had seen little more of the sights than on the first day he arrived, and he had not made the acquaintance of an Italian, with the exception of the Chancery servants and an old gentleman, Signor Barbi, who came every morning to give him an Italian lesson before the work in the Chancery began. Signor Barbi was a cultivated man with a military appearance, who had fought for Garibaldi ; he had a passion for Dante, for Lord Palmerston, and Mr. Gladstone. C. wrote to Beatrice every day, and every day he heard from her. At the end of August the Lords had gone to Ireland to stay with some cousins. Mr. Lord was writing a book which was to reveal to the world some remarkable new theory and revolutionise the art of pottery. So far no winter plans had been mentioned.

His mother sent him a brief account of Julia's wedding, supplemented with many cuttings from the provincial Press.

August and September passed without anything of interest happening to C. He made no new friends and met no old ones. His life was spent between sitting in the Chancery, where, when he was not working, he wrote long letters to Beatrice, and rambling, when it was cool enough, in Rome and the Campagna. At the end of September the Ambassador came back with his daughter, Cicely, the only child of his first wife. She was fifteen, and not yet out, and the Chancery saw little of her. The staff used to have luncheon with him every day. Farr went on leave as soon as C. was considered to have mastered the rudiments of Chancery work, that is to say, a fortnight after his arrival.

At the same time as the Ambassador a second Secretary returned to his post, by name Agnew, and George Maitland and his wife went on leave, to C.'s immense relief.

A new *régime* began for C. In the first place the Ambassador asked one of the staff to luncheon every day, but Wakefield nearly always lunched at home at his apartment. Lady Lawless was still in England and was expected later.

As soon as the Ambassador arrived C. made the acquaintance of one or two Italians, and met two old acquaintances, Madame Orioli, who lived in a villa on the Janiculum, and Lady Ralph Dallington, who came back to Rome at the beginning of October.

The Maitlands went to stay at Bramsley, and George Maitland gave a good account of C. to Lady Hengrave, but he mentioned, incidentally, that it was a pity C. wasted so much time writing interminable letters, and he presumed the boy must be in love with some one in England.

Lady Hengrave at once took action. She wrote a long letter to Mrs. Lord, in which she pointed out that as they were both agreed as to the impossibility of a marriage between Beatrice Lord and C., would it not be better to clear up the situation ? She had reason to believe that her son was writing to Mrs. Lord's daughter every day and that the children considered themselves to be definitely engaged. It was interfering with her son's work and would damage his prospects in diplomacy. Had the time not come to put things on a better footing ? Would it not be better if they were to stop writing, etc., etc. ?

Mrs. Lord was upset by the letter, and did not know quite what to do. She at first did nothing and left the letter lying about, and her husband happened to read it. He made a scene, said that he had been kept in the dark, and that the whole thing was preposterous and out of the question, and he told Beatrice that she must write to C. and tell him that he must give up all thoughts of an engagement, and that their daily correspondence must cease immediately. What especially annoyed Mr. Lord was a phrase in Lady Hengrave's letter which alluded to Lord Hengrave's repugnance for Roman Catholics. Mr. Lord told his wife that he wished it made clear to Lady Hengrave that his repugnance for Protestants was equally strong. But Mrs. Lord did not allude to the religious question in her answer. She wrote back a vague but conciliatory letter, and she assured Lady Hengrave that all would be for the best. Beatrice wrote and told C. what had occurred. She said she was willing to wait, but she felt quite certain that the marriage would never be allowed, that the obstacles were too great, and that he had much better put all thoughts of it out of his mind. She had promised no longer to write to him. She asked him not to write any more.

C.'s first thought was to take a ticket for London and start that night. But just as he was thinking this over the Ambassador walked into the Chancery and said to him, " I want you to dine with us to-night ; we shall be alone."

Lady Lawless had arrived the evening before.

C. felt that he was caught in a machine from which there was no escape ; he experienced the physical pain of unhappiness.

CHAPTER XXVII

THIS crisis inaugurated a new epoch in C.'s life. All the dream of the Lords spending the winter in Rome which he had been living on during the last two months, and which he had discussed so often at so great a length with Beatrice, had come to an end. He felt like a man imprisoned in a living grave. He was indifferent to the official routine, but he detested the social life of the place, and Rome itself, with all its glorious associations and all its present beauty and living interest, seemed to him nothing more than a mouldering churchyard full of chilly ghosts. It was to him a prison and a charnel-house.

And yet he was not at first so utterly miserable as might have been expected. He was miserable, but he was not desperate. He secretly harboured for the moment an invincible optimism that made him think that all would come right in the end. The very fact that his life at Rome was distasteful to him, his loathing for diplomatic life, foreign life, Rome and everything to do with it, made things curiously easier. The big catastrophe seemed to be part and parcel of the minor daily nightmare, and consequently easier to bear. The two would come to an end together—so thought C. He seemed to be experiencing a transient phase in a dream. One day the curtain would go up ; his diplomatic career would be over, and he would find himself once more face to face with Beatrice in the world of reality. Neither had he given up hope of the Lords coming to Rome, or to Italy, in the winter, and if they were to come C. felt quite certain he would manage to see Beatrice.

Lady Lawless arrived at the beginning of October. She had been a beauty in her day, and she was still extremely handsome. She was vivacious, full of fun, and fond of flirting with the young ; but C. was in no mood for flirtations, and Lady Lawless found him silent and unresponsive. She knew, though, what was happening, for Sir Hedworth had outlined the situation to her, and they both saw that some crisis must have occurred ; so she pitied C., for she had a romantic mind. She tried to distract him by introducing him to various people whom she imagined he would find congenial, and by inviting him to entertainments. Rome began to fill up. English residents returned, and American, English and tourists of all nations began to dribble through. Sometimes people would stay at the Embassy ; and Lady Lawless would employ C. in showing her guests the sights of the place. She thought it was good for him.

C. was thrown back upon himself. By the end of September he could understand Italian well and talk it fluently. He was reading Dante with Signor Barbi, who was the first foreign teacher that C. had met with who looked upon literature from the same

point of view as he did himself and who felt towards it
in the same way. C. was able to translate passages of
the English poets with Signor Barbi into Italian, and
his Italian master never complained of a *manque de
goût* in the masterpieces of Shelley and Keats. C.
began to write himself again for the first time since
he had left Oxford—impersonal descriptive impressions suggested by Rome; and he showed some
of them to Signor Barbi, as well as what he had
written before. Signor Barbi said they were the first
steps towards the work of a poet. "*I primi gradini.*"
He encouraged him and urged him to continue.

Signor Barbi understood C. He understood him
through and through, with all his southern intuition.
He understood him as a man and he understood him
as a writer, or as a would-be embryo writer.

One day they were reading Dante. They had
finished the *Inferno*, and they had just got to the
Purgatorio; they came to the line:—

Dolce color d'oriental zaffiro,

and as C. came to the line he gasped and stopped,
overcome by the beauty of the words.

Signor Barbi's eyes filled with tears, and he
murmured "*Stupendo*," and then he cried, cried not
only at the beauty of the magnificent poetry, but
having met with response to it in the heart of an
alien, an English boy who had only just learnt
Italian, but who he saw belonged to the mysterious
freemasonry which exists all the world over between

those who love good verse and who possibly may write it.

C., too, was moved, moved beyond all words and beyond all expression ; the words not only opened for him the doors of fairyland, but in so doing they touched a thousand strings within him, and all the vibrations of all those thousand strings made one chord, which was Beatrice.

The very same night that he had read the first canto of the *Purgatorio* with Signor Barbi he dined with the Ambassador. There were about a dozen guests, a well-known Italian beauty, Donna Laura Bartolini, and an Englishman who was passing through Rome, a Mr. Dallas Wace, middle-aged, good-looking, prosperous, independent, unmarried, cultivated, a man of the world. C., although he had never seen him before, recognised by the tone of his voice, and by everything he said and did, that he was a man whom his family would accept without question, and yet there was a curious difference between him and the *habitués* of Hengrave House. Dallas Wace was not only cultivated, but " modern."

There was nothing he couldn't talk about, nothing he didn't seem to know. And yet he seemed to skate over everything as if, after all, nothing was very important. The only thing that mattered was not to be a bore, not to dwell too long on anything. He was agreeable to everybody, young and old. At dinner he sat next to Donna Laura Bartolini and talked to her in unaffected, effortless French ; on his other side was the Consul's wife, Mrs. Maclure, who came from one of the English county families and considered that she had married beneath her in accepting for husband a delightful ex-sailor who had drifted into the Consular Service. Dallas Wace smoothed her *amour propre* and fanned her sense of self-importance ; and after dinner, when the men went into a smoking-room, according to the Italian custom, he devoted himself for a time to C. ; he talked of Rome, the sights, the Italians, the foreigners, the theatres.

" Zechetti's acting—charming, charming, especially in comedy ; she hasn't the presence or the voice for drama, but she's clever—very clever."

" Madeleine Lapara ? Oh yes, of course, she's no longer what she was once—I remember her years ago in *Hernani ;* she overdoes her effect ; she rants sometimes ; it comes from playing to ignorant audiences, and in second-rate companies ; she ought never to have left the *Théâtre Français*, but, of course, she's got immense talent, and she's clever, *very* clever."

C. felt a faint echo of Hengrave House conversation here, but with a difference ; Wace's field of action was a larger one, his criterion was on another plane, more acute, more sensitive, and more modern.

Wace dismissed the subject of acting and touched lightly on opera. " Have you heard Giraldi ? She *is* a great artist, finer as an actress than Zechetti. Yes, a singer. Her *Traviata* and her *Manon* are really fine. Yes, you ought to hear her. She sings in the *Cavalleria*."

" I think that's a lovely opera," said C., who had just heard it for the first time.

" It's dramatic and effective," said Wace. " The book's good ; the music "—he shrugged his shoulders —" the *intermezzo* is pretty, but as to the rest, one has heard it all before."

Professor Fani, the archæologist who had just discovered some pre-Romulus remains in the Forum, joined in the conversation, and so did Agoura, who was Secretary at the Russian Embassy, and who spoke six languages quite perfectly.

Professor Fani deplored the influence of Wagner. He was ruining modern opera. Wace and Agoura had both been to Bayreuth last year.

" They make a great fuss about the scenery," said Wace, " but the truth of the matter is that it's very ugly indeed, heavy and German, all beer and sausage ; the way *Parsifal* is staged, for instance, is hideous."

" But after all, the music's German," said Horace Clive, a well-known musician and a passionate Wagnerite.

" Oh, the music's charming, of course," said Wace, " but that's no reason why they should stage the things so badly—those dresses, those crude colours— the design of Kundry's garden, which is like the picture on a *décadent* fan."

" But Wagner *was* a German," said Clive, angrily.

" The music's charming," repeated Wace, smoothing him down, " *Parsifal's* charming."

"I think one gets sick to death of all those motives if one hears enough of them," said Agoura.

"It's a mistake to stop for more than one cycle," said Wace.

"If you're not musical——" said Clive.

Wace deftly changed the subject, and talked to Fani about the recent excavations ; their conversation expanded, and, finally, included the world of art and literature. He quoted Renan, and in the course of the long, crowded talk Carducci, Stendhal, Turgenev and Huysmans were mentioned.

The groups of talkers were slightly reshuffled. Wace felt as if he had disposed of art and music, and turned to the Ambassador, who was discussing the prospects of the Cesarewitch with Maclure. Wace said he was sorry to miss Newmarket this year, but he was looking forward to his big game shooting. He was on his way to East Africa.

They went into the next room, and Wace went straight up to Lady Lawless and said an appreciative, appropriate and accurate word about an Old English musical clock which she had recently picked up. Mrs. Castleton-Wyse (an American) joined in the conversation, and discussed the authenticity of a Giorgione in a private collection. Wace lightly led the conversation away from the pitfalls of art criticism, which bored him, to actualities and gossip, international society, and prevented any one dwelling too long on any one item or person.

C. left the dinner party that night with a subtle

sense of blight, as if everything that Wace had touched had withered, and yet how friendly Wace had been, how good it was of him to pay him so much attention.

But, although C. felt a little depressed he was full of wonder and awe, and marvelled at the variety and range of Wace's culture and knowledge. There was nothing he hadn't seemed to know, and yet there was obviously no effort, and no pretence about him. He had talked just as easily to Mrs. Maclure as to Donna Laura, and had dealt with English county life just as lightly as with European politics and society. C. had gone away dazed, and yet at the bottom of it there was a distinct sense of devastation.

All that he thought was most beautiful and wonderful in the world, under Wace's universal appreciative touch seemed to have been turned to dust and ashes.

The inner life of the Embassy, the Chancery life, seemed to C. peculiarly curious. In a way, he was extremely intimate with Wakefield and Farr; he shared their interests, their jokes; he was at his ease with both of them. He liked them both immensely, and yet they were at the same time worlds away. Wakefield interested him the most—Wakefield, with his quiet manner, his barrier of unbreakable reserve. He was a Catholic, and C. (thinking of Beatrice) would have liked to discuss the question with him, and hear what Wakefield really thought about it all; but whenever C. got near the fringe of the topic, Wakefield gently eluded him. All he heard him say on the subject was that it was very tiresome to have to eat fish on Fridays, although easier in Italy than in England.

He discussed the question with Signor Barbi, but Signor Barbi had no patience with Catholics. He said that Wakefield had a countenance *da prete ;* that in Italy nobody went to church except women, and that one day the Pope would be sent to Malta, and that that would settle the question once and for all. Or else if there could only be a liberal Pope, who would order his carriage and drive straight to the Quirinal, then we should see a united Italy, such as there had never been before ; but, of course, he added, the Jesuits would never allow such a thing to happen. C. repeated this conversation to Farr, not to Wakefield, and Farr, who was a Protestant, said he thought that Signor Barbi was talking nonsense.

Every now and then stray Englishmen would arrive at Rome ; people who brought the bag instead of the King's Messenger, or friends of the Ambassador, who stayed at the Embassy. Sometimes they would ask C. to dine with them. Just before Christmas one of his Oxford friends, Blades, brought out the bag, and C. spent an evening with him. They sat in C.'s sitting-room in the Embassy and discussed books and poetry. When C. had been at Oxford, Blades had thought it wrong to read modern poetry, but since C. had gone down Blades had apparently broken this rule, for he talked of modern as well as of ancient literature. He told C. he had heard of his having written at Eton and at Oxford, and he asked him to show him something.

C. turned the tables and asked him if he had written anything. Blades said that he and another undergraduate intended to edit a magazine next term at Oxford. It was to be called the *Oxford Rambler* and was to be literary and serious. Blades said he had written some verse for it.

" I should like you to send us something," he said, " only I warn you that our standard is a high one."

" I expect your poetry's awfully good," said C.

" Yes, it is," said Blades.

That night, when he went home to his hotel, he took with him a large envelope containing some of C.'s typewritten poems. He brought them back the next day and said he was afraid that they were not very good, and that there was nothing which would do for the *Oxford Rambler*. " I should stick," he said, " to prose. You see, verse is so difficult, and bad verse is, as Horace says, ' impossible.' "

" Yes," said C., " quite impossible."

C. thought that Blades was no doubt right and he burnt most of the poems he had written. He felt quite disinclined to write verse, and, after all, what did it matter ?

VOLUME II

CHAPTER XXVIII

Up till Christmas, C. was convinced that the Lord family would somehow or other, by some miracle, arrive in Italy; and that he would be able to see Beatrice. This was quite unreasonable on his part, but he was buoyed up by a causeless optimism, nor did he take the story of Mr. Lord's opposition seriously. He did not take Mr. Lord seriously; he felt that all opposition from that quarter could be dealt with quite easily. But one day, just about Christmas-time, he happened to be calling on some one at the Grand Hotel, and as he sat waiting in the hall, he cast a listless eye on the *New York Herald*. The first thing that caught his attention was a paragraph in the social news, which announced that Mr. and Mrs. Lord and Miss Beatrice Lord had arrived at the Mina Hotel, at Helouan, near Cairo, and were expected to spend the winter in Egypt.

This little paragraph hit C. as though it had been a poisoned arrow. He passed from a mood of unreasoned optimism and baseless hope to one of reasoned pessimism and solid gloom. He felt that Beatrice had been taken away from him, that in some odd way he had been cheated by Providence. He retired more than ever into himself. At the same time he was determined that no one in his entourage should notice

359

anything.   He accepted invitations ; he spent a great
deal of time at the house of an American lady who
entertained largely ; he did his duty by his colleagues ;
and the Ambassador said he might make a good
diplomat.   The only moments which he enjoyed were
those which he spent studying Italian with Signor
Barbi.

Towards the end of February he caught a chill.
He neglected it and it developed into pneumonia.
He was laid up during the whole of the month of
March, and at one moment he was seriously ill.   Lady
Lawless found him an English nurse, and his Aunt
Emma, who had returned to Rome soon after Christmas, sent Lady Hengrave daily bulletins, but she was
firmly of the opinion, which was corroborated by the
doctor, that it was not necessary for Lady Hengrave
to come to Rome.   By the end of April, C. was up and
convalescent.

He returned to life a different man.   He seemed to
have shed a portion of his self.   He felt indifferent to
everything and everybody, and he looked at the
world with a calm, detached curiosity.   The doctor
said he wanted change of air, and that Rome was bad
for him.   He must on no account stay there during
the summer.   The Ambassador was suffering from
asthma, and had been ordered to go to *Mont Dore*,
a place which he detested, and which bored both him
and Lady Lawless to tears.   They suggested taking C.
with them.   The Ambassador was to stay there a
month.   C. accepted.   He did not in the least care

where he went nor what he did, and he wondered at his own indifference.

Sir Hedworth, Lady Lawless and C. arrived at *Mont Dore* in the middle of May, and they stayed there for a month in a little house that Sir Hedworth had hired. Sir Hedworth was taken up with his cure, and Lady Lawless became engrossed in a bantering, only half-serious, flirtation with a French man of letters whom she had never seen before. C., who had a room to himself, spent most of his time pretending to work. In the afternoons the whole party would sometimes go for expeditions all together, and in the evenings Sir Hedworth played patience, while Lady Lawless used to read out novels, sometimes French and sometimes English, with plenty of spirit and sentiment.

They made acquaintances among the visitors ; there were several well-known singers taking the cure. Madame Bellini (*née* Wilson), who at tea-time received guests standing on a dais in her best Balmoral manner ; several well-known preachers, among others Father Walter Hissop, a High-Church clergyman who preached eloquently on the reconciliation between science and religion, and a few French actors and actresses. C. took little notice of the life which went on around him. He spent the whole morning poring over books which he was not in reality reading, or in reading French novels, because they were, as Lady Lawless said, " good for his French," and in the afternoons he would go for long solitary walks, unless Sir Hedworth and Lady Lawless took him out for an expedition.

Lady Lawless liked C. She thought him remarkably intelligent and possibly full of promise, but she slightly alarmed him, and in her presence he would become more than usually silent ; nor did he ever approach anything bordering on intimacy with her, although he liked and appreciated her.

Both she and Sir Hedworth were kindness itself to C. They thought his depression, which was now obvious, was the result of his illness, and they did their best to distract him. C. tried to play up to their efforts, but nothing could pierce the wall of his listless indifference. He was like a numbed person suffering from permanent and deep-seated frostbite of the heart.

Towards the middle of June he went home to London. Lady Hengrave found him greatly altered. He looked older, and she said he had improved. He found his father was laid up. C. refused to go to any entertainments in London this year. He said the doctor had told him he ought not to sit up late, at present. He called at Ovington Square as soon as he arrived in London, and he learnt that the Lords were at Oxford. He called on Mrs. Roden, hoping for news. Mrs. Roden was embarrassed, and C. felt there was some new factor that was being kept from him. Towards the end of June his father got worse ; he took to his bed, and never got up, and finally died after a short and peaceful illness.

The family went down to Bramsley for the funeral. C. felt more numbed than ever in the presence of death, and the arrangements and attendant circumstances of the funeral left him with a feeling of unutterable emptiness. The non-naturalness of all concerned, with the exception of Lady Hengrave, who was sensible and dignified, was appalling. All the family were gathered at Bramsley. There were Edward and his American wife, who now made it excruciatingly clear to Lady Hengrave that she was Lady Hengrave and that Lady Hengrave was a dowager. There were Uncle George and Aunt Emma, who were so used to going into temporary mourning for foreign royalties and diplomats that they assumed a possessive air about mourning and death in general. There were Uncle Cuthbert and Aunt Fanny, who made it clear that they thought it permissible to tolerate the mythology of their epoch. There was Aunt Louisa, now a widow, who was the most human and natural of the mourners with the exception of Mr. and Mrs. Roden. Harry came from York, where he was now stationed. He had passed from Sandhurst into the Rifle Brigade. He tried hard to look solemn, but his cheerfulness would leak out. C.'s two married sisters were present, Lady Holborn and Lady Ducane. C. found both his new brothers-in-law slightly trying. Lord Holborn was amiable, but almost half-witted, and Harold Ducane was aggressively friendly, but could not help striking an undefinable wrong note, whatever he did or said.

Lord Hengrave was to be buried in the village church. The Bishop of Barminster was to read the service. A great many wreaths arrived. Lady Hengrave spent the time answering telegrams of condolence. She was quite calm, and faced the change of circumstances with dignity, and with a complete mastery of the situation which made her daughter-in-law, the new Lady Hengrave, appear indescribably wrong and out of place. Lord Hengrave had left his affairs in considerable disorder. Edward said he would probably have to sell Bramsley, and very likely Hengrave House as well, but the new Lady Hengrave, while she had made up her mind to permit the former, if necessary, had resolved to retain the London house, whatever might happen. Lady Hengrave had been left badly off, and C. had been left two hundred a year, and Harry three hundred, to enable him to live in the army. C. had the Rodens to look after him. The girls were provided for, so they had been left nothing.

The day of the funeral was very beautiful. All the neighbours and the Lord Lieutenant of the County attended. The choir sang " Now the labourer's task is o'er," and the Bishop of Barminster read out the fifteenth chapter of the First Epistle to the Corinthians. C. was standing next to Harry in the high pew, with his two sisters. In the pew in front of him were his mother, Mrs. Roden, and his eldest brother, Edward, and the new Lady Hengrave. In the pew behind him were his brothers-in-law and the other uncles and aunts.

As the bishop, with his sonorous, well-trained elocution, read the tremendous words : " For this corruptible must put on incorruption, and this mortal must put on immortality," C. felt more than he had ever felt before, that such thoughts and such words were the children of fond human hopes and desires. The words of Swinburne came back to him :—

> From too much love of living,
>   From hope and fear set free,
> We thank with brief thanksgiving,
>   Whatever gods may be
> That no life lives for ever ;
> That dead men rise up never ;

He had not yet read Catullus, and did not yet know the terser, more terrible statement of the Roman poet :—

> Nobis, quum semel occidit brevis lux,
> Nox est perpetua una dormienda.

But another line of Swinburne's echoed in his head :—

> Only the sleep eternal
> In an eternal night.

" So when this corruptible shall have put on incorruption, and this mortal shall have put on immortality, then shall be brought to pass the saying that is written, Death is swallowed up in victory. O death, where is thy sting ? O grave, where is thy victory ? "

As the bishop read these words, C. looked round the church. What did these words mean to those that were present ? What were they thinking of ? Were they giving a thought to the immortal soul of the departed ? Did they really believe there was an immortal soul appended or belonging in any way to the mortal remains now enclosed in that massive shiny coffin, which, with such difficulty, had been carried up the aisle by the faithful tenantry ? Did they believe that this particular mortal had put on immortality ? And as C. looked round the church he seemed to breathe an icy breath from a bleak, desolate country, and to be alone in a world dispeopled of gods ; and all that was going on, all the circumstance of the present ceremonial, seemed to him to be the most hollow and meaningless of mockeries.

The coffin was carried to the churchyard ; the villagers and the tenants, and the casual visitors, all strained for a last look at it. "Earth to earth, ashes to ashes, dust to dust." It was over, and C. felt that more than a chapter—the first volume—of his life had come to an end.

The following day the family began to disperse. Lady Hengrave, who had behaved with incomparable dignity towards her tactless daughter-in-law, went to stay with her eldest daughter, who lived in Suffolk. The Rodens went back to the country and invited C. to go with them. The Maitlands went back to Rome. They were taking their regular leave later. The remaining uncles and aunts went back to London. Harry rejoined his regiment, and Edward and the new Lady Hengrave were left in possession. The family lawyer, Mr. Grayshott, was to come down and discuss what was to be sold.

The night before C. left Bramsley, the footman who had been looking after him brought him a small piece of paper, on which some figures and items in pencil had been noted, the whole amounting to thirteen and sixpence. C. looked at it without understanding, and asked what it was.

" Your washing bill, sir."

C. felt that if he had to pay his washing bill in his own home he was indeed a stranger and a guest— it was indeed true that he no longer had a home. Bramsley or Hengrave House at the best of times had been a chilly home for him—a home, nevertheless, round which a thousand associations were entwined. Now he felt even this had been taken away.

He said :—

" All right, I'll pay it to-morrow."

As he went to bed he pored over the little washing bill. " Three shirts, three collars, four pairs of socks," etc., etc., and he laughed till he cried, but not in the sense that the phrase usually implies. That is to say, there was no mirth in his laughter and no happiness in his tears.

The next day he went up to London.

The programme for his future, as outlined by Lady Hengrave, was as follows : He was to go up for the first examination that occurred either for the Foreign Office or for the Diplomatic Service. Candidates, besides having to be nominated, were expected to be in possession of an income of four hundred a year. Mrs. Roden promised to supply the extra two hundred which would be necessary for C.

C., in the meantime, woke up to reality from the cold dream in which he had been living, when his future was discussed before him as a matter of course, and he made up his mind at that moment that no force on earth would compel him to enter the Diplomatic Service. He was thankful that he had been allowed to have a taste of it. He did not want to appear ungrateful to the Rodens, and he was determined, if it came to a battle with his mother, to choose his own ground and his own time for the action. His mother had asked him to go and see Mr. Spark, the crammer, on his way to the Rodens, and to consult him as to his programme of work, and as to what he should do before his term began in mid-September. C., who had heard a great deal about Mr. Spark from friends and people in Rome, determined to reveal his real feelings to him. He had made an appointment with Mr. Spark, and he went up to London.

Mr. Spark received him in his rooms at Gower Street, at twelve-thirty. He had prepared candidates for the Foreign Office and Diplomatic Service Examinations for years, and he had a power of diagnosis as to whether the candidate would be successful or no, as acute as that of an inspired doctor.

Mr. Spark received C. genially. He had heard of him from his old friend, Hedworth Lawless; he knew his Uncle George. He said a few appropriate words of condolence and asked feelingly after Lady Hengrave. Then he plunged into business.

" So you're coming to me in September. How's your German ? "

" Well," said C., " they want me to, but the truth is I hate diplomacy. They told me when I went to

Rome it would be a good thing, as I should be able to see whether I liked the life or not. I did see. I know I *hate* it. Of course, I know I've got to do something, but I don't see why I should go into diplomacy as a way of making a living—it's so expensive. It's a luxury. I've got two hundred a year of my own, and my aunt, who is my godmother, Mrs. Roden, gives me two hundred a year, and says she will go on giving it me as long as I am working, and when I get in."

"Have you spoken to your mother and to your aunt about this ?"

"No, not yet. I thought I had better see you before doing that. In the first place, I should never pass. I know French pretty well, German not nearly well enough, although I learnt it as a child ; some Italian, but none of the other subjects except Latin. I'm bad at geography and all that. I should have to live a long time abroad in Germany again. I hate living abroad, and, you see, Mr. Spark, I don't want to pass."

Mr. Spark nodded his head.

"What would you like to do ?"

"I should like to stop on at Oxford," said C., "only that's too late now. The Master wanted me to stop, and thought it a pity I should go down so soon. He wanted me to read for Honours ; but now I should like to read for the Bar," C. said, with some slight hesitation.

"Are you quite sure you would hate diplomacy ?" said Mr. Spark.

"Quite, quite sure."

" And what about the Foreign Office ? "

" I think that's almost worse."

" Did you ever discuss this with Sir Hedworth ? "

" Yes, a little ; he wasn't particularly encouraging. He doesn't seem to think it great fun being an Ambassador, and he's supposed to be the youngest and the most successful of all of them, and if they feel like that when they're successful——"

" You might change your mind later. You haven't been well. The climate at Rome is very trying. Diplomacy gives you an opportunity of seeing interesting men and interesting places under the best conditions, especially at first. You could leave it later if you didn't like it."

" Then it would be too late to do anything else. I think it is best to settle now."

" Do you think you have any aptitude for the Bar ? "

" I don't know ; I should like to try."

" Well, well," said Mr. Spark, " what do you want me to do ? "

" I want you to write to my mother and tell her it's no good my cramming, as I never shall pass. I don't mind what you say, as long as you make her understand that it's no use my going up. She will believe *you ;* she wouldn't believe me."

" But won't your aunt be annoyed ? " said Mr. Spark, thinking of the extra two hundred a year.

" No, she will understand perfectly. She has always been very good to me."

" You won't give it a trial ? "

" You see, I have given the thing itself a trial ; I know now what diplomatic life is like, and I know I would rather do anything else in the world. I would rather enlist."

Mr. Spark understood perfectly. He saw that argument would be quite useless, and that as C. felt like that about it, he would certainly never pass the examination. He didn't believe C. really cared about the Bar. He was certain he would never make a lawyer. He suspected literary aspirations, but he said nothing about that. He promised to write to Lady Hengrave, and at one o'clock he carried off C. to his Club in Whitehall and entertained him to luncheon. Two of his pupils were guests as well. Mr. Spark talked lightly on the topics of the day ; the theatres, Zechetti, Madeleine Lapara, the new books, the picture galleries, the political situation, the drawbacks of foreign travel, the obstinacy of Custom House officials ; and all the time, although he was far from appearing to do so, he was watching C. and sizing him up.

C., in his enthusiasm for Lapara, and in certain remarks on French poetry, had betrayed his tastes. Mr. Spark saw his frame of mind quite clearly.

" He could pass if he worked, but he never would work." That was his verdict. " He's not a diplomat and never will be, nor would he make a good Government servant. As for the Bar, he will never be called. However, he can try. The boy has literary ambitions and has certainly the makings of a man of letters, but he is too shy to talk about his aspirations." Mr. Spark thought of Lady Hengrave and understood. He thought also that careful treatment was necessary, for if C. were to be openly crossed at this moment, Mr. Spark felt he would be capable of doing something desperate—of enlisting, for instance.

That is what Mr. Spark thought, and that evening he wrote a diplomatic letter to Lady Hengrave. He pointed out that C., although well equipped in French, Latin and Italian, would need at least another year in Germany to attain the standard necessary for the examination ; that, of course, he had not yet even begun to face the practical subjects : geography, précis writing, etc. His French was fair, but would need further brushing up. He did not honestly think the boy's heart was in the work, and that being so, he would be unlikely to pass, in which case it would be criminal on his part to recommend a long course of studies, which could not help entailing great expense, if the whole thing was to be done for no purpose. He had discussed the matter frankly with the boy, and he felt that he was bent on reading for the Bar, which was certainly less costly, etc. ; and Mr. Spark pointed out the advantages of such a step. He ended by lightly hinting at the danger of crossing C. at this period of his development and of making him go in for diplomacy against his will. He also hinted at the costliness of diplomacy as a career, and at the possi-bility of some political secretaryship turning up later. C., at Mr. Spark's advice, made a clean breast of the whole matter to his aunt directly he arrived at Elladon, and enlisted her sympathy; and she at once wrote to Lady Hengrave, and made C. do so as well. Although these letters came as a complete surprise and were somewhat of a shock to her settled ideas, Lady Hengrave did not, in reality, mind whether C. went into the Diplomatic Service or not. She had been in favour of it because she thought it would ensure the two hundred a year being given by Mrs. Roden, since the possession of four hundred a year was obligatory for candidates; but as soon as she got Mrs. Roden's letter saying that the two hundred a year would be given to C. whether he went into diplomacy or not, and that her husband seemed to think C. might do very well at the Bar, Lady Hengrave capitulated. She wrote to C. that, although she vitally disagreed with what he said about diplomacy and his prospects in that career, he could do as he liked. His father would have minded, but as he was no longer there to mind there was no more to be said. Lady Hengrave was no longer uneasy about Beatrice Lord, for Mrs. Roden had communicated to her the likelihood of an event occurring which would eliminate that danger for ever. The event occurred almost immediately.

The day after C. reached Elladon, the Rodens' house, he received a letter from Beatrice. She had read of his father's death in the newspapers, and she wrote to tell him how sorry she was for him. She had something else to tell him: she was engaged to be married to Vincent Fitzclare.

Vincent Fitzclare was a Catholic, the son of a friend and business associate of her father's. Beatrice had met him in Egypt. He had himself been in the Army, and was now a partner in an English bank in Paris, one of the firms in which her father was interested. They were to be married at the end of the month at the Oratory. Her father and mother were overjoyed.

Although she said little in the letter and explained nothing, C. understood much. He knew that Mr. Lord had been the chief agent in this match, and that Beatrice was not in the least in love with Vincent Fitzclare. Had he received the letter a few months earlier, before his illness, the result might have been disastrous. As it was, it was like a drop of water in a cup that is already full to the brim.

C. passed through London a month later, and stayed a night with his sister Marjorie, who now had a house in Eaton Square. In the afternoon he called at Ovington Square. He found Beatrice in. She was alone. She welcomed him, and he saw that she was just the same. She was to be married the next day.

" Give it up, I beg you, and marry me," said C. " It's not too late."

Beatrice smiled sadly.

" It's too late," she said.

" No, it's not too late," said C., and he poured out a flood of argument and entreaty.

Beatrice buried her face in her hands and cried ; then she pulled herself together and said : " I can't,

C., you know I can't ; you know I would if I could. Don't make it more difficult for me than it is already, please."

C. became calmer again. He felt that he must not give way for her sake.

" I suppose people don't do those things," he said, " do they ? "

" Perhaps people who are very brave do," said Beatrice, " but I'm a coward, a fearful moral coward ; but not only for myself, but for you."

Their conversation was interrupted before it became too difficult by the arrival of Mrs. Lord, who seemed delighted to welcome C., and talked of the wedding presents.

The next day Beatrice was married to Vincent Fitzclare.

CHAPTER XXIX

AT the bottom of his heart C. would have liked to be a journalist, but he felt it was useless to suggest such a thing; and, moreover, even if he had insisted on taking up a journalistic career, where in the world of journalism would he find an opening? What were his credentials? What had he got to show?

But on the same day that Lady Hengrave had outlined to him the programme of his future at Bramsley, he received a letter from his Oxford friend, Gerald Malone, telling him that he had taken his degree (a second) and was coming up to London to read for the Bar. He was to work in the chambers of a friend of his father. He suggested that if C. was going to live in London they should share rooms together. The word "Bar" came to C. as a heaven-sent suggestion, and he acted upon it, as we have seen.

C. would willingly have accepted the proposition with regard to the rooms, but it had been already arranged that he was to live with his mother. She had taken a small house in Gloucester Place, and he was to have the use of one room on the ground floor as a sitting-room, as it was thought necessary for him to have somewhere to work. Lady Hengrave, after spending some time with her married daughters in the country, came up to London, took the house, engaged servants, and by the middle of September, when C. arrived in London—the day before Beatrice Lord's marriage—she was established in her new home and ready for C. It had been arranged that he should work in the chambers of Sir Shreeve Mellings, who had been an acquaintance of her husband's. C. went to his chambers in the Temple, had luncheon at various restaurants in the Strand, and sometimes dined at home. Gerald Malone had two rooms near Fetter Lane, and they had luncheon together every day.

Sir Shreeve Mellings was a portly, unctuous man, who smoothed the creases out of his lips after every word he pronounced and seemed to taste them with succulent relish. He remarked with pain that C. did not seem to take to the law as quickly as he would have hoped. Gerald Malone seemed to take to it even less well.

On the other hand, Gerald was thoroughly at home in the Bohemian precincts of the London half-world, and the principal cause of his neglect of study was a passionate relationship he had formed with a certain Cissy Tilden, who was a pupil in a dramatic academy, learning to sing with a view to the stage. Cissy Tilden was a gay Cockney, with fair hair and laughing blue eyes, and a quick temper. C. made the acquaintance of a friend of hers named Ivy Darrell, and sometimes a *partie carrée* would be arranged, and the four would spend the evening at a music hall and

have supper afterwards in Gerald's rooms ; but these
entertainments were not a success, as Cissy Tilden
invariably quarrelled with Ivy. Ivy, who was the
less clever of the two girls, but the more sensitive, and
certainly the more unwise, exasperated Cissy by letting
her feel that she considered C. to be vastly superior to
Gerald. This was more than Cissy, who was passionately fond of Gerald, could bear, and the inevitable
crisis came about one night in Gerald's rooms. Ivy and
Cissy quarrelled over the pronunciation of the word
" waltz " ; they flew at each other and had to be
separated, and the result was that Ivy quarrelled with
Cissy for good, and then with C., who she considered
had not taken her part sufficiently. She demanded
that he should break off all relations with Gerald,
which he refused to do. Ivy went out of C.'s life for
good, and shortly afterwards, Cissy announced, not
without triumph, that Ivy was engaged to be married.
Gerald's relationship with Cissy was considered, both
by himself and by C. at that time, to be permanent
and enduring, and Gerald announced his intention of
marrying her as soon as he should be called to the Bar,
an event which seemed for the moment to be infinitely
remote. After the quarrel with Ivy, C. kept clear of
all serious entanglements, and his love adventures were
fleeting and casual, and left no impression whatsoever
on his feelings.

Several of his Oxford friends were now living in
London. One day he met Wright in the street, who
asked him whether he had written anything. C.

replied negligently that he had quite given up all that, but he said he was still interested in books, and that he craved for an entry into the world of letters, which was still surrounded in his eyes by a nebulous aura of romance. Wright shared his desire, but did not know how it could be fulfilled. Before long C.'s wish seemed to be near realisation. He spent a Sunday at Oxford, and at the Junior Dean's dinner table he met Mr. Clement Horridge, whose wife was better known as Charles James Clarke, the authoress of several popular psychological novels, one of which, *Equality*, had been translated into French and had appeared in the *Revue des deux Mondes*. She was not staying at Oxford herself. She rarely indulged in social excursions, but she received her friends at her comfortable house in Bryanston Square, and Mr. Clement Horridge, who was well known in the financial world, and who was nothing if not affable and "social," asked C. to be sure to come to luncheon any Sunday he should happen to be remaining in London. He would meet some interesting people.

"I say it who shouldn't," he said, "but we do know every one worth knowing in the world of art and of letters, and my wife will, I am sure, be delighted to make your acquaintance."

She was somewhat of an invalid and rarely went out, and she found the strain of writing very great; nevertheless she was always glad to see people in her own house, especially the young. During the summer they lived a great deal at their house near Dorking,

He asked C. to give him his address, and a few days later C. received a note from Mrs. Horridge's secretary asking him to luncheon on the following Sunday. He accepted, although Lady Hengrave expected him to have luncheon at home on Sundays, a day when a few people usually looked in, and the luncheon was just as good as it used to be at Hengrave House, and the guests the same, namely, Mr. Dartrey and Cecil Whitelaw (on alternate Sundays), and sometimes an uncle, or an aunt, or a sister. When C. said he was going to have luncheon with Mrs. Horridge, she asked with surprise who that might be.

" She's Charles James Clarke," said C.

" Oh ! " said Lady Hengrave, " I've just been reading her new book, *Tribute*. It's well written," she said with a sigh, " but too long, I think, in the second volume. But they say the third volume is interesting."

C. went to that luncheon with high hopes. He imagined he was going to walk straight into a magical country. Who knows ? Mr. Swinburne might be there, or Mr. Meredith. Neither of them was there, however. He found Mr. and Mrs. Horridge, their eldest son, James—a silent youth, who was working at Spark's for the Civil Service Examination—an affable clerk from the Foreign Office, and Miss Launceston, an old lady who was shabbily dressed in a black poke bonnet. She did good works in the East End and prided herself on speaking her mind with the unvarnished frankness of the eighteenth century.

Charles James Clarke herself was a timid, handsome
lady dressed in floating black robes, and with pre-
Raphaelite reddish-gold hair, who was passionately
fond of classical music and absorbed in the study of
Russian, which she was learning so as to read Turgenev, her favourite author, in the original. She
received C. kindly. She knew his Aunt Fanny and
remembered having seen him as a little boy at one of
his aunt's musical afternoons. They still went on,
did they not ? C. confessed that he did not care for
classical music.

" You are a Wagnerite, I suppose, like all the rest
of us," said Mrs. Horridge with a sigh.

" We're all going to Bayreuth next year," said Mr.
Horridge cheerfully. " You'd better come with us.
We're learning up the motifs," and here he hummed
something faintly resembling the sword motive.

Charles James Clarke's new book was mentioned.
The reviews were pouring in. They had been highly
complimentary. *The Times* had given the book a
whole column, and the *Speaker* had said that Charles
James Clarke was the most subtle English novelist
since George Meredith. C. sat between Miss Launceston, who knew his family well and talked of them, and
a Mrs. Leonard, who was a queen in the modern
painting world, and a patron of impressionist artists.
She took little notice of C.

C. came away greatly disappointed. Instead of
having effected an entry into the magic world of art,
he had been immersed into the very atmosphere he

was pining to escape from, and in a less pleasant setting. However, he was perhaps to succeed better a little later, or at least to try again.

His old friend, Lady Harriet Clive, asked him to luncheon on another Sunday, and there he met Mr. Leslie Goldsmith, who was the senior partner in the old publishing firm of Ludgate & Sons. Leslie Goldsmith was pouring new wine into the old bottles of the firm as hard as he could. He was publishing novels translated from the Swedish, the Spanish, and the Dutch, and verse by young writers, and a magazine called the *Curlew*, with startling illustrations and a cover designed by a revolutionary A.R.A. He asked C. to look in one evening the following week at his house in Cheyne Walk.

C.'s heart beat faster when he received this invitation. He felt that at last he was going to enter the magic portals. He entered them when the appointed day came about ten o'clock, and found himself in a large, square, empty room papered with brown paper. On the walls were a few etchings by Whistler and a sketch by Degas. There was not a trace of a book anywhere. The room was crowded with a heterogeneous collection of men, some of them in velvet smoking jackets, some of them in tweeds, some in frock coats ; all of them in day clothes, and most of them smoking pipes. One burly man had a black-and-red check necktie round his collarless neck.

Mr. Leslie Goldsmith was an alert, dark little man with a quick, beady eye. He gesticulated, as he talked, like a foreigner. He greeted C. immediately, and presently introduced him to a man whose name C. did not catch. He was a middle-aged baldish man, with something scholarly about him, but he did not altogether suggest a scholar. He wore spectacles and seemed to be looking on at the world from a remote post of observation. He talked to C. amiably and pleasantly, with a cynicism that was not bitter and a condescension that was evidently assumed. He told C. who the people were.

"The man with the flannel scarf is a footballer. He plays Rugby football very well. He also writes verse. I can't tell you what it's like; I've never read it. I seldom read any verse. In any case, it's no good reading verse when it's new. You must keep it, like wine. If it hasn't gone bad in twenty years, if it still exists after twenty years in the cellar, it's perhaps worth trying. But there are plenty of poets about now, because poetry apparently pays. That is so, isn't it, Goldsmith?"

Goldsmith had come to see how they were getting on.

"Yes," said Goldsmith; "the modern poets, too, are admirable men of business. You must get rid of all the old-fashioned ideas on that subject."

"Perhaps," said C.'s new acquaintance, "that means not that poets have learnt to become good men of business, but that good men of business have learnt to write bad verse."

Goldsmith laughed.

"You mustn't say that before Harrison," he said, and he darted off to another group.

"Are there a lot of poets here to-night?" asked C.

"A lot. But they don't all look like poets. Besides the footballer, that little man with a large head and serious eyes, like a wise owl, is a poet, but I'm not sure whether he writes in English or only in Latin— possibly in Hebrew. That very pale man sitting on the edge of the sofa is an etcher, and is said to be very clever. The man in a frock coat who looks like a City man is a poet too. Some one must be paying him a compliment, because he is visibly bridling."

They had talked on various subjects for about ten minutes; the stranger continued to banter C. lightly, and talk to him as if he were absurdly young, but not in an offensive way, and C. enjoyed the conversation. It amused him; it was the last thing he had expected at Goldsmith's house, but it was different from any- thing he had as yet experienced. Presently the stranger said :—

"I must be going home. I can't introduce you to any one because I know no one."

He slipped away, and Goldsmith, at once noticing that C. was left alone, drew him into a group which was at the time being dominated by the man who the stranger had said was an etcher.

The other members of the group were a rather tall man with vague blue eyes and fair bright hair that stuck out round his head and reminded C. of the pictures of Swinburne, Goldsmith himself, and a dark, saturnine man who was smoking an enormous pipe.

They were discussing Zechetti. The dark man said he preferred Zechetti to Lapara. She had more charm for him.

" She never walks through her part. She never imitates herself, and one cannot help falling in love with her."

" I prefer Lapara," said the etcher, who looked, on closer inspection, emaciated and worn in spite of his great youth. C. thought he must be consumptive. " There is something to me drab and dull and prosaic about Zechetti. I feel no thrill when I see her, whereas when Madeleine stalks on to the stage in *Fédora*, or any part, looking gorgeous and strange, like a tired peacock, then I am carried away."

" They are both women of genius," said the fair-haired man.

Goldsmith asked C. what he thought.

" I like Lapara best," said C., blushing and feeling incapable of explaining why.

The group split up again. A little man with spectacles joined in and began rather fiercely to dogmatise on the French stage. Goldsmith led C. into the next room and offered him a whisky and soda.

C. took the opportunity of asking him who the people were he had been introduced to.

" The man I introduced you to first," said Goldsmith, " is Johnstone-Craye. He's been in the Home Office for years. The man sitting on the edge of the

sofa is Basil Lee, the etcher. He's a genius, but his
lungs are bad. The tall, fair man is Walter Mason, the
poet. I'm bringing out a new book of his next week.
It is to be called ' Silver Woodways.' A good title,
and Lee has designed a wonderful cover. The large
paper edition on India paper has been sold out before
publication. The dark man is Jeremy Lowe, also a
Civil servant. He has done me a book of essays on
Spanish Cities—very fine. We are going to call it
' Pomegranates from Granada.' "

In the next room there was another group of men,
in the centre of which was the little man with the large
head. " That's George Bede, the poet," whispered
Goldsmith. The group were discussing French poetry.
A man with a silken beard and a suave, refined utterance was saying that French poetry was never on the
first line. " No French verse affects," C. heard him
say, " my *sensorium* in the same way as Goethe, or
Dante, or Shakespeare at their finest."

Bede protested, and quoted some lines of Victor
Hugo.

" Yes, very pretty," said the man with the beard.
The argument proceeded with quick, short attack and
counter-attack, and the man with a beard launched
into a short monologue. C. could not catch all of it,
but he heard the final sentence—" . . . English,
German and Italian poetry so incomparably above
French is the co-ordination into a total mood as
distinguished from the charm of metaphors or
descriptions."

After a little more argument Bede said that he was certain Victor Hugo was one of the greatest poets of all time, and a wonderful painter.

" So was Byron," said the man with a beard.

" Oh, Byron," said Bede, " he's dead."

Bede, C. reflected, seemed a frail and anæmic creature, compared with even the thought of Byron. He thought of Professor Kaufmann saying that Tennyson was a dwarf beside Byron, who was a giant. If Tennyson was a dwarf, what was Bede ?

" Burstall," some one said, " says that in thirty years' time there will be a great Byron revival."

" Poor Burstall," said the man with a beard. The mention of Burstall's name had been like an electric shock to C. He felt himself tingling all over.

Bede, apparently tired of the discussion, walked into the next room. The group dissolved. C. told Goldsmith that he was afraid he ought to be going home. Goldsmith led him to the door. Several of the guests had gone home. C. asked the name of the man with a beard.

" That," said Goldsmith, " is Arnholm, the art critic."

Goldsmith said good-bye to him, and said C. must have luncheon with him at his club, the Gainsborough Club in Dover Street. He had luncheon there every day.

On the doorstep he met Bede. Bede asked him which way he was going and, as they were going in the same direction, proposed that they should go home together. C. felt a little shy, but he consented, nevertheless.

On the way back, as they were passing through St. Leonard's Terrace, Bede said. " I live here, come in a moment. I'm not going to bed. I am really only just up. I only live at night."

He led C. upstairs into a little room full of books. He poured him out some whisky and they both sat down. He asked C. about his life and education. They talked of Oxford. Bede had been a Cambridge man. They compared impressions. C. told him how bitterly he regretted having gone down so soon. Rome was mentioned.

" Are you a Catholic ? " asked Bede.

" No," said C., and the question, bringing as it did thoughts of Beatrice, hurt him.

" I'm nothing——"

" Of course not, if you're not a Catholic," said Bede. " There is either that or nothing. There is no third course."

" And one can't very well *become* a Catholic," said C.

" Why not ? " asked Bede.

C. stammered and did not answer ; what he was thinking was that converts always seemed to him rather tiresome, and never quite the same as real Catholics ; but then he reflected that Bede was very likely a convert himself, so he refrained from saying anything. It was not, however, necessary, for Bede poured out a stream of argument and exposition to the effect that Catholicism was the great reality ; the only thing that mattered ; the only thing that counted ; the only creed a thinking man could adopt ; the only solace that satisfied the needs of the human heart ; the only curb to the human passions ; the only system that fulfilled the demands of human nature and into which factors such as love and death fitted naturally ; the unique and sole representative of the Divine upon earth. The English had gone wrong because they had fallen into a rut from the straight road of their true inheritance : Catholic England, Chaucer's England, to which the whole of Shakespeare's work was the dirge.

"But do you believe it all ? " asked C.

"You are in a muddle about the meaning of the word *belief*. You use the word *belief* in the sense of thinking something is probable or improbable in itself. When we say we believe in a dogma, we mean we are giving credit to something which is guaranteed to us by the authority of the Church. Religious belief is a mystery and an adventure. But if, like Pascal, you wish to bet on it, you have nothing to lose if it turns out not to be true, whereas the other way round——"

"I should hate to do it from fear. I have the greatest contempt for death-bed repentances ; for men who have blasphemed and rioted all their lives, and then at the last moment have sent for a priest——"

"That means you are not a Christian, that is to say not a Catholic. (Catholicism *is* Christianity. It's the same thing—and nothing else is.) Well,

Christianity is the religion of repentance : it stands against fatalism and pessimism of every kind mainly in saying *that a man can go back, even at the eleventh hour*. A man may quite well hold the opposite opinion and die nobly, stoically—heroically, if you will—but he is *not a Christian* if he does so——"

" I don't want to be a Christian, and I must go," said C. They had been talking for over two hours.

Bede walked downstairs with him into the street. They passed a cabman's shelter. Bede peeped in and bade C. do the same. At the table, with a cup of coffee in front of him, a little pale man was scribbling in a notebook.

" That's Henry Dixon, the poet," Bede whispered. " We mustn't disturb him ; he's writing."

Bede left C. at the corner of the street.

CHAPTER XXX

It was thus that C. entered the portals into the literary world. He wondered as he left Bede whether he would ever see any of these people again. He did not have to wonder long, for the next morning, as he was walking to the chambers in the Temple where he worked, he passed the British Museum, and just in front of the entrance he met Johnstone-Craye, the first person whom he had been introduced to at Goldsmith's party. Johnstone-Craye greeted him with a chuckle, and said to him : " You had better come in here with me ; it will be good for your mind." C. followed him into the Museum, and Johnstone-Craye led him to a marble bust, a Greek head with a broken nose.

" In thirty years' time you will be able to appreciate that," he said. He then led him to another bust, which was still more dilapidated. " And perhaps when you are sixty—mind you, I only say *perhaps*, you will be able to appreciate *that*."

They then left the building. Johnstone-Craye had to go to his office, and C. to the Temple.

C. met Goldsmith frequently during the next months. He was proposed by him as a member to the Gainsborough Club, and elected. There he met Walter Mason, Basil Lee and others, but he did not become intimate with any of them. Bede, who had interested him most, he did not see again ; for the time being he had, he heard, left London and gone to live in the country. C. asked Goldsmith if he knew Burstall. Goldsmith knew him, but had no idea as to his present whereabouts ; he had, he thought, quarrelled with his wife and started on a prolonged voyage to the South Seas. After the evening spent at Goldsmith's one of the first things C. did was to buy the works of some of the poets he had met. They rather disappointed him. And it was after reading their works more than after meeting the authors in the flesh that he thought that he had not yet come across a circle of men such as Shelley, Keats and Coleridge.

He felt less inclined for further adventure, but, nevertheless, he would not yet admit to himself that he was disappointed in the literary world. What if there was no Shelley or Keats at present in London, yet all these people were interested in interesting matters ; they were interested in intellectual and artistic problems, in ideas.

Concurrently with this thread which led him from time to time to Goldsmith's house, to the Gains-borough Club, and sometimes to the Café Royal with Mason and others, his life with his family went on in the same rut as before. Twice a week he dined with his sister Marjorie in Eaton Place. Julia was away, and was staying in the country till after Christmas. But the only real intimacy which he experienced was that which he enjoyed with his Oxford friends, with

Malone and Wright. He spent Christmas in London with his mother. Julia had asked them to stay with her in the country, but Lady Hengrave did not wish to go to a large party, and C. pleaded the necessity of work. On Christmas Eve he and his mother dined with Marjorie and her husband, where they met his eldest brother and his wife. Soon after Christmas, C. met Blades, who asked him to dinner with his people. There he saw another facet of the intellectual world : the Bishop of Christminster, who had just published the last volume of his brilliant history of the Dukes of Athens ; William Farren, who directed archæological research in Rome, rarefied, remote and silent ; Hodgkinson, the critic, amiable and acute, witty and gay ; and a Mrs. Airlie—enthusiastic, but pointed and critical—who had read all the latest French novelists and poets. Nothing but literature and books was discussed.

" I suppose you never read novels," Mrs. Airlie said to the Bishop.

" I read little else," the Bishop replied.

Modern writers were discussed : the forthcoming production of a play by William George, the novelist, at one of the West End theatres, of which great things were expected.

" But will it be a success ? " asked Mrs. Blades plaintively. Having been a *Liedersängerin* she knew the surprises of the footlights.

" It *must* be a success," said Hodgkinson.

A comedy by Maude, the notorious Irishman, which

had just been produced, was mentioned. Mrs. Hodgkinson said it was so curious he should have written a goody-goody play. Mrs. Airlie said all his epigrams were stolen from other people and his technique stolen from the French. The Bishop remarked that he wondered more playwrights didn't steal their technique from the French. A poetical play was about to be produced, and the author, a young Cambridge poet, had read his play aloud to William Farren and his wife a little time ago.

" Is it in blank verse ? " asked Mrs. Airlie, with sympathetic interest.

" Well, it's blank——" said Farren.

" William is so naughty," said Mrs. Farren.

Ibsen was mentioned. A hot discussion ensued. The Bishop could not abide Norwegian literature. Hodgkinson made every one laugh by describing how another Norwegian poet had mistaken at his house General George, who had just returned from a victorious expedition against the hill tribes in India, for William George, the shy psychological novelist. C. was sitting between Mrs. Farren (an American and ultra-cultivated), and Mrs. Airlie, so he could not complain of the conversation not being literary. Mrs. Farren talked to him incessantly of the adventures of her soul among masterpieces—of Rome, Florence, American architecture, and the sins of Italian archæologists. Mrs. Airlie patronised him, and when he ventured to say that he did not appreciate Russian novels and couldn't read Tolstoy, she said : " It's a very good thing for the young not to have good taste."

After dinner, the Bishop and Hodgkinson held the table. Style was discussed and young Edmund Blades staggered the company by saying that he thought the two worst living stylists were Stevenson and Pater. His father said that the habit of paradox was becoming a positive disease in young England, but Edmund Blades stuck to his point, and Farren, to the surprise of everybody, said he thought the boy was quite right. Hodgkinson said it was a comfort the young should admire anything. C. took no part in the discussion. But when Farren asked him point-blank what French prose writer he most admired, and he answered Renan, Farren became interested and they discussed Renan's works, which C. was saturated with at the moment. From French they got on to English literature. C. spoke to Farren of the so-called renascence that was supposed to be taking place in English verse, and asked him if he thought there were many first-rate English poets alive. Farren said he thought that among the more modern younger men there were only three who wrote good verse, and of these two were Irishmen. There were some good poets alive, but they belonged to a much older generation.

" They say that Byron's work is dead," said C. " Do you believe that ? "

" I think," said Farren, " that Byron is one of the greatest of English writers, the greatest English poet

of the nineteenth century, that the sweep of his wings
was larger and stronger, although Shelley had as much
genius and a greater mind. But I can tell you one
thing. Those young men can say what they like, but
there is not one of them who would be sorry if he found
that by accident he had written one of Byron's even
second-best lines."

English poetry led them back to French poetry.
Farren scoffed at the want of appreciation of French
verse in England, just as Burstall had done. "They
might just as well say the Persians had no poetry," he
said. C. asked him if he knew Burstall. "Yes, I have
met him," he said. "Very brilliant, but he's wasted
his gifts. He's frittered away his intellectual capital
in the newspapers." He had no idea where he was.

When the men went up into the drawing-room, after
some pressing Mrs. Blades consented to sing. She
accompanied herself. She sang a setting to the words
of Byron :—

> So we'll go no more a-roving.

"And they say," said Farren, when she had finished,
"that the man who wrote those lines is not a poet."

It was the words more than the music or the singing
that struck C., for Mrs. Blades's voice was long past its
prime, and at its best she had been more remarkable
for taste than for inspiration. But she was much
applauded. Only, as she knew that some of her guests
were restive under music, she refused the encore that
was asked of her.

She talked a little to C. and asked after Mrs. Roden and his Aunt Fanny, and wondered she had not seen him at her musical entertainments. C. confessed that he was unworthy of difficult music. Mrs. Blades smiled tolerantly. Mrs. Airlie again looked at him patronisingly, as if she were once more approving of bad taste in the young, and then C. went home.

Three nights later he dined with his brother, Edward. Bramsley had been let, and Hengrave House also, for the moment. The new Lord Hengrave was living in a small house in Grosvenor Place.

It was a small dinner party—one or two Members of Parliament and an American relation of his sister-in-law who had come to London for the first time. The new Lady Hengrave patronised her, and when the coffee was served, offered her a cigarette, saying, " Oh ! we all smoke here now."

After dinner C. found himself with the Members of Parliament. They were discussing some legal Bill with which an eminent lawyer had had something to do. His name was Sir William George. At one moment some one said, " It was very foolish of William George to behave like that," and C. thought they meant William George the novelist, whose play had been produced two nights before, and after the performance of which there had been a *fracas* caused by the appearance of George himself, who took his call.

" It wasn't his fault," said C., joining in the conversation. " They made him appear." He was full of the topic, and thought the whole of London was thinking of nothing else.

" He doesn't mean him," said Edward impatiently. " We're talking of the House of Lords."

C. felt deeply ashamed of himself and realised in a flash how little one half of the world knows what the other half are talking about, and he felt that he was condemned to the half which interested him the least.

A little later, upstairs in the drawing-room, they did discuss books : the newest books of the day, an English novel by a well-known novelist. C. was asked whether he had read it. He said no, but that he had read a story by the same author, alluding to one of his earlier works.

" Oh, but that's quite *old*," said young Lady Hengrave with the utmost disdain, and in a manner as if it were a disgrace to mention something that was not brand new. Again C. felt that he had committed a solecism. And yet, he thought, why should one not mention a story just because it had been out a few years ? Here was a difference between this world and the new literary world into which he had just peeped. In the literary world, at least, you could mention a book of any epoch, it did not matter if it was old or out of date. You would find response. Here it was looked upon as a blot and a sign of being behind the times, which, apparently, was unforgivable. Truly the values of the two worlds were different, and C. felt saddened, not by this discovery, that such values can be and are different, which he had, indeed, made years before, but by the sense that the new world, which he had so longed for, had not after all proved quite so radiant as he had expected. But he consoled himself with the thought that he *had* enjoyed his conversation with Johnstone-Craye and Farren, and that he had made the acquaintance of Bede. There were others, too, whom he might get to know in time.

At any rate the new world was alive. Books were being written and pictures were being painted by people who were keen and young. There was a world, which was in touch with realities, even if it possessed less glamour than he had expected it to have. One day Goldsmith asked him to luncheon to meet a very famous author and scholar whose fine, witty work in criticism and whose grave, melancholy verse he had admired even when he was at Eton. The luncheon took place, as usual, at the Gainsborough Club, and there were several authors present : a successful writer of romance, a French novelist, and the editor of one of the evening newspapers. C. sat next to the Frenchman, who was delighted to find some one who could speak French without an entirely English pronunciation. C. suddenly remembered that the author whom he had been longing to meet, namely, Angus Cole, was one of the many to whom Calmady had written from Eton, and C. also remembered he had on one occasion been persuaded by Calmady to append his signature with Calmady's to a letter, lyrical in enthusiasm, that had been sent to Cole. He was so appalled by this recollection that he did not dare say a word to the object of his hero-worship.

He needn't have worried. Angus Cole had probably entirely forgotten the incident, and even if he had remembered it he would never have connected it with C. at this moment.

C. listened to the conversation of his hero with the writer of romance. The latter asked Cole's advice as to whether it would be wise to write a sequel to a romance which had lately been published, and which had been a great success. Cole was against it. He said sequels were never quite satisfactory, even the best of them.

"I should leave your hero and heroine in their kingdom and think of something else."

"I expect you're right," said the novelist, but C. felt that he was determined to write the sequel, and he was right, for the sequel appeared a year later, and was just as successful, and deservedly so, as the first book. "I wonder why people ask for advice," thought C. to himself, "when it is quite obvious that they do not mean to take it."

CHAPTER XXXI

The Rodens had taken a house at Florence for Easter and longer. They had taken it for two months. It was a large palace on the Lung' Arno, and they asked C. to come and stay with them. Towards the end of March he had not been well again and had a sharp attack of influenza, and the doctor said that a change of air would do him good, so he accepted the invitation with alacrity.

The Rodens were there, their two daughters, and Hester Carteret. Wright had been sent to Florence to rub up his Italian, and the Rodens had made him move from a *pension* to their house.

C. arrived at Florence just before Easter and found the city basking in sunshine and sweet with the smell of flowers. They spent the mornings doing the sights and the afternoons in expeditions to Fiesole and other places. The sight of the Tuscan country in the spring was a revelation to C. The wild tulips, the blossom, the brown hills, the young corn, the early roses, the burning April sun, the delicate shapes of the budding trees, the clean and coloured buildings seen through the " live translucent air, as the sights in a magic crystal ball," were a wonderful solace and a divine surprise after long months spent in the gloom of a cold and foggy London winter. The sights of Italy and the sound of the Italian language brought back the nightmare of Rome to him, and the thoughts of Beatrice indeed, but no longer with actual pain. He felt as if he had been dead and were gradually coming to life again. He felt he could no longer enjoy himself as before, as in the Oxford days, but nevertheless, unbeknown to himself, something was sprouting inside him and his youth was reasserting itself. He was, as the doctors say, mending. From Hester Carteret he heard news of Beatrice. She had attended the wedding. After the wedding the Fitzclares had gone to Ireland for their honeymoon. Later on they had gone to Egypt, where Vincent Fitzclare had business to transact, and thence they returned to Paris. C. asked a few questions about him. He was, it appeared, the only son of an Irish squire, but he had an uncle who owned mines in Yorkshire and was immensely rich. This uncle was childless and was expected to leave everything to his nephew. C. asked what kind of man was this Vincent Fitzclare. Hester Carteret said she really didn't know. He was good-looking and was said to be doing very well in his Paris business, which was important and lucrative. Beyond that she knew nothing. She had merely shaken hands with him at the wedding. C. could talk about it quite calmly now. It seemed to him to have happened infinitely long ago.

There were a great many English visitors at Florence that year, and the Rodens entertained frequently.

Wright spent all his mornings studying Italian and working at his other subjects. In the afternoon he and C. would sometimes go for long walks to San Miniato, to Careggi, to Fiesole, to Bellosguardo, or drive to La Gamberaia and other picturesque places.

They went for a short expedition by themselves to Perugia, where they spent a few days, and visited Assisi. When they returned they found Florence was fuller than ever. The first person C. met the day after his return was an old acquaintance, Lady Ralph Dallington. She had taken an apartment for a month in the Borgo San Jacobo and she asked C. to luncheon the next day and told him to bring Wright.

When they got there they found the lofty *salone* full of guests. Some of them C. knew already. Agoura, one of the Secretaries of the Russian Embassy at Rome, two Italians whom he had met at the Rodens' already, one of them a young man and the other a lady who was one of the beauties of Florence, and an old Russian lady with an unpronounceable name. The first person C. was introduced to was Mrs. Bucknell. She was there with her husband, who was in the English Foreign Office. There was also present another Englishman, a neat, little, dark, dapper, well-dressed, nice-looking man with soft eyes, to whom C. was introduced. His name was Sir Wilfrid Clay, Bart.—a Leicestershire family. At luncheon C. sat between an Italian lady, Countess Montecchi, and an elderly Miss Brooke, who possessed a lovely villa, and who was one of the permanent features of the English colony

in Florence.   He wondered where he had seen Countess
Montecchi before, and then it flashed suddenly into his
mind.   She was the Miss Burke he had heard sing at
Vegas' studio in Paris.   He remembered what Madame
Orioli had said about her.   Her prophecy had proved
quite correct.   She had not gone far in art, but she
had made *un beau mariage dans le monde*.   Her
husband was not there.   How different she looked,
thought C., in spite of her being the same woman.
She was dressed with a simplicity which can only be
achieved by great wealth, but that was not the only
change.   She no longer looked English.   She looked
like an Italian, and she spoke like an Italian, without
any effort or pose or pretence, but with perfect
naturalness and ease.   Mrs. Bucknell was sitting on
the other side of the table to C., between an Italian
and Agoura.   C. had felt a slight shock on being introduced to her, as he recognised her as being, firstly, the
Leila whom he had played with in Hamilton Gardens,
and, secondly, the lady who had not recognised him at
Stuart House.   However, she smiled at him very
graciously on this occasion, and introduced him to her
husband.   While he was carrying on a stereotyped
conversation with Miss Brooke about the visitors at
Florence this year, the sights, the gardens, and what
one ought to see, and what one ought not to see, he
watched Mrs. Bucknell.   She was, he thought, beautiful ; much more beautiful than he remembered her
to be.   She was really small and short, but, although
nobody would have called her tall, nobody would have

classed her in the category of the tiny, delicate Dresden
china shepherdess type, in spite of a china-like delicacy
there was about her. She was so well proportioned
that she looked just the right height, and on the
stage she would probably have seemed as tall as
Ellen Terry. She was dressed in black, and she
wore a large bunch of fresh yellow roses. There
was something plaintively delicate about her little,
slightly pouting face, something liquid and appealing in her eyes, something in the extremely rare
texture and whiteness of her skin, and in the elegance
of her line and the finish of her beautifully modelled
hands that seemed to make you want to take her away,
and put her out of reach of the rough possibilities of the
world, and to guard her in a crystal shrine. One could
not bear the thought that she might be buffeted or
damaged or ruffled in any way. C. compared her with
the other women present in his mind, with his neighbour who was undoubtedly a real beauty—a face for
painters to rave about—and with another, a real
Italian, who was sitting opposite him. They had the
more obvious attributes of beauty, whereas Mrs.
Bucknell's beauty was far less easy to define, grace was
so important a part of it, and undefinable lines and
curves, the ripple and changing lights of the chestnut
hair under the large black hat, the slanting downward
look of the eyes, the very long lashes—was it these that
seemed to spread a powdery light, a kind of star-dust
over the eyes ? or were there in the eyes themselves
specks of a golden colour, for what colour were they ?

C. had always thought of Leila, as a little girl, as having violet eyes, but now he could not tell, they were like that strange gem, the Alexandrite, which is violet in the daytime but which at night, and at certain times, changes its colour and reveals sudden golden glints, so that C. thought of the title of one of Balzac's stories, *La fille aux yeux d'or*.

Undefinable, too, the nose, turned up without being short, and the way the head was poised on the neck, like the bell of a proud flower, but what flower? thought C. What flower was she like? A golden flower. But where was it to be found, and where did it grow? In what forbidden field, " in what hidden way," in what secret high-walled garden? It was, perhaps, he thought, a strange flower that men seek for all their lives, and never find, the hopeless quest of fairy princes; it haunts the dreams of poets, and teases the brush of artists, and dances before the blank score of the brooding musician, for ever just out of reach.

C. remembered a line of Greek verse he had read at Oxford which said, " I have a fair daughter, Cleis the beloved, in aspect like a golden flower." What flower was that? What had the Greek poetess been thinking of, something fabulous and out of reach in Elysium, or in the garden of the Hesperides, or something exquisitely common, like the yellow poppy or the saffron crocus?

Soon his other neighbour claimed his attention. C. recalled the party in the studio to her, and she laughed and told him about her youth in Paris, and how she had dreamt of being a great opera singer, and how the masters had ended by telling her that she had not a shadow of talent, but might accomplish something by immense hard work. It had been a series of disappointments, but great fun, and now it seemed so far away.

C. detected a slightly wistful note in her voice. He wondered whether she regretted it, and he wondered what her husband was like. He wasn't there. She asked him to come and see her. "Come to *déjeuner* any day you like ; we live in a large, hideous Palazzo in the modern part of the town, near the tram line." They talked of the improvements that were being made in Florence, the threat that was in the air of the whole of the old houses on this side of the Lung' Arno being pulled down.

"Foreigners are so tactless about these things," said Miss Brooke ; "they talk of Florence and Rome as if it was their country, and, of course, that irritates the Italians."

"Yes, that is true," said the Russian lady, who had caught the topic, "but when you Italians," she said, addressing Mrs. Bucknell's neighbour, whose name was Scalchi, "say you are making these improvements to attract and please us foreigners, I wish personally to make a protest, and to say, 'Don't bother to do it for me. I am quite happy without an arcade at Florence.' "

"Ah ! you are an Italian—more Italian than any of us," said Scalchi.

Lady Ralph, on the other hand, told her Italian guests quite plainly that she had no patience with what they did to their towns.

" You all want to make an artificial and second-rate Paris," she said, " and you can't do it."

Miss Brooke got red in the face with anger, and said the Italians had a perfect right to do what they liked with their own cities, and that it was most impertinent of foreigners, especially a foreigner who lived in Italy, to interfere and to criticise.

" But you, too, are an Italian," said Scalchi. " Too Italian to judge."

" More Italian than any of us," said the dark Italian lady.

" Miss Brooke speaks such wonderful Italian."

After luncheon they walked out on to a large, shady loggia, and drank coffee and green *Certosa*. C. had hoped that he might find himself next to Mrs. Bucknell, but Sir Wilfrid Clay absorbed her attention. Lady Ralph talked to C., and asked him after his mother and his sisters, and his aunt. " Your mother ought to spend the winter in Rome," she said, " next year. I'm sure it would be good for her and that she would like it. You've given up diplomacy ? I suppose it's a pity, or that I ought to say I think it's a pity, but I don't. I think diplomacy is an awful life. I oughtn't to say that before Agoura, but he's used to me and doesn't mind. I congratulate you. What are you going to do instead ? The Bar ? That's interesting, but dreadfully difficult—you'll become one of those

K.C.'s who are dreadfully clever and cross-examine people, but please don't develop into one of those funny judges who make jokes and tell stories. Let me give you one piece of advice : if you want to get on in the world, *never* tell a story. Nothing is so tiresome as a *raconteur*, and there's no such thing as a story one hasn't heard before."

Mr. Bucknell joined the conversation. He belonged rather to the stiff than the smooth type of Foreign Office official. He had overheard Lady Ralph's conversation, and he said he was extremely sorry to hear that C. had given up trying for the Diplomatic Service. He would have found life and the work extremely interesting.

" I don't think I should ever have passed the examination," said C.

" The truth is," said Lady Ralph, " he has just confessed to me that he didn't want to be an ambassador."

Mr. Bucknell snorted. " There would probably be very little chance of that," he said stiffly.

" If Mr. Bramsley speaks other languages as well as he speaks Italian," said Scalchi, " it is a great pity he has not gone into the Diplomatic Service."

" Ah, you speak Italian ? " said Bucknell. " That's always useful, although nowadays Spanish is more useful, as so much business is done in Spanish. And, of course, if you had learnt Russian you would get an extra hundred a year. It's not yet too late, you are quite young, you will still have time to pass the examination. I think you will find it wiser to go on once you have begun."

"But I'm reading for the Bar," said C.

"Oh, the Bar!" said Bucknell, and he became stiffer than ever.

"The Russians are such wonderful linguists," said Lady Ralph. "Look at Agoura."

While this conversation was going on Mrs. Bucknell and Sir Wilfrid Clay had withdrawn to the end of the group, and their conversation, which had been going on in an undertone, seemed to have increased in pace, as if some divergence of opinion had occurred. This was perhaps the case, for it came to a sudden break. Mrs. Bucknell left Sir Wilfrid abruptly, and sat down next to Lady Ralph and C.

"No, alas! we're not staying on," she said in reply to a question of Lady Ralph's. "Terence has got to go back. They get so little leave, and they're so hard worked at the office. Terence never gets home till half-past seven and is often late for dinner. Aren't you coming to London this summer? What a pity! Yes, we live where we used to, the same poky little house in Upper Berkeley Street. You must come and see us when you are in London," she said to C., smiling. "I wish we were going to stay. I dread the thought of the whole summer in London. The dinners and the balls and the fearful rush. Last summer was awful. I had to go to Aix to recover from it. This year Terence has to go to Carlsbad. Aix is awful now, quite spoilt. Everything is spoilt.

Good-bye, dearest." She kissed Lady Ralph on both cheeks. "We've got to go ; we promised to meet my cousin Elsie at the Bargello." She shook hands with C., and gave him a melting smile.

"Usen't you to play in Hamilton Gardens years ago ? " she asked.

"Yes," said C. "I thought you didn't recognise me."

"I remember you perfectly, a little boy with curls and brown holland knickerbockers. We used to play flags. I know your brother Edward. How are they all ? Well, I must go. Don't forget to come and see me." She made for the door, but before going she said she had one word to say to Lady Ralph, and they walked together to the door, and their last farewell lasted for more than five minutes. Sir Wilfrid Clay walked after her, as if he wanted to say something, but she took no notice of him at all. She seemed to talk through him, and she called her husband, and said they must be going, as they were already late, as if he was being the cause of the delay.

"What a good-looking boy that is," were her last whispered words to Lady Ralph. "Georgina Hengrave's son. He is much better-looking than his brother Edward, who has grown so fat. It's funny, I remember him a little boy with curls. Well, good-bye, darling ; and if you do happen to come to London, don't forget us, and come to luncheon any day. Yes, we go to-morrow, alas ! alas ! Good-bye."

CHAPTER XXXII

C. STAYED at Florence till the middle of June. He stopped, on his way back to London, in Paris for a week, at the little hotel where he had once stayed with Pelly. Wright left Florence with him, and they went together to see Lapara, who had just produced a poetical play by a young poet. C. was slightly disappointed with the performance. The poetry seemed to him stagy, and Lapara had hardly anything to do. In the interval after the first act he was startled by suddenly catching sight of Beatrice. She was sitting with a party of people in the box next to the stage. She had seen him, and beckoned to him to come round. After the second act he went round to her box. She was obviously pleased to see him. She introduced him to her party, which consisted of two elegant ladies from the Argentine Republic. They were friends of Vincent Fitzclare. C. was introduced to him also. Beatrice asked him to luncheon on the following day, but C. was going back to London, and, having announced his arrival to Lady Hengrave, he did not dare to change the arrangement. They talked of the play, the acting, Florence, Italy, and it seemed so strange to C.—as if they had crossed one of the rivers of Death, and were talking in a new world. He was shocked by the great change in Beatrice's appearance. It was not that she had lost her looks, but the change was in her expression. C. had the impression that she had been washed by oceans and oceans of salt tears. She was just as beautiful as she had been before, but the look of happy radiance, as of apple blossom, had gone.

In the course of conversation she said, " You probably didn't hear that I was rather ill for a time. It is only three weeks ago that I was allowed out, and this is the first time I have been to a play for weeks."

Vincent Fitzclare was most amiable to C. He was good-looking, a little florid, with a certain Celtic volubility of language, and melancholy eyes with a dangerous glint in them at times. He made on C. the impression of a not altogether reliable collie dog that had the appearance of being well-bred, with a streak of something not quite well-bred.

Beatrice talked and laughed as easily and as naturally as usual, and begged C. to bring his friend round during the next *entr'acte*.

C. did so, and this time he found the box empty, save for Beatrice, as Vincent Fitzclare and another male guest of his, who had arrived in the meanwhile, had taken the Argentine ladies to the *foyer*.

Beatrice talked of the acting and the play. She was, she said, enjoying it greatly. She asked C. after his family, and talked to Wright about the Rodens, and they all three compared notes about Florence. C.

asked her if she was coming to England. " Perhaps, later in the autumn," she said. " We will probably have to go and stay with Vincent's uncle. We shan't stay in London."

She asked C. what he was doing, and was not surprised to hear that he had given up all ideas of diplomacy. Vincent Fitzclare came back, and C. and Wright said good-bye.

The next day they returned to London. This brief interview left C. profoundly sad. But the saddest thing about it was that he felt incapable of feeling. He had expected to suffer, and as it was he felt perfectly numbed, as if his heart were dead.

When he arrived in London he found that his mother was being greatly worried by the behaviour of her daughter-in-law, who had made scenes about the removal of some of the bedroom furniture from Hengrave House. Lady Hengrave had refused to argue, discuss and wrangle, and had told her daughter-in-law she could keep whatever she chose. Edward was apparently much distressed at his wife's behaviour, but had no influence over her. She would not hear of Hengrave House being sold, and she vehemently urged the selling of Bramsley rather than of the London house. She had announced her intention of doing up Hengrave House, and entertaining there next year. Edward did not want to sell Bramsley. He managed to temporise and to obtain a compromise for the moment. It was let for another six months, and no immediate decision was necessary. Edward and his wife had violent quarrels on the subject. She hated the country as much as Edward disliked London.

"It is a pity," said Lady Hengrave to C. with a sigh, "that Edward has married a vulgar little American."

Both C.'s sisters were in London.

Julia lived in Curzon Street, and seemed happy. She had already a one-year-old son and was expecting another baby. Marjorie lived in a large, dismal, pompous house in Eaton Place. She had no children and did not pretend to be happy. She loathed her husband, who, save for being antipathetic, gave her no cause for complaint, and thus probably made matters worse. Harry was in Ireland, but was expected to come through London later.

C. called on the Carterets as soon as he arrived in London. Lady Elizabeth told him the news. She was guarded in her references to Beatrice, but she conveyed to him, nevertheless, that the marriage did not seem to have been as satisfactory as was expected. Beatrice had been very ill after a baby was born in April. It had died almost immediately, and this must have been a great sorrow for Beatrice. Mr. Lord was delighted, of course, and Mrs. Lord accepted everything with patience, but—but——

"But what?" asked C.

"Well, they say he has violent outbursts of temper," she said. "And some people say he drinks, and that he's very unfaithful. That may be all gossip, he is certainly very well off and does well in business."

Julia and Marjorie got C. some invitations to dances, but C. refused to go. They were boy and girl dances, and C. protested that he knew no one. He was wondering whether he would ever see Mrs. Bucknell again. She had told him to be sure to come and see her, but he did not dare take such a step.

C. felt it difficult to settle down to work. Malone's uncle had died, leaving him a small legacy, and this had led him into extravagance. He had given up his rooms in Fetter Lane and had taken rooms in Ryder Street. He was supposed to be eating his dinners.

Had he received the legacy six months sooner he would certainly have married Cissy Tilden, but as it was they had violently quarrelled about six months before his uncle's death and she passed out of his life, not to come back. Malone was doing nothing, and C. followed his example ; he had no wish at the present to make adventures in the literary world and still less any desire to go into the social world. He spent his time dining with Wright and Malone, going to various restaurants and theatres, and spending his Sundays sometimes with the Carterets on the river, and sometimes with the Rodens, who had returned from Florence.

It was at Mrs. Roden's he met Mrs. Bucknell again. Mrs. Roden lent her house one afternoon for an amateur concert in aid of a charity and begged him to come. He did. For an amateur performance the music was passable, and a celebrated actress recited *The Last Ride Together* by Robert Browning.

After the concert was over there were strawberries and iced coffee in the dining-room.

As C. walked into the dining-room the first person he saw was Mrs. Bucknell.

She appeared to be delighted to see him, asked him when he had come back, talked of Florence and Paris, and other things, but she did not repeat the invitation she had made him at Florence. She said nothing about his coming to see her.

As she was going away she just asked him casually if he was going to the Stuart House ball.

" No," said C. " I'm not asked."

" Oh, that will be all right," and she said good-bye.

C. felt, as she left the room, that a ray of sunshine had gone with her. She had looked so cool in her fawn-coloured gown, a chain of pearls round her neck and a large bunch of dark red carnations at her waist ; she had seemed so super-refined and delicate in that crowd of rather faded, æsthetic ladies, philanthropic spinsters, and stately dowagers.

This fleeting vision danced in front of C. for the rest of the day.

The next day he received an invitation for Stuart House. He told his mother, and she said he must certainly go. She was in mourning and went nowhere.

He felt as he walked up the staircase of Stuart House that he was years older than when he had entered the house two years before. Everything seemed exactly the same as before, he knew hardly anybody. Not even his sisters were there, not even

Lady Harriet Clive.   He walked through the crowded
rooms not admitting to himself, but nevertheless hoping
at the back of his mind, that he would come upon Mrs.
Bucknell.   He did at last catch sight of her.   She was
dancing in the ballroom.   He stood for a moment in
the doorway.   He then caught sight of his sister-in-
law coming towards him, and he fled.   He went downstairs to a room in which there was a buffet and
refreshments, and there he found one or two men
friends—among others, Wright.   He then went up the
staircase again, and this time he found Mrs. Bucknell
sitting in the gallery with a tall young man who had a
white gardenia in his buttonhole.   He wanted to ask
her for a dance, but he did not dare.   As he was
hesitating, his sister-in-law caught him this time and
introduced him to a shy girl, whose first ball it was.
C. determined it would be better to dance it than to sit
out and he got through the dance without doing very
much damage.   When the dance was over, he noticed
that Mrs. Bucknell was dancing with Sir Wilfrid Clay,
whom he had met with her at Florence.   He despaired
of ever getting a word with her.   The Roden girls were
there enjoying themselves immensely.   They were
both fair-haired, blue-eyed girls with immensely high
spirits and great simplicity.   The eldest, Alice, came
up to C. and told him she was so fearfully hungry and
that nobody suggested taking her down to supper.
He offered to do so at once.

" Well, after this dance," she said.   " I am obliged
to dance it, and, if you like, I'll find you a partner."

"No, please don't," said C. "I'll wait here."

After the dance was over they went down to supper. At one of the round tables Mrs. Bucknell was having supper with Wilfrid Clay. The rest of the seats at that table were nearly all of them empty. As C. and Alice Roden passed the table, Mrs. Bucknell made him an almost imperceptible sign to sit down next to her, which he did. She smiled at him quickly, and said, "How do you do?" and then went on with her conversation with her neighbour. Presently the table began to fill up. Mrs. Bucknell said a few words to C. "I think you treat your old friends very badly," she said. "You have never asked me to dance with you."

"You were always dancing," said C.

"I'm a little bit hurt—C. Are you still called C.?"

C. blushed, and said it was so. He looked at her admiringly. She was a dazzling vision in grey and silver, with silver lilies in her hair, and she wore a large bunch of stephanotis on her shoulder.

Her neighbour showed signs of impatience, but Mrs. Bucknell took little notice, and said to C.: "Do you remember Hamilton Gardens? I used to be so jealous because I thought you liked Freda better than me. You used to make me cry."

Wilfrid Clay, at that moment more impatient than ever, said something about going upstairs. Mrs. Bucknell and her partner left the dining-room. Before she left she turned back and said to C., "Come and see me any afternoon at 116, Upper Berkeley Street."

"Who is that?" said Clay as they walked upstairs.

"Oh, that's only a boy I used to know when we were children. One of the Bramsleys. Lord Hengrave's son."

When C. took his partner back to her mother he noticed that Mrs. Bucknell was again dancing with the young man with a gardenia in his buttonhole, and he didn't get a chance of getting anywhere near her. He came across Wright, and they decided to go home.

"Come back to my rooms for a moment," said Wright.

They talked over the ball. "I heard you being discussed," Wright said to C. "Some one asked an old lady who you were, and she, after giving the facts said that you were a remarkable person, full of promise ; that you were going to be a writer and were very clever. When she mentioned your name it caught the attention of that lady we met in Florence— Mrs. Bucknell—who was standing quite close, and she at once began to listen with great interest to the old lady's conversation."

"Oh!" said C. "I used to know Mrs. Bucknell a long time ago, when I was a child."

The London season was nearing its end. The Eton and Harrow match had come round once more, but C. did not go to it this year. He was thinking of Mrs. Bucknell and whether she really meant him to go and see her. One afternoon he did screw up his courage to go to her house at six o'clock. He rang the bell and waited with expectant trepidation, and at one moment he almost ran away. They were a long time answering the bell, and he rang twice, and at last a maid appeared, who said that Mrs. Bucknell had left the day before for Carlsbad and would not be back in England until September. Lady Hengrave had been ordered to go to Bath by the doctor for her rheumatism, and she was going there with her sister Louisa; Mr. Dartrey was going there as well. C. had been asked to join a reading party consisting of Malone, Hallam, Wright, Wilfrid Abbey, Blades, and some other Oxford men.

They were going there at once for a month to stay at a house near Lynton which Blades had been lent. C. decided that he certainly did not want to stay in London any longer, and he accepted the invitation.

C. enjoyed himself ecstatically at Lynton. The dawn of a new life seemed to be breaking. He bathed, he rode ponies, he went out sailing in a boat, he read books, he sat up all night talking with Malone, Hallam and the others. The days passed in a flash, but he did no work whatsoever. No more did the others. They lived in a little house at the top of a cliff, and every day they bathed in the rocky sea. Sometimes they spent the whole day on the moor, and sometimes the whole day sailing.

C. began to take a keen interest in literature once more. He began to think of writing himself, and he was no longer overawed by the criticism of Blades. He realised that Blades was not infallible, and it was a short step from thinking that, if he was not absolutely right, it was just possible that he was absolutely

wrong. C. even began to write a little verse, and he
looked at some of his old poems, written two years ago,
which he had not destroyed. They seemed to him
very bad. One day he showed the small typewritten
sheaf of poems which he had preserved to Hallam, to
which he had added a new poem. Hallam read them
in silence, and said nothing at the time.

An evening or two later they were all of them
discussing what constituted good or bad verse, and
were talking of poets in general.

" Nobody writes good poetry now," said Malone.

" Well," said Hallam, " I read a modern poem the
other day, by a young writer, that I thought frightfully good."

" Who by ? " asked Blades.

" I forget his name, and I can't quote it, but it was
good." He looked at C. as he said this.

" Who do you think is the best poet ? " Wright
asked Wilfrid Abbey.

" Homer," said Wilfrid.

" Yes ; but the next best ? "

" Shakespeare."

" All the same, it's all rot," said Wright, " to say
there is no good modern verse. What about a line like
this :—

> The wind of death's imperishable wing ?

" Rossetti," said Blades with a slight sniff. " Just
compare that with this :—

> You, who men's fortunes in their faces read,
> To find out mine, look not, alas, on me.

" Is that Elizabethan ? " asked Wright.

Hallam interrupted and said : " Do you know this ? "—

> It is not many miles to Mantua,
> No further than the end of this mad world.

Nobody knew, and Hallam said he had forgotten.
That conversation remained in C.'s mind and had a considerable effect on him. He knew now that Hallam had thought his poem good, and from henceforth he knew that he would not care a pin for what Blades or any one else might say.*

* One poem of C.'s which appears to belong to this period, although it may have been written later, was found in Malone's papers :—

> A song is sighing in the breeze
>   And in the wind to-night ;
> Beyond the hills, across the seas,
>   It calls to me : " Take flight,
> And follow the soft singing breeze."
>
> Around me in the darkling air
>   Its echoes call and float :
> Sad as a tear, soft as a prayer,
>   And now a mocking note
> Is bidding me Beware.
>
> " Beware and pay no heed to me,"
>   So sings the mocking tune ;
> " Beyond the hills, beyond the seas,
>   Beneath the phantom moon,
> There's worse than Death awaiting thee."
>
> O ! Song, to peril I am blind,
>   I'll wander o'er the earth ;
> For I shall seek and I shall find
>   The voice that gave thee birth ;
> The lips that gave thee to the wind.

CHAPTER XXXIII

In September, after staying for a fortnight at the Rodens', C. came back to London and resumed his legal studies, and continued to eat his dinners at Gray's Inn. His life slipped back into its old groove; he saw a certain amount of his relations, and a great deal of his Oxford friends. He did not feel inclined for any fresh venture into new worlds, literary or others.

One day, in November, when he was walking down Bond Street, he met Mrs. Bucknell.

" I think it's too bad of you never to have been to see me," she said.

C. stammered something.

" Well, come to luncheon to-morrow; you will find an old friend of yours, Maud Dallington."

Mrs. Bucknell had an appointment at a hairdresser's, and went into a shop.

The next day C. went to Mrs. Bucknell's house in Upper Berkeley Street. He was shown up into a rather small, crowded drawing-room, where he found Mrs. Bucknell, Lady Ralph Dallington, and a Captain Redford, whom C. recognised as being the young man with the gardenia whom he had seen dancing with Mrs. Bucknell at Stuart House, and a Mrs. Tryan, who was Mrs. Bucknell's eldest sister, and

who was about four years older than she was. There
was a great resemblance between the two sisters, but
the eldest sister, although equally elegant, had none
of the younger sister's beauty.

There was something rather dark about the house,
especially about the dining-room, in which there was a
large, heavy mahogany sideboard.   Over the chimney-
piece there was a portrait in oils of Mrs. Bucknell (just
the head and shoulders), which at once caught C.'s
attention.   It was an amazingly competent, clever
and bold piece of work by a French artist, famous
in Paris, but who had not yet been heard of in
London. It gave an idea of her beauty and her
grace, but C. felt, nevertheless, that it was inexpressibly inadequate and it seemed to lose all its
life as he turned from it to the reality, to Leila Bucknell herself, who looked more than ever like a rare
shining flower in this dark setting.   " She looks always
just right, whatever her surroundings," thought C.
And, indeed, not even the nearest and severest friend
of Mrs. Bucknell would have denied her the talent of
dress.   There was nothing startling nor remarkable
about her clothes ; but she could not go wrong, and
her female friends said she knew exactly when and
where to put a pin ; what to wear and what not to
wear on every occasion, and every day, not only taking
the circumstances, but the weather into consideration,
and doing all this easily and almost unconsciously.

On this occasion she was in harmony with the bright
autumnal weather, and her soft velvet jacket—" Mrs.

Bucknell looked charming in flame-coloured *velour
miroir* trimmed with beaver," so " Miss Maud " in
Fashion described it—was of the colour of rowan
berries and trimmed with fur.

The room was full of white, yellow, and russet
chrysanthemums and the pears and the grapes on the
dining-room table were magnificent.

C. sat between Mrs. Bucknell and Lady Ralph.
The latter was passing through London on her way
back to Rome. She had been spending two months
in Scotland. Mrs. Bucknell said that they had been
lent a house in Brighton for the next two months.

" Terence," she said, " hates London. He would
rather go up to the office every day by train than live
in London. We are going there next week. You
must come down one Sunday."

The Bucknells had no house in the country but they
were often lent a house.

All through luncheon C. could not take his eyes off
Mrs. Bucknell. He thought he discovered new beauty
in her every time she spoke, every time she lifted her
eyebrows and turned her little head towards him.

At the end of luncheon Lady Ralph said something
about the magnificence of the pears and how much one
missed English fruit abroad.

" Uncle Freddy Marryat always sends us fruit from
Sillworth," Mrs. Bucknell said.

She was extremely amiable to C. She made him
tell her everything he had been doing. How she
envied him his life at Lynton ! They had had a dreary

autumn. First of all a cure at Carlsbad, which she hoped had done Terence good, and then a round of duty visits to relations. Terence was so fond of shooting, but they had had so little this year. She adored the country, but she got so little of it. She did not call staying with people living in the country.

Lady Ralph asked Mrs. Bucknell whether she would be likely to come to Rome in the winter or the spring. Mrs. Bucknell said it was extremely unlikely. They couldn't afford an apartment and it was hardly worth while just spending a few days in Florence, as they had done last year—the hotels were ruinous.

"How I envy you living in Rome, Maud!" she said, and a soft shadow veiled her eyes.

"*Dolce color d'oriental zaffiro*," thought C.

"Don't envy me," said Lady Ralph, "I detest it. I only live abroad for economy's sake. It is much cheaper if one lives there regularly. But, frankly, I hate the people. There is not a soul one really cares to be friends with."

"But you see such a lot of English people."

"The nice ones never stop. I like Paris for a time, but I really detest every other place abroad."

"I adore Paris, the shops, the restaurants," said Mrs. Tryan.

Captain Redford, too, put in a word for the Paris restaurants.

"I grant you the restaurants," said Lady Ralph. "It's extraordinary that there should be no such thing as a decent restaurant in London."

"The new café isn't bad," said Captain Redford, talking of a restaurant that had just been opened.

"We dined there the other night," said Mrs. Bucknell, "and at the next table to us there was that *awful* woman, Cynthia May. They oughtn't to allow that sort of person to dine there." Mrs. Tryan and Lady Ralph joined in the chorus of indignation. Cynthia May was a leading light in the *Demi-Monde*, but she was not on the stage.

Terence Bucknell asked C. whether he had changed his mind about the Foreign Office. C. said he had not.

"You are quite right," said Mrs. Bucknell smiling. "I assure you that to be in the Foreign Office is a slave's life. I never see Terence from morning till night, and when he comes back from the office in the evening he is too tired to speak."

Terence Bucknell left in a hurry immediately after luncheon and took a hansom back to the office. Mrs. Bucknell said she was going to a concert after luncheon. It was a Saturday afternoon. Eugene Franck was playing at a Chopin recital and she never missed an opportunity of hearing him play. "He's the only man who understands Chopin, I think," she said, and she looked serious—No, her eyes are violet, thought C.

"You are, of course, musical like all your family. Your aunt has such beautiful music at her house."

C. had to disclaim once more the inheritance of his aunt's knowledge and of his mother's taste in these things.

"I know all about you," said Mrs. Bucknell. "Lady Harriet Clive told me you know all about these things."

Captain Redford looked at C. with suspicion and hostility. C. said firmly that he was not at all musical and that he didn't know a note of music.

"But you know all about books," said Mrs. Bucknell. "I know," she added mysteriously and smiled, and then changed the conversation so as not to embarrass him.

"How tactful she is!" thought C. "How understanding!"

Just as C. was going a messenger boy arrived with a note for Mrs. Bucknell. She read it. "Wilfrid has missed his train," she said to her sister; "how tiresome!" She turned to C. and asked him whether he would like to take her to the concert. It was at St. James's Hall. He accepted with fervent alacrity. The Chopin recital turned out to be a ballad concert.

Helen Brunesi gave an impassioned rendering of *Abide with Me* and some luscious settings to Persian Lyrics, and Eugene Franck played Chopin sometimes so loudly that you feared for the instrument, and sometimes so softly that he was almost inaudible. C. enjoyed the concert rapturously and he kept the programme as long as he lived. He had marked on it the songs that Mrs. Bucknell preferred.

C. stepped along the streets with an elastic step that afternoon after he had dropped Mrs. Bucknell at her house. It was not owing to any particular thing that

Mrs. Bucknell had said to him, but he felt, nevertheless, that he had been given a sip of nectar.

About a week later she asked him to spend Sunday at Brighton. There was no one there but Terence Bucknell and a vague, diaphanous friend, a Mrs. Evelyn, the widow of a general, who lived on the memory of the man whom she had been forbidden to marry. He had afterwards died of typhoid fever. Terence Bucknell delighted in her society, because she seemed to listen to every word he said. In reality she was absent-minded, and was generally thinking of other things. She was shrewd and observant, however, in spite of her absent-mindedness. Leila Bucknell had been the friend of her youth. Mrs. Evelyn was genuinely fond of Leila, but harboured no illusions as to her character.

Leila told her friend everything, and Mrs. Evelyn repeated these confidences to all whom it did not concern but whom it might interest ; not because she was purposely mischievous or indiscreet, but because she found Leila's adventures a fruitful topic of conversation and was convinced that the discussion of them didn't matter. Without her unconscious aid this part of the story, as they say in dedications, would not have been written, or would have been written less fully.

Mrs. Evelyn liked C., but she told Leila at once that the boy was visibly head over ears in love with her and did she think it wise ? Life was already complicated ; C. was absurdly young. Leila pooh-poohed the whole matter.

"Yes, but what will Wilfrid do?" said Alice Evelyn.

"Wilfrid is sensible," said Leila. "Far too sensible to see anything in it but what there is."

"Sensible men are sometimes the worst of all," said Alice with a sigh. "I know it's no use giving advice, but if I were you I should stop it before it's too late."

Leila laughed.

"My dear Alice, I've known that boy ever since we were children."

She appeared to be determined to renew and cement her old acquaintanceship. Terence Bucknell had to go up to London on Sunday afternoon, and Leila took C. for a long walk on the downs and their old acquaintance ripened rapidly into the beginnings of intimacy. Leila enjoyed C.'s undisguised adoration. She did not admit to herself that it was serious, still less that she would ever be to him anything else than an older, sympathetic friend. As for C., his heart and his mind were now full. When he returned to London he wrote almost the longest *Collins* ever penned to thank Leila for his visit, and Leila, thinking that the progress was being a shade too rapid, wrote him a cleverly worded short letter pointing out how fatal exaggeration was to *true friendship*. Nevertheless, the next time she came up to London for the day, she let him know, and they had a brief interview in the British Museum, of all places. Leila saying that she wished to renew her acquaintance with the Elgin marbles.

Christmas came. C. was obliged to spend it in London, but directly after Christmas he was invited to stay with Mrs. Tryan, Leila's sister, who had a large house in Gloucestershire. It was a hunting party. Leila was fond of hunting, and C. enjoyed the sport for the first time in his life. He was well mounted. Horace Tryan, Leila's brother-in-law, was in the Household Brigade, a gentleman of means; he had an admirable stable, and C. was intoxicated by the long rides home, and thought there was no more pleasant flirtation than that of the hunting field. Not so Wilfrid Clay, who spent a few days at Bridlington House. He had a fierce scene with Leila. She laughed at him and said he would mind her seeing her nephews in the nursery next! She had known C. all her life. They had practically been brought up together. They were like brother and sister. In any case she was going to see whom she chose. Wilfrid Clay said that every one was talking of it and that every one thought it ridiculous. She was making herself ridiculous, and it was a shame on the boy.

"Who is every one?" she asked. "Have they said anything to you?"

No they hadn't, but he knew quite well what they were thinking.

As for C., he had entered a new world. He no longer wanted to go near the literary world, but all sorts of plans and ideas for poems, lyrics and sonnets, all on the subject of Leila, buzzed in his head. He invested her with every good quality, every attribute of the head and the heart, every virtue, every grace. There was nothing, he thought, she did not know and did not understand, did not guess, did not feel.

Terence Bucknell was quite unconcerned about the matter. He did not give it a thought. He spent a Sunday at Bridlington, but he went up to London on the following Monday. He did not hunt. Leila had never had any bother with him.

After this Christmas party was over, they all went back to London. Harry came up to London after Christmas. His regiment was starting for India and C. went down to Hounslow with him the night before he started for Southampton. Lady Hengrave said good-bye to Harry in London. She showed little outward signs of emotion, but C. was made aware by one or two little incidents that she was taking his departure very hardly. He heard her say to Miss Hackett that Harry's socks were in a dreadful state and that she had better go to Alderson's in Bond Street and buy him two dozen pairs of the best thick woollen socks, and before Harry started, she gave him his father's watch, a repeater, which she had kept hitherto as a sacred relic. C. knew that in doing this she felt she would never see him again. At Hounslow, in the barracks, where a deafening sound of hammering was increasing, and where soldiers were rushing about, hurling things into packing cases, and where every scrap of unnecessary furniture and importunate object seemed to be in the process of being packed, C. had the same presentiment himself, and still more so at

Southampton on the quay as he watched the troopship get under weigh. He saw Harry waving to him, and an icy feeling went down his spine, a real shiver from the shores of death. Harry looked so radiant, so young and so happy. As the troopship departed and the last cheers died away, C. felt that a portion of his life had gone, gone never to come back again.

Harry, himself, had left England in tearing spirits; he was young, strong, good-looking, healthy, fancy-free, and not twenty-one, and all life and all India were before him. He was looking forward to his five years there with the utmost impatience.

The first thing that C. did when he got back to London was to go and see Leila, but she was not at home. Leila, although she had determined that nothing in the world would make her drop C.'s acquaintance, or take steps to damp the ardour of his adoration, nevertheless felt that for the moment it was best to proceed carefully and prudently. Wilfrid Clay came to see her every day of his life; and then there was Lord Marryat, an older admirer, of another generation, with reddish hair and grey whiskers and a slight air of the 'eighties about him. He had known Leila as a child, and he treated her paternally. She called him " Uncle Freddy," although there was no relationship. He was easy to deal with, but he was a factor of no little importance in her life. He was a widower and extremely well off, and he supplied Leila with everything she wanted in the way of fruit, game, and, in an indirect way, clothes and

other objects of ornament and use. He was a man
of taste and knowledge. The French portrait of Leila
in her dining-room was his gift. Little Christmas
presents and birthday presents and mementoes " just
to mark the day " took the form of cheques. If she
gave a dinner, he lent her his plate and his cook, and
he sent her flowers from the country once a week. He
accepted Wilfrid Clay, whom he looked upon as a
docile slave, necessary to Leila's comfort ; but he had
his particular days, his particular hours, and on
certain nights in the week he came to dinner and
played patience after dinner, and on these occasions
he resented the presence of strangers and newcomers.

Leila had during the last season one other admirer,
in the shape of Captain Redford, but soon after she
made the acquaintance of C. she began to find him
wanting, and finally she dismissed him. He was
penniless, uninteresting and rather sulky. At first she
had thought him good-looking and attractive. He
had thought at the end of the summer that he was
getting on well. The autumn had brought him a
harvest of disillusion, and one day, when he had
ventured on a declaration and suited the action to
the word, Leila had turned on him with immense
dignity and said, " I'm not that kind of woman."
After that she had forbidden him the house. He went
away disconsolate and discomfited and penitent, but
it was too late. Leila gave him to understand it was
all over.

C. was now the chief excitement of Leila's life. She

played up to him, although she found this difficult, but the difficulty added to the excitement. She cared not a rap for any of the things that C. cared for. She never read a book, except the novels of George Ohnet and such books as she received from the circulating library, which were chosen for her by the man behind the counter. The only poetry she cared for were the words which were married to certain sentimental songs she was fond of. She copied out some of these in a book bound in pink which had a gilt lock, and which she was far too wise to show to C., but she gave him to understand that it was a storehouse of all the rarest poetry in French and English. C.'s conversation when he talked of such things was Hebrew to her, but, nevertheless, she never committed herself to a foolish comment, nor to an incriminating revealing criticism. She encouraged C. to talk, to abound in himself, and while he was pouring out fervid quotations from Browning and Keats she mentally added up her bills or thought out a new ball gown. She sometimes took C. to the South Kensington Museum, not because it interested her, but because she was not likely to meet any of her friends there ; and sometimes she took him to a concert, where she cried whenever the music was soft. She could cry easily, as she had a natural fund of sentiment. She honestly enjoyed C.'s society at this time. In the first place, looks always attracted her, and C. had blossomed out under the influence of his passion. He seemed to have broken his shell. He was a different person from the shy boy who had returned from Rome so listless, and who Lady Hen-grave had thought was going to develop into a social recluse, a kind of literary Diogenes.

He had dressed carelessly, had not given a thought to such things until now since he had left Eton ; but now, under Leila's influence (she subtly and tactfully took interest, approved—it was not necessary to advise : he had his father's instinct for such things— interest sufficed), he looked different, and he reminded Lady Hengrave of his father when he had been young. He was becoming almost as good-looking as Harry. And now, instead of being sullen and shy, he was in high spirits and had become talkative and gay. He went to a gymnasium three times a week, and fenced. Sometimes he got his brother Edward to lend him a horse, and he would ride in Rotten Row in the morning. There, sometimes, he would meet Leila.

Leila would sometimes get up parties of four to go to the play, and take her sister or Alice Evelyn, who now accepted the fact of C. and understood that the time for remonstrance was over. It was far too late.

The change in C. did not, of course, pass unnoticed either to Lady Hengrave or to his sisters. Lady Hengrave guessed what was happening, and soon understood who was the agent. She said nothing. She never criticised. She considered that it was a matter, like getting the measles, that young boys had to go through, and that it would soon be over. She was thankful that it was Leila Bucknell, the daughter of some one she had known as a girl, and not an actress. She was devoutly thankful it was a married woman. " It will prepare him for marriage," she thought. His sisters took a different line. They told him he was making himself ridiculous and that Leila was laughing at him and taking him as a joke. This, of course, fanned the flame of his passion still more. He quarrelled with Julia and with Marjorie and thought about Leila all the more. He began sending her poems which, although addressed to anonymous beings, had a strong personal accent. Leila encouraged this at first, and said that she had copied out some of his beautiful lines in her sacred pink book, in which she only copied the most beautiful things, her most treasured favourites, but as the poems increased in fervour and in outspokenness, she became slightly uneasy. She did not like things to be expressed so crudely; she disliked dots on the i's, and she once more administered a slight check and said that the best poets treated friendship with greater reserve. She not only did not understand his verses, finding them full of obscure classical allusions which meant nothing to her and turns of phrase which puzzled her, but what she did understand (except when it was directly flattering to herself, and even then not always) she did not like. She wished his poetry were more like that of Lord Henry Somerset. She agreed with the dictum that verse should be simple, sensuous and impassioned. She vaguely guessed C.'s effusions to possess the last-named qualities, but to her taste they lacked simplicity, and she sometimes suspected them

of being coarse, which, to do them justice, they were
not. What she would have liked would have been love
poems written in the style of the *Christian Year*.
Leila never missed going to church on Sunday.
She had a strong Low Church streak in her nature,
but she sacrificed her personal inclinations to what
she thought, considering all things—Terence and
public opinion and the rest—was most proper and fit
by going to a church with a broad, colourless flavour
near Oxford Street, where there was a popular-
preacher. One Sunday she took C. They walked to
church with Terence and her two children, a little
boy and a little girl (aged eight and six respectively).
She sat in the pew between her two pretty little
children, dressed in black with a fur boa round her
neck, a touch of violet in her fur toque, and a large
bunch of violets very deftly pinned and arranged in
the fur of her jacket, and she followed the service
with rapt devotion. During the hymns and at a
certain allusion to the unhappy in the sermon her
eyes were wet and seemed to be like wonderful dark
flowers with dew upon them. C. thought that he
was indeed in the presence of an angel, a creature
who had been banished from some brighter clime
and condemned to a term of imprisonment in a world
that was alien to her and altogether too hard and too
rough for so rare and exquisite a being.

CHAPTER XXXIV

Things went on more or less like this until Easter, when C. was asked to stay with the Rodens. He said he was unable to go, as he had promised to go and see his old friend Madame Maartens, in Paris, who was not at all well. She was, in fact, seriously ill, and as she was very old one never knew what might not happen. She had expressed a wish to see him, and, of course, he must go.

It so happened that Terence and Leila Bucknell were going to spend Easter in Paris as well. They were staying with a French friend of theirs, a Madame de Volnay, who had a charming little house on the other side of the river. C. stayed in the little hotel in the street off the *Rue de Rivoli*, where he had always stayed before. He went to see Madame Maartens directly he arrived, and found her more or less convalescent after a severe attack of influenza. She was overjoyed at seeing him, but, after he had been with her for about ten minutes, he saw that the effort of talking was becoming too much for her, and he said good-bye. M. Maartens, as he said good-bye to C., broke down and said, between his sobs, that he knew there was no hope. What would he do without her ? But he would not—that was one consolation—survive her long. C. promised to return again shortly.

Leila was engrossed in the serious business of buying clothes, a duty she performed with scrupulous conscientiousness and unflagging energy, and with which she let nothing interfere. But in the evenings she let her hostess take her to all the interesting plays that were on, and C., who had been introduced to Madame de Volnay, joined the party. Madeleine Lapara was not in Paris, but they saw a rather bitter emotional comedy in which Réjane was playing, and which Leila said she thought "*horrible*, so *cynical*," and a play by Sardou that was creating some stir and in which Coquelin had the leading part.

Madame de Volnay was a widow; she was dark, practical, inquisitive, and well-off, with a good deal of knowledge, culture and intelligence. She read the story of C.'s heart in one moment.

Two days after his arrival C. called on Beatrice, but he was told that Madame and Monsieur had gone to Rome for Easter. The news made C. laugh bitterly. She could go to Rome now quite easily. However, it was no use thinking of that—and, indeed, he had little desire to think of the past. He was absorbed in the present.

Every day Leila said they must really go to the Louvre, but every day the visit to the picture gallery was put off, as the visits to the *Magasin du Louvre* and other shops proved to be so time-taking, but one day Madame de Volnay, Terence, C. and Leila drove to

Versailles (Easter was late that year) through a
stretch of opening blossom; it was a world of blossom,
blossom everywhere, sheets and flakes and delicate
traceries, as of frozen foam. C. was in the seventh
heaven of happiness. They had luncheon at the
Hôtel des Réservoirs, and after luncheon, C., Leila,
Terence and Madame de Volnay, who tactfully
took charge of Terence and led him away, wandered
in the park, which brought back to C. many memories
of Burstall. He told Leila all about Burstall. She
realised from C.'s description that he was just the kind
of man whom she could not endure and who would
bore her to death, but all she said was : " How I
should like to know him ! I wonder where he is now ? "

" Nobody knows," said C. " Somewhere in the
tropics, at Tahiti or some such outlandish place."

" When he comes back you must bring him to Upper
Berkeley Street," said Leila. " I'm sure I should love
him, although I should be frightened to death of him,
and I don't think he'd like me."

This expedition to Versailles was the only occasion
on which C. had the opportunity of having any talk
with Leila alone. All the rest of the time she had
either been shopping or out with Madame de Volnay
and Terence, and C. made the most of his opportunity,
and intoxicated as he was after the beauty of the spring
drive, began not only to be lyrical, but direct in his
declarations, so that Leila had once more to check him.
She felt he was going too far, and she did not want
that. She begged him not to spoil everything. The

word *friendship* was again employed with dexterity. Up to now *friendship* was the only word which Leila allowed the use of when their relation was mentioned. As far as she was concerned there was at present nothing inaccurate in its use, but it was a wild under-statement of C.'s feelings.

C. accepted the rebuke, and Leila began to talk of herself and to convey, by a series of delicate hints and suggestions and reticences, that her life was a very difficult one, it was a long struggle with poverty, with unsympathetic and critical relations and "in-laws," unpleasant surroundings, difficult conditions, and dis-tasteful duties and want of understanding on all sides. She had thought that in C. she had at last found a friend who understood, and she did hope he was not going to disappoint her. She was so greatly in need of help and sympathy. She had really no friends. Terence was wonderful, of course, a tower of strength, but he was so engrossed in his work and so harassed by it, and so unfairly treated by the Office. He ought to be in the Diplomatic Service and to be given a Legation. But then, could they afford it ? No. She saw nothing for it but for him to remain in the office, and after years he would perhaps be an Under-Secretary. He could not afford to exchange into the Diplomatic Service. Of course it was a pity. He would have made an ideal Ambassador. Then there was Wilfrid Clay. She owed him a lot, more than she could ever repay. He had been a devoted friend and had helped her in every way. Whenever she went abroad he looked out her trains for her, as Terence was far too busy and was bad at Bradshaw, but Wilfrid understood all those things, and he was so good to the children. He understood children and always remembered their birthdays, which was wonderful of him. He was so faithful, so devoted. He had had such an unhappy life, too. He had never married. He had wanted to marry, but he had been cruelly treated by a horrid girl; a girl to whom he had been engaged and who had broken off the engagement at the last moment. One must always remember that. He had suffered greatly, and he had a heart of gold. She, none the less, gave C. to understand that although Wilfrid had a heart of gold, he had a great deal of lead in his composition as well, and that he was one of life's burdens which had to be borne with patience. The day before they left Paris, Wilfrid Clay arrived in person, so as to travel back with them and see they had everything they wanted. He was a director of one of the railway companies, and he saw that Leila had a carriage and a cabin to herself. Leila explained to him that C. had come over to see a great friend of Lady Hengrave's who was dying, and she suggested to C. that he should spend his last day at Versailles while Wilfrid helped her to do her final shopping. C. called once more on Madame Maartens, but she was in bed and could see no one. M. Maartens was with her, and did not come down. C. left a message. The next day they all travelled back to London. Leila had again been lent a little house for the summer by Lord Marryat. She had let her London house for the season for a high rent, too, the business having been managed by Wilfrid. This time it was a house on the border of Surrey and Berkshire, not far from Ascot. Terence, she said, could not endure summer in London, and although Leila confessed she did enjoy going to balls sometimes, and dining out, she was only too ready to give all that up, and she could always go up to London for a week or so at the end of the season and stay with her sister. She invited C. to spend a Sunday at Twyford, which was the name of the house, soon after they returned. He went, and there he found Lord Marryat, Wilfrid Clay, Mrs. Evelyn and Mrs. Tryan. He had hardly any talk with Leila at all, who devoted herself entirely to Wilfrid Clay and Lord Marryat, giving C. to understand by her looks that she was performing a necessary, but uncongenial, duty.

C. began to receive invitations to go out. Mrs. Tryan said he must go to a dance that was being given at a house in Manchester Square. C. went to the dance, but there was no Leila, and he felt utterly forlorn and disconsolate. Mrs. Tryan introduced him to several people. The dance was not for girls, but for young married women, and was said to be very " good."

C. was asked to take some one down to supper, and he went down with a Mrs. D'Avenant, to whom he had been introduced that evening. She was handsome and gay, and enjoyed the society of the young. They talked on and on. C. interested and amused her by his violence and his outspoken opinion of persons and things ; his strong likes and dislikes. She was attracted by him ; he was something new, and she resolved to keep her discovery to herself.

The ballroom had begun to thin, and the supper-room was almost empty.

Mrs. D'Avenant had asked her sister to wait for her and take her home just before she met C. Her sister came to fetch her, and was indignant at having been kept waiting.

" It is ridiculous," said the sister, " for you, at your age, to sit talking for hours to those young school boys."

Mrs. Evelyn watched the scene with interest from the table where she was sitting.

C. went to one or two other entertainments, and Mrs. Evelyn reported the facts to Leila.

" C.," she said, " is going *everywhere* to *every lighted candle* and is enjoying himself *immensely*. Some one is sure to get hold of him soon."

This was a gross exaggeration. He had been, at the most, to two or three balls, and where there was no Leila there was for him no enjoyment ; but he went because he sometimes saw people who knew her, and he had the chance of hearing her name spoken or of saying her name, of talking to Mrs. Evelyn or to Mrs. Tryan, or to Mrs. D'Avenant, with all of whom he could mention Leila. He wrote to her regularly, and his letters had got to the stage of omitting a beginning.

Leila, as soon as she heard this, became uneasy. She felt an unexpected, irrational wave of jealousy and fear. She suddenly realised that she could not bear the thought of C. being taken from her. This could not, must not, be. She asked him down to Twyford on the following Sunday. Wilfrid Clay had been coming, and Leila put him off. She explained that some tiresome "in-laws" of Terence's were coming. As a matter of fact, there was no one there at all except Mrs. Evelyn. Terence had been invited to a political party at the Foreign Secretary's to meet some Colonial Premiers.

Wilfrid Clay had accepted an invitation to stay at another country house not many miles from Twyford, and, having nothing better to do on Sunday afternoon, he bicycled over after luncheon to see Leila. He found Leila and C. sitting on the lawn. Mrs. Evelyn had gone to lie down. She had a bad headache. When Leila saw Wilfrid approaching, she showed the utmost *sang-froid*. "Go for a little walk in the kitchen garden," she said to C. "I will be back directly."

She walked indoors with Wilfrid into the little drawing-room whose French windows looked out on to the garden, and which was full of nick-nacks, books and flowers, and had an original picture by Mason in a prominent place. The owner of the house was artistic.

"Well?" said Leila.

Wilfrid Clay poured out the vessels of his indignation. He was a prim man, exceedingly correct in everything he said and did ; he was as honest as the day, and inexpressibly faithful and loyal. Moreover, he had loved Leila for years, passionately, and at one time, at any rate, she had returned his love, and during the rest of the time, up to the present, she had pretended to do so. He had slaved for her, there was nothing, big or small, he had not done for her ; no wish of hers he had not guessed and forestalled ; he had thought of nothing but her ; he had never looked at any one else. She was his whole existence.

He had had many disappointments and ups and downs ; she had often treated him cruelly. He had borne everything, accepted everything, forgiven everything ; but this was too much, that she should have taken the trouble to deceive him in this manner, for the sake of this boy.

Now, as he thought how often C. had been with the Bucknells, his anger grew. She had been deceiving him all the time. He spoke his mind with great bitterness.

"So that was all a pack of lies about Terence's in-laws," he said. " I might have known."

Leila looked at him icily.

"Of course," she said, "if you like to call me names——"

" I didn't call you anything, but I do think——" And the tide of indignant remonstrance and protest swelled and rose, and then subsided once more. He begged her not to treat him like this, and not to play the fool with this boy.

Leila looked at him with a colder hardness.

Wilfrid's rage, which had spent itself for the moment, suddenly took on a new lease of life. Past grievances arose. The manner she had treated him last year ; her behaviour with Redford (and here he had done her an injustice—Leila had never given Redford a chance) ; the way she had behaved about Paris, how she had prevented his coming there till the last minute, until it was too late.

" Too late ? " said Leila. " What do you mean ? "

" You know quite well what I mean."

" Well, and what if I do ? " said Leila. " What if things *are* what you think, what you *choose* to think ? What business is it of yours ? "

" What business is it of mine ? Oh, let's stop this ridiculous wrangle ! Say it has all been a mistake."

" Say it's all been a mistake ? " she echoed. " What has been a mistake ? What have I said that I have got to retract ? You come down here, you force yourself into the house, you insult me, and you expect me to apologise, just because I happen to have asked a boy to the house whom I have known all my life and whom I am very fond of."

" You are too unfair."

" Unfair ? " She laughed ironically.

" The sooner you get used to C. the better ; because you will see him here very often. I have promised his mother to be kind to him."

" Leila, don't——"

" I like people who are civil, and he is civil. I don't
like being treated as if I was . . . as if I was . . . I
don't know what . . . in that way. I'm not used to
it. Don't you think you had better go back ? Nothing
is so rude as to go away from a party when one is
staying with people. I'm sure Mildred will think it
rude."

" Leila——"

" Please go away; I've got a headache. You've
given me a headache. I am so—so tired——"

" No, I shan't go away," said Wilfrid, suddenly
losing his temper. He was a meek man as a rule,
extremely good-tempered and well-mannered, with
great self-control, and a great sense not only of the
decencies of life, but profoundly sensitive to the
conventions of society and to the amenities of intercourse. He loathed scenes, and would sooner have
died than make one in public, but at this moment he
was goaded beyond human endurance. He was
stung, wounded to the quick, injured, and he felt
capable of anything. During this conversation he
had been walking round the room in an agitated way,
lighting cigarettes and throwing them away as soon
as they were lit. Near a chintz armchair there was a
little red three-legged stool, painted with Aspinall's
enamel, and on it there was a bowl of roses. He took
the bowl and flung it on to the floor. It broke in
pieces.

Leila lay back in her armchair and cried silently.

Wilfrid felt ashamed of himself, and he rushed

towards Leila, but she waved him away with a gentleness that was decisive.

"Don't," she said faintly and shuddering, "don't come near me, please."

Wilfrid poured out apologies. He was not a violent man. His act had been entirely out of keeping with his usual self, and he could not, he did not know how to proceed on the same plane. It was against his nature. He was full of more than repentance, of acute remorse. Leila knew this well, and exploited the situation to the utmost.

"I beg of you to go," she said.

She got up and left the room slowly, still crying. She went up to her bedroom and locked the door.

Wilfrid knew there was nothing to be done. He waited half an hour, then an hour. Tea was brought out to the lawn and Leila's maid came down and said to Wilfrid that Mrs. Bucknell had told her to tell them that she had a bad headache, had gone to bed and would not come down.

Wilfrid took his bicycle and went back to his party.

He had not been gone long before Leila said she felt better. She had a cup of tea in her bedroom and then had a long talk with Alice Evelyn in her bedroom; she recounted every detail to her friend, who received the story with the tenacious receptivity of a gramophone record.

"Wilfrid is impossible," said Leila. "He is always making scenes. I shall be obliged to give up seeing him altogether."

Alice Evelyn was sympathetic but wise, and urged her to do nothing rash. Leila remained talking to Alice for about half an hour, and then she reappeared in the garden. She asked C. to read to her; she felt, she said, very tired.

"What shall I read?" asked C.

"I should like you to read me something quite simple. One of Hans Andersen's fairy tales. There is a copy in the drawing-room, the children left it there this morning."

C. fetched the book.

"Which story shall I read?" he asked.

"Oh, the *Ugly Duckling*," said Leila.

C. thought it was adorable of her to like fairy tales and he read out the story of the *Ugly Duckling*, as they both lay back in garden chairs.

Leila lay back with closed eyes, but in spite of her eyes being closed she had the appearance of listening. She was not listening in reality. She was probably making up her mind as to how inconvenient it would be for her to break with Wilfrid altogether at this moment, and carefully weighing the pros and cons. At any rate he must be taught a lesson that he would never forget, and she made up her mind either then, or soon after, to break for the present. After all, she knew she could always get him back just whenever she chose, and she smiled to herself.

Leila said nothing to C. about Wilfrid, except that he had come over from a neighbouring party and had had to go back. Alice Evelyn came down to dinner.

She was feeling, she said, a little better ; she was, in fact, exhilarated by the drama that she felt was going on in the house. She had done her best to dissuade Leila from bringing about such a situation, but now that it had happened, Alice could not help being interested, and enjoying it to the full. She was not yet, she said, quite well, and would go to bed early. It was a lovely June night ; breathlessly hot, and there was a smell of syringa in the air. C. suggested a walk in the woods. Leila acquiesced, but they never got as far as the woods. They wandered, in fact, the other way in the garden, and they stopped to listen to the soft orchestra of the darkness, and C. poured out to its accompaniment all that he felt, in a tremulous stream of whispers. This time Leila no longer checked him.

Although Leila often made a great show of resistance, and did resist what she did not share, for a time ; and could resist what she had ceased to share, indefinitely, and with a stubbornness that had the force of steel ; she could never resist a new love, if it were expressed with sufficient force and ardour. On such occasions she yielded at a touch, and let the great river swiftly bear her to the main. She now felt no wish to resist C. On the contrary, she responded to his passion with every chord of her sentimental soul and every fibre of her soft pliant voluptuous temperament.

.   .   .   .   .

The next day C. went up to London, not without having made arrangements for meeting Leila in the immediate future, and Leila spent several hours composing a letter to Wilfrid. It was a masterpiece, an unconscious masterpiece, when it was finished. It put him entirely in the wrong and it was nicely calculated to wound every nerve in his being.

She received several telegrams from him and a long letter by the first post. These she threw away. They had often had many scenes and quarrels before, partings and reconciliations, and Wilfrid felt quite certain that it would be all right in a day or two— acutely as he was suffering for the moment—but the days passed and no sign of reconciliation was made by Leila. He went down to Twyford and she was out. He went down a second time and she refused to see him. The week after she came up to London for the Arlington House ball. C. was invited to it and Leila sat out with him in the garden most of the night and had supper with him as well.

Wilfrid Clay was there. Leila said " How do you do " to him civilly, as though he had been a stranger she had once met at some watering place and whom she remembered quite well, and she talked through him as if he were not there.

CHAPTER XXXV

THE summer seemed long in the same way the epochs of childhood seemed long to C., and yet when it was over it seemed to have gone by in a flash. It was for him a see-saw epoch alternating between complete ecstasy and utter despondency. Leila came up to London very often, and he saw her constantly, and every now and then she allowed him to come to Twyford, not as often as he wished. In July, she often stayed a night with her sister, Mrs. Tryan, and C. went to any entertainment where he knew he would find Leila, but this was not an unmixed pleasure, as she had to devote a certain amount of time to other people at these entertainments, and C. suffered acutely when she spoke to others for any length of time. But as far as their personal relations were concerned, everything seemed so far to be going smoothly. Probably Leila found it a strain ; he was so young and so serious, and he could not take things lightly. Every now and again C. would send her poems that he wrote, and she ended by treating these like bills ; they got lost almost before she had looked at them. Leila took no steps to make up things with Wilfrid Clay, who was reduced to pulp. Finally he left London for a month's yachting. Leila showed no signs of minding. At the end of the season, in August, Leila told C. that Terence had again been ordered to Carlsbad, and that she was going with him. He suggested coming there, too. That, she said, was impossible. He might, if he liked, meet them at Bayreuth, where they were going to stop on the way to hear one of the cycles.

C. met them at Bayreuth. Mrs. Evelyn was with Leila, and they had all their meals together. Leila confessed to her friends that the music bored her, and she resolved, after the first two performances, not to stay for the rest of the cycle ; she made up her mind to sell the tickets for the remaining performances. She was, perhaps, wondering how she would explain this act to C., without letting him know that she found the music quite intolerable, when C. received a telegram from his sister Julia, telling him to come home at once, as Lady Hengrave was seriously ill. Leila was relieved and intensely sympathetic. She said they would meet in the autumn as soon as she came back, and he must write to her every day.

When he got to London he found that his mother had caught a chill, which had developed rapidly into double pneumonia. The doctors took a grave view of the case. He was taken into his mother's room. She looked very ill, but she was just the same. She asked who had been at Bayreuth, said nothing about Leila, but told him that she had heard from Sir Shreeve Mellings, who said he was dissatisfied with C.'s attendance at his chambers during the summer.

" I told him," she said, " it was the first summer you

had been out, and that you would work harder in the autumn."

This was the last time he saw her but one. The day after she was worse, but, nevertheless, she expressed a wish that C. should come to her room for a minute. She was coughing badly when C. went in. She smiled, as if apologising for her bad manners. When the paroxysm was over, she whispered : " Look after Harry." The nurse then whispered to him to go. He never saw her again, and she died early the next morning. Just before she died she asked for Gilbert, her ne'er-do-weel son, whom she had never been known to mention since he left in disgrace for Canada.

She was buried, according to her wish, at Bramsley. Bramsley was still let to some American friends of Edward's wife, and the family went down for the day and drove straight from the station to the church and straight back to the station when the funeral was over. They none of them went near the house. Mrs. Roden took C. back with her to Elladon. He was moody and depressed. This, of course, seemed, under the circumstances, quite natural, but although with his mother's death he felt as if a large part of the background of his life had gone, and although it added to his melancholy, it was not the real reason of his sadness. The real reason of that was not so much the absence of Leila, as the dawn of a suspicion that she had not been so sad at his departure as he had expected.

The day of the funeral he received a few lines from her.

"*I am thinking of you all the day,*" she wrote. "*I know you will be brave. It is so true that the darkest hour is the hour before the dawn. Last night I was reading some beautiful lines, and I thought of you—*

> Only the dead hearts forsake us never ;
> Death's last kiss has been the mystic sign
> Consecrating Love our own for ever,
> Crowning it eternal and divine."

The Bucknells came back to London at the beginning of September. Leila let C. know the date of her arrival and asked him to come and see her the evening after, at six-thirty. He was already back in London. His mother's house was to be sold, and he took furnished rooms next to Gerald Malone's and Wright's in Ryder Street.

Leila appeared overjoyed to see him. She told him about her time abroad, how dull it had been. In the course of the conversation she said that Wilfrid Clay had come out. He had been ordered by the doctor to go to Carlsbad, and they had travelled back together. C. had forgotten the existence of Wilfrid Clay.

"Poor Wilfrid, he means so well," she said.

She told C. her plans. Terence had to go back to the office. She was going to Scotland to stay with some relations. She would be away for the next month.

"Then I shan't see you for years," said C.

"I shall be in London all the winter."

At that moment the butler walked in and announced Lord Marryat.

They exchanged a few banal remarks, and then C. left the house.

Leila went to Scotland. She was to stay there a month; as it was, she stayed away two months, until the end of October. Nevertheless, C. saw her once before she came back. He travelled up to Scotland to have ten minutes' conversation with her at Inverness Station, where she was stopped to change trains on her way south to Glasgow.

In November, she came back from the north for good and settled down in London. C. was working hard for one of his law examinations. Leila, to his surprise, had not let him know the exact day she was coming back, and it was only after her arrival that he received a note from her saying that she was back in London. He found the letter on his table when he came back from the chambers in the evening, and he flew round in a hansom to her house. Mrs. Bucknell was at home. She had finished tea and was sitting by the fire. Every time C. saw Leila after a period of absence she seemed to him more beautiful, and more beautiful in a different way. Never had she looked more radiant than on that November afternoon. A life of open air and exercise had given her a bath of sunshine and rest and youth, and she seemed to be still glowing from the effects of it.

" Why didn't you tell me you were coming ? " he said.

" There wasn't time; I came away a day sooner than I expected, and I missed the post. You couldn't have heard sooner."

There was a slight pause.

" Tell me everything you have been doing."

" What have you been doing ? "

" Leila, you're different."

She laughed.

" What nonsense ! "

The butler came in and announced : " Mr. Dallas Wace."

C. had not seen him since they had met at Rome at the Embassy. He thought to himself, " He won't stay long." But he was mistaken. Mr. Dallas Wace had no intention of going away. He, too, had been in Scotland, where he had met Leila. They had known each other for a long time quite slightly, but in Scotland they had evidently made friends.

Dallas Wace was civil to C. He remembered having met him at Rome ; he asked after his sisters, and tried to rope him into the conversation. C. was boiling with inward rage, and refused to be roped in. He sat gloomy, sullen and silent, answering in mono-syllables. Dallas Wace, realising the situation, then ignored C. altogether, and talked to Leila as if he were not there, as if he were a child or a schoolboy to whom one has done one's full duty once one has flung them a word.

But C. was determined to sit him out. He sat on without saying a word, answering in monosyllables when Leila said something to him, until half-past six, when Terence returned from the office.

Then Wace got up and took leave of Leila.

" Don't forget to-morrow night," she said, as he was going. " Dinner at half-past seven, here. We've got tickets for the Gaiety. They say it's very good."

Terence greeted C. cordially, and then the children were brought down to say good-night, and C. left the house. He wrote Leila a long letter of passionate reproach that night. She didn't answer it. In the morning he had received a letter from Lady Elizabeth Carteret, asking him to stay with her in the country from Saturday till Monday. If Leila was going to be in London, he thought he would not go. He went to see Leila again in the evening. She was at home and by herself. She said nothing about the incident of the day before and was natural and friendly. C. asked her what she was going to do on Sunday.

" We are staying with the Stonehenges," she said.

Lord Stonehenge was the Foreign Secretary at the time, and Terence's chief. Tea was brought in.

" Wilfrid's coming to see me presently," Leila said with the utmost naturalness, " and when he comes you must leave us, because I've got to talk business with him. He's trying to sell some land for my mother."

" You can't want to see him," said C.

" I can't help it, one's life has to go on," said Leila plaintively. " You must understand that certain things have to be done. You make things so difficult. You must be a little patient."

C. got up.

" The truth of the matter is," he said, " that you

don't care for me any more. You're changed ever since you came back from Scotland."

Wilfrid Clay was announced, and this time C. went away. Perhaps he was wrong, he thought, as he reflected afterwards.

He wrote Leila a long letter that night, saying how sorry he was he had behaved in such a foolish way. Couldn't he see her before she left the next day, which was Saturday?

She sent him round a note by a messenger boy in the morning, saying that she was having luncheon out and that she and Terence were going down to the country directly after luncheon. She would see him on Monday.

On Saturday afternoon C. went down to the Carterets. They no longer lived on the river now, but in the New Forest. To his great surprise, who should C. find there but Beatrice. She and her husband had been spending two months in England in the country. He had been obliged to go back to Paris more suddenly than he had expected. She was going back on Monday. Beatrice looked a little better than when C. had seen her in Paris, but she had not recovered her radiance, and there was a hunted look about her. They went for a long walk on Sunday afternoon. They talked of everything under the sun, as they used to do, but C. said little about his life, and Beatrice nothing of hers. They each of them avoided vital issues. But C. felt, nevertheless, that Beatrice knew exactly what he was going through, which, indeed, she did, and would have done even if Lady Elizabeth had not told her the facts and painted them in no uncertain colours.

Lady Elizabeth was an old friend of Terence's, and liked him. She knew Leila slightly and disliked her intensely, and she had told Beatrice that Leila would no doubt ruin C.'s life. This meeting with Beatrice was just at this moment like balm to C. He felt that she understood everything, and he knew that she would say nothing that would jar or would hurt. She was catching every word that he did not say, every shade that it was unnecessary for him to indicate.

On Monday morning they all travelled back to London together.

C. found a letter from Leila telling him to come round at six. He found her alone, and she asked him about his Sunday.

" Who was there ? " she asked.

" Only just the family and a Mrs. Fitzclare."

" Mrs. Fitzclare ? "

" She lives in Paris. Fitzclare is in a bank in Paris."

" Was he there ? "

" No, he had gone back."

Leila talked of her party. It had been large and rather official.

" Terence enjoyed it," she said. " The Stone-henges are very kind. She's such a nice woman."

They discussed plans for the future, and especially

Christmas plans. Terence and Leila were going to stay with some people in Northamptonshire whom C. didn't know. He was going up for his examination in December, and when it was over, Wright, who was also going up for an examination, wanted C. to go to Paris with him. After Christmas, Leila was going to stay with her sister. She would get her to ask C.

Terence came back early from the office that evening.

"I have just met Lady Elizabeth Carteret in the street," he said to Leila. "I hadn't seen her for ages. I've asked her to luncheon to-morrow. That's all right, I suppose?"

"Oh, yes," said Leila, "but I've got no one to meet her."

"Won't you come?" said Terence to C.

C. was engaged. He was having luncheon with his sister-in-law.

"It doesn't matter," said Leila, "I'll get some one."

On the following evening, when C. got back from his chambers, he found a little note from Leila, written in pencil. C. read it quickly and burnt it at once, but the sense of it blazed in his brain in letters of fire. It was to this effect: she had not thought she had been mistaken in *him*, but found that she had made a mistake; that she had no wish to be an obstacle, and that he must cut her out of his life altogether. The letter seared him like a piece of hot iron. He did not answer it, but the next morning, early, he went round to Upper Berkeley Street. Leila was out shopping. In the evening he went round again. This time she was not at home. He walked up and down the street not knowing what he was doing, like a man in a dream, revolving all sorts of things to say and to do. It was incredible, that was the main idea in his mind. It could not be true. She must have meant something else. There must be some monstrous misunderstanding somewhere. What could have happened ? What could be the meaning of it ? If only he could see her he felt it would be all right in one moment. So he thought at one moment, the next he would be boiling over with rage. What right had she to write to him like that, to say things like that ? He would never see her again as long as he lived. He would forget that she had ever existed. What did he care ? She was not worth a thought. And then, again, he realised that this was, oh, how untrue ! He admitted how dreadfully he cared. He would force his way into the house ; he would strangle her, he would kill her, he would force her to shriek for mercy and beg his pardon on her knees. And then, again, he felt that these were the ravings of a lunatic. The truth was she was tired of him. Nothing had happened. It was simply a pretext. She had evidently been meaning to do this for some time. And yet only the day before, that last evening, how gentle she had been to him, how softly her sad eyes had shone upon him, what silent, rapturous electricity had been in the touch of her hand when she had said good-bye to him, and how divine had been her smile at that moment. He felt certain there had been nothing wrong then, no shadow between them. But what could it be, and what was the meaning and the cause of it ? As he walked up the street and down the street, round Portman Square, and then up the street again, all these thoughts raged and revolved in his head. As he walked up the street for the last time he saw some one on the other side of the street stop at Leila's door. It was not Terence. He rang the bell. It was now dark. The door opened, and the light from inside the house lit up his face. He was allowed admittance. It was Dallas Wace.

CHAPTER XXXVI

FOR three days C. was like a madman. He wrote
Leila a long letter in which he used the most violent
language, but underneath the violence of the language,
which had the ring of sincerity, there was an apparent
basis and residue of sense. He imagined that some one
must have made mischief, and he suspected Lady
Elizabeth. He suspected her with reason. She did not
disguise the fact that she had tried her best to make
mischief; in fact, she boasted of having succeeded,
even to C.'s friends. The friends repeated this to C.,
and he communicated what he had learnt to Leila.
The quarrel was made up. C. went up for his examination, spent Christmas with the Rodens, and after
Christmas he stayed for a week with Mrs. Tryan, and
once again hunted with Leila.

In the beginning of the following year, a diplomat
who had been appointed as Second Secretary to the
Embassy at Paris, and who was unmarried, had a great
longing to spend two years in England, and tried to
find some one in the Foreign Office who would like to
go abroad and exchange with him. He asked Terence
Bucknell. Terence consulted Leila, who was all for
going to Paris but for the question of expense. It
then turned out that Lord Marryat had taken a flat

in Paris and that he no longer wanted it, and he proposed to Terence and Leila that they should keep it warm for him. He would be unable to go to Paris for more than two or three days during the next year, and as the flat was there and doing nothing, they might just as well use it. The Bucknells accepted this kind unexpected offer, and it was settled that they should go to Paris in February.

C. was despondent when he heard the news, but resolved, nevertheless, to go to Paris as soon as and whenever he could.

He passed his examination, but there were still several other examinations for him to pass which would entail a considerable amount of reading. Terence and Leila Bucknell left London at the end of February. The night before they had started, C. had dined at Upper Berkeley Street, and Terence had told him he had better spend Easter in Paris ; he wished there was room in the flat to put him up.

C. spent the whole of the winter in London working. He wrote to Leila every day, and he generally received either a letter or a note or something from her every day as well. She liked Paris, she said ; the Ambassador was very kind, there were some nice secretaries at the Embassy, and often friends from England came through. She had not made many great friends in the French world. A little later she wrote to say she had made the acquaintance of the Fitzclares. Mrs. Fitzclare was so *very* pretty and *so* much admired, and Vincent Fitzclare was quite agreeable.

C. and Wright both went to Paris for Easter. Wright had failed to pass his examination, but was going to have a second try. Beatrice and Vincent Fitzclare had gone to Italy for Easter. Leila told C. that at the end of July she was going to take a small house for the children in the Forest of Fontainebleau. C. spent a very happy fortnight in Paris. He saw Leila all day long and there were no disturbing elements ; no Wilfrid Clay, no Dallas Wace, nobody and nothing to interfere with his happiness.

In order to read for his next examination and not to be distracted by London, he, Wright and Malone took a small house together which was to be let for the summer at Chiswick. They stayed there the whole summer, and had a boat of their own, in which they used to spend the evening, and sometimes the night. C. went to no entertainments, balls or parties that summer. As Leila was not there, there was no one he wished to see, and he did not even now want to hear her even talked about by other people.

At the end of July, C. went to Fontainebleau to stay with Leila. There he spent the most radiant and bliss-ful fortnight, alone with her and the children. Terence was kept at Paris by the press of business ; they were so short-handed, but he was coming down later. C. roamed, walked and bicycled all day with Leila in the forest. It was like a dream that seemed too good to be true. Never had she been more beautiful, more charming, more gentle, more radiant, more adorable.

C. liked to see how the French people admired her,

and one day, when he heard the old cook, Adèle, who looked after the house, say, " *Madame est comme un rayon de soleil*," he could have kissed her.

Leila indeed seemed to be shedding the sunshine and the sympathy that come from great overflowing happiness.

On C.'s last evening at Fontainebleau they went for a bicycle ride after dinner, and as they were bicycling Leila teasingly said to C. :—

" In spite of everything you say, you know quite well that if I were to do anything you didn't like you would never speak to me again."

" You couldn't do anything I should really dislike, because, if you did, you wouldn't be you."

" I could do all sorts of things that would shock you, that you would hate, that you would never understand and never forgive."

" There is nothing in the world that you could do that I should mind—nothing, nothing ! "

" Take care, C., take care ! Don't say such things ; it's tempting Providence."

" Don't you see that what I love in you is *you*, and whatever you have done or might do in the world would never affect *that*? I love you because you are *you*, not for anything you think or do. That is nothing to do with it."

" I wonder," said Leila pensively.

They were bicycling slowly along a broad, dark avenue of tall, cool trees. It was a very hot evening, but in the forest it was cool.

" I don't think you will go on caring for me, C. After all, you were in love with Beatrice Fitzclare. You wanted to marry her."

" That was different."

" I wonder who it will be next, and what it will feel like. You will marry, you will be sure to marry. I shall hear people saying, ' I have asked the Caryl Bramsleys.' How odd that will sound ! I suppose I shall get used to it. One gets used to everything in the world."

" But don't you see that you are quite different from other people, and that after one has been with you, other people are so hopelessly—well, what shall I say ?—nothing ? After reading certain books one simply can't look at others."

" What kind of books ? "

" Well, for instance, all love poetry after Heine ; all music after Wagner."

" Oh, Wagner ! I wonder where we shall be when we meet again ? I don't think we shall stay very long in Paris, not more than a year. We shall never have a time like this again as long as we live. I feel that. It is the kind of thing that so rarely happens in life. Life, especially my life, is so crowded with tiresome things I have to do, and tiresome people I have to see. And yours will be some day. But just every now and then one sometimes has an escape like this fortnight at Fontainebleau. It is a sort of treat that is given one, but I'm sure it happens very seldom. Oh, C., don't forget me quite when you go away ! I shall be *so* lonely."

" You generally have too many friends about you."

" You know, you really do know, don't you, how little they count ? "

" Haven't you made any new friends in Paris ? "

" Not one real friend. I go to people's days. I leave cards. We are asked out to dinner perpetually. We go to large official dinners ; Embassy dinners, Rothschild dinners ; dinners with Foreign colleagues, or with Terence's racing friends. We sometimes dine at restaurants with London friends who are passing through, and go to the play. We sometimes dine with one or two French people or with English people, and Americans who live here—like the Fitzclares— and so it goes on. So as far as *friends* go, the only friends I have seen are the English people I have seen before. The French are very civil, of course, and sometimes very amusing, but one could never be friends with them."

" I'm sure they must admire you."

" They don't admire English women. They have got quite a different standard. They think we are, all of us, too tall and thin and scraggy, and they think, with reason, that we are badly dressed."

" But you are not tall and scraggy, and they couldn't think you badly dressed."

" You don't understand these things. There are degrees. I am well dressed for an English woman, well dressed in London, but here it's different. They take much more trouble. They know more."

" Nothing will make me believe they don't admire

you. I can see it by the way they look at you here. I know it by what Adèle says."

" They think it rude not to flatter one, not to pay compliments and make up to one ; that is, of course, a convention. But I could never be really friends with a French person, either man or woman. I feel I am too different."

" Has Dallas Wace been in Paris this year ? "

" No, not once. It's funny you should dislike him so. I think he's so agreeable."

" I hate him, hate the sight of him."

" I wonder what we shall all be doing this time next year."

They got off their bicycles. The moon had risen like a large tawny shield ; they pulled their bicycles up on to the grass under the dark stems of the trees, and they lay down on the grass, and drank in to the full the magic of the August night. It was the culminating moment of C.'s youth. He felt as if he had stepped off the edge of the planet into an unutterable, incredible, indescribable, unending eternity of happiness. This, he thought, could never be again. If the fleeting moment could only stay. For it was so fair, so very fair . . .

He left Fontainebleau the next morning. The parting was agonising. Leila drove with him to the station.

" Think of me to-night," she said, " if you see the moonrise. I shall be so very lonely without you. Perhaps you will stay the night in Paris ? "

"No, I shall go straight through, by Dieppe, to-night."

Leila was expecting Terence to luncheon that day. The train by which she expected him to arrive was due shortly after C.'s train left. As they were waiting on the platform, and just before the train started, a little boy in a blouse, who did the odd jobs in the house, arrived with a telegram in his hand. He said it had come almost directly after they had started for the station, and he had pursued them on his bicycle.

Leila opened it.

"It's from Terence," she said.

At that moment the guard blew his little horn and shouted, " *En voiture, Mesdames et Messieurs.*"

C., after one last hurried good-bye, jumped into the carriage. Leila waved at him as the train steamed out of the station.

When he got to Paris, he found the town insufferably stuffy, dusty and hot. He left his luggage at the Gare St. Lazare, in the cloak room, and he began to wander about Paris in search of a place where he might have luncheon. He walked until he reached the *Place de la Madeleine*, and then he turned into the *Rue Royale*, and went into one of the cafés, where he had luncheon by himself, thinking over his first visit to Paris and everything that had happened since. He drank his coffee outside ; he asked for some paper and a pen, and he wrote a long letter to Leila. Just as he was going out of the café whom should he meet but Freddy Calhoun, whom he had not seen, except for a moment

at his father's funeral, since he had left Eton. Freddy
Calhoun had preceded him at Eton (Albert, the second
boy, had gone to Harrow), but they had, nevertheless,
known each other ; and after that, Freddy had been to
Cambridge for a short time, and then had passed into
the Diplomatic Service, and was now Attaché at Paris.
He was the eldest son and extremely well off. He had
grown up into an extremely amiable, friendly, good-
natured, good-looking young man, whom every one
liked, and C. laughed to himself when he thought how
he had dreaded his company as a child.

Freddy was genuinely pleased to see his old
neighbour.

" I say," he said, " you simply must come and dine
with me to-night."

C. explained that he was passing through Paris on
his way back from Fontainebleau, where he had been
staying with friends, and was leaving Paris for London
by the night train *viâ* Dieppe.

" Are you in a desperate hurry to be back ? "

" No, I'm not, but now I've settled to go I suppose
I'd better, all my luggage is at the station. I haven't
got a room at an hotel."

" I never heard such nonsense. You must stay
with me. I've got a flat not far from the Arc de
Triomphe, and a spare room and spare bathroom.
Of course, you must come. Directly I get back to
the Embassy I'll see that your luggage is sent for."

C. was tempted to stay another night in Paris ;
there might—one never knew—by some kaleidoscopic

shake of circumstance, be another chance of seeing
Leila once more.

"Well, if you really mean it," he said, "I will; only
don't you bother to send for the luggage, I'll do all that
myself if you tell me where to take it to."

"No, no, you'd better let me do it. You see, the
fact is, I don't live alone, I'm *en ménage.* I suppose
you don't mind that, only I must let Thérèse know
you're coming."

"Oh, I'm sure it's inconvenient."

"If it was I shouldn't have asked you; we often
have some one to stay, and there's nothing Thérèse
likes so much. You'll like her. She's great fun, and
it really is doing her a service. It's a dull life here for
her in summer; I want to send her to some watering
place, but she won't go by herself, and I can't get
away just at present. The best thing for you to do
is to come round to the Embassy at half-past five.
Give me your luggage receipt now and I will have all
that arranged for you."

"Are you quite sure it's all right?" C. asked a last
time.

"My dear fellow, my dear old C., I shouldn't hear
of your leaving Paris without stopping a night with
me. I wouldn't hear of it. I can't tell you how glad
I am to see you. It's such a comfort to see some one
here who belongs to something one has known before,—
some one I can understand. I don't understand these
people here, and I don't pretend to. I never go out.
I live entirely with Thérèse, so it's all right, but

if it wasn't for her, I don't know what I should do. Well, I've got to go back to the Embassy now, we might walk down that way together, if you've got nothing better to do."

There was such an obviously genuine ring in Freddy's voice and a look of such undisguised pleasure in his expression at having met C. that the latter was convinced that he really was wanted, and he had no afterthought of doubt, as they strolled towards the Embassy. He was in no particular hurry to get back. He was expected by the Rodens towards the end of the week, but they had told him he could arrive any day he liked ; if he would telegraph the day before ;—that would be sufficient. And who knows ? There might be another chance of seeing Leila again. Life was full of surprises. Little did he know, as such thoughts flitted through his mind, how true they were going to prove presently.

He walked back with Freddy to the Embassy, and left him there. He was to call for him again at half-past five. Until then, he spent the time wandering about the streets and sometimes sitting outside cafés.

CHAPTER XXXVII

FREDDY drove C. home to his flat, which was on the
north-east side of the Arc de Triomphe and not far
from the *Avenue du Bois de Boulogne.* It was on the
third floor ; it was clean, tidy, neat, and elegant.
There was a drawing-room with light grey Louis XV.
boiseries, a cottage pianoforte, and two little book-
cases, full of a collection of modern French poets,
bound in green, a great many flowers, and everywhere
you felt the influence of a feminine touch ; there was
a spacious, comfortable dining-room, and a sitting-
room for Freddy, which was also used as a smoking-
room, and which had large green leather armchairs in
it and a huge writing table.

Thérèse was out when they arrived. Freddy had
warned her of C.'s arrival, and she had gone out to
buy a few things—some accessories to her clothes.
C.'s luggage had arrived, and he found all his things
had been put out ready for him by Freddy's English
servant.

Thérèse came in about half an hour later, and C. was
introduced to her. She had chestnut, wavy hair and
soft brown eyes. There was an air of refinement about
her. Dinner was discussed. Where should it be ? It
was too hot to dine indoors. Why should they not

dine at *Malmaison*, a café far out in the *Bois de Boulogne?* Freddy assented—supported by Thérèse —but suggested the terrace at *Bellevue* as an alternative. Thérèse voted for *Malmaison*, which was, she said, cooler. She would invite Jaqueline, she said.

" Why ? " asked Freddy.

" *Parcequ'elle est toute seule ce soir, et nous serons quatre, c'est plus gai.*"

She would send a note, she said, but, as a matter of fact, as it turned out afterwards, she had asked her already.

Jaqueline was a friend of Thérèse. She was the unofficial wife of a rich banker who lived with his legitimate wife and family in the Boulevard Hausmann. C. had a bath, and Thérèse spent an infinity of time in dressing and appeared towards eight o'clock, very simply dressed, but looking ravishing in a large black hat with one flower in it. They waited for Jaqueline. She was late. She was older than Thérèse and larger ; she was dark, with something frank, honest, engaging, and not super-intelligent about her expression. She was delighted at the idea of this sudden, unexpected treat. Freddy's carriage, an elegant brougham, which was driven by an immobile and immaculate English coachman, was waiting for them, but Thérèse said that as it was so hot they would go in an open *fiacre*, so they all drove off together, the two men sitting on the little seat. The restaurant was far off, but when they got there it was at least cool. They chose a table in a secluded part of the garden, under a large tree. There were but few diners. Paris was at that moment quite empty. All the French frequenters of this kind of restaurant had gone, that is to say, all who could go, and there were not many foreigners, and no English. The diplomats went to their regular haunts not so far off, or stayed at home.

Freddy ordered dinner and champagne. Thérèse liked dry, and Jaqueline sweet, champagne, so they had to have two bottles. C., out of politeness to Jaqueline, said that he, too, liked sweet champagne. At the beginning of dinner Thérèse and Jaqueline talked to each other without taking notice of the men, as they exchanged rapid items of information as to who were the diners—who the female diners were " with," punctuated with comments, plentiful and frank, as to what they were wearing and who had probably paid for it. Then the conversation, after this purely technical episode was over, became general, and they talked gaily on various topics.

In a line with their table, but half concealed from them by the stem of a tall tree, there was another table, at which a party of four were sitting : two women and two men. Thérèse asked Jaqueline who was sitting there, in the middle of the general conversation and in a different tone, as of one expert questioning another before people who did not understand. Jaqueline said she could not see very well, but she thought it was . . . (and the name escaped C.) and *La Bucknell*, with her back turned towards their table. C. felt a cold shiver down his back. For the moment he couldn't even try to look. He drank a whole glass of champagne at a gulp.

"*Elle est sans son mari, naturellement*," said Thérèse.

"He's gone away," said Freddy.

"That's why he wanted to dine here," said Thérèse, pointing at Freddy mockingly. "You know," she explained to C., "she's his new flirt."

Freddy got scarlet. "What nonsense!" he said.

"*Avec qui est-elle ce soir?*" she said to Jaqueline, once more in the confidential expert tone.

"*Fitzclare, naturellement*," was the answer.

C. felt the place swimming round him. He bent to the right, and sure enough he had a glimpse of Vincent Fitzclare, sitting with his profile towards their table, next to Leila, who was sitting with her back to them. He did not know who was her *vis-à-vis*, nor who was the man on her left. Jaqueline enlightened them. Now, she said, she could see them all: it was "Bob" and, of course, Madame Ibanez.

"No wonder Freddy insisted on coming here," said Thérèse. "I proposed *Bellevue* and lots of other places, but he insisted on coming here. *Simplement pour voir le bout. . . .*"

But Freddy interrupted her. It was quite monstrously ridiculous, he said. He had suggested their dining wherever *she* liked, and it was she who had chosen *Malmaison*. "I didn't care where we dined, did I, C.?" C. nodded. He wasn't listening. The conversation seemed to be happening in another plane, infinitely far off.

"*C'est parfait!*" said Thérèse.

"Bucknell's had to go to London to-day," said Freddy. "His mother's very ill. He left this morning suddenly, in a hurry——"

Thérèse laughed. "*De mieux en mieux*," she said. He would really be able to enjoy himself now. The only drawback was Fitzclare. Ah! he was a drawback. "*On ne badine pas avec celui-là.*"

"They hardly know each other," said Freddy, irritated.

"*Mon pauvre petit, tout le monde sait qu'il est son amant. Tout le monde sauf son pauvre mari; elle ne le cache pas.*"

"All this is because I had the misfortune to say one day to Thérèse," Freddy explained to C., "that I thought Mrs. Bucknell dressed better than most English women."

Thérèse appealed to Jaqueline. She assured her, on her word of honour, that Freddy had been lyrical on the subject of Mrs. Bucknell, not only on her dress but on her beauty and her charm——

"Well, if it comes to that, I do think she is very pretty," said Freddy. "Everybody thinks so."

"*Écoutez, écoutez. Voilà, voilà bien les hommes*," said Thérèse. "Once the *mot d'ordre* has been passed round, they all say the same thing. But you can be the most beautiful woman in the world, and you won't attract the faintest attention without this *mot d'ordre*.

The fact is men don't admire beautiful women. They admire women who take them in, and how easy that is to do ! *Cette Bucknell*, for instance, what has she got ? Eyes—yes—one could admit that, and a figure which isn't bad ; but then, who hasn't ? But her hair is *impossible*, is always done anyhow. . . . Freddy, of course, admires that . . . *et ce nez trouvé dans un accident de chemin de fer !* And as for her clothes, anybody can have nice clothes if you have so many people to pay for them."

Freddy interrupted her. C., he said, knew the Bucknells, and probably liked them very much, and they were, at any rate, friends of his family.

Thérèse apologised, but C. was hardly conscious of what she was saying. He was stunned by the bare fact of Leila sitting there at that table, not fifty yards off, laughing and talking to Vincent Fitzclare. Leila, whom he had left this morning in tears at Fontaine-bleau !—his Leila ! It was so impossible that it was comic. He laughed out loud. Thérèse thought he was laughing at her violence. She laughed too.

" But you see," she explained, " it is trying some-times, you must admit. One does take infinite trouble to try and make oneself look nice, so that Freddy shouldn't be ashamed of one, and so that he might even be a little bit *proud* of one, but does he ever notice it ? No, never. He never notices if I have a new hat or a new cloak, or, in fact, anything—I might wear anything—he takes all that for granted, but if he sees some complete stranger, or a new friend, a new flirt—*La Bucknell,* for instance—in one of last year's fashions that nobody wears any more, he comes home raving about it."

"They're all the same," said Jaqueline. "Arthur is just the same."

"Thérèse can't bear one to mention another woman," Freddy said, laughing. "Isn't it true?" he said, taking her hand.

At that moment the party at the next table got up to go. They walked straight out, and did not pass near Freddy's table because their way out lay at right angles to it.

C. had a good view of all of them as they went out. Leila went first. She had on a white satin and black lace cloak—it was lovely (that is to say he thought so)—and a black hat with white flowers in it. Then went a lady who looked like a Spaniard and who may have been, he thought, one of the Argentine ladies he had met with Beatrice at the play the year before. Then there was Vincent Fitzclare, very *galant* and full of attentions, and another man, a dark, foreign-looking person whom C. did not know by sight. Leila did not look in their direction, nor did the others; she walked out of the restaurant as though completely unconscious of the presence of any other people there.

"I apologise," said Thérèse to C., "if I said anything rude about any friends of your family. The worst of me is that I am terribly frank. Freddy will tell you this is true. When I instinctively feel antipathies or sympathies, I can't help saying so; *c'est plus*

fort que moi. Je suis comme cela ; and that is just
what I feel about that woman. She has done me no
harm. She doesn't know I exist, and she never will
know, probably ; but in spite of that, I don't like her—
I can't bear her. She is antipathetic to me in the
highest degree. I feel that she is *rosse*—that there
is no trick she wouldn't play you—and then she's *hard*.
Oh ! la la la."

" Let's talk about something else," said Freddy.

" I was only explaining," said Thérèse.

C. seemed to have split into a double personality :
one half of himself was listening to Thérèse, and the
other half was miles away. They had finished dinner
now, and were drinking coffee and smoking, and
Freddy had ordered some yellow Chartreuse. C. drank
several glasses of it. Then he began to talk quite gaily,
to chaff Thérèse and Jaqueline. They thought him
delightful and so *en train*. He had, Thérèse said to
Freddy, none of the stiffness that was usually the mark
of an Englishman.

They stayed late. It was, so Thérèse said, so cool.
Jaqueline drew attention to the moon, which was full ;
she thought it was the full moon, or was it last night
it had been full ? C. laughed. He was thinking of
Leila's words of the night before. And then he drifted
back to the dream stage. Everything about him
seemed unreal, like a scene on the stage. Freddy
Calhoun—why had he met him, and why was he with
him in Paris, out of doors, with two French women ?
That was the kind of thing that happened in a dream

and did not happen in real life. It couldn't surely
happen in real life? He would wake up and find
himself—where would he find himself? In London
or in Rome, or at Fontainebleau? And while he
was thinking all this he went on talking quite gaily,
laughing, chaffing, answering, arguing, as if he had
been wound up like a musical box. It was some
one else doing that, not himself. He himself was
somewhere else; perhaps he was dead. Perhaps this
was the next world. Perhaps it was Hell. That was
what Hell would be like, he had so often thought. It
would be a place with an appearance, a false air of
gaiety about it, and plenty of champagne, and small
tables. It was a hot night. This was the coolest place
in Paris, and even here *he* thought it was stifling.
One could hardly breathe.

"*Il a l'air fatigué,*" said Thérèse to Freddy, talking
of C.

After a time they made a move. Jaqueline proposed
their taking two cabs this time. She and C. would go
in one, and Thérèse and Freddy in the other. Before
they left, Freddy whispered to C. that it didn't matter
how late he was.

C. and Jaqueline went for a drive round the
Bois. Jaqueline became sentimental and confidential,
and poured out her troubles, which were intensely
commonplace and soothing to C. under the circumstances. Jaqueline's was an intensely *bourgeois*
domestic nature. She ought to have been the mother
of a large family, with a complicated household to run

and affairs in the village to look after. She had missed her vocation. And she made vain efforts to try and shine in the world in which she lived. With C. she made no such efforts. She talked of her life—the trouble she had with servants, how she had had to send away the cook the day before. How she wanted to go to the country. She was going, of course, but she did not yet know where. She would like to go to the seaside, but to some quiet place. She hated the ordinary smart *bains de mer*. She would like to go to some small quiet place—*le Crotoy* possibly. Or, failing the sea, somewhere near a river, the Oise for preference. But all this depended on Arthur. Arthur was very good, and he always let her go away in the summer, but it had to be somewhere where he could come for a few days if he could get away. Life was very difficult. Thérèse was a fortunate girl to have found Freddy ; he was so *gentil* and so *comme il faut*, and then so well-off. Of course, she didn't suppose he would stay in Paris very long. At the most two years. And then. . . . He had not been here a year yet . . . there would be time enough to think of such things then. He was a charming boy, and very faithful to Thérèse—*très sage*. Thérèse was jealous ; that had to be faced. It was her only fault. He didn't really give her cause for jealousy ; that was all nonsense about Mrs. Bucknell. It is true he did admire her. Of course, seeing her at the Embassy, and she being that kind of woman, how could he help adoring her ?

" What kind of woman ? " asked C.

" *Vous savez très bien,*" she said. " For a real bad woman commend me to a *femme du monde.* They are much worse than *nous autres. Nous autres, nous avons le cœur grand comme le monde, mais celles-là quand elles commencent! Oh ! la la.*"

" Do you think she is very bad ? " C. heard himself ask.

" *Je ne le crois pas. J'en suis sûre,*" said Jaqueline. " Just think how she treats that wretched husband of hers ; *et non seulement son mari, et son amant ; mais son amant de cœur, car elle a un amant de cœur.* And then, what does she live on ? *Pour mener la vie qu'elle mène.* It's money she cares for. Where does she get those pearls, those emeralds, those hats, and those *sorties de bal?* We go to the same dress-maker," she explained, " and so I *know* what she orders and what she spends, and I assure you that she spends immense sums, and it's always paid. She's very careful, very *casée ;* her bills are always paid at once. But *she* pays them herself. For instance, she had a new necklace, a new row of pearls, last month. Vincent Fitzclare gives her money. He is very rich, and he spends what he likes *now* . . . well, he doesn't care ; he knows he is finished. He hasn't long to live. I don't know what's the matter with him—some heart disease, or perhaps worse. So he is making the best of it. His wife, poor thing, he has treated her very badly. They say she used to be pretty. Now she's nothing ; *sympathique,* yes. *Bonne comme de l'or,* probably. Just the sort of wife a man like Fitzclare would have ; he is a real *viveur*, a real *Parisien. Il a fait une noce à tout casser maintenant il est plus que vanné ; il est fini !*" He had been ruined twice, but he had always made money again. Now he was said to be richer than ever. He had an extraordinary flair and talent for business, and a very good post. His situation was *solide ;* Arthur had told her so, and Arthur knew. Arthur was a *sommité* in *le monde des affaires*, and he admired Vincent Fitzclare. It was in his youth that Fitzclare had been imprudent. Now it didn't matter. He would leave no children. They had only had one child, and it had died. It was just as well. The children would have had *un triste heritage*.

C. said he would drive Jaqueline back to her *appartement* before he went home. She lived in a street out of the *Rue Montaigne*. When they got there, she asked him to come in for a moment. He did. He found a strange comfort in Jaqueline's society. He thought that her heart, in any case, was *grand comme le monde*. And when they got upstairs, and she offered him a citronade or some whisky, she saw that he was sad, and she felt that something had happened. She did not, of course, bother him with any questions either about that or about anything else. She talked and soothed him and told him every kind of thing, and treated him like a tired child.

It was very late when he got home. It was broad daylight. Everything seemed more unreal than ever to C. He walked upstairs and threw off his clothes and fell into a deep sleep. He did not wake the next morning till ten o'clock. Freddy had told the servants not to disturb him. When he woke he did not at first remember where he was, and then he felt a horrible undefinable sensation. He knew that something disagreeable had happened, but he had forgotten what, and then, in a flash, it all came back to him, and he buried his face in the pillow and tried to put away the vision and the thought of the monstrous nightmare.

CHAPTER XXXVIII

FREDDY came into his room and told him not to bother to get up till he felt inclined. He would be back to luncheon. Of course he must stay a few more days, but C. said this was impossible. He was expected at his aunt's, and he was late already. He insisted on going back by the night train *viâ* Dieppe.

Freddy and Thérèse saw him off at the station.

" You must come again," they said. C. promised he would.

The C. who returned to England was a different person from the C. who had started for Fontainebleau. His boyhood had been burnt away in a night. He felt not only a hundred years older, but a different person ; as if he had shed one personality and taken on another. Or, rather, as if he had passed through a furnace and a part of his old self had been burnt away.

When he got to his rooms he found nothing from Leila awaiting him.

He went down to Elladon in the afternoon. It was a Friday. The following Monday he received a letter from Leila from Fontainebleau, dated Friday. It ran as follows :—

> *I have had no word from you since you left—since you said good-bye to me at the station. If you had*

gone to London straight after leaving me on Wednesday night, as you said you were going to do, I could have had a letter on Friday. I should have been surprised not to have had a telegram, but, as it is, I quite *understood. I went up to Paris on Wednesday later to try and see Terence before he left for London, but I didn't catch him. And quite by chance I dined with some friends of mine (and of yours) at the* Bois de Boulogne. *There I saw you with your friends. I couldn't believe my eyes at first, but Mr. Fitzclare told me who you all were. I think you will agree there is nothing more to be said. I* quite *understand why you found it difficult to write.*

C. sat down to answer this letter. He wrote several letters, but he tore them all up. He felt that letters were indeed useless. He found life at Elladon impossible at this moment, and he made an excuse to go to London. Malone had gone to Norway with a friend to fish, and Wright was rubbing up his German with a German family at Heidelberg. There was no one in London whom he knew. At the same time, he was happier alone than with people whom he knew well, and with whom he was supposed to be cheerful.

He said to himself that he would concentrate on work, and pass his next examination brilliantly, but he found that he was totally incapable of concentration ; he read, but after reading four or five pages, he found he had retained nothing, and the vision of Leila came between him and the printed word—an image which inspired him with love and with hate, alternately and simultaneously.

A vicious circle of argument was burning in his brain. He didn't believe, he assured himself over and over again, a word of what those French women had said about Leila. But why had she been there? Why hadn't she told him she might be going to Paris? He was there when the telegram arrived, and she said it was from Terence. It was true the train was just starting, but there was time to say that he was going away. She might have travelled with him; but she had no luggage, and then she wanted to stay the night. But again, if what she said in her letter were true, she knew she was going to stay the night. Then, in that case, why didn't she come with him? Why didn't she tell him? But, after all, supposing all she said were true, supposing he had done her the grossest injustice, supposing it were quite by chance that she had gone out to dinner that night; all the same, he knew, he knew by her face—as he had seen it then—by her manner, by her whole attitude, that she was not the same Leila whom he had left at Fontainebleau. Did he know that? Was that true? She might be wearing a mask, just playing up, as people did in life every day. No, she wouldn't have been there at all, if she had felt what she had pretended to feel. There was nothing odd about her dining out; of course not, if she had been in Paris—of course not. But what was odd was her silence, her not telling him. If she had thought there was a chance of her going to Paris, there was no reason why they should not have had dinner together. As it was, she had said nothing. Perhaps Terence had telegraphed twice. The day after he arrived in London he wrote to Leila again and said he had remained in Paris quite by chance, having met Freddy Calhoun, whom he had known all his life, in the street. Freddy had insisted on his staying the night, and he had been stunned by the sight of her in the *Bois de Boulogne*. He had thought that if there had been the least chance of her being in Paris that day she would have told him. She had told him nothing. He begged her to write, if only a letter of abuse ; this silence was driving him mad. Leila wrote to him again :—

I always thought you might change, but I never dreamt it could happen so quickly and so soon ; it is so strange that nothing I say now seems to have any effect on you. I tell you the simple truth and you don't believe me ! I don't know what you believe, but I am not going to defend myself to you, as if you were a lawyer or a judge, or as if I were in any way in the wrong. I didn't tell you I was going to Paris, because when I said good-bye to you I didn't know. I had no idea I was going to Paris myself. If you remember, I hadn't even time to read Terence's telegram before your train left. I had just opened it when they bundled you into the train, and I only just had time to say good-bye. When the train left I read his telegram. He told

me that he was going to London and I thought he
meant by the night train, of course. That was, it
turned out, his original idea, but he found he could
catch the earlier train, so he went by it. I went
straight to Paris by the next train and missed
him. But I met Vincent Fitzclare in the street and
he asked me to dine with them and I accepted. Later
I got a message that Beatrice had gone to bed with a
bad headache, but they were all dining at Malmaison,
and that I was still expected. As I was alone, I
was glad to have somewhere to dine. There was
nobody at the flat, and the cook had taken her evening
off, thinking there would be no one there. Of course,
I had no idea you were still in Paris. Well, that is
all. There is nothing more to say. There is nothing
to be said, as I told you before. You have shown
me, proved to me, what you really think about me,
what you really feel for me, and it is just as well
this should have happened now—just as well for
you as for me. I already thought this once before,
but then I was weak, and thought that perhaps I had
been wrong. Alas! I was right—you, too, have
made a mistake about me and I want you to realise
that. You think I am the sort of person who will
endure anything. That you can blow hot and cold,
but no. It is true I was very fond of you—too fond
of you; foolishly, madly fond of you, no doubt.
It was silly of me! I am older than you, and I ought
to have known that such a friendship was not likely
to last. I ought to have known better. It was really

impossible, I ought to have known what people were likely to attract you. However, I was foolish. I didn't think. I just lived in the present and now I am being cruelly punished. Please, please don't write to me again. When I see your handwriting on an envelope it gives me a curious pain in the heart, like neuralgia. I put the letter by for a little—it hurts me to open it.

But C. did write again. He wrote a long letter and impassioned defence, and at the end of it, he implored Leila to forget the whole thing. He had been wrong;— he admitted it to the full; but it was only the intensity of his love that had caused him to act as he had acted. . . . He wrote burning words, and they were alive and fiery with sincerity, and yet they came from a different part of him than the same words would have come from some months ago. Something in him had been broken, which could not be mended, and poisonous seeds had been sown—although he would not have admitted it. He had torn out the plants that had grown up from these seeds, torn them out violently by the roots, but the seeds were there, nevertheless, and fresh weeds would grow from them in the future.

When he left the Rodens they expected him to come back in a few days, and he had left them under the impression that he was coming back. He intended to go back if nothing unexpected happened, but he felt that he must remain for the present in London. He was nearer Paris. He could, if he wanted to, start at

a moment's notice for Paris, and without explana-
tions : whereas at Elladon there would be all sorts of
difficulties, and he would have to explain. It was the
evening of his fourth day in London when he met
Wakefield at a music hall—Wakefield, his former
colleague in Rome. They talked together in the
foyer, and when the performance was over, Wakefield
walked back with C. to his rooms. Wakefield was, he
said, no longer at Rome, he had been at Paris since the
beginning of the year.

"I was at Paris the other day," said C. "I had
dinner with Freddy Calhoun."

"And Thérèse, I suppose ? "

"Yes."

"I like Thérèse, only she's rather tiresome on certain
subjects."

"What subjects ? " asked C.

"Oh, all that *femme du monde* nonsense."

"Yes, I suppose all that *is* great nonsense."

"Of course, there's nothing she doesn't say about
any one in that category, especially if they are English,
and, after all, she has only seen about two of them in
the distance—English women, I mean—in her life."

"Do you know a friend of hers called ——"

"Jaqueline ? "

"Yes."

"I should think I did. She's a very good sort,
but rather *cramponne*, very difficult to get rid of."

"Of course you know Terence Bucknell," said C.,
tentatively.

"Of course. I like them so much. They are a great addition."

"I wonder if he will try and exchange altogether ? "

"I should think it improbable, they've got so many friends in England."

"But I suppose they've got a lot of friends in Paris by now."

"Of course, but that's never quite the same thing, is it, for people who are used to living in England ? And then Paris is different from other posts. They wouldn't be able to stay in Paris. They would have to go somewhere like Rio or Tokio."

"Yes, that's the worst of it."

"You've quite given up all idea of trying for it now ? "

"Quite."

"I daresay you're right, but I don't think it's worse than other professions."

"Oh, I suppose not."

"And if one makes up one's mind to like it, there's a good chance of getting on."

"When are you going back to Paris ? "

"Not just yet. I've just come away on leave. I shall be back in about a month."

"Do you happen to know a man called Fitzclare ? "

"Oh, yes, the man in the Egyptian Bank. I know him and his wife. He's very ill just now."

"Really ? "

"He's not expected to recover. He dined out of doors last week and fell ill the next day."

" What is it ? "

" I don't quite know, it's all sorts of things and something to do with the heart, I think, and a chill into the bargain. He's always been very imprudent and never taken any precautions."

" Do you know her ? "

" Yes, quite well ; they've both of them been very good to me."

" I suppose she is very anxious and unhappy ? "

" Ye—es—yes, of course."

That was all that Wakefield said about the Bucknells and the Fitzclares. C. thought he was guarded and wondered whether he had heard anything. A few days later he read in *The Times* that Vincent Fitzclare had died in Paris. He was buried in the *Père la Chaise* and a requiem Mass had been said for him at *Saint Philippe du Roule*. C. wrote to Beatrice. He then thought it would be as well for him to go back to Elladon, but when the moment for starting came, he felt he could not really face that cheerful, boisterous atmosphere just at the moment. But what was he to do, and what was he to say ?

Every day he expected a letter from Leila, but as the days passed he came to the conclusion that she wouldn't write now. He began to think, too, that he had been monstrously to blame. How could he have listened to the conversation of those French women for one minute ? But he wasn't listening ;—he was stunned by seeing Leila ; and then the old argument would begin once more to go round in his head; the whole vicious circle of accusation and justification of herself and himself. Would there never be an end to it? Evidently she was not going to write. What should he do? He reflected that six months ago he would have taken the next train to Paris, and now he was not doing . so. Why not? Finally, he settled to go back to Elladon. He couldn't work in London, and it would be better to be there with people he was fond of, than alone in empty London, pretending to read, and in reality doing nothing. And who knows? the nightmare might lift suddenly when he least expected it.

C. stayed at Elladon till the beginning of the September term, when he came back to London once more to resume reading for his law examinations and to eat his dinners. He lived, as before, with Wright and Malone; but the establishment, or rather the partnership, was to be partly broken up before long. Malone's father died that autumn, leaving Gerald quite a decent competence. There were no brothers or sisters; Gerald's mother had died a long time ago. He was alone and independent. He had nearly finished eating his dinners; he had passed two examinations, but had several more to pass. His father's death and the inheritance that came to him from it had the effect of underlining his distaste for the law. He would certainly have gone to the Colonies at this moment, or set out on some distant travels, if he had not fallen in love with the daughter of a professor of physical culture who had left her home, and who had now a small walking-on part in a spectacular piece that was going on at the Alcazar Theatre.

Her name was Esther Bliss. She had copper-coloured hair and long grey eyes, and the first thing that Gerald did with his inheritance was to buy her some pearls. He left his rooms in Ryder Street, and moved into a flat in Knightsbridge; and there, during the winter months, he lived a life of great gaiety and extravagance. C. and Wright both took part in it. Gerald's rooms were on the top floor in a street that was an off-shoot of Sloane Street. One night Gerald gave a sumptuous dinner to his old Oxford friends. Wright, Hallam, Wilfrid Abbey and others were there. There was a good deal of music and song. After dinner some one strummed on the piano . . . tunes that reminded them all of their Oxford days.

At the height of the fun C. walked out on to a balcony. Round the table, in the dining-room, there was a loud argument going on as to whether Eastern philosophy were superior or not to Western philosophy. In the sitting-room, in one corner, some one was telling Wilfrid Abbey a very long, detailed story, and Abbey was listening with quiet attention. Some one else was playing a song at the pianoforte—a song called *The Truthful Lover*—and Gerald was singing it at the top of his voice. Some were listening, and some were not.

The balcony belonged to the sitting-room, and from

it C and Wright leaned out and looked up at the stars and down on to the glistening pavement. It had been raining.

They stopped in their talk and listened to the music. They had often heard the song before.

"That reminds me of Gerald's rooms at Oxford," said Wright. "Do you remember that time when. . . ."

The flood-gates of reminiscence were opened—

> Once you were fair as a flower, dear,
>   Tender and sweet and kind,
> And every fleeting hour, dear,
>   Closer our hearts entwined ;
> And I was brave and true, dear,
>   A hero of chivalree,
> But *I* have found out *you*, dear,
>   And *you* have found out *me*.
>
> And so we have played our parts, dear,
>   On the lines that we chose to take ;
> We have not broken our hearts, dear—
>   Hearts like *ours* don't break.
> I fear our love was not true, dear,
>   I know we are glad to be free,
> For I am *tired* of you, dear,
>   And you are *tired* of me,

sang Gerald.

Wright and C. paused in their talk.

"How easily one could fall or jump off this balcony !" said Wright. "Shall we do it ?" He meant it as a joke, but C. astonished him by saying quite seriously :

"Yes, let's do it. That would be far the best

solution, and the quickest. I will if you do." He began to climb to the ledge. Wright pulled him away.

"Don't be an ass! We'll throw out a bottle instead!" And C. threw out a bottle of champagne, and narrowly missed hitting a policeman.

CHAPTER XXXIX

C. WAS never called to the Bar. He went up for some more examinations and failed to pass them. Sir Shreeve Mellings told him that he had not the legal mind, and that he would be wise to find something else to do. His brother Edward got him the offer of a billet in Australia, a secretaryship to one of the Governors, but nothing would induce C. to even consider the question of leaving England. In the meantime, the Rodens, so Edward said, had suffered financial reverses. They were not, of course, ruined, nor anything like it, but they were embarrassed, and it was doubtful whether Mrs. Roden would be able to continue the allowance that she had hitherto been making to C. (As a matter of fact, she did, for the Roden reverses never materialised outside Edward's imagination.) It became imperatively necessary, he said, that C. should find something to do.

At last—again through the good offices of Edward—a billet was found for C. in a Government office. It was a small office, to be found in Westminster, and which I will call the Sardine Fisheries Department, although that was not its name, nor had it anything to do with fish or the sea.

" Of course, it leads to nothing," Edward said. C.

said he was quite indifferent to that. It was a billet at any rate. C. took up his duties at the beginning of the New Year. The work was not burdensome, the hours were not overwhelming, the work was not less interesting than could be expected, the fellow officials were friendly. C. preferred it to the City, that is to say, to the thought of being in Edward's office. His life now settled down into a regular groove. He had given up definitely any ideas of literary work, although he once or twice contributed prose articles to the provincial Press—he had an Oxford friend on the staff of a large provincial newspaper, the *Northern Argus*, and his friend sometimes sent him books to review, and he printed, too, a descriptive article of C.'s. C. rather liked routine work at the office. It distracted him. He lived a kind of double life. One side of him got through the work of the day mechanically and not unhappily, the other self lived in a world of dreams, but that world was still suffering from the fearful havoc that the thought of Leila was making there.

He had never heard from her again, and he had not written himself; he felt that it would be useless. He thought he was getting over it; he thought he was forgetting her, that in a few months' time he would be completely healed once more.

In February, he heard that Beatrice had come back to London. She was staying with her father and her mother in Ovington Square. C. went to the house. It was just the same. Terence, the butler, was still there. Mrs. Lord was just the same, and asked him

if he was still at the Embassy at Rome. Mr. Lord
was just the same, only he looked far more prosperous. He had just invented, he said, a marvellous
device which would enable the whole population of
England to dispense with coal fires altogether.

Beatrice appeared to be delighted to see him. She
was looking, curiously enough, ten years younger than
when he had last seen her, although there was something infinitely sad in her expression. But it was as
if some dreadful weight had been lifted—some fiery
ordeal at an end. She was moving immediately, she
said, into a small house of her own. She intended
spending the summer in London, and then perhaps
she would go abroad. Her father and mother wanted
her to go to Switzerland with them. She had not yet
made up her mind. She asked C. to look in whenever
he liked at her new house. He went there one evening
the following week, and found her in and alone, and
they had a long talk about old times, and her life in
Paris. She talked of this in detail, superficially, but
she was quite reticent as to her husband. She did not
mention Leila, nor did C.

This was the beginning of a new phase of intimacy
between Beatrice and C. It was not in the least like
what had been before, but they were beginning to
be friends again. She understood C. perfectly, and
C. found rest, pleasure and solace in her company.
He wasn't in love with her as he had been before, nor
even in a new and different way. That faculty seemed
to have been burnt out of him ; but he preferred her

society to that of other people, and he looked forward to seeing her.

She was spending Easter with the Carterets, and C. was asked as well, and accepted. Lady Elizabeth thought the old romance had begun again, and she was thrilled at the prospect. There was nothing now, she said, to prevent them being married. Beatrice had been left well off, but not too well off, there were no children, and it would be a pity if she were to waste all her money on her absurd, sponging father. It would be the sensible—the only sensible—thing for her to do . . . after a decent interval, of course. Lady Elizabeth discussed marriage with C. in the abstract. She told him he ought to marry, and urged him not to let the Heaven-sent opportunity slip should it present itself. " I don't mean propose to the first person you see, but I do mean don't be a fool, don't think that things will happen if you do *nothing*, don't think, if you love some one, she will mind your telling her, or any nonsense of that kind, or that she will think you unworthy."

The thought of marrying Beatrice, which had not entered C.'s head, now crept into it, just as Lady Elizabeth had meant it to do. He did not, at first, think it possible, but at the same time he did not think it inconceivable.

Beatrice had taken a little house in Westminster, in Palace Street, out of Buckingham Gate, but she did not seem to be making it into a permanent home. At least there were no signs of that about it. She

had only taken the house for six months, and she had
few of her things there ; they were all of them, she
said, still in her flat in Paris, which she had not yet
got rid of.

One evening—it was towards the end of May—C.
was sitting with Beatrice in the drawing-room of the
little house, and they were talking of some friend, to
whom what at the time had seemed an overwhelming
calamity had brought great eventual happiness.

" It was all the time a blessing in disguise," said C.

" Yes, I wish those blessings could be labelled
' blessings,' " said Beatrice, " so that when they came
disguised as calamities one shouldn't worry quite so
much."

" Yes," said C., " that would be a good idea," and
he wondered whether his separation from Beatrice and
the whole of the Leila episode had been a blessing in
disguise, and whether he would end by marrying
Beatrice and living happily ever afterwards. But he
said nothing at the time. That evening, when he got
back to his rooms, he found a message from his brother
Edward, saying he wanted to see him at once. He
went round to Hengrave House. The house had been
redecorated during the winter for the London season,
and the new Lady Hengrave had found her heart's
desire. A French firm had been employed to do the
work, but the house now looked neither English nor
French. It looked cosmopolitan, like a smart modern
hotel. A lift had been put in. She had not yet got her
way about Bramsley. It had not yet been sold, but it

was still let; they tried in the summer a smaller, a more convenient and altogether more modern house which they had acquired on a lease. It had the supreme advantage of being only ten miles from London, and next to a golf course. This was "so convenient for Edward." It would have been still more so had Edward been a golf player.

C. was shown into the Blue Room, his father's old sitting-room. It was now called the "Blue Drawing-Room," and Edward had a smaller sitting-room in the back part of the house. All the old furniture had gone, the rather shabby, comfortable, old chairs, the prints on the walls of Morland and Hogarth had given way to framed photographs of Lady Hengrave's friends. Over the chimneypiece there was now, instead of the dignified picture of the fourth Lord Hengrave that had been there before, a large pastel portrait of the present Lady Hengrave by a contemporary artist. The portrait was as lifelike as it was lifeless.

C. found Edward standing in front of the fireplace smoking a cigar. He offered C. a cigar and told him to sit down. He looked grave and somewhat weather-beaten. He was getting fatter, C. noticed, and more Early Victorian every day, and he had a great look of his mother.

"We've had bad news," he said, after a pause.

"Is Harry ill?" said C., with a flash of certain intuition.

Edward nodded. C. read the worst in his face.

"We had a telegram from his colonel this evening. He died yesterday. The regiment had been sent into camp for cholera. I suppose, but he doesn't say, it was cholera. He says fever. It must have been very sudden. Poor boy!"

"Do Julia and Marjorie know?"

"Yes, they both know. They'll——"

At that moment Lady Hengrave came in. She was dressed smartly in black. "Is this all right?" she said, giving Edward a letter. "How do you do?" she then said solemnly to C. "It's dreadful about Harry—dreadful. Edward is greatly upset." She paused. "I think it's odd, I must say, of Julia and Marjorie not to have come here."

"I saw them together," Edward said. "Julia is not well, she's lying down, and Marjorie said she would stay with her."

"They never think of others," said Lady Hengrave.

"I think that's rather unfair, Marie," said Edward.

"No, they don't," said Lady Hengrave decidedly. "They knew, for instance, that we were going to have our house-warming dinner . . . you were coming, C., afterwards, weren't you? . . . to-morrow night, and they knew that I would have to put off twenty people at a moment's notice, and write twenty letters, and they never thought of even asking to help me. I've not finished them yet. I must go back to my work at once. In fact, I just came to ask you whether this would do," and she pointed to the letter she had given Edward, which was addressed to a Royal personage.

"We will have a memorial service on Saturday, at St. Luke's," said Edward, as C. left.

C. said good-bye. It was a lovely evening. Portman Square brought back the scenes and episodes of his childhood to him vividly, and now Harry, the source and centre of his fun as a child, was lying cold and dead far away from home, in a camp, in the hills in India. Perhaps his body had been burnt. He would never see him again. Never! Never!

As he drew near to Oxford Street a barrel organ was playing a song from the *Geisha*; cabs were beginning to take people out to dinner and to the theatres. London seemed very gay. He crossed Oxford Street, and walked down Upper Brook Street into Park Lane, and down Park Lane to Hamilton Gardens. He looked through the bars. There were no children playing. If children still played there, it was too late for them. At Hyde Park Corner, he took a bus to Victoria, and he walked quite naturally to Beatrice's house. It was nearly eight o'clock when he reached her house. She was at home.

"May I have dinner with you?" he said, as he walked into her drawing-room: a "furnished" room with pictures of *The Soul's Awakening* and *Diana or Christ?* on the walls.

"Yes, if you don't mind there being almost nothing to eat." She rang the bell and made arrangements when the servant answered it. C. sat down on a sofa and told her the news.

"I knew it would happen," he said, "when I said

good-bye   I knew quite well I should never see him again."

Beatrice had always known exactly what C. felt about Harry.   He had talked to her so often about him.

"Dear C.," she said.   "I'm sorry for you, with all my heart.   I'm not sorry for him.   He's had a happy, cloudless life ;   nothing in it he wouldn't be ready to have all over again.   But you, how you will miss him. It is cruel for you."

C. couldn't trust himself to speak.   All the past came over him in an overwhelming rush, and the burden of life seemed to him to be "Too late " and " No more."

Presently they went down to the dining-room, and during dinner Beatrice talked quietly of other things : about her father and her mother, the Carterets, and Hester Carteret's marriage to a Polish pianist.

After dinner they went upstairs again.

"You believe in a future life ? " C. asked.

Beatrice nodded.

"I know you do, officially, of course, but I mean, do you feel it ?   Does it mean anything to you ? "

"It's not a thing one can define or explain to one-self, or to any one else," she said.   "One can't imagine what it will be like ;   I only know that I feel certain that it will be, that it *is*."

"But you don't believe it will be the same as this life, and if it isn't the same, what is the point of it ? The point of this life is—I think—its imperfection.

The point of human beings to me is that they are full of faults and weaknesses and wickedness—it is because of all that that they are human, made up of a thousand things : defects, qualities, idiosyncrasies, tricks, habits, crotchets, hobbies, little roughnesses and queer pitfalls, unexpected quaintnesses : unexpected goodness, and unexpected badness ; take all that away, and what is left ? Nothing that I want to see again. Take Harry, for instance. I was fond of Harry as he was ; rather boisterous, sometimes rash, full of high spirits, gay, fond of the things of this life, with a temper that flared up quickly and subsided more quickly still, leaving no rancour behind it ; his laughter and fun, his way of blushing and talking quickly, falling over his words when he was shy, his obstinacy . . . but I can't imagine an improved Harry, a perfected Harry, with all the faults left out, Harry without his stammer . . . that to me would not be Harry at all . . . it would be some one else, and then I can't imagine Harry in Heaven—in any kind of Heaven——"

" That is because you have got the conventional idea of the next life you learn in the nursery—hymns and crowns—but can't you imagine, can't you take on trust, that the next life might be better than this one, and that the best and essential part of human beings may survive, or that they may for the first time be complete, complete in body *and* soul ? We can't think out, here and now, how that could be, nor what it could be, but we can take on trust that it will be better than the best of this life. Isn't that enough ? "

" It's too much for me," said C.

> Your chilly stars I can forego,
> This warm kind world is all I know.

You know the poem, *Minermus in Church*. The last lines—

> But, oh, the very reason why
> I clasp them, is because they die—

that sums up what I think.   It is because things and persons are perishable, and mortal, and fallible, and human, and partly bad, if you like, that I love them. And what's more, I don't believe in anything happening twice.   I believe that Nature never repeats herself ; and that every note that is struck in the universe is struck once only, and for ever."

" And yet," said Beatrice, " every year there is blossom in spring, flowers in summer, corn in autumn, rain and snow in winter."

" My point is this," said C.   " I daresay immortality is true.   I know one can't prove that it is untrue.   But I don't want it.   The events of life seem to me irreparable.   Nothing can make up for certain things that have been.   Nothing can be again exactly like what it was."

" It can be better—there can be another life which is as different from this one as a peach from a pear."

" That won't make up for the past—for the pear. At any rate, I don't want that consolation prize.   I don't want the peach.   I want to go out like a candle when this life is over."

" You can't help thinking that, if you have no faith."

" But you, with your faith, do you want things to go on ? "

" Yes, because—and not only because—I am taught that this is what I should believe, and not only because I accept this belief among other dogmas guaranteed by the authority on whose mast I have nailed my flag, but because my own heart tells me it *is* so."

The following fragments of letters from Beatrice Fitzclare to C. are appended here, as they belong to this date and are connected with this and similar conversations which C. had with Beatrice at this time. They throw light on C.'s frame of mind at this moment. They were copied out by C. in a notebook in which there were also notes of other conversations, on similar topics, most of which, however, are illegible.

No. 1

" Your faith must be a wonderful thing."

Yes, faith is a wonderful gift. But it is a gift ; one must always remember that. It may always be taken away. That, to me, is the greatest mystery in the world. I mean, why some people have faith and others not.

No. 2

. . . When you say I must have felt in touch with something beyond and outside me, something super-natural, and that you have felt that kind of thing in

looking at a landscape, or when hearing certain pieces of music, or reading some things for the first time—in Dante, for instance, and in Shakespeare.

But that is surely only delight and pleasure in beautiful things?

I know what you mean ; but there is something else. I know what one feels face to face with a glorious landscape, or a wonderful piece of music, or a poem—or, if you like, a flower in the garden, a ray of sunshine in a dusty street. But there is something else. There is something I have only felt at Mass, and that is a sense of final calm and absolute content, as if one had got beyond all obstacles and had been released from everything—all chains ; as if one had come into a wide, calm, shining harbour after a long and stormy voyage ; and that no harm could happen to one ; as if nothing could hurt or disturb or reach or touch one any more ; as if one had been put to sleep in a safe cradle ; and as if that little cradle were all eternity and all infinity. . . . I can't describe what I mean. One can't describe these things, but I mean it is something more than all the beauty and all the art in the world can give, something beyond and above art. You see, I think the reason why great art is great is because there is in it a message from Heaven ; it is a spark of the Divine given to us in fleeting glimpses and transitory hints ; through a glass darkly, through an imperfect medium—landscape or pictures or music or poetry. But at Mass I think the message is there, directly transmitted to us, if we are in a state to receive it.

But I may be talking nonsense. Lots of people feel nothing like this at all, and yet are saints, bursting with faith.

No. 3

I will try to answer your letter and your two points. You say, " I respect your religion, but I can't help thinking there is something shut about it, something about your services and churches that is walled up and stuffy, something that shuts out nature and life— the sun and freedom and joy ; something cold, hard and exclusive." Yes, there is something hard and cold and exclusive about a door when it is shut, especially if you are standing outside it, on a cold night when it is freezing and snowing, but if you turn the handle and find it opens quite easily, and that inside there is a vast, endless room, full of lights and blazing fires. . . . . . . what I feel with regard to our Mass, for instance, is the exact opposite of what you think you would be bound to feel. I feel at Mass as if I were breathing the kind of air you breathe on the mountains in spring, or in a wood, or in the fields at dawn on a spring day ; something where the freshness is fresh beyond all sweetness : it is more than sweetness, it is simply fresh—unspeakably fresh . . . that is all, and that is enough. . . . What I want you to understand is that this is quite separate from and independent of beautiful surroundings, and accessories—I mean it doesn't necessarily happen in cathedrals, with music and ritual ; it may happen there, too, but not because of that. It is just the same in the tin tabernacle, or shed, or barn, in any village church where there are the cheapest coloured statuettes of St. Joseph and the Sacred Heart and sham stained-glass made of coloured paper, and images of Our Lady like penny dolls dressed in tinsel . . . and all these things help, I assure you; they don't hinder, because, don't you see, where the object represented is Divine and indescribable in human terms and by human means, the image is none the worse for being childish. After all, the best picture by the greatest artist in the world of something like the Crucifixion, is just as inadequate as a child's picture, and a child's picture is often more satisfactory, not as art, but as an image of the Divine, where the beauty is beyond human reach; the more frankly unpretentious and naïve the attempt at representation the better; it becomes then a symbol, and I think that the people who make a picture of God as an old man with a beard are nearer the truth than the philosophers who write tomes on the nature of the "Supreme Director" or the "Prime Mover." But all that is a side issue—to tell you, to try and explain to you, why these things to me not only don't matter, but help rather than hinder.

You can say: "What I can't understand, and what I think a lot of people can't understand, is why you want all that; why isn't a buttercup in a field enough for you to believe in God and worship Him? Why do you want churches, priests, statues, images, rosaries, holy water, confessionals and scapulars?"

Well, you see, that is the sacramental view *of life, and the sacramental view of life is there, before us, like the Ark ; nobody can help noticing it, everybody knows if some one is a Catholic ; they may know nothing else about a person, they will be sure to know that. Nonconformists, atheists, agnostics, Jews, Turks, all admit that the Ark—our Ark—is there. You may dislike it, but you cannot deny its existence ; and the flood, namely, human life, is an undeniable fact too. So, to us, the people who say they have no use for the sacramental system are, as I once heard a priest say in a sermon, like a man who would refuse to go into the ark because he knew how to swim.*

No. 4

You say you understand that to me the Church is the Ark, the one and only refuge, but to you it's different, for two reasons :

Firstly, you don't mind being drowned ; and secondly, you have no reason to believe my ark is real, that it isn't a phantom ark. Call it an arc-en-ciel. *Why not believe in it as that ? But please, never say again : " You had better let me drown in my own way."*

CHAPTER XL

Beatrice and C. talked on that evening till late. It was past midnight when he left her. He went back to see her the next day, the day after, and very frequently during the next week.

One evening, when he was with her at tea-time, he said :—

" Lady Elizabeth Carteret has asked me to go and stay with her next Saturday week. She says that she is going to ask you. Are you going ? "

" No," said Beatrice, " I am going to Paris almost at once."

" But not for good——"

" I shall be going away for good, but I'm not going to stay in Paris. I am only going there to make arrangements about my flat, my furniture, and other things, and to get through some business that Vincent left behind——"

" And after that ? "

" After that I shall go away—for good."

" What, abroad ? "

" Perhaps——"

" You mustn't go," said C. " You are all I've got left in the world now, and you mustn't leave me. You can't. We mustn't make the same mistake over again. I believe it *was* perhaps a blessing in disguise that we didn't marry before—we were not allowed to do it then, I think, so that we could do it *now*. I'm not going to let you go a second time."

" You want me to marry you, C. ? "

" Of course I do. You know it. I'm not going to explain anything. You know all there is to be said."

" Yes, I do," Beatrice said gravely and sadly. " I can't marry you, C.," she said. " It's too late. If, before I had married Vincent, you had insisted ; if you had taken me by main force and made me go to the registrar's office, or to the first possible church, or any sort of Gretna Green, I should have done it, but I can't do it now. I know you couldn't do it reasonably then, but I think the reason you didn't do it, in spite of all, in spite of its being impossible, was because you didn't really love me. You loved me then just as you love me now, but you weren't really in love with me in the sense that breaks down all barriers. You thought you were, but it wasn't a thing that filled your whole self, in spite of yourself, beyond all control, and all reason. That has happened to you since. You know what I mean. You think that is all over ; that you have got over that and forgotten it, and that it can all be as though it hadn't been. But I'm sure, and I know with every fibre in my being that I'm right about this, and that you're wrong, that it *isn't* over. It might begin again any minute—it will begin again, I am positive—and think how terrible that would be, if it happened after we were married. I should never forgive myself, nor would you. How miserable you would be!"

"You're wrong, Beatrice," C. interrupted. "You really are wrong. That *is* all over. It's broken in a way that nothing could mend. I'm like a person drowning, and you are there in a life-boat, and I am calling for help; you surely can't refuse to pick me up—— ?"

"That is just it," said Beatrice. "If it was the real thing you wouldn't be calling for help; you would be climbing into the boat."

"Well, that's just what I mean to do."

"No, because I can't."

"You mean you don't love me."

"You know perfectly well, C., what I feel. It's not that, it's partly because of what I have already told you, and partly for other reasons."

"What other reasons?"

"Well, I'm not sure I can *tell* you my other reasons. I might be able to write them, but I'm not even sure of that. They are personal reasons to do with my own life, with the inside of my own life. It's too difficult to say all that I have to say; I might be able to write it. I'm not sure, but whether I can or not, it all comes to the same, which is that I know it's impossible. You mustn't ask me. It's impossible for you, and impossible for me. It's too late, much too late. You see, I'm not the Beatrice I was when you first knew me, and you're not the C. you were when I first knew you."

" But if we are just as fond of each other, what does it matter ? "

" Because, C., you are fonder of some one else, even if it is against your will.   I say this without any bitterness or envy, I promise you.   But it is the sad and simple truth, and you know it."

" But, Beatrice, I swear——"

" Don't, C.; remember St. Peter. Don't—don't say anything rash. I *do so* understand. You needn't say anything more. I know exactly what you are feeling, and I want you to believe, even if all *that* hadn't happened to you, it would be still impossible for me *now*. I couldn't do it, however much I might want to. If she were dead I couldn't do it."

" Will you think over it for two days ?   That isn't much to ask, is it ? "

" If you like, but it won't make any difference.   It can't, I promise you."

" It can't matter to you.   It is, after all, not much to ask."

" Very well, and if I can, I will write to you. I shan't be able to explain things properly in a letter, but I may be able to give you an inkling of the position I am in. You mustn't think me selfish, C. Promise me that whatever happens, you won't think me selfish ; or think me as selfish as you like about everything in the world, but not selfish about you. I want you to promise me that."

" But how could I think you selfish ? "

" You probably will when you get my letter.   You

won't understand ; if you don't understand, don't try, but just trust me ; just believe in me, just say *Credo*— that is all I ask of you."

At that moment Father Blacklock was announced, an oldish priest with serene eyes, white hair, and a cheerful smile. Beatrice introduced C. to him, and C. sat on for a few moments talking, while Father Black-lock was given a cup of tea, and then he went away. Beatrice went down to the door with C., and said :—

" If I think it over for two days, you mustn't come and see me during those two days."

" Very well," said C. ; " and promise me something else, Beatrice. Promise me that whatever you settle, it will be you, yourself, that will settle it ; you won't do anything because you are told to do it by one of your priests."

Beatrice laughed.

" They wouldn't think it a crime. On the contrary, they would be delighted," said Beatrice.

" Who is that priest ? " asked C. suspiciously.

" He is a very old friend of mine. He knows, or, rather, knew, a friend of yours called Burstall."

" How do you mean, *knew* ? "

" Didn't you know that Andrew Burstall was dead ? He died last year at Versailles. He was received into the Church a year before he died."

" Do you mean to say he was in France last year ? "

" Yes, on and off, he was never there for long at a time. I used to know him quite well. He often spoke of you."

" He never wrote to me."

" He was very busy and had great troubles. His wife was ill ; she got better. I must go back. I'll tell you about him another time."

Two days later, in the morning, C. received a letter from Beatrice :—

I wrote to you yesterday a very long letter. This very long letter (fourteen pages) didn't take very long to write, but when I had finished it, I tore it up and tried to write you another letter in which I tried to say just the same thing on half a sheet of small writing-paper. That took me all day. I tore that up too. I am now writing without any plan at all. So für mich hin. *This is, dear, dear C., what I have settled to do. As soon as I have got through my business in Paris, which won't take me long, I am going into a convent. This doesn't mean that I am necessarily going to become a* nun. *It means that I shall live in a convent for a year as something more than a paying guest. I shall be called a* postulant ; *after that I may or may not become a* novice, *in which case I shall be a novice for two years. After that I may or may not take what are called " simple vows "— and those are not " final vows "—but I needn't go into that at present. I shall not do anything final unless I feel certain that my vocation is to leave the world and not to live in it. I have told you enough for you to understand that I am not doing anything irrevocable at present. You must look upon me as some one who* is taking a rest cure of the spirit. My spirit, C., has been broken. I don't know that it can ever be mended. I can't go into the Why? and it doesn't matter. Perhaps you will think this very selfish and very self-indulgent of me, only you must remember this: If I am to be of any use in the world, I must be in possession—in full possession—of my spiritual faculties, just as a hospital nurse, say, to be any good, must be in full possession of her physical faculties. I mean it would be no use her accepting work—hard, important, anxious work—at a hospital at the time she was suffering from a severe physical breakdown. It wouldn't be fair—any more than it would be fair for a man to offer to play in an important football match if he knew he had a sprained limb. I think there may be still some use for me in the world—the outside world, I mean. I don't know. On the other hand, I may be meant to leave the world and live apart from it. This would be (for me personally) far the nicest course, the happiest and the best, but I don't know whether it will be my privilege. You see, it is not an easy thing to be a nun. It is like, in the business world, trying to be a Rothschild—many are called, few are chosen. But although I don't know, although I may not know for a year, or for much longer— not, perhaps, till my noviciate is over, and not, perhaps, even then—I shall, I am sure, ultimately know.

I am going a long way round to answer what you asked me to think over for two days: whether I

*could marry you or not. I think perhaps I have
answered it already. I know this : I couldn't make
you happy now as I am ; I wouldn't have the power,
the strength, or the life. But even if I felt I had all
that, I'm not sure I should try, because I don't think
that even with me at my best and strongest and happiest you could ever be happy* now. *I think I know
you better than you know yourself. I think that in
about six months' or a year's time you will say to
yourself that I was right after all, and that you will
regret nothing. That is all for the moment. I
shall pray for you every day of my life. You
will never be far from my thoughts, and others far
better than myself shall pray for you too. Of course
you think this is all unessential, but we think there is
such a thing as direct answer to prayer—that, although
not all prayers are answered, there is no prayer that
is unheard. I wish you would pray for me, just
mechanically, although it may mean nothing to you,
just because I ask you to. I wish you would say every
night before you go to sleep :* " Mary, Mother, pray
for Beatrice." *I would rather you would pray for
yourself, but I feel that you would not do that. Perhaps you wouldn't mind doing both together? There
was an old Italian who used to be a friend of Father's.
He was a great sceptic, and he believed in* nothing,
*but he took the trouble to go to St. Anthony's shrine in
Padua, and to put up a candle there. This surprised
his friends.* " Cela ne peut pas faire de bien," *he
said.* " Mais cela ne peut pas faire de mal." *Look*

at it in that light if you like. Lastly, I want to tell you that I have decided on this course by myself. *I did not speak of it to a priest or to any one else until I had quite made up my mind that I wanted to do it. I told Father Blacklock about it the day before yesterday, just after you had gone away. I had not said a word about it to him before, although he is a very old and intimate friend of mine, and although I do not mind what I say to him. You would like him, by the way, and you can safely go and see him if you would like to talk about ideas and people and human nature, without fear of being " got hold of." He has infinite delicacy of perception, infinite tact, and a wonderful sense of what not to say. He is, too, a* great *friend of mine, and I know he is fond of me. That is all for the moment. Don't come and see me, because I shan't be here. I felt I couldn't face another meeting just now. I go to Paris to-morrow for a few days; then I come back and go straight to the Convent. That is why I have gone away without saying good-bye. God bless you.—B.*

" Evidently," said C., as he read this letter, " I am not going to be thrown a life-belt from that ark."

And the old feeling of numbed indifference came back to him, mixed with an indefinable feeling of resentment and opposition.

" Damn those priests! Damn those Catholics ! " he said to Wright, as he read the letter at breakfast.

After all, what did it matter ? Beatrice was pro-

bably right. He doubtless would have made her
unhappy. She would certainly be better off in a
convent than in the world—who wouldn't ? Only it
was a little hard now, just as he thought ; . . . but
that was, of course, a selfish, a purely selfish, thought.
Why should one expect to be happy ? The ancients
were far more sensible. The best thing, they said, was
not to be born, and the next best thing was to die as
soon as possible. But then, after all, why live ? An
overdose, and the whole thing was settled, the problem
solved, the trick done. And if you didn't believe in a
future life, what was the obstacle ? Why not ? Well,
there were several reasons. Beatrice, he felt, would
mind—might feel responsible. If only on account of
her he couldn't do it, and then—who knows ? Who
knows ?

He dined with Wright that evening. Wright had
passed his examination into the Diplomatic Service,
and was now serving his apprenticeship at the Foreign
Office. They discussed suicide.

" Do you think it is very cowardly ? " asked C.

" My feeling is," said Wright, " that short cuts are
no use. I feel it wouldn't solve the question, that one
would find one had to begin again somewhere else at
another end of the stick, that one had been sent back
to the bottom of the class, and that would be *awful*.
I think it would be awful to kill oneself and find oneself
in another Mayfair."

" It all comes back to the *Hamlet* theory : ' To
sleep, perchance to dream.' Personally, I can't think

it cowardly.   My old Italian master used to say that he thought the courage it needed to take one's own life was *desperate*."

"Well," said Wright, "I don't think *I* could do it. I should be too interested in what is going to happen next."

"I don't care a damn what happens next," said C.; "not a damn."

This was a rash statement, as it turned out.   They had been dining in a small restaurant in Soho, and they walked home to their rooms past the theatres in Coventry Street, out of which people were beginning to pour.   They passed the doors of the Imperial Theatre, where a successful American comedy was enjoying a startling success.   The play was just over. There was a crowd at the doors : commissionaires, playgoers in evening clothes, men running to get hansoms, and women standing on the steps in opera cloaks and shawls and lace veils.   C. and Wright pushed their way through the crowd slowly.   Standing up near the side of one of the open doors, on the top step of the theatre entrance, C. caught sight of a figure that he fancied was familiar to him.   He looked again and caught sight of some one dressed in black and wearing a black coat—you had glimpses of, and the impression of a cloud of black tulle.

It was Leila.   There was no doubt about it.   With her was Mrs. Evelyn, looking patient and *distrait*. Wilfrid Clay appeared in the crowd.   He waved to them.   Evidently he had been sent to fetch a cab, and had performed the task successfully. As soon as they began to move it became apparent that there was also another man belonging to the party. A tall, good-looking, middle-aged man, with a military upright appearance, with a look of a Lawrence picture about him, with brown, smiling eyes and dark hair.

He was talking to Leila.

C. pretended to be lighting a cigarette, so as to have an excuse for a slight delay, and by the time his long-drawn-out process of lighting it, which entailed lighting and blowing out the contents of almost a whole match-box, was over, Leila and her party had passed through the crowd to their cab, and C. had enjoyed a complete view of them. He and Wright were not, as far as he knew, observed by them.

C. felt his heart beating very fast. The colour, when he first saw them, rushed to his face, and he was shaking slightly all over, so that no pretence was needed to make the lighting of his cigarette a long business.

A line of Dante came into his head :—

D'antico amor sentì la gran potenza.

He was thankful—it was a rueful admission—that Beatrice had stopped him in the middle of his rash protestation ; but although he had been prevented, just in the nick of time, from voicing a formal denial, he felt that *morally* he had been guilty of one, and he wished to go out into the night and weep bitterly, although he had no remorse as far as Leila was concerned, but remorse in general, because he had been proved untrue.

That is why, perhaps, he was so silent as they walked home to their rooms, and why, when he got home, he said he was too tired to sit and smoke even one cigarette. He must, he said, go to bed.

CHAPTER XLI

THE next morning C. got a note from Mrs. Evelyn asking him to luncheon. It was not a party; she would be quite alone, she said; there might possibly be her brother. C. went with a beating heart, because he felt, although most likely he would not have admitted this, that Leila might be there. She was there, and there was no one else except a brother of Mrs. Evelyn's who was working in the Foreign Office. Her husband always had luncheon in the City. Leila greeted him in a friendly manner with an expression as of some one who had suffered immensely, but who had got over it, of some one who had borne a great, irreparable injury, but who bore, nevertheless, no malice; she seemed to talk to him across a gulf that nothing could bridge, although, at the same time, there was nothing in the least hostile or cold or alien, or even unfriendly, in her manner.

She conveyed what she wanted to convey with the unerring spontaneous precision of a great artist, and C. was acutely conscious of every shade she wished to indicate.

After luncheon Mrs. Evelyn took her brother into the back drawing-room, leaving Leila and C. in full possession of the drawing-room that looked over Manchester Square.

Leila said a few words about Harry. " I am so sorry," she said, very softly. She asked a few questions about it. She had seen in the *Morning Post* that there was to be a memorial service at St. Luke's. She would certainly go to it. " It's to-morrow, isn't it ? It was terribly sudden. And one is glad in a way that your dear mother was spared the blow and the separation. They are happy now together . . . above."

" Yes, if you believe all that," said C. savagely. " I'm afraid I don't."

" All what ? " said Leila, genuinely surprised.

" About a future life and the resurrection of the body. I don't believe a word of it."

" But we know that it is so. We are told so in the Bible," she said in a tone of outraged dignity.

" I suppose we are," said C., as if this were a surprise to him, but in reality wishing to avoid argument. " How long are you going to stay in London ? "

" Only a day or two. I'm here alone, without Terence."

She had come over to see her mother and her relations. She was staying with her sister Emmie (Mrs. Tryan). She was obliged to cram in a great deal in a very short time. She talked to him exactly as if they had not met since their first meetings in Florence and London, treating him, that is to say, as some one she liked the look of, and knew about, and was ready to like, but whom she did not know at all. Nor was C. able to break through the intangible barrier which she erected between them. He was conscious of one thing, and of one thing only—however much she might have changed with regard to him, he had not changed with regard to her. He loved her as much as ever—perhaps more than ever—nor did he know or care what she had done, what her attitude had been with regard to him. He only knew that he loved her now. After they had been talking for a very short while she got up to go.

"May I come and see you," he asked, "before you go away?"

"I should love you to, only I am dreadfully full up. Let me see, this afternoon is impossible. To-morrow I'm engaged all the morning. I'm having luncheon with Emmie, and I'm driving with her in the afternoon. After tea I'm engaged right up till dinner, and then we are all dining out. The day after to-morrow we shall be in the country all day, and the day after that I go back. It's a pity we can't meet to-night at the Cleveland House ball, but you're in mourning, of course . . . it's most unlucky. However, if you come through Paris you must look us up. Good-bye," and she gave him one of her most engaging smiles, and then, turning to Mrs. Evelyn, she said, "If Wilfrid doesn't come soon I shan't wait for him."

"He's sure to be here in a minute."

C said good-bye, and as he walked downstairs he crossed Wilfrid Clay, and for the first time he felt jealous of her friend. He had never felt jealous of him before.

The next morning at eleven-thirty he went to the

memorial service for Harry, which was held at St. Luke's. There he met his two sisters, his brother Edward, his sister-in-law, Mr. and Mrs. Roden, his Uncle George and his Aunt Emma, who were in London on leave, his Uncle Cuthbert and his Aunt Fanny, Mr. Dartrey, Albert Calhoun and his two sisters, and various other friends of the family, among them Leila Bucknell.

The church was a perfect example of the eighteenth century Georgian church architecture ; there was a gallery all round it, and high shut pews in the nave.

The congregation was not large ; it consisted of Lord and Lady Hengrave's relations and friends, some of Edward's city friends, and some of Harry's Eton friends. The hymn *Peace, Perfect Peace*, was sung at the beginning of the service ; the ninetieth psalm was sung by the choir ; the lesson from the Corinthians was read, and the service ended with another hymn, *O God, Our Help in Ages Past.*

C. had luncheon with his brother Edward. Julia and Marjorie were there, and Uncle George and Aunt Emma, whom he had not seen since Rome. They talked of the service.

" It was very beautiful and dignified," said Aunt Emma, " so different from the memorial services abroad . . . we have to go to so many of them. . . . They are so tawdry, so theatrical."

That night when he came home from his office C. found Malone waiting for him in a dreadful state. He had spent all his money. It was impossible for

him to live in his rooms in Knightsbridge any longer.
He would like to go to the colonies, but there was
Esther. How could he leave her ? It was imperative
for him to find something to do.

As they were talking Blades was announced, and
Malone went on discussing the matter and expounding
the situation. They all three of them discussed what
job Malone could possibly find in London. He had
certain qualifications and assets.

At Oxford even the Dons had thought highly of
him at one time. He had taken a First in Mods.,
but his degree had been a disappointment.

" Why couldn't you be a publisher's reader ? " said
C. " Perhaps Leonard Goldsmith would give you a
job."

Blades said that his father knew Goldsmith intimately, and he would ask him to see him about it, and
to do what he could.

C. wrote to Goldsmith as well, and the result of this
was that Malone was given work as reader, on approbation at first. He was to read novels.

During the rest of that year C. saw practically no
one but Malone and Wright.

He did not see Leila again that year, nor did he hear
from her. He was in London during the whole of the
year, going every day to his office, and working there,
with the exception of one short holiday in August,
which he spent partly at Elladon with the Rodens
and partly with his sister Julia.

Christmas found him living in London with Wright

and Malone. Malone had given satisfaction to Mr.
Goldsmith. Novels bored Gerald to death, and
perhaps that was the reason that he was able to do the
work successfully. Whether this was so, or whether
it was merely chance, the fact remained that he
showed an extraordinary flair for what pleased the
novel-reading public. He reported favourably on
a book called *Eastern Windows*, which dealt with
the struggles — religious, conscientious, financial,
emotional and amorous—of a curate in a London
parish. The book had been refused by three well-
known firms. Goldsmith published the book on
Gerald's recommendation. Gerald recommended it
because he knew it was exactly the kind of book that
would please Esther. The book was published, and
sold in its thousands, and Esther enjoyed it
immensely. After that Gerald's position was secure.

After Christmas, Wright went to his first post,
namely, Paris, and Gerald Malone was the only friend
that C. had left to him in London.

C. did not hear from Beatrice again, and the thought
of her was not in the foreground of his mind. Leila
still occupied that place. He wondered who the man
was whom he had seen with her at the play. The
thought of her never left him for a moment during all
those autumn and winter months, although he tried
to drive it away by every kind of distraction. But it
was quite useless. Leila was holding him, although
absent, and although she never once wrote to him, as
with a poisoned hook.

Early in January, C. received a letter from Wright, in Paris, giving him his impressions of diplomatic life, and telling him the news of the Embassy. His impressions were much like those that C. himself had received during the short time he had spent in Rome. As for the news, there was one item which blotted out all the rest, and that was that the Bucknells were coming home.

Wright had seen a good deal of them. He wrote in great detail about Leila, knowing how deeply the topic would interest C. She had gone out of her way to be civil and kind to him; and he said—what was quite true—that she would be greatly missed in Paris, both at the Embassy and outside; that the French liked and admired her, and that the Ambassador thought her charming. He did not mention one fact which he imagined he had noted: that Colonel Wilmot, the military attaché, was wildly in love with her, and was waiting impatiently for his time in Paris to be over, which would not be until the autumn, so that he might go back to England.

Wright recognised him as being the man they had seen with Leila coming out of the play. Nor did he mention another little thing which only struck him as being significant much later. On one occasion, when he and Leila were talking of C., a third person had broken into their conversation, namely, Freddy Calhoun, and he had abruptly asked Wright whether C. was married yet. Wright had said that he had not known there was any question or likelihood of C. getting married.

"Oh!" said Freddy. "I didn't mean he was engaged, or anything of that sort, but a fellow like C. is bound to get married soon. He's sure to be snapped up. I hear he's in love with a girl now."

Leila had listened to this conversation in silence.

The Bucknells arrived in London before the end of January. Wright reported the hour of their departure to C., but C. did not like to make any move. Wright reported that Leila had spoken of C., not only with friendliness, but with eagerness; in fact, she had talked of him constantly. Wright knew, of course, of the break in the relations, and he was convinced that Leila wished to close the breach. Whether that would conduce to the happiness of C. or not, was another matter; that was not his business; he was merely a spectator. His conjecture proved to be correct.

Not long after Leila had arrived in London, C. met her, by chance, at a dinner given by Mrs. D'Avenant. It was a small dinner-party of ten people. Leila and Terence were late; and C. did not have the chance of speaking to her before he went down to dinner. He sat at dinner between Mrs. Evelyn and an older lady, but opposite Leila. He thought she looked younger and prettier than ever. She was dressed, so some one said, not like people who get their clothes in Paris, but like people who live in Paris; and her clothes, her flowers, her jewels, the way she did her hair, everything about her, seemed to obey the subtle rhythm of her personality. C. could not take his eyes off Leila during that dinner, and he was strangely *distrait*.

Mrs. Evelyn guessed the reason, sympathised, and left him alone, concentrating on her other neighbour, who was her host. C.'s other neighbour, a middle-aged, hardened diner-out, did not need to be talked to; she only wished to talk, and she never noticed if any one listened or not, and she was perfectly satisfied with C.'s seeming silent attention, and unconscious of the fact that he was worlds away.

Although he had exchanged no greeting with Leila, except a smile across the drawing-room upstairs, C. had a feeling that the barrier between him and her was no longer there; he had the same impression during dinner, although she hardly ever looked at him, and concentrated her whole attention on her two neighbours.

When the men went upstairs, after dinner, the guests fell into groups, and Leila was sitting on a sofa at the end of a small back drawing-room. C. went straight up to her and sat down beside her. They began to talk; and C. was at once aware that his instinct had not played him false. The barrier had gone. It was the same Leila, the Leila whom he had known at Twyford and Fontainebleau, who was now speaking to him.

C. was like a man who wakes up after a long night-mare, and realises that the agony he has been through, and the catastrophe that has overwhelmed him, is nothing but a dream. The load that had been on his heart, ever since his return from Fontainebleau, had been magically rolled away in one supreme second.

He was alive once more; he was sandalled with wings, and he felt as if he was sailing through the blue of an infinitely radiant space. They talked till it was time to go. What did they talk about? C. would not have been able to tell even had it been a question of life and death. No human power could have made him unwind that happy inconsequent tangle of talk. Before he left, Leila had told him that they were back in their old house. He must come and see her soon.

"May I come to-morrow?" he asked. Leila reflected for one brief instant.

"To-morrow? Yes, I am going to stay the night with my sister Emmie; she's got a little house at Windsor, where Horace is quartered. If you would like to come down for the night, I can arrange it. Terence won't be there; he's got an official dinner."

It is needless to say that C. accepted that invitation.

When C. got home that night he found Malone in his rooms. Malone plunged *in medias res*, without a moment's delay.

"I'm going to be married to-morrow morning," he said, "and you've jolly well got to be best man. I'm marrying Esther, of course, and we're going to be married at the Catholic church in Maiden Lane. You see, it's a mixed marriage."

"You're going to be married as a Catholic?"

"Of course."

"Yes, of course, I suppose; but I thought you **didn't care. . . .**"

" I don't believe in it, if you mean that . . . but if one is to be married in a church, and Esther won't be married at the registrar's office—for some reason or other she doesn't think it is legal—well, then, I couldn't be married in a Protestant church. I was baptised as a Catholic, and I shall be buried as a Catholic ; but I admit it's only a clannish feeling with me, mixed with a fanatical hatred of Protestant religious institutions."

" That always seems to be the worst thing about Catholics," said C., " they pretend to believe in a super-natural, Divine revelation, which necessitates an Infallible Representative on earth. That representa-tive is the universal Catholic Apostolic Church. (Stop me if I am saying anything wrong.) I didn't even say Roman, you see, so as not to confuse the issue, but I now add Roman, Roman in that it is centred, that the visible head of it is the Bishop of Rome, the direct successor of St. Peter, the Vicar of Christ upon earth. Well, here, you say, is our Catholic Church ; any one can belong to it ; it's open to all, and open to all in the same way ; it is the same *everywhere* and *everywhen*, ' *Quod semper, quod ubique, quod ab omnibus.*' ' *Securus judicat orbis terrarum,*' etc. In China, in Africa ; yesterday, to-morrow ; in the cata-combs of Rome, in the Roman villas in Britain, in the cathedrals of the Middle Ages, in the palaces of the Renaissance, in the taverns of London, in penal times ; in tin tabernacles at Aldershot or in India ; in an Austrian village, an Australian shanty, a Canadian

shack; a village in the outer islands of Scotland or in
the South Seas; there it is, always the same, and always
ready to receive any one.—Don't, for God's sake,
interrupt me yet.—Soldier, sailor, tinker, tailor, rich
man, poor man, ploughboy, thief . . . well, that is
your claim; that is the claim I have heard made by
your people;—and yet in practice, what happens?
If I were to say to you: 'I've been converted, I'm
going to be a Catholic to-morrow,' you would look
on me as the kind of man who calls himself Irish
because he stays a few months every summer in
Ireland, or even, let us say, has a house of his own in
Ireland.

"It's never the same, you say, and mind you, *I
quite agree*. My sister Julia has several friends among
the old Catholic families of England, and the other day
I was having tea with her, and Lady Hurstmonceux
was there, who belongs to one of the oldest English
Catholic families, and they happened to mention Mrs.
White, a friend of father's, who had a villa in Cannes
for years. She has become a Catholic. Julia
announced this piece of news to Lady Hurstmonceux,
thinking, I suppose, it would please her. She gave a
slight sniff, just as old men do, just as my uncles do
when they hear that a *nouveau riche* has been elected
to their favourite club. That is what I mean, they
treat it as a *club*, a hereditary, aristocratic club into
the bargain, and I quite agree with them that they are
right. I quite agree with them that converts, especially English converts, are impossible; but if this is

so, bang, surely, goes the universal *semper ubique*
. . . *orbis terrarum* claim !

"But, as a matter of fact, I don't think you—I mean
your people—are sincere when they say it is necessary
to be *born* a Catholic, or when they imply it, because
they are *delighted all the same to make converts*, so
where is the logic ? The moment you begin to be
logical you stop being sincere—isn't that so ?"

"The Church is, I believe," said Malone, "often
accused of faults that contradict one another. Most
people complain of the Church being too logical ; but
all I've got to say is this—now that you have finished
proving to me, what I knew before, that the English
are incurably snobbish !—I'm going to be married in
a Catholic church, in Maiden Lane, to-morrow at
eleven o'clock, and you are going to be my best man,
and a lot of jolly nuns are going to pray for Esther and
me ; but what's made you so argumentative, C. ?
What *has* happened to you ? Why are you in such
good spirits ? Are you going to be married, too ?" And
he hummed the tune out of *Iolanthe*—

> For I'm to be married to-day, to-day,
> For I'm to be married to-day.

C. answered by whistling the tune with even greater
gusto than Gerald.

CHAPTER XLII

MALONE was right, C. was in good spirits; he thought that life was about to begin again for him, that the blots of the past had been wiped out, and the future seemed to wear a rosy mist.

Circumstances, too, seemed to be favourable. Terence was engrossed in his work. Foreign affairs were peculiarly complicated at this moment. Wilfrid Clay had gone to America.

Everything lately had conspired to make it easy for him to see Leila. During the first weeks of February he saw her often, but at the end of the month she fell ill; she was threatened, so she said, with bronchitis, and the doctors said she must at once go to a milder climate.

A friend of hers, Lady Wendover, had a villa at Nice. She could not *lend* it, she could not afford to, but she did want to let it, and if possible to a friend, it was so tiresome to have to let one's house to a stranger. Lord Marryat, Uncle Freddy, was going to Nice, too, and several of her acquaintances. Under the circumstances it seemed madness not to take Lady Wendover's villa, which was comparatively cheap. The climate of Nice, her doctor said, would be exactly right for her.

She left London at the beginning of March. Mrs. Evelyn went with her, and she took her little girl with her. Basil, the boy, had gone to school.

She wrote to C. every day. In one of her letters, she mentioned that Lord Marryat was ill, and just as she was about to start home at Eastertime, she wrote to say that alarming symptoms had developed. She could not possibly leave Nice as long as he was so ill ; he was in danger. Then came news that the crisis was over, that he was out of danger, and, finally, that he was convalescent.

The Easter holidays by this time were nearly over, and Leila was expecting to be back shortly. C. suggested meeting her in Paris, but she explained to him that she was coming straight through. She let him know, later, that she changed her plans at the last moment, as Terence wished to spend a day in Paris and was coming to fetch her. As matters turned out, she was able to stay a few days at the Embassy ; Terence didn't come to fetch her until the day before she left. He was, at the last moment, unable to get away sooner. They stayed at the Embassy, and Wright met her there one day at luncheon.

Wright still thought that Colonel Wilmot was in love with Leila, although he had no positive evidence of the fact beyond his own surmise, and several intangible incidents and undefinable signs : for instance, Wilmot had spent some days at Nice—but there was nothing very unusual in that. During Leila's stay at the Embassy, although she and Wilmot met, nothing occurred which lent any colour to Wright's supposition, and yet he was more convinced of the matter than ever, and he suspected that Leila had lost all interest in C.—all real interest.

Colonel Wilmot was not married, but he was living with a Mademoiselle Angèle Durcis, who was a well-known personality in the highest spheres of the *demi-monde ;* most refined and most austerely elegant, she hardly ever wore a jewel and was never seen to eat or drink. She was extremely quick, as well as extremely jealous ; so if the Colonel were meditating or practising any infidelity, he would have to be careful if he wished to deceive her.

Leila was escorted home by Terence and by Wilfrid Clay, who had just come back from America, and when C. realised this fact (and it was Leila who told him) he burst into an ungovernable fit of passion.

" You never tell me anything," he said. (This happened in Mrs. Evelyn's house, where Leila had asked him to meet her, as Alice was in the country—her own sitting-room wasn't quite ready—towards six o'clock, the evening after she returned.) " You told me a string of lies about Paris. You said I couldn't come, and then that you were coming straight through, and then, after all, you go to Paris and stay there nearly a week because, you say, of Terence—but Wilfrid Clay comes to fetch you ! "

" Of course, if you're going to be jealous of Wilfrid——" said Leila.

" Then why didn't you let me come too ? "

"Because Terence would have minded. He, of course, doesn't mind Wilfrid, but he would mind you."

One grievance led to another. He believed the reason she had stayed in Paris was to see Dallas Wace. She had mentioned in her letters that Dallas Wace was at Nice, and was perhaps going to Paris. Leila laughed.

"Dallas Wace? Yes, I believe he *was* in Paris, but I never set eyes on him. I saw him at Nice, it's true, quite often; and why not? You are so silly, so absurd."

She laughed and C. laughed, and they talked of other things.

But C. soon realised that a new era had begun. It was not that she was not charming to him; it was not that she did not see him quite often; it was not that she did not make plans for the future, for their future; but he felt there was something behind it all, something he didn't know. She was all the time subtly, intangibly *different*. He felt that they were dancing on a volcano, and that at any moment the gay merry-making of their relation might be interrupted by a formidable catastrophe.

Leila had not been long back in England before an event happened which upset her profoundly. Lord Marryat, whom she had always called "Uncle Freddy," whom she had known ever since she was a child, whom she had always looked upon as more than a godfather, and as being certain to leave her his country house, possibly his London house in Berkeley

Square, and a substantial income, and certainly the family jewels, as he had no family—only a few relations whom he hated—startled the world by marrying the nurse who had looked after him during his illness at Nice, and by selling his London house, and buying a villa at Cannes for the winter. Leila told C. about it.

" I knew that nurse was a horrible woman from the first moment I set eyes on her," she said. " I could see she was determined to get his money. Poor Uncle Freddy! It was such a shame to take advantage of him when he was in that state. You know he was almost unconscious. Of course, it's only for him I mind, although I once thought he was interested in the children, and would probably do something for them some day. Of course, *now* all that's out of the question."

It was indeed. The weekly supplies of fruit and flowers which hitherto used to come from Lord Marryat's country house ceased altogether. He was remaining for the present at Cannes, and he intended to spend the summer in Scotland. Leila had written to him, and all she had received in return was a coloured postcard of a youthful couple coming out of church, and written underneath the following words :—

Ring the merry wedding bells.

" *She* chose that ! " said Leila when she showed the picture postcard to C. " It's just like her ! So vulgar ! "

Leila entertained a great deal that summer. She was constantly giving small luncheon parties, and sometimes little dinners (never more than eight people, as her dining-room did not hold more).

One of the most frequent guests was Sir Alfred Rooter, of Johannesburg, a middle-aged man, who had made an immense fortune in the South African diamond mines. He had built himself a large house in Kensington. He was not socially ambitious, as his wife was anæmic and delicate and disliked going out ; she was cultivated and musical, and lived entirely in the musical and artistic world. But Sir Alfred liked power. He was not averse to intrigue, and he owned a weekly newspaper, and contemplated buying a daily newspaper. He had the reputation of being immensely able.

Leila had got to know him through one of her impecunious female friends, who had a sure nose for finding out the whereabouts of money. She at once introduced him to Terence. The conjunction was perfect, as Terence was delighted to make the acquaintance of this bluff (as he thought), honest, rough diamond, who could give him excellent advice about his investments ; and Sir Alfred was delighted to make the acquaintance and win the friendship of so distinguished—and so discreet—a Government servant. Leila was charming to him, and he appreciated beauty and grace when he saw them, especially when they were allied to wits. He consulted her about buying a country house in England. He wanted a large house, but not *too* large a house, in which he could entertain fourteen or fifteen people if he wanted to. He wanted a house with a large room, as his wife was fond of music and had set her heart on a music room, and he didn't mind a good tune either if it was decently played. He didn't want the house to be too far from London, and yet he did not want anything *suburban*. An hour and a quarter's journey would be about the limit; it must not be longer.

Leila asked C. casually what had happened to Bramsley. Had it been sold yet? No, not yet; it had been let to an American family; but this family had gone back to America. His sister-in-law, Marie, was anxious to *sell* the house; but Edward still clung to it, although he probably knew that he would never be able to live there.

"And what do *you* feel about it?" asked Leila.

"Oh, I don't care a rap," said C. "I'd just as soon any one had it as Marie. You see, if she had it she would spoil it entirely. You have only to look at what she has done to the house in Portman Square."

"Yes," said Leila, pensively, and it is more than probable that she thought Marie Hengrave had been quite right in carrying out such improvements as she had made; she had not, perhaps, even gone far enough.

"Then you wouldn't mind if Edward sold it?"

"I should be sorry for Edward; and if Harry had been alive I should be sorry for him, he loved it; but otherwise I really shouldn't care a rap. And I believe Edward is quite used to not living there *now*, and to living in the suburbs—he hated it at first. And, at any rate, he's reconciled. He knows he can never live at Bramsley."

A few days after this conversation, Sir Alfred Rooter called on Lord Hengrave one morning in the city. The day after his visit he went down to Bramsley. Bramsley had been evacuated by the American family which had rented it some time. This family had had enough of English country life to last it a lifetime, and the place was now to let again. But Sir Alfred had no wish to take a house on a lease ; he would either buy it, or not have it at all.

The present Lord Hengrave, however, had no wish to sell, although let he must. Sir Alfred called and made a tentative offer. Lord Hengrave did not mention Sir Alfred's visits to his wife. Sir Alfred visited Bramsley again, this time with Lady Rooter ; and after this visit, he called on Lord Hengrave again, and made another offer, an offer still more handsome than the first, which had been no mean one.

Lord Hengrave met Sir Alfred's second and more than handsome offer for buying the house, with a civil, but final, *Non possumus*.

Sir Alfred was convinced that Lord Hengrave meant what he said, and he reported want of progress to Leila Bucknell. She understood where the difficulty lay in a moment.

"Do you really want the house ? " she asked.

"More than anything. My wife has seen it, too, and it's the only house in England that she fancies. And she knows——"

"I'll get it for you," she said.

Sir Alfred shook his head.

"He won't part," he said. "Believe me, I know when a man's bluffing, and that man's not. He's not after the dollars ; it's the house he wants to keep ;— family pride, and all that. I don't blame him."

"I'll get it for you, all the same," said Leila.

Sir Alfred laughed.

"You don't know what I've offered him. After my wife saw it I almost doubled my offer. I've offered him far more than the place is worth, far more than he'll ever be able to get. I tell you the man is mad on the subject ; he won't part."

"Yes he will," said Leila, "in two days it will be yours."

"Well, if it is, all I can say is that you're . . ." and he didn't know what she was.

Leila took immediate action. She called on Lady Hengrave, who showed her over the improvements she had made in her house, and they had a long, long talk. Leila asked her to luncheon the next day. There she met Sir Alfred Rooter, who sat next to her.

"Edward," she said to him, "has been telling me all about your wanting to buy Bramsley. Of course, it will break our hearts to have to sell it, but one really feels for the children's sake that one would almost not have the right to refuse a really good offer . . . only, of course, when one feels as *we* do about it, one has the right to ask a fancy price."

" And what do you consider a fancy price ? " asked Sir Alfred.

" Oh, don't ask me those sort of conundrums," said Lady Hengrave, " I know nothing about business, you must ask Edward."

" But Lord Hengrave, when I last saw him, told me he had absolutely decided not to sell, there was nothing doing," said Sir Alfred.

" Yes, I know," said Lady Hengrave, " it was all my fault.   He'd promised me *never, never* to sell, whatever the price offered, because the last time there *was* an offer, and that wasn't long ago, and they—American friends of mine are still longing to buy it—I made *such* a fuss ; but now I've been thinking it over, I really do see that it is unreasonable, and I told Edward yesterday, last night, in fact, that he might think it over and write to you."

They talked a great deal more about Bramsley, and during the conversation Lady Hengrave understood exactly what had passed between Sir Alfred and her husband.   She took the opportunity also to mention some of the less well-known good points about Bramsley—the Romney on the staircase, the Raeburn, the Laurence and the relics of Charles II.

That evening she mentioned the sale of Bramsley to her husband for the first time.

At first Edward was firm, but his wife had too powerful weapons in her armoury, and he knew that capitulation was only a matter of minutes. He saw he was beaten from the start.

"But, of course, you must ask for more," she said, "you must ask *double*."

"My dear, that's not possible," said Edward, "one couldn't do such a thing."

Lady Hengrave laughed.

"That's why you're such a shocking man of business. The more you ask the more a man like Alfred Rooter will respect you. He'll think it's part of the game, and that you meant to sell at the time."

"But that's just what I don't choose him to think— what I won't let him think," said Edward.

"But it *is* so silly, mixing up sentiment with business."

"Very well, I shan't sell at all," and Marie saw a peculiar, obstinate, mulish expression come to her husband's otherwise pliant and somewhat weak face; a look which she dreaded, as she knew when it was there, there was nothing to be done, and that all further argument was useless. She knew that there is nothing in the world more insuperable than the obstinacy of the weak.

"Very well," she said, "have it your own way and accept the lowest offer. But remember, I think it's madness."

"The lowest offer!" said Edward. But he wrote to Sir Alfred, nevertheless, that night. He had been thinking things over—he was ready to reconsider.

The next day the bargain was concluded.

Sir Alfred called on Leila in the evening, and his first words were :—

" Well, you're the most wonderful little woman that's ever stepped ; and you'll have to come and help us to entertain, when we give our first house party. But how in the world did you do it ? "

" The Bramsleys are very old friends of mine," said Leila. " I was brought up with them. We have always been very great friends. Julia and Marjorie, Edward's two sisters, used to go to the same dancing classes as I did. I knew all the brothers, too. Caryl, the youngest but one, is a great friend of mine. Terence likes him so much, and says it's such a pity he's not in the Foreign Office."

Before Sir Alfred took possession of Bramsley, C. went down one day and spent a few hours at his old home by himself. The house was uninhabited, except for a caretaker ; the morning room had been stripped of its oak panelling, which had been sold ; the late tenants had painted the mouldings gilt and pink and blue in the Adam breakfast room ; almost all the pictures were gone. The bedrooms empty—some of the furniture had been removed to London or sold. What remained was heaped up in the middle of the rooms, and covered with a sheet. The garden had been utterly neglected and was full of weeds; grass was growing on the drive; and when C. reached the kitchen-garden he could bear it no more, and he left the place. This was his private memorial service for Harry, but he had broken down before it was ended.

CHAPTER XLIII

BRAMSLEY was sold to Sir Alfred Rooter, and he lost no time in getting into it. He was going to carry out considerable structural alterations, but they were to be done by degrees, and in the course of time. For the moment, he was content with the house as it stood. In the autumn (when he meditated a trip to some French or German watering-place) he would have the house thoroughly done up, repainted, and a number of bathrooms inserted, which were as yet painfully lacking. He contented himself for the moment with getting a little new furniture from the emporiums of the Tottenham Court Road to brighten up the house, which was, he said, sadly in need of brightening. Electric light would be put in later. Leila chose the furniture for him, as Lady Rooter took no interest in the kind of furniture he liked, and was far too delicate for the bustle of those big stuffy shops.

Leila had made friends with Lady Rooter. She dined with her and went to her musical evenings. She introduced C. to her, and he was invited at once to a musical evening, on the following Wednesday.

He told Leila that he detested that kind of entertainment, but she said it was no matter, he must come.

He went, and found himself in a palatial house. There was a large hall paved with marble, and a marble staircase, and a banister of wrought steel.

Lady Rooter received her guests in a low and slightly stuffy, panelled drawing-room, which had a certain affinity with the sleeping carriages of the Orient Express. Beyond this long, low room, which was full of heavily upholstered chairs, there was a large vaulted Gothic room, and at the end of it a platform, on which there was a large Steinway Grand.

Lady Rooter was slim without being in the least thin, and short, without being stunted, with dark hair, and a complexion as white as ivory. She had been painted by Lembach, and she was one of those people who seem living proofs of the paradox that Nature imitates art. She looked as if she had been created by Lembach. She was languorous-looking, delicate-looking, and there was something indefinably foreign about her accent as well as her appearance. She was dressed in ivory satin, and round her neck there was one row of large pearls which supported a pendant consisting of one large yellow diamond.

In the room there was a sprinkling of celebrities, but the majority of guests were the connoisseurs and hangers-on of the musical and artistic world.

There were two well-known painters, one famous novelist, and one famous American architect. There were several of Sir Alfred's city friends and their wives, and a certain number of people who had been introduced into Sir Alfred's life by Leila, and a host of people, some of whom were genuinely musical, and others who pretended to be.

C., after exchanging a few words with his hostess, suddenly caught sight of Mrs. Lord in the opposite corner of the room, and he at once went and spoke to her. He asked after Beatrice. Mrs. Lord said she was exceedingly happy. She was not far off, and she went to see her every now and again.

" It's such good air," Mrs. Lord said, " so good for the nerves, after Paris, which is so noisy and dusty."

A man got on to the platform, and Leila at that moment, swept past the door where C. was standing, and carried him away into a smaller room called the library—although the only books in it were *Ruff's Guide to the Turf* and the *Strand Magazine*—where they could talk without disturbing any one.

They talked uninterruptedly there, without being heard or seen, while Eugene Franck, a short-haired pianist, with the face of a bull-dog and the fists of a prize-fighter, made the pianoforte sigh like a ghost. He was succeeded by a handsome contralto, who sang some songs by Frantz and Fauré, and she was succeeded by a famous flute player and some music for flute, strings and harpsichord.

Leila and C. took no notice of the music. They were quite unconscious whether it had begun or ended until Dallas Wace strolled into the room, walked up to Leila and said that he had been asked to take her down to supper.

C. looked at him with disgust, and walked into the music room, which was now gradually growing empty.

Sir Alfred, who had disappeared during the music, now re-appeared, and was shepherding the guests down to supper. He caught sight of C., and said :—

" You've missed a treat," and he winked. " After all that talk you'll want some food. You'll find the balloon-juice on the table. Will you take down Miss Haseltine ? You don't know her ? not know Miss Haseltine ? Why, she's the jolliest girl in London."

Sir Alfred led him up and introduced him to a girl who was talking to the pianist.

Sir Alfred was right, thought C., she had an amazingly amusing face ; the charm of it was quite undeniable, although no one would have called her pretty. She was no longer quite young ; she was short, she had a rather turned-up nose, a laughing mouth, and laughing, but sometimes very serious, eyes, and there was something radiantly honest in her expression ; she had a neat figure and a little head.

" Go on downstairs," said Sir Alfred ; " don't be shy, I'll lead the way," and he led the way, escorting a dark lady, who was the wife of Count Anzoni, the First Secretary at the Italian Embassy.

In the dining-room, supper was being served at round tables, and C. and Miss Haseltine found themselves at the next table to Leila and Dallas Wace. Leila's other neighbour was a dark, rather sleek, young man. C. enjoyed his supper immensely. His companion amused him ; she teased him, she chaffed him, she read his thoughts. They understood each other, and began to have great fun, and all this did not pass unobserved by Leila, who, although just out of reach of hearing, watched them while she pretended to be enjoying an artistic conversation with Dallas Wace into which her other neighbour, whose name was Harold Wraith, kept on languidly breaking in.

" Do you come here often ? " asked C.

" Lady Rooter always asks me when there's music, as she knows I like music, especially the music she has here. You see, it's not the ordinary professional kind, nor the sickeningly bad amateur kind, but there's always something rather unusual and interesting about it. For instance, those songs that Ella Leishmann was singing to-night, that song of Frantz's, and then the Purcell on the harpsichord."

" You know, I'm not musical ; I only like tunes."

" I'm the same ; perhaps I'm worse. I'm not sure I don't only like *bad* tunes. I like street songs. Only singing, when it's dramatic, always fetches me, and Ella Leishmann is dramatic. One trembles——"

" For Mr. Leishmann ? "

" He doesn't mind, but there's an unattached Herr Curtius, also a musician. He's the man to be——"

" Pitied ?

" Yes."

" Is he here to-night ? "

" Yes, he's over there at that further table, talking to the lady in red velvet."

" But you're not a musician, then ? "

"No, I'm an artist. I paint portraits for a living, not for choice, and I live all alone with a friend, a cousin of mine, who is a pianist. We have got a studio in a place you've probably never heard of, called Hammersmith Mansions, near Walham Green. You must come and have tea with us one day."

"And you know the Rooters well?"

"Oh, yes, very well. I have known her for a long time. She is half a Dane, and has French blood too. But she was brought up in Germany. We were at the Slade together. She is a very wonderful woman, so cultivated, so kind, too, and so generous. She is very good to us artists. She was an artist herself when she was young, and she was very poor, and she knows what that means."

"And I suppose he's a very wonderful man?"

"Yes, he is. His career is almost like a fairy tale. He started life as a street boy. He sold newspapers in the streets, and was a bootblack. He taught himself to read—and everything else; and after that he was every kind of thing—a prize-fighter, and an acrobat in a circus, and an engine driver. You must ask him to tell you his story. I should only spoil it. He loves telling it. There's no pretension about him. That's what I like. He doesn't want to be thought anything but what he is."

"I expect he's good-natured too?"

"Yes; but I shouldn't like to cross him. Do you notice those lines between his eyes, those very thick black eyebrows that almost meet, and the steely quality in his dark eyes ? You wouldn't have noticed all that. I have, because, you see, I have painted his portrait."

" Really ? "

" Yes ; it was exhibited at the New Gallery last year. Lady Rooter has got it now in her sitting-room."

" I should love to see it."

" You must ask her to show it to you some day. I don't know if it's good, as a picture, but I think it's got something that's right ; I mean I've tried to give the idea that those who would treat Sir Alfred as the bluff, hearty, uncultivated boor might one day have the surprise of their lives. You see, I think he's in some ways the *cleverest* man I've ever seen. Nothing escapes him. He sees all the little things he's no business to see."

" Is he very fond of her ? "

" I think he always takes her advice about every-thing."

At that moment Leila tapped C. on the shoulder.

" I'm going home," she said, and she walked upstairs with Dallas Wace.

" I must go, too," said Miss Haseltine. " Will you take me upstairs ? "

As they were walking upstairs she told him how to find her house, and to be sure to come and see her some time. He said he would.

When they got upstairs he found no trace of Leila. He went into all the rooms, and then he ran downstairs, into the cloak-room and the hall, where the front door was wide open, as the guests were beginning to go. There, he caught sight of Leila driving away alone, in a hansom cab. Dallas Wace was at the door. He had been helping to get her a cab.

The evening after that party C. went as usual to Berkeley Street. Leila received him icily. After they had tea, a meal during which they behaved like two Chinese mandarins, so perfectly polite they were, the matter was broached, and each of them stated the case with violence, and at the same time Leila burst into tears. C. walked round and round the room like a caged tiger. Ultimately they made it up just before Terence came back from his office.

It was from this date that a new and curious phase started in Leila's London career. She began to go out in the artistic world. She saw a great deal of Lady Rooter, and went out for drives in her victoria in the afternoon. Through Lady Rooter she got to know one or two of the leading lights of the artistic world, that is to say, a sculptor, who was better known in Paris than he was in London, Mr. Bernard Wilkes ; Bellamy, the novelist, Eugene Franck, a pianist and composer, and Harold Wraith, whom she had met at the Rooters, a young man who was immensely well-off, and seemed to have no particular profession. He went to all the principal race meetings ; he had a flat in the Albany ; he collected Greek coins, and was said to be an authority on Italian pictures and English prints. Dallas Wace came frequently to the house, and Leila gave C. to understand that now as far as literary and artistic matters were concerned, she was well supplied, perfectly equipped, and in possession of information that came from a better stable than his. She had made friends, she gave him to understand, with real " professionals," and so he, being a mere amateur in such matters, had no right to look down on her. The truth being that she suspected that C. had once or twice found her not so much unresponsive as inadequate in matters of art and literature, and she had suspected that he talked of such matters in a different way with people like Miss Haseltine, for instance, than he did with her. It was, indeed, the case. Leila therefore took pains to protect herself. Dallas Wace enjoyed her society very much, and he gave her the latest news from the international world of cultivated and intellectual gossip, namely, what was being said in Paris, Rome and St. Moritz, about books, pictures, music, and the stage ; whereas Bellamy, who found her an adorable listener, poured out all his theories to her, and she gathered, by the opinions of others which he quoted and held up to her ridicule, what was being said by the whole of literary London on all contemporary topics of that kind ; while Harold Wraith, who was extremely cultivated and utterly *blasé*, gave to the salad of opinions that Leila was busy concocting, the necessary *soupçon* of indifferent cynicism and cautious scepticism. He pointed out to her how little there was in the modern world to admire, or in the ancient for that matter. He talked of C. to her as being the crudest of Philistines, an utterly ignorant boy. C. found this new world of Leila's frankly unendurable. He loathed Wace ; he hated Harold Wraith with a still fiercer hatred, and indeed, they could scarcely carry on a conversation for more than five minutes without almost coming to blows. And the worst of it was that C. felt and knew that Wraith was horribly competent on his own subjects. He was not a *poseur*. He really knew about Greek coins and prints and pictures. He really knew about racing. Everything he did he did well ; and he was an admirable card player.

But what was more than he could endure was to notice how gradually Wraith's sceptical and *nil admirari* attitude was being absorbed by Leila, and how she let him have the benefit of the reflection, letting him feel that *he* knew nothing of such things, whereas she, if she didn't of herself, was nevertheless in a position to be able to consult the real authorities whenever she was in doubt.

As for Bellamy, the novelist, he took no notice of C. at all ; but he took little heed of any one, so busy was he propounding his own theories and recounting his own impressions.

Leila entertained her new friends at little dinners, and more often still to little luncheons. To the latter she never asked C. It was difficult, for one thing, for him to get away late enough, as Leila had luncheon at two, and C. had luncheon at one with his fellow officials at a club in Westminster. Neither did she ask him to her literary dinners. But she gave him to understand that they took place, and that she didn't ask him because she knew these things didn't interest him. She went out a good deal that summer as well, and she liked meeting C. at balls. She gave him to understand that he was all right in that setting. But even in these surroundings he suffered from the presence of Harold Wraith and Dallas Wace, who neither of them ever missed going to a big entertainment, and, if they did, never failed to monopolise a certain amount of Leila's time.

Sir Alfred took a house at South Ascot that year for the races, and he invited Leila, Terence, and Harold Wraith to stay with him. C. was invited as well, and he went up to London every day to his office and back again to Ascot in the evening. Leila went to the races.

By the end of June Bramsley was ready to receive its new owners, and Sir Alfred gave a party to celebrate the occasion. Terence and Leila were invited, Dallas Wace, Sir Wilfrid Clay, several of Sir Alfred's city friends, and some of Lady Rooter's artistic friends, Bellamy, some musicians, and Colonel Wilmot, who had come over from Paris for a week's leave.

C. was not asked. Leila broke the news that she was going to Bramsley to C. at a dinner-party at her sister's house. He was sitting next to her.

"Lady Rooter asked me if you would like to come," she said to him, "but I told her I thought it would be painful for you. I thought it would revive too many old associations; and Emmie quite agreed."

"What nonsense!" said C.; "one has to get used

to these things. After all, everything in life changes. Nothing remains the same, and all good things come to an end."

" How true that is ! " said Leila, " how terribly true ! "

" I shall probably have to go there some time or other, so the sooner I get used to it the better."

" It's too late for me to do anything *now*, I'm afraid," she said. " They're full up, I know. If I had thought you'd feel like that I would have encouraged them to ask you, but I was so sure you wouldn't like to go there."

" You know perfectly well," said C., " that the only thing I care for is to be where you are. But I believe you did it on purpose. I don't believe you wanted me to come. I believe you like being with those people, Wace and Wraith, without me. You think I spoil your fun."

" It's not that. I think you dislike them so much that you make it all very uncomfortable. You see, although you've read such a lot, you don't understand the people in that world. Of course, I know how fond you are of poetry and all that sort of thing, and how clever you are at writing verses and guessing acrostics. But those people—people like Robert Bellamy and Bernard Wilkes—they are different. They are *professionals*, you see."

" And Dallas Wace and Harold Wraith, are they professionals ? " asked C.

" No," said Leila, " but they know all about art

and books, just like professionals. Robert Bellamy
said he would rather have Harold Wraith's opinion on
a picture than any one's, and that he thought Dallas
Wace was the best judge of a book he knew. You see,
they are artistic as well as literary."

"And I'm neither," said C. "Thank God, thank
God, I'm neither."

"I didn't mean that; you know quite well I didn't
mean that."

But C. was too angry to speak, and Leila turned to
her other neighbour, who was old and deaf and greedy,
and they talked about food till dinner was over. C.
went away as soon as he could after dinner, and did not
say a word to Leila. It would be the first Sunday
since her return from France that they would not be
spending either partly or wholly together, and C. felt
that there was something behind all this that he had
not fathomed. He was madly jealous, but jealous of
an unknown quantity.

CHAPTER XLIV

C. SPENT that Sunday alone in London, and he took the opportunity of paying Miss Haseltine a visit in her studio in Hammersmith Mansions. He found her at home, and she showed him her pictures, which he thought were bold and original. She asked whether she might do his portrait. He said he was afraid he would not have time to give her sittings. He had to be at his office all day.

" I shouldn't want many sittings," she said. " I would do what's called an ' oil sketch.' Two sittings of an hour and a half each would be ample. If you could give me more, so much the better."

C. laughed. " I could give you that," he said.

She wanted him to come on the following Tuesday, but the difficulty was to arrange a time when the light would be satisfactory.

" Would six o'clock in the evening be too late ? " he said. " I could be here punctually by that time, or, if you would rather I came in the morning, I could come quite early before I go to the office, but I'm sure that would be too early for you, as I have to be there by eleven, at the latest."

It was arranged that he should come in the evening at six. C. stayed a long time in the studio, and they talked about every sort of thing. Towards tea-time, Miss Haseltine's musical friend arrived; she was a little dark girl, an admirable pianist, and she was at present studying at the College of Music; her name was Eileen Pratt. They all three had tea together, and they boiled some eggs and made toast. C. enjoyed himself like a schoolboy, more than he had done for years. It was settled that he was to come back on Tuesday afternoon.

He had arranged to meet Leila on the Monday evening after her return from Bramsley at a little dance that was going to be given at a house in Bruton Street. Leila had asked for him to be asked. But just before dinner there came a note from her in which she said she was not going to the dance. She had a bad headache and did not feel well enough. She would see him soon, and would let him know when.

The next day he received another note asking him to come at six. That was just the time he had fixed for his appointment with Miss Haseltine, and he did not like to disappoint her, as he knew she was busy, so he told Leila he couldn't come at six, and suggested that they should meet some other time the next day. He said this in a telegram. She answered this by a telegram, and said in it: "See you at Wessex House Ball."

The Wessex House Ball was to happen on Wednesday night. It was one of the great events of that season. C. kept his appointment with Miss Haseltine on Tuesday, and she got through a satisfactory amount of work. She would, she said, want only one more sitting. She was dining that night with the Rooters. Would he be there?

" No," said C., " they haven't asked me."

" I think Lady Rooter has asked you," she said, " because she asked me for your address and whether I thought you would mind being asked at so short a notice. I said I was sure you wouldn't mind that, but that you would probably be engaged."

" No," said C. " I'm doing nothing. I shall dine by myself."

As they were saying this a messenger boy brought a note for Miss Haseltine. It was from Lady Rooter. She had, she said, asked C. to dinner by telegram, answer paid, early that morning, but had received no answer. If he was there, sitting for his portrait, wouldn't she bring him to dinner? They would dine early—at a quarter to eight—and go to Earl's Court, or somewhere, after dinner; or, if they felt it was too hot, they could sit in the garden, and have some music. He needn't dress. Would she send answer by bearer?

Miss Haseltine read out the letter, and C. said he would be delighted to go. He had not received the telegram. He had started very early for a walk before going to the office, and then he had come straight from the office by Underground to the studio. He asked if he might write a note to Lady Rooter. He explained matters and said he would be delighted to dine. By the time the sitting was over it was time for them to start, and they took a bus to the Albert

Hall, and from there it was only a few minutes' walk to the Rooters' house.

"Eileen is coming, too," said Miss Haseltine; "but she will meet us there."

Sir Alfred greeted C. with boisterous cheerfulness, and made him a cocktail. Lady Rooter looked rather tired, and they had dinner on a veranda which looked out on the large garden behind the house.

There were no other guests besides C. and Miss Pratt.

"How's the portrait getting on?" Sir Alfred asked.

Miss Haseltine explained that it was only a sketch, and that it would be finished the next sitting.

"How long would it take to make a *pukka* picture?" Sir Alfred asked.

"Oh, much longer. I couldn't quite tell exactly."

"But you could finish it by the end of the summer?"

"Oh, yes, of course, I think so. It depends on the sittings;—how often, and what sort of sittings. I don't think he's a very difficult subject."

"Well, it shall be a *pukka* picture," said Sir Alfred. "I give you an order for it, and it's no good messing about with sketches. If you are to paint a portrait, you may as well paint a real one. Don't you agree, Adela?" he said to his wife.

Lady Rooter agreed.

"But Mr. Bramsley won't be able to sit to me," said Miss Haseltine. "He's too busy."

"Rubbish. If it's too far for him to go to your

studio, he can come here, and you can paint him upstairs, in the empty room."

C. was extremely embarrassed. What he could not explain was that six o'clock was the time he kept for seeing Leila. But he did not want Miss Haseltine to lose the commission through him.

" I could come in the mornings, quite early, to your studio ; perhaps that would be more convenient for you ; I'm not always sure about my evenings," he said.

" Joan, you had much better come here in the mornings," said Sir Alfred, with a wink, " just as you used to do, when you were painting me. Young men never are sure about their evenings."

Finally, it was settled that C. was to come to Sir Alfred's house early, in the mornings, at nine o'clock.

After dinner, they all went out into the garden, but presently Lady Rooter took Joan Haseltine and Eileen Pratt upstairs and left the men to have a smoke together. Sir Alfred gave C. an enormous cigar. Before long, as they sat in the garden, they heard the sounds of music.

" You can't flog my old Dutch from the piano. We'll let them play. It pleases them and doesn't harm us; or perhaps you'd rather go upstairs and listen."

C. said he was very happy where he was, and that he understood nothing about classical music.

" Then you're just like me," Sir Alfred said.

First of all he talked about the picture.

" That girl's a topper," he said. " She told me she wanted to paint you, and thought she could make a big thing of it. That's why I took action. So far she's only done a few fancy things, and a portrait of yours truly. But they gave her some fine notices, and hung her well in the New Gallery, and what's-his-name thinks highly of her, but she hasn't got many orders. They say she's too damned realistic, and that puts people off. People like being flattered ; they like the chocolate-box style, and that's not Joan's line. It's a pity it isn't ; it would be a damned sight more lucrative. On the other hand, any one can see with half an eye that the girl's got a punch. She gets it across, and I hope she'll make a hit with your portrait. She'd deserve to. She's a topper. She used to support her aged Ma, a quarrelsome, querulous old —— but she's dead, that's one thing——"

Sir Alfred suddenly paused in his talk as he was looking at C.

" I say, you haven't got a relative in South Africa, have you ? "

" Not that I know of," said C.

" It's funny, you remind me of a chap. A chap I used to know quite well—— Yes," he went on, " it's a hard, tough job for a girl like that to take on the professional business and compete, not only with other artists who are all as jealous as a swarm of hornets, but with the men into the bargain. They get precious little chivalry shown them, I can tell you. It's a question of get on or get out, and the survival of those who push hardest. But, you see, Joan made good, and they say she'll go right to the top of the tree, unless she marries a crook who drinks, or bets, or gambles, and gets away with it somehow, and that's what does happen, nine times out of ten."

" I suppose she's got very little to live on," said C.

" Damned little now except Press notices and promises. But mind you, I've no children of my own, and no relations worth a cent. I regard her as my child, and I shall see that she doesn't starve. But it's not that. I want her to make good all round. I want her to make good at her painting job and to make good in the world—in life—too. However, there'll be time for that. Joan's one in a thousand."

They got on to other topics. Bramsley was mentioned. Sir Alfred said :—

" I suppose you wouldn't care to come down there sometimes. Too many associations."

C. said he would be delighted to come any time Sir Alfred asked him. " It's nonsense expecting things never to change," he said.

Sir Alfred asked him about his work, and was surprised that C. should be tied down to a job in a small Government department which could not possibly lead to anything.

" It's queer, damned queer," he said " Why, I started life by selling papers."

He told C. the strange epic of his life, beginning when he was a bare-footed street urchin and which had now reached the phase when he was a millionaire with this huge house in London and the owner of the Bramsley estate redeemed from mortgages and restored to some of its pristine glory.

"Don't you feel you would like to strike out a line for yourself ? Haven't you any ambition ? "

C. told Sir Alfred of his early adventures. How he had wished to be a journalist; how he had not liked ever to mention it, knowing his parents' invincible prejudice to anything of the kind, and also because he had nothing to show, no assets to procure him an entry into Fleet Street. Then his trial of diplomacy and his attempts to become a barrister.

"But would you like to be a journalist now ? "

"Yes, I would ; but I should never get a job."

"Have you tried ? "

C. told him of the work he had done for the *Northern Pilot*.

"The *Northern Pilot !* You've written for the *Northern Pilot ?* That, in my opinion, is the only paper in this island worth reading, and I'm seriously thinking . . . however, we'll talk about it later. In the meantime, do you ever read the *Saturday Despatch ?* "

Yes, C. did.

"That's my paper, you know, and I can do what I like with it. I'll tell you what, you shall write an article about anything you like . . . a race meeting, a cricket match, a play ? "

C. said he would prefer something theatrical.

"Well, I tell you what," he said; "there's

Madeleine Lapara. She's acting all this week and the next. On Thursday night, so Adela says, she's playing something big and classical, for one night only. You understand French. You shall go and write about that. They say it's her best part. If you can write about it in a way that makes *me* want to see her in the part I shall know what you can do. Adela and I are going another night, when she's doing something more modern. You just describe the whole thing. We've got a dramatic critic, but he probably doesn't understand the lingo, and we've had nothing about her so far. At any rate, you shall do it, and he shan't. Let me see. It's the day after to-morrow. Thursday night. Can you go ? "

C. said he could.

" Capital! that's fixed. And if you make good over that, I'll try and get you something else, and something better. Now I think we'd better join the ladies, or we shall get it."

They went upstairs.

Sir Alfred led the way to the large, dark, cool music-room, and when they got there he asked Miss Pratt to oblige with selections from Gounod's *Faust* and from the *Geisha*, two works to which he was extremely partial, and which C. listened to without difficulty. Lady Rooter talked to C. and spoke to him about Bramsley, and said she so wished not to touch it, not to alter anything. She knew it would be so much wiser to leave it exactly as it was, but that Alfred was a fanatic for modernity. He

could not understand a house without electric light
and a bathroom to almost every bedroom. She didn't
think he would be really happy till he had installed an
electric organ. It was really so comfortable as it
was. She thought the guests had been quite comfortable on Sunday. It was a pity he had not been there.
She had wanted to ask him, but had not liked to. C.
once more explained that he had no wish not to go to
Bramsley, and that it was a comfort to him to think
it was not all falling into decay. "And then, you
know," he said, "you'll think it very odd of me, but
I wasn't very happy at Bramsley, as a child—or, at
least, most of my time there. There were nice
moments, of course——"

Lady Rooter laughed. "I had the same kind of
experience," she said. "I was brought up in a large
castle in Denmark, and I hated it—hated it. My
father was a Dane. He died when I was seven years
old, and my mother married again—an Englishman
who had business in Hamburg. We lived there, and
then all the business went wrong and I went to London
and studied at the Slade School. I had some talent for
drawing in those days—not much, not such as Joan's,
but a little—and I thought I could make a living that
way; and then I met Alfred, quite by chance, one
year, and we were married a month afterwards. Alfred
always makes up his mind about a thing at once, and
once his mind is made up he never changes. He's
made up his mind now that Joan is to paint you here,
and that it is to be her masterpiece."

C. stayed on till about eleven o'clock, when Joan and Eileen said they must be getting home. It was settled that C. was to come to Sir Alfred's house in the morning in two days' time for his first real sitting, and then every day; the sketch was to be scrapped, and a real portrait was to be begun in its stead.

As he left the house, Sir Alfred said :—

"Don't forget the play; you'll get the tickets to-morrow; two—so as you can take a pal, and write us some good stuff. And you must come here again soon."

C. thanked him and left.

He did not see Leila till the Wessex House Ball, the following night. It was a large ball; and the house, with its wide staircase, and square gallery going right round the landing, on the first floor, its fine pictures and furniture and books, looked noble and dignified.

C. did not catch sight of Leila for a long time. At last he found her sitting in the corner of a long room, looking her very best in a golden tissue,

> Robe d'or et rien ne veux,
> Qu'une rose à mes cheveux.

and talking to an old politician.

"Ours is the next," she said.

C. waited impatiently, absent-mindedly nodding and saying "How do you do?" to friends and acquaintances, and exchanging conventional remarks till the music should begin again, and as soon as he heard the strains of the *Monte Cristo* valse strike up its light, heady melody he went to the corner where Leila was sitting, and they walked away till they found a convenient spot right at the end of the gallery.

" Shall we sit here or dance ? " he asked.

" We'll sit here," she said, " for the present."

" Well, tell me all about the party," said C.

" Oh," said Leila, " it wasn't so bad. I like her so much. I must say they haven't done any harm to the house, *not yet*, but I'm fearfully afraid they will spoil it. I had luncheon there to-day, and they told me all about your picture that is going to be painted by Miss Haseltine."

" It's only going to be a sketch," said C., blushing.

" I think it's such a good idea. Sir Alfred said that Miss Haseltine thought you were one of the most interesting subjects to paint she had come across. And he said he thought you had a capable-looking head, but that it was a pity you were wasted in one of those silly little offices. He said you ought to go out to the Colonies."

" I daresay I ought," said C. ; " but I would rather die than do it. What should I do in the Colonies ? "

" I think you would soon make your mark. Sir Alfred thought so too."

" Do you mean you want me to go ? "

" Of course *I* don't want you to go ; I was thinking of what would be best for you."

" Well, you know why I *couldn't* go, couldn't want to go."

" I shouldn't like to think I was spoiling your life." She smiled at him.

" Spoiling it ! Good gracious ! "

At that moment, as they caught the opening bars
of the *Valse Bleue* there was a slight stir and a
rustling of skirts near them of people moving, getting
up and finding fresh partners.

A young Guardsman came up to Leila and reminded
her that it was their dance.

Before she got up, she said :—

" We'll dance not the one after next, but the one
after *that*, and we'll *dance* it.   I shall be near the door,
and, by the way, before I forget it, I want you to dine
with us to-morrow night, *very particularly*."

She went off.   C. smiled his assent.   " Of course,"
he said.   Then he remembered it was the night he was
going to hear Lapara.

C. looked round. It was a lovely sight. The
gallery was crowded with beautiful people.   He felt so
differently now than he used to feel on these occasions ;
now he knew almost everyone by sight.   How things
had changed, he thought, in the last six years !   Both
the Roden girls were married.   He caught sight of
a *débutante* cousin of his, whom he had been introduced
to that year.   She was sitting solitary and melancholy-
looking (next to her aunt, an old lady with a high
tiara), so pretty and young, with a wreath of gold leaves
in her hair.   He asked her to dance, and they whirled
round the ballroom.   C. was not a good dancer, but he
could dance just well enough not to run into people,
and not to tread on their gowns.   When the dance was
over, they walked downstairs to a large room, where

there was a table with lemonade and tea. It was the library; all round the room there were shelves full of rare editions and wonderful bindings. The library opened on to a garden which was lit up with little coloured lights, hanging in festoons from tree to tree. Both C. and his partner were very hot and out of breath. They drank some lemonade and then they strolled out into the garden.

"How delicious it is here," she said. "I should like to stay here all night."

They sat down on two chairs and watched the people go by, and their conversation proceeded more or less on stereotyped lines. "Are you going to So-and-so's and to So-and-so's? No, but to So-and-so's. It's sure to be good," etc., etc.

Presently they heard the music beginning again, and the girl leapt to her feet, saying, "I'm dancing this."

CHAPTER XLV

C. WENT upstairs and sat out the next dance with Mrs. D'Avenant, and after that he went to look for Leila, and they danced a valse together, but she was slightly critical of his dancing to-night, which, as a rule, she used not to be.

" I think you really must have some more dancing lessons, C.," she said, as they walked into one of the large rooms. " It's such a pity not to dance as well as you might. You could dance perfectly if you just had one or two lessons."

" I shall never be a very good dancer," said C. " Let's go down and sit in the garden."

They walked downstairs. Supper had begun. They passed several couples going down to supper. At the corner of the staircase a very tall figure was standing by herself, waiting for some one. It was the famous Lady Vanburg. She was dark, her head was very small, she was dressed in white satin, and wore many rows of pearls round her neck. She had the quality and the authority of *absolute* beauty about her. It was impossible to say exactly where her beauty lay; whether in her features, or in her eyes, or her skin, her shoulders, her figure, or her expression—the only thing certain was that the effect was overwhelming.

" Isn't she beautiful ? " said Leila. " Still much more beautiful than any one else."

" Yes," said C., absent-mindedly, " quite beautiful," he agreed, but he thought Leila was far more beautiful.

" Let's go and have supper," said C.

" Not now, later ; we'll go into the garden for a moment."

They walked out.

Leila looked like a lovely ghost, C. thought, in the warm darkness, so faintly lit by the twinkling coloured lights. Her eyes were like stars to-night. They talked almost in a whisper. They talked, were silent, and talked again, but there was nothing wanting, nor empty, nor embarrassing, nor tedious (so C. thought) about their silences. Their silences (again in C.'s opinion) at least were far more expressive than their words. Time seemed to rush by, and C. felt sad—" sad from the whole of pleasure," but he did not experience the shadow of satiety. This, he thought, is too good to last, but oh ! how delicious ! Oh ! how wonderful !

A remark of Leila's suddenly recalled him to earth.

" You will come to dinner to-morrow, won't you ? "

C. explained that he couldn't. He was obliged to go to the play to see Lapara.

" Can't you come with me ? "

" No," said Leila, " that's quite impossible ; besides, I've got a dinner party. Surely you could go to the play another night ! "

" I can't," said C. " It's a special night. Lapara's

doing *Phèdre* for one night only, and I've been given tickets."

"But surely you can go and see her any night! And who wants to see her *now*, in any case? She's old and *passée*. *Do* come; I want you."

"I'm afraid I can't, really. I've promised to go."

"Who made you promise?"

"Sir Alfred Rooter has given me tickets."

"Oh, I see; you're going with Miss Haseltine!"

"No, I'm not, I swear," said C., getting scarlet.

Leila laughed. "I see," she said.

"He's given me tickets because he wants me to write about it in his newspaper. I've not got any one to go with me yet. I shall try and get Gerald Malone."

"Well, I think you might put it off, as I ask you to. I don't often ask you to do anything for me. Do, C., please. To please me."

"Any other night I would, but not *this* night. I promised Sir Alfred."

"But I'll arrange that with him. I'll make it all right."

"No, I can't, Leila. I can't, really."

"Oh, very well!"

"You see, he wants me to write an article in the *Saturday Despatch*."

"I quite understand. You're quite right. Of course, you must go."

"Of course, if you really insist, I will come."

"I don't want you to come if you don't want to. That's the last thing I want. I wouldn't hear of it."

" All right, I'll come."

" No, C., I don't want you to. I promise you, I'd rather you didn't."

" Please let me. I'll write and tell Sir Alfred I can't go that night."

" No, no ! I really don't want you to. Let's go upstairs. I'm dancing the next dance."

They walked back in silence. Up to that moment everything had been to C. like fairyland : the music, the people, the garden, the lights, the soft warm night, the flowers, the smell of the fruit in the supper-room ; but now there seemed to be a blight on everything. The lights seemed to be dim, the flowers faded, everything tawdry, sham ; all those dazzling people, in coloured satins and jewels, were now, he thought, like a gallery of waxworks. The very music seemed unreal. And yet, not five minutes ago, how intoxicating it had been when he was whirling round the room with Leila, and whispering in the garden ; and Leila in that galaxy of beauty had seemed to him the queen of the evening, the centre of the festivity, in her shimmering gold satin gown with the one pink rose in her hair and the single row of chosen pearls round her lovely neck ! Never had he felt so near to her. And now, instead of being his own, she seemed far away, further than the furthest star ; inaccessible, aloof, and separated from him by æons of time and infinities of space.

He tried one final appeal.

" Don't," he said, " don't, please, Leila. You know

I'm longing to come. I didn't mean to be so silly. Do, please, let me come."

" No, no," she said. They had reached the top of the staircase. " I'm dancing this with Wilfrid," she said. " Ah, there he is ! "

" Will you have supper later ? "

" I'm afraid I'm engaged for supper."

" Well, then, afterwards—later—will you dance with me later ? "

" Yes, later, perhaps," she said. She seemed to have relented, at any rate ; C. thought that all *might* be well—presently.

He caught sight of Lady Elizabeth Carteret. He asked her if she would like to go down to supper. She accepted with alacrity. They went downstairs. Lady Elizabeth told him one piece of news after another about mutual acquaintances. After they had been at supper some little while Leila came into the room with Colonel Wilmot. C. did not know who he was, but recognised him as being the man he had seen with Leila coming out of the theatre. He was longing to ask who he was, but he noticed that Lady Elizabeth looked at them with the look of the hungry but now satisfied gossip-hunter, and he could not bring himself to ask—he was afraid of what the answer might be. He said rather abruptly :—

" I must go upstairs. I've promised to dance with one of my cousins."

They left the dining-room. C. danced with one or two people he knew ; the whole time he was waiting

and watching for Leila to come back, but he saw no
sign of her. It was getting late. The rooms were
less crowded than they had been, but it was evidently
going to be a very late ball. The people, however,
showed no signs of going away. C. walked down the
stairs and looked into the supper-room. He could not
find Leila anywhere. He walked through all the rooms
downstairs ; he saw no sign of her there. He went
upstairs again. There was no one he wished to talk to
or to dance with. Once more, he had the sensation of
blight ; as if some one had put out all the lights, and
had stopped the spring that gave life and gaiety to the
entertainment. Sitting all round the room, the tired
chaperons looked more than ever like waxworks, he
thought, and the dancers, too, were they not all of them
mechanical toys wound up for the occasion ? He felt
a sense of immense weariness and disgust. They
evidently did not share this sensation ; they were
intoxicated with enjoyment. The ball reached its
climax at that moment. A new dance was just
beginning, and as the first bars of the valse *Sourire
d'Avril* were played Leila came into the ballroom with
Colonel Wilmot, and they began to dance.

That tune, *Sourire d'Avril*, was the most popular
of all the dance tunes that summer, and no sooner
were its opening bars heard than there were clappings,
and a buzz of applause, and people came into the
ballroom from all the other rooms and began to dance ;
and the room was once more crowded, almost as
crowded as it had been at the beginning of the

evening. Nearly all the dancers now were really good dancers, and dancers who were dancing because they enjoyed it. There were at least four remarkable beauties—not counting Leila—and a number of extremely pretty girls.

C. noticed at once that George Wilmot's dancing was in a very different category from his own. He noted bitterly what a wonderfully graceful couple they made. George Wilmot was one of those rather inarticulate people who are born not only musical, but with an infallible sense of rhythm. They are common enough in Austria, but rare in England. He couldn't go wrong; he danced as if the music had been composed especially for him, with absolute certainty and, at the same time, without any stiffness. Round and round they went. Would the dance never come to an end? But when the valse did finally stop—and the band had played it as if inspired—the dancers clamoured for more, and the band acquiesced and began the same tune again. C. could hardly bear it; he had only one thought—to find out the name of the man who was dancing with Leila; and as he watched her and her partner from the doorway he felt he would have given worlds if, like Samson, he could have pulled the whole ballroom down and overwhelmed Leila, himself and every one in a common destruction.

Who was there who would know? At that moment Freddy Calhoun came into the room.

"Why aren't you dancing?" said C.

"Hullo, how are you, C., old man? I can't dance

any more. I'm so hot I can't breathe. I've been dancing all the evening like a dervish." They both walked to the window.

" Are you on leave for long ? " asked C.

" Not very long, only a month ;—here, that's to say. I'm going to spend the rest of my leave with Thérèse in the Pyrenees. She's at St. Sebastian at this moment."

" How is she ? "

" Oh, awfully well. She often asks after you, and why you don't come and stay with us. You haven't been to Paris at all lately, have you ? "

" Not since that time I stayed with you."

" Hullo, there's Mrs. Bucknell. Do you remember how jealous Thérèse was because I said she was pretty ? She *is* pretty, too, isn't she ? I think she's the best-looking woman here."

" Who's that she's dancing with ? "

" Don't you know ? I suppose you wouldn't. That's George Wilmot. He's our Military Attaché at Paris. He's only over here for a few days." Freddy laughed.

" Why are you laughing ? "

" Well, you see, his *chère amie* is Angèle Durcis. You haven't heard of her ? She's a great person in Paris, in Thérèse's world. The other women all hate her. Thérèse won't speak to her. And they're fearfully jealous of her. She's the last word of what's *chic* and *nouveau jeu* and all that. But she leads poor old George rather a life, don't you know. She's rather difficult and all that. Always flaring up and making scenes, what ? And can't bear him to look at any one else, and always suspecting him even when he isn't. I was laughing to think what she would say if she could see him now."

" Yes," said C., nervously.

Freddy lowered his voice.

" They say old George has been in love with Mrs. Bucknell all this year, and that he's quite mad about her."

" Oh, really ! " said C., and there was a strain in his voice. "But they can't have seen much of each other ! "

" Well," said Freddy, " he went to Nice, only for a day or two, this year, and they say he went just to see her, as he hates the Riviera like sin, and Angèle never could get him to go there as a rule."

" But she let him go this year ? "

" Well, he arranged it like this : he's a great pal of the——"

Here their conversation was interrupted. The dance had come to an end, and Freddy was caught by one of his relations and taken into the next room.

Leila and Wilmot had walked out on to the landing.

C. waited a reasonable time, standing out on the balcony. It was not yet daylight, but the sky had that peculiar, intensely jewel-like blue which precedes the earliest dawn,

Dolce color d'oriëntal zaffiro,

thought C., and there was a breath of freshness in the air after the great heat of the night.

As soon as the music began again (and there were not many dancers now) C. walked up to Leila, and said :—

"This is our dance."

"Is it ?" said Leila. "I believe it is. I'm too tired to dance, but we'll go downstairs, and I should like just one glass of lemonade or a little hot soup before I go. I'm going home."

She then said good-night to George Wilmot, who in return said "Good-night, I'm going home," in a matter-of-fact tone of voice, which slightly reassured C.

"I think we'll go into the supper room and I'll have a little soup," said Leila.

There were still several dancers having supper, and the men were beginning to smoke cigarettes.

"Well, you have been beastly to me," said C. "What have you been doing the whole evening ?"

"I'll tell you exactly," said Leila. "I danced with Harold Wraith and Bobby Redford, and then I had supper with Fritz Adelberg, and afterwards we had a dance ; then I went out into the garden and we sat there for a little, and then he left me and I talked to Dallas Wace and to Wilfrid. Then I had to be civil to Sir Alfred Rooter for a little, because I got him asked, and he didn't know any one. Then I danced with George Wilmot, and that's all. Now you know."

"I didn't see Sir Alfred to-night."

"No, he only stayed a very short time. She wouldn't come, she said she'd got a headache, and she loathes going out to balls or to anything big."

"Well, I think you might have been a little bit kinder to me," said C. "I was looking forward to to-night. I haven't seen you properly for days. You treat me like dirt. You dance the whole evening either with foreigners or with Wilmot."

"But, my dear C., I love dancing, and you must admit that I seldom get a chance of it when I'm at a ball with you; and Fritz Adelberg and George Wilmot both of them dance quite divinely."

"He's in love with you."

"Who, Fritz?"

"No, the other one."

"Is he? I do hope he is. I like him so much—to dance with, that is to say—of course he never speaks; he's quite silent. But, as a matter of fact, he's more in love with a beautiful person called Angèle Durcis than any one has ever been known to be in love."

"Everybody says he's in love with you."

"Who's everybody?"

"I don't know, the people in Paris."

"Your lady friends you mean, those people I saw you dining with at *Malmaison*. Yes, I know the kind of thing they say about all of us, especially about Englishwomen. But, my dear child, if you were a little bit older, and a little bit more a man of the world, you would know what all that counts and how little it means."

"But why has Wilmot come over here now?"

"He always comes over to see his friends. He's passionately fond of racing, too."

"But he went to Nice, to see you."

"You probably don't know that Uncle Freddy Marryat is his great friend, and when Uncle Freddy was said to be dying they sent for him. Directly he was out of danger, he went back. But really, my dear C., you are impossible with your questions and your suspicions. You're mad. I must go home."

"But you will let me come to-morrow night to dinner, won't you?"

"I'm very sorry, it's too late now. We can only be eight, and now I have filled up your place. Besides which I talked to Alfred Rooter about you, and he said he particularly wanted you to do that article; so it's just as well. It wouldn't have done at all for you to chuck that."

"And what about Saturday?"

"I think Alice Evelyn is expecting us both," said Leila. "I'll let you know definitely about that to-morrow."

"But when shall I see you?"

"If you would like to look in to-morrow quite early, on your way to the office—about half past ten."

"I'm afraid I can't," said C. "Can't I come at six?"

"Not to-morrow. I'm selling at a sale of work. I shall be there till seven."

"Can't I come to it?"

"You'd better not. I shouldn't be able to talk to you. There'll be a large crowd, and nothing but women. I think you'd really better not."

" Then, when shall I see you ? " he asked savagely.

" Saturday, at any rate."

" I must see you before Saturday."

" Yes, you shall, some time on Friday. I'll let you know. Are you going to the Eton and Harrow match on Friday ? "

" I can't get away."

" That's a pity, because I'm going to the Calhouns' box, and as you know them so well you might have come too."

" I can't possibly."

" Well, anyhow, I'll let you know, and I'm going to bed. Terence went away ages ago.   Fortunately, I remembered the latch-key. Perhaps you'll get me a four-wheeler."

They went into the hall. It was daylight now ; one star was shining very brightly in the luminous blue of the dawn. The guests were going fast ; the ball was nearly at its last gasp, although a few couples still remained on in the supper-room and you could still hear the sound of music.

C. had never enjoyed himself so much and so little in the space of one evening. He swore that he would never go to a ball again as long as he lived. It was not worth the acute misery. It is the kind of rash vow that is often made and that is rarely fulfilled by those who make it. In C.'s case he spoke truer words than he knew, and had he been told, at that moment, how literally his wish was to be fulfilled, he would have been astonished. It was as if he had been overheard in

Heaven, and taken at his word, for he never went to another ball.

The next morning, before he went to the office, he received a note from Leila saying that she begged him to come to dinner. It was a kind letter. He answered in the affirmative, and sent back the tickets he had received from Sir Alfred, saying that he had hoped to be able to get out of a dinner engagement, but had not found it possible to do so. He hoped he might be given another chance of writing something for the *Saturday Despatch*. He was free to see Lapara act on any other night.

C. thought that Leila wanted to show that their reconciliation was complete. Perhaps she did, but it was also true that some one had failed her, as C. afterwards learnt, and she was for the moment a man short.

CHAPTER XLVI

C. DINED with Leila instead of going to the play.
He was surprised when he arrived at her house and
realised the nature of the dinner and the guests, but
he thought that she had really wished to ratify their
reconciliation, and he did not regret having come.

There was at that moment in London a " Foreign
Mission," which had arrived from Japan It was
being entertained by the Foreign Office. Nobody
quite knew why. They had been received by the
Queen, at Windsor, and Terence was attached to them ;
and wherever they went, he went, too ; he had felt
bound to entertain certain of their members, and that
was, no doubt, one of the reasons why Leila, after
Harold Wraith had thrown her over, was especially
anxious that C. should attend this dinner, as the
" Mission " spoke English imperfectly, and preferred
French as a vehicle of communication. Leila had
asked none of her literary acquaintances. The dinner
was political and social.

C. was quite happy ; and it was settled that evening
that they should both go down together to Mrs.
Evelyn's house on Saturday afternoon. Mrs. Evelyn
had taken a house near Oxford. Terence would not be
able to come, as the Foreign Mission were being

entertained by the Prime Minister during the week end. Madeleine Lapara was giving a *matinée* on Saturday afternoon, and C. suggested that they should go to that first.

Leila said she would rather not.

" You see," she said, " I saw Madeleine Lapara years ago, the year after I married, and she was so wonderful then that I wouldn't have the impression I had of her, as she was then, spoiled ; no, not for anything in the world."

" Yes, I understand that," said C. " I only heard her recite, and that was seven years ago."

" They say she rants now," said Leila, " and that her voice has gone. What is she doing on Saturday ? "

" It's *La Dame aux Camélias.*"

" Oh, such a silly play ! "

Saturday came, and just before C. started for the station, he got a note from Leila, sent in a hansom, saying that she might miss the train ;—there were complications. She had to wait to see Terence, but she would come by the next train, or later ; in any case, in time for dinner ; but he must on no account wait ; Alice was sending to the station to meet him, and he must explain matters to her. She would send a telegram as soon as she knew what train she could arrive by.

When C. arrived at Mrs. Evelyn's house he found that Leila had telegraphed to say that she would not be able to come at all. Terence's sister was not well, and she had promised him that she would look after her, as he was obliged to go away. It was nothing very serious, she hoped, but they were rather anxious.

Staying with Mrs. Evelyn there was no one but an old friend of hers and Leila's, an old man with white hair, who belonged not only to another generation, but to another world. He had been a secretary to a well-known politician in the days of Lord Palmerston. Alfred Evelyn, Mrs. Evelyn's husband, who was in the City, was there, too, and her younger sister, who had married a sailor.

C. had a long talk with Mrs. Evelyn on Sunday afternoon. They talked of nothing but Leila, and C. poured out his troubles. Mrs. Evelyn was sympathetic and did not consciously make matters any worse than they were already, but she did actually. She liked every one she knew to think that the whole world was in love with Leila, and when C. mentioned Wilmot, and remarked that, of course, all that was nonsense, that it was well known that he was madly devoted to Angèle Durcis, Mrs. Evelyn couldn't help saying that she *had* heard in Paris that Colonel Wilmot *was* in love with Leila. It was not to be wondered at. After all, Leila had lived two years in Paris, and he must have seen a great deal of her. It was unlikely that he should not have been attracted.

" Then you think he is in love with her ? " said C.

" I would think it very odd if he wasn't. Leila is, of course, quite unconscious of her power. And, after all, she is far more beautiful than any of the French-women one sees, and so much more attractive.

"However, he won't be here long. He can't be, can he?"

"They say his time in Paris is up this autumn."

"Oh, I suppose he'll come back for good then?"

"I expect he will."

"But you don't think she cares for him?"

"Oh, no," she said, laughing. "You needn't really give it a thought; but it's no good pretending we don't all of us like admiration and devotion, and Leila especially. You can't blame her, can you? And he *is* very devoted. You see, he went to Nice, just to see her for five minutes."

"Did Leila tell you that?"

"Yes, of course she did. She told me the whole thing. She often talks about it. Of course, it all means nothing to her. It just amuses her. She doesn't care for him at all; in fact, she thinks he's rather a bore. She says he dances very well, but that's all. And then he's got a very bad temper and makes scenes. And Leila hates scenes. But don't you be so foolish as to mind, or don't look as if you minded, or don't show it if you *do* mind. That would be a great mistake, it would only irritate her. Men are so silly, they *never will* let well alone. Nobody likes being bullied and worried and suspected."

"But how can I help minding if she sees so much of him?"

"She sees very little of him."

"She danced with him all night the other night, at the Wessex House ball."

" She told me she only danced with him once, and she said you had been so unkind to her. People are so unfair about Leila. Look how disgracefully Lord Marryat has behaved to her."

" By marrying ? "

" Well, when one thinks of all that Leila had done for him ;—if it hadn't been for her he would probably have died of drink years ago. She *saved* him. She brought him back to life. And now he's married that common woman, and he won't probably leave Leila a penny, and after all he *is* her godfather ;—when one thinks how angelic she used to be to him, and how she put up with him for years and let him come and do his horrible patiences in her house, which wasn't great fun for her ! He's the most selfish man who has ever lived. But you are all just the same. You would be just the same, C. You are ready to suspect Leila at the slightest provocation, and everything she has done for you in the past would suddenly go by the board and not count. You are all of you terribly spoilt and ungrateful."

" I'm not ungrateful to Leila, you know I'm not ; but it drives me mad when I see her surrounded by all those sham literary people."

" You can't bear her to talk to any one but yourself. Of course, I understand that in a way, and in a way it's quite right. It's as it should be. But she must talk to other people sometimes, and what does it matter, really ? "

" No, I suppose it doesn't—if only——"

" Of course it doesn't, and I only pray and beseech you not to be foolish, and never to do anything foolish."

" If only she would tell me the whole truth about things."

" There you go again. How can people tell you the truth ? You simply force and drive them into telling lies by not letting things that don't matter alone. Why can't you have more tact ? How would you like to be perpetually cross-examined and suspected ? "

" I'm not suspicious, only some things are forced upon one's notice."

" I think that Leila has shown wonderful patience with you, sometimes. If any one else had done and said the kind of things to her that you have done and said, she would never have spoken to them again."

" What kind of things ? "

" Oh, you know quite well what you did in Paris that time."

" That really wasn't my fault. It was quite an accident."

" It never is your fault. However, all I say is, be careful and don't try her too highly."

The result of this conversation—and, of course, it was far longer and more detailed—was that Mrs. Evelyn, instead of having done, as she thought, a great deal of good, instead of having eased the situation, had really made matters far worse. A few casual words she had dropped had made C. far more jealous, far more suspicious, far more irritable and far more miserable than ever.

Mrs. Evelyn liked C., but she liked C. as an appanage of Leila, and she thought it the duty of every Englishman and every Frenchman to be slavishly in love with Leila, and she took a fearful joy in dramatic developments. She did not suffer from jealousy, and although Leila was her best friend, she had made a scientific, lasting and final conquest of Terence, who worshipped the ground she trod on. Leila knew it, and although she said nothing, and, indeed, found it convenient, it irritated her.

Mrs. Evelyn liked C., but she still considered him to belong to the schoolboy, calf-love category, and she had deplored Leila taking him at all seriously. She was in her heart of hearts thrilled by the Wilmot episode. Colonel Wilmot was just such a lover she considered Leila ought to have, and she expected the worst with a pious hope. She knew that C., too, was very violent-tempered, and she felt that the situation was fraught with dramatic possibilities.

On Monday morning C. went back to his office, and on Monday afternoon, he went to see Leila. She appeared to be delighted to see him. She had, she said, spent a miserable Sunday, sitting with Terence's sister, who lived in a gloomy house in Eaton Square. She was much better and quite out of danger. They had known she was out of danger on Saturday night, and she had been able to send Terence a reassuring message early on Sunday morning. So really she needn't have stayed. But it was just as well she did. One never knew. She had thought of coming down to Oxford on Sunday morning, but the trains were so bad. They talked about the party, and C. said he had been miserable without her, and had missed her during every moment of the visit, which had seemed to him to be interminable. Leila had a box at the opera that night, and asked C. to come. She and Terence were taking two members of the Mission, and there would be room for him at the back of the box.

It was at the opera, during one of the *entr'actes* of *Carmen* when Terence had taken the Japanese Emissary to smoke, that Leila gently broke the news to C. that she was going to Newmarket for three days.

C. was on the point of saying, " To see George Wilmot ? " but, remembering Mrs. Evelyn's advice, he refrained. If it were not so, why disturb the state of their relations, which had just become once more peaceful after a storm ? He said nothing more than :—

" Will you come back on Thursday or Friday ? "

" Thursday, I hope."

" I'm staying," she said, " with Uncle Freddy and his wife. He begged me to come, so I thought I must. They say she's really quite a nice woman, and one *must* be civil to her."

" I didn't know he'd a house there."

" Yes, he's always had a house at Newmarket."

" Is Terence going too ? "

" No, Terence has still got these people to look

after. They stay till Wednesday. But he couldn't get away in any case."

" Well, then, I shan't see you for three whole days."

" I shall try and get away on Thursday. I will let you know."

Terence and his Japanese charge came back into the box, and C. did not have any more talk with Leila that evening, and during the next *entr'acte* Wilmot, who was in the stalls, paid her a visit.

The next morning he went early to Sir Alfred Rooter's house for his sitting. He was there at nine punctually, and he found Miss Haseltine waiting for him, and everything ready in a large empty room which had a splendid light and a square canvas fixed on an easel.

" I'm only going to do your head and shoulders," she said, " like the sketch I began."

C. sat down in a chair. He was made to try several positions. The light in one place was compared with that in another; but Miss Haseltine made up her mind rapidly, and she had soon finished arranging him as she wished and had begun to work. For some time she worked in silence; then she began to talk a little. They talked of various things, among others of Madeleine Lapara.

" There was a *matinée* on Saturday afternoon," she said ; " Eileen and I went together. Sir Alfred gave us a box. They went down to the country early, or at least they said so. I don't believe they ever thought of going—at least I don't think he did—and they went one night last week. I think they got the box as a treat for us. They are always doing that kind of thing."

" It was *La Dame aux Camélias*, wasn't it ? "

" Yes."

" Did you enjoy it ? "

" I thought her wonderful, and I thought she looked wonderful. Everybody was crying at the end, even the other actors on the stage. She's got such a wonderful face, I think. I've never seen so expressive a face. I did some sketches of her while it was going on. Only one can't draw her ; at least I can't."

" Sir Alfred wanted me to go the other night and write something about her for his newspaper. Unfortunately I couldn't."

" I know ; he told me."

" Was he annoyed ? "

" Not a bit. He said you must go another time. You ought to go this week. She's acting every night, and I think it's her last week."

" I must."

They talked of other things. When half-time came she said he could get up and walk about if he liked. He got up and smoked a cigarette. He walked up and down the room. Near Joan Haseltine's hat, cigarette case and other belongings, on a table, was an oblong sketch book.

" Are these your sketches ? " said C. " May I look ? "

" Yes," she said absent-mindedly.

He opened the book. It was full of sketches of heads, and now and again there was the outline of a house or an interior, and sometimes a bit of landscape.

" We were sitting in the stage box," she said, " and I could draw in the corner without any one seeing me. It was most convenient. Of course, these are only the roughest of sketches, and it's impossible to get her expression."

There was a striking sketch of Lapara, looking into a hand looking-glass. C. had seen a photograph of her in this pose, and he thought the sketch vastly superior to the photograph. There were one or two other rough indications. One faint suggestion of the head, in which you saw the eyes turned up to heaven with all the sorrow of the world in them.

" That's marvellous," said C., " she looked just like that when I saw her."

He turned over the page. On the next page there was a series of heads.

" Oh, those are nothing," she said ; " those are only some sketches of a few heads of the people in the stalls that I did in one of the *entr'actes*." There, among the sketches of strange people, there, quite unmistakably, was the head of Leila, or of her double.

Joan took the book from his hands rather abruptly.

" They're not worth looking at," she said, " and now we must go on." She laughed a little nervous laugh.

C. felt somehow at that as if he were made of glass, and as if Joan could see the very pulse of his machine.

But he said nothing. He did not ask whether she knew who the original of that sketch was. He knew it was Leila, and he knew that she knew that he had recognised her. He felt she had forgotten it was there. He also knew that she knew about his feeling for Leila. She had probably met Leila quite often at the Rooters. Leila was always talking of Lady Rooter, and saying how nice she was, and driving with her. But C. did not say a word. The rest of the sitting passed in comparative silence. There had been other heads next to the one of Leila, heads of men; but Joan had taken the book from his hands before he had time to look at them. He was haunted by the fear that he might have recognised one of those male heads.

That night he dined with Gerald Malone and Esther at a restaurant in Soho.

Esther was in one of her worst moods; peevish, and on the defensive. She tried to flirt with C. and to annoy Gerald. Gerald took no notice. He was only too well used to her tantrums, and he scented the dawn of a familiar scene. C. kept on wondering to himself whether, if Leila had been in the same circumstances as Esther, she would have been just the same kind of woman. There was a strange likeness and affinity between them, he thought. Esther felt that as C. was looking at her he was comparing her with some one else—and unfavourably, and she resented this. She ceased trying to cajole him and began to try and annoy and exasperate.

"We never see you now," she said to C., "do we,

Gerald ? You're far too much taken up with all your grand friends. We saw you last night at the opera, didn't we, Gerald ? You didn't see us, you didn't choose to see us, you wouldn't look at us, would he ? "

" I wish I'd seen you," said C. " Where were you sitting ? "

" We were in a box, right up in the top circle, complimentary, too."

" It was a jolly opera, wasn't it ? " Gerald interrupted, wanting to change the conversation, " and I think Dalbiac is a ripping singer, isn't she ? "

Esther ignored the interruption, and went on :—

" He was far too busy to take any notice of us, wasn't he ? Far too busy with the beautiful Leila. You were going it, and the husband and a Japanese gentleman there, and all. I wonder what he thought of it ? "

" Oh, shut up, Esther," said Gerald. " We've had enough of that. It's so boring. Have a glass of fizz and let's talk about something else."

" No, I shan't talk of something else," said Esther, getting red with passion. " I mayn't mention Her Royal Highness now, mayn't I ? But *you* may talk about her as much as you like ; *you* may admire her, too, and tell me all about her, and her goings on ; but if I put in a word I'm put in my place. I may tell you," she said, turning to C., " that Gerald dragged me to Kew Gardens on Sunday afternoon, and there we spent the whole blessed afternoon looking at the plants. Oh, beautiful they are ! A treat ! Only I've been there with Gerald till I know the whole place better than the keepers, if that's what they're called. Well, as we were there, inspecting the *Phyloxera maxima*——"

"Oh, stop," said Gerald, "for pity's sake, stop!"

"Oh, it's 'stop' now, is it? Well, that's better than 'shut up,' but I shan't stop nor shut up neithei. While we were there, as I was saying, who should pass by but Mrs. Bucknell, the beautiful Mrs. Terence Bucknell, and not her husband, oh dear no! and not, as I should have expected, the Honourable Caryl Bramsley, but a handsome military gentleman, and I said to Gerald, 'Who's that?' I said, and Gerald said——"

"The whole thing's a lie," said Gerald savagely, and he kicked Esther hard under the table.

"It's no good kicking me," she went on relentlessly. "And Gerald said: 'That's the new man Leila's got hold of, he's the military attaché at Paris,' he said: 'Poor old C.!'—that's what Gerald said—'Poor old C.!' he said."

Gerald turned white with rage, and looked as if he could kill her; he looked fit and ready for murder.

"That's all a damned lie," he said, with deadly, icy quiet, "and you will own up that it is, now, or else, by God! I swear I'll kill you."

He meant it, and she knew he meant it.

It was Esther's turn to grow pale.

"I only said it to tease," she half whined. "Don't be so silly," and as in her fright she said this phrase, the fundamental commonness of her nature seemed to attain its full and complete expression.

CHAPTER XLVII

C. RECEIVED a telegram from Leila the next day telling him that she would not be back till Friday, and that she was going to stay at Bramsley from Saturday till Monday. "Hope to see you there," she said. He inferred from this that he would be asked, but so far he had heard nothing from Sir Alfred, who was at Newmarket, nor from Lady Rooter.

He felt that the crisis had come in his relations with Leila. He felt that, even if Esther had invented that story about Kew from beginning to end, it was true all the same, morally true. Far worse than that had been Miss Haseltine's embarrassment when he had found the sketch of Leila in her book. He felt that she had divined the situation, and that, therefore, the situation was there to divine; and now that he had pieced everything together, it was all so plain. She was in love with George Wilmot. He had better face it. And as he thought of her, he was overwhelmed by a surging wave of hate, and at the same time he felt certain, if he were to see her, to see her even for two minutes, that he would forget all this, perhaps, or perhaps he might kill her. Who knows? His head was in a whirl. He did not answer her telegram.

This was the first time in his life that he had not answered a communication from Leila within five minutes.

Nor did he write; but he received a little letter from her saying that Uncle Freddy's wife was *quite* a good sort, and that it was very hot, that there were a lot of people she knew, and that she had won £10. There was a faint scent of stephanotis about this letter — Leila's favourite flower and favourite scent — that went to his head and made him dizzy with love, and hate, and memory; terrible questions, unbearable wonder, and excruciating perplexity. The letter ended: "*Could you bear to come to Bramsley, or would it be too* painful? *I should like to be there with you. I think Sir Alfred is going to ask you. I threw out a hint. But he has said nothing* definite. Do *come if you can. There won't be many people, only some of his city friends, who don't matter, and Lady Rooter's pianist, and possibly Dallas Wace! You won't mind him* now! *Write.*"

C. went to his club, meaning to dine by himself that night. He met Freddy Calhoun, who had been to Newmarket for the day.

"Are you dining here?" he said. "Let's have dinner together."

They dined together. Freddy said he was going back to Paris the next morning. "So is George Wilmot," he said. "He says he's got to go back to be present at General Valmont's funeral, which is the day after to-morrow, but I expect the real reason is that Angèle has got wind of his goings on, and is putting on the screw."

" Yes," said C. blankly.

" You see," said Freddy, " she's as sharp as a needle, and, although she knows nobody here, you can bet she guesses exactly what is going on. And then there are some Frenchmen at Newmarket, and all that news gets round in Paris so quickly."

" What news ? " asked C.

Freddy suddenly remembered that some one had said something before him about C. and Leila ; he couldn't remember quite what, and he did not know the story, but he was suddenly frightened of having put his foot in it, so he said :—

" Oh, only his having a good time ! You see, he used to be frightfully in love with Lottie Playfair, and Angèle knew all about it, and I daresay it's still going on. You see, Lottie Playfair was at Newmarket to-day."

" Staying there ? " C. asked listlessly.

" Oh, no ! She has to get back in time for her evening performance. Let's go and see her. She's acting in the *Girl from San Francisco*.

" All right," said C. " We might try."

He felt a vague curiosity to see the person who had preceded Leila in George Wilmot's affection. They hurried through dinner, and drove to the Leicester Theatre and managed to get two stalls at the end of the first row.

When Lottie Playfair came on and sang her first song—

> I'm naughty little Susie
> From the port of Vera Cruzie,

Freddy Calhoun said :—

" She is a taking woman, isn't she ? No wonder George is still in love with her ! "

Freddy thought, in his naïve way, that he had put things right. Unfortunately, C. knew more about Lottie Playfair's love affairs than he did, and he knew that her present protector was Sir Alfred Rooter's partner, Mr. Felix Hershell, but he said nothing of this.

The next morning he received a telegram from Leila ; it ran :—

> " *No letter to day.   Write.*"

C. did not answer this either.

On Thursday night Lady Rooter, who did not go racing and who was alone in London, asked him to go with her and Miss Haseltine to see Lapara, who, it was announced, would give an extra and final performance of *Phèdre*.

C. dined with them first at Lady Rooter's house, and during dinner Lady Rooter said :—

" Alfred tells me I am to ask you whether you would like to come to Bramsley on Saturday ; there will be a few people, not very many : Mrs. Bucknell, Mr. Dallas Wace, Eugene Franck, and a few friends of Alfred's ; but he says perhaps you would rather come next

Saturday, when there will be no one except ourselves;
and I must confess to you, also, that Joan is very
anxious for you to stay in London this Sunday;
because she thinks if you could give her a sitting on
Sunday, she might finish the portrait, and she's going
away to Germany for a holiday to Bonn with Eileen,
who is desperately anxious to see Beethoven's birth-
place, and she wants to finish the picture before she
goes."

C. said he would rather go to Bramsley on the
Saturday after, when there would be no party.

" Oh, I'm so glad! " said Lady Rooter. " We shall
have so much more fun when there is no party. I do
so dislike parties when I have to give them in my own
house. I'm always so afraid of the people being bored,
and Joan will be so glad. She was so longing to finish
the picture."

They went to see Lapara and sat in a large box
opposite to the Royal Box. C. was swept off his feet,
overwhelmed by the beauty of the performance, and
Joan Haseltine was in tears. Lady Rooter admired it,
too, but she was slightly more critical.

" I don't say she's too old," she said; " because
there's no doubt she does act it better than she did
when she first came to England in 1879, and I saw her
then. She's more force and more experience; but I do
think that, on the whole, I prefer Zechetti, and still
more the acting at the *Burg* Theatre at Vienna."

C. and Joan were too much moved to argue.

When C. got home that night he sat down and wrote

an account of his impressions of the performance.
He stayed up till half-past two writing, and, when he
had finished, he sent off what he had written to the
editor of Sir Alfred's weekly newspaper.

On Friday morning he received a short note from
Leila in pencil, which ran :—

"*C., what is the matter?*"

He did not answer this either ; but he did not tear
it up. He locked it up in the despatch box in which
he kept all the letters that Leila had ever written to
him.

On Friday he received a telegram saying : "*Shall
be in at six.*" But C. did not go. It is true that he
took a cab and told the cabman to drive to Upper
Berkeley Street, but when he got as far as Portman
Square he told the driver to stop, and he got out and
walked home.

On Saturday he received no letter from Leila.
That Saturday, and, indeed, all the days that immediately followed, were to C. like a vague dream. He
remembered going to the Rooters' house and sitting to
Joan Haseltine for the last time, and he had a dim
recollection of a dignified and austere lady arriving
towards the end of the sitting and congratulating them
both on the picture and taking them off to luncheon at
Hampstead ; and there he met rather a fierce-looking
scholar with a hatchet face and clear grey eyes who
made one remark that stuck in his memory ; they
were discussing the situation in South Africa, and Joan

said Sir Alfred Rooter thought there would be a war, and the stranger agreed and said that that would mean the end of England.

" Do you mean," Joan had asked, " that we should be defeated ? "

" No," was the answer. " I mean that we shall win," and he had buried his face in his hands, and C. had the impression that he was in the presence of one of the most unaffectedly and completely sad men he had ever met—a soul in exile ; but these were after-thoughts. At the time, he had taken no interest ; he had not joined in the conversation except mechanically with the outward part of his mind.

On Monday morning he received a short letter from Leila. She quite understood, she said, and she was all in favour of his marrying Miss Haseltine, who was a charming girl, and would make him an admirable wife, besides being a great heiress.

He sent no answer.

On the following Monday, he received a note from Sir Alfred Rooter asking him to come and see him. Sir Alfred told him that his editor had sent him the article he had written about Lapara ; he had thought it good and well worth publishing ; unfortunately, that week they had had a " middle " about Lapara—they couldn't very well have another ; it was just too late.

" But," said Sir Alfred, " don't worry. It's served its purpose. I can see that you can write." In a week's time, Sir Alfred told him, he was starting for

Aix-les-Bains for a month. Lady Rooter was going to stay at Bramsley. If C., Sir Alfred said, cared to go down to Bramsley on the next Saturday, he would be welcome ; he would be there himself, as he was not starting for France till the following Monday. There might possibly be one or two other friends, but no party.

C. said he would like to go.

He received in the evening his article on Lapara from the editor of the *Saturday Despatch*. He tore it up and threw it into the waste-paper basket. He spent the whole of that week in solitude. He did not even want to see Gerald Malone.

He heard nothing from Leila, and life seemed to be singularly empty, as if he had been through a moral earthquake, and nothing of the former buildings, the tall palaces, the stately temples, the well-known streets and squares, had been left, nothing but a heap of smoking ruins, and he knew it was his duty to set about, out of all this rubbish, to try and build a little hut ; only he hadn't the energy, he couldn't begin— not yet.

On the following Friday evening, he had been to see his brother Edward, who wanted to see him on some business matter of no great importance. After his interview was over, and he walked out into Portman Square, he could not resist walking up into Upper Berkeley Street. He passed Leila's house and as he looked at the front door his heart seemed to beat in a peculiar way. The house did not look as if it were shut up. Almost mechanically, as if not he himself, but his subconscious self, were acting, he went up to the door and rang the bell. It was answered almost at once.

" Is Mrs. Bucknell at home ? "—the phrase seemed so natural, the answer had always been such a matter of course, and it seemed unbelievable that Wilkins, the butler, would do anything else than silently assent.

But to-day he said that Mrs. Bucknell was not at home, in his most formal manner, and then, after a slight pause, he said :—

" Mr. and Mrs. Bucknell are leaving to-morrow morning for Aix-les-Bains."

C. said " Oh ! " and made a step back.

" Shall I say you called, sir ? " asked Wilkins.

" Oh, it doesn't matter."

On Saturday afternoon he went down to Bramsley.

Bramsley was, as yet, unchanged structurally. Sir Alfred had bought it lock, stock and barrel, but the difference in the interior of the house was immense and indescribable. Even such furniture and pictures as Edward had not taken to London looked now quite different. But C. minded seeing it as it was now far less than when he had seen it empty. It had seemed then like the old home derelict and full of ghosts ; now it was a different house.

The bedrooms had been smartened up by a few pieces of modern furniture, and Lembach's portrait of Lady Rooter hung in the drawing-room, where there

had once been a portrait of one of the Hengraves by
Lawrence.

The drawing-rooms were smartened up by modern
cushions from Liberty and a few rather gaudy stand-
up brass lamps.

The guests besides himself were Sir Alfred's partner,
Felix Hershell—Miss Haseltine had started for Germany—Joshua Jones, the editor of Sir Alfred's weekly,
Hiram Sykes, a racing friend, and Eugene Franck, the
pianist.

It was, of course, an extraordinary sensation for C.
to find himself once more in these familiar surroundings under such different conditions, and, indeed, it
seemed to him the kind of thing that only happens in
an absurd dream. It was all the same, and yet so
different. You could not have had a sharper contrast
than that between his father and Sir Alfred at the
head of the table, between Lady Rooter and Lady
Hengrave. The card tables in the drawing-room,
Sir Alfred and the other men playing bridge while
they smoked cigars . . . cigars in that drawing-
room ! . . . and Eugene Franck playing Wagner on
the pianoforte in the hall, which had been converted
into a sort of living-room and modernised, seemed to
strike such an alien note. The Romney on the staircase
was no longer there. Although the present Lady
Hengrave had made so much of it in her description,
it was entailed and could not be sold. It was now in
Portman Square, and in its place there was a life-size
portrait of Sir Alfred by Bonnat.

After dinner C. and Lady Rooter listened to the music.

" Eugene," she said, " is one of the few people who can play Wagner on the piano ; he gets the sound of the instruments."

C. looked as if he were listening intently ; but he was far away. The place was far too full of ghosts and unheard melodies for him to listen to any audible music.

The men sat up late discussing the political situation in South Africa. They all agreed that war was inevitable.

The next morning Lady Rooter asked C. whether he would like to go to church. He said he would, and she took him. The other guests remained behind. The church looked at first sight the same. They sat in the Hengrave pew. The large red prayer-books were still there, but the old clergyman, the Reverend Stephen Hawley, who never missed a meet if he could help it, and who had such beautiful, clean hands and polished nails, and such a dignified white tie, and who preached in a black gown, was dead ; and he had been replaced by a young High Church vicar who turned to the east when he said the Creed, and had surreptitiously introduced a coloured reproduction of the *Madonna del Gran Duca* into the side aisle, and whose ultimate ambition it was to convert the south-eastern end of the church—where the school children still sat—into a Lady Chapel.

The choir no longer consisted of schoolgirls, but of

little boys in cassocks ; they intoned the responses and struggled with an elaborate *Te Deum* and an all too complicated anthem. The sermon, instead of being read from a book, was now extempore, breezy and topical, with allusions to Ibsen and a new novel that was being talked of—*The Perilous City*—which left the congregation cold. The Communion table now boasted of a green altar-cloth. There were several broad green ribbons hanging out of the prayer books. There was a brass lectern—an eagle with carbuncles for eyes—at which the vicar read the lessons, and a special reading desk for the Litany in front of the chancel steps. The wheezy harmonium had been replaced by a " positive " organ, on which the new organist played a voluntary from *Parsifal*. The hymns sung had tunes taken from the *Hymnary* and the seven-fold *Amen* was sung at the end of the service.

The hatchments which had been put up in the memory of the various members of the Hengrave family had disappeared.

After church was over, C. walked by himself in the garden, and spent an hour rambling about familiar places. This time he carried out his memorial service to Harry to the end, and the familiar sights no longer gave him pain. He found the summer-house, in front of which Harry and he had their gardens as children, completely buried in ivy ; otherwise the garden was much the same.

After luncheon they all sat in the garden. A rather

languid game of croquet was being played, which Franck, the pianist, took very seriously. They all had tea in the garden, and after tea Sir Alfred took C. for a stroll. He told him he felt quite certain there was going to be a war in South Africa. He also told him, in confidence, that he had just engaged in an important negotiation. He was going to buy the *Northern Pilot.* The deal was not actually done, but it was practically done.

" And," he said, " if this comes off and if there's a correspondent, you shall go. I shall see that you lose nothing. Even if they won't take you back at your miserable office when the war is over, which I think, as a matter of fact, they would do. But if they don't, I will see that you get a job. Would you like to do that ? "

" I know nothing about war," said C.

" That's just what I want—a man who has never been to a war, who knows nothing about it, and *knows* he doesn't, but who can write. You are the very man I want for the job."

C. said that nothing would please him better than to leave England for good, and never to come back.

Sir Alfred looked at him curiously as he said this.

" Well," he said, " I shall be away for the next month, unless I'm called back on urgent business, and I may stop a few days in Paris as well, but I expect to be back in London by the end of September, and I'll let you know what happens."

CHAPTER XLVIII

C. STAYED on in London. He refused to go and stay with his eldest sister in Wiltshire, or with his second sister in Berkshire, or with his eldest brother in Middlesex. He explained that the arrangement of the clerks' holidays in his office was such as necessitated his remaining, this year, in London during the month of August. At the beginning of September Wright arrived in England for two weeks' unofficial leave, and he and C. went down to Cornwall, and stayed for a fortnight in a village not far from St. Ives, where they enjoyed some sea-fishing and bathing.

Wright, from what he had heard, surmised more or less what had occurred between C. and Leila. He knew there had been a breach, and, although he did not know the immediate cause of it, he knew it must be connected with George Wilmot. After staying a month at Aix-les-Bains, Leila had taken a small house at Chantilly for a month. Terence had returned to London. Sir Alfred Rooter was staying on in Paris. He had business there, and as he had a flat in Paris of his own, he could go backwards and forwards from London to Paris without inconvenience and at the shortest notice.

C. asked Wright whether he had seen anything of

Leila, and Wright was truthfully able to say that he had seen nothing of her in Paris. George Wilmot had been away, he said, at Luchon with Angèle Durcis, but he had now come back.

C. asked him whether people in Paris thought there was going to be a war, and Wright reported the usual eddies, fluctuations and conflicts of opinion.

Wright asked C. whether he had given up all thought of literature. He said he had, although he still looked upon journalism as a possible refuge.

" I wrote," he said, " a lot of poems, but I've thrown them all away."

When they returned to London from Cornwall, Lady Rooter asked C. to bring Wright (who had met Sir Alfred in Paris) to Bramsley. They spent a few days there, and met Miss Haseltine. Sir Alfred was away during most of C.'s visit, but he came down for one night. The *Northern Pilot* was now his own, and he said to C. : " I have not forgotten my promise to you in the event of war—and there will be a war. Don't forget to keep your pen sharp ! "

At the end of September, Wright went back to Paris, and C., after a few days with the Rodens at Elladon, was once more at work at his office. He no longer thought there would be a war, in spite of what Sir Alfred said, and he had dismissed Sir Alfred's promise as one of those dreams that never come true ; so that, when war was declared in October, what many people had for so long said was inevitable came to him with a shock of surprise.

He received a telegram from Sir Alfred, asking whether he could start at once as correspondent for the *Northern Pilot*. He answered " Yes."

Sir Alfred instructed him to go and see the editor and the business manager of the *Northern Pilot*, whose headquarters were in the north, at Barminster. C. spent the night there, and arranged everything with the editor and the business manager. He met Sir Alfred there, too, who gave him many hints and instructions. He was to start as soon as possible. Gerald Malone helped him to buy his kit. C. was in a state of excitement and elation. He had taken leave of his chief at his office, who had kindly offered to keep his place for him. He had announced the fresh and unexpected revolution in his career to his brother Edward, who was mildly surprised, but who did not venture to criticise it, or to make any special comment, and to his sisters, who thought that it was a pity to go to such an outlandish country when you had a safe job in England.

" It's not as if you were a soldier, like Harry," said Julia.

Mixed with the feelings of exhilaration and excitement that he was experiencing, there was also at the back of his mind, and at the bottom of his heart, a dull, leaden sediment of misery. He felt like a child who is being banished from home, and sent to a school full of unknown boys, and where every situation would be new, and like a child who would not even have the satisfaction of missing those whom he left behind : a

homeless child going into a larger, stranger home-
lessness.

And then, through and in, and behind and over
everything, there was the thought of Leila.

How he longed to see her before he started! She was
in London, he knew. He had walked past her house
in Upper Berkeley Street, and he had noticed that it
was occupied. He wanted to say good-bye to her.
He wanted to see her face again. What, after all, did
all the rest matter? What did anything matter? He
might not come back . . . that, indeed, would, he
thought, be too good to be true . . . but if he didn't—
he would like to see her once more, if only for a minute
. . . but would she see him?

He wrote and told her what he was about to do.
He begged her to see him, if only for one moment,
before he left England. He only wanted, he said, to
say good-bye to her. He was sailing on Thursday.
He wrote this on Sunday evening. She answered it in
a hurried pencil note. She said that she was full up
with engagements, and that she could promise nothing,
but that if he cared to look in on the chance she might
possibly be able to see him for a minute on Wednesday
at six. Wednesday at six!

C. could not understand from her letter what she
was feeling, nor how she was disposed towards him.
The letter had no beginning, and was signed " L."

But, Wednesday at six! How familiar that phrase
seemed to sound! Just as in old days, when everything was so happy, when everything was different.

As C. walked past the Marble Arch to Great Cumber-
land Place, the newspaper boys were shouting
the winner of the Cambridgeshire. The dates of the
Cæsarewitch and the Cambridgeshire had always been
landmarks in the Bramsley family, and to C. they
marked the seasons more than anything else; they
meant for him the actual approach and presence of
autumn and winter.

He bought a newspaper, and saw that Irish Ivy
had won.

Here he was at Leila's door! How strange it seemed.
Had he been dreaming these last months, and would he
now suddenly wake up? He rang the bell, and Wilkins
opened the door, just as usual, and in his most impres-
sive manner said that Mrs. Bucknell was very sorry
she would be unable to see Mr. Bramsley. Lady
Fairleigh was with her at present.

The same evening he received a long letter from
Leila. It ran as follows:—

UPPER BERKELEY STREET.
Monday.

DEAR C.,

 I was, of course, most *awfully surprised to hear
from you after all these months! and to hear your
news! I confess that I was, and still* am, *altogether
puzzled by your behaviour! I couldn't understand
it at the time, and cannot understand it now! I suppose some one made mischief, but I really do not think
that is an excuse,—You cannot expect me to under-*

stand and to bear *such sudden changes! At first I suffered* dreadfully *and went through a great deal! I* wasn't well at the time, *and the doctors were quite frightened, and they said they were sure I must have had a severe shock! Of course I said they were wrong,* but it was only too true. *I was very ill, later and all that time at Aix* ———. *I don't suppose you suspected this for a moment, for you never even once asked after me and, at the time, I* did *think it rather thoughtless and callous and cruel of you. Now I am gradually getting over it, but, in a way, I feel quite* dead, *and I* do *find it hard to take an interest in anything. I wish I could have seen you just for a minute, to have one word with you before you leave on that long journey, and go to meet Heaven only knows what dangers and difficulties in that dreadful Africa! I should have liked to see you just for a moment to say one good-bye, although, of course,* nothing *can or could ever be the same again as before, as you know very well yourself, but it was* you *who did not even give* me *the chance of seeing you by not telling me till the last minute—till it was, in fact,* too late—*that you were going away. I could not guess, could I? that you would be likely to go to the war! Indeed, it was the last thing I thought* likely *ever to happen. I tried to keep a moment on Wednesday evening free, but Mother wanted to see me so badly all that evening and I had promised, and Terence was coming I knew at seven, and I felt that if I saw you at all, I* must *see you alone. But, perhaps, it is all for the best. After all, the past is the past. You broke*

*our friendship, just as you might have broken a
valuable piece of china.   Nothing,* nothing *could ever
mend it again* in this world, *and it could never be the
same again, but in spite of that, from the poor broken
pieces of china there is* still something there, *just a
faint breath from the past happy days, which I shall
never be able to forget* quite.   *I wish you all possible
good luck and happiness, and I hope that everything
may go well with you, and that you will take care of
yourself, and be a great* success.   *We will all take
in the* North Pilot, *and look forward to all you
write.   Terence says it's a very good newspaper.   He
thinks very highly of Sir Alfred Rooter.   Well, I've
nothing more to say, except that I feel* very, very
tired.   *In old days you would have understood.
Good-bye,* C.

> *Your friend,*
>
> *L.*

> *Ah, Love! could thou and I with Fate conspire*
> *To grasp this sorry Scheme of Things entire,*
> *Would not we shatter it to bits—and then*
> *Re-mould it nearer to the Heart's Desire.*

C. dined that night—it was the night before he was
to sail—with his sister Julia; Marjorie and her husband,
Edward and his wife, were there, as well as other
guests. The only incident of the dinner that he
remembered, was a conversation between his brother,
Tommy Holborn, and one of the other guests, as the
men were drinking port after dinner. Some one said
that George Wilmot had come back to London, and

some one else had said, " I suppose he is going out to South Africa ? "

" No," said Tommy Holborn, " he's got a job at the War Office now. Leila Bucknell won't let him go to Africa."

After dinner, C. got away as soon as he could, and drove round to Gray's Inn to see Gerald Malone. He found that he, too, was longing to go to South Africa, but that Esther would not hear of it. They talked about the war. They both were inclined to think that the cause of the Uitlanders was not a cause at all, and that our dealings with the Boers were those of the wolf and the lamb.

" I wish we were fighting for any one and anything else," said Gerald. " For, after all, if they hadn't discovered gold there, all this situation wouldn't have come about."

" But we're in for it *now*, and there's nothing to be done. It may turn out that we were right, after all, in the long run. We have an amazing knack of doing the right thing in the wrong way—*in the long run*."

" Yes," said Gerald, " but it all looks pretty bad and beastly at present ; I wish I could go out, all the same. I'd give my eyes to."

" Perhaps you will be able to come out later,"

" No," said Gerald, " not as long as that goes on," and he pointed to the next room in which Esther was singing a song from a new musical comedy to her own accompaniment. " And the worst of the matter is, I can't live without her. I hate her, hate her like hell, but I can't live without her, because I love her ! Can you understand that ? "

" Yes," said C. " I can understand that."

C. said good-bye to Esther and went home. When he got home he thought he would like to write to Beatrice, and he sat down and wrote her a letter, of which the following passages are extracts :—

There is one thing—I want you to know in case I shouldn't come back . . . although that, in a way, would be too good to be true . . . too easy a solution . . . These things don't happen. . . . When Andrew Burstall died in France, or rather some time after, his wife sent me a small parcel, and in it was a copy of the Imitation *in Latin and the* Dies Irae, *copied out in his own scholarly handwriting (that looked as if it had been written by a monk), and a slip of paper, asking me to go to a Requiem that was to be said for him every year at the church in Maiden Lane on the day of his death. He asked me, too, to buy a penny copy of the Mass for the Dead, and to read the prayers at the end. As you know, he's only been dead a year, so I've only been once. But I bought the penny book and studied it enough to follow the service. . . .*

I had always heard my Protestant relations and friends criticise your services, and especially your funeral services, comparing unfavourably what they called either a " theatrical " or " meaningless "— [word illegible]—with the simple dignity of the Angli-

can rite. . . . *I used to agree, or think there was
something in it, although, at the same time, I always
felt there* must *be something in* your *service that
escaped us, or that we didn't understand, and you used
to speak of the want of, as you used to say, " Everything that mattered " in ours. And certainly, at my
mother's funeral, and still more at Harry's memorial
service, I felt there* was *something wanting. Well,
when I read that little penny book, and especially the
prayers at the end of it, I seemed to begin to understand what you meant*—[four words undecipherable]
—*the reason Protestants thought as they did, or, rather,
received the impressions they received, when they went
to Catholic services was that they had not the slightest
idea what it was all about. It was to them a meaningless and rather tawdry or depressing Punch and Judy
show. They did not know what a Mass meant ; they
did not understand that in a Requiem the dead person,
the soul of the dead person, plays a real part, and that
it is a means of communication . . . a kind of divine
telephone . . . between the Living and the Dead, and
not a beautiful external tribute—or—[?]—like a
concert or a—[?]—paid* once *and* for all *to the
memory of the Dead Person. You used to tell me
when people criticised your services because they were
in Latin and not everybody could understand and
follow the words of the Mass, that it didn't matter
whether they did or not ; that the Mass was a* Drama,
*and the people did not need to follow the words in their
book ; they could follow the action and say any*

prayers they liked. When you used to say this, I wondered what you meant. . . . After reading the penny book, I began for the first time to have an inkling, and especially after that Requiem for Andrew Burstall. (It was after Harry's memorial service I first really began to realise what was wanting in ours.) So what I want to ask you is this. Supposing I die in Africa (or anywhere else), would it be possible for you to have a Requiem said for me? Or is it impossible . . . heretic? . . . If I could believe in anything, I think I should believe in your Church. I feel it is a solid fact, a reality, something different from all the others (. . . " Authority, not as the Scribes "). The moment I go into a Catholic church I feel this (wherever it is—[unintelligible words]—Rome, Paris, or Maiden Lane) but, at the same time, I couldn't belong to it now myself, *as I really don't believe, well, in what? In God? I certainly don't* disbelieve *in God. I don't suppose any one over twenty-one does? When Faust asked Gretchen whether she believed in God, you remember . . . " Wer darf Ihn nennen? " etc. . . . not the dogmas I find difficult, least of all those peculiar to your Church—I mean if people can believe what they say when they repeat the* staggering *affirmations of the Nicene Creed, as my relations and acquaintances do every Sunday in church, the extra little stretch to one's Faith in believing, say, in Purgatory (when you've already got to believe in and swallowed Hell!), or in the Immaculate Conception or Transubstantiation, or the Infallibility of the Pope's decisions*

(i.e., *guidance of the Holy Ghost, when you have
accepted the Trinity—gnats after the camel), would
be nothing. Nor do I think the dogmas, the main
dogmas common to all the Christian churches, especially impossible; there is nothing, to my mind,
unthinkable in the idea of* Hell, *once you accept the
idea of the Christian revelation. But*—[unintelligible]
—*There's the rub. Can I accept the idea of this*
particular *revelation, this unique claim? Can I
believe this and this only is true; truer in a different,
more special way than, say, Buddhism or any other
of the hundreds of religions, philosophies and creeds,
that have been woven out of the dreams and desires of
mankind in the huge, rolling, endless stretch of time
that lies behind us . . . India, Nineveh, Mexico,
Egypt, China, Tyre, Rome, Carthage, Etruria, At-
lantis? God knows how many more!*—[words
missing]—*not a question with me of* this *difficulty, or
of* that *doubt or of the stock problems—free will,
predestination and Grace, or of the problem of Evil
. . . God Almighty and All-Good permitting—evil,
sin, punishment—eternal. " Ihr führt ins Leben uns
hinein—Ihr lässt den Armen schuldig werden."*
[Unintelligible] *beside the point—real point to me—is
that I can't respond to the appeal . . . my heart
doesn't tell me that the thing is true, it doesn't help my
reason. My reason is quite willing to be convinced and
my heart remains neutral. It doesn't, that is to say,
play up—it doesn't* answer. *And although, with all
my* will, *I should like to share your Faith, the result is,*

try as I may, I can't.   You will say I haven't got the gift.   What can I do to get it?   Pray that I may get it some day, for at—[words scratched out)—*in a ship that is without a rudder*—[unintelligible]—*I only wanted to be allowed to drown in my own way.   That will have to be my fate unless . . . unless I could suddenly be convinced that what* you *think is the Ark is* the Ark, *and, of course, I would. . . . It has taken me all this time to unlearn what I thought I knew about your religion.   I find that all that I thought I knew was wrong.   If it had been right (and I suspected this when I first knew you), you* could never *have been a Catholic all your life long, nor could a man like Andrew Burstall have possibly been a convert.   And, after all, what was my authority?   Where had I got what I thought I knew about your Church?   My only authority the traditions of the nursery and what I heard Protestants say at dinner*—*that was my authority*—*and a few remarks from school history books*—[three lines scratched out]—*because I have found out, because I am convinced that all that I had taken for granted, all that so many people take for granted about your religion and your co-religionists, is all wrong, that doesn't make it any easier for me to assent to what is the corner-stone of your religion*—[illegible sentence]—*I find there is a thing called the Catholic Church in the world.   I am aware of this when I am quite small in the nursery.   My nurses tell me it is wicked.   Later, my governesses tell me it is not always nor altogether wicked, but misguided or, at any rate, partly mistaken. At school I am told that it is historically wrong ; that it is not a tree, as it claims to be, and as you might think it looks like, but a distorted branch, and that what was once only a branch is* now *the real tree. At the university I am told that it is an entirely exploded superstition, that one needn't bother about it, that no one who has ever dipped into Kant can take it seriously, and that the only people who believe in it are women, foreigners, priests or fools . . . [as] life goes on I come against the fact myself that there are Catholics who are not necessarily either* (a) *foreigners or women or priests, and* (b) *if they are either foreigners, priests or women, they are not necessarily and by no means always* fools, *and that people I know and respect either for their characters or their—[?]—and sometimes for both, actually become Catholics of their own free will, at great personal inconvenience. Well, I make the acquaintance of some of these—R. for instance . . . what do I find out ? I find out that all I have thought to be true about this Catholic Church, all that I have taken for granted . . . is not true. I find I have to make a clean sweep of all that, as an outsider, I have been taught to hold true about it. But granted I can do this, that I have done it . . . and I have done it . . . this is my— [word illegible]—I say to myself : " Here is a Church in which I was told people worshipped plaster images " . . . I know now that they don't, that they worship God (as Dr. Johnson said, ' Sir, they believe God to be there, and they worship Him '), but that doesn't*

make it any easier for me now that I have discovered
and realised this mistake, this mistake in public
opinion outside the Church, about the Church, it
doesn't make it easier for me to believe in the dogmas
on which the Church is founded, for me to believe that
God came down from Heaven and was made Man,
died upon the Cross, rose from the Dead, and will
come again to judge the world. That, and not in the
efficacy of wooden images, is what you believe. That,
and that God is there, present to-day and every day
in the Sacrifice of the Mass in every Catholic Church
all over the world and, if one can believe the first
proposition, the second, and all the others, are child's
play, I think ;—but I can't believe in the first. . . .
Do I want to really? That is the point. I used most
certainly not to want to. I used to long to be drowned
in the nothingness, the Néant, Nirvana, whatever you
call it. Nox est una. Lucretius, etc. But now,
to-night, I confess I would like to feel there was
a bridge between me and something else . . . across
the abyss which seems to be everywhere ;—above,
below, in front, behind. . . . Is it fright? Not
entirely, I think.

> Ay, but to die and go we know not where,
> To lie in cold obstruction, and to rot.

How does it go on? Something about the " delighted
spirit "

> To bathe in fiery floods, or to reside
> In thrilling region of thick-ribbed ice ;
> To be imprison'd in the viewless winds.

Did Shakespeare, do you think, read Dante ? because this is like a summary of the chief elements in the Inferno, *especially the " viewless winds." Paolo and Francesca* — [illegible sentence follows] — *Beatrice Cenci . . .*

> *No God, no Heaven, no Earth in the void world,*
> *The wide, grey, lampless, deep unpeopled world. . . .*

Pray . . . one day find the Bridge or the lamp. . . . Pray with all your might . . . because I . . .

C. never sent off this letter. It was found in Gerald Malone's collection of papers. It was all of it difficult to read and had evidently been hurriedly written, with many words scratched out, and here and there an afterthought put in. Some sentences it is impossible to decipher or even to guess at. Other passages have been left out. The letter was in a large envelope directed to Beatrice Fitzclare in her convent, and marked " To be forwarded." But C. did write to her that night a few lines which he sent off, asking her to pray for him, and to pray that he might one day learn to pray for himself.

The next morning, before he started for Southampton, he received not an answer, but a letter she had written him spontaneously. She had heard he was going from her mother, who had heard it from Lady Elizabeth Carteret. In the envelope there was a little medal with an image stamped on it of *Notre*

Dame des Victoires, and with it a slip of paper, on which was written :—

> *Thou shalt not be afraid of the terror of the night— of the arrow that flieth in the day, of the business that walketh about in the dark, of invasion, or of the noonday devil.*

C. left that morning for South Africa, and Gerald Malone saw him off at the station.

CHAPTER XLIX

EXTREMELY little is known about C.'s life in South Africa, nor is it possible from his despatches to the *Northern Pilot* to reconstruct anything of his personal history. His work consisted almost entirely of telegrams. He rarely wrote a postal despatch, and then only of the most impersonal kind—the distance made things so easily out of date. The editor of the *Northern Pilot* was thoroughly satisfied with his work, which he considered to be unexpectedly professional and competent. Telegraphic news, too, was what he wanted. C. wrote a certain number of private letters to Walter Wright, and to Gerald Malone; but in these he did not mention the war, nor his own war impressions or experiences. He wrote about books and common acquaintances. His letters were extremely short and scrappy.

He was slightly wounded at Spion Kop, but he only remained a short time in hospital. Later on, he had a bad attack of enteric, and he was nearly six months in hospital at Cape Town. He came home to England in the winter before the end of the war. He took a room in the top floor of a lodging-house in Bury Street.

When C. arrived, Sir Alfred and Lady Rooter were in London, and C. informed Sir Alfred of his arrival.

Sir Alfred asked him to luncheon at his club the same day. He welcomed C. cordially.

" You did well," he said, " damned well, and now I've got another job I want you to do. I want you to go as Special Correspondent to Berlin for us."

C. said he had thought of going back to his office. They were willing to take him back.

" Office be damned ! " said Sir Alfred.

" I want to stay in England—for a bit."

" Well, stay in England for a bit. I'm in no hurry. Stay a few months, till you're sick of it ; and then I'll see what I can do for you; but it probably won't be Berlin. I can't promise. I've got to fill up the billet as soon as I can—I mean if I find some one else who suits I shall have to give it him. Think over it till to-morrow, and let me know." Then they talked of other things.

Miss Haseltine's portrait of C., Sir Alfred Rooter told him, had been greatly admired. It had been hung at the New Gallery in a good place.

" It's at Bramsley now," he said. " She's doing very well. But she's not married yet."

" Is she in London ? " asked C.

" Well, no, not at this moment. At this moment she's in Germany—Munich, Dresden, Leipzig—all over the place,—I think; with her friend Eileen Pratt. They'll be back in the summer."

Sir Alfred said he was taking his wife to the Riviera in a few days' time. He had taken a villa at Cannes for the winter.

" Believe me," he said, when C. said good-bye to him, " you'll make a great mistake if you stop in England."

That evening C. had dinner with Gerald Malone. They dined together, that is to say, at a restaurant in Soho by themselves. Esther, Gerald said, was engaged till ten. She was rehearsing for something.

C. discussed Sir Alfred's offer.

" You see," he said, " I'm not a journalist. I don't care a fig for news ; and I've no ambition. I used to have, or thought I had, a kind of ambition to write. But that's all over. On the other hand, I don't particularly want to stay here. The office is as dull as ditch water. There's nobody here I want to see, and I daresay Berlin would be interesting, — the job would be well paid, and I should live comfortably while it lasted. So, perhaps, it would be rather foolish to say 'No.' But I should like to stay here just for a little, not go abroad at once. All this sounds contradictory. It is."

Gerald said he didn't think C. need hurry ; he was sure that if in six months he were to be sick of London Sir Alfred would be able to find him a job.

" But you wouldn't go," said C., " if you were offered the job ? "

" I should, if it wasn't for Esther," said Gerald.

C. gathered that there was no change in that situation. Indeed, towards ten o'clock Esther walked into the restaurant herself, and sat down at their table. She was, C. reflected, intoxicatingly pretty, and very

charming when she chose. That night she chose. Later
on they all drove back to Gerald's rooms at Gray's Inn.

"It's quite like old times," said Esther, and sat
down at the pianoforte and sang them her new song.

C. slept on the problem that night, and when he
woke up the next morning he made up his mind to
accept the offer. He wrote to Sir Alfred to that effect
before he had breakfast.

As he was glancing at the newspaper, two bits of
news caught his eye. One was, that Lady Holborn
had been safely delivered of a boy at her house in
Curzon Street. This was, C. reflected, her fourth
child. And the other that Mrs. Terence Bucknell was
leaving London for the south of France. He then
threw the newspaper away.

He looked at his letters ; they appeared to be mostly
bills. There was one large envelope directed in a
slanting, slightly illiterate handwriting.

"Another bill," thought C. He opened it, but it
was not a bill ; an enclosure, another letter, fell from
the envelope. It was a letter originally directed
"care of the Editor of the *Northern Pilot*." It had
been sent from the *Northern Pilot's* country office to
their London office ; from the London office to his
club ; from his club to his office in Westminster ;
from his office to Lord Hengrave in the City, and
from the City to Hengrave House, where the butler
had put it into a fresh envelope.

It was in Leila's handwriting, and there was a faint
smell of stephanotis about the letter. It was written

in pencil.   She had heard from Sir Alfred that he was
on his way home.   This was a little word of welcome.

> *I am just leaving for Cannes.   Alice Evelyn and I*
> *are going to stay there with Adela Rooter at her villa.*
> *We start on Thursday, and if this reaches you in time*
> *do come and see me.   I shall be in every evening—*
> *late, after seven——*

He took up the newspaper again to look at the date.
It was Friday's newspaper.   She had started the day
before.   Her letter was dated Monday.

C. tore up the letter he had written to Sir Alfred and
wrote another.   He said he did not feel he wanted to
go abroad at once.   He would like, after being away
so long, to stop for a little while in England.   If a little
later Sir Alfred still had a job which he thought he
could do successfully, perhaps he would be kind enough
to think of him.   He was not ungrateful, but . . .

He asked Sir Alfred to give him his direction at
Cannes.   Sir Alfred wrote back and said :—

> *It's as I feared.   I think it's a pity, but we'll see*
> *whether you're just as anxious to stop in London in*
> *six months' time.   And whether anything can be*
> *fixed then.   Our address is "Villa Beau Site,*
> *Cannes."   We shall stay abroad till after Easter,*
> *and we may put in a week or two in Gay Paree*
> *on our way home.*

C. at once wrote to Leila telling her that her letter
had arrived too late for him to act upon it.

A fortnight later she sent him a postcard, thanking him for his letter. "It's lovely here," she ended, "and we all wish you were here, too." C. wrote again, but she did not write back to him; and there the correspondence ended for the time.

C. went back to his office life. He saw his family; he dined with his sisters and with Edward; he stayed with the Rodens and with the Carterets; and soon he began to feel that he had never left England at all.

It was one day in April that he found a note from Lady Elizabeth Carteret saying: "Come to luncheon on Sunday. I have got a surprise for you."

The Carterets had an elaborate house near Regent's Park. It had a green marble staircase, a drawing-room with black walls and a silver ceiling, and a dining-room painted in tempera by Gabriel Carteret himself. The first person C. noticed as he walked into the room was Beatrice. He was immensely surprised. At luncheon he sat next to her.

"I won't explain anything now to you," she said, "I will write to you to-night, and then you can come and see me. I've got a house in Kensington, near Campden Hill. I'm looking after a sister of Vincent's who has been fearfully ill. I'm generally there all day, but I get away for a little every now and then. I'll write and tell you when to come."

Beatrice was changed, but changed for the better. C. thought she had never looked more beautiful, although she looked different. She had not the youthful, dazzling freshness she had had when she was quite young at Oxford, but there was now something serene about her, and something radiant and infinitely soft. The look of weariness and of strain had left her. There was still an immense sadness in her expression, but a softer sadness; there was nothing of the worn-out, battered look which had struck him the last time he had seen her in London, nor the hunted look in her eyes which he had noticed with pain when he saw her in Paris. The conversation was mostly general at this luncheon, and there were one or two well-known literary people present, but as C. left to go back to his office Beatrice said :—

" I'll write to you to-night, and you shall come and see me."

Lady Elizabeth seemed gratified and satisfied as C. said good-bye to her, like a person who feels she has done a good piece of work.

The next day C. received a letter from Beatrice.

I finished my period of postulancy, and my noviciate at the convent, and I decided not to take vows, but to leave the convent and to return to the world. I want you to know all this . . . these main facts, before we meet again. . . . It will make everything much easier. It will be just as difficult for you, I expect, to understand why I am leaving the convent now as it was for you to understand why I went there at all . . . if that was difficult. The simple truth is I was too happy there. I liked it too much. If I were to say that to some people, and even to some people I am very fond of—to S., for instance—they would say (and I have heard them say it, not about me), " Of course, that's what we always say about nuns; *they have far too easy a time, sheltered as they are from the world and everything in it that is disagreeable and difficult," but I don't mind telling you, and I expect you know already that it isn't so. A nun's life isn't easy in the way they think. It may be radiantly happy; . . . that's another question. . . . But, of course, it's no use trying to explain this to people; some things you must experience from the inside to understand at all—marriage, for instance. In fact, I never would dream of trying to explain, only I want you to know. I came to believe and I was finally certain that my vocation lay and lies outside that (for me) citadel of happiness . . . at present, at any rate."*

C. went to see Beatrice the next day. He did not allude to her convent life, except to say that he had quite understood what she meant, but they talked of everything else, and he found that he was able to take up the thread of intimacy without any difficulty at all, and to go on just where they had left off. Walter Wright had been moved from Paris to Berlin, and C. heard from him frequently. In one of his letters he mentioned that he had met a charming English artist, a Miss Haseltine, who had come to Berlin to see the picture galleries, and they had talked of him.

" She told me," he said, " that she's painted your

picture. She and a Miss Pratt are living together at a *pension*. Miss Pratt is working at the *Hochschule* (music), and they are both of them going to stay here for the rest of the year."

C. soon fell into the habit of seeing Beatrice quite often ; but after Easter she was leaving London, as she had to move her sister-in-law, who was better and had been ordered country air, and so she had taken a house for them both near Farnborough.

C. was not looking forward to the summer in London. He decided that it would be quite impossible for him to begin once more the old routine of balls and parties, the life of which Leila had been for him the centre. For, although the thought and, still more, the hand-writing of Leila affected him strangely, he, neverthe-less, felt that this chapter in his life was definitely and finally closed. He did not hear her name mentioned much. Lady Elizabeth had conveyed to him that George Wilmot was still devoted to her. She had told him that George Wilmot was at the War Office, " and just as sad as ever, poor man ; he did so want to go to the war."

C. met Freddy Calhoun one day, but Freddy had learnt wisdom and had acquired experience, and no longer burnt his fingers over that topic. He had left Paris and was now at the Embassy at Madrid. The Thérèse idyll was over, but he had left her well provided for ; she had found consolation and sub-stantial support and protection. He was taking, he said, a little well-earned leave. But, although Freddy did not mention Leila, some unconscious train of thought in which Leila was evidently a link, led him to tell C. that Wilfrid Clay, who had gone out to South Africa in the Yeomanry (C. had come across him once or twice in Africa) and had been seriously wounded and invalided home a year ago, was now in London.

Just before Easter, C., to his surprise, met Mrs. Evelyn one morning in St. James' Street.

" I thought you were at Cannes," he said.

" So I was, but I had to come home because of Jimmy (her husband). I was sorry to come back ; it was so delicious there. Leila was enjoying it. She was ordered to go by the doctors. It was doing her so much good, too. She was very ill while you were away at the war."

" Really ? I had no idea of that."

" Yes, she was ill twice, once very badly."

" What was it ? "

" Only influenza—both times—but the after-effects were so bad. It left her so terribly weak."

" Some one told me that Wilfrid Clay has come back."

" Oh, has he ? " she said, with a frigid indifference.

" I thought he was a friend of yours ? " C. laughed.

" He was, but after the way he behaved to Leila——"

" What did he do ? "

" Leila *made* Wilfrid Clay. Without her he would never have existed. And now he never looks at her. He's over head and ears in love with a horrible little

South African woman called Mrs. Weltheim. It's really unbelievable, isn't it ? The more one sees of men——"

Mrs. Evelyn left her sentence unfinished.

" Come and see me some time. Leila's not coming back till after Easter. Terence is going out to fetch her, and they will probably stay in Paris for Easter."

C. felt that Mrs. Evelyn looked upon him with disapproval. He had the feeling that she considered him also to belong to the class of men who had been created by Leila and who had not shown any gratitude to their creator. This casual meeting convinced C. that whatever happened he could not stay in London. On the other hand, he had to be at his office every day, so what was to be done ? While he was pondering over this problem it was suddenly solved from the outside by what seemed to be the direct intervention of Providence.

Miss Haseltine had two married sisters, both of whom C. had met frequently while she had been painting his portrait. One was the wife of a Norfolk country gentleman, who lived almost entirely in the country, and farmed ; and the second had married a sailor called Gambier, who had just come back from South Africa, where he had taken part in certain operations in which the Navy had been concerned. They had a house in London and a small house near Farnborough ; they were relatively well-to-do, and had one daughter. Gambier came back from South Africa suffering from some slight lung trouble, and was advised by a doctor to stay for a month or so in Cornwall, which he decided to do. They were going to stay with some cousins who had a house near Falmouth.

Mrs. Gambier, who had seen C. quite often and liked him, had heard of him still more often from her sister, and had now heard of his return from Africa, where, at the beginning of the war, he had met Captain Gambier and made great friends with him. C. met Gambier at his club and Gambier asked him to dinner. The Gambiers lived in a little house in Cheyne Walk. They discussed the past and the future, their plans and prospects. Mrs. Gambier talked a great deal about her sister, and what fun she was having in Germany, and how she was going to have a permanent studio in Munich, and all the interesting artists she had met; and C. told them of the work he had been offered in Germany, which he had refused because he wanted to stay just a little while in England, after having been away such a long time.

"At the same time," he said, "I loathe London. I have to be at the office all day, and when I get out of it I hate everything and everybody. I would give anything to live in the country, even if I had to come to London every day. I shouldn't care how long the journey was."

"Why shouldn't he live at Holmhurst?" said Mrs. Gambier to Gambier.

"Why not?" was Gambier's answer.

They explained to C. that they had got a little house. There was a housekeeper who lived there, and who knew how to cook. They were not going to let it. They had no one they wished to let it to, so that if he cared to go and live there for a month or two he was welcome to do so.

Finally it was arranged. He was to go there as soon as he liked and stay there all the month of June and possibly July as well. They might come back in the middle of July, but not before. It was a short journey to London. The trains were excellent. The house was full of books. There was a garden. The air was very healthy. He would be quite happy there, and there was a spare bedroom, if he cared to ask a friend to spend Sundays, or any night with him.

C. was delighted at the idea, and soon after Easter he found himself established at Holmhurst.

He would have the great advantage, he thought, of being near to Beatrice Fitzclare. But until he got there he did not realise how near she would be. She lived actually next door, and the Gambiers' garden was not a hundred yards from the garden of the house where Beatrice Fitzclare was living with her sister-in-law.

CHAPTER L

C. KEPT his relations in the dark about this arrangement. He told them that he was staying with Gerald
Malone in the country, but was coming up to London
every morning, and he had all his letters sent either
to the club or the office. Beatrice was exceedingly
surprised to see him. Her sister-in-law was making a
slow recovery. She had a trained nurse to look after
her as well as Beatrice, and she sat in the daytime for a
few hours every day in the garden in a wheeled chair.
She went to bed before dinner in the evening, and
liked to be left alone then, so that Beatrice had her
evenings to herself, and either C. would stroll over to
her house or she would stroll over to his. Sometimes
Malone would come down and stay the night, if he
could arrange matters with Esther. Malone was
delighted to see Beatrice again, and the three old
friends spent some delightful hours together. Sometimes Malone and Beatrice had talks together alone.
They were both of them struck by C.'s reticence about
South Africa and his life there. He never seemed to
wish to talk of it at length, and seldom alluded to it.
They wondered whether he had disliked the life there
very much. He never told them. Nor did C. ask
Beatrice any questions about her religious life, and her

experience at the convent, nor did he ever allude to his own religious beliefs or disbeliefs ; nevertheless the old intimacy between them was renewed, and it began to ripen quietly in a way it had never ripened before.

C. arrived there at the end of May, and May and June went by quickly. The Rooters had come back to London, and C. presumed that the Bucknells were there also. He wrote to Sir Alfred, and told him he was living in the country, and Sir Alfred discreetly asked no questions. Towards the end of June, Walter Wright came back from Berlin on leave, and intended to spend the rest of the summer in London. It was the first long stretch of leave he had had since he had been in the Service. C. asked him to spend a Sunday at Farnborough, and he accepted. As they were talking together on Saturday evening, after dinner, Walter Wright asked him whether he had had any very interesting experiences in South Africa.

" I had one extraordinary experience," said C.

" What was that ? "

" I met my brother."

" What brother ? Your brother Edward ? "

" No, my second brother, Gilbert. One you have never heard of. He got into some money scrape when he was quite young, and working for the Diplomatic Service. He quarrelled with my father, and he was sent out to Canada. My father would never see him again. We never heard him spoken of. I believe the lawyer used to send him a remittance every now and then. He never came back to England. He was my mother's favourite son, all the same."

" Did she like him better than Harry ? "

" Yes. She tried to think that Harry did as well instead of him, and she gave all she had to give to Harry, but the one she was really fondest of was Gilbert."

" How did you meet him ? "

" At Cape Town, at the bar of the Mount Nelson Hotel. He just walked in, and I thought I had seen a ghost at first. You see, I was about nine years old when Gilbert went away. And he was at a public school and at a crammer's or abroad, when I was still in the schoolroom, and we seldom saw him, even in the holidays. I think he must have left school early and been sent abroad to learn languages, and then I never saw him again nor heard him spoken of till the other day. This man looked extraordinarily like Harry. He'd got all Harry's looks—he's awfully burnt and hard and fit and strong, only——"

" Only what ? "

" I don't know. There's something wrong about him, something just a little wrong. Especially when he talks. Of course, he's knocked about so much that he doesn't talk like an Englishman."

" Did he recognise you ? "

" At once. I don't know what he was doing. He was selling horses, I think. He's a great man out there in some ways. He's very rich, they told me, *very* rich indeed. We had some talk. He told me he meant to come back here when the war was over."

" How extraordinary ! "

" Yes, it is ; and he's had an extraordinary life. He didn't tell me much about it.   He hadn't time."

" Did you see him again ? "

" No, I didn't.   I was leaving the next day, and he was leaving that night.   Somebody once told me that it was fearfully bad luck on him—that scrape, I mean —and that really he had done nothing ; only, you see, the suspicion was enough for father."

They talked of other things.   Wright gave C. news of Miss Haseltine.   He liked her very much.   C. discussed Rooter's proposal.   Wright strongly urged him to come out to Berlin, if possible.

" I'm afraid it's too late now.   He's probably got some one else."

Wright did not mention the Bucknells nor George Wilmot.   He had heard in London that George Wilmot was still desperately devoted to Leila, but C. surprised him by talking of the Bucknells in the calmest and most natural manner.   They had come back to London, he said, but he had not seen them.   Wright wondered whether all that was over and whether C. was definitely cured.   The next day they went to see Beatrice.   She was busy with her patient, but she sent them a message, asking them to look in after dinner, which they did.   Wright was delighted to see Beatrice again, and he thought that she and C. seemed perfectly happy and comfortable together ; were they too comfortable for it to lead to anything satisfactory ? That's what he wondered.   Otherwise, what a perfect solution it would be if they could be married ! Wright couldn't help thinking that C. must be looking forward to such a possibility at the back of his mind. But then there was Leila. He wondered whether she knew anything about it. In London, during the next few days, he met several of C.'s friends, but they did not seem to know anything about him nor of his movements.

"He never goes out now." "He's disappeared completely." "He's not been well since the war." Those were the remarks one heard made about him.

One night, towards the beginning of July, Wright went to a dance that was given at a house in Belgrave Square. He had been there some time, and he was sitting in a sort of hall with his partner when he caught sight of Leila Bucknell in the distance, talking to some one on the staircase. It was, he saw, George Wilmot. He was talking quickly and vehemently, and she was listening with a look of great calm and patience. Wright admired her greatly. She had, if anything, improved, he thought, as time went on ; there was something finished about her, something that seemed to belong to the periods of refined elegance ; Louis XV. or Charles II., which was it ? Versailles or Hampton Court ? He saw her at both ; on the Thames in a barge, all ivory satin and pearls and point lace, or he saw her equally well and appropriately, in Watteau-like scenes :

Frêle parmi les nœuds énormes de rubans,

. . . but all this reverie, carried on while he was discussing a play with his partner, was suddenly cut short.

George Wilmot had evidently asked her to do something which she had refused to do; for, quite suddenly,
he left her by herself in the middle of the staircase,
walked downstairs, at an abnormal rate, made a dart
for the cloakroom, and walked straight out of the
house with his coat in his hand, and did not wait one
moment, although it happened to be raining hard at
the time. Wright could not see what happened to
Leila, as there was rather a crowd of people on the top
of the staircase, and she had evidently gone upstairs
again. But presently, before the next dance began,
the supper doors were thrown open, and the host
and an ambassadress went down to supper arm in
arm; others followed, and presently Leila walked down
on the arm of Sir Alfred Rooter.

Later on in the evening, he had a very little talk with
Leila upstairs on the landing. She asked after C., and
said :

" He's living in the country with a friend, isn't he ? "
" No, he's alone, he's been lent a house."
" I thought his friend, Gerald Malone, was there,
too."

Leila asked him to come and see her . . . to come
to luncheon any day he liked. It would be nice to
talk over old times in Paris.

Two days later, Wright heard at the Foreign Office
that George Wilmot had accepted the post of Military
Attaché at St. Petersburg, and was going out there
almost directly.

In the meantime, Mrs. Gambier wrote to C., and told

him that they would be obliged to come back to their house for the last week in July, so C. made arrangements to go back to London at once. He spent his last evening at Farnborough with Beatrice, and stayed on for dinner. He talked of the past and how strange everything had been; how widely their paths had diverged. They had each of them seemed to be going off in entirely opposite directions, and yet Fate or Providence had brought them together again.

" Wouldn't it be silly for us to throw away this third chance ? " he said. " So few people are given even a second chance, and we have been given three. We never took them. I own it was *my* fault, entirely my fault, but perhaps if you had said ' Yes ' before, the second time, perhaps all would have been well ; and yet, somehow, I feel that it was all meant to happen as it has happened. I think you were meant to go into the convent, and to come out again, and I think I was meant to go to the war, and to come back again. I think we were both of us meant to travel all round the world of life, in a way, and then to come back, to a still calm harbour, before we could be happy together."

" Do you think you have reached that still calm harbour ? " she asked.

" I feel sure of it. I'm cured. I thought I perhaps wasn't till I came down here, I mean even after I came back from the war. I wasn't sure when I first came back. I wasn't sure when I refused to go to Berlin whether the real reason wasn't that I wanted to stay here because . . . because I wasn't cured . . . but now it's different. I know,—and I believe that was meant . . . that it was providential that I didn't go to Berlin just at that moment. Could you do it? Could you marry me, Beatrice?"

" I don't know. I feel I am *mended* to a certain extent, and that, in a way, I could and can and must begin life all over again. I feel quite sure and confident about all that. On the other hand, I don't feel sure about you. I mean, I know you mean what you say now, but I feel, all the same, it would be wrong for me to say ' Yes.' And even if not wrong, I don't know that I could. . . ."

" I know it's asking, oh! such a lot!"

" No, it's not that . . . I'm afraid—what I am afraid of is bringing about some great calamity for you."

" You mean you feel as you did before you went into the convent?"

" Yes, only this time I have the extra knowledge that I was proved right by experience."

" Yes, only it was different then. I wasn't cured. You see, I've been away now, how long? Nearly three years. That's a long time. Besides which, you must remember you left me to my own devices before."

" Were you left for long to your own devices?" she asked, with a smile.

" It's all so different now. I'm much older for one thing. I've been through a long, long tunnel, and come out at the other end. Don't send me back into it. Don't say ' No.' "

" If it hurts you that I should say ' No,' this is what I will do. I will wait till next year, and if you still want to then, I will say ' Yes '; but, but, promise me this ; don't be sad nor ashamed of yourself, nor miserable if in a year's time you no longer want to ask, and in that case *do nothing* and say *nothing;* don't blame yourself ; just say to yourself, in that case, that it was *I* who said ' No,' and it will be true, because, you see, the only reason why I don't say ' No ' *now* is that I am *quite* sure, quite convinced, that in a year's time you won't want to ask me."

C. was about to say something.

" It's not that you will have forgotten me. You will never quite forget me. You have never forgotten me. You would always like to come back, but you will find, you may find, that all sorts of things that you thought dead after all, or that new things, things you didn't suspect, you couldn't dream of, nor guess at, are suddenly there, and that all is suddenly different. I know I am right. I'm sure if it had been meant to be it would have happened before. I feel quite certain it is not meant to be, but I won't shut the door for you now. I will leave it open for a year, and if in a year's time from to-day, if at the end of July next year you still want to marry me, I will marry you, and I think it would be best for us not to see each other, and not to write, and if at the end of next July I don't hear from you, then I shall know."

" But why can't we make certain of things now ? One fact, one *fait accompli*, prevents a thousand others."

"I love you too much to do that. I couldn't. Don't ask me any more, C., because the temptation is almost stronger than I can bear."

"If that's so," he said triumphantly, "you must say 'Yes,' and here and now; twice in our lives we have behaved like fools, and twice we have been punished; don't let's make fools of ourselves a third time. That one couldn't possibly expect the gods to forgive, could one?"

They had been sitting in low basket-chairs in the garden. It was a soft, warm June evening. C. remembered the evening on the river long ago near Datchet, and before that the evenings at Oxford. All that seemed to have happened a very long time ago. He felt that now he ought to be able to convince Beatrice, to sweep her away, to carry her off her feet, as he had wanted once to sweep her away on the torrent of his love . . . and yet he no longer had the necessary driving power at his command, much as he wanted to. He suddenly saw there in front of him, here and now, the possibility of real true happiness, love and peace, security and final content—ideal married life. There it was for him to have and to hold, for ever. He had—it seemed—but one little step to make to grasp it, and it would be his for ever.

"Say 'Yes,'" he whispered.

"No, no," said Beatrice. "I can't; I mustn't."

"It's nothing to do with *mustn't*," said C. triumphantly. He felt that he had now been given what was lacking before. Now nothing could impede him; he would carry everything before him ; he would break down all obstacles and all opposition.

" You can, and you shall, and you must ! " he cried out exultantly as he got up from his chair and walked towards her.

At that moment the parlour-maid came out of the house and said to Beatrice :—

"Miss Fitzclare would like to speak to you a moment, ma'am," and then, turning to C., she handed him a telegram on a little tray, saying :—

" They've brought this from Holmhurst. It came last thing."

" May I open it ? " said C.

Beatrice nodded and said :—

" I must go and see what Mary wants. I'll be down directly. Don't go away."

She went into the house and C. opened the telegram, but it was too dark for him to read in the garden, so he went into the drawing-room, where there were two lamps burning. He read the telegram. It ran as follows :—

> *Please come and see me as soon as possible. If possible, to-morrow at six ; in great trouble.—L.*

C. tore it up and threw it into the fireplace, and said to himself : " I'm damned if I will." Then he laughed. " That," he said to himself, " just proves it."

In the meantime Beatrice had come down from seeing her patient.

" It was nothing," she said as she came into the

room. " She only wanted a book that she had left downstairs."

She looked at C., surprised to find him there in the room, and not out of doors. Then she looked at the fireplace and saw the crumpled telegram there, and she remembered. There was a slight pause. She thought C. looked white and strange, and his teeth were clenched with an odd kind of determination in the dimly-lit pitch-pine drawing-room.

" Not bad news, I trust ? " she said.

C. laughed.

" Oh, no, not bad news, not bad news at all, but good news, very good news ! Beatrice, you're wrong. If you like to make this absurd condition, you can, but I swear it's unnecessary. I shall come in a year's time from to-day, if we are both of us still alive, and insist on your keeping your promise. Do you agree ? "

" Yes," said Beatrice very sadly. " I agree. Of course, I agree. It was, after all, my idea. And now I must go up to Mary, because I promised to read to her a little before she goes to sleep. You're going away to-morrow—to-morrow morning, so it's good-bye. I shall be here till the end of August. Then I'm going to Switzerland with father and mother. I shall be back in the autumn in London. I've got a lot of work I've promised to do, but I shall be living where I was living before in Kensington, near Campden Hill."

The parlour-maid came back.

" Could you come up to Miss Fitzclare ? " she said.

" She says that's not the book she wanted, and she would like to speak to you herself."

" I'm coming," said Beatrice.

" Well, then, it's good-bye."

" Good-bye," said C., " and don't forget your promise."

" I shan't forget . . . and don't forget . . . everything I told you. Good-bye."

C. walked back to the garden of the Gambiers' house and climbed over the railings into the garden, of which he was, for the last time in his life, the temporary tenant.

CHAPTER LI

C. DID not answer Leila's telegram. At first he
decided that nothing would compel him to go and
see her. He would write and make a civil conventional excuse. But then, he thought, wasn't it very
cowardly not to go ? Was he afraid of her and of
himself ? If it was impossible for him to risk seeing
Leila, if he couldn't meet her on natural terms, well,
wasn't Beatrice right ? No, he would go, and he
would prove to Beatrice that she was wrong once and
for all.

At one o'clock, just as he was leaving his office for
luncheon, a messenger brought him a telegram :—

> *Very sorry cannot see you after all this afternoon.*
> *Leaving to-morrow for Salza Maggiore. Writing.—L.*

The next day he found a letter in that well-known
handwriting on the table. He looked at the envelope
and wondered what an expert in character reading by
handwriting would say about it. There was nothing
cryptic about it ; nothing subtle or mysterious about
the rather florid curves and long flourishes, and it
went smoothly on at the orthodox angle and slope ;
there was something candid and ingenuous about it
. . . so thought C. He opened the envelope, and

what was lacking in the handwriting was compensated by the aromatic hint of stephanotis that came from the paper.

It was a short letter.

> *Terence and I had been going to leave a week later, but it was more convenient, owing to things at the F.O., for Terence to go* at once. *We shall be there about three weeks, at the* " Grande Bretagne." *After that plans are uncertain. I have been through a* dreadful *time. I won't go into it now, but I* did *want to see* you. *However, as things turned out it was quite* impossible, *as last night Terence wanted me all the evening, and there were other complications. Must stop.—L.*

C. read the letter calmly, so he said to himself. It seemed like the lilt of a forgotten tune, a page out of a chapter that is finished.

Two or three days later, Sir Alfred Rooter asked C. to luncheon. He told him that his wife was going to Venice.

" I shall spend a few days there, too, very likely, but I hate the place at this time of year, it's too smelly."

He asked C. whether he still wanted to stay on in England or whether he had had enough of it. The Berlin vacancy was filled. C. regretted now that he had not gone ; but it was too late to think of that. So he said that, for the moment, he was quite happy in London. They talked of South African affairs, and

C. mentioned his brother, Gilbert, and told him of his meeting with him. Rooter was puzzled at first.

" Your brother Gilbert ? "

C. explained how and where he had met him, who he was, and the whole story.

" Oh ! " Sir Alfred said, suddenly understanding. " Now I know who you mean, and now I know who it is you have always reminded me of."

" You know him then ? "

" Yes, I used to know him very well in old days, but he used to call himself Gilbert Gordon then."

" Gordon's his second name. He said he was coming back to England next year."

" To England ! Oh ! "

Sir Alfred said nothing further on the subject of Gilbert, and C. felt that he had been surprised at the news.

C. heard nothing further from Leila. He spent the month of September partly at his sister's houses and partly with the Rodens, and in October he was settled in London once more.

It was in the middle of October that he went down to Eton for a Saturday and Sunday. He was staying with one of his Eton contemporaries, Bentham, the boy with whom he and Calmady had written a book of verse when they were boys, who had now become a master. He had not yet got a house. On Saturday night they had a cheerful dinner, discussing old times, and on Sunday morning C. went to chapel ; in the afternoon he went to tea with his tutor. He was shown into the well-known drawing-room with the books he knew so well ; those which used to be lent to the boys when they were staying out by the matron (*Treasure Island* and *Oliver Twist* and *Peter Simple*). His tutor greeted him with the same slightly satirical, bantering tone, but now C. found him charming, and wondered why he had ever felt alarmed or annoyed by him. They had not been talking for long when the butler announced Mrs. Bucknell. Her son, Basil, was at Pringle's. It was his first half, and he shyly escorted his mother into his tutor's drawing-room. It was the first time C. had seen Leila since the war, and it was quite useless for him to pretend that he felt she belonged to the past or to a closed chapter. She seemed to him to belong more undeniably, more superlatively to the present than ever ; there was, too, a look of melting sadness in her eyes, that became her better than anything. She greeted him naturally without a hint of any reservation in the background. They all talked except the boy, who remained mute as a stone and blushed scarlet whenever he was spoken to. He was the image of his father, and already showed signs of having a bureaucratic mind. Mr. Pringle and Leila discussed him, and Mr. Pringle said :—

" He's doing well, far better than that scamp did when he first came to me." He pointed at C., and the boy giggled.

" I daresay," said Leila, " C. gave you a great deal of trouble. I knew him as a little boy, before he went to school at all, and he was a *dreadfully* naughty boy. He used to play with us and pull our hair."

They talked on various topics, and they had tea, but before Leila went she said to C. :—

" Are you staying till Monday ? "

C. said he was going back that evening before dinner.

" By the six o'clock train ? "

" Yes."

" We'll travel together. We'll meet at the station."

Leila went off to the boys' part of the house with her son. C. went to fetch his things and to say good-bye to Bentham. He was pleased, pleased with himself and with the world ; he had seen Leila and all had been well. He had felt no sadness and no regret.

" We shall just be able to be the best of friends," he said to himself, " and everything will be all right and quite comfortable."

He met her at the station, and they travelled up in the same carriage. There was nobody else with them. Leila said she had been abroad. She had passed through Venice, and then she had stayed with her sister till the holidays were over, and she had taken Basil to Eton.

" I had a terrible time at the end of the summer," she said, and tears came into her eyes. " I can't tell you about it now. I may some day."

" Tell me now," said C.

Leila looked at him with wonder.

" I didn't think you would care any more about anything that could happen with me. I thought all *that* was finished, done with for ever, and that you had quite forgotten."

" I have never forgotten anything."

" I used to think that whatever and whoever changed you would always be the same—and then you . . ."

" I never changed."

" Didn't you ? "

" Never."

" Have you forgiven me ? " she asked very softly.

" Yes."

" I was so, so sorry. I *am* so, so sorry."

C. took her hand. He felt once more the touch of Leila's hand in his, and everything that had happened since he last saw her, either between them or to him, or between him and Beatrice, was forgotten, flung away, annihilated. He only knew that he loved her to distraction, that he didn't care what she had done, or what had happened, or what he had gone through. He loved her here and now, and as she was. How foolish it was to want people to be perfect, to be different from what they were ! and who was he to judge her ? After all, did he know her side of the question ? He was probably just as much to blame as she was. It had been his fault ; he had been young, silly, oafish, but what did that matter ? That was all over and done with now ; now what mattered was that Leila was in his arms once more for him to love and worship as he had always loved her.

He drove Leila home. Terence was away playing

golf with the Evelyns, and was not coming back till late. He was expected at eleven. C. stayed to dinner, and after dinner Leila and he remained together for long, and, as in old days, time was annihilated for C. ; only he felt that his love then was nothing to what it was now. Then he had felt like a child ; now he was a grown-up man. He was never going to let anything childish spoil their relations again. When he got home a reaction set in. He thought of Beatrice, and he seemed to feel that she knew already that it was all over. How clear-sighted and how far-sighted she had been ! Then he seemed to see her sad, tear-washed, celestial blue eyes looking at him, those soft, soft eyes, full now of an unearthly radiance. They were looking at him without reproach, but with infinite sadness, and, like Saint Peter, he felt inclined to go out and weep bitterly. Then he thought about Leila, and he saw the whole of their past unfurl before him like a pictured scroll. There was no doubt that, making every possible allowance, she had treated him abominably ; and there was no doubt that she had at one moment got tired of him and had simply loved some one else ; but that was not his fault . . . but even then . . . however that might be, he had no illusions now with regard to her. He did not know why she was behaving now as she had done. Perhaps George Wilmot and she had quarrelled ; perhaps she was lonely ; perhaps she was acting out of revenge . . . there might be a thousand motives and reasons, but he didn't care . . . he didn't care whether she was in earnest or whether it was all only a game. He knew only that he adored her, and that he was not going to, that he couldn't, however much he wanted to, resist the tide that was carrying him away.

Then he sat down and wrote to Beatrice :—

"*I am worse than you thought*"—he began—

Then once more he cursed himself. "I ought to be shot," he thought. The future appeared before him, with all its ghastly possibilities. He knew now, only too well, what Leila was capable of. "Even if she loves me now"—and he was convinced that she loved him now, just as he had been convinced, and was still convinced, that she had loved him when he had first known her the summer when she had lived at Twyford—"even if she still loves me now, she may love some one else next week, and she will throw me away like a broken toy. It's not her fault. She's made like that, and she's beautiful enough for it not to matter." But yet, at the thought of Leila loving some one else now, he felt himself trembling and shaking all over. Of course it would happen. It had happened already how many times ? She had probably loved Vincent Fitzclare, she had certainly loved George Wilmot, and then there were all the others, all those others who must have been there before he knew her—Wilfrid Clay, for instance. And then C. felt himself get cold all over, cold with a sudden feeling of hatred for her. How had she dared be so cruel ? How had she dared to behave like that ? How had she dared to go on,

to trifle, to pretend, to lie ? She was a tissue of
lies . . . her life was one long lie, everything she
said and did was a lie. She was the queen of liars.
She was *the* liar, the type of all women, just as
Meredith's *Egoist* was the type of all men. And
then he felt he hated her. He would like to kill her.
What a pity it was they weren't living in the past
when people did such things ! But they did sometimes now ; after all, one read in the newspapers of
such things . . . they were rarely people you knew,
but there were dramas, passionate, bitter, vital dramas,
for all that—sordid, if you like, but dealing in life and
death, and sometimes in poison and murder.

Then he laughed at himself ; laughed at the thought
of thinking that he could kill Leila.

"Why," he thought, "if she came into this room at
this moment, I should be on my knees to her." And,
after all, why not ? What was he fussing about ?
Why need he be so complicated ? Why couldn't he
take the gifts the gods gave and pass on ? Because—
and that was just it—he couldn't pass on. He was not
built like that. Why should he be flattened out and
broken ? Perhaps because there was something
wanting in him. If he had had some little extra thing
he would have been different ; he would have been a
stronger personality—if he had only been made of
sterner stuff. But he wasn't, and there was nothing
to be done. He was what he was, and Leila was what
she was, and there was no help for it. No help ; and
it would always be like that, he felt and he knew, till

he died. Nothing to mend, no cure for this disease.
All sorts of strange thoughts passed through his mind.
A rhyme kept on buzzing in his head about the parson
pocketing his fees, and he said over and over again :

> Canst thou not minister to a mind diseased ?

He went into his bedroom and began to undress,
and as he sat down on his bed he burst into tears,
those bitterest of all tears that are witnessed by none
but the angels and the devil—by the angels with pity,
by the devil with interest, for who knows what they
may not lead to ?

And he thought of Goethe's poem :—

> Wer nie sein Brod mit Thränen ass,
> Wer nie die kummervollen Nächte,
> Auf seinem Bette weinend sass——.

That was what Goethe meant. Goethe knew. It is
sitting on one's bed in the silence of the night that
these moments occur. If only, like Beatrice, he could
see daylight somewhere . . . if only there was for him
a bridge. But there was no bridge ; there was at least
an exit, a way out. Why not make an end of it ?
And he remembered the evening at Malone's rooms,
when they had leant out from the balcony and thought
of jumping out into the street. If he had done that
then, all would now have been over, and there would be
nothing to bother about. It was such a quick way.
He looked out of the window. Was it high enough
up ? Yes. Should he do it, and finish everything once
and for all ? Would it *finish* everything ? He

remembered Wright saying, when they discussed the matter, that short cuts were no use, and that suicide might mean beginning again further back, being sent to the bottom of the class. Well, even if one did have to begin again, even if it meant making everything longer, one would, in any case, get out of this. It would cut this particular knot, even if there were a worse one in store for him elsewhere.

Was he afraid to do it ? How could he do it ? He thought of a little case of medicines he had been given by one of his sisters to take to the war with him. It contained medicines in little flat squares of paper, stuff looking like thick postage stamps. One of them was cocaine ; another laudanum. He felt that if he took five or six squares of either of these it would probably do the trick. But that was too decisive. He would rather have something in which chance had a chance, something which might be fatal or might not be, so that, if it were not, at least he might have the satisfaction of thinking that he was meant to live.

And again he thought : " That is all wrong. If I really feel like that, and if I really have made up my mind I don't want to live, like the old Romans used to do when they felt the moment had come, I shouldn't leave a possible loophole." His thoughts again went back to Leila. " If only," he thought, " she loved me *best*, how little I should care what she had done, or what she did, but I feel she never *did* love me best, and never will, and that, even if she loves me now, there will be another best soon. How soon ? And then, at first, I shan't know, and then the old torture will begin again, and I shall be imprisoned once more in the vicious circle of protest and recrimination, and suspicion, and explanation, and quarrel, and reconciliation, and alternate love and hate, and finally of simultaneous love and hate." Could he bear that all over again ? Would nothing ever set him free from this chain ? Would nobody take out the thorn from the flesh, and cleanse his bosom of the perilous stuff ? And then, at the thought of this, he cried out in the dark : " I don't want to be cured. I don't want the thorn taken out. I don't want to be released. Oh, Leila, deceive me, deceive me once again ! "

He had got into bed and put out the lights, and all these thoughts were racing through his mind, and the image of Leila was never absent.

" What a fool I was to think I could ever be cured ! " he said to himself. " Nothing can cure me except death, and as that cure is here ready to my hand, here in this room, within my reach, it proves, if I don't make use of it, that I don't want to be cured."

He remained awake about two hours, and then drowsiness began to steal over him, and at last he fell asleep murmuring, " I don't want to be cured."

The next morning he tore up the letter he had written to Beatrice. " It's useless," he said to himself. " I feel certain she knows already."

CHAPTER LII

AND now began another phase in the history of C.'s and Leila's relations. She was kinder to him, more loving and gentle, and altogether more adorable than she had ever been, and her whole nature seemed to have mellowed and deepened by an undefinable hidden sadness. Yet she did not allow him to see her nearly as often as before. She did not appear, as far as C. knew, to see other people either. She stayed in London all the autumn, and she spent Christmas with her sister, Mrs. Tryan, in Somersetshire. C. spent a few days there—as long as he could stay—after Christmas, but this year Leila did not hunt. She did not, she said, feel quite up to it. In January, she came back to London, and, loving as she was to him when they met, he found it increasingly difficult to see her. Terence was far more to the fore than he used to be for one thing. Mrs. Evelyn had not been well, and owing to this he was rather at a loose end. But there was something else, something that C. could not fathom, which from time to time seemed to be erecting an invisible barrier between them.

Leila seemed to manage and arrange their meetings—so far—more carefully than ever before. It was as if they were being fitted into some plan of which he knew nothing. Not that he suspected her of any infidelity. Whom should he suspect ? There was nobody there. Dallas Wace never came near the house now. Leila was bored to death with the artistic acquaintances she had made through him, and said so openly.

Wilfrid Clay she saw very seldom. George Wilmot was in St. Petersburg. She had, as far as he knew, no new friends, and yet her life, which on the surface seemed to be much emptier, was in reality fuller than ever before. It was a mystery to C., and he did not attempt to solve it. As long as she was nice to him what did it matter ? And yet he was from time to time caught as by the shadow of coming possibilities, and he would feel cold all over. It was in a way too good to last, and yet at the same time it was so profoundly unsatisfactory and unsatisfying ; do what he could, and in spite of everything Leila could do and did, the relation for C. was one of unceasing anguish and permanent torture . . quite apart from anything he might suspect or dread or anticipate. At the end of January, she had a slight bout of bronchitis, and was advised to go abroad. Lady Rooter came to the rescue, and offered to put her up at their villa, which they had again taken for two months. C. wanted to go out there, too, if only for a few days, but Leila said that, for one thing, there wouldn't be room in the villa.

" I could stay at the hotel," he said, but Leila said it would be a pity, as he had so little leave, to waste it in driblets. He had much better save it up for the summer.

He saw Sir Alfred Rooter once or twice. He was keener than ever now on sending C. abroad for his newspaper, and said that if he liked he could go to Paris. He could not give him the job of first correspondent there, at once, but he could work under the man who was there now for a year to begin with, and then, later, if he made good, he would send the other man to St. Petersburg, which he had long wished to do. But this time C. was quite decidedly sure that he did not wish to go abroad. He was quite certain that he wanted to stay in London. Sir Alfred was almost annoyed ; he spent over two hours one night at his house, after dinner, trying to persuade C. to accept the post, explaining to him what a wonderful offer it was ; how lucrative to begin with, how interesting in the second place, how conveniently near to London he would be in Paris ; in fact, it had every advantage. But C. was as obstinate as a mule. He said he had no vocation and no talent for that kind of journalism ; no " nose " for news, and that he was quite happy where he was in his office. So Sir Alfred gave it up. Miss Haseltine, C. learnt, had left Berlin and was now in Paris, where she had a studio. She was going to stay there for two or three years, and she was said to be doing very well, and to be making a name for herself in the Paris world of art.

Leila left for the Riviera in February. Lady Rooter had gone out there already. Sir Alfred was to join

them later for a short time. " Just for a few days,"
he said. Terence remained in London. Leila came
back for the Easter holidays, which she spent with her
children at the Rooters' at Bramsley. She told C.
that Sir Alfred was certain to ask him, too, but Sir
Alfred did nothing of the kind.

" I can't understand it," said Leila. " I think you
must have annoyed him."

" Yes, I have," said C., and he told her the whole
story of the correspondentship.

" Of course that's it," she said. " It's just the sort
of thing he can't understand."

She stayed at Bramsley for a fortnight.

It was at the end of the Easter holidays that C. got
an urgent summons on the telephone in his office from
his brother Edward.

C. went round after the day's work was done and
found Edward in a state of excitement.

" Do you know what's happened ? " he said.
" Gilbert's turned up from South Africa, and, what's
more, he's a millionaire, and has bought a house in
Park Lane."

" I knew he was coming," said C., and he told him
of their meeting in Africa.

" Why the devil didn't you tell me this before ? "

" Because if Gilbert was ever mentioned in the
family there was such a deadly silence that I never
dared talk of him."

" The question is, what are we to do ? " said Edward.

C. said nothing.

" We shall have to see him."

" I think," said C., " it's more a question of what he thinks about us than of what we think about him. I don't think he will feel at all embarrassed or shy."

" No, quite," said Edward, " and after all, it was a very long time ago, and he's made good, and they say nothing against him in the City."

" But what did he actually do ? " asked C.

" I'm damned if I know, really. All I know is father said he did something which no son of his could do and expect him ever to see him or to have anything to do with him again. In any case, he lost ten thousand pounds, and father had to sell the tapestry, and then, whether he was in the wrong or the right, he was foolish enough to get angry and to quarrel with father."

" But people have told me that it was most unfair, that he was accused of doing something he hadn't done."

" He said so at the time, but father didn't believe it ; and if father didn't believe a thing there was nothing to be done. Perhaps he had done other things that father knew about. Perhaps it was all about something else."

" But that's all a private matter, and it doesn't concern the world."

" Oh, not in the least. Well, I shall ask him here, and I hope he'll come."

Edward appeared to be relieved at C.'s attitude. He had thought that perhaps C. was going to maintain the necessity of carrying on the tradition of his father's attitude to the end.

As it was, Edward needn't have bothered. London received Gilbert Bramsley with open arms. It was said there had been some unpleasantness at a club years ago; but it was when he was quite a boy, and it was very doubtful whether he hadn't been the victim of jealous spite. He had quarrelled with his father; but it was well known that Lord Hengrave was as obstinate as a mule; all the Bramsleys were that, but he was the worst of them in that respect. He would certainly never have admitted that he was wrong. He was a martinet, too, and a man of ungovernable temper. In fact, he belonged to another age. At any rate, Gilbert had made good. Nobody said a word against him in the City; and there he was, a man who had started as a remittance man, and who, entirely owing to his own wits, grit, determination and hard work, had become a millionaire; although he had had everything and every one against him, and had started with every possible disadvantage.

That was what the world said; and people were only waiting to be asked to the large house in Park Lane that Gilbert had taken. But Gilbert did not appear to be particularly eager to see any one, and he certainly had no social ambitions. He called on his brother Edward in the City, and he asked C. and his sisters to luncheon. His sisters disapproved of his colonial expressions, his strange accent, and of his too easy manners ; but he stood no nonsense from them, and he chaffed their heads off, and ended by giving each of them a large diamond, in return for which they forgave him his alien ways and unfamiliar vocabulary.

The only man who did not seem to be over-enthusiastic about the return of the prodigal was Sir Alfred Rooter, who, when C. mentioned the news of Gilbert's arrival, merely said :

" I knew him very well," and made no further comment.

The first time C. saw Gilbert the latter mentioned Bramsley, and when he heard that Rooter had bought it he swore in the most unmeasured terms and with a wealth of picturesque abuse.

" Do you hate him ? " said C. " He's been very good to me."

" I don't hate Alfred Rooter, I've known him all my life ; but what I say is : Alfred Rooter has no business to own Bramsley, that's all. And he shan't own it for long, what's more." Gilbert looked grimly determined. Then he chuckled to himself. " Fancy mother's feelings," he said, " if she saw Alf there at the head of the table. However, we'll get him out, don't you worry."

Gilbert laughed immoderately, and there was something about his laugh that C. did not altogether like.

C. told him of his personal relations with Alfred Rooter, and how it was owing to him he had been to Africa, and what he had done for him since.

"That's all right," said Gilbert, "Alf's a white man. The only knock I've got on him is that he lives at Bramsley. It's not his house, it's ours."

Edward and Marie asked Gilbert to dinner, and Gilbert said he would come on condition it wasn't too pompous and too swagger an affair. After much deliberation, a small dinner party was arranged, to which the following guests were bidden : Lionel Mells (Edward's partner), representing the City, and his wife, a pretty Irishwoman ; Terence Bucknell, representing the Foreign Office, and his wife ; Lord and Lady Holborn, representing the aristocracy and the Bramsley family as well ; Mr. Dallas Wace, representing the cultivated man-in-the-street ; Lady Harriet Clive, the past generation ; Walter Wright, youth and diplomacy ; and Mrs. Evelyn (without her husband), the essence of London.

Lady Hengrave was proud of Hengrave House that night. It had suffered a third partial "doing up" last winter, and the style had been slightly changed ; but the French influence predominated still ; the large pastel of herself had disappeared and been replaced by a portrait in a more modern style by an Austrian artist.

C. had been asked to dinner ; he was engaged, but he was to look in afterwards if he could. Walter Wright had just come back from Berlin, and had exchanged for a year into the Foreign Office. He and C. had decided to share rooms, and C. had moved from Bury Street into a flat over a shop in Baker Street.

The dinner went off well. Marie Hengrave had not disguised her apprehensions to her husband before Gilbert's arrival.

" I hope," she had said, " that he won't do anything *odd*."

" Why should he ? " said Edward. " After all, he was brought up at home and at Eton, so I suppose he ought to know how to behave."

" Yes," said Marie, " but he has been away for so long and in such dreadful surroundings, with such awful people."

When Gilbert entered the room, however—he came rather early, before the other guests—absolutely at his ease, and as if the house belonged to him, Lady Hengrave was slightly taken aback. She was taken aback, too, by his extreme good looks ; although she disapproved of the black pearl stud in his shirt-front, which she thought was too large.

She had meant to introduce a *soupçon* of coldness into the friendliness of her greeting, as much as to say : " Although we are killing the fatted calf for you, you mustn't take advantage of it ; and you must remember that you are here on approbation, that it behoves you to be careful."

But Gilbert, whether he was conscious of this or not, swept it aside with a breezy familiarity. He chaffed Edward ; he told him he was growing too fat and should try Swedish exercises or a month on the veldt ;

and when he was introduced to the other guests as they arrived, he was just as much at his ease with them. It was clear that he was *chez soi*, and his sister-in-law was rapidly obliged to revise her policy. The projected attitude was frankly of no use. At dinner he sat on his hostess's right, next to Leila. She had on her other side Tommy Holborn, who was not famous for conversation. Leila talked to him feverishly during the soup and the fish; and she then left him to his charming and pretty Irish neighbour, with whom he was quite happy, and roars of chaff soon came from the middle of the table. Then Leila turned to Gilbert, who was being riddled with questions by his hostess. He was puzzling her by answering them in a way which baffled her; she never knew whether he was serious or not. Just at that moment Lionel Mells, who was at her left, was telling Lady Holborn an anecdote that seemed to amuse her, in a loud voice; he evidently wanted an audience, and Lady Hengrave could not help listening; she turned towards Lionel Mells for a second, and his laughing eye and infectious laugh roped her into his conversation. Leila took advantage of that moment to snatch Gilbert's attention, and from that moment she talked to him without stopping till the end of dinner.

Wright was sitting next to Mrs. Evelyn, and he asked her whether she thought Gilbert was like C.

"They are all rather alike, the Bramsleys," she said, "but I think he is more like Harry: the one who died; as a matter of fact, he's less like his father and mother than any of them, I don't think he's at all like his mother.   He is very good-looking, very—*in a way*, isn't he ? "

" What do you think is wrong ? "

" Well—everything—in a way. I think there's something a little bit—I don't know what—flashy, second-rate, about him, which is very odd, con- sidering——"

" He seems to be getting on very well——"

" Leila can't resist good looks," she said with a sigh, and added, " Why isn't C. here ? "

" He's coming afterwards.   He couldn't dine, as he's dining with some Italians who were kind to him in Rome."

Leila seemed indeed to be enjoying herself im- mensely, and so did Gilbert. The fact of the matter, Wright thought as he watched them, although he did not say so to Mrs. Evelyn, was that they suited each other far better than Leila and C. did. Gilbert had all the qualities she liked in C., with an added dash; an added spice, a touch of the devil, something reck- less and wild and break-neck; and then he had none of the culture, the mere hidden presence of which Leila found a difficulty. It was a thing she felt she had to play up to. It made her uncomfortable, and she didn't like it. She disagreed with C.'s taste, whereas with Gilbert everything was plain sailing. There was no hidden culture ; and there was a certain amount of undisguised, unvarnished frankness in his conversa- tion, and something more than frankness and less than coarseness. He went further than other people ; and yet there was something engaging about him. And then she was, as Mrs. Evelyn said, highly susceptible to looks, and Gilbert's looks were just the kind that appealed to her most :—the dark, rich, bronzed, tanned, rather florid kind. Besides all this, he was new and unexpected. His strange experiences and his roving life had given him an odd flavour, and a curious mixed, picturesque vocabulary in which the slang of all nations met. Added to that, there was the Bramsley soil in his character as a foundation ; an element which she had already found most attractive and which she was used to.

She found Gilbert frankly irresistible. He also had an asset which she was certain to prize, Wright reflected. He was immensely, carelessly rich, and he meant to spend his money. Mrs. Evelyn's attention was presently caught by her neighbour, Terence, and Julia Holborn was still talking, or rather listening, to Lionel Mells, so that Wright had ample time for observation and reflection ; and he concluded that a perilous situation was being prepared ; not only was he aware that Leila was finding her neighbour attractive but there was a look in Gilbert's eye that meant something very definite. It was a look in which there was a blend of Bramsley obstinacy, reckless desire, and the determination to get, and acquire, and possess at all costs ; and by all means, whether fair or foul, mixed with a slightly cynical appraisement. He seemed to be appraising Leila at her just value, without illusion, and in the coolest manner, in spite of his feelings.

But Wright was startled from his reverie by his other neighbour, Lady Holborn, who asked him if he was going to Ascot this year.

When the men were left to themselves after dinner, Mells and Gilbert moved up to the other end of the table to be nearer Edward, and Wright listened while Gilbert, deftly cross-questioned by Wace, exposed what he considered would be the future of South Africa now that peace had been declared. Wright noticed that Gilbert seemed to anticipate Wace's skilful questions, and while he appeared to answer them with a frank volubility, in reality he said nothing.

When they went upstairs, two bridge tables were arranged. By this arrangement it happened that Leila, who seldom played, Gilbert, and the host and hostess were left out. Edward took Lady Harriet into the back drawing-room ; Lady Hengrave took Wright into a corner and began to discuss *la haute politique* with him ; and Gilbert and Leila were left.

" Wouldn't you like to cut in ? " Lady Hengrave said to Gilbert.

" Oh, no ! " he said, " I never play cards for money."

C. didn't appear, after all, that night, and when Wright got home he was not yet back. He came in later, saying that he had been taken to the play and his party had insisted on having supper at the *Savoy*.

CHAPTER LIII

C. ASKED Wright about the dinner. He wanted to hear every detail. Had they been nice to Gilbert? Where had he sat? When he heard he had sat next to Leila he said :—

" I'm sure she was nice to him."

That afternoon he went round to Upper Berkeley Street, when he left the office. He had said he was coming, but he found a note from Leila saying she was obliged to go to Mrs. Evelyn, who wasn't well. The next day he got a letter from her saying that she was taking Mrs. Evelyn down to Brighton for a few days' change of air. It was the only thing, she thought, that would cure Alice of her constant headaches. She would be back before the end of the week. But the end of the week came, and there was no sign of Leila. C. telegraphed to her : " When are you coming back?" She answered : " Terence is coming here till Monday. Hope arrive Monday." After once more putting off her arrival for a day, she did come back the next week, and she asked C. to dinner the night after her arrival. C. went ; and there he found Mrs. Evelyn, a girl who was a cousin of Terence's, Anne Bucknell, who was pretty, and who had not been out long ; and Gilbert.

Leila managed to find the opportunity of explaining to C. that she thought it would be such a good thing if Gilbert married Terence's cousin, Anne, who was so pretty, so nice, and quite penniless.

After dinner, Leila played the piano and sang, or, rather, hummed, the words of a French song, slurring over the difficulties of the accompaniment, and by an adroit use of the loud and soft pedals sometimes alternately and sometimes both together, concealing a certain sloppiness and uncertainty in the bass—

> Allez chercher loin dans l'espace
> Les perles d'or ;
> Je ne veux rien de ce qui passe ;
> J'ai mon trésor.

" That's very pretty," said Gilbert, " but sing something English."

" I can't sing," she said, " but what would you like me to play ? "

" Oh, any old thing ! something old."

" Do you know this ? " she said, and she began to play and to hum *The Garden of Sleep*, and after that a song of Lord Henry Somerset's, and then Tosti's *Good-bye*, only the accompaniment of the latter proved a little too difficult towards the end, and she had to end abruptly before the climax.

C. was left to talk with Terence's cousin, while Leila and Gilbert sat and made music ; but he hardly knew what he was saying as he had such a splitting headache. Terence and Mrs. Evelyn were talking in the next room. When Gilbert and C. left, Gilbert suggested taking C. round to his house for a moment and having a drink. They drove there in his electric brougham.

"Pretty little woman that," said Gilbert, "and cute, too, damned cute."

C. said nothing.

"She's staying at Bramsley next Saturday!"

"Who? Mrs. Bucknell?"

"Yes—funny, isn't it?"

They talked of other things. Gilbert told C. some of his plans and projects.

"If Rooter goes back to Africa," he said, "I'll buy Bramsley."

"But is he thinking of going back?"

"I guess he will. Do you think Edward would feel badly if I bought it?"

"No," said C. "I'm sure he wouldn't. He could never buy it himself, and even if he could, Marie would never let him. She hates the country—that sort of country, at least."

"It's just as well to be put wise."

They had reached the house in Park Lane. It had belonged, after passing through various hands, to a South American who had lately gone bankrupt. Gilbert had bought it just as it stood, and it was full of rather startling pictures and bright gilt furniture.

"I shall change all this, of course," he said. "Have a high-ball," and he poured out two generous doses of Bourbon whisky for himself and C.

"Here's how," he said, as he drank, looking C.

straight in the face. "I say, you don't look at the top of your form. Feeling like thirty cents—mouldy?"

"I've had a splitting headache for the last three days."

"Get outside this," and he poured out another dose of whisky for C., who took it and drank it mechanically.

"Yes," Gilbert resumed, "as I figure it, Rooter will beat it."

"What?"

"Beat it, fade, quit, what we used to call 'do a bunk' at school."

"But why should he?"

"One can't have two lions in one cage."

He didn't explain this cryptic remark, and C. said good-night. Gilbert sent him home in his electric brougham.

C. couldn't sleep that night and the next morning he felt so seedy that he allowed Wright to send for the doctor. The doctor diagnosed a violent form of influenza, such as C. had had once or twice before in his life. For three days he was very ill with a high temperature, and at moments he was on the verge of delirium. Then the fever subsided, leaving him very weak. He was, the doctor said, to stay in bed. He was not to make any exertion or see more people than was necessary. Wright looked after him, and his sisters came to see how he was every day. Leila wrote to him as soon as she heard he was well enough to read letters, and sent him fruit and flowers. She told him what she had been doing. She spoke of Gilbert and

said that every one liked him so much.　She thought
he would have a great success.

*I want him to give a ball, but he won't ; he's too
shy! He is very shy really, although people don't
know it.　He ought to marry a nice girl.　It would
be a great thing if he could marry Anne Bucknell,
she is so nice.　I'm going to Bramsley on Saturday.
It's such a pity you're not well.　Sir Alfred would
certainly have asked you.　I saw Lady Rooter in the
park and she was sorry you were ill, and wanted to
know whether there was anything she could do.*

She wrote to him from Bramsley.

*It's delicious here ; so cool after the fearful heat
of the last few days, which must have been very
trying for you.　It's a nice party, not too big.　Several
of his friends and of hers and of yours—Maud
Dallington.　We had some lovely music last night.
Eugene Franck played the whole of Tristan, while
the others played bridge.　I had a long talk with
Adela.　She asked after you a good deal, and is so
glad you are better.　She says you must go down to
the sea to get strong.　Your picture has been lent to
an exhibition in Paris.　Miss Haseltine, she says,
is coming home.　I have been walking about in the
garden this morning wondering which were the spots
where you used to play, you, Marjorie and Julia.
How strange it seems! They're calling me now so I
must stop.　Get well quickly, and don't quite forget*

me. I shall come and see you as soon as I possibly can and am allowed to when I get back.

C. hoped to be up early the next week, but he was more ill than he thought, and the doctor kept him in bed during the whole week. Gerald Malone came to see him often. Leila looked in to see him once; but his sister, Julia, was there; and she was very severe if visitors stayed more than a few minutes. Then came Ascot, and Leila went away. Gilbert had taken a house there. He asked C. to come, but he couldn't. He had invited Leila and Terence, who could only come down for the night, Edward and his wife (Edward couldn't go, but Marie was going), Julia and her husband, Marjorie and her husband, Mr. and Mrs. Evelyn, and young Freddy Calhoun, who was over on leave, and to whom Leila had introduced him. Just before Ascot Leila wrote to C. as follows :—

The Rooters have taken a house in Ascot too, and Sir Alfred is annoyed at my not staying with him. But I never told him I would, and because I stayed with him last year, no, not last year, I didn't go, but the year before last, it is too silly to think I must stay with him every year. He only sprang this on me two days ago, at the last minute, when I had made all my arrangements. Don't you think it's silly of him? Besides which, Adela hates the races and she's very tired, and I think it's doing her a kindness not to go. I mean the fewer guests she has the better.

She wrote just a line from Ascot saying there was no time to write, but that Gilbert was being a perfect host and enjoying himself very much. When Ascot was over she wrote to him, saying :—

I've been asked not to see you yet. They say you've seen too many people, and that it puts you back, so Julia says. Sir Alfred has been rather tiresome. I am afraid I shall be obliged to drop him altogether. He had made a scene at the races and you know I can't bear scenes. Surely I can stay where I like. Marie Hengrave and Edward asked me as a favour to be kind to your Gilbert. As he is your brother I would of course want to do anything I could for him, and Edward and all your family have always been so good to me. Besides that, I like him for himself. I I think he's very original, and so full of life. Sir Alfred seems to think that an invitation from him is like a royal command, something one can't refuse. I will come and see you directly they let me. It was all great fun, but I missed you.

As C. lay in bed thinking over things he was filled with longing, melancholy and apprehension, and a dread of he knew not what. Life seemed to have an extraordinarily bitter taste just at this moment, and the one short glimpse he had had of Leila, followed by a prolonged absence, made things worse. He felt that, in spite of her kindness to him when she saw him, (perhaps because of it), her thoughtfulness (she sent him flowers and fruit every day), that she was slipping, or had slipped, away from him. Something had happened ; what was it ?

There was some barrier ; something he didn't know. She was, for some reason or other, worlds away ; and it was as if she were putting off the moment of letting him know it. If he could only get up, and be well and about, he would soon know. These kind of thoughts made him brood and fret ; and then the thought of Beatrice used to recur to him, and fill him with shame and self-loathing . . . how right she had been. . . . The doctor saw that he was worrying, and told him that if he worried he would never get well, so he made a supreme effort not to worry, and after he had been in bed a fortnight, the doctor said to him :—

" To-day you can get up for an hour or so, and then we'll get you out, and then to the seaside, as soon as we can manage it."

What was worrying him most, of course, was not seeing Leila. Unfortunately his sister came just at the only moments when Leila could have come, and Leila wrote saying how increasingly difficult her life had become ; the thousand things she had to do, and how plain Julia and Marjorie had made it that she had better not visit him.

There was nothing to be done, C. thought, but to get well as soon as possible ; as long as he was kept in bed, he was at the mercy of the doctor and of his sisters. They had wanted him at first to have a nurse. There was, however, no room in the house for her ; and the doctor said it wasn't really necessary if he didn't want it, and C. wouldn't hear of it.

The evening of the day he was allowed up, Freddy Calhoun came to see him. But he had gone back to bed and was asleep when Freddy arrived. Wright was in the sitting-room next door. Freddy sat down and talked to him; the door between the sitting-room and C.'s bedroom was open, and Wright asked Freddy to wait. "He's sure to wake up presently. He will have his dinner presently and he'll be very angry if I let you go without his having seen you."

"How is he?" asked Freddy.

"Oh, he's getting on very well."

"But he was very bad, wasn't he?"

"Just the first two days, but I don't think the doctor was anxious. He was really afraid there might be after-effects, but there don't appear to be so far."

"Has he got up yet?"

"Yes. This morning for the first time. To-morrow he's going out for a drive with his sister. And then he's going down to Brighton."

"I suppose he's not seen many people."

"No, not many."

"I've been staying with his brother, at Ascot."

"Oh, yes, of course! What was it like?"

"Oh, I enjoyed it; but, I say, he is a rum fellow. I've never seen any one quite like him. Awfully decent to me, don't you know. I mean awfully anxious to do one well, and all that."

" Yes, I know. I've seen him once or twice. He's been here to see his brother. Who else was staying there ? "

" Nearly all the Bramsley family, and the Bucknells."

" Gilbert gets on with her, doesn't he ? "

" Yes, by Jove ! she's met her match there. But poor old Alfred Rooter is taking it awfully badly; and, I say, it's lucky that her little affair with C. is all over, isn't it ? George Wilmot was at the races ; he's over on leave, and she didn't look at him, so poor old C.'s well out of it, what ? And I think we needn't pity the brother. He can take care of himself, what ? "

" Hush ! " said Wright, pointing to the open door. " You'll wake him up."

A few moments later C. called to them and insisted on Freddy going to see him. Wright wondered whether C. had heard what Freddy had been saying. He thought not, for he was obviously only just awake ; but he had heard the conversation. He told Wright so some time afterwards ; only he was not certain at the time whether he was not dreaming. He heard it, and it seemed to belong to his dream, because he had been dreaming about Leila. In his dream, oddly enough, he had seen Leila sitting at the head of the table at Bramsley, and Gilbert sitting at the other end of it. Sir Alfred Rooter was handing round the port, dressed as a butler. And then his dream had changed, and he was at the café in the *Bois de Boulogne* with

Freddy and Thérèse, and his two sisters; and Leila had walked in on the arm of a stranger, and had said to him : "I am going to be married ; let me introduce you to my new husband," she had pointed to the stranger, and the stranger had changed into Gilbert. And then Sir Alfred Rooter had appeared, and Gilbert had said to him : "Beat it, fade, get back to Africa!" And in the middle of all this the people had literally faded ; and only Freddy and Thérèse and himself were left, and he seemed to hear the conversation, or a fragment of the conversation, which he did hear, and then he woke up definitely, and called to them. At the time, he said to himself, "I was dreaming," but it was a dream which opened out a whole vista of new possibilities. Oddly enough, instead of making him feel worse, it braced him up with a sense of possible action, of something to be done. He was determined to get well. The next day he got up and dressed about eleven, and he sent round a note to Leila's house telling her that he was getting up. Could she come and see him ? He mentioned times in the morning or evening ; he was going out driving with Julia in the afternoon. Leila wrote back to say that the afternoon was her only possible time. She would try and arrange something for the next day.

He went out for a drive with Julia in the afternoon, and in the evening who should call to see him but Sir Alfred Rooter.

"I've been wanting to look you up for some time,"

he said, " but I was told by your relations that the fewer people you saw the better. I'm glad you're all right again."

C. asked after Lady Rooter.

" She's fairly well, but the truth is, the life here doesn't suit her. It's too much for her ; the doctor says she must absolutely stop entertaining and all that, and as she hates it, and as I don't want her to do it, and as we only do it for a crowd of greedy, ungrateful sponging hangers-on who laugh at us behind our backs, what's the use of it ? So I've made up my mind to chuck the whole bally business."

" What, are you going away ? "

" Yes. Back to South Africa, and for good this time. Of course, I may come over to England again, from time to time, but I shan't live here any more."

" And what about Bramsley ? "

" I've sold it. To your brother Gilbert. That's all as it should be, isn't it ? Poetic justice has been done."

" And what about your newspaper, the *Northern Pilot?* "

" I'm keeping that for the time. Armstrong can look after that all right for me. But I've got a proposition to make to you. Why not come with us right now ? I'll find you plenty of jobs out there. It will set you up again, and don't pretend to me you're not sick of England, for I'm sure you are. Come with us. Chuck this silly, rotten life you're leading here, and I'll find you plenty to do out there. You can go back if you don't like it. They say you want sea air ; come for the voyage, and see how you like it."

" It's too late," said C., " too late. I can't now."

" I thought as much," said Sir Alfred, with a sigh. " Well, my last words to you are these—If you stay here, don't be a fool, but marry Joan Haseltine."

" Miss Haseltine ? What could have put such a thing in your head ? I don't suppose she'd ever dream of such a thing."

" Yes she would. She would marry you at once if you asked her. Adela says so, and Adela knows. She's a good girl, and a clever girl, and as straight as steel, and she's fond of you ; and you like her, and if you think you have not got enough to live on, well I shall fix that as far as she is concerned ; because I regard her as my daughter, and even if I didn't, I guess your brother Gilbert would fix it, because he'll soon be glad to get you fixed."

" What do you mean ? "

" Only what I say ; that he'll be glad to get you fixed ;—married, settled down for life instead of work-ing at that miserable office—what's it called, ' Sardine Fisheries ? ' or some such damned tomfoolery—when you're a man with brains and capable of doing all sorts of things, and you know how to write."

" It's awfully good of you to tell me all this, but I don't want to marry, and I don't want to leave England."

" That may be, but if the time comes presently when you should change your mind, and if you'd like then to come out to Africa, and take a real rest, and think things over, you're welcome to come to us ;—you've only got to cable ; and if you think of the other proposition, let me know ; but, of course, if you wait too long it may be too late. And now I've stayed here long enough. Good-bye. We sail in a fortnight."

CHAPTER LIV

THAT evening C. sent round a note by hand to Leila, saying that he would go to see her the next evening at six o'clock. She didn't answer, and he supposed that he was expected. He went round at six, and asked if Leila was at home. Wilkins said that Mrs. Bucknell was not at home to any visitors.

" It's all right," said C., " she's expecting me," and before the butler could do anything he ran upstairs and opened the door.

There was in Leila's house a drawing-room with three windows looking on to the street, and a small back drawing-room. The door on the landing led into the front drawing-room. As C. opened the door he saw no one in the front drawing-room, but his eye caught the tall looking-glass framed in gilt, a wedding present, Leila used to say, from Uncle Freddy (in that case it must have been a belated one), which hung between the two windows nearest to the chimney-piece. In this looking-glass he saw the reflection of two persons— a man and a woman who were in the back drawing-room. The man was the taller of the two, and he was looking down and holding the hand of the woman, who was looking up at him with an expression of mute ecstasy. They made an interesting picture. He was looking down at her, and his expression was unmistakable, too. The woman was Leila, the man was Gilbert. All this lasted for the flash of a second; as they heard the door open, Leila drew away her hand with a swiftness in which there was no clumsiness, and in a second, her expression was changed. She was another woman; she walked into the front drawing-room to see who it could be disturbing her at this moment.

"C. !" she cried out in intense astonishment.

"Weren't you expecting me ?" asked C., and there was a curious strain in his voice. "I sent round a note by hand, last night, saying I was coming round here, and telling you not to answer if it was all right. I got no answer, so I came."

"I never got it," said Leila, and then she turned to Gilbert and said, as he came into the room : "This is a surprise, isn't it ?"

"I guess it is," said Gilbert, and the accent with which he said the words jarred horribly on C.

Gilbert was standing near the tea-table.

"Do smoke if you want to," said Leila to Gilbert, handing him a silver box full of cigarettes.

"Thank you, I only smoke cigars," he said, "and I won't smoke now, any way."

"I don't mind cigars," said Leila. "I like them."

C. was still standing up in the middle of the room. Leila sat down on a little sofa which was behind the tea-table, between the windows.

"Do sit down," she said, smiling.

Gilbert sat down near the tea-table. C. looked all round the room, and took in every detail with one quick glance, and in his mind he registered another picture that could not be forgotten. He had already registered one as he came into the room.

There was Leila, cool and soft and lovely, in the thinnest of muslin, with a rope of pearls round her neck. The room was full of rather too 'expensive' pink roses, and pink carnations. There were masses of them everywhere. Outside in the street a barrel organ was playing *The Soldiers of the Queen*. It was a very hot June evening; and the newspaper boys were yelling " Special ! " with regard to a piece of news of public importance.

There was Gilbert sitting in a chair, equally cool. He was wearing a grey frock-coat, a white waistcoat, and a black satin stock tie, in which he had a very large emerald pin, and a large white carnation in his button-hole. And as C. looked at him he was certain, with that perspicacity with which only brothers can read each other, that Gilbert knew that he knew ; and also that Gilbert knew exactly what he was feeling, and why. He also felt that all his past relation to Leila in the last minute had been as suddenly revealed to Gilbert, as surely, as certainly, as Gilbert's present relation to Leila had been revealed to himself, at the moment when he had caught sight of them in the looking-glass.

All this flashed through his mind ; and he was convinced of something else ; something that he felt

with all the intuition of a lover, especially when a
brother is concerned, and that was that Leila loved
Gilbert ; and loved him as perhaps she had never
loved any one else. He saw, too, in a flash what the
world would say . . . the glib summing up of the
situation as the capture of a millionaire . . . and he
felt that, whatever Leila might have done in the past,
whatever might have been her guilt in that way ;—
supposing everything, for instance, that Freddy's
French friends—Thérèse and Jaqueline—had said that
night in the *Bois de Boulogne*, were true, and more
than true,—it was *not* true, he felt, in this case. He
knew that she loved Gilbert with all her being ; and
he would have persisted in believing it even if an angel
had told him the contrary.

"Well, the end has come at last"—he said to himself in the brief moment during which he stood
in that room—"I knew it would come. I knew it
was coming soon," and the words that he thought
he had dreamt, that Freddy Calhoun had said to
Wright, as he lay in bed, came back to him. "By
Jove, she's met her match!" This was about Leila
and Gilbert. He understood now, and, what's more,
he agreed. She had met her match ; of that he felt
certain.

She would have no control over Gilbert. It would
be he who would be able to do what he liked with her.
Had she guessed what he knew, what he was feeling ?
He was not sure ; but he was sure of this ; that, even
if she had guessed, she would not, she could not possibly,

care. Leila was a person who thought of one person, and only one person, in one particular way, at a time; and as she only looked upon every human being in one light, it was easy to know what she was thinking of now; at least so he thought. All this and more passed through his mind in a few seconds, but he said, in the most ordinary voice :—

"I can't possibly stay. They make me go to bed early. I only came to say I was going to Brighton to-morrow."

"That will do you good," said Leila. "I'm so glad. You look so pulled down, doesn't he, Mr. Gilbert?"

C. admired the phrasing.

"Yes, he does," drawled Gilbert. "To-morrow afternoon?"

"Yes," said C.

"Then I'll be looking in on you to-morrow morning at twelve," he said, and he got up and said good-bye, as if it were an understood thing that in that house he was the person who stayed, and C. was the person who went.

C. went home. He felt quite light-headed in a way. He had no sense of the reality of things, and he felt very tired, and a hundred years older. Also, he experienced a feeling of relief, as if an impending catastrophe which was surely expected, but whose nature was known, had at last happened. He knew the worst, so he thought. As a matter of fact, he did not know the worst.

When he got home, he found Wright sitting in an armchair and reading the newspaper.

As C. came in Wright said to him :

"You look fagged. You've been doing too much too soon. You'd better go to bed."

"Yes, I am rather tired to-night," said C., and he went to bed. He couldn't eat anything, but he drank a pint of champagne. He slept that night the sleep that schoolboys sleep when they have arrived at school for the first time; a sleep the numbness of which has no equal. His awakening the next morning was like the awakening the morning after the first night spent at school, with the little interval of grace in which the mind wanders in limbo before it is definitely aware of what is the disagreeable thing that has happened. He stayed in bed late. When the post was brought, the first thing that he noticed was a long letter from Leila ; at least he thought it must be long, as it was fat. It *was* a long letter, and at first he thought of not reading it, and sending it back unopened. He then reflected that would be *crude* indeed. Whatever move the rules of the game demanded, that, he felt, would be the wrong one. He began to read the letter. It was different from anything he had expected. Here it is :—

My very dear C.,

You must have thought it so strange of me, so thoughtless and horrid *not to have made* every *effort to see you while you were so ill, or at least as soon as you were allowed visitors, but I was really waiting till you were better to tell you something which I have known I had to tell you for a long time. Only it was so difficult! It still is very, very difficult. I don't know how to begin. There's so much to say, and words seem so helpless. I felt I couldn't say it, and now it's just as difficult to write. I have been thinking everything over lately, and while you were ill I had some long talks with Julia and Marjorie, and with Sir Alfred Rooter, who has always taken such an interest in you, before he became impossible. Julia and Marjorie are very anxious that you should marry some time, and they think our friendship is a mistake now—they thought it was all right before—but they think, and I do think they are right, that it would be a pity for you to depend so much on me, and in the long run it is very unsatisfactory, isn't it? It is so little I can give you. I can, as things are now, hardly ever see you. Terence usen't to mind my seeing you, but that was when you were younger and quite a boy! And now he does mind it so, and I don't like him minding things. Everything is different now for me, and for you, and I think it's more honest to face things, to face everything, and to tell the truth. You and I have never been afraid of that, have we? And I have always told you the truth, and you have always been so truthful. We have nothing to be ashamed of. I feel perhaps I was wrong ever to let our friendship start, or get so far, as nothing could come of it, but then you know one is so weak one doesn't think and calculate, and I was and am so, so fond of*

you, and I can't regret anything, or look back on it all
without a pang of great, great *thankfulness*. It was
all so *beautiful*. We had ups and downs and a few
little misunderstandings, but these were like specks,
weren't they ? *Specks in the sun?* You always understood *afterwards, and I think I did. After all, no real
friendship can exist without these ups and downs,
otherwise it means that the friends don't care, that
they're not friends at all. Well, it's all very sad when
one looks back, but you must remember that I'm getting
old ! my children are growing up. I've got a boy at
Eton now, but you are still so young, still quite a
boy, and the world is still all before you. You are only
just beginning life. You will have many more friends
and love many more people I'm sure, and I'm sure, too,
that one day you'll marry and be very happy. Of
course, when that happens, I shall not be able to help
feeling a pang of sadness, but that must be faced.
That's life, isn't it ? I shall always look back on everything with joy and thanksgiving, and always thank
God in my prayers that He let me know you, my dear,
dear C. I won't say to you " Don't be sad," because I
know you won't be able to help being a little sad, and I
should feel rather sad myself if you didn't feel anything at all. But I do ask of you to think of it all
in the same way, and to think of me as I shall
always think of you. I have thought over this a long
time, and I feel, I know, my dear, dear C., that I'm
doing right, however hard, and it is always so hard to
do right.

Do you know these verses from the " Triumph of Time " ?—I think they are so true.

I wept that all must die—
" Yet Love," I cried, " doth live, and conquer death——"
And Time passed by,
And breathed on Love, and killed it with his breath
Ere Death was nigh.

More bitter far than all
It was to know that Love could change and die—
Hush ! for the ages call
" The Love of God lives through eternity,
And conquers all ! "

Whatever happens to you afterwards, I only ask you to keep one little tiny corner in your heart where I shan't be quite forgotten. That's all I ask. I needn't tell you that it has cost me a good deal to write this letter !

The cord is frayed—the cruse is dry,
The link must break, and the lamp must die.

I, of course, shall never forget. How could I ? Dear, dear C.

Your friend.—L.

That was Leila's letter, and C. read it and re-read it several times. Then he put it away in a box where he kept such papers as he did not wish to destroy.

Gilbert came to see him punctually at twelve. He asked C. first about Brighton. He wanted to take rooms for him there. C. thanked him very much, but he had made other arrangements, now. Their aunt,

Mrs. Roden, wanted him to go there, and he was going. He would be more comfortable than in an hotel, and the air was very good at Elladon. So he had given up Brighton altogether.

Gilbert sat down in a chair and smoked a cigar.

"If ever you want any cash you've only got to ask. But—sorry—that's a mug's speech, isn't it? Nobody does ask. At least, not your sort. Well, I've bought Bramsley. That's fixed."

"So I heard," said C. "How did you do it?"

"Well, it was this way. I've known Alfred Rooter for years; we were mates; in Africa years ago, and we never parted rags in the ordinary course of things. But there was one queer thing about our intercourse, and it was this. We more than once got fond of the same girl, and in those contests I came out top, and he came off second best. Do you get me? There seemed to be some fatality about it. If ever he loved some one, I would be sure to love her, too; and the girl would be sure in time to turn him down for me. Quaint, wasn't it? And, mind you, it weren't my fault. I never tried to butt in. I did nothing. It just happened so. It happened more than once. I guess he was rather sore once or twice, but he never bore malice. Alfred Rooter's white all through. Then he went home and married that Danish girl, and so that was all. They say she was a high-stepper when she was young, maybe. I guess she was, or else Alfred Rooter would never have married her. But her game wasn't his game. She was on in the high art act :—Wagner-stuff, impressionist pictures and Norwegian plays about doctors with tuberculosis and nervy women in the suburbs of Spitzbergen. That wasn't Alfred Rooter's act. Then he comes here to England, and buys Bramsley. Then I butt in, too late to buy Bramsley, after having worked all my life with that one object in view, and I say to myself, ' It's up to me to get it, all the same, and to get it without making Alfred Rooter feel sore or envious, or he'd stick to it like a horse-leech.' Get me ? So I say to myself, say I : ' Why is he in London, anyway ? ' Not ' Why did he come ? ' but ' Why is he staying ? There must be some reason, some pretty good reason, otherwise Alfred Rooter would never come to London, and buy a London house and a country house, too, with his wife an invalid and hating all society except that of pianists with hair like monkeys, and sea-green painters who paint puce portraits of has-beens.' So I figured out there must be a girl in the matter, and, of course, there was. I nosed around to find out who it might be. I didn't have to look long. It wasn't harder than looking for St. Paul's Cathedral near Ludgate Hill. Well, I needn't tell you who the girl was. Every one knew it and all about her. She was married, good-looking, and poor. Her husband was all right, but a four-flusher and a tight-wad. But in other affairs she had a regular protector, who provided her with all she needed. It appears he was an old guy ; I don't know and don't care. Anyway, that had come to an end,

and Alfred had come along, and he'd fallen to her in
no time, and he was just what she needed. He fixed
up a little flat for her in Knightsbridge, where she could
do the double-life stunt when she pleased, but she didn't
please quite often enough to please Alfred. However,
for a time, all was merry and bright, and nobody a
penny the worse, and the tight-wad none the wiser,
and never stopping to think where it all came from.
But I guess she was clever enough not to let it show,
and to keep up appearances and all that stuff. Besides
which, she was the sort that spends a thousand dollars
on sleeve linings no one ever sees. You may wonder
how I came to know so much. Well, Alfred Rooter
could never keep anything hidden from me, and that's
all there is to it. And I said to him : ' Aren't you
scared, Alfred, of the old ju-ju working, the old
fatality ? ' He said, ' It won't work this time,' and
he laughed. ' What do you bet ? ' I asked. ' I won't
take your money off you,' he said. ' It won't work
this time for a very good reason ; she may get sick
of me any day—I'm not saying she doesn't—but she
won't go for you. There's reasons for that ; she's
been inoculated against Bramsley fever,' he said,
whatever he might mean by that. ' Very well,' I said
to him. ' You let me make her acquaintance, and you
see.' ' You can make her acquaintance whenever you
like and be damned,' he said. ' You won't get me to
introduce you. But I tell you one thing, Gilbert
Bramsley,' he said, ' if you do get to know her and
the old game comes off this time, I'll quit. I'll sell

Bramsley and leave England.' 'Done,' said I ; ' and if you sell Bramsley, will you give me the refusal ? ' 'I will,' he said. 'Done,' I said. Well, then I met the goods, without any difficulty, and then what happened ? Alfred was fired at Ascot. He got it good and plenty, and he owned up that he was beat, down and out, at once, and he kept his word, and he sold me the house and the estate ; and, between ourselves, he's thankful. None of it was in his line, neither Bramsley nor London nor the girl. But they're all in my line . . . for the present, at least. So that's all there is to it. Good-bye for the present, and I shall see your account never gets too high—on the wrong side of the ledger."

Gilbert left. C. had said good-bye, and saw him out. He had listened to the whole story in silence, and he had no doubt of its truth. When he came to think of it, he realised that he had really known it all before, or most of it, although in a way, till the night before, he had not really known any of it. It had been a gradual process. But whenever he had acquired an extra piece of knowledge, whenever the curtain had been lifted for a moment, he had pulled over the newly-revealed prospect a curtain of his own making.

Now he knew everything; and the first thing he did was to laugh—it all seemed to him so comic, so utterly fantastically comic ; but there was little enough mirth in his laughter. And as he looked out of the window, he thought to himself : " There's the world, and life, waiting for me, and I've only just begun; and yet I feel and know that for me it is over, irrevocably over. *La commedia è finita*, and yet I've got to go on. I've only just begun."

In the meantime the Rodens had asked Wright to Elladon. He couldn't go during the week, but he was going down on Saturday. C. wrote Leila a short note. He thanked her for her letter and her good wishes, and he reciprocated them; he said that he quite understood everything. He thanked her, too, for the verse, which was new to him.

CHAPTER LV

C. WENT down to Elladon the next day. There was no one there but Mr. and Mrs. Roden. Both their daughters were married and in London, and the Rodens themselves now rarely came to London. On the following Saturday Wright joined him, and they had long, long talks together. C. couldn't do very much at present, and he sat on the terrace and talked to Wright. It was there, during these days, that C. told Wright as much of his story as he ever told any one, and that was not much—a few glimpses into one or two chapters: stories of childhood, detailed full reminiscences of school and Eton:—about his later life, only a few illuminating details and suggestive silences.

He stayed at Elladon a month. That brought him very nearly to the end of July. He wrote to Beatrice and told her that she had been right, and that, although he was now free, and everything that might once have been an obstacle was no longer there, he realised now that he was finished, and the whole sad truth. He was incurable. He had always been incurable, but only she had known it.

She wrote to him and implored him not to worry as far as she was concerned. She was at present in

Ireland, with her sister-in-law, and she was going to take her in the winter to Algiers, as she was not strong enough to face an English winter.

"*Don't,*" she wrote, "*ever think that you are in any way to blame. I couldn't have done it either ; and the only reason I did not shut the door last year was because I knew it must shut of itself, as I think I told you then. You see I'm incurable, too, in a way. It was not meant to be.*"

C. was more or less well again at the end of July, but he was advised not to go back to London, and it so happened that he was able to take a month's holiday at this moment without difficulty, so, after staying a month with the Rodens, he went for a short walking tour with Gerald Malone in Devonshire. By the middle of September, he was back again in London. Gilbert asked him to come to Bramsley during the autumn and shoot partridges, but C. said he could not get away. Gilbert had a large family party at Christmas, and C. was asked to that, but he and Wright had both promised to stay in Paris with Sir Hedworth Lawless, who had just been appointed Ambassador there. Sir Hedworth Lawless told him that if he would like to come back as Honorary Attaché, or even Private Secretary, at any time, he would be delighted to have him ; and C. seriously thought of accepting the offer later on.

There was no one at the present moment on the staff of the Embassy that C. knew. There was a First

Secretary called Napier, whom he liked and got on with easily. Lady Lawless was extremely kind to him. She scented something of a romantic adventure, and this gave him a special prestige in her eyes. He got to know her now better than he had ever known her before.

Beatrice Fitzclare passed through Paris while C. was there, on her way to Algiers, and she was asked to dinner at the Embassy. Lady Lawless was an old friend of her mother's.

When C. saw her as he walked into the drawing-room, it was a shock to him, a shock as of meeting some one on the other side of a gulf, a gulf of the irreparable. He felt he was no longer the same person he had been when he last saw her—not that he had changed with regard to her; it was the universe which had changed.

She sat next to C. at dinner. It was rather a large dinner-party, with several French people, a well-known man of letters, and some of the staff of the Embassy, as well as one or two English people who were passing through.

Beatrice and C. were not able to have much conversation during dinner, because they were near the end of the table, and they were involved in a general conversation which was dominated by a French official belonging to the *Quai d'Orsay*, who described a house he had recently purchased in the environs of Paris, at the greatest length; beginning with the attics, and ending with the drains, till Beatrice and C. could scarcely keep their countenances. They did manage, however, every now and then to get a few words in to each other;

and C. was once more aware of the delicious balm of Beatrice's sympathy. She felt, she understood everything. He told her Gilbert had bought Bramsley, but she asked no questions about him. She was so skilful and clever, too, in making the most of the general conversation into which they got caught at every moment. She made it amusing and she created out of the unpromising material intimate personal fun between her and C.; and all this, to C., was pain, unmixed pain, infinite bitterness, and a tragic Shakesperean realisation of the pity and waste of things.

After dinner, several other people looked in, and Lady Lawless had some music. A pianist played " to get," she said to C., " people used to it ; he doesn't expect you to listen." Whether he did or not, the audience certainly took but little notice of the noise, but it attuned them to what was to come, and prepared them, as Lady Lawless said, for hearing what was to come. She considered that the art of entertaining, like that of writing plays, was the art of preparation.

When he had finished, Foscoli, the composer, sat down at the pianoforte and sang some songs. His opera *Ninon de Lenclos* had just been produced at the Opéra Comique. He had not a strong voice, but its quality, its timbre, was warm and captivating, and his singing was exquisitely appropriate, his phrasing, his interpretation unobtrusively right, whether he sang a song of his own, a Neapolitan street song, or an air of Mozart, a song of Schubert or of Brahms.

He started by singing a Neapolitan song, the song

of an excruciated lover; desperate, sick, mad with
love ; the singer gave just the right nasal sharpness
and metallic tang which expressed the bitter sweetness
and sweet pain of the utterance.   After that he sang a
song from Mozart's *Seraglio*, then *Maid of Athens* in
English, and then Fauré's *Tristesse*.

As he sang :—

> Avril est de retour.
> La première des roses,
> De ses lèvres mi-closes,
> Sourit au premier jour ;
> La terre bien heureuse
> S'ouvre et s'épanouit,
> Tout aime, tout jouit,

Hélas !   J'ai dans le cœur une tristesse affreuse !

> Les buveurs en gaité,
> Dans leurs chansons vermeilles,
> Célèbrent sous les treilles
> Le vin et la beauté ;
> La musique joyeuse
> Avec leur rire clair
> S'éparpille dans l'air.

Hélas !   J'ai dans le cœur une tristesse affreuse !

Did ever singer, thought C., combine before such
exquisite lightness of manner with so heartrending an
interpretation of the sad business that lay behind and
beneath, the sorrow that hurt, the passion that seared ?

> En deshabillés blancs,
> Les jeunes demoiselles
> S'en vont sous les tonnelles
> Au bras de leurs galants ;
> La lune langoureuse
> Argente leurs baisers
> Longuement appuyés.

Hélas !   J'ai dans le cœur une tristesse affreuse !

C. remembered hearing it years ago at the first
Bohemian party he had ever been to in his life, at
Vegas' studio in Paris, when he was living at Versailles.
How different were the two experiences. They were
as different as the interpretations of Foscoli and the
young painter who had sung at the studio—C. could
barely recall his name—then it came back to him.
It was Dorant. His light, youthful, fundamentally
careless interpretation revelling in the *sentiment* of
sadness had exactly suited C.'s frame of mind then.
How *he* had enjoyed the sadness of it then ! How he
had wallowed and revelled in the luxury of those idle
tears ! But now it was a question of recognising by
and through his own experience that the words were
true. And if there were tears now, they would be
tears of recognition. His first experience of the kind
had been, he now remembered, his last chapel at Eton,
but that was only a faint shadow of this.

> Moi, je n'aime plus rien,
> Ni l'homme ni la femme,
> Ni mon corps, ni mon âme,
> Pas même mon vieux chien.
> Allez dire qu'on creuse,
> Sous le pâle gazon,
> Une fosse sans nom.
> Hélas !   J'ai dans le cœur une tristesse affreuse !

It was the wonderful appropriateness of Fauré's
tune which made these words so unbearably, so painfully poignant; and as Foscoli sang them they became
more poignant still . . . he phased the inner soul of

the pain, and seemed to seize the unseizable. It was, C. felt, unbearable . . . the song brought everything back to him . . . the whole miserable story . . . the whole of his broken, wasted life—Beatrice—Leila. The sharpness of death, the bitterness of life, of the world, *lo mondo senza fine amaro*—infinite, unending, indescribable bitterness.

When Foscoli stopped, the audience were too greatly moved to applaud, and he went straight on and sang a song of Gounod's, *Ave Maria de l'Enfant*, and C. felt transported from a pagan world of bleak desolation, a dry, illimitable desert and a starless universe, into a serene, sunlit white space, the spaces of Fra Angelico, and Heine's *Wallfahrt nach Kevlaar* and Dante's *Paradiso*. He looked at Beatrice, and he knew what she must be feeling; and this sharp, sudden, unexpected contrast, which was quite accidental on the part of the singer, was the most unkindest cut of all. The very balm and relief, the serenity and simple *naïveté* of the second song was too much; more than could be borne after the heart-wringing anguish and desert air of the first song. It created too fierce a reaction; too decided a *détente*. C. felt that the mainspring of his being must snap. He was on the verge of a real breakdown, and needed all his self-control not to sob. He was thankful, when it was over (and Foscoli sang it twice through without stopping, as if it had only caught his attention as he sang it the first time, and as if it were only the second time that he was really in his stride and really singing it), that Foscoli sang no more that night.

Everybody streamed into the next room, where there were refreshments. Lady Lawless congratulated Foscoli with tears in her eyes, but said she would have liked a few more love songs.

" I so enjoyed the Byron," she said.

" You are going away to-morrow ? " said C. to Beatrice as she said good-night to him.

" Yes, to-morrow evening, and I am travelling straight through. I shall be away till Easter. *Au revoir*, C."

" *Au revoir*, Beatrice."

The next day, she telephoned to him before leaving her hotel, and said " Good-bye " and " *Au revoir* " to him once more. She felt she would never see him again. And when they spoke on the telephone, she told Gerald Malone a long time afterwards that she felt as if C.'s voice were coming from another world. It seemed to have a curious unearthly quality. Two or three days later C. read in the *Morning Post* that " The Honourable Gilbert Bramsley, who had recently purchased Bramsley Hall, the seat of the late Lord Hengrave, had been entertaining a large party for the New Year. Among the guests were Lord and Lady Hengrave, Lord and Lady Holborn, Mr. and Mrs. Evelyn, Mr. and Mrs. Terence Bucknell, and the Honourable Freddy Calhoun."

C. stayed in Paris till the end of January. Sir Hedworth wouldn't hear of their going away sooner.

He travelled back to London with Wright, and they had a very bad crossing. The day after his arrival C. felt seedy; he had a headache. The next day this developed into a splitting headache, with pains all over him: the regular and usual signs of his attacks of influenza. He went down to the office feeling ill, and when he came back he felt feverish. He thought he had probably caught a chill during the crossing; but when the doctor came the next day, he said it was influenza, and was likely to be a severe attack, and that this time C. *must* have a nurse. C. protested, and said it was impossible. Where could she live? The doctor said he ought to be moved to a nursing home. C. said that nothing would induce him to move. The doctor appealed to Lady Holborn, who arranged for him to have a nurse during the day who would sleep at Hengrave House, which was quite close. The doctor said that a night nurse would be necessary too.

For three days he had a very high temperature, and he was delirious. He talked a great deal about Paris and Burstall and Madame Maartens, and recited fragments of poetry, and kept clapping and calling for Lapara. He thought he was once more living through one of her memorable performances.

Then his temperature subsided, and again it went up; and so on for a few days; then it finally subsided, and he became extremely weak. It was then the doctor grew anxious and said that the illness might prove fatal. It all depended now on himself and on his will to live. If he could make the necessary effort he would pull through. If he couldn't, they must fear the worst. His sisters took turns in looking after him; and he had an excellent nurse as well, also a night nurse. Many people came to ask after him: the Rodens, the Carterets, Lady Harriet Clive, the Calhouns; and Leila called and inquired often, and sent flowers and fruit; but he saw no one except his sisters and Walter Wright. He made no effort to live, and every day he grew weaker. He did not seem to take any further interest in anything. He recognised his sisters, and smiled at their efforts; as if he were looking on a child trying to prevent the sea invading the moat of a sand castle. Sometimes odd ideas came into his head.

He said suddenly to Marjorie :—

" I'm sorry I killed Joséphine, but then you *did* spoil my farm, and I did get my roof on first."

He saw Wright every day, but he did not talk much. There was a tired look in his eyes, as of a man who is not prepared to face the light of day after having been near the valley of the shadow of death.

One morning—it was the fourth after the fever had subsided—he asked for Wright.

" I must see Gerald," he said ; " ask him to come round to-day."

Gerald Malone came about one o'clock. The nurse told him he mustn't tire him. " He's very ill," she said, " far worse than he knows."

Gerald Malone sat by his bed.

" Well, C., old man," he said, " you're better."

"Am I?" said C. "Perhaps I am. What Gilbert calls 'fine.'" He laughed a little. "You needn't bother, you know. *You* needn't play up. I have to play up to them. They think I don't know. I humour them. One has to. It's the only fun they get, after all. I wanted to see you," he paused and sipped a little barley water, "to tell you I'm leaving you some papers . . . in case. Only scraps and things . . . I don't want any one else to have them. I couldn't burn them, and I don't want any one else to see them. I don't mind you or Walter. There's nothing 'so damned private' about them. Do you remember that story? The man in the bathroom and his brother, the High Church clergyman." C. laughed. "If I don't get well, tell Beatrice, if you should see her, that I felt the *bridge* . . . felt there *was a bridge* . . . that's as far as I got . . . no further . . . I hadn't time for more . . . I meant to think it all out some day; I'm too tired now. She'll understand . . . and tell her it *still holds good*."

He was rather exhausted after this spurt of talk, and Gerald thought he'd better go.

"Won't you have a cigarette?" C. said. "There are some somewhere," and then he smiled and said to himself, hardly audibly, "'the rottenest of all rotten poets' . . . true, but not about him."

He couldn't speak any more. He smiled at Gerald and made a slight movement with his hand. Gerald went out.

Gerald saw Wright in the next room.

"I'm afraid he's very bad," said Gerald.

"Yes, very."

C. lived through the night. The next morning was St. Valentine's Day. C. said he felt better, although he said :—

"I had an awful night. I had the *steamer* dream, what I used to have in the nursery. I wonder if I'm going to get well, after all. That would be hard. I don't believe one ought to do that, when one gets so far ; it's a mistake to come back, like going down to Eton after one's left . . . I mean directly after one's left Eton. 'What do they know of Eton who only Harrow know?'" And he hummed to himself to a funny high tune : "Phœbe, Phœbe, sausages, Rowlands, Browns !" His voice was fainter : "Phœbe, Phœbe, sausages, Rowlands, Browns !"

Outside in the street, an old-fashioned barrel-organ began to play. C. smiled. He loved barrel-organs, especially the old-fashioned sort.

"Don't send him away, for God's sake don't send him away," he said, with all his force. "Throw him some pennies or pounds, and tell him to play. Is he an Italian ?" And he said :—

> It is not many miles to Mantua,
> No further than the end of this mad world.

The nurse, who was next door, had already begun to take steps to send the organ-grinder away, but Wright stopped her, and she understood.

"Walter," said C., suddenly, "what day of the month is it ?"

" It's the fourteenth of February."

" St. Valentine's Day."

" We must remember to send Hackey a valentine."

Outside the barrel-organ played an old-fashioned dance tune, one of the valses of the 'eighties—*Estudiantina*, by Waldteufel. C.'s face lit up with recognition.

" Leila," he said, " do you remember that tune, the night in Hamilton Gardens, when you——" but Leila wasn't there.

When the nurse came into the room about a quarter of an hour later, C. was asleep, and he never finished his question.

C. was buried at Bramsley, but there was a memorial service in London at St. Luke's Church, at which there was a considerable attendance. The Foreign Office was represented by Terence Bucknell. Mrs. Bucknell was much affected, and broke down when the choir sang *Lead, Kindly Light*.

That is all the story as I was able to construct it from the papers by Gerald Malone, and from what I had myself seen and heard from C., Gerald Malone, Mrs. Fitzclare, Mrs. Evelyn, and others. I am aware, now that I have finished it, that it leaves everything out, and it gives no idea, no real idea, of C. It leaves out all the one thousand little things which made him C.

One day, several years later, after I had left the Diplomatic Service, and had taken to journalism, I was passing through Paris, and had luncheon with Sir

Hedworth Lawless at the Embassy. It was in the summer, towards the end of July. Paris was quite empty, and Sir Hedworth was having luncheon by himself. Lady Lawless had gone to Dieppe for a few days.

I thought Sir Hedworth looked aged and ill. We talked of various topics, the possibility of war—not the European war, it was before that—and in some connection or other the Hengraves were mentioned, and C.'s name cropped up.

" That was a waste," said Sir Hedworth.

" Do you think he ought to have stayed in Diplomacy ? " I asked.

" Oh, dear no," he said, " nobody was less fitted to be a diplomat. But his life was a waste. He was born to be a man of letters ; but he got into the wrong rut, and his whole life was *a conflict of values*. If he had been a Roman, in the days of Augustus, he would have been a poet like Catullus or Calvus."

" I don't think that would have made him any happier," I said.

" Certainly not," said Sir Hedworth, " but something would have come out of it."

" He did write at one time," I said, " quite a lot of verse, and when he was at Oxford it was his ambition to be a writer."

" Did he ever show you anything ? "

" Hardly anything, but Andrew Burstall saw several of his early poems, and said they were good—really good. And Hallam, do you know him ? Hallam saw a few of the later ones—and he thought the same."

" What happened to them ? "

" He burnt everything, and what wasn't burnt was lost." *

" Lost ? "

" By the person to whom the poems were written."

" I see," said Sir Hedworth, " *Lesbia illa*." He understood that sort of thing.

" Yes," I said. " *Illa Lesbia*."

" Poor C. ! "

" Poor C. ! "

* I read the poem printed in the Appendix for the first time when I went through Gerald Malone's papers some years after this conversation took place.

FINIS.

APPENDIX

THE following poem, besides his Eton *Vale* and the song which I have already quoted—is the only composition of C.'s that is extant. It was written on the death of his brother Harry, probably just before Bramsley was sold. It is only a rough draft, and has been put together from the MS. with difficulty. The MS. consists of twenty-six pages quarto, closely written on both sides of the paper in ink and pencil, corrected and re-corrected and amended in every direction. Although there were (as far as I can judge) in the poem no actual gaps, I have had to choose between alternative readings, and sometimes I have been denied even the choice, only one of two or more readings being decipherable. The MS. was with the rest of the papers left by Malone.

W. W.

I. M. H.

This is the house we used to know so well ;
    This the front door,
And locked.   I had no need to ring this bell :—
    Never before.

Where is the sundial with its sphere of gold ?
    The vane's bright comb ?
All gone ! but from the bank the soft black mould
    Still whispers : " Home."

Those paths, once cared for, are now choked with grass ;
    They've stripped the tower
Of ivy, and exchanged for costly glass
    Our trellised bower.

The old we knew is crumbling in decay ;
    The new gives pain ;
The soul of home has fled too far away
    To come again.

The door is open : what is this strange face ?
    " I'll show you round."—
" I think I know the way." Ah ! here's the place ;
    " Tom Tiddler's ground."

I walk through empty rooms ; she tells her tale :
    " They used to smoke
Here, after dinner. Here, before the sale,
    The walls were oak."

Upstairs. " Sir, mind the step,—this used to be
    The nursery floor."—
There is but one thing left that speaks to me :
    A creaking door.

And here, once more I breathe while shadows fall,
    The smell of hay ;
The pictures come to life upon the wall ;
    My prayers I say.

But hark ! what wondrous bird is this that sings
    So sweet a tune ?
Now I am borne away on elfin wings,
    Beyond the moon.

The morning sun is streaming through the blind :—
    " They come, they come !
The soldiers ! Hark ! ' The girl I left behind !
    The fifes ! the drum ! "

Back to the garden . . . here we used to hide . . .
        Where is the spot,
The summer-house ? his garden by its side,
        My rival plot ?

A forest now of grass with weeds entwined.
        Ah, there's the mouse !
Ivy ! I crawl beneath it, and I find
        Our summer-house.

And here, with buttercups and watering-can,
        We made a brew ;
Beneath that tree we called " Fort Caliban,"
        A toadstool grew.

The kitchen-garden. Here's the stagnant tank,
        The floating mole ;
The pond with dock leaves and with nettles rank,
        The rat's dark hole.

All is the same.   But all is not the same :
        For he is dead.
The well-known cry : " Hurrah ! I've won the game ! '
        The curly head,

The laughing eyes, the angry, stammering speech,
        The heart of gold :—
All that is far away beyond our reach,
        Beneath the mould.

He lies not here, but far away beyond
        His native land ;
Beneath the alien rose, the tropic frond,
        The burning sand.

His life was like a February day,
        Too warm too soon :
A foretaste of the spring that cannot stay
        Beyond the noon.

As the swallows, when September pomps conceal
      A frosty spell,
Fly low about the horses' heads, and wheel,
      To say farewell,

So he, at some sure summons in the wind,
      Or sky, took wing,
And soared to the gold South.   He stayed behind
      When came the spring.*

They say we'll meet in some transfigured space,
      Beyond the sun.
I need you here, in this familiar place
      Of tears and fun.

I do not need you changed, dissolved in air,
      Nor rarefied ;—
I need you all imperfect as you were,
      Here, at my side.

And yet I cannot think that Death's cold wind
      Has killed the flame
Of you, forever, and has left behind
      Only a name,

That mortal life is but a derelict ship,
      Without a sail ;
The soul no stronger than a farthing dip
      Matched with a gale.

I ask, I seek, and to the empty air,
      In vain I cry ;
The God they worship, if He hears my prayer,
      Makes no reply.

Lord, give to me the grain of mustard seed,
      That moves the mount :
Give me a drop of water in my need,
      From Thy full fount.

* These last twelve lines were scratched out in the original; but a *stet*
in the margin seems to correct the word "Omit."—W. W.

Around me, and above me and beneath,
     Yawns the abyss ;—
Show me the bridge across the gulf of Death,
     To banks of bliss.

Cast the dumb devil from my tomb of grief ;—
     Help me to say :
" Lord, I believe, help Thou my unbelief."
     Teach me to pray.

But if the fault be mine, then, Lord, forgive ;
     My heart is dry ;
So bitter is the world I cannot live ;—
     I dare not die.